Mark of the Profane

By: Kyle Belote

Copyright Page

Edited by:
Jonathan Oliver
https://reedsy.com/#/freelancers/jon-o

Book Cover by:
Ivan Zann: https://www.bookcoversart.com

Author Website:
http://www.outpostdire.com

Dedication

This book is dedicated to two individuals in no particular order.

To David Williamson: You've been a rock, a champion of fantasy, a springboard, and a steadfast companion through many years of writing together. I am blessed to call you friend.

To Julie Albini: In many ways, you were my first beta reader ever, and I was just an awkward fourteen-year-old boy writing crappy poetry or other haphazard ramblings filled with misaligned, youthful angst. You didn't sing praises, but you didn't judge me either—not out loud. In a way, you gave me hope by not crushing my dreams. So, twenty-five years later and a little too late, let me say, thank you. It meant the world to me.

It still does.

Acknowledgments

To my beta readers and acquaintances across the years. I couldn't have done it without you! Take a bow for braving the frontier on numerous occasions. For this volume, I'd like to highlight three in particular: Christina Fulwider, Carlos Carrasco, & Dwayne Demastus.

To Sarah Bickel: without you, book 1 wouldn't have been published, so thank you for the push. You've been an inspiration in countless ways, and I can never repay the debt of kindness or honor.

To my Ko-dons on Substack: SHould and Ioleta. Your support keeps me going.

And most especially to you, dear reader. Welcome back to Ermaeyth. Thanks for being a part of where stories are born, worlds are shattered, heroes are slaughtered, and villains win.

Oblus ina'ti Sepan Eti.

Terms

Fortnight—Two weeks
Moon turn—One month
Season—Three months
Tour—Two years (generally for military and government term)
Score—Twenty years
Epoch—100 years
Era—500 years
Age—1,000 years
Legend—10,000 years
Fathom—100,000 years
Revolution—Ten Fathoms

Titles:

Arysto—a title for someone of noble birth, a male, with an undisclosed name or House, the same as saying Sir to a knight or lord to nobility.

Arysta—a title for someone of noble birth, a female, with an undisclosed name or House.

Mage—another common title like wizard, except while everyone can be technically called a wizard, a mage is someone of magical skill that pursues a career in magic beyond school level.

Madam—proper title of a lady, regardless of birth, a mother.

Sire—proper title of a man, regardless of birth, the head of his house, a father.

Lady—woman of noble or minor noble birth.

Lord—man of noble or minor noble birth.

Sorcerer—an evil Rumigul user, a person who can do magic without incantations.

Warlock—a Rumigul user, a person that can do magic without incantations, but is not evil.

Wizard—general term used for all people with magical abilities.

Witchen—an evil magical user but not a Sorcerer, Witchens must use incantations and generally use Derengi magic.

Dramatis Personae

Main Cast:
Starriace—Female, Unknown
Xenomene—Female, wizardkind, Krey
Judas Lakayre—Male, wizardkind, Rallocan, Warlock/Exile

Krey:
Daniel—Male, wizardkind, The Heir of Valin
Tiny—Male, wizardkind
Bitcher—Male, wizardkind, Forgotten Islander

Supporting:
Norek—Male, traveling scholar
Ava—Female, fairy
Rusem—Male, spirit / Risen
Harold the Hermit—Male, Unknown
Lily—Female, wizardkind, Rallocan
Kam—Male, wizardkind, Forgotten Islander

Kothlere Council Members:
Meristal Raviils—Female, wizardkind, Advocate of Law
Daylynn Reese—Female, wizardkind
Sedrus—Male, centaur

Antagonist:
Callum Godfrey—Male, Forgotten Isles king
Xilor—Male, Sorcerer/Dark Lord
The Betrayer—Male, wizardkind

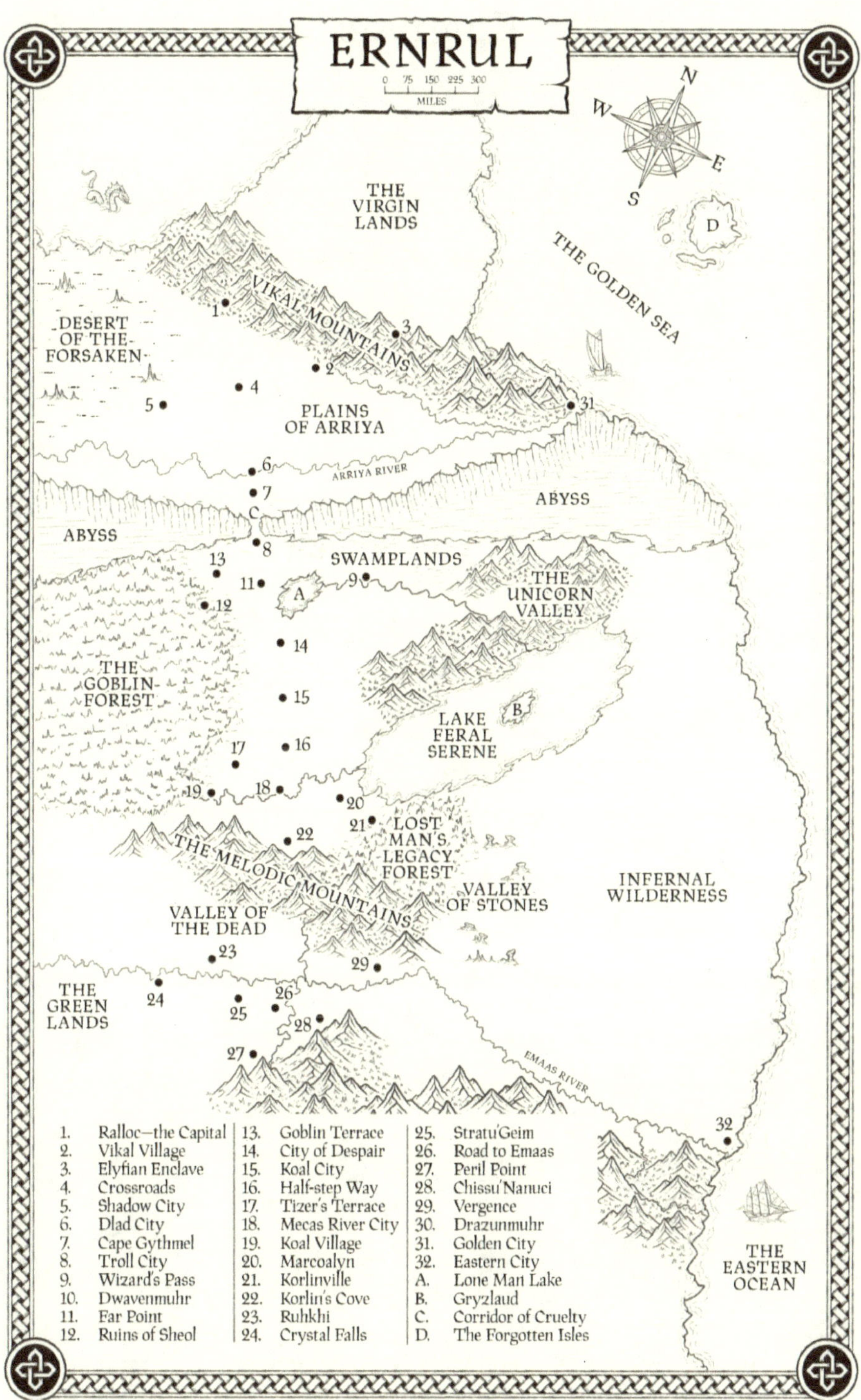

ERNRUL
0 75 150 225 300
MILES
N
W
E
S
THE VIRGIN LANDS
D
THE GOLDEN SEA
VIKAL MOUNTAINS
DESERT OF THE FORSAKEN
PLAINS OF ARRIYA
ARRIYA RIVER
ABYSS
ABYSS
C
SWAMPLANDS
THE UNICORN VALLEY
A
THE GOBLIN FOREST
LAKE FERAL SERENE
B
LOST MAN'S LEGACY FOREST
THE MELODIC MOUNTAINS
VALLEY OF STONES
INFERNAL WILDERNESS
VALLEY OF THE DEAD
THE GREEN LANDS
EMAAS RIVER
THE EASTERN OCEAN
1 2 3 4 5 6 7 8 9 11 12 13 14 15 16 17 18 19 20 21 22 23 24 25 26 27 28 29 31 32
1. Ralloc—the Capital
2. Vikal Village
3. Elyfian Enclave
4. Crossroads
5. Shadow City
6. Dlad City
7. Cape Gythmel
8. Troll City
9. Wizard's Pass
10. Dwavenmuhr
11. Far Point
12. Ruins of Sheol
13. Goblin Terrace
14. City of Despair
15. Koal City
16. Half-step Way
17. Tizer's Terrace
18. Mecas River City
19. Koal Village
20. Marcoalyn
21. Korlinville
22. Korlin's Cove
23. Ruhkhi
24. Crystal Falls
25. Stratu'Geim
26. Road to Emaas
27. Peril Point
28. Chissu'Nanuci
29. Vergence
30. Drazunmuhr
31. Golden City
32. Eastern City
A. Lone Man Lake
B. Gryzlaud
C. Corridor of Cruelty
D. The Forgotten Isles

Epigraph

Justice is in the mind; revenge is in the heart.

Prologue

The not-too-distant future…

A minuscule splash sounded in the obscurity, her only companion.

Her body lay broken, twisted, agony lanced through her ribs as she gasped. The sharp inhales brought tears to her eyes.

Only the silence kept her company, holding her close. Mortal life bled away, and the darkness stood as witness.

Another tear ran down her face. The constricting cocoon of suffering enveloped her body. Coldness made the misery … more.

What am I doing here? Where am I?

Despite the desperate thoughts, nothing returned. Her mind stood like a blank canvas, without a hint of shade, shadow, or shape.

Being paralyzed on the stone floor gave her the sense of vulnerability.

Helpless.

The darkness devoured her like a ravenous animal, mute, voiceless, never revealing its secrets.

Drip…

The small splash echoed in the deep. Was she somewhere deep underground?

Within the confines of her dark prison, a new hush crept over the air. Something stirred beyond the edge of her vision.

Her spine tingled.

A new predator stalked her, one she couldn't escape. As the panic grew, her consciousness slipped beyond the precipice…

Chapter 1: Norek

Apor rose in a blue blister of fury; its heat lashed out against the tiny Forgotten Isles. Hot gusts of wind laced with wisps of water tore through the beach, making their way to the heart of the small island.

Norek sat in the limited shade of his small hut. Salty sweat dripped from his tanned, naked flesh.

Thatched houses of reed and local wood called spear grass encroached upon the thick vegetation, and wildlife ran like an untamed fire through the forest.

Ocean water, dust, and humidity filled the air, a demon masked in reprieve.

Norek stayed on the coast, far from the interior where the monarch resided. Foreigners weren't granted sanction to visit inland. Living near the docks, he could survey each incoming ship, some hailing from the Golden City, a mere ten-day voyage away. Others ventured from the Eastern City, an arduous, three-week trip. Sometimes, the voyage took longer if the weather turned.

Elysys, the next largest city beyond, doubled that distance. Unfortunately, some ships never reached port again. Even though the climate turned treacherous this time of year and hammered the eastern coast of Marcoalyn's realm, most ships still dared the journey.

If the elements didn't get them, sometimes pirates did.

The people of the Isles called Norek "a man of many talents," chosen each morning as a hired hand. The peddlers and dock workers took note, and so did the jungle keepers and the farmers.

A foreigner picked first was uncommon.

The sound of footsteps crunching on the white sand made him perk up. Who would violate the period of rest? During the hottest part of the day, all Islanders went home to escape the heat. By the sound of padded footfalls, a small group headed his way.

The first person broke his line of sight, and Norek knew him as the herald of the king. As the custom dictated, he lurched to his feet before taking a knee. When the herald visited, he did so by the monarch's order and merited the same respect, minus the bowed head.

In the other cities south of the Melodic Mountains, where monarchs still ruled, heralds wore elaborate, silk robes, House emblems, and jewelry to display their power, wealth, and status. In the Isles, the herald wore linen in the colors of his lord—forest green.

"You may rise," the herald said.

Like most Islanders, he had light hair and pale eyes. The indigenous had either blond hair or a light shade of red, and their irises ranged from gray, green, hazel, amber, and blue.

Norek stood. His dark hair and matching goatee contrasted with the group around him.

"How may I be of service to you, sire?" Norek asked, his eyes lowered.

"Herald will do, and I'm not a sire yet, Outsider."

Most foreigners considered the term rude, but the Islanders resisted external influence and used the word as a constant reminder.

"His Eminence requests your presence; however, you're unsuited dressed as a worker. We brought you a change of clothing. You'll bathe before entering the king's presence."

"As your king commands."

The group ushered him to the public bathhouse where the forest gave way to the beach. The water trickled downhill from the center of the island, near the castle.

The bath was a fresh reprieve from Apor's sweltering heat. Norek bathed in haste, and two women came to dry and clothe him, dressing him with a thin, almost sheer, white linen. Tying the vestments at his sides, the women draped a slightly heavier outer robe around him in the king's color. The cloth, though cut short, wasn't meant to fully close.

With dyed leather, the ladies shod his feet. When presentable, the girls covered him with powder and oils to obscure any residual stench.

Norek grabbed the only two possessions allowed, refusing to part with them—his staff and his brown leather satchel.

Exiting the bathhouse, they traveled up a worn path through the forest. Tall, thick grass claimed the edges of the road. Spear grass—a fibrous wood, strong and sturdy, but hollow at the center—claimed the forest in innumerable multitudes.

The herald set a silent, moderate pace up the sloping trail. Several times, segments of the path became steep, and Norek tried to take in the scenery, since it was his first, and probably last visit inland.

When the castle came into view, it sat on a small plateau on the highest point of the island. Norek had read about the Kothlere Castle in Ralloc, but this would fit into its courtyard. Considering the scarceness of resources, the feat here seemed rather impressive.

A curtain wall, barely deserving the name, lacked fine masonry work. Massive boulders stood cobbled together with globs of mortar, the strength of many men, and sheer desperation. Beyond, the gate proved no different. How they managed to level the wall, Norek hadn't a clue. While the barrier boasted enormous stones, the interior relied on smaller rocks.

The castle doors, surprisingly, were made of wood, no doubt shipped in from one of the coastal cities.

The herald pushed the doors open, and a not-so-tremendous great hall greeted him. One hearth sat at the back of the room.

Probably unused since the day it was crafted.

The room lay twenty feet long by ten wide, far smaller than most great halls he'd visited; four tables with benches lined the outer walls. A throne of spear grass and rock with a few scant precious gems found on the island adorned the chair.

A brooding man with a stern expression sat upon the unyielding seat.

"My Lord Eminence, may I present to you Norek, the outsider, wayward traveler, hard worker of your people. Norek," the herald turned to him, "you're in the presence of His Eminence, King of the Forgotten Isles."

Norek stopped with his procession and knelt. The monarch glanced up from his contemplation and cold, blue eyes appraised Norek. The king's short, strawberry blonde hair flecked with gray and the closely cropped beard matched.

When the king spoke, his voice was almost monotone, as if bored to state fact, but it came out clipped and quiet.

"No outsider has set foot within these halls within the last legend."

Norek swallowed.

From the first sentence, he knew the ruler did not mince words nor waste breath on frivolities. He stated facts, offering cold silence for a companion—almost as frigid as his expression.

Then, why did you bring me here?

"You honor me, Your Eminence."

"I don't honor you. Your very presence here defiles this hall. If I didn't need you, you'd still be on the beach."

Grimacing inwardly, Norek tried a different tactic.

"How may I be of service to you, Your Eminence?"

"You may rise. You may address me as King Godfrey."

"As you wish, King Godfrey. What do you require of me?"

"I understand you're a man of many talents."

A hint of admiration entered his voice, or was it just Norek's imagination?

"Even those you keep hidden. I recognize a mage staff when I see one. Tell me, what's your specialty?"

"My specialty?"

Godfrey rolled his pale blue eyes.

"Don't play coy, it's unbefitting of a man. Coy is a woman's game, one well-played here. Tell me, has a woman of the Isles graced your bed?"

"No, King Godfrey."

Norek's brow frowned at the odd question.

The monarch smiled at this, then his face returned to the typical scowl.

"It's unfortunate you haven't tasted the flesh of our women. Even if you did, I worry not about you spreading foul seed among us. But back to my original question: what's your specialty?"

"I possess many, but my primary skill lies in the art of orb gazing."

"Ah," Godfrey smiled again, "an Owlen mage."

From Godfrey's expression, Norek surmised he already knew the answer.

I must be careful with this man.

Since setting foot in the Isles, Norek abstained from calling on magic unless need demanded it. As of yet, no such incident arose. If Godfrey ferreted out his hidden side, Norek must assume that all questions were potential traps, and he didn't know what repercussions awaited if he lied.

And I don't want to find out!

"I've always heard of Owlen mages but never met one. Would you care to demonstrate your abilities?"

Norek almost laughed, but controlled the foolish urge. Scrying the future didn't work the way people assumed.

"King Godfrey," Norek began, "perceiving what's to come isn't always assured. Many times—"

"It's not the future I wish to know," the monarch interrupted. "I want to test your abilities. Scry the past. What's my given name?"

A smile twitched upon his lips.

Norek fumbled for his leather satchel, and spears lowered, poised to kill. The lord waved them away, and Norek withdrew his crystal orb. A white fog filled it, but the center remained clear. He palmed the sphere, the size of a small orange.

Norek knelt, his right hand dancing over it in a clockwise motion. The crystal ball floated, the dull fog glowing pearl. Norek breathed a few words, hot breath fogging the surface. The color changed to a bright red cloud before returning to its previous state.

Raising his eyes, he spoke.

"Your given name is Callum; Callum Godfrey, second son of Edmund Godfrey."

A satisfied grin crossed the king's face, but it didn't reach the eyes.

Nothing genuine has come from that man in ages I'm willing to bet.

"Well done. Another test, why do I rule and not my eldest brother?"

Again, Norek muttered his words, and his bulb glowed and shot red, then returned to the pearl sheen.

"He reigned for three years before being afflicted with a malady. There isn't a treatment for him, and he never returned. Therefore, the throne fell to you."

The king's grin froze on his face.

"And this malady?"

Norek swallowed hard.

"Bloodlust is the most common term."

"Where do people go for the bloodlust malady?"

The king's eyes twinkled with malevolence.

"To the Black Tide of House Eti. He's Krey now."

"I hear there's a war in your realm, is this true?"

"Begging your pardon, King Godfrey, but it isn't *my* realm."

"Oh, come now," he chuckled. "Your hair and aristocratic features give you away; you're born of noble blood. You definitely came from Ralloc or one of the other great cities."

"I'm an orphan, King Godfrey. My parents died in the Wizard's War. I've been traveling many years."

"Nevertheless, I know your kind, and now you do, too. So, tell me, is it true? Ralloc's at war?"

"Yes."

"Did you gaze that from your orb?"

"No, King Godfrey. That was common knowledge when I left port to come here."

"Then, gaze into your orb and tell me the fate of my brother."

Again, Norek peered within, but this time, it showed him something different. It showed him more than what he wished. The king's brother flashed through, but the last thing he glimpsed was a woman with hair the color of flame. Ensuring he kept any expression from his face, his surprise and a spike of hope, Norek looked back up to Callum.

"Your brother still lives."

The king's fond scowl deepened at the news. Whatever answer he searched for, Norek failed to deliver. Godfrey rose, and as was custom, everyone knelt.

"You'll dine with me, the queen, and my children tonight. Once we've feasted, and I've asked more questions, you'll return to the beach."

The king left the hall in a silent storm. Norek watched him go, only rising after his departure.

If I'm still alive on the morrow, I'm boarding the first ship out of here.

Godfrey hadn't lied when he spoke of a feast, and Norek hadn't eaten so well since…well, he couldn't remember. A roasted pig lay in the center of the table. Imported potatoes from the Eastern City were mashed and mixed with goat's milk—the same goat later slaughtered for the feast.

Leafy Isle greens were steamed and mixed with a white grain grown on stalks like corn; carrots, broccoli, and mushrooms augmented the rest. Servants passed out spiced rum stored in oak casks with ginger root. Norek had never seen a clearer vintage. It went down smooth but smoldered in the pit of his stomach.

All the lords turned out for the feast, few as there were. Norek didn't take the time to find out their names. They only offered customary greetings. Even the captain of the guards and the herald sat in at the feast. In the municipals far to the south, the courts would never allow the herald to attend.

With so few at the king's gathering, exceptions were made.

Afterward, they'd gorged themselves with pies of blueberry, blackberry, and koja, a fruit only indigenous to the island. A dull royal blue skin covered the bright crimson interior. The koja was a sweet fruit, almost tart, and juicier than a tangerine.

More rum flowed with each course; clear, amber, and dark infused with spice, ginger, and other local fruits. Each tapped cask boasted a different wood for flavoring and aging.

Deep in their cups, Callum called Norek forward to conduct a show. Lords asked random questions of the past. Norek tried to figure out why Callum would make him put on a show for his guests, but he refused to ask or reveal how much it bothered him.

When they had their fill of laughs and curiosities, Callum held a hand for silence.

"Norek, tell me of Ralloc."

"I can only tell what I know from books. I haven't seen Ralloc with my own eyes."

Callum grunted.

"I have no use for a description of their sprawling spires, I shall witness that soon enough. Tell me, who runs Ralloc?"

Norek turned to his globe. This time, the pearl glow sputtered and shot through with purple, then black before returning to its prior state.

"I see a woman with amethyst eyes and red hair, pale skin like snow, and the wrath of gods tearing the sky asunder."

This news gave Godfrey pause as his cold countenance measured Norek.

Then, as if he hadn't spoken, the king raised his cup and toasted.

"To the full moon!"

Norek, not privy to the meaning, stood with his brow frowning. Perhaps he'd played a part of something elaborate for the king. Godfrey allowed the lords to pose their questions, perhaps validating Norek's gifts, and now that he'd proven himself, it solidified something for the king.

Godfrey, seeing Norek's confused expression, focused on him.

"On the full moon, we sail for the Golden City, then onto Ralloc, where we'll demand to become part of their domain. From there, I shall lay claim to my right."

His men cheered, and Norek couldn't figure out what the man meant. What right did he have? Why would Ralloc accept the Isles? Plus, Islanders were isolationist, and they lacked wealth and materials. With nothing to offer Ralloc, Norek doubted their acceptance.

I'm missing something. There's more than just this simple move.

"Outsider," Godfrey said through the cheers. "You've defiled our hall long enough. Take your leave; on the morrow board a ship, and don't return."

"As you command."

He bowed low, making sure he gave no slight and left briskly. The soldiers intended to escort him to the beach, but Norek shrugged them off, telling them that he could find his own way.

By the time he left the castle, Nykron and Faellon had risen, and a black velvet covered the sky. The cool, irritating sand managed to find the space between his toes, and he cleared the grit by shaking his feet out to the side. The sound of crashing waves encouraged his haste.

He reached his small hut, and a blonde woman with emerald eyes awaited within.

"What are you doing here?" Norek barked, startled by the woman's presence.

She smiled.

"The king sent me to you with a message: 'no man should go without a woman of the Forgotten Isles.'"

Norek nodded, thinking before he spoke.

"Tell the king that I thank him for his kind gift, but it's unnecessary."

"Refusing His Eminence will be a terrible dishonor to him and his family."

"I mean no disrespect—"

"It'll be perceived that way, and he won't take kindly to rejection. It won't go well for you, Outsider."

Norek chewed his lower lip, debating his options. When no obvious choice came, the woman continued, taking his silence as a refusal.

"The last clan who refused a gift were expunged."

"He exiled them or erased all written record of them?"

She laughed, a bright and cheerful noise.

"No, Outsider, he had them cleansed. The whole family was put to death."

Norek swallowed.

"How do you think he'll look upon me and my failure?"

He was set to leave in the morning, and disrespect meant death. He eyed her. The woman was gorgeous, and he didn't need much encouragement. Still, it seemed like a trap of some kind.

Eating the last of his resolve to refuse, Norek nodded.

"Very well. I accept the king's gift."

Chapter 2: Xenomene

Xenomene leaned over the desk, poring over orders and summaries of Dlad City and its fortifications. Her candles burned low, and the crisp, cool air of hushed night rustled through her window.

At least I got an upgrade!

At the start of the war in Cape Gythmel, the Krey lived in tents, but after the retreat to Dlad City, she improved their living conditions. The Krey were allotted a small four-story inn near the north side of town, and it lay furthest away from the Grand Royal Army, which suited both sides.

She appreciated the savvy tactic.

The smartest move the army's officers made thus far.

Once again, the tasks of daily camp life and fortifying the defenses reverted to the army. Only she, her second in command, Tiny, and the Mind, were allowed into the camp proper.

The inn, called Traveler's Respite, stood almost taller than its length. Xeno took the entire fourth floor, and the squad bedded down on the second, leaving the third floor as a buffer. The first floor stood as their mess hall and the third as storage for items not readily needed, like recovered armor from Raven and Two-Tons. Due to the accord struck between Xilor and the warlock, Judas Lakayre, they were allowed to collect their dead unmolested.

Monsters have honor?

She turned her attention back to the detailed maps and accompanying orders. Most seemed straightforward, but every time she voiced her opinion, it'd been turned aside like she hadn't spoken at all. Did the problem arise because she was female or Krey?

Probably both.

The thought tasted bitter in her mouth.

Bitcher's face floated before her eyes.

Damn him to the Underworld!

Nearly a month ago, he took her in Islander Fashion at Cape Gythmel. She'd retaliated, seeking justice for his transgression, but her thoughts dwelled on him. She didn't harbor resentment, but rather affection, which surprised her.

He'd awakened something in her, something she'd been missing but couldn't articulate. It wasn't the deed itself, but how it was delivered.

Much to her chagrin, it reinforced the Krey's way. They never turned their nose up at anything, least of all experiences of the flesh. Any Rallocan would've shunned their acts, but her fellow Krey? They would've pulled up a bench and cheered the performance.

And they'd think no different of us.

Her cheeks flushed with color.

Both she and Bitcher were stuck at a crossroad in their relationship.

Relationship? What the fuck? I'm actually thinking of this as a relationship?

If it was, it was one-sided.

Bitcher had sulked since his punishment. In her mind, the deeds were done and over, but he perpetuated his penalization by avoidance. He never looked her in the eye anymore, and when she approached him, he sought out nearby people, avoiding her in one-on-one encounters.

Even Tiny, her second, commented on the odd behavior.

"He's less bitchy."

Tiny wasn't privy to Bitcher's punishment, nor the fact that Bitcher fucked her. She liked Tiny as her steadfast rock, and faithful supporter, perhaps a friend, but the big man fostered aspirations for romance. She couldn't crush his hopes by saying it'd never happen, let alone tell him the truth.

That night, what passed between them, kept replaying in her mind. As much as she hated it, she enjoyed it, too.

"Have you come to 'bury your face in it'?"

"That, among other things."

She shook the thoughts away and returned her attention to the documents. The smallest parchment leaf sat folded, and she picked it up again, much to her annoyance. She unfolded the paper and reread the heir's message.

What the fuck is wrong with you, cunt? You refused each pair of replacements I sent you. You better fall in line, or I swear by the Lord of the Underworld, I'll come down there and strip you of your responsibilities. I don't give two shits of a fucking prostitute if they look funny, stink, seem too small, or too young! They're Krey, and so are you, so fucking act like it! You'll take these two I sent, and if I hear another word of protest, so help me by the dwaven gods, I'll suck out your soul after I let your squad rut you into oblivion!

Xenomene smirked, and a quiet chuckle rumbled in her belly. The heir didn't understand her. She implemented each pair he sent, five in all, and none fit. They disrupted the meld. Krey needed to function as a seamless, cohesive unit.

"Have you come to bury your face in it?"

She ground her teeth at the stray thought and wadded up the heir's note. A small knock sounded on her door. She tossed the paper into the corner behind her desk.

"Enter," she snapped.

Tiny entered, a towering man with a thick shadow of stubble on his face. He bowed his head so he wouldn't hit the threshold. He, like her and the rest of the Krey, dressed in camp attire, a simple black tunic with ties on the side and shorts. Xeno, however, cut the excess length of her britches and the sleeves of her shirt.

Mauler, upon seeing her alterations, did the same.

"Are you ready to see them?" Tiny asked.

"Yes."

The big man turned to leave.

"Oh, and Tiny? Wake Bitcher. He can stand by outside until I'm done with the two virgins."

Virgins were the nickname all Krey carried until they bloodied themselves in battle. In Cape Gythmel, just a month prior, Xenomene was a virgin herself.

"Is that wise?"

"Are you questioning me?"

"Not at all, but since you two…"

"He can't hide forever. Whatever is between us must be resolved before battle."

"As you command, Do-don."

Tiny left, and the two virgins filed into the room. Her second closed the door, his footsteps growing quieter.

"Oblus Eti," they courtesied.

"Oblus ina'ti Sepan Eti," she returned their informal greeting with a formal one: Live and die by the sword.

She came around the desk, and both men glanced down at her crotch and legs, noticing her…alterations.

"So, you're the two new virgins? What are your names?"

The one with the meticulously kept goatee and green eyes spoke up first.

"I'm Slurp, Do-don. He's Smokey."

Xenomene couldn't help but stare at the former. Slurp embodied the pinnacle elements of attractiveness for her: pale skin, blond hair, an athletic build, and just a few inches taller than her. She fought the urge to imagine him without clothes.

Smokey, by contrast, had thick, curly facial hair—a beard flecked with dark blond and brown—reaching past his collarbone. His pot belly hid the belt beneath. Smokey mirrored Slurp in paleness but with blue eyes and hair a shade or two darker.

Xenomene stared at the contrasting men for a moment before returning to her seat.

"Where do you hail from?"

"From the Isles," Slurp supplied.

Xenomene hesitated for a fraction of a second before she reclaimed her seat. Bitcher's declaration and the salacious act that followed flashed through her mind.

"Good. Another member of our squad is from the Isles, so you'll at least have some companionship as you recall your homeland."

"We may," Slurp said. "Then again, we may not come from the same area or island."

"True."

She looked them over.

"Tell me about yourselves."

"I'm from the main island, the big one."

Slurp's words seemed a little forced. He jerked a thumb at Smokey.

"He comes from the smallest island; I don't remember the name. We always called it Speck, like a mote of dust."

Xenomene glanced at Smokey.

"Are you a fucking mute?"

"I speak," Smokey said, his accent thick.

Xeno almost retorted, *"Better if you don't."*

She suppressed a smile, realizing she had an opportunity to embarrass them.

"Tell me, is it true what they say about Islanders?"

Slurp nodded, but Smokey's lower lip protruded.

"I'd fuck your ass," Smokey blurted, giving her a wink.

Slurp rolled his eyes and shook his head, flushing brightly.

"I bet you'd fuck anything, even a turtle," she said.

"A turtle? That doesn't—?"

She waved his comment away, exasperated.

"It's the only thing I could think of at the moment."

She turned her attention to Slurp and raised an eyebrow.

"Aye, it's true."

"Why?"

"Why do you care?" Smokey growled. "You're not from our culture."

"Hey, I genuinely want to know why y'all prefer…that. Never heard it explained. You got to admit, it's…different."

The thought of asking Bitcher crossed her mind, but he avoided her.

Slurp seemed both defiant and abashed.

"The truth? We overpopulated our islands. A king, I don't remember his name because it happened so long ago, decreed that all intercourse was to be done in this manner to curb our growing population. The men of our islands are not renowned for showing…restraint at the crucial moment, and our women are quite fertile. It's been that way ever since."

Xenomene nodded, hearing his words.

"How long ago was this?"

Slurp shrugged.

"Three or four legends ago."

She did the math.

"Thirty to forty thousand years ago?" she blurted.

That was an impossibly long time, and those changes were ingrained into their culture for good. Just to reverse the effects would take ages, maybe even a legend or more.

She leaned back in her chair.

"According to the heir, I have to accept you, but *you*," she said, pointing to Smokey, "I'd send back for your lack of tact. I don't like you very much right now. Fix that."

"Aye, Do-don."

"Did you receive quarters?"

"Yes, Do-don," Slurp answered.

"Very well, on the morrow, we'll add you to the meld. I hope by the scrotum of gods you aren't fuck-ups like the last few groups the heir bestowed. You may retire for the evening."

They turned and left, half walking, half fleeing from her. She heard Slurp say, "I kind of like her," as they retreated.

Her door almost shut when Bitcher's hand caught it, and he shuffled in, eyes downcast, steps timid.

"Close the door," she ordered.

Bitcher complied with wordless, meek movements. He stood a few paces from the desk, his eyes on the floor.

I fucking broke him.

Bitcher had become a pitiful shell of his former self.

Where's the fire?

"What the fuck's wrong with you?"

Bitcher shrugged and moved his eyes to a new segment of the floor. Xenomene leapt from her chair and bounded around the desk, her pixie form moving with agile grace. Bitcher didn't even flinch. She reared back and slapped him in the face.

"What the fuck's wrong with you?"

Bitcher's cold, gray eyes found her for a moment, and then he regarded the floor.

"You," he whispered.

"Me? Me, what?"

"You...you cut off my fucking testicle!"

His eyes found her again, and they were hard, filled with hate and anger.

"Yeah, and I had the Heart put it back!"

"You cut off my testicle!" he repeated, his voice finding his inner fire.

Finally, something!

She hoped for some rise, some emotion that showed he wasn't beyond repair.

"I told you there would be consequences. Did you think I was joking?"

"If it was without your consent, you would've stopped me."

Xenomene didn't want to concede the point, because it was true. She'd let him take her. He'd told her to lay on her side so he could fuck her ass, and she complied, knowing full well what was going to happen. She could've screamed, and Tiny and the Krey would've stormed the pavilion in a torrent of violence, tearing Bitcher apart.

But she didn't scream, didn't resist, and she'd punished him for it.

Well, the oil. That took away my agency.

"Damn it, Bitcher. I don't get you! What happened to the man who always complained about everything? Where's the asshole we all know and love and hate?"

"What the fuck would you know of love?"

"Nothing."

She shook her head.

"Love's frivolous and fickle at best, a notion for people who are dumb enough to believe. It isn't the Krey way."

"Not the Krey way?"

Bitcher laughed, a harsh mocking in his tone.

"The Krey are all about love. The love of war and bloodlust, of death, drink, and sex. We love it all."

Again, Bitcher had a point, but she wasn't willing to avow to it aloud.

"What would *you* know of love?" she countered.

His laughter died.

"I loved someone once, from afar."

He cast his eyes to the floor.

"Then, she cut off my balls."

He glared back at her.

Xenomene's eyes widened in disbelief. She shook her head, the proclamation sinking in. She stumbled to the desk's edge, staring at the wall, trying to find her voice.

"What?"

She glanced at him.

"How? When? Why the fuck would you love me?"

"Loved," Bitcher corrected.

The past tense usage hit like a troll's club to the chest. She hadn't known, not in the slightest. He never spoke of affection. As a loner, she relished the comfort of isolation, but do-dons couldn't indulge such luxuries.

His revelation took her wind. Knowing she destroyed his affection compounded the guilt.

Since when do I start caring about his fucking affection?

She gazed into his pale gray eyes and saw hate and pain and mistrust.

I did those things to him. I made him what he is.

That epiphany killed her the most.

She broke the man. Xenomene could feel the disconnect between them, and she always would unless she fixed it. Could the warlock erase the memories? He'd find out what really happened.

When they had sex, he'd drugged her. He couldn't deny that fact, and that was why she punished him. The oil did something to her. The effects were an altered state, making everything euphoric, and destroying her inhibitions.

Or did it?

The oil came after the fact, smoothing his entry.

She shook her head, trying to clear the memories away, how he took her, the way he cupped her breasts and smacked her ass. His exploring hands between her legs…

I have to fix him, but how?

The answer came unbidden and almost immediately. She resisted the solution at first, but it only grew stronger as more time passed. Swallowing her pride, she disrupted the quiet between them.

"Look…I enjoyed our time together."

His disbelieving eyes stared back at her.

"The Underworld may damn my soul if I'm lying, but I can't stop thinking about you."

"What cruelty is this?"

She shook her head.

"It's not a trick, Bitcher."

She didn't want to say the next words, but she needed to, had to. She had to take accountability for her actions and voice the truth.

"You're right," she confessed.

"About what?"

She swallowed.

"I could've stopped you, but I didn't. The battle—" Her voice caught in her throat, "—wasn't as I expected."

"Shades, are you fucking crying?" Bitcher asked.

She smiled.

"Fuck you."

Xenomene took a moment to collect her thoughts.

"I always imagined that killing people would be different, how we trained for it. All those bodies I cut down…"

"*We* cut them down," Bitcher corrected.

He took a step closer.

"We followed our training, and will do so again. Afterward, all who survived will be merry, and we'll drink and fuck pretty girls and whores. In Smokey's case, maybe a goat."

Xeno chuckled, and he continued.

"I'm sure everyone felt the same. You shouldn't focus on the deaths, but the lives you saved."

Her eyes widened.

"Bitcher…that's very optimistic of you."

She searched for the word.

"Almost kind."

"Yeah, well, don't tell anyone."

She smiled again, and he almost seemed his old self. Xenomene bowed her head to hide a lone tear from him.

Snap out of it, you're squalling like a child without her dolly.

She wiped the tear away and glanced up at Bitcher again, their gazes locked.

"I'm sorry."

"What?"

"I said I'm sorry. The punishment was too severe, it didn't fit the crime."

She shook her head.

"I let my anger find a justification after the fact, and that was wrong. I'd do it over, if I could."

He grinned at her.

"Do what over? The deed or the punishment?"

Her brow twitched upward.

"Both."

He leaned forward and kissed her, quick and passionate before breaking away.

Emotions flashed through her: aggravation, shock, embarrassment, lust, pain, and disbelief.

"Have you come to bury your face in it?"

That, among other things.

He can do whatever he wants to me.

He paused, waiting. She nodded, and he was on her before she could suck in a breath. In moments, he had her bent over the desk, shorts around her ankles, and bare ass in the air. They didn't have the mind-altering oil this time, no lubrication other than what they could provide. It was rough and frantic and a touch painful as they returned to their dynamics from their first encounter, and that made it enjoyable for her.

Xenomene awoke to the rooster's call the next morning.

An arm draped over her as Bitcher spooned her naked form. Last night returned in a chaotic jumble. Sex in a proper bed was better than a pallet in a tent, but the possibility of them being discovered heightened the enjoyment.

But behind a locked door, they were able to do so much more.

Blinking a few times, she noted the mess on the floor, the contents of her desk lay scattered. Vaguely, she recalled throwing everything off as he bent her over the surface, sodomizing the hell out of her.

Great, just more shit I've got to clean up on top of my ass being sore.

The rooster crowed, and she glanced out the window, the sky noticeably lighter.

"Fuck!"

She rushed to her feet, searching for her discarded clothes. Bitcher awoke with the near-shout and hurried to gather his trousers and dressed.

"What are you going to say if they catch you coming back in this late?"

He grunted.

"Are you daft, woman? I'll tell them I went to use the chamber pot."

Good!

"You'll need to wash me off you. They'll smell the sex."

"This isn't the first time to let my sword fly from the sheath. I'd rather not."

"Do it anyway."

He swept from her room, mocking her with bows before shutting the door behind him.

What the fuck did I do? Do I want this?

Yes, she did—at least, what they shared, but maybe not him long-term.

If Slurp could do the same things…

But Bitcher made her feel alive, something she hadn't felt since her near-death experience when Mauler's blade lacerated her face.

I can't let anyone find out that we're sleeping together.

A half-moment later, she recanted the sentiment.

Who cares if they find out? If Krey aren't fighting or training, we're fucking.

Chapter 3: Meristal

Meristal rolled her amethyst eyes in disgust as strands of her flaming red hair flapped in the breeze.

The gust rippled through Ralloc's crowded streets. Heavy footfalls of the Royal Guards echoed off the buildings, and her horse's shoes resounded from the cobblestones. The streets overflowed with commoners, merchants, and nobles, hindering Meristal's escort.

When she left the castle that once housed both royal bloodlines of Kothlus and Kothlere, two squads—twenty men—of royal guards accompanied her. Today, the war council came, and the five generals dragged their guards along, too.

In addition, Meristal's personal retinue brought up the rear: the Master of Commerce, the Lord of Coffers, and the Steward of Disbursement. Their total troupe comprised one hundred soldiers, Meristal's guards, the five jyneruls with one scribe apiece, and Meristal's entourage.

A sigh of disdain slipped from her as her horse shifted through the crowded streets.

To make matters worse, she agreed to help Judas with a pesky problem and inherited his vexation: Todd Wynters, the young and overly excited journalist. Now, he hounded her as much as Judas. Since Judas kept away from the capital, she had shown Todd a small thimble of kindness, and he clung like a babe at the breasts.

At one point, she barred him from certain castle sections, mainly the council's chambers, but that only made it worse when she slinked away. He smothered her like the blackness that swaddled the celestial bodies at night. He jumped on any business outside the castle grounds, and he recorded everything with his quill and parchment.

The war council complained of all they lacked, but one stood at the top of their long list: armorers for their two hundred thousand members. With the start of the war, Cape Gythmel's fall, former Consul Kayis Dathyr's death just weeks prior, the army's ranks swelled with conscripts.

Meristal hunted for the skilled laborers, but economics hindered all efforts. Blacksmiths made much more money than they would if recruited into their ranks. When she came calling, most laughed them out of their forge. With what they were offering for their services, she couldn't blame them.

However, they didn't come away empty-handed.

The apprentices saw an opportunity to continue their desired trade and make more money by enlisting. Any apprenticeship received the lowest wages in Ralloc except servants, but servants enjoyed free lodging and meals. With an immediate increase in funds, a rank above normal conscripts, and the choice to retire from the army, the apprentices clambered to serve. Meristal cast a far-reaching net for masters of the craft but came away with workers of minor experience.

Reaching the Anvil of Thunder, the consul dismounted and stretched out her saddle soreness—the last stop inside city walls. Without acquiring this blacksmith, or any others, they'd turn to hiring outside the city, and the costs would soar with moving fees. This smith remained her last sliver of optimism which dimmed by the minute.

As she entered his shop—a barn-like structure easily three times bigger than any she visited yet—a blast of heat rebuffed her. Young men worked, oblivious to their entry; hammers smashed against glowing steel. A quick headcount revealed twice as many apprentices or helpers as the last.

A young man's eyes went wide in recognition of her and the jyneruls.

Today, she wore official robes which echoed those of her royal escort. The inner robe of white silk was covered with an over robe of black and silver stripping. The phthalo blue sash holding the robes closed completed the ensemble. The boy dropped his hammer and iron in his haste to greet them.

"Lady Consul, Jyneruls, how may I be of service?"

"I'd like to speak to the master of the smith," Meristal said.

Though tired and disgruntled, she kept up a gracious appearance and soft voice.

"At once, my lady."

He hurried off, and moments later a mountain of a man loomed before her. His entire body gleamed with sweat, his shoulders were like cannonballs, his chest and back like slabs of iron.

His gray eyes peered through a sweat-coated brow. It took him a moment to recognize them, and then he courtesied.

"Lady Consul," he said.

He reached down and kissed her hand.

"Unhand her, commoner!" Master Jynerul Tyku snapped. "You presume too much!"

The jynerul's hand immediately went for his sword, but Meristal waved him away.

"I don't think he means any harm, do you, Master Jynerul?"

She turned back to the blacksmith.

"That's the nicest greeting I've received today. What is your name, kind sire?"

"Kam, if it pleases you, my lady, though I'm yet a sire."

"Very well, Kam. What's your family name?"

"Vebbek."

"Vebbek."

She frowned.

"I'm unfamiliar with this name. From where do you hail, Kam? May I call you, Kam?"

"Call me anything you wish, my lady. I'm from the Forgotten Isles."

The jyneruls grumbled at his proclamation, and Meristal blushed a shade of light scarlet. She fought for control before speaking again.

"Tell me, Kam, you courtesied and speak as eloquently as a lord of a noble house. Are you of a noble bloodline?"

"I'm of a minor noble bloodline, a distant cousin to the Godfrey family that rules the Isles. As for the standards of the Ralloc though, I'm no more than a commoner."

"I see," Meristal said. "Consider me impressed."

"Thank you, my lady. What brings you to my forge this fine day?"

She smiled.

"You even lie like a nobleman. I'm sure you saw the rain coming down."

"As you say, my lady."

Meristal sighed.

"Alright, enough with proper talk and all that nonsense. It's terrible outside. It's raining buckets, and I'm like a cat when thrown in the horse trough. I hate the rain and whatever gods decided it had to be today."

Kam choked back a laugh at her abrasive demeanor. She imagined the jyneruls shook their heads behind her. Meristal took a breath before continuing.

"Let's be blunt, Kam. I had high hopes when I set out this morning, but I was refused at every turn. You're the last forge in the city, and I have a feeling that I'm wasting my time and yours. So, I won't praise or cajole, I'll just say it. I need men of your profession for the army. Would you be willing to consider joining our ranks and working for us?"

Kam's eyebrows drew downward.

"I find it hard to believe that someone would deny a woman as beautiful as you, my lady."

"Okay, Kam, we are past the flattery and flirting. Let's sidestep that pile of manure and get on with it."

Kam smiled.

"As you wish. I'm not surprised they turned you down. Anyone who took your offer would be mad. On average, blacksmiths make slightly less than you, Consul."

"Last I checked," Meristal corrected, "you make about an ingot less a month, not including expenses and supplies."

An ingot was a small gold bar worth six thousand scepters—or ten gold coins called bright eyes.

"That's a correct assumption, my lady. However, I'm not most. I make more than they do because my products are of higher quality, and I do more business. Moreover, I can barter down my supplies because I buy in bulk and return for more business more quickly. So, in truth, I make nearly as much as you do per month. But you didn't come to argue incomes; tell me what you wish."

"I wish for you to join our ranks as the Master Blacksmith."

Kam grinned at her words.

At least he didn't laugh, that's to his credit.

"I'm sure you appreciate my position, but I'd be a fool to accept, a fact you're well aware of. Out of curiosity, what would you grant me?"

Master Jynerul Tyku came forward and spoke.

"The rank of Master Sergynt, a most generous of offers."

"Generous? That's an insult."

"Contrary," Jynerul Vikal spoke up. "You have no prior military service, no training in arms of war. You'd be in charge of a platoon of fifty men."

"What need do I have of men?" Kam countered. "I need apprentices, not soldiers. Just as I have no time in your army, your soldiers lack experience in the forge."

He pivoted and spoke to Meristal.

"I'm sorry you came all this way to receive a no, but that's my answer."

He turned away when Meristal called out.

"What would it take for you to consider joining?"

He paused in mid-stride, then turned around. He was silent for a moment, his eyes rolling up and to the left as he thought.

"For starters, a larger place, twice as big as this."

"Done."

"And I get to keep it after my time is done."

Meristal paused in consideration as Tyku spoke up.

"If that's the case, you relinquish your hold on this building."

"Agreed."

"What else?" Meristal inquired.

"An officer commission."

A jynerul barked a laugh, but Tyku spoke up.

"You're common born; you can't receive a commission."

"We were making an exception when we offered you Master Sergynt," Jynerul Mecas added.

"Make another," Kam muttered.

"What rank?" Meristal asked.

Again, the jyneruls growled at her back.

"Kernoyl."

"Outrageous!" Tyku barked. "That's for noble houses, and you're a commoner."

"Actually," Meristal held her hand up. "He's a cousin to the Godfrey bloodline, who is king of the Forgotten Isles. At the very least, he's a minor house."

"Still," Jynerul Vikal said.

"I can wave that exception, but you'll not receive the rank of kernoyl," Meristal spoke. "You'll be escalated to the rank of kaptyn. Does that suit you, Kam?"

Kam stood silent for a moment before shaking his head.

"No, the pay cut would be too great. Good day."

He turned to leave.

Damn it! Shades, we were so close.

Too close to just walk away.

"What do you want to compensate for your commission?"

"Consul, I must protest," Master Jynerul Tyku said.

"Either be silent or go away," Meristal hissed. "In case you forgot, we need him, and much more."

She turned back to the blacksmith.

"Well, Kam? Name all your terms."

He was silent for a moment.

"If I'm a kaptyn, then I want the ability to advance in rank. Additionally, I'd like the privilege to do enough work on the side to make the same amount of money that I'm accustomed to. I'll run my work from the new forge here in Ralloc; you will, of course, be providing all the supplies I'd need. If you want a smith in the field, I'll send apprentices in my stead."

"What apprentices?" Jynerul Vikal laughed. "You don't have enough!"

"I'll take all the apprentices that joined your ranks today."

Meristal smiled as she finally caught on.

"You knew we were coming."

"Of course. After you cleared out the other blacksmiths of apprentices, they showed up and tried to bribe mine with better wages."

"I agree to all your terms," Meristal said.

A collective gasp came from those who accompanied her. She held a hand up to silence them. "All except the supplies part. Making additional armor to sell for personal gain will come from your purse."

Kam dipped his head.

"As you command, Consul."

A true smile spread across Meristal's lips, the first of the day.

"Then, it's good to have you in our ranks, Kaptyn Vebbek."

Chapter 4: Starriace

Blood and urine pooled at her feet.

The black fog thinned. The whites of her amber eyes glowed a faint red, echoes of the last torrent—uncontrolled and near fatal.

Her back ached. White-hot pain stabbed her neck as she lifted her head. Bound to a chair, ropes held her prisoner, and the cold metal seared her naked flesh. She noted the dried blood on her breasts, trailing rivulets down to her belly.

A foul odor wafted through the stale, dirty air, and she fought the urge to gag.

But this echoed something from before, and panic flooded her. She swore the voice of Mr. Pleasure reverberated in her ears, along with his haunting laughter, but the room remained devoid of the fat, bald man.

She let out a gasp of relief.

The skin bled where the bindings held her, the flesh raw. She lifted her head, her honeyed hair cascading into her face, obscuring her vision.

Where am I? What happened?

Images raced through her mind in a chaotic burst. Facial hair: gray, red, and black; crooked teeth with dirty smiles leered through the obscurity. No further details bled through, but her captors had numbered three.

Her throat burned. An ache permeated her cold feet, soaked with urine. She jerked to the side and emptied her stomach on the earthen floor.

How long have I been here?

A ringing silence filled her ears; the stillness accentuated each heartbeat. She eyed the shambled stone walls that hemmed her in. Animal traps on rusted iron hooks clung to the walls. Skinning knives, browned with dried blood, lay on shoddy tables. Rotted slats were tacked on overhead, and dirt lay underfoot.

A hunter's cabin?

Her face ached, even her teeth.

Whoever her captors were, they tied her up and left her to die alone.

She scanned the room again for anything she might've missed.

The contents of her backpack lay strung out; the coin purse was gutted. The robes from Judas's manor were strung about. The garments she'd worn lay in tatters next to the skinning knives.

Her gaze swept to the far side of the room, and more chaotic images flashed through her head, each as painful as a physical blow.

Out of sheer rebellion, she yanked against the bindings until her skin bled anew. Hopelessness sank in as her addled mind scrambled to think of a way to free herself. Desperation turned to despair as the faces of all the people she'd never see again flashed through her mind: Lily and Kam, Meristal and Judas, Rusem, Fife…even her short-lived familiar, Ava.

Ava!

Happiness ripped the desolation away. Starriace was their Head of

Creatures; her familiar, Ava, had to come when called.

Ava? Ava! AVA!

"Once is enough, Mistress," the small creature said as she materialized.

Her chiming-bell voice was a sweet melody in the terrible silence.

"By the gods, what happened?"

The fairy fluttered up into Starriace's line of sight.

"You look like shit."

"Thanks."

Starriace's voice sounded hoarse to her ears.

"Who did this to you? How?"

"I don't know, but I can't get out."

Starriace swallowed, afraid to admit she needed help.

I was weak and helpless.

"Free me."

"I can do that."

Ava's hands grew bright with white luminance, and the bindings fell away as she touched each one.

Starriace tried to stand but fell out of the chair. Dirt and grime covered her naked, sweaty body. Sharp pains shot up her legs. Bone grated against bone as she landed.

She cried out.

Ava fluttered down beside her.

"What's wrong?"

"I don't know," Starriace admitted through tears. "I think my legs are broken."

"Can't you heal yourself?"

Starriace reached out with her essence, a lesson she learned with Fife Doole, but a void took its place. In a desperate attempt, she reached out to her surroundings the way Harold had shown her, but she only sensed emptiness.

Even with Ava, she perceived nothing.

The panic returned. She had just learned to call upon her essence, and now, it abandoned her.

"I can't feel my magic. It's not there."

"Whoever did this to you has blocked it, but it's only temporary. To my knowledge, no one's able to block abilities permanently. Most likely, it's an herb or drug. You'll have to wait until it flushes from your system."

An herb or drug?

Starriace's eyes went wide.

"Ava, I need you to find someone for me, bring her here. Can you do that?"

"I can do whatever you ask, if it's within my power."

"There's a woman named Lily; her husband's a blacksmith named Kam, and they live in Ralloc. I can't remember the street name, but they live within the third tier. Are you familiar with Ralloc?"

Ava nodded.

"Bring Lily here. Tell her I sent you, but say Julie asked for her, not my real name."

"But Julie *is* your real name."

Damn, that's right. Ava has only ever known me as Julie—she wasn't there when I accepted who I really am.

"Not anymore. There's no time to explain. You must bring her here. If she has trouble remembering, tell her that she met me at Far Point. She'll remember then."

"And her husband?"

Starriace wanted to see them both, but it was hard enough to let Lily come to her like this. Kam would only salt the wound.

She shook her head.

"No, not him. Not now."

"What if she won't come without him?"

"Tell her my life is at stake. She'll come. Check my pack, there's a letter with directions. Go! Hurry, before they come back."

"As you command."

Ava fluttered over to the pack and rummaged through until she found what she needed. Unfolding the parchment, she read it before leaving in a flash.

Starriace laid her head down as the exhaustion washed over her; shivers and hot flashes taxed her strength. She tried to stay awake, but fatigue carried her to the reclaiming blackness. Gentle hands woke her, and Lily's face and cascading blonde locks swam into view.

"You came," Starriace said, her smile as weak as her voice.

"Of course I did. What in the Shades happened to you?"

Instead of answering, Starriace tried to stir.

"I didn't know if you'd remember me. Why is it so dark?"

"Of course I remember you. How could I forget? You're the only Julie I've ever met. Not a common name around these parts. And it's night."

"Night? When Ava left, it was daylight."

"Yes, I'm sorry, Mistress. The Corridor…there's an army of goblins and trolls there. Did you know?"

Starriace shook her head.

"We need to get her out of here and cleaned up," Lily said.

She turned to Ava.

"Do you think you can take us to Far Point?"

"Yes." Ava nodded. "I have enough to take both of you, but it'll tax me. I'll need to rest afterward."

"They robbed me."

"I'm sure they took more than your money, sweetheart," Lily said, her voice laced with sympathy.

Starriace wasn't sure whether she welcomed or hated the sound. Lily nodded to Ava, who reached out to touch them both. In a flash, they were gone from the small hovel and reappeared in the center of the street in Far

Point. Lily scooped Starriace's naked body off the ground and carried her a dozen strides to a familiar inn.

On her last visit, Starriace, Lily, and Kam had stayed here.

Traveler's Haven remained unchanged from the brief view Starriace managed to snatch. She heard indistinct raised voices, one belonging to Lily who spoke with urgency. Strong hands lifted her and carried her upstairs. The hall seemed as dark as the memories she held dear, and both fostered secrets they'd keep forever.

A door opened, and after a few steps, someone gently placed her on the floor. Footsteps retreated, and the blackness took her again.

When she awoke again, darkness still lingered outside, but warmth embraced her. She found herself lying in a tub of warm water with Lily washing her with gentle strokes, inspecting wounds and chafed skin.

A soft cloth caressed her face.

"What—?"

"Shh, don't talk. Conserve your strength," Lily soothed. "You've been unconscious for a while now. Sorry, I took the liberty of bathing you. The innkeeper was kind enough to lift you into the tub. I think your legs are broken."

"They are."

"Here, drink this."

Lily pushed a warm mug into Starriace's hands. She drank greedily.

"Easy, not so much."

The heated liquid spread through her body. Her woes eased, but her body still throbbed. The contents of the cup made her sleepy.

"Where have you been, Julie? What happened to you?"

"That's not my name," she breathed.

Her eyelids grew heavy.

"What?"

"That's not my name…not my—"

When she awoke again, a dark sky filled her window, but she found herself dressed in sleeping attire. Blankets drew up tight around her. Fever wracked her body.

Lily slumped in a chair beside her. The feather mattress and soft, linen sheets seemed like bliss after her ordeal. A blanket of heavy wool and a large fur pelt lay on top. Starriace stirred, and Lily snapped awake.

"Don't move!"

Lily rushed over to keep her still.

"It's still dark?"

"You slept for two days. Whatever drugs or herbs they used, they used a lot. It might be Oblivion. Kam shook with fever for days when he quit using it. Your shakes reminded me of his recovery."

Starriace smiled at the good news.

"He quit using?"

Lily returned her smile.

"Yes. After we met you, he quit. I think you were the catalyst. It's hard to break the addiction. I think your body is going through withdrawals."

"I can't feel my essence. You once told me about something that can inhibit magic."

Lily nodded.

"Rakette. You think they used that?"

"Maybe. Like I said. I can't feel my essence."

"Hell, most days I can't either, but I don't possess exceptional gifts."

"I do. I've done things, seen things…I can heal myself."

"Perhaps, but you won't be able to do it until the oblivion or rakette is out of your system. I've prayed to the One that you aren't pregnant."

"Pregnant?"

"Shh, don't worry about it now. We can talk later."

Anger smoldered in her gut like the coals of an iron stove, giving her strength.

"We can talk now. What do you mean? Who is the One?"

Lily sighed.

"The One is the god of my religion. I'm not much for it, but when the situation is dire, I renew my faith. I prayed for you. What I mean by you being pregnant…" Lily's eyes misted, "…while I tended your wounds, I discovered that you had …"

"What?" Starriace snapped.

"You showed signs of someone forcing themselves on you."

"How'd you come to that conclusion?"

Lily took a deep breath.

"When I worked for Lord Brenton, some clients liked blonde women, some liked brunettes. Some men liked certain aspects of particular girls. Some tied them up and dominated them. A select, rich few, had darker desires. I've been on the receiving end of that scenario more than once, as have some of the other girls. I know *they* violated you because you carry the same markings."

Starriace fell silent for a moment. The shock twisted into a bright flash of anger and resentment.

Damn it! Now, I feel terrible for snapping at her.

"I'm sorry," she whispered.

As the temper fled, the energy drained from her body, and Starriace shivered.

"Here, drink," Lily said, pushing a mug into her hands. "I'll get you some food."

The woman left, and Starriace sipped the mug. The liquid was cold, but it still warmed her insides like before. The pain retreated, and her shaking subsided. Lily returned shortly with a plate of food.

"It's not much."

Lily handed her a plate of hardened toast, a porridge of oats, and three strips of bacon.

"Thank you." Starriace moved into a sitting position.

"Scoot over."

Lily climbed into the bed. She sat vigil while Starriace ate, and her strength returned. Her stomach lanced with hunger pangs, and she shoveled her food faster.

"What did you mean by that's not my name?"

"Huh?"

"The other day, I called you Julie, and you said it wasn't your name."

"Oh."

Starriace swallowed.

"It's a long story."

"We've got time."

Starriace conveyed the tale, starting after they'd parted ways. She continued with the run-in with the nine elyves and Ava. She recounted the temple inside the City of Despair and her time with Fife, but she omitted his name.

Recounting the sheol attack after leaving Fife's brought a shudder from Lily. Starriace concluded her story with omissions of Rusem but conveyed the battle with Xilor—though not the end. Lily might think her mad if she claimed to be among archangels.

The next thing she remembered was waking up in the hovel, but how she got there remained a mystery.

Lily sat in silence, and Starriace noted the disbelief in her eyes, but what she found most difficult to comprehend was her new name. When asked, Starriace elaborated.

"I've been told that I'm a Wcic, that I come from the *Other Side*, but that's not true. I was born here."

"The *Other Side*? As in, the world with Xilor's followers?"

"Yes. I don't remember anything, though. That's the odd part. I can't remember the life I lived, only from when I woke up."

"That must be awful, to live somewhere else and never remember anything."

"Other than a mild curiosity, it's not that bad. I can't remember, so you can't miss what you've never had."

"True enough."

Lily surmised the events of the war. The Krey mobilization, Cape Gythmel, Warlock Lakayre, the retreat to Dlad City, Meristal as the consul, and Kam joining the Grand Royal Army.

Weariness took Starriace after spending an hour recounting her tale and listening to Lily. Both women fell asleep after, and Lily held her.

When Starriace awoke the next day, her magical essence lingered on the edges of her awareness. Daring to hope, she reached out and caressed Lily with a gentle mental probe and rejoiced at the touch.

Starriace spent the rest of the day, and most of the next, healing herself, starting with her legs. Embarrassment controlled her actions, ashamed each time Lily carried her to the chamber pot.

Mobility became the priority.

After she mended and knitted her bones, she worked on her raw skin and internal bruising.

By the fifth day, her physical injuries were almost gone, but she couldn't heal the mental trauma. Though recalling only flashes, the memories came back as the drugs wore off.

On the sixth day, Starriace made ready to leave. Lily came back from eating in the common room to find Starriace clothed and packed.

"You're leaving?" she asked.

"Yes."

Starriace did not elaborate; it was best if she didn't.

"I wish you weren't. Why don't you come back to Ralloc with me? You can stay with me and Kam until you're ready to do…whatever you do."

"I'm ready now. I'd love to stay, but I need to do certain things."

Starriace closed her eyes and considered how to best tell Lily without revealing too much or hurting feelings. Once before, Lily implored Starriace to come with her, and she never knew how close Starriace came to giving in. She treasured Lily with a zeal that rivaled her cravings for knowledge, and as her only friend, Starriace couldn't afford nor wanted to lose her.

The mage opened her eyes and hugged Lily before pushing her down on the bed, seating her.

"There's a war going on. I missed the start, but I'm strong and should help."

Lily's brow furrowed.

"How strong?"

Everyone possessed magic and used it to some degree, but most relied on their own hands and skills.

"Exceptionally. Perhaps someday I'll rival Warlock Lakayre. But I'm lacking, my training is incomplete, and I need to discover a better way to tap into my abilities. I plan to join the war and stop Xilor."

"You'll die," Lily blurted. "Don't do this!"

"I can't," she shook her head. "I can't turn my back on people in need. People will die, are already dying. The quicker this war can end, the more people we'll save. You, Kam, me, everyone. If I can help stop Xilor, if I can destroy him…I have to try. I can't explain it; it's a compulsion. A *duty*."

Lily shook her head.

"I understand what you're saying, but why you?"

"If not me, who?"

To this, Lily said nothing. Starriace reached down and kissed Lily on the forehead.

"I care for you. You're my dearest friend. If anything were to happen to you…"

Starriace wasn't good with expressing feelings.

"You and Kam. If anything happened to the two of you, I don't think I'd ever stop blaming myself if I didn't try."

Lily's eyes misted.

"You're always welcome in our home. Promise me that if you ever come to Ralloc, you'll visit."

"I promise."

The young woman reached down and kissed the older on the cheek. She broke the embrace as fond memories of Kam resurfaced, and called to Ava. The familiar answered promptly. Ava stood on the bed next to Lily. "Ava, I want you to take Lily back to where you found her. And when you're done, I want you to return to the Melodic Mountains. Don't come back to me."

"But I want to go with you. I'm supposed to."

"Where I'm going, you can't follow. When I'm done, I'll call you, I swear. But I have a request, Ava."

"What?"

"I want you to go to Lily if she ever has dire need."

"You want me to answer her call? It doesn't work that way. We only respond to the Head of Creatures, not to everyone who wants to see a fairy."

"Ava."

Starriace knelt to be eye level with the fairy.

"Lily's my dearest friend, and I'd want to help if she were in peril. I'd be greatly distraught if I never knew. So, will you do this for me? Lily would never call unless the need were dire."

"It's not supposed to work like that."

"Do it for me, and I'll owe you one."

"Owe me one?"

"Yes, if you do this for me, later when you ask something of me, I'll do it for you."

"But you are supposed to, you're the Head of Creatures."

"I meant in regards to something personal."

"Oh."

"Please?"

"Very well, if you insist, but you owe me."

"Yes, I owe you."

Starriace rose, and Lily stood from the bed. The two embraced, long and fierce.

"Thank you."

"No thanks is required. You'd do the same for Kam or me. You're a good person."

No, not really.

But some things were better left unsaid.

Ava touched Lily, and in a flash, they were gone, leaving Starriace alone.

She sank to the bed, her knees weak. It was the second time Lily left, and for the second time, a hole formed in her chest. She heaved a deep breath and fought back tears of loneliness and despair.

With Lily's absence, ire swelled inside her, the hovel returning in grisly flashes. Lily's words rang with the truth. Her captors had violated her.

How long was she captive? She couldn't guess. The most painful part: she'd been powerless to stop it.

You were weak and helpless.

She ground her teeth as resolve anchored in the pit of her stomach. She drew on that power, teleporting away.

When she came through to the other side, the insides of the hovel filled her vision. She retraced her steps, detecting a concentration of her essence like a dog hunting unseen prey. But more than her essence, she recognized the presence of the three men.

They defiled you!

She ran a light hand over the makeshift tables, the chairs, the tools, traps, and knives. Though faint, she sensed them, like a scent lacking strength from the passage of time. Her fingers touched the rough surfaces, the leather, the metal, and more memories hammered her.

And it eroded all doubt.

She jerked her hand away as if shocked by lightning, their faces filling her mind. What she sensed was more emotion than physical, and perhaps the drugs blocked it out.

The difference was between knowing it happened and reliving it.

Her simmering resentment turned to rage. Her eyes burned, itched, festered, and the crackling power beneath her skin screamed for release.

And she would, on this place, on them.

In that moment, she lost control. All around her, the furniture shattered. A table flung across the room, slamming into the wall, a new permanent resident. The chains glowed red-hot and melted; the leather that once bound her burst into flame.

In moments, the hovel was engulfed. The roof groaned and collapsed, but her mageshield held the flaming debris at bay.

Destroying the hellhole empowered her, but it wasn't enough.

What those men did to you, they will do to someone else.

Enough of their essence lingered for a trace. She sensed them to the north, just past Far Point.

Damn it! I was just there!

She wondered how they managed to get so far just by walking or horseback.

They'd left her for dead.

Drawing on her power, she teleported south of their position, and ensured they wouldn't detect her arrival. Without knowing for sure if they had magical abilities, she erred on the side of caution.

Praema touched the southern horizon, with Apor already well below. The darkness deepened and soon her glowing eyes would shine like beacons.

With quiet care, she foraged through the foliage, bypassing branches where she could. She drew up to a broad cedar tree and peeked around. When she saw the men, crimson filled her vision. Her hand yearned for her wand.

Rounding the tree, she marched for them, her footsteps sure, a storm of energy and malice building in her wake.

The men sprang to their feet. One drew an arrow and let it fly.

Starriace batted it away with a wave of her wand. While he knocked another, one man drew a sword and rushed forward.

Calling upon her power, she melted the sword, the liquid steel melted and pooled like mercury.

By this time, the archer loosed another arrow. A barrier flared between them, and the projectile shattered apart. The third man attempted to sneak up behind her, circling wide. She pivoted, slamming an invisible fist into his chest, and he doubled over.

The swordless man almost took her by surprise.

She spun from his grasp and lashed out. Her sweeping arm sent a surge of power that tore his head free of his shoulders.

The archer let a third arrow fly.

Her splayed fingers stopped the projectile in mid-flight; it quivered mere inches from her face. She peered at the shaft of wood, then it faded into a mist of granules, breaking down to the molecular level.

The archer dove for another arrow.

The man she knocked down sprang to his feet and charged.

A stone as big as her fist caught her eye. Her power flared, and she drove the stone through his chest.

A massive cavity of red pulp remained.

Starriace turned to the sole survivor who abandoned his bow, knowing the futility.

"Sit!" she commanded.

She felt the malevolence pouring from her, and damn it felt good.

"I believe you owe me something."

Chapter 5: Judas

Judas sat in his assigned room. The commanding officer, Kernoyl Tyku, ensured he received adequate quarters. The hotel, *The Royal Scepter*, was ostentatious by design, built to pamper the elite. Silk sheets, rare art, antiques, and ever-present attendants came standard. The Grand Royal Army commandeered the establishment for its senior ranks.

Luxury lived low; prices fell with each staircase. In Dlad City, like Ralloc, status was measured by the distance traversed. Budget-conscious patrons lugged up the stairs.

Judas's room stood adjacent to the kernoyl's quarters on the first floor.

The warlock sat, nursing an imported drink from the Isles. Koja rum comforted the aging exile, but he missed the quiet of his home. Upon first sampling, it reminded him of a rum hailing from the Stratu'Geim domain. The amber liquid remained his first choice, a smooth swallow of peaches and vanilla with a hint of spiciness beneath.

In truth, the hotel offered the same amenities of home but not familiarity.

A low fire crackled in the hearth.

His cool azure eyes drooped with weariness as he paused reading the dull volume about dwaven and centaur conflicts. He'd read many on the subject; this volume, written by a maghai historian, had dry prose that matched numerous religions.

With a sigh, he closed the book and rubbed his eyes. A lock of his long hair fell free from behind his ear before he swept it back in place.

A knock on the door shattered his fragile cocoon of solace.

"Enter."

The door opened as Kernoyl Tyku swept in like a gust of spring wind. Judas rose from his seat.

"Kernoyl, how may I help you?"

The kernoyl stayed silent for a moment, taking in the room. As far as Judas knew, every room held soft rugs, stained hardwood floors, stark white hearths, and feather-stuffed indulgence.

The officer took a chair opposite him and broke the silence. Judas mirrored him, taking a sip of his rum.

"Why doesn't the Krey do-don attend our meetings?"

Judas snorted.

"I thought that obvious."

"No."

"Why would she? Your men are jackasses."

Tyku blinked.

"What?"

"You heard me; your officers are jackasses. They treat her as inferior because she's a woman. In reality, she could kill them all without an exerted breath. If she endured any more, she might go nuts."

He took another pull of his drink, rolling the liquid over his tongue before swallowing.

"I'm half-tempted to watch the debacle."

"My officers brought it to my attention. They're worried the Krey aren't being watched closely enough."

"Watched? What are they? Impotent children? Half of your battle preparations originated from Xenomene."

Tyku blanched.

"I doubt that!"

Judas chuckled.

"You can lie to yourself, but not to me. I was at those meetings. Each time she presented an idea, your men distracted you. When she quit coming, her suggestions were regurgitated by your underlings."

Tyku looked distant for a few moments.

"She needs to come back."

"Why? So they can mock and regard her with disdain again? Leave them be. I'll admit, I used to look down on them, the ones inflicted with the bloodlust 'malady,' but they dove in front of your men while Xilor's horde poured through the wall. The Krey saved your army, not me."

"You held the dragons at bay."

"True, but they saved your men from immediate death. The enemy would carve a swath through you, but the Krey stopped them. You didn't call them, they came of their own accord, hearing me shout 'stand to.' It should be them in these rooms, not us, half of which haven't seen battle yet."

"If what you say is true, then, so be it. I'll take the meyjours and the kaptyns to council and dismiss the leftenants."

Judas shook his head.

"We have three brigades here, maybe more. It should be you and the other two kernoyls. Trust your men to be officers and let them inform the others."

Tyku shook his head.

"They'll never go for that."

"I thought you were in charge. You make the call, not them. Besides, rumors say a jynerul will be headed here soon. Have your men in hand before he arrives."

"A jynerul? That means a division and fifty thousand more troops. Where are we going to put all of them?"

"I reckon we build additional quarters. I'll talk with Xenomene, but I strongly advise you keep your council small."

"What about you?"

Judas's lips twisted.

"I'm not a man of warfare. Strategy and fortifications are best left to those who live it. If it comes to mystics, well …" he took another swig of his rum, "… that's my department."

Tyku stood and cleared his throat.

"I'll consider what you've said. The kernoyls and I are opening up a case of my cigars from the Forgotten Isles. Would you care to join us?"

Judas studied him. He rarely did anything spontaneously, but there were occasions.

"Yes, I think I will."

The warlock stood and froze. His eyes grew distant for a brief instant.

"It can't be …" he muttered.

"What?" Tyku asked.

Judas blinked as if surprised to see the kernoyl there.

"I felt her."

"Who?"

"My apprentice, Starriace. She's angry. No, that's not the right word. She's furious."

Judas turned his gaze south, in the hearth's direction. With his mind, he searched beyond the walls of stone.

"She's nearby. Just beyond the Corridor."

"You can't be thinking of going. Xilor has minions all over the place!"

Judas waved the younger man's concerns away.

"I'm not worried about goblins and trolls."

Judas gathered up his travel cloak and the small leather satchel he had carried on his person since the Battle of Cape Gythmel. In battle, it was difficult to find a sliver of mirror to cast a Psimond spell. He downed the rest of his drink and set the glass on a small, white, marble stand.

"I need …"

The warlock searched his room in haste, checking his robes and bag.

"What?"

"I need some investigators. You wouldn't happen to have any, would you?"

"You mean criminal investigators?"

"Yes."

"Of course, we're a division strong. Crimes happen, but why would you need them?"

Judas paused and turned to him.

"My apprentice is young and determined, mentally and emotionally unstable because of the Corridor of Cruelty."

Tyku frowned.

"Then, why did you let her go?"

"I didn't; she left in the night. I can only feel her when she's close or experiencing a potent emotion. I felt her hate, her…malice. Whoever wronged her may die or is already dead. I need investigators."

"When did you become a pessimist?"

Judas stopped and glanced at the man.

"I'm a realist. They can look for clues where she might have headed, while I search with my magic. Bring them to me, I'll take them with me when I teleport."

Tyku nodded and fled the room.

Judas pulled his small mirror from his bag. With a wave of his fingers, the surface swirled green. Meristal's face materialized on the other end.

"Judas?"

"Meristal. Are you busy?"

"Yes, I'm about to finish my meeting with my War Council. Do you need me?"

There was something in her voice, almost a plea.

"Yes, whenever possible, I need you to meet me."

"Dlad City?"

"No, south of the Corridor. Can you make it?"

She nodded.

"Yes."

"I'll see you, then."

Judas cut the communication and tucked the mirror back into the bag. Tyku burst through the door a moment later with three young wizards in tow. The warlock looked them over.

"Any of you investigated before?"

They nodded in unison. Judas glanced at Tyku.

"Aye, they've done investigations, but nothing like you're thinking."

Judas nodded.

"Very well. Grab hold."

They teleported from the room to the mouth of the Corridor of Cruelty—a narrow strip bridging the Abyss—behind Xilor's massive camp. They went unnoticed, as he could teleport without the telltale signs of a swirling blue mist. Judas saw the effects, but those of lesser power wouldn't be able to.

He entered the Corridor with the three young wizards on his heels, and by the time they emerged on the other side, the sunless sky engulfed the land in darkness. Once again, the others held on as he teleported away.

When they stepped through the last teleport, smoke and the smell of charred meat—the latter not quite right—filled the air. Judas cleared the last of the foliage hiding the campsite. As it came into view, the wizards bustled into a flurry of activity.

He walked among the campsite, examined the bodies, checked their clothing and armor, weapons, and bags. Evidence suggested that at least four people were involved, maybe more, and three lay dead.

The fourth was nowhere to be found.

An unsettling cloud hung in the air, an acrid scent that turned his stomach. Judas hadn't endured the uneasy queasiness since the Wizard's War as a young man, a clash of all races that started before his birth. By the time Judas reached the Age of Maturity, the Great War had spilled out and engulfed the entire realm. Old scores became fresh wounds. Most battle lines were drawn along the races with very few coalitions until the end.

During the carnage emerged Xilor, dubbed a dark lord, and his presence sent shock waves through Ermaeyth. Instead of creating more disorder, the races consolidated against the new threat.

Xilor might've started the war, Judas suspected, but had he remained hidden until every race wiped each other out, he might've succeeded.

Pride became his undoing.

Many souls perished in Xilor's fall. When they finally met face to face, Xilor's arrogance only saw Judas as a nonthreatening boy. Only at the end did Xilor take him in earnest.

And Judas defeated him.

Under duress, Judas could slow time to a crawl. Every use terrified him. Even now. But the day he faced Xilor, he chose terror over annihilation.

Memories scattered as someone slammed into him—a group of someones.

"Warlock Lakayre!" a young man exclaimed.

Judas eyed him.

How the hell did he find me?

It seemed like a lifetime ago that young Todd interviewed him in Dlad City. Beyond him, wizards in many different colored robes set about the place, working in tandem with the investigators.

"Who're you?" Judas teased him.

"It's me. Todd! From the *New Suns Times*, the paper in Ralloc, remember? We started your interview but never finished."

Judas gave a single shake of his head.

"No."

"I interviewed you at Dlad City. You invited me."

"You showed up hours before the scheduled time!"

"Oh, so you do remember?"

Todd smiled, catching Judas in a trap.

"I—" Judas closed his mouth and opened it again. "Yeah, I remember. What do you want? Why are you here?"

"I followed Meristal's entourage out of the castle. Hey, when are we going to be able to finish the interview?"

"Not now, Todd, I'm busy."

He pointed to the carnage around them.

"Catch me in Ralloc; we can set up a time then. Now would be inappropriate, like trying to continue the interview in the middle of a funeral."

Judas marked the embarrassing flush across Todd's face as he glanced around the carnage.

The warlock walked toward the crime scene and focused on the nearest wizard standing close by.

"What happened? Find anything yet?"

"We're still gathering information," answered the younger man.

Judas's lips thinned as his gaze fell to the campsite, searching for anything amiss—their possessions, the way the bodies lay, where their horses were supposed to be. Two were missing. At least he assumed so and vocalized that.

"Yeah, it's strange, one horse? They wouldn't travel with two walking and one riding. Maybe if one were a woman or a child, but that's not the case. Perhaps one was sick?"

"No, they traveled with three horses. Two are missing. Whoever they happened upon was most likely traveling by foot and took the horses for faster travel. Check the horse for a branding so we can track down the other two."

Judas didn't voice his suspicions, but this unfortunately reeked of his apprentice.

The younger man did as instructed, grabbing an aide and checking the horse. The investigators clustered together before making their way to him, and he had an idea of what they were going to say before they spoke.

"What did you find?" he asked them.

"Well," the woman spoke, "whoever did this isn't powerful."

"What makes you say that?"

"Because they wouldn't need the horses, and they could just teleport away."

"Okay."

Judas didn't follow her logic, but in normal circumstances, she might be right. He turned to the younger man.

"What about you?"

"I'm not sure what to think. Nothing makes sense. We can't even get a lead on these people. We don't know anything about them or how they died."

"I thought it obvious. That one right there," Judas said, pointing, "is missing a head. It's pretty obvious how he died. The middle one was killed by a wound to the chest with a blunt object. Maybe a hammer or a magically propelled object like a rock. Whatever it was, the wound isn't consistent with a stab wound, thrown or otherwise. The third is charred beyond recognition, most likely burned alive, but let's not rule out any possibilities just yet."

As he finished his sentence, a woman teleported into their midst. Everyone who noticed her gave a quick bow before continuing with their tasks. Judas bowed, too, but for different reasons. He knew the importance of position and rank.

"Judas," Meristal said.

A warm smile crossed her lips but faltered when she saw the slaughter.

"Gods and homugons! Who did this?"

Meristal's haunting features turned to abhorrence, but even then, Judas still found her beautiful. Not a single lock of her reddish-orange hair was out of place. Her wide amethyst eyes swept the scene. Her dark robes made her porcelain skin stand out.

"I have theories."

"Give me a report?"

She looked from Judas to the young investigating officers.

"Nothing solid yet, Consul," the young man spoke in a rush, fumbling over the words. "The man on the left died by decapitation, the middle one by a blunt object of considerable force, and the third most likely burned from the fire, but we aren't ruling anything out yet."

Judas gave the young man a long look, silently amused that he repeated everything he'd stated. The girl took the opportunity to speak up.

"That horse has no identifying marks, it's possible the other two didn't as well."

"And my work here is done," Judas said with a hint of lilting sarcasm.

Meristal grinned, eyeing the workers and him.

"I must say, Judas, good work on the findings. What do you think happened?"

The warlock mulled over his thoughts before he chose to speak, growing older and wearier as he said it.

"The two unburned bodies are wearing lightweight, dark armor. If you kick them now, their armor won't jingle or make a sound. This type of armor is usually made for and worn by assassins, so they won't be heard as they go about fulfilling their contract. Assassins aren't the only ones who use this armor. Highly skilled thieves do, too."

"Thieves?" the young woman asked. "You mean like from the Sleight of Hand Society?"

"Yes, the same. There are other guilds and factions that we don't know much about. It's possible a rival ambushed them, and their loot was confiscated."

Inwardly, Judas cringed. He didn't lie necessarily, he theorized, but it skirted too close to that horrid feeling. What did these men do to anger Starriace…his daughter?

"Interesting theory," the boy admitted. "I would've never made that assessment. It's a shame you're not part of our investigation squad."

The young man and woman left when a superior called them away. No doubt they were telling their peers the warlock had already solved the case. Meristal eyed them before turning back to Judas.

"Now that we have the public's take and what facts are going in the official report, what aren't you saying?"

Judas exhaled slowly.

"Someone with a better than average understanding of magic did this. There was something the mage wanted, something important. That burned body wasn't consumed by their fire. It isn't hot enough to burn the skin completely off or char the bones black."

"So, a mage is responsible, but what's their possible incentive? How can you be sure it was a wizard? It could have been a witchen."

A witchen was a vile mage who relied on the fourth form of magic: Derengi. Their conjury relied upon necromancy, reincarnation, pestilence, and dealing with the souls of the Underworld. Most users turned evil, tainted by their gifts, and relied upon incantations like the Plotus, Mussari, and Owlen branches.

He looked at the burned body and shook his head.

"That body was blasted by a fire spell which burned the body. Derengi played no part in this. The bodies show blunt trauma where a witchen would've disintegrated the person and armor, like acid eating flesh."

Meristal sighed with relief.

"Okay, so one attacker, not a witchen. It's better than searching for two."

"There could have been two."

"What?"

"See that man's rib cage? It is pushed out from the body. He wasn't attacked from the front but from behind. The force of impact pushed his rib cage out."

"You think there are two murdering wizards?"

"No, I never said there were two wizards. I said that one was killed by a wizard. This is pure speculation, though. I could be wrong."

"So…this person is psychotic and intelligent? That's a deadly combination."

A darkness flickered within Judas. The pang he endured by Meristal's words cut to the core of his soul. Did she really think his daughter was a monster?

If you only knew.

"Yes, it is a deadly combination, and that worries me."

"We can look back on the files at Ralloc for possible suspects which will take a lot of time. Any ideas on who it might be?"

"Only one, my dear, and it's not good."

"Who?"

How much do I divulge? It'd hurt Meristal if she finds out I wasn't honest. But if I'm forthright, Meristal will have me teleporting all over creation.

"Are you aware of anyone who might be semi-powerful with more than average knowledge of magic? One who might be traveling on foot and smart enough not to teleport away from the scene of the crime because of recognizable signs of teleportation?"

"Mother of gods, don't tell me…"

"I told you it's not good."

"We have to find her, Judas. Find her and bring her back before she does anything else."

"If she wants to be found."

"We must try, for her sake."

"If I know anything about her, after this, she'll stay as far away from me and Ralloc. South would be my guess, this side of the Corridor. In fact, I don't think she'll ever willingly set foot in the Corridor again."

He sighed.

"If she did this, I'm sure she feels remorse. Guilt will keep her from resurfacing for a time."

"You must find her! Promise me you'll make an effort to find Julie before she does something like this again!"

Judas didn't reply.

His eyes found hers, and at that moment, each knew the other's fears.

Xilor was bad enough, but now, they could be watching the origins of a second dark lord.

Chapter 6: Norek

The heavy smell of salt clung to the air as the rickety ship rocked from the swells below. Every small change in the water made the vessel groan and shudder as if it would break into a thousand pieces, but it would hold.

It better hold.

Norek had taken King Godfrey's advice and fled the tiny islands.

Perhaps advice is too kind of a word. Commanded, more like.

Sound advice, nonetheless.

The king's eerie, cold gaze still sent chills down Norek's spine. A beast lay within Godfrey, scarcely under control. Norek realized how much of a monster the king was when the woman relayed the tale of a family's gruesome end.

The woman.

The thought of the blonde brought a smile to his face. He'd been with women before, most of the time because he loved them on a certain level. However, Norek was jaded in those matters and no longer saw an emotion but an illusion.

He'd given up on those foolish notions.

Still, there were times when he'd feel the call of flesh and visit brothels. Norek had been intimate with enough women to know what to do, what he liked, and what he didn't. With her, however, the king's gift brought about a novel experience. Norek wanted to ravish her, but she wouldn't let him. He'd never been with a woman like that before.

Every culture was different, but Islander perversion horrified him at first. The wandering mage encountered many societies in his travels. Once, in Merlul, across the Golden Sea in Cronele, he made love to a woman with his mind, their bodies never touching.

After finishing with the Islander woman, he moved to dress like he would in a brothel, but she remained for the night. Each recurrence came just as fascinating as the last.

At dawn, she left.

When he asked for her name, a giggle escaped her, and she walked out without a word. For all he knew, she could have been a whore or servant, even the king's own daughter, but he doubted the last.

The pounding of running footsteps sounded above. Ropes scraped as sailors hauled them across the deck. Shouted orders rang clear no matter the distance between the topside and his small, cramped cabin.

Norek took a berth below the crew quarters. In all honesty, Norek was closer to the ocean than topside. Below Norek lay the cargo hold, vast stores of non-perishable items and the iron tanks of drinkable water.

The galley claimed its home two decks above Norek, the mess deck and the wardroom for the officers. The kaptyn resided in the next deck above, his cabin, sitting room, and sleeping quarters.

Another flight of stairs took him topside.

Each day Norek spent at sea, he practiced his Owlen skills, a dying art. Legends ago, back when Ermaeyth was riddled with prophecy, Owlen users were as abundant as Plotus users. As time wore on, the prophecies were left untended, either repressed or assumed inert, and the art began its slow death. Now, there were probably only a few thousand Owlen mages left. Of those thousands, only a couple of dozen held enough power in foretelling or battle.

But that didn't deter Norek. He grasped many things with his ability that he otherwise wouldn't. When he told the king that scrying the future was difficult, he didn't lie. However, Norek found that as he viewed his own destiny, it transpired more than not. Sometimes it altered slightly with his foreknowledge, but most of the time, it happened as envisioned.

He did, however, lie about his parents. He believed they were alive.

Many times, he scried the past, searching for the day of his birth, and was successful only once. Despite that, he remembered the woman who held him. She cried tears of joy and told him that she loved him before someone took him from her arms. Only the woman filled his orb, her face permanently etched in his mind. He never saw the vision again, nor did he spy his father to his knowledge.

Though he always believed his mother lived, now he was certain.

Lying in his swinging hammock, Norek tried to doze through the day but rarely succeeded from the noise, intense heat, and humidity. Fat droplets of sweat clung to his brow. His body never acclimatized to the harsh weather despite time spent on the Isles. The oppressive weather was nearly unbearable, and he only ventured topside during the first and last rays of light.

The crew complained to their kaptyn, expressing fears he might be a vampire due to nightly excursions. True, Norek preferred nights when on a ship or in big cities. At sea, the night cooled considerably, and in the city, nightlife was full of surprises, excitement, and lively entertainment—not only plays and stage performances, but vices, too.

And Norek loved his vices.

He stirred in the hammock, reaching for the small glass orb on his night table. He shook it and blew hot breath over the surface before whispering as if to caress it awake. The globe brightened, and a fog swirled inside before revealing what he sought.

Inside, an image appeared—of a beautiful woman he'd never met but whom his heart longed for.

When the king asked him to scry Ralloc, Norek was rewarded with a glimpse of the past: his mother. Her face filled his vision and his one sacred memory.

But another image of a woman appeared, too, beautiful but far younger.

My age?

The second image frustrated him. He first scried her over two seasons ago. Sometimes she'd be clear and resolute, other times faded or incorporeal.

Every day since leaving the Isles, he scried his future and saw the younger woman, a constant in his fate. Generally, when something appears every day for a period of time, it is considered a constant. Nothing short of his or her death would change the fact that she'd show up in his life. He didn't know her—his new constant—any more than he knew his mother.

When he first scried the young woman, she manifested resolute and unwavering. Now, her image darkened to a silhouette, and he could no longer distinguish her features.

Each scry showed the duo side by side; now, the shadowed woman loomed in the distance, encompassing the glass sphere in darkness. Everything darkened by her shadow, everything but his mother. He reflected each night on this woman, and in the end, only one hypothesis rang true.

She's going to kill me.

It was an unsettling thought. He strove to be kind and caring, wronging as few people as possible.

But that's why women walk all over me.

He sighed, frustrated, and turned his thoughts away from the darker shadow and focused on his heart's desire. She was beautiful and alluring. Driven by passion, he set out to find her. Norek discovered her name and where she resided, but would she be there when he arrived?

He hoped so.

He first discovered his mother when he wandered far from Ralloc's domain. Across the sea in a cluster of small islands—not the Isles—he trained under an ancient sect of wizardkind. Unsure of how venerable they were or who their ancestors had been, and assuming it rude to ask, he left the question unvoiced. These islands lay beyond all domains, and nobody claimed sovereignty.

It didn't bother him that they may not be wizardkind; on the contrary, he loved spending time with those outside his race. Wizardkind, to him, insinuated boredom. Rude, obnoxious, self-centered, quick-tempered, judgmental, an unending and less-than-important list.

There were a few small outcroppings of wizardkind he did want to meet—one had been the Islanders, another would be the people from the city Stratu'Geim. His lifetime goal was to meet the Krey, the Black Tide of Outpost Dire.

He turned his thoughts back to his mother. When he discovered her again in the presence of King Godfrey, he smothered his immediate joy. He could sense her presence through the orb, giving him a general direction, and boarded a vessel for the Golden City.

The kaptyn took him reluctantly. The ship's master studied him with wise, brown eyes, wisdom attained from years on the seas. Norek realized the kaptyn didn't intend to take him, so he doubled the offer.

"Any man who's willing to pay that much for passage is desperate and running from something."

He informed the kaptyn that the king commanded him to leave and never return. More sympathetic, he agreed at twice the price.

Norek formulated his plan by the moment. He needed to reach Ralloc and warn them of the Islander's impending arrival. Though the ship wouldn't take him directly to the capital, the Golden City was the closest port. From there, he'd travel across the northern peninsula, steering clear of the Vikal Mountains and the elyves within.

Ralloc lay due west.

He let his thoughts of the long journey go and turned back to his mother.

She seemed somber now, and he wondered what troubled her. His own spirits soared. He found his mother at last, and nothing would keep him from finding her and getting to know her. His heart thrummed with anticipation; his face lightened with a warm smile as he spoke her name.

Foreign, but it felt so right, fitting.

"Meristal Raviils."

Chapter 7: Xenomene

The two virgins the heir sent turned out to be not-so-useless after all.

Xenomene was impressed, even with Smokey, despite his ecstatic announcement regarding her backside. He was actually good, though his weapon choice was odd: a two-handed war hammer.

When they entered the battle meld, the squad functioned smoothly with the newest members—like a well-worn shoe, almost as if they'd always been a part of their group. The Mind ran them through drills and formations, switching the leader, and reshuffling personnel.

Bitcher returned to normal, which everyone both hated and loved, like having a sick, detestable sibling return to full health. At times, he pissed her off so bad that she wanted to crush his throat with her boot.

I can't believe I slept with that asshole again!

But the murderous moments were fleeting. Other times, she couldn't wait to bed him.

Xenomene tried to infuse herself into the War Council consisting of Warlock Lakayre, the ranking kernoyl, and all subordinate officers, but they never accepted her. Judas listened and agreed with most of her suggestions, such as digging pits and fortifying the gates with interlocking iron arms. The junior officers distracted Kernoyl Tyku with woes of low supplies, the forge smashing out new armor, and estimates of out of service scabs due to illness, or with their own fortification ideas.

Not long after, she quit attending.

They just want me to jump in front of them and die.

Their days consisted of drilling, mock-fights, building and running an obstacle course, and maintenance on their armor. Nights became regular with visits from Bitcher. One night, she entered her office and noticed the additions of several mirrors, no doubt confiscated from the third deck. Bitcher staged them so she could watch him penetrate her.

She had to admit that it turned her on.

Of course, she reminded him to avoid discovery by the others. She didn't necessarily care, but she preferred privacy. Who wouldn't? She knew they'd find out, but until then, she craved the secret intimacy.

The secret didn't last long.

Two nights after she dragged Bitcher from his rack and slapped sense into him, they were caught. The Mind swept into her office while they enjoyed the rhythms perfected by the gods, literally catching Xenomene with her pants down and bent over her desk. Bitcher had either forgotten or intentionally left the door unlocked.

The Mind's sudden entrance made both turn; however, Bitcher didn't bother to stop.

"Shut the fucking door!" she snapped.

Instead of leaving, the Mind entered, closed the door, and locked it. He attended them for a spell, and with the mirrors, she watched the excitement dance across his face. She also noticed the bulge in his trousers.

Who invited him to join, she could never remember, but she desired it. Zeal on the Mind's part hurt her more than she imagined.

After the Mind left, Bitcher, in an unexpected move, pulled Xeno close and held her.

"I'm sorry, I shouldn't have offered you to him, but I saw you watching. I didn't think he'd hurt you. If we ever invite anyone again, I'll never offer what isn't mine. I was trying to make sure you were satisfied. We'll take a break so you can recover."

He didn't say anything else; he didn't have to. She was grateful that he wasn't a complete asshole. He held her until she stopped trembling, and after a while, he shifted to leave.

"Wait. We do this every day, and I don't know your name."

Bitcher's brow flickered downward.

"Does it matter?"

"To me. I want to know."

"It's Jakeb."

He left.

True to his word, they took a break. Dewgrass, the multipurpose herb for pain, swelling, fevers, and chills, quickened recovery. Three days later, at her behest, their conjugal sessions resumed.

Xenomene, despite the worst of her exchange with the Mind and Bitcher, enjoyed the congress, especially when Bitcher mounted her from behind and she lay pressed between them.

She spied the Mind the following day after their tumble; they shared a smile, but both kept their distance.

The last thing I want is for my men to start treating me like the team whore.

The cons far outweighed any advantage.

Days peeled by in mock combat; most members tested the virgins and their unorthodox weapons. Surprisingly, the recruits held their own quite well. Xenomene even engaged them, smacking them down with playful disdain, insulting them with superior mastery.

Mauler had inflicted the scar on Xenomene's face, but she was no longer in the same league of swordplay. Xenomene's skills surpassed most in the House Eti—the House of the Sword—if not all, and she had trained with elyfian. She wasn't infallible, but thus far, remained undefeated.

One of these days, I'm going to lose, and it'll be the death of me.

While she battled the virgins through a rolling peal of laughs from her squad, she tried teaching the newest additions. If they didn't learn by the end of their first battle, two new faces would replace them. She taunted their faults with japes and slaps of the blade, but drove the point home with sharp words and clipped tones when left exposed for a killing blow.

After an hour with both, she let the other Krey take turns. When finished, their attention turned to weapon and armor maintenance.

It'd be shitty timing if battle started now. Good way to die.

Guilt wracked her. The deaths of her brothers-in-arms at Cape Gythmel still haunted her. Two-Tons fell with an unlucky and fatal shot, but he wasn't the only one who perished.

Raven, their do-don, died when a troll had snuck up the mountain of bodies. She and her squad responded in kind, sending the troll tumbling down the hill in seven pieces, but the damage was done. Xenomene could accept a death by the sword, but death by an arrow was a dishonorable stain, not for the Krey who fell, but for the coward who wielded the bow.

With armor maintenance behind them, they enjoyed their midday meal and took an hour of reprieve. She used this time to catch up on correspondence with the heir and whoever else deemed her worthy of letters. She even received a short and formal parcel from Consul Meristal Raviils, offering condolences for the fallen Krey, and praise for their efforts against the invading army.

The letter closed with a saying, "Thank you for saving countless lives with your service and sacrifices."

Xenomene had never met the woman but was drawn to her. She'd taken the time to write the letter herself instead of having a minion pen it. The signature matched the rest of the body.

Warlock Lakayre also wrote to her, even though he was in the same city. He kept her apprised of all the proceedings of the meetings held in her absence.

After their reprieve, the Krey spent the next several hours conditioning, maneuvering their obstacle course, running a set distance, or lifting heavy objects for repetition. Xenomene was the weakest in weight training, other than the Heart. Even Mauler, who boasted more mass than Xenomene, lifted circles around her.

To everyone's surprise, Mauler could lift more than the Heart, Xeno, Wrath, and Patch.

Where Xeno floundered in one aspect, she excelled at the others, such as the obstacle course and running, loving the former but loathing the latter. In battle, she relied less on brute strength and more on agility. A sharp blade made her untouchable. Dexterity played a huge part; speed, both in short bursts and long distances, allowed her to strike in the blink of an eye.

Every Krey learned the first two forms of sword fighting. Form I, the Novice, focused on just the sword, learning to defend and deflect and attack. Form II, the Guardian, incorporated sword and shield, group tactics, and footwork.

Most stopped their progression there. A few others learned the different forms depending on their weapon of choice, but she also used Form VIII, the Zealot, which was for people like her who relied on speed, alacrity, and acrobatic tactics. To be fair, she could use the latter while in a wedge formation.

The Krey broke for dinner after conditioning. Whether by bad luck or planned shunning, the Krey were served last; the army came before them, ensuring fights didn't occur. The Krey could enter the bloodlust and annihilate a quarter of the Grand Royal Army before the Mind could bring them under control.

Whenever Xenomene traversed the camp, her second, Tiny, and the Mind went with her. The A'uri joined the squad as they ate. After they had their fill of fresh vegetables, grains, and freshly butchered meat, the Krey returned to their building and buried themselves in their cups, or retired early, or in the case of the two virgins, practiced their technique.

She took this time to file the nightly reports for the heir. Each evening, the Heart would carry her letter to the heir by teleportation. Her limited power provided an additional problem: she lacked the prowess to carry company.

Letters would have to suffice.

Every night, an hour before the suns set, camp hands delivered scalding bath water. It cooled while she read and wrote reports. Afterward, she soaked the day's sores away. Meticulous scrubbing became a necessity, not that she was careless before, but in expectation of Bitcher's arrival.

One night, the Heart returned early from her trip to the Hive. She teleported outside Xenomene's door and knocked. The red-haired do-don bade her to enter. The Heart swept in to find Xenomene still bathing. She glanced up as she scrubbed.

The Heart didn't avert her eyes. She began talking as if she were clothed.

"The heir sends a message. He said for you to be ready to receive more Krey."

"More Krey? I thought we weren't supposed to deploy in massive numbers. How many are we talking about?"

"He said two more squads would join your ranks, and you are to assume command."

Xeno grimaced.

"Assume command?"

The Heart glowed with her smile.

"That's not all, he's elevated you to the rank of ko-don."

Xenomene was silent for a moment, choosing not to rejoice at the news.

"Aren't others more senior?"

The Heart rolled her eyes.

"You know better than I how things work within the Krey. It's all about how well you handle the sword."

"But ko-don?"

Xeno frowned, then laughed.

"What? Did somebody die?"

The Heart schooled her features.

"Yes. Ko-don Bear passed in his sleep."

That shut her up.

"Shades. He should've died with a sword in his hand, not like some plush noble in Ralloc."

She sighed and stood inside the tub.

"Hand me my towel, please?"

The Heart grabbed the cloth and stepped within arm's distance before she stopped, dropped the towel, and backpedaled.

Xenomene's brow furrowed before she reached down to the floor and plucked up the cloth.

"What's wrong?"

The Heart heaved rapid breaths; her face flushed.

"I'm sorry."

"About?"

"The lust…it hit me just now."

"The lust?" Xeno echoed but remembered about the mages. "Oh, that lust…"

Xeno chuckled.

"Find me attractive, huh?"

"No."

The Heart blushed.

"It was purely the lust. It's also been known to emerge around those who are highly engaged in sexual activity."

Xenomene toweled herself dry and wrapped the cloth around her body. A thought crossed her mind.

"Does the lust work on the Krey?"

"Yes, though the Krey's is weaker than ours; you have magic of a different kind, but it works the same. Weaker was a poor term, it's just different. I'm surprised you guys aren't having orgies more often with all the Krey and A'uri crammed up in the Hive."

Xenomene nodded and switched subjects.

"So, Ko-don Bear is dead, and I've assumed his rank."

Xeno plopped herself into the chair behind her desk, her towel tucked tight around her.

"Wonderful, I'm sure all the men here will be thrilled."

"Since when do the Krey care what others say?"

"I don't like it when you make sense."

Xenomene wadded up a paper and threw it at her, then sighed.

"Alright, I'll tell the squad on the morrow."

She meant it as a dismissal, as she expected Bitcher at any moment, but the Heart remained.

"Something else on your mind?"

"Yes…the night with Bitcher in the desert."

"We don't need to talk about that, it's taken care of."

"No, we *do* need to talk about it."

The Heart exhaled.

"I can see that he's returned to normal, and I assume that's your doing, but you broke your vow to the warlock. If he finds out, he'll kill us both, not to mention breaking a vow altogether. None in the Krey would look kindly upon that. You know the penalty is."

Xenomene twitched her nose left and right.

"He won't find out, and, like I said, it's taken care of."

"This is also my life you are playing with, Ko-don."

Xenomene let out a breath.

"He's of no consequence. He's not Krey, not the do-don, the ko-don, or the heir. He's not of the Black Tide and never will be. It's not for him to decide who's punished and how. I admit, in hindsight, that the punishment was too severe, but Bitcher wasn't permanently disfigured. You were able to heal him. I don't see the problem."

The Heart was silent for a moment. She swallowed.

"I'm not Krey, but I'm part of the Black Tide. I know what matters to us, honor, integrity, discipline, war, pleasures of the flesh. You dishonored yourself, me, and the Krey when you broke your vow. That's an oath breaker. Never again ask me to help you with your personal fancy, Ko-don."

"I told you, the warlock—"

"—Is of no consequence, yes, I know! Until you set this right between you, the warlock, and Bitcher, you have the taint of dishonor on you. I'll not be a part of it."

Xenomene narrowed her eyes.

"Are you refusing to obey orders?"

"Orders? No. To help you break vows? Yes."

Xenomene sat still, her ire simmering. The Heart was right about breaking the vow, but she didn't understand the flip side of the argument. It wasn't the warlock's decision, it was hers, and she knew beyond a doubt that the heir would back her. This was another stress she didn't need.

"You're dismissed," Xenomene bit out.

The Heart was taken aback by the hostility, but nodded, and left without a word. The door closed. Xenomene slumped in her chair and blew out a breath.

This is all I need, another problem compounding all the other ones.

She leaned forward and massaged her temples when the door burst open with a thundering crash. She leapt from the chair as Bitcher bounded over the desk, a hand clasped around her throat. He slammed her into the wall. Her feet left the floor far behind. The towel fell away. The impact of her head against the wall nearly made her black out.

"You fucking cunt!" Bitcher hissed, his spittle flecking her face.

Xenomene's eyes rolled as darkness threatened to take her. He released her, and she fell to the floor. She coughed, struggled to rise, and his right hand smashed across her face. She could feel each individual splayed finger tingling across her cheek.

"Wait!" she pleaded.

Bitcher buried his fist in her gut, driving the wind from her lungs. Kneeling, clutching her abdomen, she fought the dry heaves and to reclaim her breath.

Bitcher's fingers snaked through her short, dark red hair, and jerked her naked body from the floor before slamming against the desk.

"You fucking whore! How could you?"

He spun her around and slapped her with such force that she sprawled to the floor. She tried to crawl away, to the door, but a boot caught her in the stomach and ribs, the latter cracking.

She doubled over, sucking in to no avail. The worst part? No one would hear, not with an empty deck between them.

Bitcher jerked her by the hair, a series of slaps: once, twice, three times, and she crashed back to the wood-slat floor. Blood leaked from her nose and split lips, her cheek and eye swelled, threatening to close. He was in absolute control, and she was helpless to stop him.

Another quick wrench brought her face up, and his hard knuckles met her soft flesh. An audible pop and a sharp, icy pain radiated from her jaw.

Another heavy blow, and her cheek crumbled.

She lay in a useless jumble on the floor, at his mercy and anger. Blood pooled beneath her. Another boot snapped out. Her face and head bounced off the floor. Blood smeared the deck.

He heard everything!

His hand seized her by the hair again, her scalp afire. Dragging her up to her feet, he slammed her face-first into the desk. Her hips drove hard against the edge of wood. The furniture slid from the quick movement and her weight.

Splinters stung her naked hips. Quills scattered and parchment flew as her chest skidded across the top. Blood and sweat smeared her letters and maps. An ink bottle spilled, its black contents covering a portion of the surface, seeping into her hair and staining the side of her face.

He turned her head, exposing the right side, and he pummeled with the meat portion of his fist, breaking her other cheek bone. Vision blurry, a blade of hot pain shot through her eye socket and her sight restricted.

"You fucked with the wrong person, cunt! You fucked me over, were told not to disfigure me!"

His weight slammed down on top of her, one hand yanking her hair, the other closed around her throat. His hand tightened like a rapidly-closing vise. Blackness took her, but his pummeling knuckles reawakened her.

The desk held her upright as she sagged against it, her legs hanging uselessly beneath her.

A blunt force rammed into her backside and sex, his knee driving up into her, stealing her breath again. Her lungs seized, and her body shook in shock and rebellion. She sucked in a ragged breath, desperate to breathe again.

"You'll pay for this, bitch!"

He kicked her legs apart, and she heard him opening his trousers. Bitcher rammed into her without grace or kindness. Xenomene thought she was dead to pain, her body numb from the inflicted wounds.

She was wrong.

She felt as if she had been split open. Rage drove his repeated thrusts, invading deeper each time.

Xeno tried to fight back but couldn't. She sagged back to the desk, helpless. His hands returned to her hair and stars peppered her vision when he slammed her face-first into the desk, her nose crunching.

She saw bright light when it did.

Xenomene dangled between the cusp of sweet unconsciousness. Her body shuddered underneath Bitcher, and when his violations finally ceased, his hand clamped around her throat pulled her from the desk, suspending her upright.

Her feet swayed as the darkness took her. Sanguine fluid and ink caked the side of her face. Fresh blood and semen trailed down her legs from the darkness between her cheeks.

Unable to breathe, she passed out, but when her back slammed against the desk, it snapped her awake as she crashed to the floor.

The last thing she remembered was the door closing and footsteps receding. And then, she waited to die, as she deserved.

Chapter 8: Starriace

The sky sparkled above Starriace, like twinkling diamonds in the dark expanse. After dealing with her captors, she rode east to obscure her trail. Others would come looking.

For nigh a week, she kept her course, reaching Lone Man Lake. Arriving, she teleported to random destinations leading away from Far Point. After several jumps, she sat in a heap against a cluster of trees, sweat trickling from her brow. She intended a momentary reprieve, but exhaustion overcame her.

A blood-red evening welcomed her. Praema slinked low in the south. Disoriented, she stood, her back and neck protesting. Utilizing Fife's teachings, she eased her pain, healed her body, and the last of her pangs faded. With a stretch, her back popped.

A grumble in her stomach reminded her of the many days of neglect. She sustained her body with magic throughout her journey, eating sparingly. After a quick rifling of her pack, she found herself without.

"Shades."

With her reclaimed money, she could port to any city and eat, but more important tasks gnawed at her. Her essence eased the pangs. Magic had its limits, and eventually it'd fail regarding sustenance; the more she staved off hunger and sleep, the quicker the need for both would return.

Something cold and metallic brushed her sifting fingers. Grasping the small object, she withdrew a ring. Recollection shot through her.

Rusem!

The ring had been a gift from the spirit, an echo of his former self. Simple in design, the band would teleport her to and from the temple in the City of Despair. Between her confrontation with Xilor, her rescue by the archangels, and the heinous captivity, his gift had slipped her mind.

Is he still in the temple?

The once-prosperous metropolis now lay cursed and barren. Only one structure remained within the ruined walls. With cunning, she tricked Rusem's spirit into taking physical form, and she leeched his essence and drained him of magic before channeling it back into the lifeless, corporeal form.

He'd been born anew.

Risen.

She slipped the ring on her finger. Her vision blurred, swirling, then the insides of the temple manifested. Rusem stood near the pedestal in the center. He turned as she closed the distance. Other than his sallow skin and lifeless eyes, he appeared unchanged. His movements were spastic, having lost fluid grace from before. Starriace eyed him warily, uncertain.

She reached out for his presence but found nothing.

I need to test him, find his limitations.

"Kneel," she commanded.

I obey, his thoughts filled her mind.

His response seemed simple and lacked the cognitive capacity he once possessed. With the same jerky movements, he knelt.

"Rise."

I obey.

Is he having difficulty breathing?

She watched for a sign of a rising and falling chest. It didn't.

Dead, yet alive.

Bound, he answered.

"Bound?"

Bound between…

Bound between what?

He remained silent.

"Bound to my commands?"

Bound to obey.

Starriace allowed herself a small smile. She'd compelled Rusem, could she bind others? If so, they'd all answer to her will.

"Come, Rusem, let's be gone."

He lumbered forward, and she put her arm through his. Replacing the ring on her finger, she returned to her previous location. Her bag still lay next to the copse of trees, almost impossible to see in the darkness. Belongings gathered, she hooked arms with Rusem and teleported away.

Far Point lay to the north, a week by foot or days by horse. With silent purpose, she climbed up the sloping hills, disappearing into the thick trees and shallow crags.

Soft footfalls marked their presence; tumbling rocks punctured the comfortable, country silence. Sweat broke between Starriace's shoulder blades and across her temple. The cool night felt hollow, void of sound except for the intermittent chirps of scattered insects or the hoot of an owl.

A gentle breeze caressed her face, a welcome companion. The treetops swayed, gentle sighs in the night.

Her thoughts turned back to her actions after slaying the men. She suspected that Judas would come searching for her. If he attempted, he would've caught up with her by now. She wrestled with it until the early hours of the morning.

A spirited pace whittled the hours away. The hunger pains returned as the magic faded. She could no longer afford to put off eating. Her eyes drooped with exhaustion. Sleep crept up on her as a close second. Dawn threatened the night's solemn hold in the north.

She passed an entrance to a cave and halted. Tendrils of her mysticism rushed forward to probe the vacant hollow. A trail weaved a short, sloped path to a room no more than two dozen feet from the opening. She entered, and Rusem lumbered in her wake.

Calling upon her abilities, she rendered him unconscious. The temple restricted his movements, but here, he could venture out. She'd leave him while returning to Far Point. An undead creature would raise questions, and the hermit, Harold, wouldn't understand.

The cave lay between Far Point and the Ruins of Sheol and provided an appropriate place to keep him nearby. Though nearly a mindless monster, some intelligence lingered within. Just how much influence did she have over him? What were the limitations?

Will distance affect it? Is it permanent until I die?

Starriace waited a day to make sure the slumber would hold. After building a fire, she passed the time meditating, exploring new rips in her tattered robes, and inspecting her scant possessions. Judas had bought her these robes; Lily's gifted clothing stayed tucked away in her pack, prizing them above the warlock's. Stained, ripped, and reeking, they outlived their usefulness like her former teacher. These clothes represented the last reminders of the life she'd forsaken.

She'd get a few new sets, ones more optimal for her needs and style. A darker color would blend in well at night, and, if need be, conceal her in the brush during the day.

Why should I hide?

You know why, the voice answered.

It was always with her now.

They'll come after me. They found the bodies, I know they did, and if Judas was summoned, he'll figure out at least half of the truth.

Still, half of the truth, as monstrous as it was, was better than unequivocal. She relived the scenes and shuddered. Tears threatened to well up, stinging her eyes. She rubbed them away.

I wish I could forget them.

They were animals. They deserved death.

Starriace had no misconception: murder was murder; self-defense was something else entirely. But she delivered justice.

Well, it was revenge, too.

She focused on the justice aspect. They came against her with arms, and she defended herself. They deserved retaliation for leaving her for dead. She went to their camp with the intention to hurt them as they hurt her. Murder happened to be a byproduct.

Or was it?

She pushed that away, fixating on Harold's home. He had a trove of knowledge. No one could help on her quest, which is why she traveled alone.

She rummaged through her bag, finding a decorative belt made of black leather and studded with aquamarine gems. She pulled the item out, a treasure taken from the lawless men. The belt radiated beauty and uniqueness, sellable for a handsome coin.

She started to stow it when she noticed a faint aura.

The tingling filled her head, tickling her memory. The sensation was familiar and faint. Dropping the belt, she fumbled through her tattered bag for the one possession that held any sentimentality. The book Judas bestowed in the swampland came free.

While Judas remained a bitter memory, his gift wasn't.

The book emanated power and was written in a lost language. Sometimes the pages were blank. Other times, text appeared in an unreadable form. Regardless, the book spoke, opening for her in the swamps. The tome had called her the Bearer of Secrets.

She thumbed through the blank pages, looking for writing. The trickle of power was meant to ensnare her. It wanted to show her something. Halfway through, she found a page littered with a tiny scrawl. The strange words shifted to Myshku, her language.

Of all creatures that walk Ermaeyth, only one race holds the vast secrets of charging stones with power. The elyves are the gifted race in this matter, and even the most elementary secrets elude us. More can be read about this in the elyfian book Du' Garuaex.

Intrigue ensnared her as she tried to recall vague facts about the race.

Starriace had her own brief encounter with an assorted group of nine elyves. The motley group was comprised of males and females. Most seemed reserved, but the leader of the group, Iddrial, greeted her and assured no ill intentions. The momentary occurrence ended with the nine fading into the foliage.

"Why show me?" she asked aloud, but the book didn't answer.

Her gaze fell back on the belt. Snatching up the item, she looked between the two.

"Did you mean this?"

Again, only silence greeted her.

Where would she find the book *Du' Garuaex*? Certainly, Ralloc had it, but she couldn't go there. Judas would most likely be within the city, and she wasn't ready for that encounter, for good or ill. Harold had an extensive book collection, and she was already headed there. If an extra copy floated around, the hermit would have it.

With conviction, she stowed both items, stood, and stretched.

The movement made her sway. Drowsiness washed over her. When was the last time she slept? Days? Weeks? She couldn't remember. She rarely slept anymore. Most of the time, she opted for a meditative trance. It took less time, and she wasn't as vulnerable.

An hour of meditation freed up the rest of the day for searching, reading, and training. Sleep provided the best rejuvenation, but a little discomfort was an acceptable price for productivity. Only genuine rest restored the full breadth of her abilities.

Despite the reckless behavior, her essence grew stronger. She often pondered the reasons, but thus far, the answers eluded her.

"You never sleep, do you?" a voice called out, startling her.

Eyes snapping to the cave entrance, she projected her aura out.

Someone stood outside.

Her wand materialized in her hand. Fear spurred her into action. The air shimmered, a defensive barrier encompassed her, and she exited the cave. With the opening behind her, she called out into the night.

"Who are you? Show yourself."

She searched for his presence, but pinpointing his location required finesse.

"I mean you no harm."

She perceived movement. A soft crunch reached her ears. The man came forward. When he stepped into the light, she sucked in a breath. A man in black robes with a white, skeletal face materialized.

No, a mask.

He loomed close enough for Starriace to see the dark skin of his neck. He stayed well out of striking distance. Did he intend to attack or run?

"What do you want?"

"You've come to our attention."

"*Our*?"

At the mention of others, she searched, but only found the man in the immediate vicinity.

"I'm alone. But we are a group of people, somewhat like you, who carry out recompense when needed."

While he spoke, Starriace stretched out her awareness, expanding further than ever before. Every life form that fell within her sphere of influence was an animal. The man spoke truth. Satisfied, Starriace turned her attention back to him.

"Who are you?"

"Who am I, or who are we? I'm the Summoner, one of the Embrace, a sect of the One."

Her face remained expressionless. None of the names made sense to her. She crossed her arms.

"I'm not familiar with you."

"This is expected. No one finds us; we find them."

"Then, how did you find me, Summoner?"

"We've been aware of you since the caravan when you traveled to Far Point. A member of our sect was there, returning from a mission in Ralloc's domain."

"What does this have to do with me?"

"We kept tabs on you in Far Point, but when you left, our man lost your trail. He abandoned hope until he saw you again—the men's camp? He tracked them after they bragged about what they'd done in Far Point, but you arrived before he acted."

He still hadn't answered her question, so she remained silent.

"The Embrace extends an invitation to join our ranks, to dispense rightness where others have failed."

She shifted on her feet.

"Vigilante work? Mercenaries?"

"That is such a…harsh assessment. We hand out justice where corrupt judges and inept law enforcement blunder their duties. We stand for the helpless."

Her lips drew into a line.

"Where were you when I was in need?"

The bitterness bubbled up. The familiar itch returned to her eyes.

"Ah, you are referring to…"

His eyes rolled up as he searched for the words.

"…your unfortunate predicament. We can't stop every ill deed. Do you feel better now that you've obtained your revenge, or did they receive true justice?"

Though a question, the accusation stung. Anger simmered within her.

"They got both."

Behind her back, Starriace clenched her fist, her knuckles turning white.

"Go away, I'm no murderer."

"Neither is the Embrace. We're the extension of law. You have done what we do. You know you were justified."

"I'm not interested."

"There are innocent people who are just as helpless as you—"

You were weak and helpless!

Starriace lashed out. With a deft swipe of her wand, the Summoner slammed to the ground.

"Innocent people?" Starriace screamed, closing the gap between them. "You think I'm helpless? Innocent, helpless, lame, it's all the same to you! I managed without you! I survived. I saved myself!"

Even as the words left her, the last sentence lingered as a lie. Ava and Lily had saved her. The Summoner lay motionless, held by her essence.

"I got my justice and revenge. That's enough, don't you think? Shall I kill everybody and everything until I am alone? Should I start with you?"

She let go of her hold, and he stood. The ebony-skinned Summoner stared up at her.

"Start with me, if you wish to become like them."

His words smothered the fire within her, and her energy dissipated. She stowed her wand and turned back to the cave, monitoring him with her gifts in case he attacked.

He didn't.

"You have an amazing gift," he said. "Few of us possess such potent abilities. I'm one of the strongest of the Embrace, and no one has ever handled me like that. You'd be a great value to us. Help us; help them by joining us."

Starriace entered the cave, retrieving her bag. Returning, she fastened her pack, vowing to not lose control again. Why had his words angered her? She found that it wasn't him, but the three men, proving that she was still helpless. Though she survived Xilor, she was still too weak to stop them.

But they probably used Rakette like Lily said. They blocked my magical abilities.

"I'll think about it," she said at last, "but I don't promise anything. More important things require my attention."

"What could possibly be more important?"

Her eyes narrowed.

"In case you missed it, there's a war going on. Xilor must be stopped. Is that good enough?"

"A noble cause."

His tone didn't imply he thought it so.

For the first time, she detected an emotion from him: resentment.

"Foolish and wasteful but noble. There's no defeating Xilor; even the Embrace knows that."

She bit back a retort, and he continued on.

"In one moon turn, we'll change locations, leaving Far Point. If you wish to join us, come to Crystal Falls, near Ruhkhi, south of the Melodic Mountains. If you come, we'll find you. If you haven't sought us out by the end of next season, the Embrace will consider it a refusal."

Starriace tightened her straps on her pack.

"Like I said, I'll consider it."

He dipped his head.

"Let your journeys be far and fair."

He took a step back, and another, and kept backing until he faded into the darkness. Starriace tracked him with her magical awareness. Once he faded, she called upon her essence and teleported away.

When she emerged, a familiar town greeted her. Far Point: the place where her life began.

Judas may have awakened her, but she started to live once she met Kam, Lily, and Harold. The village lay in a shallow valley. A gush of nostalgia ran through her. In a way, Far Point distinguished itself as her home.

Setbacks hindered a swift return and altered her fate, but perseverance arranged a long-awaited homecoming. She ground her teeth at the memory of the men.

No more. I won't think of them again! That part of me is vanquished. They don't deserve my tears, my soul, or my thoughts. I'll bury them and forget they ever existed.

As she finished, she restated the original mantra that comforted her in the darkest of times.

I'll never be weak, I'll never be powerless. I'll never be that vulnerable again.

Then, she added to the chant.

I control my destiny.

The reflections receded, locked behind walls of iron resolve. She kept many things interred there, including the other half of her banished conscience. The warring within took its toll, and she partitioned her mind, barricading the weaker side away.

The disobedient thoughts darkened her mood, but the proximity of Harold's home banished her exhaustion. The sagacious hermit, though quiet and withdrawn, was kind. Why did she keep him in high regard compared to Judas and Fife? Perhaps because she had so little time with him yet learned Shadowcasting. Or perhaps because he never angered her. Many factors weaved through the conundrum, and none presented a complete answer.

He was always nice, but so was Judas.

She inhaled the crisp air.

The changing of the seasons weaved through the breeze. Seven months ago she had awoken in Judas's manor at the end of spring. She spent the summer months and half of autumn in the Melodic Mountains with Fife Doole.

Winter approached.

The gnomling has skill. My training wasn't a complete waste of time.

Grand Maghai Fife Doole's training, bizarre and sometimes cruel like his sharp words, facilitated her learning. His teachings enhanced her minuscule understanding, but he refused to teach what she craved, denying her knowledge of offensive magic.

Her confrontation with Xilor pointed out the weakness. Luck kept her alive.

A gentle gust stroked her face, dancing through her hair like a lover's fingers. She closed her eyes at the sensation. It brought memories back of Kam and Lily. Starriace's heart mourned again for having to say goodbye to her friend, but Lily couldn't be a part of her plans.

Starriace could never live down seeing Lily's horror; she could take Judas's condemnation, Fife's contempt, but not that. The warlock held no morality after letting the Corridor destroy her mind. A part of her would wither if Lily likened her to a monster.

The memories of her intimate times with Kam made the dark reflections fade. Her face reddened, and her pulse quickened. A sense of wrongness clung to her, enjoying another woman's husband, but Lily encouraged their coupling.

The carnality faded as the humble village filled her eyes. Notions of calling the place home filled her. Why? Because nothing bad happened to her here? She spent more time with Judas and Fife, but the fondness she fostered for Kam and Lily originated here.

It was home, at least for the interim.

She set off at a brisk pace. Fatigue riddled her joints. Each step made her body ache. The magic no longer helped as before; the pangs returned almost immediately.

She'd reached her limit.

The faint glow of light pushed up into the night like a hazy dome hovering above the small village. Loose stones clamored when she stumbled. Each tumbling rock disappeared into the darkness before it lay still and quiet. Obstinance kept her moving forward, her body falling into a steady, mindless rhythm.

Adrift in a thoughtless and exhaustive murk, the gate materialized much quicker than anticipated. She stood next to a tree, catching her breath. Her head throbbed, and her withering magic sputtered, sluggishly responding to soothe away the anguish.

Her aura warned her of another's presence. A guard reclined in his chair, teetering between the cusp of slumber. His consciousness rose and fell like gentle waves. Starriace waited for a recession before she implanted the suggestion to sleep. The persuasion took effect, and she stumbled toward the gate.

While the gate remained locked, the guard's door—an opening cut into the wall with a narrow tunnel leading into the city—was not. Without opening the gate to relieve sentries, changing of the guard became a quieter affair.

Her vision swam, blurring like a drunkard's. A hand on the wall helped steady her befuddled steps. Breath held, she passed the sleeping form. His hand clutched a spear with loose fingers. His head leaning against the wall lolled. Soft snores escaped through his half-opened mouth.

She passed him by, through the small opening.

The sleeping sentry's presence faded as she continued to the Enchanted Allure Guild. She stumbled up the steps, sagging in relief against the door frame. No one in the city could detect the building swathed in a graveyard illusion. The final resting place of ancestors tended to bring curious people or bereaved relatives, but the effect carried a foreboding sense of damned souls entombed within.

Her hand clutched the cold, brass knob. With a slight turn, it opened. As before, only scant candlelight lit the dim interior. An eerie quiet settled over her as if the house watched and waited.

Perhaps Harold slept like the rest of the city?

The faint and familiar aroma hit her nostrils after three cautious steps inside. Harold was awake. Like her last visit, he sat in his chair with his back to the door and smoked a pipe while reading. But more than that, it was his presence, his aura, that she latched on to. Of course, she'd felt it before, but now it became something tangible, recognizable, and beyond that, something else bothered her. She could've sworn she'd felt it before, but not here in this house.

"Well, come in already," Harold said.

He sounded just as she remembered, warm and inviting. She rounded his chair and saw a book in his lap.

"Let me get a good look at you."

His wide smile beamed up at her, his gray-blue eyes soft and receptive. A fondness surged in her chest, an emotion she hadn't experienced since Meristal's arrival in Cape Gythmel. Harold's smile faded with a curious glance. The luster of his pale gray-blue eyes waned.

"What happened?"

"What do you mean?"

She feared what the question meant, and while mild mannered, the question made him sound demanding and judgmental.

How can he know? He doesn't.

"I can sense the taint of death upon you. You were near someone who died. The only alternative is murder. It's not a sense that won't go unnoticed in my presence."

Panic stirred in her sluggish mind, but the lack of food, water, and sleep kept her from blurting out explanations or lies. How could he sense death? Would it affect eventual dealings with others if they could sense the trail of bodies upon her?

Would Kam and Lily sense it?

More like a unique specialty that Harold alone commanded.

The Summoner didn't appear to be affected. Did that mean that Harold had never killed anyone? What could she possibly say to tame his inquiry?

"I fought Xilor after I left your place," she blurted.

Her statement remained true, contingent upon a technicality. She hoped he sensed honesty in her statement.

"I almost died. Perhaps it's that you feel?"

"You know more than you're telling me, don't you, young one? No, I sense a majestic presence, too. This demise I feel, it's as much yours as someone else's."

Starriace couldn't bear the thought of lying to him. His eyes brought it out of her, and his presence that she couldn't quite pinpoint destroyed the emotional walls she'd kept in place.

She collapsed in silent tears. In a heap at Harold's feet, she spilled her story. The terrible weight crushing her eased as she confessed. She no longer carried the burden alone.

Still, in defiance of her admission, they deserved their fate, maybe not by her hand but death for their atrocities. Her hands would've remained clean had someone else executed them, but to forgo watching them suffer would rob her of closure.

Harold's hand touched her hair tenderly. She looked up, tears streaking her face. He smiled, one that empathized with her pain. His eyes misted over as his huge, warm hands cupped her face.

"I don't judge you. That's not my job in this world. I can never imagine the anguish you went through no more than you can imagine what it is to be an old man. Do I agree with what transpired? Yes and no. They did deserve death, but not by you. The appointed law should carry the burden of rendering guilt or innocence, not you the victim or the mindless masses. From this ordeal, take this from it: what's done can never be undone.

"Now, the hardest part is yet to come: to forgive yourself. I find heart and faith in your remorse. That means you're not hopeless...yet."

He paused and drew a heavy breath.

"But heed my words: you are lost, child. Pain and death is your life to come, but I didn't think you'd find it so soon. I pray you find yourself before the end."

She sobbed.

"Is that my only future?"

"I don't have the heart to tell you."

"Please! Tell me it's better than this!"

"You know not what you ask. To know one's fate darkens the remaining days, but if it's truly your wish…"

She nodded.

Would knowing help ease the anguish she suffered? She'd endured more in the short span of weeks than most did in their entire lives. Defiled, invaded, abused, victimized, those men took something from her that she'd never get back, and killing them crushed everything else.

Harold sighed.

"The Underworld will claim your soul. One of your companions will die. A thing you most cherish will turn against you, and you'll lose it forever. A bed of stone awaits you, graced with an angel."

He stopped, and she choked back her tears.

Perhaps he's right, it's better to not know.

He reached out and lifted her tear-streaked face.

"But, before that comes to pass, you'll find a family member. I also see the arms of a man you'll come to love, and three sets of arms that love you beyond comprehension."

His eyes grew distant, and he sucked in a breath.

"A tenebrous figure haunts your future, unchanged by time. And stones of tremendous and harrowing capability."

Starriace wiped the tears away with the back of her hand and breathed a sigh of relief. He knew her future, what she was supposed to do.

Rusem came to mind as Harold's words settled. He mentioned stones, and so did Rusem. The tenebrous figure? Xilor's shadowy silhouette filled her mind. Even as she tried to navigate the forthcoming events, the hermit had nullified it by the laws of Shadowcasting. He changed her subsequent outlook twice, once because he peered into the future and twice because he revealed what he saw.

Hope sparked within her.

"Tell me what I must do."

"No!" Harold said with a sudden harshness. "You'll never find out what you need from me. I'll never mark out your steps. That's for you and fate to decide."

He ran his hand through her honeyed hair and gave a kind smile. He leaned forward and kissed her forehead.

"Upstairs, on the third floor, you'll find a room and some clothes. Take a bath and rest; more than your soul is weary. When you wake, we can discuss why you've come."

Starriace left Harold sitting in his chair. He lit his pipe as she walked away. He always sat there, his natural element, like the house developed around him.

The first time she came here, he left his chair for a few brief moments to fetch her a book. And this time? In the wee hours of morning, he remained unchanged.

She climbed the rickety stairs. The faded white railing stained by time ran smooth under her fingers. The stairs were the same kind of wood as the floor, a lyptus lumber with a dark stain finish.

The hermit's words echoed in her head.

How old is Harold?

"One of your companions will die."

Did he foreshadow his own fate?

"Is Harold the companion to die? Stop it! Prophecy's greatest gift is to sow doubt."

If Harold was the companion to die, so be it. She couldn't change tomorrow...but perhaps Harold had. By telling her, he skirted death, changed the outcome with just a few uttered words.

Or had he?

Harold embodied the best qualities of a friend. Kind, nonjudgmental, patient, the opposite of everything she despised in wizardkind, but everything she needed in her life.

Harold's words drummed through her mind.

"I also see the arms of a man you will come to love..."

Her pulse quickened.

Was that Kam or someone else? Was it literal or figurative love? She just hoped it never happened until after the war. If she defeated Xilor, then she could have a life without fear of reprisals, like the tragedy visited upon Judas and Meristal.

A stray feeling of misplaced thoughts flickered through her mind.

Something about Judas...

Then, it hit her, burning in her mind.

Both Meristal and Judas lost a child. Perhaps their children were taken on the same night, a coordinated attack? What were the chances of that? Judas once told her that Xilor's followers held both prominent figures to blame. A failed coup for retribution?

Meristal had come to them in Cape Gythmel. Starriace noted the chemistry between the two, a lifetime of friendship, of hardships endured together. But still, something about the thought nagged at her.

If they both lost a child...and on the same night...perhaps it was the same child?

Judas said he had a daughter, and Meristal, a son.

Did they both lie to protect the identity of the child? Was it me?

She tried to shake that thought away, but it resonated within her. The more she dwelt on it, the more she couldn't deny how right it felt. Like when she accepted her name, her true lineage, the magic swelled with a resonance.

It did now.

Maybe I am his daughter, and he doesn't know it.

Starriace entered the first room to the right. A few lamps lit the room in a soft golden hue. On the bed, she found a fresh set of robes, a thin, linen inner robe of an off-white color, followed by a cotton outer robe of forest green. A traveler's robe of black, forest green, and off-white was folded next to it.

Did Harold know she was coming? She dismissed the notion. Why would he take the chance of altering the future?

On her first visit, Harold introduced her to Shadowcasting, a way of seeing upcoming events. Peering into elements altered the outcome in small, subtle ways. The hermit did admit that the ability could alter dramatically, but such incidents were rare.

Sometimes, she thought the skill as useless, but why would he teach her? In the Melodic Mountains, she used the ability to peer into her own future. She only glimpsed her imminent death. Each instance changed, but the outcome endured.

Under Fife, she studied the art of scrying, but it seemed a waste of time, and she gave it little attention. It was a lesson taught in between her more important ones. Fife revealed people could scry, but it was near-impossible to find a legitimate seer. Scrying revealed aspects, not the full picture.

Whatever you did perceive often led to a wrong conclusion; Shadowcasting revealed a much more precise revelation but with the possibility of the shifting inevitabilities.

Starriace rubbed her eyes and shed the torn robes. She caught her reflection in the mirror, horrified by her unkempt hair and the dirt and grime marring her face. Upon closer inspection, the whites of her eyes were almost clear, only a trace of the scarlet glow lingered.

In the privy, she filled her tub, stepped into the steaming water, and the warmth soothed her body. Before long, she scrubbed the filth from her body and hair, drained the tub, and filled it again. Hot water soaked away the soreness, the tension in her neck and shoulders melting. Three times during her bath she fought off sleep. She nearly drowned, her face falling forward into the water.

Exiting, she drained the tub again, dried off, and crawled up in bed. The soft linen sheets felt cold to the initial touch against her bare skin, but she liked it cold when she slept.

Harold hadn't laid out any sleeping clothes.

Guess he doesn't have any.

She didn't remember falling asleep, but it seemed as if she had just closed her eyes when she opened them again. She took a moment to remember where she was. Harold's provided comfort and safety, a respite. Standing, her legs buckled.

I must've slept for a long time.

An unattractive yawn escaped her lips as she stretched, and the urgent need for the privy quickened her wakefulness. Relieved and awake, she dressed in haste, completing Harold's outfit with the belt she acquired from the three thieves. The fresh robes boosted her spirits.

A pitcher of cold water sat on the dresser next to a shallow basin. Calling on her essence, she raised the temperature of the water the way Fife had taught. When she reached for her magic, it lurched at her call. Within seconds, the water radiated warmth. She toweled her face dry, ran the brush through her hair, and hurried downstairs.

She found Harold in the kitchen with a plate of food awaiting at the table. Harold rummaged through the cabinets, preparing to make tea.

"Feel better?" he asked.

"Much better! Thank you."

He grunted and set the cup in front of her.

"You slept for a day."

He poured a dark liquid from the kettle. She scrutinized it, frowning as he doled out milk and sugar from his cold cabinet. The black liquid turned a light brown. With two spoonfuls of sugar, he encouraged her to drink.

"Harold? Isn't tea supposed to be a lighter color like brown and not black?"

"It isn't tea. It's coffee, an import from the Forgotten Isles."

With the mention of the Isles, Starriace's mind raced back to a flattering image of Kam. Color rose in her cheeks, and she ducked her head to hide the embarrassment. Mastering herself, she eyed the coffee before taking a cautious sip. To her surprise, it was delicious, and she finished the cup before touching her food.

"More?"

"Please."

Harold retrieved the pot as she dug into her plate of steak, eggs, toast, and some form of ground grain with water, the latter sweetened by honey.

Harold returned with her cup and added the milk and sugar, then sat opposite her.

"I knew you'd be back, but you're earlier than expected. What brings you my way?"

She swallowed her food.

"I found this belt on…the men. There's an aura emanating from it, and I wished to learn more about the skill."

"So, you put on a stranger's belt that's emanating power without testing it to make sure that it wouldn't kill you?"

Never thought of it that way.

She took a bite of the eggs.

"And what does this belt or the aura have to do with me?"

"I intend to research it, duplicate the process, if possible. You have the most extensive collection I know of besides Ralloc, and I hoped to use your library."

She cut into her steak, stuffing her mouth.

"You can use my library anytime, though I don't know if it's the most extensive. Maybe the most eccentric…."

He gave a wolfish grin.

"Great!"

Starriace was careful not to reveal her complete motivations. She hadn't lied, just been less than forthcoming. She danced on a precarious precipice and didn't want to destroy any good will she'd fostered.

"I'd like to start with the elyves. I heard somewhere that they're most adept at performing these kinds of arts."

"Hmm," he muttered after a few moments. "Any book in particular?"

"Yes."

Starriace drew a deep breath and swallowed.

"*Du' Garuaex.*"

Chapter 9: Starriace

In the week following her arrival at Harold's, *Du' Garuaex* or any related material eluded her diligent search. The one book Harold lacked. According to the hermit, elyfian books—like anything elyfian—were rare. If *Du' Garuaex* turned out to be a rare elyfian tome by their standards, what did that make it for wizardkind?

On the first day of searching, hope and excitement filled her. As the days trickled by, she became disillusioned and overwhelmed by Harold's collection. She searched room by room, book by book, page by page, speed-reading almost every hardback cover to cover. She didn't bother to skim *Extinct Creatures and Races of the Realm*, *What's on the Other Side?*, and *The Rise and Fall of the Kings of Old.* Oddly enough, she discovered several volumes written by Fife Doole and Judas Lakayre, both coming as a surprise.

One book written by Fife caught her attention, though she didn't read it. *The Great Wizard Council.* Judas wrote a follow-up to the original, but in between Fife's and Judas's, another was written by Scholar Tyku called: *The Mythical Truth of the Great Wizard Council.*

Fife's work took an unvarnished stance, Tyku argued the group's existence, and Judas delivered conspiracy—a hypothesized council and their demises.

Harold took note of her interest and commented on each one.

"Fife's was pretty accurate, but he should know. He founded the council."

Just those few simple words made Starriace pondered on how much Harold knew. More importantly, *how* did Harold know?

"Tyku took a condescending tone, and the coins that followed proved its popularity. He probably thought he deserved a seat at the table, if they existed."

Harold didn't say anything more on the subject until Starriace found Judas's book.

"Judas hit the mark on the whole. He tried to peel back their tragic, untimely deaths, never suspecting how close to the answers he came."

Harold shrugged.

"But that was before the Wizard's War. Now, people just speculate on Xilor's involvement."

Harold's house provided many distractions, and every diversion taught her something new—all snippets inhabited little clues to a three-dimensional puzzle. Much to her delight, Harold gave her leave to read anything she desired. She would've never been able to search at leisure under Fife's or Judas' tutelage. They'd quip "that's forbidden," or "you're too young to comprehend the vastness of…"

The list expanded each day.

As she riffled through the texts, certain subjects caught her attention. Magical forms, hand-to-hand combat, weapon fighting and forging, and creatures—especially dragons—she devoured.

Each page revealed how little she knew of the dragons. Massive, muscular, and deadly, war dragons reached incredible heights in excess of thirteen meters, with a length one and a half times greater—the latter a general criterion for all.

Opposite to the war caste, the harbinger class grew twice as thick and heavy, but didn't amass the same in height and length. Though second largest, their wingspan was somewhat longer than normal.

The most populated clan was the Chimera class—established as the breeding class—their numbers tripled the nearest clan. Chimeras were considered "normal" size, reaching between seven to nine meters high and one and a half times as long.

The last clan, the Cyclone class, embodied speed. The smallest, they flew faster, higher, and further while carrying loads equal to the war dragon's mass. This clan made up the smallest faction. As the gentlest, they companioned well with other species. Head-to-ground ranged from three to five and a half meters, and head to tail no greater than nine, but their wingspan stretched twice their height.

Starriace wanted to delve deeper, but prior engagements mattered. With reluctance, she put aside the misplaced devotion.

Like in her travels, she abstained from sleep or food, living off her magical essence. Training ceased unless she picked up something along the way. Forgoing personal knowledge and advancement became the price of diligence. She'd continue her training when time and focus were allotted. Leaving all books that didn't pertain to what she needed, she continued to search elsewhere in the house.

Whenever she couldn't find something, she pestered Harold with numerous questions and references. He'd either answer or direct her on the right course. At one point, she had asked if he ever read all the volumes in his enormous house.

"No," he answered, "but I'm getting close."

If Harold hadn't finished, what hope did she have? She completed searching the upper floors after three days, most of which were stacked from floor to ceiling. Then, he showed her the basement, the sub-basement, and the deep basement. All mirrored the rooms upstairs.

Beneath the first floor of Harold's house, it reminded her of catacombs.

No wonder he hasn't read every book.

If he had all these books, why didn't he have *Du' Garuaex*? Was it so rare that it eluded his procurement? Either way, he didn't have it.

Du' Garuaex, Harold speculated, was a volume solely on the charging of power and storing it in objects or stones. He recalled a book in the sub-basement. Sifting through the endless editions, she retrieved the publication.

Boredom ached through with each banal word; a dry, droning text reminded her of Judas's teachings. Enthusiasm spurred her to skip over the dedication, author's note, table of contents, but the emotion subsided with small blips about charging stones or other objects. The tome revealed a considerable amount about elyves, but how would she apply that to her life?

Elyves chose their names once old enough, a name that echoed their natural talents and skills, a stark contrast to wizardkind who named newborns at birth. Children were referred to by their house name: kahun for boys, and salaa for girls.

In regard to elyves, Starriace had several blank segments in her memory, a byproduct of coming from the *Other Side*. To cope with the new world, Judas used the Essence Transference, moving knowledge from publications he carefully selected to her mind. The Transference was meant to copy from texts to parchment. Attempting the same on a living person had been daring and foolish.

Like dragons, elyves had many subcultures. Some lived near Ralloc in the Vikal Mountains. Those bore the closest resemblance to the people of the region with a fair complexion, hair, and eyes. The Enclave in the Vikal Mountains boasted the biggest assembly, though not all from the same subculture.

The Vikal clan—mountain elyves—considered themselves the warrior caste. Other subcultures focused on different aspects and skills.

Long ago, a special breed of warriors called the Jaikari—elyfian knights in Myshku—ran rampant. Jaikari manifested not through hard work but were born with the innate nature of combat. Spotted in their youth, they remained peerless in flawless victories.

A Jaikari hadn't been born since before the Great Wizard's War.

Other, smaller subcultures existed. The forest elyves possessed the most potent magical abilities, their wild magic grounded in nature, and conversed with elementals. These elyves carried earthly tones in their hair, eyes, and skin tone. Forest elyves made bows and arrows from a Giving Tree, and the book hinted at sentience. Each bow took a moon turn to craft.

Another prominent subculture was the nocturnal and subterrestrial night elyves. Their skin took on a spectrum of colors ranging from a faint blue to black. Their eyes took on the most drastic change, ranging from a radiant green, yellow, or gray hue. Their eyes allowed for perfect vision in darkness, a mutation that enhanced over time with their elaborate tunnels and cities beneath the soil.

Other elyves existed, but each subsequent entry became smaller than the last.

To Starriace's relief, at the end of her first fortnight, she stumbled onto a passage. Similar to what she searched for, the section directed her back on course: the stones Rusem spoke of. The book mentioned another, which referenced another. After a series of tomes, she unearthed the answers she sought.

There's an ancient power hidden across Ermaeyth, created long ago by majestic magic with the potential to destroy the world. The pull for power is strong, too strong for some as they slip forever into madness. Hagen succumbed to his foolishness.

Creatures from above came to Ermaeyth, angelic beings, benevolent and compassionate, gods of grace and power. These archangels took pity upon Ermaeyth and restored order by destroying the mightiest and darkest of us: Hagen, the Father of Magic. Saddened by their deeds, they chose never to interfere with the affairs of mortals again. The aptitude Hagen possessed caused tremendous harm, taking eons to heal and could possibly destroy most, if not all, life on Ermaeyth. As the story goes, the gods took his unique abilities and segregated it into seven brimstones.

Individually, these brimstones hold immense forces. Legend tells that if combined, the possessor would become a god, reaching through time and space and all the spaces between. No actual record of these events occurring exists, but the accumulative knowledge of all races through their myths, legends, memories, and stories brought this information to bear. Since the creation of the brimstones, many have searched, but none have been found.

Brimstones! Finally!

Now, Starriace had a name. She attained tangible evidence that they existed at one point. She didn't dismiss Rusem's mumblings, but now, she had empirical proof.

Seven stones.

The pedestal in the temple had seven carvings! She needed to find them, but where would she search?

They've been found before—the brimstones! It can be done again.

Starriace began a frantic search for anything referring to brimstones, only finding hints and tidbits. All clues pointed to *Du' Garuaex*, as the premise for charging stones with power came from the tales of brimstones. There was only one place where it might be: Ralloc.

She paused, weighing the outcomes, but the risk was worth the rewards.

Rushing upstairs, she packed her meager belongings. The tattered robes Judas provided found their way to the refuse. His book, however, survived the purge, tucked deep in her bag. Slinging the backpack over her shoulders, she dashed downstairs, halted by the hermit blocking the path.

"Harold?"

"I have three things to bestow before you leave. The first is a journal containing all my personal notes on the elyfian society. From experience, mind you, not that useless junk you sifted through. I noticed you reading about them."

"I don't know what to say!"

He placed the thin, threadbare journal in her hands. Once again, his kindness caught her at a loss for words. She'd treasure it and treat it with as much dignity as Judas's volume. Eyes glittering, she tucked it away. Silent thanks was all she could give, not trusting her voice.

"The second is a warning: Rumigul is the counter to Derengi."

Perplexed, she opened her mouth, but he cut her off.

"That's all I'll say, for it's all I know."

She nodded. Perhaps it had something to do with Shadowcasting?

"The third is a promise," Harold waved a hand, indicating the house. "All that is mine will be yours upon my departure."

His gray eyes also threatened to betray him.

"Departure? You're leaving?"

"I can't stay here forever. Eventually, I must go home. When I leave for the last time, I know you won't be here to see me off."

The warmth of his voice belied the gravity of his words.

"But don't worry right now. I return there every once in a while, as I will this visit."

"Home? Where's home? Can I visit?"

"No. For when I'm home, I'm not who I am now."

He combed his thick fingers through her hair and cupped the side of her face. She could no longer hold back, and one long tear streamed from her eyes.

"Fear not, I'll return, and so will you. No more words, no goodbye. Where I'm from there is no goodbye, for no one is truly gone. There we say 'Live free, go unburdened, return unhindered.' So, that's what I shall say to you."

She hugged him.

His large, warm arms held her tight for a moment. A sense of safety washed over her, and so did the nagging feeling that she'd sensed his aura before. She pushed it down. Leaving a haven and returning to the world that hunted her didn't seem like the smartest decision. Breaking away, Starriace took a slow step back.

"Live free, Harold. Go unburdened and return unhindered."

Chapter 10: Norek

Strong winds battered the cargo vessel just days after departing the Isles. The storms came on without warning, or so the sailors said. The boat, a medium-sized ship built for speed, bucked over the giant swells.

Norek felt minuscule in the vast waters.

While dwarfed by warships, it was built to outrun them before ever coming within range of their cannons. The slick design meant less wood, less support, and less protection from the roiling water. Every breath that went by, the mage prayed in silence, beseeching whatever gods listened.

The storms raged for ten days of their normal fourteen-day voyage, pushing back their port call by half a week. More than once, Norek wondered whether King Godfrey had sent him with foreknowledge of the storms. He dismissed the notion out of hand, but with each hammering blow, the thought came back anew.

Norek's tall, thin frame came in handy while the boat rocked, latching onto ropes or beams overhead. He kept his brown hair cropped short, the ends sneaking past his earlobes, but the rain matted it to his face, getting into his dark brown eyes. A matching goatee rounded out his appearance.

Since hearing the crew's complaints and suspicions, Norek made a point to come out more during the day. At least until the storms started. While topside, he helped with odd jobs that required little skill. Conversing gave him vague insight into their lives, and their attitude towards him changed, but then the storms came.

From there on, he stayed below decks. In the galley, between mouthfuls of food, they retold stories of their perils and adventures on the Golden Sea, the Eastern Ocean, and the lands that lay beyond.

On the tenth day, the tempest calmed, and a thick fog obscured the remainder of their trip. Past due at port, the winds confounded their problems and antagonized the weary sailors.

A call to arms broke through his light doze. The book he'd been reading lay against his chest. With a crisp, audible snap, he shut the book, discarding it with a toss. Clutching his staff and satchel, he hurried through his cabin door only to be knocked down by crew members making their way topside. Norek almost reached his feet before the second stampede shoved him back down.

"Gangway, gangway!"

Norek followed in their wake, climbing the slick, narrow stairs, gripping the railing to keep from slipping. Though the storm passed, nasty swells pestered the ship. Several times, Norek made acquaintances with the walls, and usually face-first.

Breaching through the last door, land tickled the edge of his vision. The haze started to break, and in the distance, Norek detected a brown-gray blot on the horizon.

Golden City!

Above and behind their destination, a massive sheet of blue-gray hung, the impressive Vikal Mountains tipped with snow. His gaze dropped level, and several ships stood between them and the port.

"Kaptyn!" he called. "Kaptyn? What's going on?"

"Pirates! Hard about! Take us back into the fog."

"We'll never make it! They've seen us," a young sailor cried.

"We were built for this. Evade. Even if we can't outrun them, it doesn't matter, we can lose them in the fog. Hurry it up lad!"

"I can help," Norek offered.

"Help? Fine! Go to the crow's nest and tell me how many ships there are."

The man above had impeccable timing.

"Thirteen ships, Kaptyn!"

Norek couldn't blame the kaptyn. The officer knew someone was stationed in the crow's nest but wanted Norek sequestered. The mage could contribute more than they knew. Stepping to the guardrail, he planted his staff on the deck and held out his arms like an embrace. Eyes closed, Norek sought the well of magic within him.

Norek's affinity marked him as rare, but not as rare as a Rumigul user. He was a combination of two branches of magic: Owlen, his primary, with Mussari as his secondary, a broad-based power commonly referred to by all staff-wielding mages, for whom the staff served as a focal point. Wands enabled acute and delicate work with pinpoint accuracy. The rod endowed the user with the ability to wield power over a wide area.

Norek dug deep, knowing his stunt would expend most of his energy. It'd either drive the buccaneers away or give the vessel time to escape. He could do more than one, but if the pirates boarded, he'd need a reserve.

Less is more.

As it was, the raiders turned to give chase. Finding his breaking point, Norek opened his eyes and waved his staff.

Five of the leading vessels exploded. The wood bowed and rippled, like a heat mirage, gushing out like petals of a blooming flower. Cannon powder ignited in a secondary explosion, flinging debris and shrapnel in all directions.

The ships broke apart, some cleaving in the middle, others opening up at the bow and nosediving into the water. Shattered wood cartwheeled through the air, soaring almost as high as the oily black plume. Mangled bodies and barrels floated in the water.

Judging by the distance of the other ships, the wreckage would sink long before the pirates closed. They were in no position to help their comrades. Now, the question remained: would they stop to help or give chase?

Shouts of awe filled the air behind Norek, the crew enthralled. Though suffering the loss of almost half their fleet, the marauders never faltered, determined to seek revenge on the merchant craft.

Norek's knees went weak and he grew lightheaded, the sudden rush of power leaving him drained.

"That was bloody great, lad!" the kaptyn cheered, clapping him on the back. "Can you do it again?"

Swaying, the mage shook his head to clear his vision.

"Damn!"

"Wait, there's one more thing I can do. Send one of your men to my quarters. In the trunk under the bed, there's a giant glass orb. Bring it to me."

The kaptyn turned and relayed the instructions. The shipmate disappeared below.

The nearest vessel broke away from the pursuing fleet, intent on catching them before they reached the haze. Fast and small, similar to their own, it meant the outcome would come down to moments.

The advancing vessel was almost upon them when the crewman returned, bursting through the doors with a large sphere the size of a cannonball. In a minute at most, the pirates would be able to pull alongside and board. Norek held no delusions that the merchants wouldn't be able to repel the invading force.

"Finally!"

He took the globe in his hands.

"I need a few volunteers, three will do."

Tentatively, three stepped forward, including the kaptyn.

"Not you. I need you to have your wits about you."

The officer stepped away and another took his place.

"Place your hands on the orb," Norek instructed.

They complied, their hands palming the glowing sphere before they collapsed to the deck.

"What the bloody hell was that?" the kaptyn barked.

"Necessary."

"Are they going to be alright?"

"In a few hours, a day at most. They'll be fine."

"What did you do to them?"

"Kaptyn, you're distracting me. If you want your men to see tomorrow, stop heckling me."

With his free hand, Norek fumbled in his satchel for his palm-sized orb.

"I leeched their life energy and converted it to magical energy. I made it into a bomb."

With the smaller globe in his hand, he released the larger. It floated, hovering. Guided by his rod, the larger one rose, sailing above the mast. With a gentle coaxing, he manipulated the floating crystal toward the nearest pirate ship. The smaller sphere acted as a guide, relaying a bird's-eye view of the larger. Once aligned, the orb plunged.

The sphere ripped through the deck and exploded outward with blue energy.

A bubble expanded and formed around the vessel, and bent inward like a giant hand folded it in half before exploding out. The concussive blast was powerful like before, and the black powder burned with a frenzy. A dark, oily plume of smoke and ash rose as another marker of destruction.

The shock wave buffered against the merchants, some falling to the deck. Norek gripped the railing, steadying himself. By the time they recovered, only the churning of water remained, the ship devoured by the deep.

Norek turned to the man at the helm.

"You there!" he said, pointing. "Turn us back to the heading to the Forgotten Isles."

"Belay that order," the kaptyn yelled.

He turned to Norek.

"I give the orders. We're not going back to the Isles."

"I know that, Kaptyn. I have one more trick, a simple deception. If you'll permit me?"

After his initial hesitation, the officer nodded, and Norek repeated his order. The helmsman complied instantly and Norek, with the kaptyn at his side, watched as their adversaries altered course to engage.

"Good. They're falling for it," Norek muttered.

"Now what?"

"Now, Kaptyn, we wait for nature."

"Underworld's Homugons! What are you talking about?"

"The fog. It'll obscure us from view. They'll think we're headed to the Isles. Under cover, we can alter course."

The minutes trickled by. Sometimes it seemed as if they weren't moving at all, but Norek could no longer distinguish the Golden City against the thin ribbon of coastline. Even the Vikal mountains diminished.

The pirates closed the distance but still out of cannon range when the first wisps of fog reached out with its tentative embrace. In short order, the fleet was swept from sight.

"Hold course for half an hour and then hard to starboard. Take us south!"

Norek witnessed a grin crawl across the kaptyn's face. They showed the buccaneers they were running back the way they came. The misdirection would have them sailing for a ghost quarry on an incorrect heading, and it'd be more than a day's worth of travel before they realized they were duped.

"Interesting tactic," he complimented. "I haven't the knack. Never was a military man."

"Let's just hope it'll work, and we won't encounter any more today."

"Indeed," the kaptyn agreed. "Helmsman, after half an hour, lay in a course for the Eastern City."

"The Eastern City?" Norek balked. "No, no, Kaptyn. My stop was the Golden City, I must reach it. To take me to the Eastern City would put me well behind schedule, two months of extra traveling I didn't plan on."

There'd be no way to reach Meristal in time to warn her of King Godfrey's intentions. He had to arrive before the vile man descended upon her unsuspectingly. The added urgency of meeting his mother didn't temper his disquiet.

The kaptyn nodded.

"I understand that was our original deal, but we can't while it's blocked by pirates. I'm sorry to inconvenience you. Truly, I am. Our original destination was the Eastern City, and we altered our plans to accommodate you. Since we're unable to keep our end of the bargain, I'll return half of your fee once we reach port. The men have already been paid. That's the best I can do unless you want to jump and swim, but you'd freeze to death before you drowned."

Despite not wanting to agree, the kaptyn was right. With his energy depleted and the cold water, the effort would usher him to an early grave. Had Norek not expended himself, he might've tempted fate. But he couldn't. It'd be foolish and reckless.

The officer turned and left.

Damn. So close.

He sighed, resigned, and returned to his hammock below.

Chapter 11: Bitcher

Cold gray eyes stared at the red hair resting on her soft face.

A small scar traced from the split of her lip to the right mid-cheek. Regardless of the beauty, the blemish remained. Emerald eyes hid behind her closed lids. She drew deep and slow breaths while she slumbered.

Bile rose in his throat, and he yearned to lash out. The physical scars were healed, and her back mended as she slept. Of all the luck in the world, he underestimated her resolve to live and left her for dead.

A fitting end.

Hearing her confession to the Heart had killed whatever affection he felt. Xenomene dominated his mind from the first glance, even though she ignored everyone and treated him the same.

Many tried to crawl into her bed, and she refused almost everyone. In fact, he couldn't remember a time when a man claimed such a sweet victory. He, like many others, wondered what lay beneath teasing clothes.

Then came Cape Gythmel.

That was then.

Now, he hated and loved, but which won out? He'd teetered on killing himself the night of the attack. His sword's hilt lay against the ground, his gut pressed into the point, ready to impale. He'd join her in the afterlife, where lies and deceit of the flesh couldn't touch them.

If she realized how much he had loved her…

But she didn't, not until his revelation. Shock riddled her face, not horror, but recognition. She made an effort afterward.

It was all a lie.

He remembered the first time he partook of her body. The smell of her hair was like a fine wine; the silky touch of skin intoxicating, the faint, sweet taste of flesh…he shuddered at the memory. She'd given him the honor of her body. He, in return, poured all his emotions into their tangled forms.

He thought she loved him, too.

What a fool I was.

She punished him by removing his testicle, a barbaric and abusive use of power. His love turned into ashes of resentment. She'd spit in the face of his culture when she marred him.

She made an effort to talk to him, to win him back. Hope flirted within the gray clouds of emotions. Remorse had filled her eyes and shaky voice. She opened to him and melted the steel around his heart, then offered her body again.

That was twice you partook of me and never offered your love or devotion.

His feelings were stronger than hers, and he loved her enough to make her happy. He remembered, with slight embarrassment, that the Mind walked in on them. Krey weren't modest, but he dishonored them both by being caught. As a boy, and later as an adult, he remembered watching people have sex in the Isles and at House Eti. Those that usually did were not lovers, but people answering the call of lust, a typical behavior with an audience. It was a mark of strength for an individual, or if a couple engaged, a sign of devotion to their relationship. However, he and Xenomene never discussed that aspect, and the shame of dishonor stung by being discovered without invitation or forewarning.

The Krey side of him didn't care. He remembered that night. She had been deep in her carnality, loved watching in the mirrors. A sexual animal writhed within her. Lust turned into an inferno as she stared at the Mind.

Bitcher wanted to scream.

I fucking shared your flesh!

Once Islanders became a couple, their promiscuity customarily ended with other people unless their relationship was built around that. He witnessed her want and relented to share. It was hard at first, to see her head bob up and down on another man, but she craved it.

Her happiness mattered most.

If you were happy, I was delighted. Gods! Why couldn't you see that?

He even let the Mind penetrate her. Xeno's lust drove Bitcher's, and he yearned to sate her desires. He didn't claim her sacred virginity, only ending the renowned, self-imposed celibacy.

Then came the horrible night he overheard the Heart's conversation. He hid in an adjacent room and listened. Xenomene never loved him after all. She pitied him and sought to fix him so that life could go back to normal. Xenomene's voice gave away her true emotions. If she didn't speak in dry, deadpan, and sarcastic tones, something caused her turmoil. As they say: this is how the fool loved with his heart cut out.

She promised Warlock Lakayre not to disfigure him or her life was forfeit. Honor and discipline mattered most to the Krey, and she spat on both by misleading the warlock. She took Bitcher into the desert knowing she never intended to keep her word. He remembered her warm hands before the cold bite of steel. The Heart healed those wounds, but his screams irritated his throat for the next three days.

The warlock could claim her life, but Bitcher took it upon himself to carry out the sentence. She'd defiled the vow she swore, her confession cut out his heart, and the broken bond left him cold.

She was dead to him, dead to the Krey.

He didn't know what hurt worse: the fact that she pitied him, didn't love him, or that he was an oath breaker.

Breaking a vow was enough to strip her of rank permanently. An oath breaker was the lowest a person could sink in the Krey. Slaves enjoyed a higher status.

At minimum, she'd wallow in a life of servitude after reneging, living and serving on her knees, scrubbing floors, hemming clothes, washing laundry, preparing meals, and cleaning armor. The black collar of oath breakers would never leave her neck, branding her lower than the dogs, and like an animal, she'd take meals on the floor. Even the vermin ate better, and from a bowl, too.

She'd serve two purposes: slave and whore. Once the collar closed, the Mark of the Profane—the punishment for oath breakers—she'd service not only House Eti, but the flesh of the Krey within. No one would dare release their seed within her, and her womb would wither as the years rolled by.

All Profane lost their tongues. Lies weren't welcomed. At first, the tongueless cowered, but when enough time passed, defiance would kindle in their eyes. The Krey took that, too. Blind and voiceless, most would prefer death. If the broken vow was severe enough, they'd torture a Profane to death, denying the sweet release until the spirit broke.

And that fate awaited Xeno when she woke: the Mark of the Profane.

Bitcher's hand ached as he clenched his fist until the nails dug into his flesh.

She deserves that fate!

He remembered the rage, not quite bloodlust but close. He poured his hate and discontent into each landed blow. He meant to kill her, and that was a kindness.

Stubborn bitch doesn't die.

He had partaken of her flesh one last time; the anguish he felt fueled each malcontent thrust. In his own way, Bitcher showed mercy, knowing the awaited fate. He acted to save her from the collar and the dishonor. Had she died, the grave would hold his agony, torment, and her secrets. Her betrayal drove him to take his life, but stubbornness stayed his hand. He had to be certain she perished.

I did it because I loved her. I can't *bear to see her suffer that fate.*

She would undoubtedly wake, and when she did, she'd speak. Animosity and vindictiveness would urge her. When she did, Bitcher's life would be forfeit along with hers. Dying together didn't seem so bad. What if they killed him and left her to the collar?

He needed to ensure her silence.

It would've *been better if you had died...my love.*

Which brought him full circle to her bedside.

A faint sound came from behind, the opening and closing of a door accompanied by the whisper of cloth. Even the footfalls were silent and measured. Tiny sidled to Bitcher and stared down at the pixie-like woman. Neither man spoke for a time. Bitcher knew why Tiny was here. As if on cue, the big man placed an enormous hand on Bitcher's shoulder.

"We need to talk."

He didn't command, but it was implied. Bitcher nodded, and the two left the room.

Bitcher followed in silence all the way from the Royal Scepter—where Warlock Lakayre demanded Xeno be placed—to their barracks. They ascended four flights of stairs and down the long hall to Xenomene's room where Tiny assumed the duties as leader. He didn't take up residence, but he occupied the place most of the day. He opened the door and ushered Bitcher in.

Bitcher noticed the Mind and the Heart's presence as the door swung open. They stood in front of the replaced desk.

Where it all started.

The door closed behind him, almost thudding shut. Tiny moved his large frame around the three members and took the seat at the desk. In the small chair, the big man dwarfed the table and looked like a hulking brute behind a small slab of wood.

Tiny sat back so his knees wouldn't smash the underside. The big man cleared his throat.

"You can guess why you are here."

It wasn't a question, but the implied threat gave Bitcher pause. After Bitcher had left Xenomene, he climbed down the stairs. When noises arose from the second deck, he investigated. Much to his shock, he had stumbled into a perfect alibi.

"Yes," Bitcher answered.

"Tell me, then."

"You're here to question me about the night Xenomene was attacked."

"Sounds like you knew this was coming," the Heart commented.

Bitcher turned to her. Her bronze skin clashed horribly with the dark amber robes. The black sash and hunter green striping along the cuffs of the sleeves, shoulders, and the openings of her garments brought the only relief.

"I knew this was coming. You've questioned others. Though, I'm surprised you didn't come after me first."

The Heart glanced at the floor with her almond-colored eyes.

"Oh, so you wanted to."

He peered at the other two men present.

"That implies you decided my guilt. So, you played a little game to make it appear that I wasn't your only suspect."

"Are you guilty?" Tiny asked.

"Of what?"

"You know damn well what."

"I'm guilty of many things, but not for what you're seeking."

"Looks to me like a lover's quarrel gone too far," the Heart said, her eyes lifting from the floor.

"Are you practiced in the art of a lover's quarrel?"

"Answer her question," Tiny demanded.

"She didn't ask anything."

Tiny rolled his eyes.

"Answer her *accusation*."

"I thought I had. I'm not guilty."

He focused on the Heart.

"We had no lover's quarrel."

"Are you sure?" she countered. "Perhaps this was a fight of jealousy. You caught her with another man and aimed to kill her."

Bitcher sighed.

"She's been with another man, and I wasn't jealous, so why would I hurt her?"

The Mind shifted his feet. Bitcher regarded Tiny and raised a brow.

"Anything else?"

"Who?" the big man asked.

"Who what?"

"Who was this man that she was with?"

"I'd rather not say."

Tiny lurched to his feet, his voice thundering.

"Out with it, damn you! I'm in command while she is unable to serve! This is an order."

Bitcher said nothing, but his eyes slid to the Mind as the A'uri spoke.

"I'm that man."

Startled looks came from the Heart and Tiny. The Mind was a tall man, taller than Bitcher but nowhere near the height of Tiny. Where Tiny was clean shaven, the Mind had a trimmed beard of dark brown hair. His ear-length tresses held just the faintest traces of curls.

"What?" Tiny breathed.

"Why didn't you say anything before?" the Heart inquired.

"Because it didn't matter."

Bitcher smiled inwardly. The fact that he hadn't told Tiny of his involvement with Xenomene cast doubt on the Mind and off Bitcher. It couldn't have worked out better.

The Mind sighed.

"Back before the first battle at Cape Gythmel, Xenomene quested me."

The revelation shocked Bitcher as much as the others. He hadn't known that part. The Krey referred to the threesome in this office.

"Is that all?" Tiny inquired.

"No."

The Mind glared at Bitcher.

"I also had her here, in this office."

"Is that all?"

The Mind cringed, not wishing for full disclosure.

"No, I had her *with* Bitcher."

Bitcher could feel the Heart's and Tiny's gaze on him before flickering back to the Mind.

Tiny's voice held an edge of menace.

"What do you mean *with*?"

"It was consensual, if that's where your dark thoughts tumble. I came to talk to Xeno about Cape Gythmel, but when I came in, I saw…"

He turned to Bitcher.

"Yes?" Tiny drawled.

"I saw Bitcher fucking her," the Mind finished.

The Heart spoke next.

"Was he penetrating her vagina?"

Worry flickered through Bitcher. She had to be searching for a clue or a theory's conclusion they'd started. Tiny's quick glance in her direction confirmed his suspicion. The burly man's eyes found the Mind again. This wasn't a simple question to get jolly on the details, but an investigation they took seriously.

"No," the Mind answered. "He…took her in typical Islander fashion."

The Heart and Tiny turned their scrutiny to Bitcher. A flicker of emotion passed over the big man's face. The enmity and petulance always lingered, but now something else passed over him. Perhaps the flames of jealousy? Lust? Did he love Xenomene or desire to exert his dominance by claiming her?

"That's all that happened?" the Heart prodded. "You witnessed them having intercourse?"

The Mind's hands clenched his robes in embarrassment and frustration.

"No. Xenomene glimpsed me and told me to shut the door."

"I believe," Bitcher clarified, "she said, 'shut the fucking door.'"

Tiny glowered.

"Really? You interjected to make such a small clarification?"

"If you're going to investigate this matter, it should be done in a thorough and unbiased manner," Bitcher said. "The details are important, even if you and the Heart have already determined my guilt."

He turned and addressed the Mind.

"Continue. Don't feel any shame."

With Bitcher's words of encouragement, the Mind spoke.

"I closed the door, but I came inside. I admit fault on my part. It was almost as if…" he searched for the right words.

"The lust took over you?" the Heart supplied.

"Yes, that's it exactly. How did you know?"

He waved the question away.

"I pulled up a chair and attended. I was turned on. It took all my self-control not to join in."

"Did you?" Tiny asked.

The Mind nodded.

Bitcher explained the next part.

"Xenomene had been watching through the mirrors. She ached to watch. When the Mind came in, she no longer viewed herself but him. She lusted for him."

"Is this true?" Tiny asked the A'uri.

"Yes. Bitcher moved her in front of me, but she partook of her own accord. I don't know how or when or why, but I took her to the bed."

"Is that everything?" the Heart inquired.

The Mind shook his head.

"Bitcher joined us, too."

"Ouch," Tiny commented.

The Heart rolled her eyes. An emotion rippled across the big man's face, one that Bitcher couldn't catch.

An epiphany hit Bitcher, and he crafted words to cast further doubt on the Mind. The Krey picked up the story where the A'uri left off.

"I asked him if he fancied to take her in Islander fashion. He did. He said it was his first time, and I believe him."

"Why?" the Heart asked.

"He was …" Bitcher let his eyes flicker to the Mind and back, "… unsure. He hurt her more than pleased."

"How do you know?" Tiny asked.

"I watched her face as he *ravaged* her."

"Ravage is a strong word," the Mind protested.

"Maybe, but it's accurate. I glimpsed the pain dancing across her face. By the time you were done, she was rubbed raw and bleeding. We had to wait a couple of days before having sex again. In fact, I'm sure if you go to the apothecary, they can confirm that she received doses of dewgrass."

Tiny and the Heart exchanged a look before returning to the Mind.

"Is this true?" Tiny asked.

"Somewhat. I don't agree with Bitcher's choice of words, but what he describes is accurate."

"Very well," Tiny said with a weary sigh.

Bitcher and the Mind just threw their entire investigation into the chamberpot. They were confident of their guilty suspect, but now, he'd fogged their reality.

"Where were you the night that Xenomene was attacked?" the Heart continued, not willing to give up.

"I'd rather not say."

"Why? Guilty?"

"No, I was with other people, but I'd be violating an unspoken trust."

"What you say here is kept in confidence," Tiny assured.

"No, it's not that. To speak would be like becoming an oath breaker."

It took all his will not to stare at the Heart, who straightened at his words. She, too, faced dire consequences if the word got out about what she and Xenomene had done. She'd bear the Mark of the Profane, a collar similar to Xeno's, but with magical properties inhibiting her ability to control the mind-melding, rendering her helpless to thousands of voices in the Hive.

She'd go mad. That is, unless, they killed her.

Tiny sighed.

"Very well, in front of witnesses, I bid you to speak, to break your silence without fear of recourse; from this day to the end of your days, you won't be sought after for penalty or retribution."

Bitcher sighed and put on a show of hesitation, but not enough to irritate Tiny. He shuffled his feet and exhaled a slow breath.

"I was having sex."

The Heart burst out with a laugh.

"Xenomene not enough for you? With whom?"

"With a camp hand."

"I don't believe that for one minute!" she snapped. "If you're going to lie, you should at least have a plausible one."

"Let him finish," Tiny said.

Bitcher waited a few moments.

"I was having sex with a camp hand, as was Slurp. Smokey took his turn once we finished."

Disgust flashed across the Heart's features. He couldn't tell if it was because he slept with a camp hand and Xenomene, or for joining Slurp and Smokey.

Tiny's lips thinned.

"So, you brought a whore into our barracks?"

"Did I fucking say that? No, I didn't bring her in, and a camp hand isn't a whore."

"Camp hand, whore, damsel, call her what you will. She sold herself for sex. You lot are all Islanders, correct?"

"Yes, as was she."

His eyes darted between the gathered people.

"We took her in the manner that I take Xenomene. The way the Mind took Xenomene."

He added that crucial line to cast suspicion back on the A'uri. The other two glanced at the Mind.

"Was it consensual?"

"Yes! Do you think I'd rape a camp hand with old pals from the Isles? I don't even know them. Yes, it was consensual. I'm tired of your wordless accusations. Either speak them, or shut the fuck up! Yes, I fucked Xenomene, and I screwed a camp hand with Slurp. What may be considered taboo for you uptight, prudish Rallocans is an everyday commonality where I'm from. Don't judge me or my culture because you are too closed-minded, you fucks!"

Tiny leaned back in his chair, the corded muscles in his neck tight with restraint. The Heart took his words personally as she bit back.

"I'm not from Ralloc, nor prudish. I don't judge you by your sexual preference."

"Have you lain with an Islander?" Bitcher counted. "With a Toshii? A dwaven?"

She shook her head in horror.

"Then, you are. Hell, you're probably still a virgin. Every time a sexual question was asked tonight, I could see your cringing face. Shades! You fucks are supposed to be finding out who did this to Xenomene, not dissecting my sexuality, you cunts!"

"Enough!" Tiny roared.

He took a deep breath. His voice was under control when he spoke again, but Bitcher could see his tense body, his muscles bulging underneath the thin cotton material.

"You won't talk to me or anyone else that way, Bitcher! Have I made myself understood?"

"Yeah. Step in to rescue your second floozy. When Xeno denies you, you need a contingency."

Frustrated, Tiny ran his fingertips through his hair.

"Xenomene may tolerate you, but I won't. Until she resumes her duties, what I say matters."

He took a moment to pause and collect himself.

"We'll check into your story. If what you say is true, we'll consider other suspects."

"You can't be serious!" the Heart interjected. "You know he did it!"

Tiny held up his hand to cut her off. His eyes bored into her.

"Bitcher may be crass with his words, but it doesn't make them any less truthful. We've been biased. Even now, your attitude shows this truth. His tale of a consensual threesome with Xenomene has been corroborated by the Mind's testimony. If the story of the whore is halfway accurate, then we must consider alternatives."

He turned to Bitcher, the ice of his eyes belied the heat in his voice.

"However, it should be easy enough to prove if you are lying, Bitcher. I've never heard of a camp hand bending over, let alone for three men."

You've never heard of a camp hand bending over 'cause you've never been to war!

"I'll question Slurp and Smokey, and we'll search for this woman," Tiny continued. "Without her, your story is meaningless. If she confesses to your activities, then you'll be absolved. If you're lying, the gods better help you. I'll behead you myself, not from guilt, but because I don't like you. Am I understood?"

Bitcher searched Tiny's face, measuring the words of the man.

"Fuck you!"

Bitcher turned and stormed from the room.

Chapter 12: The Nine

Iddrial eyed the glittering jewel before him.

The deep night embraced Tizer's Terrace, a slight and minuscule settlement that sparkled with a few lights after the suns slinked past the southern horizon. Small but elegant, the town doubled the size of outposts like Cape Gythmel or Crystal Falls.

Iddrial found it amusing that he even thought of the little village Crystal Falls. Several ages had passed since his last visit, and he had no intent to return. Perhaps he thought of the place because their charted course through the Stratu'Geim domain would bring them close.

Iddrial and the other eight accompanying him were exiles of the Vikal Mountain's Elyfian Enclave. They hadn't set foot there or communed with elyves in over three legends.

He missed his home.

Perhaps it has been longer? So long, that even I can't remember.

None of that mattered now, only his life and that of his companions.

A voice spoke out to him, almost inaudible.

"I speak with truth."

He smiled.

"Then you can live in peace," he replied. "It's best not to let the others hear you speak that phrase, Ama. They wouldn't understand."

The elyves, Iddrial and his companions, were cursed, called dark elyves or dafs as a derogatory term. Each elyf within Iddrial's company had pale amethyst skin and crimson hair, but his carried black undertones. Their eyes varied, all unnatural—his amber among their spectrum.

Her soft voice carried like a whispered caress of the wind.

"True," Ama Ka said. "But I wanted you to know it was me."

"I knew."

He took his eyes off the glass case before him and glanced at her. He touched his nose.

"Your scent."

"Are you saying I'm foul?" she asked in mock-hurt tones.

"I can pick up your subtle scent anywhere. There's no sneaking up on me, for you, at least."

He saw a smile flicker across her lips and turned back to the glass case.

"I used the phrase to show I held no deceit in my heart."

To this, he said nothing, knowing what she sought. He couldn't give it, not until he was sure. It wasn't a secret what she fostered in her heart, and he knew the same of everyone else they traveled with. Those thoughts whisked him away for a few moments.

"Where are you?"

"What?"

"You left, I felt it. Where did your thoughts and memories take you?"

"It matters not. To a long past that can't be undone. Have you heard from the others?"

She shook her head.

"Not yet. Cal said he'd let us know when they finished. The local depository proved no challenge for Ru Sol and Fir Fera. Their execution went undetected, and they carried away a nice sum."

"Good."

Iddrial studied the glass case once more. Inside lay a gold, jeweled crown, one of the rarest finds in Ermaeyth, priceless beyond measure, and protected with magic. The gold was so pure that it could not support the weight of jewels. A mage from long ago imbued it to strengthen the soft metal.

It was a pity that it'd be no more after tonight.

Iddrial and his group were going to melt the crown down, place the jewels in the reformed gold, and make rings and necklaces to sell. If auctioned off, they wouldn't receive as much, and the chances of being caught rose. He thought of ransoming it back to the owner, but the steward of Tizer's Terrace didn't have the means to repurchase it. The loss of a precious, historical artifact would be the cost of their gain.

Invisible wards swirled around the valuable item. Iddrial could feel the tang of magic. An almost undetectable force surrounded the glass case. Iddrial stilled himself and let the small flows of magic settle around him, which gave him a clearer picture.

The glass couldn't be lifted or shifted.

A movement caught Iddrial's eye. He risked a glance. An owl landed on the ledge of the window he'd left open. Its head turned, jerked to the side, and gave a single hoot. Ama held up her arm, and the bird fluttered over to her outstretched arm.

"They're away," she said.

He nodded and turned back to the beautiful crown.

"It's a shame I don't have time to sketch or paint this masterpiece."

Ama nodded and patted his arm. He looked at her, and she gave a small, knowing smile. Bending, he grasped the large stone twice the size of his closed fist, raised it above his head, and dropped it on the glass.

Other than a loud clatter, nothing happened.

Iddrial and Ama Ka kept silent, listening to see if they awoke anybody. Surmising they hadn't, Iddrial grabbed the rock, ascended the spiral stairs, and held the stone aloft. A startled voice cried out.

"What are you doing?"

Iddrial's head snapped to the right, seeing the steward holding a candle and in his sleeping clothes. Iddrial let go of the stone. The plummeting rock smashed the glass barrier and crushed the crown, bent and warped beyond repair.

"Give the crown to the bird and go!" Iddrial said in Thymulous.

Ama Ka plucked the crown from the glass fragments, and the bird clawed the headdress and flew out the window. Ama, still on the ground level, ran over to the window and leapt through, following after the bird.

"By the gods, you destroyed the crown!" the steward yelled.

Iddrial took a step toward the staircase.

"No!"

The steward lunged. The elyf vaulted over the tackle, then over the staircase railing. Landing, he made sure no one bore down on him to catch him unawares. During the few moments he checked for pursuers, guards busted in the door behind him. The screams of steel leaving sheaths drowned out the clank of their mail.

"There he is," one sentry shouted.

The guards pursued, but no wizardkind could catch an elyf. Iddrial dashed for the window and jumped through headfirst like Ama Ka. He tucked, somersaulting through the air, and landed on his feet. The impact made him stagger, and his joints protested.

"Not as graceful as you once were," Ama teased. "Getting old?"

He pressed his lips together but said nothing. He took off, leaving the steward and his grounds behind. Ama followed, hurtled past buildings and houses as they closed on the ten-foot-high town wall, an easily obtainable reach for Iddrial. He lengthened his strides, picked up speed, and bounded. His feet touched the top long enough for him to vault over.

He landed harder than expected, falling forward to his knees.

Blessed stars, I am *getting old.*

Shouts rang in the distance behind them, guards rousing for pursuit. It was foolish and a waste of time. They'd never catch them—a night pursuit through a forest? It was foolish. Elyves could run twice as fast as wizardkind over short distances and had the stamina to run from sun up to nightfall. The guards would give up once they grew tired.

Iddrial and Ama pelted through the forest, whispering by trees, a blur among the shadows and swarthy bushes. The plant life swayed by their passing, ghosts in the darkness.

Their long hair trailed behind them like silk in the wind. Iddrial slowed his pace as he neared the group's location. A long and arduous journey lay ahead of them. So, he paced himself.

As tonight proved, he was advancing in age, and it wouldn't get any easier. he scenery changed from dense woods to sparsely wooded hills with rolling terrain, from grasslands to rocky. The stars had rotated in the sky by a quarter when Iddrial and Ama Ka finally met their fellow elyves.

"You made it," Ahn Bael said.

Iddrial doubled over, winded from the three-hour journey.

"Of course. Why wouldn't I?"

"Well, it's been a long time since, you know…you've done any real work."

"Is that an attack against my decisions and past actions?"

"Not at all."

Ahn shied away.

"I'm concerned for your health, that's all."

He gave his leader a wolfish grin.

"Cute."

Iddrial straightened and eyed the group.

"Why isn't camp broken?"

"We were waiting on you," Fir Ki replied.

"The wait's over. Let's go."

"Where are we headed?" Ru Sol inquired.

Iddrial appraised the woman.

"South. Past the Melodic Mountains."

"Are we going to the Green Lands?" she asked, hope in her voice.

"No. Stratu'Geim. Has the crown made it back yet?"

"No," Ahn reported.

"Cal!" Iddrial called out. The man came running up, puzzlement etched on his face. "Where's that feathered friend of yours with our loot?"

"He isn't back yet?"

"Obviously not. Call to him."

Cal spent the next fifteen minutes calling to the owl, but the bird never came. Worry spread across his face as he told Iddrial.

Iddrial sighed.

"We need that crown. Break camp. Let's search for it and be on our way."

It didn't take long for Iddrial and the other eight elyves to find the crown. Ama called for her pet, Qui-Ri, a female dragon of the Cyclone class, and the search went much faster. Astride the immortal beast, it augmented Ama's abilities and senses, heightened by the inherent magic of all dragons.

Sleek and slender, the impressive wingspan helped it glide in silence, much like an owl. Moreover, dragons resembled cats more than lizards. Their mannerisms resembled the small, furry mammals: stealthy, attentive, and at times, they purred, too.

When Ama Ka and Qui-Ri landed, the elyf handed him the bent and twisted crown. It was a shame the others didn't see it beforehand.

"We have what we need," Iddrial said. "Our journey lies beneath the Melodic Mountains."

"Well, let's get moving," Ahn said. "The sooner we move, the sooner we can stop."

He eyed Iddrial.

"You'll be owing us some comforts on the other side."

Iddrial didn't say anything as he bounded away, but he couldn't help but think how right Ahn was.

Chapter 13: Xenomene

Her emerald eyes opened.

She squinted at the light coming through the window. Dark, fuzzy shapes filled her vision as silhouettes returned before color did. Something shifted in the room. She turned, searching. They loomed closer, and the image became clear.

The blood drained from her face. A sharp gasp escaped her as Bitcher's face came into focus.

"Xeno."

She shifted, lurching away from him, creating distance between them. The bed's headrest wouldn't allow an escape. He snatched her by the wrists and overpowered her, pulled her close. She opened her mouth to scream, but his hand stifled any noise.

"Quiet!" he hissed. "I'm not going to hurt you. I just want to talk."

She quit struggling, but her eyes couldn't hide the fear. Her body trembled with sharp, short breaths. He moved back and removed his hand.

"Xeno."

"Get away from me."

"Shades, Xeno. I'm sorry, truly I am…"

How could he sound so calm?

"Not as sorry as you're going to be."

"That's where you're wrong."

Bitcher's voice held an edge of menace, and it sent a quiver of worry through her.

"There's so much to say, I don't know where to begin."

"It doesn't matter where you start, you'll be dead by sundown."

"And your pretty head will be right there with me."

The words gave her pause.

What's he playing at?

"What are you talking about?"

"Xeno," he searched for the words but ended up blurting it. "I love you. I have loved you for a long time, and I can't help myself around you."

"You're fucked in the head."

"That…I wasn't myself when that happened. I was angry. After what you did to me…I thought you loved me back!"

Xenomene almost laughed aloud but thought better of it. Bitcher had attempted to kill her before, any misconception of a slight might set him off again.

"You…"

Anger filled his voice and face. His pale gray eyes smoldered. Xenomene tried to make herself small against the gaze, but with her back against the headboard, she couldn't flee.

"You lied! You broke your vow to the warlock, your word as a Krey. You had him send me to the desert so you could mutilate me. And you didn't do it once, but three times! Then, you left me to sulk. You played games with me and invited me back into your bed. You shared yourself with me. Do you have any idea what that means to Forgotten Islanders? And I even shared you! I don't share, but you wished for it, so I did to make you happy."

He shot his fingers through his blond hair.

I was never yours to own or share.

Prudence stifled the blurt.

"Do you know what happens to you if you break your oath?"

Xeno nodded, not trusting her voice.

"Obviously, you don't! Let me remind you what happens to oath breakers, to the Profane."

Xenomene finally spoke, finding her voice.

"I'm not a Profane. The warlock isn't Krey."

"That doesn't matter."

"Yes, it does! Receiving the Mark of the Profane is only for breaking oaths to other Krey."

"You fool!" he said with vehemence. "How the hell did you become ko-don and not know our own laws and customs? The last person to receive the Mark was Regina the Butcher. Have you forgotten the tale? She refused to fulfill a paid contract, took the money but didn't satisfy the obligations. Then, she turned her sword on the man and killed him and his family. For their murders, she was awarded death, but the heir made an example of her. He abstained and gave her the Mark. He made it law for anyone who broke an oath, regardless of the situation. You'll receive the Mark if you talk!"

"Regina was a long time ago, there's no way the heir—"

"I didn't say *this* heir. It was his predecessor."

Xenomene cradled her legs to her chest and laid her head on her knees.

"They'll take your tongue first, you know that, right?"

Enmity flared in her green eyes.

"What do I care of a tongue? After what you did, they'll take your cock and your balls!"

"Your eyes, too!"

"As long as I see them geld you and string you up, I'll be content."

"What about being a whore to all the Krey? There are some you detest. They'll take you, and that's after a long day of scrubbing pots, wiping down armor, oiling swords, and cleaning chamber pots. Then, when you crawl upon your pallet at night, if they even give you one, they will spread your legs and ravish you for hours."

After his words, the anger and defiance fled her face, leaving her empty. She scrounged up the bravery to whisper before despair took her.

"Just imagine what'll happen to you."

Bitcher shook his head as if bewildered by her quiet defiance.

"That fate awaits not only you but the Heart, too."

Xeno jerked her head up, eyes wide with questions left unvoiced.

"Yeah, that's right. She'll be punished as an oath breaker, too. May not have broken the oath, but she acted as an accomplice. Equal guilt in the eyes of all. And that's not the worst part for her. The collar inhibiting the ability to eliminate the voices will be. That special A'uri talent will torture her until madness."

"Enough."

"And I forgot to even mention the torture."

"I said enough," she whispered, heartbroken. "What do you want, Jakeb?"

"I want you safe and whole."

"Then, you should get as far away from me as possible."

He shook his head.

"No, not going to happen. I loved you, and some part of me still does, the part that won't see you become a Profane. Gods be damned, Xeno, as much as I hate you, I can't bear the thought of a future like that for you."

"What do you really want?"

"I want your love."

She shook her head, lips twisting in disgust.

"That'll never happen."

Umbrage contorted his features.

"Then, let's commence with your fate and talk to the warlock and the heir."

Fear and desolation smothered her features.

I swear by the scrotum of all the gods that you'll die screaming.

"That's what I thought," he muttered. "You don't want to die any more than I do. And you sure don't want the Heart's fate on your conscience."

She shook her head again.

"I can't give you what you ask. I can never love you, not after what you did to me. If it's my body you want, fine. If you want to be my husband, then we'll be married. But I'll never, ever, love you."

"You better learn to fake it and fast. By now the entire squad—if not the army—knows you and I are a couple. They'll be watching us."

A thought came to her.

"How the hell did they not place the blame on you?"

He smiled, but nothing warm.

"I placed the blame at other people's feet, and subtly let the Heart draw conclusions for guilt and fear. In a way, she realizes I know she's an oath breaker. The Mind is under suspicion, too, and Tiny knows he hurt you."

"You told them!"

"Don't be modest! You fucked him in Cape Gythmel. We just took it to the next level."

While his words angered her, the truth didn't.

Now everyone is aware I quested the Mind, and both took me together. Perfect!

"If you don't sell this act, a lot of people are going to be Marked. I, for one, will go down fighting. They'll take you and the Heart, and just to be safe, the Mind, too. Their fate will be yours, as will the fault. Can you live with that?"

She let the emotion drain from her eyes, couldn't give him the satisfaction of knowing he broke her.

"When did you become so heartless, Bitcher?"

"The day you cut it out."

Is it true? Did I do this to him?

"Kiss me."

"What?"

"Kiss me."

"Fuck you!"

"Perhaps you didn't catch the part where you play this out like nothing ever happened. We'll go on as if nothing has changed. Lives are at risk."

She rolled her eyes, leaned forward, and kissed him. With haste, she pulled away.

"That was fucking pathetic. You better improve, or there'll be three collars for you, the Heart, and the Mind."

She spat in his face, a fine mist.

"I fucking hate you."

He wiped the saliva away, only looking mildly annoyed.

"Well, pretend you love me. You're good at that, right?"

She gritted her teeth and thought back to a time when she had felt something for him. She'd always found him humorous when his attentions were not directed at her. He was comical, witty, even kindred with sarcasm. There had been a time, once. She tried to put a finger on the elusive sentiment.

She thought back to the first time Bitcher had taken her. He had made her feel so alive, an unaccustomed feeling from years prior. It wasn't love, just fucking. She never had any complaints there. Perhaps because she'd chosen to remain celibate, and broke the celibacy with the Mind, was why she didn't resist Bitcher laying claim to her.

She loved it.

The Mind didn't compare to Bitcher. Lust and need compelled the quest with the Mind. Bitcher was something else entirely.

Guilt kept her company in the aftermath of his punishment.

I pitied him. But that's not why I took him to my bed again. Why?

Bitcher's words held truth. She could fake and pretend, but she hadn't with him. She *had* loved him and never realized. It was the only explanation, surely. Had she not felt something for him, she would've never screwed him a second time. Had Bitcher not overheard the fateful conversation, how different things would've been?

She swallowed.

Now, it was an act, a challenge to dig deep for those buried emotions. More than her life depended on it. Xenomene suspected she didn't value life as much as she should, most Krey didn't, but being responsible for the fate of others? She set the boundary at any life beyond her own.

Bitcher had cornered her, and the Heart's involvement was Xeno's fault. How could she live with the Heart relegated to a mentally deranged whore?

She'd have to find another way to save them.

Bitcher had to die.

While the thought of Bitcher perishing made her stomach flutter with giddiness, it wasn't a helpful emotion right now. She might've been fond of him at one point, a fact not worth denying. Now, she had to embody that fleeting emotional state and live it every day through word, thought, and action. That meant kissing him when he asked and fucking him when he wished.

But first, she needed to believe it again.

Clinging to that emotion, she reached for Bitcher and kissed him. She poured the memories of those feelings into the embrace, her warm, velvety tongue breaching past his hot, moist lips. The passion whirled in his mouth. That's how it'd been, that's how she'd always kissed Jakeb.

When she pulled away, she noted Bitcher's flushed face. A quick gander spied his arousal.

Fucking Shades of the Underworld, already?

She pushed away, rolled out of bed, and reached for her clothes. A gentle hand grabbed her wrist. Acutely aware that only a night shift kept him at bay, she withdrew.

"Not now," she said, trying to hide the mix of ire and fear. "You'll have plenty of time later. With two more squads coming soon, there are things I must attend to."

"They're here. Arrived this morning."

"What? What time is it?"

For the foreseeable future, she had to lock the fear and acrimony away and plot.

To make them believe, I must believe.

"It's another hour or two 'til the midday meal. They arrived right before you woke up. You're not going to believe what the heir sent."

She dressed facing away from him, but even that was a gamble. He'd see her ass and want to fuck her, but she hid the rest of herself. She heard the smile in his voice.

It must be funny, but I can't laugh. He doesn't rouse those feelings anymore.

The fate awaiting her and the Heart forced a smile on her face.

I don't hate Bitcher, I love him.

"What's so funny?"

"One squad is half men and half women. The other squad is all females, including the A'uri."

The last statement startled Xenomene.

Has the heir lost his mind? He sent a flock of females into a camp full of men.

"How long ago did they arrive?"

"I don't know, right before you woke up. Maybe half an hour?"

Xenomene abandoned all modesty and tore the shift from her body, exposing herself as she speedily dressed.

"This won't be good."

Clothes in place, she bolted for the door with Bitcher nipping at her heels.

His footsteps sent a spasm of fear lancing through her, expecting his hand around her throat, another rape, and additional blows to the face. Her heart pounded, hammering against her rib cage.

Panic threatened to overtake her.

I don't fear him.

Her hand closed around the doorknob, and she flung it open. Her room dumped out into a hall, and she spied the exit with ease, ignoring the turned heads and startled exclamations. She sprinted by the time she exited the building. Bitcher managed to keep up but only for a few moments.

His pace slowed, no match for her conditioning.

She ran through the door of their hotel-barracks. The jarring sensation slapped her in the face, powerful enough to knock the wind from her lungs.

Lust.

All members of the three squads pursued the throes of passion. Naked flesh gleaming with sweat all about the room. The lust cut a swath through the air like an all-encompassing tangible scent, and Xenomene's blood boiled with need.

A fleeting gander revealed dozens of vivid scenes. Sometimes, multiple men took a woman or vice versa. Some coupled off in the corners with tangled limbs; perhaps they were two people who harbored feelings for each other? Most piled together in a massive orgy of fluids, skin, and pent-up energy.

She saw more pairs of balls in one day than she wanted in a lifetime.

Lust filled her eyes, simmered in her blood, as people were bent and folded into recognizable positions to the bizarre.

Tiny was the easiest to spot, as no one matched his height. She saw four women ogling him, but she quickly discerned why. His looming manhood swung between his legs like the handle of an axe buried deep in the heart of a tree. Endowment aside, the overwhelming urge to mount him didn't arise.

Perhaps personal feelings did play a factor in the lust?

The maddening sensations snatched her up. Xenomene pulled the constricting shirt free. Running footsteps sounded behind her. She turned to meet Bitcher's pale, gray eyes, and the lust sparkled within.

All the harbored hate absconded. Only lust remained.

She launched herself at him, and they embraced in front of everyone. Hot and wild kisses flashed over him as she tore his shirt away. He ripped her trousers off. Being exposed to everyone seemed trivial when his fingers entered her.

She dropped to her knees and jerked his trousers down. His hands snaked through her red hair as she charmed him, a veneration that elicited a moan. His calescent flesh set her insides ablaze. Fervor fluttered through her stomach, and she trembled with a lecherous itch.

Her pace quickened.

Someone stepped close and stood in her peripheral vision. She pulled away from Bitcher long enough to see Tiny's fifth limb. Her eyes bulged, but she didn't suffer the same urge as with Jakeb.

One beautiful woman from another squad that Xenomene didn't know knelt and reached for Bitcher. Jealousy lurched within Xeno.

Forgetting Tiny, she stood and whispered in Jakeb's ear. With a nod, they waded deeper into the room, encircled by feverous sensuality.

The synchronous bodies amplified her lust. The sight of each coupling enthralled her. Spying Islanders in the mix, both men and women, didn't surprise her, only their growth in numbers.

Bitcher's warm hands touched her hips, and she dropped on all fours. Exhilaration from the rush of debauchery tingled across her skin. He mounted her in front of everyone. A heady sensation rippled through, wanting the others to witness. An audience heightened the pleasure, the arousal burn hotter.

Glistening flesh rocked and rolled in rhythm all around her. Some fast and frantic, others slow and methodical, each riding a unique wave of passion. Xenomene closed her eyes and breathed in the temptation, the irresistible lechery, her own lust responded to everyone else's.

Her troubles faded away. She longed to drink of everyone, yearned for them all. The number of men she could conquer, the untold women who could watch as she mounted the male squad members.

Why can't every day be like this?

Together, the Krey rode a giant swell of self-indulgence. She opened her eyes to find Slurp, arguably the most attractive man in all the squads, have his way with…the Heart? Shock rolled through Xenomene.

Slurp took the Heart mere feet away from Xenomene's face, and the A'uri enjoyed herself. Xenomene never thought the Heart capable of distraction. Xeno reached out and touched Slurp. He looked back, the desire and pleasure etched on his face. She hungered to mount him, coveted him, but the Heart drew his attention away. Xeno laid her head on the floor, relishing salacious thoughts about Slurp.

A thump sounded, and she glanced up. Tiny sat not two feet away. She rose, and he slid forward. This close, a compulsion swelled within. Tiny's apparent desire compelled the urge. Her small hand took hold of him. He pulsed in her grip.

She licked her parted lips and lowered her head.

As his manhood loomed near, a stray thought flickered to life. She didn't want Tiny in her mouth, didn't want him *in* her at all. In fact, why was she touching him? Repulsed, she released his flushed firmness. Behind her, Bitcher slowed without climaxing.

The lust, instead of swelling, receded.

What the fuck is happening? Why are we stopping?

A few moments passed, and the terror and discontent returned, knowing Bitcher buried himself in her slickness. Mingled beneath was the fondness she once bore Jakeb. Even that, too, subsided.

Around the room, the lust diminished. Most reacted the same way, in shock and embarrassment. The Heart gasped and twisted beneath Slurp, revulsion etched on her face.

"Get the fuck off me," she shrieked.

Bitcher withdrew a few moments later. On her hands and knees, Xenomene rummaged for her clothes, crawling at a frantic pace.

What the fuck is happening? We shouldn't have stopped until deep in the night. We should be fucking ourselves to exhaustion. This has never happened at the Hive!

She found the tattered remains of trousers and shirt and tried to dress in haste. The shorts wouldn't stay in place, the waistband ripped and stretched. She decided to don the tunic first. As it fell over her head, the front doors of their barracks burst open and two figures strolled in.

"If you're quite finished!" a voice bellowed.

She knew whose voice that belonged to: Warlock Lakayre. His eyes blazed with *fury*, or was it something else?

Is the lust affecting him, too?

The other figure was the heir of House Eti.

Shades!

Both held immutable faces. The heir came clad in dragon-plate armor. Warlock Lakayre dressed in a resplendent fashion suitable for nobility, in colors of dark blue-violet silk, deep crimson and orchid piping, and a traveler's cloak that matched with muted, dark gray-blue silk.

Shades, did he drop a few ingots at the clothing store?

She gaped at the pair until their eyes found her. The distinct feeling of being a madman caught in a moment of lunacy slithered in her gut.

Under the circumstances, her grace had been exceptional, standing nude in the presence of two prominent men. She let go of the shirt and trousers to salute in the Krey manner, a fist to the heart over her exposed breasts. The shorts fell past her knees.

"Oblus ina'ti Sepan Eti," she greeted the heir.

His eyes were drawn to the exhibit, a slow, lingering inspection of her entirety rather than a cursory or involuntary glance. His eyes plunged downward again.

Is that the aftereffect of our lust or his own personal desire?

The heir collected himself and returned the formal greeting.

"Oblus ina'ti Sepan Eti."

Xenomene resumed fixing her shirt.

"Warlock Lakayre, I greet you. What brings you to our barracks?"

"Your lust," he clipped.

His vehemence encouraged caution, and she kept her attention more on her commanding officer. "You have the entire camp either beginning to go into lust themselves, or they're standing outside listening to all of you… fornicating."

The heir rolled his eyes, and his lips twitched, but he didn't vocalize what he really thought.

"Thank you for your assistance."

The words were terse, and the heir's attitude reflected a silent dislike. Judas nodded and swept from the room, closing the doors behind him.

"On your feet, you fucks!" the heir bellowed once the doors closed.

Everyone leapt up, standing at attention. No one tried to cover up; the Krey were immodest. Once the shuffling subsided, the heir walked into their midst.

"Gods and demons, I could smell the sex from outside."

He chuckled, walking past Xenomene's line of sight. She could hear the heir making odd, random comments about people he passed, things like, "Who the fuck fucked you? Better suck in your gut," or "Are those breasts or pillows?"

He paused, and from his comments, Xeno knew he stopped in front of Mauler.

"Your ass is darker than the caves beneath House Eti."

His footsteps crawled through their ranks and abruptly stopped.

"Holy sweaty whores in seven hells! I didn't know you were descendant of a dragon!"

He must have stopped in front of Tiny. I can't believe I almost…

She fought the urge to yack.

"That's almost as long as a bastard sword. Shades, what do you feed that thing?"

"Redheads."

The heir cackled.

"You hear that, Xenomene?"

She rolled her eyes but didn't move.

"I hope you can run fast, or he'll impale you. Tell you what, Tiny. If she's ever choking, I'm sure you could dislodge it."

He gave a hysterical laugh, and Xenomene couldn't help but smile at the comment. It was humorous. She imagined the heir's body shaking from fits.

His feet moved again, the footfalls growing louder, and Xeno schooled her face. He paused behind her, and she felt the weight of his gaze.

In a breath almost too quiet to hear, he muttered, "By all that's holy, an ass of the divine."

A few seconds later, he pushed past her peripheral. He stood before her and looked her up and down. A quick glance. He muttered something under his breath about gods and seven hells and prostitutes.

"All right, you fucks. You've had your fun. That shit won't be happening again. The Warlock's making sure of that. Take a good look, go ahead, don't be shy. Some of you deserve a second look, fuck, some of you three."

The heir eyed Xenomene as he said that last. He smiled, his eyebrow raised.

"Some of you probably taste as good as you look."

His eyes moved past her groin to the rest of the room.

"Some of you…by the gods-unholy-fuck, don't ever take your clothes off in public again."

He sighed.

"Alright, get dressed, get cleaned up, and get the fuck out. I'm here to meet with your ko-don."

He turned toward her and held up a hand to the stairs.

"After you."

Xeno pulled up the ripped trousers, held the waistband, and walked past him, bounding up the steps two at a time. By the time she reached the fourth floor, the heir trailed by a flight and a half and labored to breathe. At the end of the long hall, she opened the door and waited outside, letting the heir enter first, as was his right as senior in rank. After half a minute, he climbed up the stairs, ambled down the hall and entered.

Xenomene followed.

She closed the door and regarded him as he scrutinized the office. After a cursory glance, he gave a nod.

"Don't mind me."

Xenomene's lips thinned with irritation, and she gave an eye roll. She crossed the room and opened the chest at the foot of the bed, digging for a new change of clothes.

"I'm glad you're awake and moving again. I came to visit you, you know?"

She hadn't, of course, but it changed her perspective of him. An unfamiliar emotion coiled in her chest. Gratitude? Appreciation?

"That first day," the heir continued. "You were a fucking bloody mess. Do you know who attacked you?"

Xenomene stopped and looked up. Her eyes found a mirror on the underside of the footlocker's lid. Doubt flickered within.

Should I tell him?

"No," she said. "Whoever they were, they snuck up on me while I was sleeping. I never saw them until it was too late."

"Them? Meaning you saw more than one?"

While Xenomene didn't want to outright lie again, she stuck as close to the truth as possible. The story would be easier to maintain.

"I use the term loosely. It could've been one."

"Xenomene? The most feared Krey with a sword was destroyed by one person?"

She paused to ponder a better answer. She slipped into her usual careless and sarcastic self.

"Well, I don't sleep with a sword in my hand, do I?"

He chuckled, but not the robust laugh from earlier. Xenomene found the last article of clothing and stood.

"Try not to drool on my floor while I change. I don't want to have to clean it twice in one week."

She turned away and stripped off the tunic, causing the heir to half-sit, half-crash into a chair. She glanced back and lifted an eyebrow at him but continued. She knew he could see the side of her breast but not her pubic region.

The heir gave half stutters and starts before finding his words.

"Well, you seem fine to me. In firm form, as they say."

As he said form, Xenomene dropped her trousers. Her eyes flickered to the mirror on the wall and caught the heir in a blatant stare.

Let the old man stare. He probably hasn't been bedded in a long time. Knowing that he came to see me when I was hurt almost makes me fond…

She bent to step into her new shorts. Her bottom loomed like a forbidden indulgence not two strides from him. The heir stuttered again.

"If there were ever another perfect woman…" he started.

She peered back at him, her brow raised in an unasked question.

"Another? What? I'm not number one?"

He shook his head wistfully and cleared his throat.

"Now that you're awake, you can resume your duties and command, unless you would prefer to be relieved."

Xenomene pulled the new pants up and turned to regard him. Usually, being relieved of duty inside the Krey meant you'd never command again, but perhaps he intended compassion and asked if she wasn't ready for the responsibilities just yet.

No, he's Krey. We're not sympathetic.

"I'm fine."

"You sure?"

"Nothing that a little rum and a good fucking won't cure. Maybe blooding my sword might help."

"Hmph."

He nodded, knowing not to ask again. Once a Krey spoke, their word as oath was never questioned again.

"Very well, let's talk about what the army wants to do with three squads of Krey. Got a map?"

Xenomene shuffled through the drawers of the desk until she found them.

"Which one?"

"The lower and east domains."

She pulled the appropriate maps out and laid them down. The heir pulled himself to his feet and leaned over the charts when Xenomene's hand stopped him short.

"What?"

"Wipe the drool from your mouth, I don't want it to get all over my maps."

The heir let out his cackle-boom of laughter and wiped his mouth greedily.

Chapter 14: Judas And Meristal

Judas set the last rune in place around the Krey's barracks and stretched.

Ever since he broke their lust, he'd crafted wards to prevent further outbreaks of en masse carnal activities. He'd never set foot in the Hive, but he understood the precautions taken with the small city.

Without thought, he pulled his goatee before nodding approval at the runes.

Outpost Dire had some in almost every building, but with their numbers, it was still possible to overpower the wards. A few types of lust plagued Ermaeyth: bloodlust and magic-induced lust. The wards would keep the Krey and A'uri from entering another passionate frenzy.

His lip twitched with disapproval.

He battled whether to alter an addendum, preventing all sexual desires based on the atrocities that befell Xenomene, but he found the decision immoral and unethical. So, he let them be.

The camp was safe now, and none would fall victim to another wave, Krey or not. How terrible would it be if Xilor marched up while their pants were down? Even Judas couldn't deny the stirrings within him, which alerted him to the incident.

I'm glad Meristal wasn't here; I don't know if I could've controlled myself.

But the yearning side of him was disappointed she wasn't.

Judas rechecked the work, probing with magic before teleporting to his manor. He touched the doorknob with his wand and the bolts retracted, breaking the magical seal. He thought back to when he and Julie left for Wizard's Pass.

Starriace, now.

Every time Judas saw Meristal, he wanted to share the news that his daughter lived, but it'd reopen old wounds, and some things were better left buried.

He sighed, feeling the weariness leaving his body.

Kernoyl Tyku suggested that Judas go home and rest for a few days. At first, he'd been adamant about staying, but after hearing the reasoning, he agreed. The Krey were to debark from Dlad City in bulk, leaving only a few behind. Xilor's small encampment around Cape Gythmel hadn't stirred, and a jynerul would soon take command in Dlad City. When that happened, there'd be no chance for a reprieve.

So, Judas left.

He did want to conduct a search for Xenomene's assailants, however. His sense of justice and duty kicked in, but he never voiced such things to Tyku. No matter how far apart the Krey were from the army, they still fell under the command of the young kernoyl.

It wasn't his business to interfere.

Judas peeled off the traveler's robe and hung it in the closet next to the door before ambling over to the table beside the fireplace. He poured a much-needed glass of his favorite liquor. The scent of vanilla and peaches invaded his nostrils as he unstoppered the decanter.

Bliss captured in an aroma.

He flipped a crystal glass upright and poured. The amber liquid almost glowed when held to the light. He kicked it back like a shot, then refilled the glass and replaced the lid. This time, he savored the flavors and fragrance.

He took the glass to the kitchen.

Fighting laziness and failing, he used magic to boil water. Judas usually did things the *mundane* way, finding it therapeutic. The water roiled by the time he retrieved the coffee grounds from the pantry. Within moments, he had warm perfection in his hands. Pulling wood from the closet, he set it inside the stove before lighting the tinder. It'd keep the coffee hot while he sat on his porch and enjoyed the midday weather. Today proved to be one of those days that melted by without realizing how much time had passed.

For once, I can be lazy.

He picked up the mug and the crystal of liquor, downed the latter, and placed the glass in the sink. Outside, he reclined in the porch's wooden rocking chair.

After months of being away, he felt peace.

He closed his eyes and enjoyed the sounds of wildlife around him, the things missing in Dlad City: birds, crickets, and other creatures of the biosphere.

"Are you going to share any of that with me?" a voice broke into his refuge.

Judas jumped, spilling some coffee on his hand. His eyes shot open.

"Meristal? I didn't hear you come through the gate. Did I doze off? Forgive me."

She stepped on the porch and gave him a sympathetic expression as she patted the burned hand, then took a seat beside him.

"Nothing to forgive. But I'll take some of that coffee now."

"Oh, right."

Judas set the mug aside and swept up into the house, coming back moments later with a cup. She accepted it with a gracious dip of her head and took a sip.

"Let's talk," she said.

Meristal sat behind her desk in the consul's chambers in Ralloc, poring over numerous documents: fund petitions, tax requests, embargo acts, law proposals, and army requisitions.

The papers piled higher each day.

This isn't what I signed up for. I didn't think there'd be this much paperwork.

She sighed. Her mind took her far away from the cold, decorous silence of the office, and found herself surprised when Judas came to mind.

With each passing day, she missed him more. During the two-year stint in Mecas River City, part of her died at not visiting him. And now, she was back, and a war erupted before she unpacked.

Vast changes took place in her absence. Judas nabbed an apprentice, the first in over two ages, then ran for Wizard's Pass. Xilor returned, Kayis had been voted out, and Meristal became the interim consul.

She rubbed her amethyst eyes with the heels of her palms and yawned. A lock of red hair spilled down to her shoulders.

Her mind flitted back to a conversation with Judas before she left for Mecas River City two years ago. She'd broached the subject of moving in with him, to which he flat-out refused.

Judas, you're too damn old-fashioned. If you only knew how much I gave up to be near you…

Far more than anyone could imagine.

But she wouldn't let herself fall to pity. They'd been an item since their youth and had done everything under the suns except wed. Meristal pushed to make them official, but her delicate and subtle nudging didn't bear any fruit. She memorized all of Judas's excuses, and if honest, she preferred his younger self to the older countenance. Had they married young, his warlock classification would've hurt her career, or so he said.

He also professed that she'd be branded an exile, too. No law, real or proposed, stated such, and no lawful excuse came to mind either. Plus, she hated Ralloc, and he remained the only reason why she stayed all these years.

She sighed and rested her head against her palm. She knew the real reason. He lived too much in the past and couldn't forgive himself for his mistake. His error angered her to no end, but the fault lay with Daylynn. Though Meristal still harbored ill feelings, they paled with the passage of time.

Daylynn tricked Judas on more than one occasion and slept with him. Judas only figured it out when Meristal walked in on Judas having sex with…

Well, me, but it wasn't. It was Daylynn.

Daylynn, like Meristal, possessed the unique and rare ability to change physical features to anything she desired. Meristal and Judas were…more than friends by that time, and would've married, but Meristal discovered Daylynn's betrayal.

Ever since, Judas shied away from Meristal's affections, finding himself unworthy and prolonging his punishment.

Judas, you've got one of the saddest lives in all the history of Ermaeyth.

He lost everything, family included. Xicx murdered his parents, his brother destroyed by Xilor himself, and he lost his only other friend, that king from Stratu'Geim, but she couldn't remember his name.

He lost his child, too. Daylynn's daughter.

Judas had impregnated both Meristal and Daylynn, and the children were born days apart. Daylynn's had died hours after birth while Meristal's and Judas's had been murdered.

As if it wasn't enough, public humiliation followed with the exile status. He loved Ralloc, but it threw him out like a stray dog. He still loved Ralloc, but the event changed him. He was no longer optimistic and boisterous, no longer blind to the insidious political arena or ambitions of others. He loved the people and the city, not those appointed to run it.

The reminiscing spurred the yearning to see him again.

She stood and walked to the mirror hanging on the wall, footsteps muted by the thick burgundy carpet. She withdrew her wand, muttering the incantation for communion between her and the mirror in Dlad City. The mirror swirled in a green-yellow tint, and a young officer appeared on the other end.

She thought she'd contacted Judas's room in Dlad City but was mistaken.

"Greetings, Madam Consul," he said with a bow. "I'm Kernoyl Tyku. How may I be of assistance?"

"Is this Warlock Lakayre's room?"

He smiled.

"Indeed; I was using it to catch a break from the bustle of camp life."

She didn't voice the same sentiments despite feeling it.

"Is Warlock Lakayre available?"

"My lady, you just missed him. He left about an hour ago."

"Did he say where he was going or when he'd be back?"

The kernoyl smile widened.

"I can do one better. I sent him home for a small leave of absence so he can rest in comfort. He should be back by the end of the week, in time to receive the jynerul. Shall I tell him you called?"

Giddiness flitted through Meristal's insides. Judas was at home and much closer. She would go to him.

"That won't be necessary. Thank you."

"As you wish, Consul. Good day."

The mirror swirled again and cleared.

Call on him? Shades of the Underworld, I'll just drop in on him.

She went back to the desk and cleared the clutter, segregating the parchment of those perused and those untouched. A thought struck her. She could get the three new appointments—her three shadows, as she called them internally—to go through these papers. Anything they didn't have the power to approve would be regulated to her, cutting back the workload. She'd set things in motion and then go.

Half an hour tops.

Vigor spurred her urgency.

Judas eyed Meristal.

The crisp morning caressed him, but the chill wasn't enough to make his bones ache. She rose the steaming cup to her red lips.

She's teasing me.

"It's an extraordinary morning."

She rolled her eyes.

"Really? The weather?"

He cleared his throat.

"I meant the part where I come home and find a beautiful woman arriving on my front porch."

He grinned, but she shot him an uncertain glance. His brow nettled. Had he said something wrong? She usually basked in his praise. Buried feelings became unearthed, and he almost spoke them aloud.

A wound that hurts too much, the cut too deep.

"I've come to ask about young Julie," Meristal said at last.

So, a business trip.

Judas reined in his feelings, and he let her continue at her own pace.

"The council's pushing for an executive order to inform the realm of her outlaw status. I can only hold them off so long before they see it as an abuse of power. Favoritism isn't allowed."

"I'm no closer to finding her," he said with a curtness he didn't mean.

He took a sip, chiding himself.

"She must've learned more than a few intricacies of magic. How else would she know not to teleport away from the scene? She must realize all magic leaves small traces from the person who casts it. The question is, where did she learn it, and why's she trying to hide?"

Meristal cocked an eyebrow.

"That's the easy part."

Judas's eyes roamed over her again.

Something bothered him, but he couldn't figure out...what. Perhaps the emotional strain, Julie in a twisted context.

"She murdered three people, that's why she's hiding," Meristal said. "It's the why I want to know. I fear she's gone insane with the power. I mean, not too long ago she struggled, am I right?"

He gave a single nod.

"And now, she savors the god-like powers—"

"—God-like?"

Meristal waved her hand.

"As she sees them. To go from struggling to some form of mastery must seem...Well, she definitely doesn't answer to anyone."

"Sometimes, I wonder if I made the right choice bringing her back from the *Other Side*."

Meristal's head jerked toward him, her expression sharp.

He shrugged.

"I won't argue—she murdered three people. The carnage appeared chaotic, yet somehow calculated and cruel. I didn't see such signs in her. Hard, yes, but not homicidal. No matter what happened to her, she isn't Xilor."

Meristal appraised him for a long moment, her expression still, then she swallowed.

"You think you got this girl pegged?"

Judas met her unflinching gaze and took a sip.

"Yeah, I do."

Meristal gave a slow nod.

"Can you find her today, or do I sign the executive order and brand her an outlaw?"

He let out a weary sigh.

"You better do it, but I want limitations and rules of engagement. There can be no blunders."

"What? Why?"

He sucked in a breath.

"Because she's my daughter."

Meristal's face remained placid, smooth, but her gaze slid out of focus.

His chest tightened. He expected a bombardment of questions by now, or an emotional response. Finally, she looked at him.

"Do you expect this to change anything?" she asked.

Of all the reactions expected, this wasn't it.

She stood, giving him another look, one he could've called cold, and left without a backward glance.

Meristal and her basket teleported outside the gates of Judas's manor.

A branch snapped in the distance, and Meristal spun to the right. Her essence flared to life; her wand materialized in her hand. What she expected, she couldn't say, but she prepared for the worst: an ambush, an assassin, trolls....

In the distance, she could've sworn she saw a woman. The door shutting at Judas's manor drew her attention back to his home.

Did he just go inside?

She glanced to the silhouette in the distance, but it was gone. Did she imagine it? Better yet, if real, who was visiting Judas?

She shook the wariness away, stowed her wand, and continued to the front gate.

In the short time she'd been back, she noted a change in Judas, a subtle shift. He seemed fine as he and Julie left for Wizard's Pass, but once the young woman turned up missing, he'd become maudlin.

When Xilor materialized in Cape Gythmel, he reverted to his old self. War brought out his youthful nature, as if born for it, and she had the feeling that the longer it went on, the more he'd change.

She pushed past the gate and ambled up the path.

There was so much going on. The army stationed itself at Dlad City, Xilor's mass moved to Shadow City, and the dark lord hadn't been seen on the battlefield for a long time.

Where in the Underworld is he?

Her thoughts returned to Judas, and what he must feel like, given that his apprentice murdered three men. Did he feel responsible, an obligation spreading like a slow poison? And all the while, Meristal nettled him, pushed him to find Julie and bring her to justice.

That must only compound the pain.

Stepping between the enormous stark-white pillars, she ascended the porch and gave a rap on the door. On the third knock, Judas answered. She thrust the basket into his arms and pushed past him.

"I brought breakfast," Meristal said. "About time you answered. It's chilly outside."

She took off her sandals as Judas preferred—something he picked up in the city of Elysys—then hung her traveler's cloak on a peg.

"What are you doing?" Judas asked.

The confusion in his voice made her turn. Disbelief etched his face. He shuffled the basket into one arm and shut the door.

"Breakfast?"

She pulled the basket out of his one arm and hurried to the kitchen. Judas followed, but in a slow, cautious manner. She peeked around the corner and gave him an unsure smile.

"I won't bite. What's gotten into you?"

He was shaking his head as he entered.

"Look, Meristal, I don't know what game you're playing, if you're here to —"

Confusion shot through her.

"—What are you talking about?"

What in the eternal Abyss is going on with him?

He opened his mouth, gaze darting away, then closed his mouth. She spoke instead.

"Look, I came to have breakfast with the most charming, handsome man in the Ralloc domain, not to mention the most intellectually stimulating, too."

Is he going to be baited and rise to the occasion or squander the opportunity?

"The Ralloc domain, huh?"

She noted a hand going for his goatee.

"Well, it's a big world. There might be a few in the Marcoalyn domain."

She set plates on the table and doled out the food. She didn't miss his calculating gaze and gave a demure glance in return, a role she had played for many years. He sat in the chair opposite her.

"So," Meristal began. "I thought ..."

Judas held up a hand to stop her.

"I don't want to talk about it."

She paused, confused. How did he already know what she came to discuss? Then again, it was Judas.

"Fine, but eventually we need to."

"Why? Can't you drop it? It's a burden weighing on me, and I want to be left alone."

Shades, what's with the attitude?

"Okay, fine!"

She bit into her pastry bought from a family-owned shop in Ralloc.

Judas sighed and leaned forward.

"I'm sorry for dropping the news on you earlier. It can't be easy to hear that Julie's my daughter."

The pastry slipped from Meristal's fingers, and her mouth fell open.

"Your daughter?"

The revelation sent tendrils through her body, something between horror and disbelief. A knot formed in her stomach and a fluttering sickness rumbled in her abdomen.

Oh, gods, that means Daylynn's baby…

While Meristal's dislike for the girl's mother manifested, she pushed it aside, focusing on the child of that union. The sweet girl Meristal knew had vanished, replaced by a murderer.

I can't *believe I almost asked him to hunt her down.*

Emotions rocked her, joy, sorrow, shock, and everything in between. The last tinge had been anger at Daylynn for lying to them all this time, saying her child died.

She hid her child. After so many years with Judas thinking she died, to find her and not know it, to lose her again.

His involvement sentenced the girl to death, and Meristal had come to ensure justice.

She swallowed.

We just lost the war.

She sat back, hooking a tress of orange hair behind her ear. Gathering her words, she made her voice soft and full of compassion.

"If you don't want to talk, I understand. This changes the way we move forward, and I'll make the decision without you."

Her words tasted like bile in her mouth.

His head snapped up, eyes narrowed.

"What decision?"

"What we're going to do about Julie."

"We already talked about that, and I told you."

"No, we haven't, and this news about Julie being your daughter is quite shocking, so I understand—"

His eyes narrowed.

"What do you mean?"

She frowned.

"What do you mean, Judas?"

He pointed to the front door.

"You sat out on my porch, drinking coffee with me, and we talked about it."

She regarded the door, then Judas, her lips thinning.

"Maybe you dreamed it."

He scoffed.

"By the gods, dreamed it? Are you mad, woman? I can show you the kettle and how much coffee is gone."

Her lips thinned.

"But I don't drink coffee."

"You drank it this morning!"

"Wait," she said, taking a deep breath, holding up her hands. "This morning? Either you're having prophetic dreams, or you're going mad. This is the first time I've been here since you left for Wizard's Pass."

His eyes, red with emotion, narrowed again. He held his tongue, but she could tell he puzzled out a conundrum. The silence allowed their tempers to ebb.

"What's going on, Judas?"

"Alright," he said, waving further conversation away. "Let's start at the beginning. This morning, you and I talked about Julie on my front porch. We both had coffee. Now, when I said my—"

"—I wasn't here; I was in Ralloc! You've known me for many, many years, all the way back to when we met in the Melodic Mountains. I can't say I've never tried coffee, but I don't drink it."

If I didn't drink the coffee, but Judas swears I did, then who was here?

The silhouette she swore to have seen came to mind.

"Who was here before me?"

"You," he said, flabbergasted. Judas leaned back, crossing his arms. "What did you come to talk about today?"

"About Julie. The council is pushing me to—"

"—declare her an outlaw of the realm?"

Her eyes narrowed.

"How did you know I was going to say that? We came to the decision late last night, and in a closed-doors session."

Judas's lips pursed as he thought.

"This means the Betrayer is active in Ralloc again. You, or someone who's very much like you, told me earlier, just before you showed up. There must be some detail I missed, but I assumed this person was you."

Meristal laughed.

"Judas, you don't know me or any woman well enough to assume anything."

"I know you better than you think I do."

"How so?"

"You still love me."

His words settled between them, and her face flushed with heat. She took a huge bite of her pastry.

Well, at least he fucking acknowledged it, and that means this whole time, he's been shutting me out, but why?

Of course, in the past, there'd been times he pursued her, and she'd done the same. Both of them were guilty.

Her thoughts focused on the important matters in front of them. Long ago, Meristal had been impersonated before, and Daylynn had slept with Judas on multiple occasions.

Meristal swallowed.

"Do you think Daylynn's the Betrayer?"

Judas shook his head.

"It wasn't her. After…the fiasco, I made it a point to recognize her essence no matter how she appeared. It's not her. I'll stake my life on it."

Meristal felt relieved.

"But now, we must turn our attention and focus on the council and the entourages. If we do, we may find the second betrayer."

"That's going to be difficult while acting like nothing's amiss. We don't know who to trust."

"Call for an emergency council meeting. Whoever turns up late is probably a good suspect."

Her brows nettled.

"What's the emergency about?"

His grim face settled as he locked eyes with her.

"What to do about your outlaw."

Chapter 15: Norek

The wind blew steady around Norek while orders were issued to the crew and dockhands, who used ropes to secure the vessel in port. Once bound, a whistle signaled the boat was secured and the plank extended, permitting the crew to debark and dock handlers to embark.

The Eastern City looked the same as the last time he visited. Each time brought a reverence. The Golden City reigned supreme in elegance, gleaming with warm colors throughout, and the harbor was secondary, with ships pulling in broadside. The Eastern City, by contrast, was built for function, its harbor the main hub of commerce. The massive bay ran the length of the municipality and could host a fleet of ships docking aft first, a laborious affair, but departures were swift.

Tall, thick walls encircling the city could withstand the autumn's ungodly storms, their width enabling two chariots to pass abreast. To craft such a monument, the stonemasons had to number in the thousands. The Eastern City ran on tariffs, which funded not only the wall but the city, too.

"Land," the kaptyn breathed as he stepped off the gangplank.

To Norek, it sounded like a foreign word in his mouth.

The kaptyn smiled at him.

"Feels weird after being afloat. The ground doesn't move and sway with the current's will. It takes some getting used to for a few days."

Norek withheld comments about previous voyages. It'd do little to ease the grumblings of the officer, and Norek needed to reach Ralloc as fast as possible.

Godfrey may have already landed and be marching on Ralloc at this very moment.

With what money he possessed, he needed to buy a horse and provisions, visit the local Commerce Guild for a map, and plot the quickest and safest passage to Ralloc.

The last of the crew left, the dock workers boarded, and Norek left the ship behind.

The kaptyn fell in step beside him.

"The depository isn't far. Not even outside the wharf. You'll have your money and be on your way."

"Kaptyn, you got me here safely, and I'm grateful to be alive. I don't want all my money returned; half of the remaining sum will do."

The other nodded in appreciation.

"Well, if you intend to purchase a nag, take one of mine. I insist. We're in my city now, just a short walk from my place. I'll have you saddled and on your way in no time."

Norek mulled over the kaptyn's generous offer. He couldn't afford to pass it up.

"Very well. I'll meet you back here within an hour. There are things I need."

"Nonsense. We'll provide provisions unless there's something other than …?" he trailed off. "A woman perhaps?"

"A map."

The officer smiled.

"We've got that too! Trust me, you'll receive appropriate care."

Leaving behind the sounds of sloshing water and thudding footsteps, they wove through the city. The breeze faltered as they passed through the wall.

Small houses with clay shingles hugged each other, encroaching their neighbor's privacy. Narrow roads—narrower than the walls—covered with cobblestone and loose dirt wound throughout. The pair dodged the milling pedestrians and departed the western gate. Norek was quickly lost in the twists and turns, and the walk, though short in distance, took them a full two hours, the city taking the brunt of it.

Rolling hills, thick, tall grass, and juniper trees hugged them from both sides. The road widened once outside the gate, and riders and caravans passed them without a second glance. The road turned caliche, and dust filled the air. They strolled into his estate as the suns rose high, and the officer called for his stableboy. Giving him instructions, the boy ran off to prepare a saddle and bring the animal to the front of the house.

The kaptyn ushered Norek up wooden steps and into the sitting room inside.

"My partner will bring you something to eat," he said, then retreated upstairs.

Norek sat in a comfortable chair, one of fine leather and wood. Looking about the room, he noted the simple yet refined quality. Sparse furnishings prevented the sense of a cluttered environment. Each painting, statue, or clock radiated an aged aura.

Antiques!

On a table sat an unfinished game. Almost all the pieces were uniquely carved with one side made of ivory and the other obsidian.

A noise drew his attention. A young man entered the room carrying a tray of food. The kaptyn had said he would send his partner, but Norek thought he meant his wife. He noted the man's age, at least half the kaptyn's. He set the tray beside the game and retreated.

Norek wolfed down the cheese, dried meats, and fruit once the young man vanished. It tasted so much better than ship food! As he neared the end of the meal, his host returned, dressed in a set of new clothes carrying a large pack.

"As promised, provisions."

He hefted the bag and handed it to Norek.

"It can be rigged to the horse, the saddle, or carried. You've got some canned foods, dehydrated fruit, and an assortment of jerky."

He passed over a rolled parchment.

"The map. In four or five hours, the suns will be setting; would you care to stay and head out in the morning? There's a guest bedroom."

"Thank you, but no," Norek replied, taking the map. "I need to start right away. A long journey in a short span of time awaits."

"Where will you sleep? On the ground?"

"No. I probably won't sleep at all 'til the next town."

"That's more than three weeks ride!"

"For normal riders, yes. We'll make good time; magic will ward me from fatigue."

"And the horse?"

The worry in the kaptyn's voice was evident.

"Taken care of, rest assured. We'll be fine, sire."

Norek used the formal term to politely inquire as to his status as the master of the estate.

The officer grunted in acknowledgment, then led him outside. The kaptyn tied the pack to the backside of the saddle and handed the reins to Norek.

"Take care of yourself. It's dangerous ground you're treading on around here. Especially at night."

"We'll be fine, sire. I'll remember you in the future, should I ever venture this far south again."

"Be sure you do. Suns and moons guide your travels."

"And may you find fair winds and parting seas," Norek bid in farewell.

The mage mounted and turned the horse down the entry of the estate and headed west. He plodded along in a walking pace until the estate fell out of sight, then picked up speed in a canter.

As promised, he made phenomenal time on the long trek to the next civilization. After ten days of following the eastern Emaas River, he finally stopped to bed down for the night, too weary to continue. He'd traveled twice as far as a normal traveler, only stopping to stretch his legs, relieve himself, or allow the steed to eat or drink.

His progress slowed at night, guided by his essence-enhanced vision. He stretched it out like a bubble around him and the horse. Their uncanny speed was only made possible by the rejuvenation spell, but the more he used it, the more the effects diminished.

He noted the horse's expressionless face, imagining its gratefulness.

They'd reached the sanctuary of the Valley of the Dwaven Kings. No predator, from his knowledge or that of the dwaven, lived in the lands. Special wards placed upon the borders kept predators and centaurs out.

Once the fire caught, he settled himself after eating his meal. He still had all his rations. Map unrolled, he plotted the next leg, eyeing each hard decision.

To the northwest lay a river he could follow, climbing over the Melodic Mountains. Who knew if the steed would make the trip, but that'd be the easiest part. On the other side, a nonexistent line separated the Valley of Stones and Lost Man's Legacy Forest. To circumvent the forest, he'd continue northwest until he reached Korlinville. After that, it was a straight shot to the Corridor of Cruelty.

The stories awakened a disquiet in him.

His other option was to follow the Emaas River in a northwest fashion until it shot off into the southwest. A smaller river with no name emerged from the Melodic Mountains. That path encroached the Valley of the Dead—not an appealing factor—and went under the Melodic Mountains to Korlin's Cove. From there, it'd be easy riding to the Corridor.

So, which is it? Lost Man's Legacy Forest next to the Valley of Stones, or the easier, longer route near the Valley of the Dead?

It was a hard decision, one he didn't enjoy making.

If that blasted kaptyn…no, it doesn't matter. What's done is done.

Rumors surrounded the Valley of Stones. Supposedly, a vast and terrible secret lay within, some sort of race kept a vigilant watch, unchanging like the stones within. Once someone entered, they never came out.

Lost Man's Legacy Forest was also a place he didn't want to wander into, the place where the Mother Centaur rebuked the dwaven for their shortsightedness and betrayed them. Supposedly, something foul and evil lurked within. He didn't want to chance it.

No path is clear.

He wished now he'd taken the kaptyn up on his offer to find a woman before setting out. To his shock, he'd ignored the feminine vice while urgency spurred him forward. In hindsight, he wished he took the offer and bought a bottle of rum or wine for the journey.

He turned back to the journey.

That left the Valley of the Dead.

He scratched his jaw.

The Valley of the Dead was where the last and greatest battle was fought in the great Wizard's War. All armies assembled there, intent on annihilating one another. The warlock, Judas Lakayre, had already bested Xilor by that point. Xilor's army was in full retreat. Without the dark lord there to spread his corrupted will upon the opposing armies, a costly but certain victory ensued.

The battle commenced with Warlock Lakayre's absence—both sides fighting without their figureheads. The conflict lasted more than a month. Norek heard tales that the Krey slaughtered in droves, but the war bled their numbers, and they still hadn't recovered from their losses.

In the end, countless bodies fell as far as the eye could see, too many to collect, to return to loved ones, so they razed the whole area.

The thought of coming so near to the haunted place made him shudder. He couldn't begin to imagine how many lost their lives during that fateful time.

If only I could teleport!

It baffled him that he couldn't. He had all the power necessary, but the craft eluded him.

The horse threw a nicker into the darkness, dragging his thoughts away. He looked up. The horse's ears were perked forward. Its tail swished at odd intervals and stared into the darkness.

"What is it, boy?"

He stood, collecting his staff, and walked over to his companion, patting him affectionately. The animal paid him no heed, continuing to gaze into the darkness, and Norek mirrored him, gazing out into the obscurity.

"How about a little light, huh?"

He tapped the end of his staff to the ground, and a bright white light illuminated the sky above the area they searched.

In the sudden light, Norek spied the encroaching figures. At first, he thought goblins advanced but dismissed the absurd notion. Then, he noted details, their stature and broadness, marking them as dwaven.

A hunting party? There must be twenty of them! Never thought I'd see one!

All the dwaven stopped in mid-stride, not bothering to seek shelter. Some glanced at the brilliant light floating above while others stared at Norek and his steed.

Those must be the older, more experienced ones. The younger would be distracted by the sudden light.

The leader, or the male in front, stopped the party with a complex arm movement. Some dwaven surged forward, surrounding Norek's camp, fanning out and setting up a perimeter. Others pushed out to the sides. The message was clear. While their leader conducted business with the trespasser, he'd be surrounded. The foremost dwaven advanced with cautious steps.

Norek noticed the war axe he clutched, a favored weapon: broad, heavy, and two-sided.

More slaughter per swing.

"Greetings," the shorter creature hailed.

He gave a quick bow, a bob of the head, not long enough for an enemy to take advantage of. The dwaven never took his eyes off Norek, a common practice among them unless greeting nobility or someone of higher rank or status.

"Well met," Norek said.

He let his eyes fall to the ground, a dwaven gesture communicating that he meant no hostility until intentions were made.

"Come, if you please, and join me by the fire. Perhaps some tea?"

Norek noted the other's grip slackened. The dwaven nodded and advanced with measured steps. Careful to make no sudden moves, Norek worked through his pack for cups and tea, his back turned. From his studies, he knew turning your back was considered one of the rudest things conceivable, signifying the person was meaningless. But in a hunting party, it was a sign of trust, showing vulnerability to your potential enemy.

Norek had studied the dwaven with a diligent fascination in his youth. He could speak some Taengrenian, but they also spoke the common tongue of Myshku. And there were rumors the dwaven crafted their own language, but he couldn't verify that yet.

Norek procured the cups and tea and faced the dwaven.

"Forgive my awkwardness," Norek said in Taengrenian.

It tumbled awkwardly off his tongue. He hadn't practiced since his youth. The dwaven's face remained placid and unreadable, but Norek got the impression he was too stunned. A sudden burst of laughter threatened to topple the other over.

"Your Taengrenian's pathetic."

Normally, such bluntness would offend, but the dwaven didn't mince words.

"I hope by Soma I never hear you try to utter them again."

More laughter bubbled out of him again.

You should meet the tyrant of the Forgotten Isles. You'd get along.

"Then, you won't."

Norek set to boiling water in his small kettle. The dwarf waved the comment away.

"What are you doing on *our* lands?"

"I'm traveling from afar and going further still," Norek said, trying to be discreet.

He appraised the dwaven. True to common belief, they were shorter than wizardkind, but not so much shorter that they seemed minuscule. Most of the males, like the one sitting across from him, boasted a stocky frame with thick chests. Their massive arms, burly and stout, extended from shoulders more akin to cannonballs. A thick, strong neck supported their heads.

"What nonsense is this? Riddles? Speak candidly so that I might mull over our options."

Norek blew out a silent, exasperated breath.

"Where I'm from," he began, "it's considered rude to pry into the affairs of others, especially strangers."

The dwaven scoffed.

"I'm Yugor, nephew to Erkon, king of the dwaven, and second in line to the throne. You'll answer my questions. We're not in your land but *ours*, and it's rude to use witty words and deceptive trickery. Only folly and flattery come from someone who spins lies with flowery speak."

He leaned in closer, and Norek couldn't mistake the fire in his eyes.

"Tell me why you're here."

Norek skirted angering the dwaven. Better to divulge some personal information than to end up in a battle.

"My name's Norek. I'm from the House of Shorn in the Green Lands. I travel to study the cultures of many races and record what I observe so others may benefit from the insight. I came from the Forgotten Isles by way of a merchant ship. The original destination was the Golden City, but the kaptyn ordered the ship on to the Eastern City when we happened upon pirates. From the Eastern City, I must travel through to my original and final destination in Ralloc."

The smaller man sat on his meaty haunches, rocking as he mulled over Norek's words.

"For someone who spoke directly, many words passed your lips."

"I didn't want to leave any room for doubt."

"There's always doubt. With honesty comes doubt. You're not from the Green Lands or the House of Shorn. You're the wrong—what's the word?—

ethnicity."

Norek felt the other's gaze, searching for any visible reaction. He wouldn't find one.

The dwaven continued.

"You look like a Rallocan aristocrat or some other noble-loaded city."

That's the second time someone said I am from Ralloc or noble birth!

"You're correct; I'm not of the House of Shorn but an adopted son. I was an orphan."

This caused an instant reaction from the dwaven.

"Forgive my intrusion," Yugor said scrambling to his feet and bowing low. This time, his eyes fell to the ground.

In the dwaven culture, it was considered an immense shame to be an orphan, not on the orphan but the society. Dwaven culture was orphan-less. All children were cared for by siblings of the child's lost parents, raised and treated with more dignity than most of the wealthiest, for their loss was greater than money and more terrible than most endured. When Norek learned of this as a child, he took an immediate liking to the culture and wished to be born among them. Since he wasn't, he studied them intently.

"Please, rise," Norek managed, almost forgetting the proper etiquette.

Yugor reclaimed his seat. Norek poured a cup of tea and handed it over before pouring himself a cup. Yugor waited, a smart custom in unfamiliar company, making sure he wouldn't be poisoned. It was on Norek to drink first. He took a long, cautious sip from the steaming liquid and let out a sigh of content. Only then did the other follow suit.

"So, mage Norek, House of Shorn, you're a traveler? Documentaries are your forte?"

"One of my many gifts, yes."

"You sound much like Warlock Lakayre when he was younger. He never ventured into our land before the war. Afterward, from what I hear, he was a changed soul."

The dwaven custom during war or truce—or like a situation they found themselves in now—was to share knowledge so you may learn something in return. While Norek wasn't considered an enemy, he was an outsider. He fell into the same category as the enemy.

"Yes, I've read about him from others and enjoyed his publications. His early work is extraordinary, but it's his works after the war that intrigues me the most. He writes about subjects no one else dares to broach."

"If you like those types of writings, perhaps another may interest you. His name's Fife Doole."

"Fife Doole? Never heard of such a wizard."

The dwarf snorted the tea.

"He isn't a wizard, but a halfling or a gnome…he is both. It's no wonder you haven't heard of him, few have. Both of their writings are similar."

"Really? That'd make for good reading, indeed."

In the short lull, the creeping wildlife filled his ears. Norek breathed in the cool, clean, open air, and waited.

"You said documentaries were one of your gifts," Yugor said. "What are the others?"

"I possess the abilities of Owlen."

"What nonsense is this mage-man? Speak so I may understand."

"Owlen is a branch of magic. Magic is like an ocean, vast and powerful and deep. There are several branches, and some have sub-branches. A conjurer is determined by how his essence works through him. We don't determine our magical abilities; thus I'm an Owlen learner."

"A learner? A mere boy?"

"No. I misspoke."

As with custom, blame rested with him in their miscommunication. By dwaven standards, people of moral character accepted blame. However, in this particular incident, Norek wasn't sure if the rules applied.

"I have advanced training. Perhaps learner is a poor term. The mistake is mine."

"Then, what term would you use?"

"I'd tell you I'm neither a master of my craft nor a novice. The best way is to see me use my abilities and determine for yourself."

"You wizardkind never cease to amaze me with your abilities to speak indirectly. You open your mouths, and shit and flowers come out in the same breath. Since you're headed to Ralloc, if you'd so choose, my hunters and I will accompany you out of our lands, and should my uncle grant it, to Ralloc itself. Few dwaven were allowed to roam outside our boundaries, but he may grant an allowance."

Norek had heard of the dwaven king, and if the stories were even half-true, he doubted Yugor would take a step out of their borders.

"I welcome your escort. However, I travel fast and don't want to be burdened by your inability to keep up."

There, that should be pointedly enough for him.

"Today marks the first time I've stopped in over a week. My abilities make the feat possible. If you don't impede my quest, I welcome you."

A look of surprise flashed across Yugor's face.

"The mage-man learns to speak properly!"

Yugor chuckled. When he subsided, he gave a small whistle and another dwaven came running up. They spoke openly to each other in a language Norek didn't understand.

Perhaps it was true. The dwaven made their own language.

When they finished, the runner vanished into the darkness.

"He'll ask for an allowance. We should hear back from him by the time we reach the other boundary. We'll take the most direct route possible, pending the way you wish to travel."

"I was just debating that when you showed up. I think the Emaas River to the Valley of the Dead and through the Melodic Mountains."

"Very well, I'll guide you at first light. But we won't follow the river. It's out of the way. I'll take you on a more direct route."

"Alright, at first light, then."

On the following morning, the mage was surprised to find he enjoyed Yugor's company. The dwaven never faltered, never slowed his travel. As promised, they crossed the Valley of the Dwaven Kings faster than by himself, cutting several days off his trip, guiding through unfamiliar territory and land Norek only dreamed of visiting.

The dwaven traveled with a singular purpose of mind, but the stout companion broke the monotony of traveling alone. Yugor was different from the rest, fostering a profound longing to experience the world with his own eyes and not through a tome's old pages. Though he'd never been granted the concession before, he held onto hope.

Yugor talked almost incessantly throughout the day, yearning to hear word of what lay beyond their land.

"As I've always said, should the king come to slumber in the Valley of Dwaven Kings, and I was appointed, I'd end our isolationist policy, take my best men, and travel."

"That'd take half a lifetime."

"Half for a mage perhaps, but we have much longer lives."

"Perhaps being isolationist isn't as bad as you think," Norek argued. "Would you wish for wizardkind to meddle in your affairs? What if they perceived you as a threat and asked you to disarm a quarter of your army? Would you still wish to commune with them? What if the elyves reject your social norms? What then? Do you acclimatize to their wishes? As of now, no one bothers you or forces their beliefs and prejudices onto your society."

They rode in intermittent silence through the cascading darkness. The stars above glittered like tiny pinpricks punching through a dark curtain. The largest moon, Faellon, with its mulberry tint, hung lonely against the black sea of night.

"I've never thought of it that way," Yugor rumbled. "Your point's well said, mage-man. Still, odd that one so free should wish for an isolated society."

"Ah, but I never said I would. I just played the part of the bantering jester, the opposite to illuminate the other half."

An idea struck Norek cold as he thought over the dwaven's words.

"You said, should you be appointed king, you'd end the closed borders. Does this mean you're a potential candidate to the throne?"

The dwarf, Yugor, gave a small huff of laughter.

Norek shook his head, amazed.

"I thought you were bluffing."

"You've become better at speaking. Yes, I'm a candidate as you say."

Norek teased him with a grin.

"And here I thought you were nothing but a lonely hunter."

Yugor gasped, eyes going wide.

"You'd make a fine dwaven indeed, mage-man. You learn fast, but not quick enough, and won't master our new tongue for years to come. Your

Taengrenian's as repugnant as a bucket of piss. Come, we must practice more. If you should come back, you may find many friends among my people."

"You keep saying that, but aren't I already a friend to your people? I mean, I'm passing through your land…"

Yugor scoffed and gave him a long look.

"Hardly! We pity you, orphan. Our bellies encouraged us to investigate your fire. Be grateful we don't eat wizardkind."

"Like the Toshii."

"What?"

Norek waved his comment away. Yugor pored over the elementary parts of their new, incorporated language. The wizard found it as difficult as Taengrenian, contorting his mouth and tongue to mimic the correct sounds.

It had taken him years to learn Taengrenian. Now, he had to start over with Akyhmri.

Their days passed in a combination of conversing and learning. It became apparent that even Yugor wasn't as fluent in Akyhmri as Norek once thought.

Perhaps they implemented it not too long ago? Maybe in a generation, they'll be better.

Yugor stopped after a time, glancing to the west with a silent stillness.

"What?"

"The Valley of the Dead."

Yugor's breath came in shudders almost too silent for Norek to hear. Even in the darkness, Norek saw what he meant.

To the west stretched a massive field. Pale, fine dirt like white powder seemed to glow with a gentle radiance as if it absorbed daylight and reflected at night. The sand reminded Norek of the beaches of the Forgotten Isles.

A strong aura stretched out and touched Norek, unseen and immutable as an ocean current. Yugor shivered, and goosebumps ran down Norek's arms as he climbed off the horse. The dwaven held no evident magic, but even he felt the call.

Taking cautious steps, the mage neared the edge of the perimeter but dared not enter. Each boot print made him quake with a myriad of emotions that accompanied war and death.

Norek knelt at the edge and paid silent respect to all who lost their lives. Yugor stood beside him, reticent as words failed him.

"There's nothing quite like it, is there?" Yugor asked.

"Yes, and no. There's another place, similar, but not the same."

"The City of Despair?"

"Yes. I've never been within the walls; no one has to my knowledge. If it could be done, it'd be an accomplishment of a lifetime."

He peered at the dwaven.

"From an educational viewpoint, that is."

Norek went to his steed.

"We best not linger."

"I can't, I'm afraid," Yugor said. "I can't travel any further and must return to my lands and people. My uncle has given voice and I must obey, though I'm loath to return when my dreams are so close."

"A pity, indeed. Have faith, Yugor. One day, perhaps you'll be king. I pray that day comes so I may see you again."

A swell of pity rose up in Norek. He couldn't imagine being a prisoner to land. That's why he never stayed on islands for very long. They were too confining.

The world didn't end at the ocean; that's where it began.

"So do I, mage-man, so do I. You've taught me much about you and wizardkind. Perhaps, if I should ever roam among them, I won't be an uncouth foreigner."

"Indeed, you won't. Goodbye, friend. Prosperity and fortune smile upon you."

"May the goddess, Soma, guide you throughout all your days."

Norek turned his horse and galloped away until the animal grew tired. He feared Yugor would defy his king if he lingered. It no doubt took all his discipline to turn back.

A thought haunted Norek as he continued on his journey.

How close did Yugor come to disobeying his king to pursue his dreams?

Despite wanting to help, the guilt would gnaw at him, and Norek had enough guilt to last a lifetime.

Chapter 16: Starriace

Tall buildings, sweeping spires, and wide cobbled streets expanded in front of Starriace. Ralloc had too many structures to count. Even at night, more pedestrians crowded the pathways than any other place she'd visited. For a long time, Starriace yearned to visit the capital, but elements beyond her control kept her away. Fear, until recently, kept her from visiting.

Somewhere along the way, she passed Sinner's Court, between the fourth and fifth tier, and once she realized she'd missed it, she didn't care to backtrack. Steeples rose like lightning rods, light gray smoke curled from incalculable chimneys, and numerous scents permeated the air, reminding her how ravenous she was. Now that she thought about it, she only ate a handful of meals at Harold's.

Probably not healthy.

She stopped by a booth—a kitchen with an awning on the side of a building—and ordered a plate of food.

Skywalks loomed above her, sidewalks connecting buildings every few levels to ease foot traffic below. Her wide-eyed ogling marked her as conspicuous.

Long, sloping streets wove through the city, but the principal road led straight from the inner gate to the front doors of the castle where the Kothlere Council presided. Ralloc was divided into seven tiers, each walled off for siege protection. The outer roads between the remaining tiers wove like a serpent.

It was a vast city of shops, houses, taverns, hotels, banks, and brothels, built up before expanding out. Outlets, stores, and emporiums cluttered the roads. The sounds of laughter and music wove through the night. Stores of cloth, silk, and other fine fabrics filled her vision.

A steaming plate distracted her from drinking in every detail. Pork ribs glistening in a sugared and spiced glaze tore her attention away. Boiled potatoes, corn, beans, and a heel of fried garlic bread accompanied the meat. She ordered a Vampire Dust when her food arrived.

"Go to a tavern if you want a drink," the cook chided.

Rudeness angered her, but the mistake was hers, and the smell of food reminded her of priorities. She wolfed her meal like a ravenous animal. Her plate bare, she left a copper bit and moved on.

Within the city, she kept herself closed off, her presence small, abstaining from magic. She didn't know if Judas was here or not. She bypassed the Corridor of Cruelty—she never wanted to set foot there again if she could help it—and took the long way to Ralloc.

From Harold's, she teleported to the sea, then up the coast to Golden City. From there, she came inland until within sight of Ralloc. It took her longer than expected, careful not to overshoot each teleport lest she find herself deep in the mountains or lost at sea. She walked the last bit of distance, the trek taking her two hours, and covering her with sweat and grime.

After her meal, Apor, the giant blue sun, vanished.

Passing a clothing store, she stepped in. The lady paid her no heed due to her state of dress, but Starriace picked a robe in her size and turned to the counter. Much to her disappointment, she didn't find silver robes.

When she inquired with the lady about her choice in color, the other chuckled and told her she'd have better luck searching in Stratu'Geim. The robe Starriace picked out came with a white linen inner robe and a silk, royal blue outer robe with black stitching. A silk, midnight-blue traveler's robe with silver embroidery depicting the movements of the three moons, Faellon, Nykron, and Auqyn, accompanied the set.

Starriace grabbed a newer pair of sandals and let the lady tally her bill up.

"One hundred and eighty scepters."

"Six chips! Seriously?"

"Leather and silk, my lady. And you are in the upper tiers of the city."

The woman must work on commission. Extortionist!

Starriace paid and left, wanting a bath before ruining her new outfit. She continued north to the upper echelons.

After a few blocks, Starriace found a bathhouse. Once inside, she spied the menu hanging above the greeting counter flanked by two men and two women. Their list of services varied as did the price, and she lost interest in reading after the first dozen.

But she was going to see Kam and Lily, and she wanted to be prepared for all eventualities. She paid the hostess twelve copper bits. The bath itself cost only two scepters, but the extras added up.

The ladies led her to a warm, private room where they took her new robes and undressed her in a methodical manner. After helping her into the steaming tub, they pointed out the different soaps and shampoos available. Lastly, they identified the small bell to signal when she was ready to resume the services.

Since this was her first visit, Starriace examined the soaps and shampoos, smelling each until finding one she liked. The shampoo she chose had a bouquet of roses, lilies, and lavender. She scrubbed her shoulder-length hair until it was full of lather and let it sit while cleaning the rest of her body. Spying a straight razor and remembering Kam's preferences, she took care of that, too.

After finishing, she rinsed and rang the bell. The ladies entered seconds after, and one attendant brushed her hair from behind while the other toweled her off and applied fragrant oil over her body. The scent reminded Starriace of flowers and fresh rain.

Finished and dressed, the ladies gathered their things and departed without a word. Starriace took her belongings in her arms and left. Outside, the air was crisp, but not as cold as the Melodic Mountains.

Glad it won't snow.

She set off at a gentle amble until she reached Lily's tier—the third tier, in the minor noble territory. Somewhere between the fourth and third segment, Starriace noted the distinct difference in architecture. Where the previous levels had been built tight and high, the minor noble territory was teeming with houses. The smaller structures had larger yards while the bigger homes encroached the road.

Squat fences made of stone or brick encircled properties while others relied on shrubs. She spied a few residences with brooks or fountains and noted that the majority of the homes were made of wood and the same materials as their fences. Lower level abodes consisted of wood except for multistory buildings. In fact, now that she thought about it, she never saw a building over three stories tall and made of timber.

She traced the map in her mind, remembering the detailed instructions given by Lily. At their front door, she steeled herself, calming the rioting nerves.

Why am I shaking?

She knocked before she could talk herself into leaving. A few moments passed and Lily answered the door. At first, the blonde-haired woman stared in shock before she smiled and embraced her.

"Starriace! What a surprise!"

Lily kissed her cheek and pulled her inside.

"Come in. I just finished putting dinner away, but you're more than welcome to it. I can put it in the oven for you."

She closed the door behind them.

"I already ate, thank you."

"You sure? It's no trouble at all! Do you need to bathe? I can get you some hot water."

"I'm fine, thank you. I just came from a bathhouse. How are you?"

"I'm great now! Where are my manners? Come in, have a seat."

Lily ushered her into the sitting room decorated in a simple, elegant style. A long chair of deep red with matching rockers, both made of mahogany, graced the den. A small round table sat between them, and a short table in front of the long chair.

The white stone hearth hosted a small fire, yet she couldn't find a speck of ash or dirt marring its pristine condition. Above hung a canvas, a ship at sea. Two small bookshelves flanked the fireplace and held perhaps three dozen books. The stain-free cream-colored rug tickled the bottoms of her feet, loose and fluffy like rabbit's fur.

Lily kept an immaculate home.

The hostess sat on the long chair, and Starriace settled beside her. Lily hugged her again, the woman's infectious grin spilling into her, and she couldn't help but smile back.

All her worries seemed to vanish around her.

Lily broke the embrace.

"Did you do whatever it was that you needed?"

"Huh?"

"Last time I saw you, you said you had somewhere to go, or something to do, and you wouldn't let the little fairy go with you. I take it since you're here, you're done?"

"Oh, er—somewhat. I finished with that part, but my travels led me here, and I promised to visit if I ever came to Ralloc. Unfortunately, I won't be here long; I'm leaving tonight."

"Really?"

Starriace heard her disappointment.

"I hope Kam gets back before you leave. I'm sure he'd love to visit."

Starriace glanced at her friend and watched a sly grin spread across her face.

"What? I'm sure he would!"

"Uh huh."

"He wants to see you almost as much as I do."

Starriace glanced around the room.

"Where is he?"

"At work. Ever since he joined the army, they have him working longer hours."

"Joined the army?"

Starriace almost laughed at the notion, but the seriousness on Lily's face stayed the outburst. Then, she remembered Lily's tale.

"Yeah, it's a long story, but the army needs blacksmiths, and he joined. The Consul recruited him."

"Meristal?"

Oh gods, how did that meeting go?

"Yeah, I think that's her name. What brings you to Ralloc?"

"A book."

Though it was an ambiguous answer, she didn't want to explain. If her friend discovered the truth, she might not want to see her anymore.

"Once I realized the book was here, I decided to come because I knew you were here."

"Oh?" Lily's eyebrows rose in a playful manner. "Did you come as a friend, or as a lover?"

Starriace was silent for a moment.

"As a friend," she revealed at last.

She watched Lily's face falter.

"And…something complicated."

Lily cocked her eyebrow.

"Does that go for both of us, or just Kam?"

Again, Starriace paused, and Lily nodded.

"Well, that answers that."

She laughed.

"Don't worry about it."

But Starriace did. She didn't want to hurt her friend, but she just didn't have those same desires for her.

"You're not upset?"

Lily scoffed.

"Why would I be? It's completely normal. And, Kam's smitten with you. I offered him another girl two moon turns ago, and he said no. That was the first time he ever refused. Shades, I even picked her because she looked like you, but he said it wasn't you, so he didn't want her."

"Really?"

"If he didn't love me so much, I'd be jealous of you! And if we weren't married, he'd be knocking on your door."

The last comment made Starriace smile, but it quickly faded.

"What?" Lily prompted.

"I feel guilty."

"About?"

"Sleeping with Kam."

"What's there to be guilty about?"

"Because you're married, and while I desire him, I don't love him. Not like you do."

Lily nodded somberly.

"Did Kam have an affair?"

Starriace shook her head.

"Did he cheat on me?"

Again, she shook her head but paused.

"What do you consider cheating?"

Lily turned her head, glancing out over the sitting room.

"Some people believe looking is wrong or admonish flirting. I was present and encouraged you. Shades, I even bought you undergarments that'd excite him."

Lily glanced at her.

"Is it guilt because you enjoyed it?"

Starriace nodded, but how could she explain it? She had difficulty explaining it to herself. If given a choice between the two for companionship, she'd choose Lily, but to be physically satisfied? Kam was the answer in ways that mattered. Did the guilt stem from enjoying that aspect of Kam, like she shamed Lily's affection or their marriage?

Lily sighed.

"Look, you have my blessing to sleep with Kam as much or as little as you want, with or without me. If you're wracked by guilt because I'm present or not, I can leave or stay. Or you don't have to do it at all. His happiness and your comfort does, alright?"

Starriace nodded. "I don't know. If you left…"

"You'd enjoy yourself more? There's nothing wrong with that! There were times when I had an audience as a prostitute, so I understand. The three of us will have plenty of time together, and we've been apart for a long while. I want to see you, and I know Kam does, too, but what do you want?"

"To see you, and maybe be with him."

Lily smiled.

"Then, that's how it'll be."

Starriace wanted to say thank you, to express how she felt, but words seemed inadequate. She leaned her head on Lily's shoulder, and the older woman ran her fingers through her hair.

She spoke of inconsequential things, and Starriace just listened. After a while, the light-headed buzz she recognized teased her, growing sharper with each moment, and she didn't have to wait long as Kam came into the sitting room, seeing them there.

Laying eyes on him, the hunger rose in her like a fire. Her pulse quickened in his presence, and she felt the tingling in her body, that of the magelust. Though the fuzzy sensation lurched in her head, the magelust wasn't as strong as before, at least, from what she could recall.

He stood shirtless, his chiseled body on display. A yearning deep inside her arced. His hair was damp; a towel lay on the chair beside him.

Wait! He bathed? How did I miss him coming in? Did I drift off?

Lily withdrew, rising.

The drunk sensation Starriace correlated with the magelust intensified. Her body felt like she was floating.

"Enjoy yourself," Lily whispered, then slipped free. She crossed the room to her husband, gave him a passionate kiss, and went upstairs.

Starriace's desire rose with each retreating step Lily took. She'd never tell the woman how much she relished her time with Kam, but she was pretty sure Lily had an idea. Still, that finger of betrayal slithered through her heart, but it all but evaporated as he moved closer. She'd do whatever he asked, including the hardest thing of all, sacrificing a relationship with both to help save their marriage.

Standing before her, he towered over her as she still reclined on the long chair. His short, dark blonde hair just as Starriace remembered, but his physique seemed bigger now, more muscular. Lily did say he was working more. Her gaze roved from his chest to his trousers, and her heart fluttered.

Her insides clenched. He stood so close; she could almost feel the body heat radiating off him, and his scent teased her nose.

She reached for him and pulled him down, kissing him passionately. The scent of sandalwood filled her nostrils. And now, without her friend there, they could pretend the secret remained unexposed.

A dizzying bliss washed over her. Her head pounded with euphoria, and he returned her affection with a blaze as hot as her own.

Before she knew it, his hands were ripping open her robes, clawing at her undergarments, spreading her legs, and breaching her in carnal hunger. She wrapped her legs around his waist, her lips never far from his, his chest pressed against her breasts, all stolen breaths at a frantic pace. It was hot and wild and animalistic.

Both were panting and sweating as they neared the end a short time later, him still hunched over her. This wasn't a joining given to exploration like the first time—only need, urgency, and directness. With time stolen between them and the risk of discovery, he took what mattered most in the passionate moment. And when it came to his release, she held him close to her body as he finished.

A dark hunger simmered throughout her body as he slowly withdrew and staggered back. With her legs finally down, she felt the tingling sensations in her hips and down to her toes. How long had they been immobile?

Her body tingled all over. Kam leaned down and kissed her once more before retreating upstairs. His wife didn't reappear immediately.

Does Lily hate me now?

As Starriace started to stir, searching for her undergarments, Lily returned. She helped find her clothes, straightening them, and helping her dress.

"Was it better?"

Starriace nodded.

Lily grinned at her.

"It sounded better."

A flush touched Starriace's cheeks.

"Do you hate me for it?" Starriace asked in a small voice.

"Shades, no."

The woman paused, a troubled, downward twitch came to her brows.

"Kam said he released in you."

When she nodded, Lily's lips pursed.

"Is that something you wanted? If not—"

"Yes, it was. I'm sorry if that—"

Lily waved her words away.

"What you two do in your time together is between you, and it doesn't bother me, as long as you both are in agreement."

Starriace drew Lily into a hug.

"Thank you."

Lily returned the embrace, and her emotions shone in her eyes.

"Come on, hun, let's get you dressed."

They set to the task in silence, and when finished, Lily guided Starriace back to the long chair. She sat, making Starriace sit as well.

"I have something to tell you. I'm pregnant."

A smile blossomed on Lily's face, and Starriace's couldn't help but be happy for her. It was only after several moments that all the implications started to arise. She kept them to herself, not voicing them aloud.

"That's great news, I'm so happy for you! Congratulations!"

"Thank you, that means a lot. If we have a girl, I want to name her Julie."

The mage's face brightened at the announcement, but inwardly she cringed.

She can't name something sweet and pure after me! I've done horrible things, things I'm not proud of.

But again, the internal conflict remained unvoiced. She wouldn't dream of ruining her best friend's moment. Anything less than absolute support would destroy their friendship. The couple was expecting, and she was happy for them. Still, deep inside, Starriace realized her time with the couple would soon expire. They'd have no time for her when the child arrived, and her activities with Kam would come to an end.

"Do you want to stay the night?" Lily asked. "We have plenty of room! I could sleep with you or Kam could."

Starriace shook her head, and her mind tilted, the buzz still receding. It was a pleasant cloying. Then, a cold rush overcame her, and it took her a handful of heartbeats to figure out what it was.

Judas was here, now, in Ralloc.

Starriace inhaled sharply.

"I have to go!"

"What? Why? What's wrong?"

"I can't explain, there's no time!"

Starriace gathered her belongings and rushed for the door.

Lily followed in her wake.

"Tell me! Help me understand? Am I pushing you away?"

The question made Starriace pause. The last thing she wished was for Lily to assume responsibility for her sudden departure. The door was so near. All she had to do was reach out, and she'd be gone, and Lily would most likely be safe.

Instead, the young woman turned back, dumped her pack, and crossed over to her companion. In a coalescent moment, she poured her desire into their embrace, crushing her in a hug.

"No," Starriace said. "I love you, both of you. You aren't pushing me away. If anything, you make me want to stay and give up my crazy plans. I came to Ralloc under cover of night and without using magic in the hopes of remaining undetected. I just realized that during my time with Kam, the magelust manifested, and I may have been drawing on my magic inadvertently. If so, they know I'm here and will come looking. They might track me here!"

"Who will? Why? Why would they search for you?"

Starriace debated what to say as she gathered up her pack. How could she explain? Would Lily even understand? The mage blurted the first thing that came to mind.

"You once said you knew they took more than my money."

Lily's eyes went to the floor as she thought, then lifted her gaze back up to meet hers.

"Yes. I was right, wasn't I? Why? Did you do something? Did you hurt those bastards?"

Starriace swallowed hard.

"Yes."

Lily stilled.

"This is what you meant when you said you had something to do, isn't it? Did you kill them?"

The mage dipped her head once, a curt movement.

"Good, I hope they suffered."

Lily embraced her again. The resolve hardening within Starriace's heart quivered. She coveted the thought of staying but couldn't afford the gratification.

"I saw what those animals did to you. It's a miracle you're still alive and able to walk. I would've done the same damn thing; don't you ever doubt that!"

A gush of gratitude lanced through her. Lily understood. She hadn't judged the deeds or actions. With reluctance, Starriace pulled away and stepped through the door.

In the cold night, Lily's voice called after her.

"I love you."

Chapter 17: Ralloc

The last light of Apor faded. A cold, northern wind slid down from the Vikal peaks. Darkness surged to claim the sky.

Judas blew out a breath, and it fogged before his eyes. The breeze snatched at his robes. He stood in the palace's courtyard, the seat of the Kothlere Council, ruling body over the Ralloc and Marcoalyn domains. Ralloc didn't meddle with allied or estranged domains, but it did restore order when faced with chaos and war.

The once imperial-turned-republic didn't govern other sovereigns but held them by a short leash, and that was the root of the problem. It was all too political: unable to act, think, or speak freely. The citizens suffered through societal bile.

Pretty soon, people won't be able to go to a tavern for a drink without offending the religious sects, and a holy man will be shunned for sharing the sacred texts.

He shook his head. Both sides were wrong.

It's like living under a monarch.

Judas befriended a king when he was young, foolish, opinionated, and headstrong, but that was before the Wizard's War, before Meristal, before he trained with Fife Doole.

Judas paced to coax feeling back in his feet; he'd been standing hours while he waited.

"Warlock Lakayre!" a familiar voice shouted.

Judas turned toward the voice, seeing a figure running toward him, robes billowing in his wake. The warlock suppressed a groan.

"Toddison, right?" he asked. "Let me guess, you want to finish the interview?"

"How'd you know? It's Todd, remember? I hate Toddison."

"Oh, right, Todd. I'd like to finish, but I can't right now. I'm awaiting the consul; we have business to discuss. Perhaps some other time, okay?"

Judas hoped his explanation was enough to sate the younger's appetite.

"Sure, no problem."

Todd couldn't hide the disappointment in his voice.

"I understand. Who can say no to the consul, right? Hey! Do you think she'd let me interview her?"

"Well, I *can* say no to her, but I don't."

Judas gave a chuckle. Then, a thought came to him.

"As for the interview, I can put in a word, but I make no promises. That's not a bad idea. I'll ask her."

Todd nodded and shuffled off. Judas watched him go, letting his thoughts drift to newer excuses in case he ran into him again at an unfortunate time.

"Judas?" a familiar voice called from the castle's doorway.

He turned to see Meristal smiling at him.

"We're ready for the War Council now. You may come in."

He nodded and started toward her but stopped in mid-stride. He paused. Something faint glimmered in his mind's eye, a sense almost acquainted.

He searched for that diminished trace.

It was there, barely noticeable. Like the softest whisper, the shortest of breaths, but the sensation remained undeniable. A flicker of warning came through his mind and settled into the pit of his stomach.

"Judas?" Meristal called again, this time much closer. "What is it?"

He glanced about but not at any one thing in particular. His eyes drifted to the city beyond the castle walls.

"She's here," he whispered.

"Who?"

"Julie."

He had yet to reveal to Meristal the name Julie had chosen: Starriace.

"Where?"

"I don't know, she's trying to hide."

"How do you know?"

"I felt her lust, the magelust. She's close, but not drawing on magic. I can feel strong emotions from her, sorrow, desire, love…it's as if she lost someone."

"As in death? Can you pinpoint her?"

He shook his head.

"Unfortunately, no. And no, I don't think someone died."

"Then, there's nothing we can do at the moment. Come, the War Council's waiting."

Together, they turned and ascended the stone steps into the castle. Every so often, he glanced back over his shoulder, wishing he could find his daughter.

As soon as she emerged from Lily's house, Starriace sensed Judas's presence, his essence bright like a shining beacon. She clamped down on her presence, drawing it tight around her.

Slipping past Kam and Lily's lawn, she crept down a darkened alley. Concealed in the shadows, she waited with a held breath.

Did he sense me? Are they coming? Will he figure out why I've come?

The last thought seemed ridiculous, the reason for the visit was as random as her return. She focused on her essence, suppressing it until she could only detect a faint speck. Would it be enough?

Fife taught her the trait of masking her aura. Rusem, as a spirit, expounded on the ability. When she turned him into a risen, a link formed between them, a way to communicate. Even now, she could detect him. Could she call him in his current state? He lost verbal communication, but she understood through the link forged between them.

She shook her head.

Rusem didn't matter now, Judas did. She felt him probing the city, searching. He lacked finesse, subtlety. His exploration trampled through, saturating the city.

She scolded herself for being careless. Regret did little for her now, and she wouldn't lament her time with Kam.

And Lily.

The possibility of Judas being within the city had always been strong, but she hadn't expected him. Possible, not probable. He wouldn't find her with her presence so small, a grain of sand among many. Unless he narrowed his perspective, which would take much longer, she'd remain undetectable.

The momentary panic wore off.

Judas sensed without discovering her location or intentions. Assured of potential success, she left the hideaway and headed to the library.

"I could've sworn she was here," Judas said as they walked to the council chambers. "I felt her, I know I did."

Doubt filled his last statement.

"What could cause this feeling besides nearness?"

"Strong emotions, but that doesn't make sense. I don't understand the cause. Earlier I felt…"

He paused. He didn't want to say pleasure, but he was almost sure it was.

"Do you really think she's here?"

Worry filled her voice, and confusion etched her features. People cleared out of their path as they walked down the halls.

"If you think so, then let's sound the guards. I don't want a murderer in my city."

Her statement hit Judas in the chest like an anvil.

"Do you believe she killed those men without provocation?"

It wasn't his voice that betrayed the emotion he guarded, but his eyes flashed a warning, and he knew she saw it.

"Innocent until proven guilty, Judas. All the same, we can't take that risk, even if innocent."

He noticed how she navigated their conversation with care. Part of him was thankful, the other, wary.

"I'll leave the decision up to you."

Judas nodded as he stretched his essence back toward the city, but it didn't yield anything new.

Resigned, he sighed.

"Alert the guard to search the city, but not house by house. I don't believe she's here to sleep. Whatever she's up to, it'll be to benefit her. We must think bigger."

His words came out slow as he pondered the puzzle.

"What does Ralloc have that she needs?"

Meristal gave a single, exasperated chuckle.

"Clothes, equipment, money, weapons, too many things to count, Judas."

"Have the guards check shops and their owners for those things. I'll check the depositories with some guards, there are many of them. But somehow…"

The answer was just beyond his grasp as if taunting him. Then, all together, it faded.

"This doesn't feel right. Doesn't feel like her. She's here for something, something either extremely big or small, but monumental all the same. Why else risk coming here?"

"We best get started," Meristal offered. "I'll cancel the meeting."

He shook his head.

"I just hope we don't find her too late."

The massive library was one of the biggest buildings in Ralloc, rivaling the splendor of the old castle. The five-story building towered with windowpanes of stained glass. Staircases of winding, white oak weaved throughout, each step decorated by various creatures intricately carved by master artisans. The gloss finish gleamed like glass.

Rolling ladders encroached soaring bookshelves that extended to the ceiling. Along the marble halls hung historic murals of the Wizard's War and at least one depiction of archangels descending to destroy one man. She noted the significance, recalling what she read about Hagen at Harold's.

Chandeliers of diamonds and glass hung from above. The largest loomed thirty feet wide in the center of the open atrium. The gold gleamed bright and untarnished—beautiful and squanderous.

But she didn't come here to ogle the riches.

Turning from the center of the room, dismay washed over her as she took in the numerous volumes. How long would it take to comb through them all? Somewhere in all that was *Du' Garuaex*.

Her eyes itched with irritation, and she fought the urge to rub them.

She watched the milling people. A frustrated young man flipping through the pile of books caught her attention. He snapped the volume shut and stalked to the counter.

Starriace followed, hovering close enough to hear the exchange.

"… so what I need is a book that would shed more light on the school. A book of the structure, and the person who built it. I need answers on its age, and if feasible, how to move or rebuild it closer to Ralloc."

"I'll see what I can find," the woman assured. "As a general rule, there isn't much on Divinity Enigumas. The sole reason is for security, but I'll look. Also, if you can't find it here, there's another library inside the castle."

"Thank you," the young man groaned and retreated to his table.

The woman at the counter wrote something on a piece of paper and handed it to a younger aide who went in search for the book.

Idiot! Why didn't I think of this before?

Without wasting more time, she strolled forward and put on a charming smile.

"Good evening."

"Good evening, citizen. How may I direct your inquiry?"

"I need to find a book. A rare one on elyves. Do you have a section just dedicated to elyves or are they scattered throughout the library?"

"We have a section on the elyves, but if it's rare, you might inquire with the rare collections. If you tell me the name of the book, I can direct you."

"*Du' Garuaex*," she revealed.

The woman's face flickered, too quick for certainty. Worried, Starriace stretched out with her aura to sense what the woman felt. Shock echoed back followed by uncertainty. Then, her mind raced too fast for Starriace to comprehend.

"Certainly," the librarian spoke with a slight quiver. "Level five. The staircase to the right will take you to the top. I'll send word so they'll have it ready when you arrive."

Starriace raced through viable options. She could turn away and leave empty handed. Judas still hadn't found her, but the longer she stayed, the more probable that outcome became. If she left, would that alarm the woman enough to call the guards? Captured or not, she'd come away empty-handed. Staying, she had the opportunity to get her hands on the book, if it was here at all.

Calm down. She doesn't know anything, and Judas can't find you. You're one person among two million.

"Thank you," Starriace managed.

She crossed to the right staircase and began her long ascent, glancing down at the people below poring over their books before tracking back to the counter.

The librarian was gone.

Her heart hammered. What did that mean? Adrenaline surged through her body and panic reigned. Hastening, she skipped steps. How many minutes remained until her time was up? Her intentions were to review the book and return it, now she'd grab it and escape.

She reached within to confirm her shielded presence. The glimmer within was hardly noticeable. Power attracted power, and both she and Judas held plenty. Unless she did something stupid, she'd slip by.

On the fifth floor, she spied a man behind a similar counter, but bars safeguarded the rarities beyond. His wizened face turned toward her.

"Ah!" he said, his voice frail but excited. "You must be the young woman I was told to expect. I haven't seen anyone up here in over a decade besides Warlock Lakayre."

She heard the disdain in his voice.

"I'm appalled they let that warmonger wander through our library!"

He shrugged.

"Where are my manners?"

Starriace refrained from responding. Judas wasn't her friend or enemy. She regarded her former master with indifference. If he arrived tonight, he'd just be someone in her way.

"The book I asked for?" she prompted.

"Yes. You may look at it over there."

He pointed to a cluster of tables and chairs to the left.

"Be warned, you may not take the book from the library. One time, about half a legend ago, this young woman came in—"

"—Thanks," Starriace cut him off and moved away.

Time was vital. How much longer until the guards arrived?

She sat down, fingering the ancient volume tattered and frayed by time. A hum of magic caressed her fingers as she did.

How old is this book? Magic must preserve it.

A commotion drew her from her trance.

"There she is!" yelled a guard.

Starriace spun out of her chair, her wand materializing in her hand. She faced a squad in cramped confines. Twenty guards advanced with gleaming swords drawn, arrows knocked and strings taut. A few carried nets.

"Get her!"

They rushed forward.

Her essence flared, and she let it take over. The chair lurched toward the men. A curling scream echoed through the building, the man's face erupting in a splatter of blood. He crumbled in a heap, his helmet clanging against the floor.

Some tried to catch him and fell, too. Teeth and blood lurched from his mouth, causing a few others to slip.

Arrows released, whizzing past the helmets of rushing sentries. The arrows broke apart before they reached her. She vaulted backward, away from the advancing men.

One guard dove for the book. The tome flew into her outstretched hand. The table burst into flames and rocketed forward. It shattered, pelting the sentinels with flaming debris. Boiled leather caught on fire, half the men incinerated by magical flames. The blockade of bodies and weapons parted, and she glimpsed her avenue of escape.

In haste, she stuffed the book in her bag and slung it over her shoulders. One guard snagged her ankle, and she tumbled to the ground. A burst of energy rippled out, a shock wave tossing him back.

Finding her feet, she made it to the top of the staircase. She nearly committed to her escape, but guards rushing up the stairs delayed her departure. One standing between the fourth and fifth floor took aim and fired an arrow.

She batted the bolt away and countered with a burst of cold air. The impact splashed around him, frosting the landing and railing. He slipped and tumbled down the stairs.

Her attack spurred inspiration. She formed a wall of ice between her and the advancing forces, towering higher than the men could climb. They hacked at the barrier, swords ringing with each strike.

Far below, sentries loitered in the atrium, blocking her retreat. A flicker of gleaming gold caught her eyes.

The chandelier.

For a brief moment, regret filled her, but it'd ensure her escape. With her essence, she felt where the bolts burrowed and froze them. Energy swelled inside her. Exerting her will, she jerked her hand in a downward motion, and the chandelier ripped free and plummeted.

Below, guards cursed and dove for cover. In a shower of gold, diamonds, and glasswork, the fixture crashed into the floor, peppering all with shrapnel. The resounding cacophony reverberated throughout the structure. Without hesitation, she followed, plunging over the balcony's handrail, dropping to the ground level.

The crash disrupted her focus for a brief instant. The floor rushed up. Just before impact, she centered her will and brought her headlong plunge to a halt. She displaced her body as Fife taught her.

Righting herself, she touched down. Bellowing shouts from above drew her attention. Most were shouts of dismay, seeing their injured comrades. Some were directed at her, their prey escaping.

They're lucky I wasn't forced to kill anyone.

In retreat, they flung themselves down the stairs with renewed vigor. Unfortunately for them, by the time they reached the first floor, she'd be gone.

An old man with wispy, silver hair opened the door to the depository.

Judas stepped inside, wand held ready. A small globe of light hovered a few feet above his head, illuminating the room. He crept past expensive, plush furniture and mahogany desks. Gold sconces hung at regular intervals along the red brick wall. A light cream-colored carpet covered the majority of the floor, easing the darkness of the walls.

The old man, the manager of the depository, padded behind him, quicker than Judas would've guessed possible for his age. The chain around his waist rattled with keys as they reached the vault.

He inserted the first key and turned it, withdrew it, then turned the wheel in a memorized sequence. He repeated the process a second time as another bolt retreated. For a third—and hopefully final—time, he did so again.

The door cracked open. The old man grunted as he strained to pull it. Two guards rushed forward to help, and the door opened at a ponderous pace. Judas rushed in, half expecting to find Starriace, but his wand lowered after a few moments.

"She isn't here."

An explosion of shattering glass sounded into the night. Judas's head snapped in the general direction of the noise, whirling around. He ran out of the depository, his eyes searching until they fell on the most prominent object he could see.

As he did, angry shouts reached him.

"To the library!" he yelled, and the accompanying soldiers took off at a dead sprint. Judas ran and concentrated. A fraction of a second later, he jumped through a swirling blue mist and teleported to the front steps of the library.

Arriving, he saw a fleeing figure exiting out the east door—the main entrance. The person scrambled hard for the south wall.

"Julie!" he yelled.

A spell of fire flung in his general direction was the only reply. The spell went wide.

"Julie!"

He took off after her. Another fire spell hurled at him with blinding speed but still not accurate.

At the southeastern corner of the building, she darted along the darkness that the library and the parallel structure provided. Judas charged after her, rounding the corner. A sinking feeling came to him; a sense of anxiety and fear crashed against him. Judas knew these feelings were hers.

His mageshield flared into existence, but it was almost too late.

Just as he entered the mouth of the alley, in the darkness between the two buildings, Starriace stood, her arm raised. A spell shot out, a tapestry of gold and amber. It nearly ripped through his shield.

As the energy engulfed him, he called upon his secret ability. Each moment passed like a thousand seconds in the single beat of his heart. The power ripped through, and the spell sent cracks through his shield. The fractures started like infinitesimal fissures; hairline breaks lurched into wider gouges, then his shield buckled as spiderwebs raced over it.

He hurried to bolster his efforts.

She broke my mageshield.

One immense blast, and his defenses almost disintegrated. He drew deep, struggling to keep the barrier intact. And then, his ability, like his shield, was ripped from him.

The blast hit him, throwing him back and across the road and into the building opposite. The strike cracked the wall around him. The wall opposite the library disintegrated, leaving a gaping hole.

For the first time since his encounter with Xilor, Judas felt fear.

It's been a long time since I've battled against power that strong.

He shook his head, trying to see Starriace through the fog of pain and adrenaline. He rose to wobbly feet, knees threatening to buckle. Shaking his head again, he charged back into the alleyway. By that time, the guards he ordered to the library had arrived and plunged headlong into the alley.

"Wait! Stop!" he warned, but the bustle of weapons and armor drowned him out.

He had to stop this before people died. Even though he was certain she'd killed those three men, he never saw her as one capable of the act.

He still thought her a novice.

After feeling her power that nearly crushed his shield, it changed his mind.

It's insane how potent she's become in a short time.

He reached the alley mouth again, and his steps slowed. Before him, two dozen men jammed together, held in place by a force field. On the other side of the alley, Starriace stood, her wand directed at the soldiers.

"Get back, Judas!"

At this distance, he glimpsed the brilliant red of her glowing eyes.

By the gods, what happened to her? She can't be Krey, too.

"You know I can't do that," he pleaded. "Stop this, there's nowhere to run. Turn yourself in, and we can work this out."

"I don't think so. Don't try to follow me."

"You must realize I will."

"And let them die?"

"I understand you, Starriace, more than you realize. You won't harm them!"

The statement made her pause. She shook her head as if dazed, but the moment passed.

"How do you know that name? How do you know *my* name?" she demanded.

Judas wanted to tell her it'd been him that named her, but she wouldn't accept it. He braced himself for the worst. He needed to save lives, to capture her, and end the mayhem.

But those hopes vanished.

Behind her, Vamor Poplu rounded the corner, surprising both of them.

"Surrender your wand!" Poplu shouted.

"Vamor, don't!"

Starriace used kinetic energy with her left hand as if to backhand him. He stood several meters away, but the blast launched him much like Judas earlier. Judas's premonition gave a slight warning, enough time to throw up a shield, but did Vamor have the chance?

Another being rounded the corner right where Vamor previously stood. To Judas's horror, he made out the small, old form of the goblin, Lagelm.

Judas, for the first time in his life, was frozen by the horror unfolding. Starriace sent a volley of fire at the little creature. Judas spied the goblin's shield, but it didn't block all the effects of the curse. Lagelm hit the ground like Vamor, his clothes smoking.

Judas advanced, but she was quicker.

"I warned you!"

She flicked her wand at the walls above the helpless guards. In an instant, they crumbled and plummeted. Her shrill voice pierced the night.

"Stay away from me!"

Judas lunged forward with his wand to stop the toppling debris. The stasis field holding them vanished. The sentinels rushed out of the alley, most heading towards the wounded council members. Judas closed his eyes in concentration and rendered Starriace's spells inert, then reversed the effects.

He opened his eyes and started to pursue, but by then, it was too late.

She'd vanished.

Chapter 18: Starriace

After the unfortunate—yet lucky—encounter with Judas, Starriace teleported numerous times. Did he pursue her? How'd she know if he did? Each surge of magic stretched her limits, each hop chaotic. The ability wasn't beyond her reach, but the finesse was.

She and Judas were able to detect each other, a skill she didn't fully understand. None of Fife's analogies she could recall helped either. The confrontation and subsequent escape should've drained her, but only the fringes of weariness nuzzled her.

Maybe it was the meal?

She wouldn't be surprised if Judas teleported straight to the Corridor of Cruelty and awaited her. So far, she was free and clear, and astonishment and relief kept her company.

Unfortunately, her erratic jumps led her to the Corridor, where her presence didn't go unnoticed. Goblins swarmed her, chasing her into the vile strip of land. Panic and need drove her to teleport at random, emerging within sight of their camps but well beyond reach.

Resigned, she settled for her second plan and pulled Rusem's ring from her pocket.

The magic swelled around her, distorted, frenzied, turbulent. Her body stretched, pulled, and pushed in different directions, a force attempting to rend her body in half.

A scream ripped from her throat.

In a sudden, concussive moment, the teleport dropped her. She slammed into the ground, releasing the contents of her stomach. Through tears, a fresh wave of pain bore into her. She blinked, realizing where she ended up.

The Corridor? Still?

Her body lurched, snatched by an unseen force as the ring activated again. The twisting, wrenching effects exploded in painful plumes throughout her body. The torquing forces threatened to rip her apart.

She was going to die.

Fighting the conflicting enchantments, she reached for the ring, and with a grunt, she pulled it free. The ground rushed to greet her, and she crashed in a heap.

Sweet air seared her lungs, but fear spiked with each thudding heartbeat. A painful fire licked the insides of her skull. She pressed her palms against her eyes as the agony lashed out unabated. Before the torment ebbed, she hurled again.

Her breath caught in her throat, realizing where she was.

Muted sounds filled the damp, humid air. Her robes clung to her skin like a sodden quilt. She wiped the beading sweat from her forehead, and her eyes searched the darkness.

I'm still in the Corridor of Cruelty! Why the hell didn't I port to the temple?

Her heart hammered with terror. The last time she'd been here, she fell victim to Mr. Pleasure. She endured countless tortures, more than she could remember.

More than she wanted to.

She wasn't as helpless as last time. Then, she couldn't perform the simplest of magic. Judas failed to recognize that she wasn't a Plotus mage. The pair of them had more in common than he realized, or that she'd admitted.

Both used Rumigul.

Incantations blocked her abilities. Rumigul's power came from within the mind, not muttered words. She also had the ability of flight, which aided her exodus from Fife Doole's mountainside cottage. If she could do it then, now should be no different.

Her need was great, as was her fear of this place.

She stood and concentrated, but the oppressive nature of the Corridor made it near-impossible. Her skin tightened around her eyes as she squinted. Gathering the air granules and coupling them with her ability to displace matter, her body levitated.

That was the easy part.

Propelling required the most concentration and effort. A prerequisite for movement was more than willing herself forward; it required insight into air currents. One slip in concentration equated to a plummeting death.

She closed her hand, using the gesture to guide her will, helping her focus. The joints of her fingers cracked, the knuckles turning white. She built willpower and conjury, molding it to her desire. Hand outstretched, she lurched forward.

The wind whipped about her face, flinging her hair and robes in the abrupt momentum. She kept her eyes closed, rocketing forward. Her aura acted as divination, sensing all around. The trees swayed as she blazed by, branches protesting and leaves rustling. Even the grass bowed in the swath she cut.

An influence pressed against her, hardening the further she went, an external force attempting to rip her from the sky. Fear hardened her concentration. It was a battle of wills, her potency against the Corridor's subjugation.

I will not break!

In a burst, the bewitchment dissipated, breaking like a rope pulled too taut. The backlash of magic sent her careening. Eyes snapping open, the ground blurred beneath as she righted herself. Eyes watered against the gush of wind. A small thrill of triumph suffused her.

She was free of the Corridor.

She gave a breathless laugh. The longer she remained airborne, the better she understood the ability. With each passing moment, she peeled back her concentration until the ability came as natural as breathing.

She was *meant* to fly.

Trepidation quickly stifled the moment. Could Judas sense her if she flew

—track her to her destination? If Judas managed to follow to the Corridor, would he pick up her trail? With reluctance, she descended.

Upon landing, she teleported away, jumping several times before heading back to Rusem. She found the risen as she had left him. Curious, she prodded with a mental command.

Awaken.

He stirred immediately. Rusem stumbled to his feet. A stench of decay permeated the shallow cavern. He was rotting, albeit at a slower rate.

"Watch for intruders," she said. "I need rest."

Whether Rusem understood tone, inflection, or actual words, it was hard to say. He lumbered forward and planted himself just inside the darkness of the den, ever still and watchful. Starriace allowed herself a small smile as she made her pallet and laid down. Waves of exhaustion washed over her. Sleep beckoned in a comfortable serenade, but too many thoughts kept her awake.

Anticipation riled her.

She'd found the book that long eluded her, and now she hungered to tear it open and devour the secrets within, but she could wait. The fight with Judas, the Corridor, and the flight left her depleted. Sleep would restore her magic. The brief conflict was the first time she hadn't held back. Judas wasn't an enemy, but an obstacle.

She noted his horror as she blasted him, and if she had hurt him, it would've devastated her.

But he'd raised a mageshield in time. If he'd died, Xilor would win. Guilt would've crippled her, knowing she caused his death.

And he wasn't young.

But more than that, she was more impressed with her abilities, how she felt his mageshield fracture, the truest testament to her growing prowess, not the games she played with Fife.

That stupid wizard snuck up from behind and almost ruined everything. Him, and the goblin.

And that's why she'd crushed the wall—to ensure she escaped. She intended to keep Judas busy, not add to the number of men she'd sent to the Underworld.

But why hadn't the ring teleported her to the temple? Was it because of the Corridor? The ring attempted it twice and failed. She might not have survived a third.

She pushed aside those thoughts and Kam and Lily's faces swam into view. Her heart ached. Lily had helped her when she needed it most, welcomed her into their home. And the moments she shared with Kam…

Smiling, she curled up on her side, and drew the traveler's cloak tight to fight off the cold.

In the shadows of the cave, she noted the subdued scarlet glittering on the walls from her eyes. Had Kam been able to see it, or was it when she drew on her power? Maybe it was connected to emotions? While he took her, he'd whispered in her ear that she was beautiful, that he loved her long, fine hair.

Doubt festered in her heart. Did he mean that he loved her honey-colored hair, or because it was similar to his wife's?

Harold's prophetic words plagued her, surfacing as she tried to enjoy the memory.

I wonder who's the man Harold referred to.

She'd love for it to be Kam, but he was already married. Even if they separated, Starriace wouldn't betray them like that. Still, in truth, she couldn't see herself with any other man.

I haven't met many.

Now that she thought about it, she didn't know if she could see herself in a relationship at all.

There had been times when she tried to imagine herself as someone's wife, but it lacked the appeal to her specific tastes. Though picky, she wouldn't settle for someone who couldn't understand her drive. Even her friend Lily couldn't. So that meant no one, friend or lover, could come before her…what?

Quest? Destiny?

Kam's scent of sandalwood comforted her as she drifted off to sleep.

Bright sunlight filtered through the dim hollow. Rusem stood unmoving in the entryway. A yawn escaped her as she rubbed the sleep from her eyes.

"How long have I slept?" she croaked.

Rusem turned. Images flared through her mind, bright and dark and fast. A sunset, a rising moon, and dawn of a new day.

"A full day?"

A sense of affirmation emanated from the risen.

Groaning, she scratched her forehead and stretched. At least she wouldn't need to rest again for a while, returning back to meditations.

The image of *Du' Garuaex* flickered through her mind, and she pulled the book out. The feeling of being watched washed over her. Rusem stared at her, and she could've sworn recognition flash through his dead eyes.

"Go play," she commanded, shooing him with her hand.

He didn't move, only stared at the book.

"What?"

Images bombarded her, places Rusem had visited, people he'd seen. The recollections flashed so fast she wanted to vomit. A flicker of fear and intrigue slithered through her. Did she just see a much younger Judas in the flashes? Starriace didn't know what Rusem attempted to communicate, but an underlying need or want teemed through their link.

"You want to know where I got it?"

A ripple of confirmation echoed from Rusem.

"From Ralloc. Why? Have you seen it before?"

Another assertion. Fragments streaked with an intensity she'd yet encountered. They spiraled faster until the imagery ended in a painful explosion and darkness.

Starriace panted, a sheen of sweat peppering her forehead.

Was that when he died? Did this book and its secrets cause his death?

"I can handle it," she said, her voice weak and shaking.

She cleared her throat and waved her fingers at him.

"Go. I don't like you staring at me."

He retreated, his presence receding, but it lingered at the edge of her awareness. Fingers brushed the tattered edges. Magic tickled her hand. She glanced back up. Rusem stood at the cave entrance, his eyes on her and the book.

"Away with you, damn it!"

She used magic to shove him out of the opening.

"Don't return until I summon you!"

Rusem lumbered away.

Discomfort irritated her eyes, festering with the rise of emotions. Alone, she could study the book and use magic to keep her awake and comfortable.

By dawn the next day, she'd read it cover to cover. When she lifted her head, a sharp pain stabbed the back of her neck. The text rarely made sense, and only a few passages referred to the brimstones. Those sections seemed to be written in poems, riddles, or just jumbled.

Frustrated, she slammed the book closed and chucked it. It clattered in a plume of dust near the cave's entrance.

Rusem stepped into view and reached for the ancient tome. He turned the book over in his hands. Starriace noticed a distant look in his eyes. A memory flashed through their link, an image of him throwing the book in frustration long ago.

Rising, she crossed to him.

"You've seen this book before? This exact book?"

Rusem gave a slight shake of his head.

Perplexed and disappointed, she turned away only to turn around abruptly.

"Have you seen another version of this book?"

Assertion permeated the link.

Excellent.

"Where?" she urged.

The Melodic Mountains filled her mind before moving to the south. The Stratu' domain. A flicker of a city ended the vision.

In the city?

Yes.

Attainable answers lay sequestered in unfamiliar land, and she'd need a guide. A gust of balmy air swept past the mouth of the cave.

"Ava?" she called.

The mage and the fairy carried a bond sealed in the core of her wand, the wing of a fairy and the hair of a unicorn. The union between Ava and Starriace was stronger than most because the wing came from Ava's mother, Fiosana, who gave up her life to ensure that Starriace became their Head of Creatures, forcing one of their most ancient prophecies into fruition.

In the swamp, Judas bestowed a book out of whimsical impulse. Little did he know that the book was meant for her, responding only to the Bearer of

Secrets. The book urged her to return to the Place of Origins, the Melodic Mountains.

Ava first appeared after she ran away from Judas and her first encounter with Lily, Kam, and Harold at Far Point. So far, Starriace had little use for the tiny creature, but the fairy had saved her life.

She owed her.

Besides, she had her own thoughts about how she could exploit her tie to the fairies in the future. All she needed was an opportunity.

An entire race at my beck and call. That could prove useful.

In the past, Starriace depended on Ava to teleport her from one place to another, but she couldn't stand the fairy's grating presence.

The fairy had her uses though.

"Ava!" she called again.

Ava's home, the Melodic Mountains, was restricted to all except Fife's plateau. She needed to find a way to circumvent the bounds and find safe passage.

Ava materialized.

"You summoned me?"

She dipped her head. Invisible wings fluttered behind her, a soft whistle hummed as she moved. Her voice was as remembered, a ballad of wind chimes.

"I need to go somewhere, and you're the only person I know that can get me there."

"You need me to teleport you?"

"Perhaps, but I need a guide."

"Where do you wish to go?"

Starriace paused, noting the creature's voice lacked the cheerfulness she once possessed.

It's almost as if she's darker…gloomier.

"South of the Melodic Mountains, into the Stratu' Domain. Is that possible?"

"Yes, but the way's dangerous. By boat would be best, slower but safer."

"The mountains would be faster. Can we go over?"

"Not over, but through them, yes. We must travel through a labyrinth of caves to reach the other side. It'll take a week if we don't stop. I strongly recommend that."

That's disconcerting.

"Why?"

"It's not safe."

Starriace waited for her to elaborate, but she didn't.

"But you know the way?"

"Yes."

"I should get a horse."

"You can't take horses."

"Why not?"

Starriace crossed her arms and waited. Ava wasn't being her typical, helpful self.

"The beast will slow us down," Ava retorted. "It'll fall and die or worse, draw the attention of what's down there. You don't want to attract attention."

"What's down there?"

"I can't tell you."

"Can't or won't?"

Ava's lips thinned.

"Only a sliver separates the Underworld from the world of the Living. The barrier is weakest there. That's all I can tell you."

The fairy's revelation seemed restrained, and it riled the mage. Did she hold back? If the fairy couldn't trust or reveal to her Head of Creatures, what was the point in having one?

"Because you can't or won't?"

"Both."

"Fine!"

Starriace stuffed *Du' Garuaex* in her bag, right next to the books Harold and Judas had given her. Though Judas's book remained silent as of late, she didn't relinquish hope.

"Let's go," the mage said tersely as she returned to the front of the cave.

Disgust directed at Rusem flitted across Ava's face, but she abstained from commenting. A swirling mist manifested, and the trio stepped through, hurtling towards the dark world beneath the mountains.

Chapter 19: Judas

"It was her!" Judas said.

That very night, his daughter snuck into Ralloc and escaped without a trace. Judas stood in the old jail, a dungeon deep in the castle's bowels, and engaged in a heated debate over whether Starriace had really come or was an imposter, like the one who visited Judas's home.

His ailments, not to mention his wounded pride, all but confirmed it for him. He hadn't realized how much Starriace had hurt him.

His shield absorbed the majority of the force, but the landing hadn't been soft. Pain throbbed through his bruised elbow, leaving his left arm dangling at his side. He suspected a fracture or break, not to mention the numerous scrapes and cuts peppering his scalp.

When he wasn't talking, he focused on healing and easing the pain.

Are you sure? Staell, the Clydesdale-size unicorn, asked through his mental projection.

His luminance brightened the dark room.

It was dark. You couldn't see her face well, could you? It's been months since you last saw her.

Judas glared at him.

"Of course, I'm sure!"

"That's not the important thing," Meristal interrupted. "Is it, Judas?"

She raised her eyebrows in warning.

He blew out an exasperated sigh.

"No, it's not. She wasn't here for money, weapons, or men. She came for knowledge. Dangerous knowledge."

"What did she take?" Scodd Yullus, the elyfian Supreme War Commander, asked.

Over the course of the last moon turn, he'd been among them in Ralloc. They managed some progress, weaning him from his full elyfian armor and into more formal robes.

"An ancient book: *Du' Garuaex*."

Scodd and Mella, his assistant, inhaled at the revelation but held their tongue.

"What else, Judas?" Meristal prompted.

When he glared at her, she returned it with a withering scowl.

"She's phenomenally more powerful than before. I don't know how, but… there's no mistake. Her essence is potent."

"Grown?" Sedrus, the centaur, asked. "I thought that couldn't happen, at least not in the terms you're talking. What you're born with is what you die with. How much growth?"

"Enough to damn-near break my personal shield. It took all my effort to ensure I didn't get hurt. Even then, it almost wasn't enough. Her power pulled my mageshield apart with hairline fissures throughout. As for her essence growing, the answer eludes me. Maybe something to do with Rumigul abilities."

"By the gods!" Sedrus exclaimed. "We need her! She should be fighting on our side, not against us. If Xilor manipulated her, what terrible fate awaits the Alliance of Races and the whole realm? Shades! Probably all of Ermaeyth!"

"Yes, we know," Meristal spoke tartly. "Is there more, Judas?"

He took a moment to collect himself.

"No one has ever penetrated my shield before, not even Xilor, but she did."

He shook his head.

"She's probably surpassed us both."

"So, you're saying…" Sedrus drawled.

"She had time to prepare and waited for me. Locked in combat doesn't allow for the same devastating effects as one who builds an attack. I was lucky, as was she. It won't happen again."

He hoped the flicker of doubt in his heart wasn't betrayed by his voice and eyes.

"How much damage was done?" Kellis inquired.

Kellis, the other goblin councilmember, wasn't there for the fight, but Lagelm's blow took fifteen minutes to rouse him. Vamor Poplu wasn't as lucky. He stayed with the healers tonight and would remain for several days with a severe concussion and a few broken bones.

But it could've been so much worse.

Judas shook his head.

"The city? Superficial, but her? The damage she can cause with the book?"

"Alright," Meristal said. "Supreme War Commander?"

"Consul?"

"Tomorrow, you'll be given official sanction to take a part of your army and move on Shadow City. The vampires have proven most resistant to political dialogue. On the morrow, a faction of your army will hike to war. Satisfactory?"

A few moments passed before the elyf answered.

"No. My entire army augments yours. Why not take my army, the whole army, and destroy Shadow City?"

"One," Meristal counted her fingers, "we're not interested in genocide. If so, we'd be no better than Xilor. Two, because an entire army takes much longer to move. The sooner you can get there, the better. Three, because half our army and the remaining half of yours will begin to fortify Ralloc's defenses should the war reach here. The other half of our army, what remains of it, will go under Judas's and Jynerul Vikal's joint command at Dlad City. We're certain that's Xilor's next target. If not, we hope to lure him there."

"That's not what I hoped for. If my army is unsuccessful, we'll have to divert more resources to rescue those in peril."

If that happens, the unicorn interjected, *we, as a race, will come to your aid.*

The unicorns rarely moved in the ways of battle, only a handful of times in history. They fought with magical power when the swords and arrows of others failed.

Scodd considered for a moment, then nodded.

"I find this acceptable."

Meristal gave a single nod.

"Very well. Tomorrow, you march to war. Gods and angels watch over you all."

Chapter 20: Xenomene

Xenomene resumed all duties as ko-don after the heir's departure. They talked for hours, going over the plans the heir was privy to at the meetings. The officers graciously accepted his presence.

He's a man after all.

The proposed plan was dangerous, daring even, and Xenomene loved it for more than one reason. The lingering shock after the first battle had washed away, and she longed to return to the slaughter. Since retreating to Dlad City, the war front remained silent. Why hadn't Xilor advanced?

Scouts reported that the enemy demolished Cape Gythmel, a sound strategy to ensure no one snuck up behind them, staving off a war on two fronts. She wondered why Xilor hadn't destroyed the insignificant settlement outright. Their spies also noted Xilor's absence, unseen on the battlefront since the Grand Royal Army's retreat.

Is he dead?

She doubted it.

His absence bodes ill.

The heir's plan involved sending a squad of Krey to probe their numbers at Cape Gythmel. A portal master would accompany them for a swift return. Their forces divided, so they were to track the enemy's movement and scout the rear element.

The heir handed me a gift. Tiny's squad is going, and I'll pray really fucking hard and promise to tickle the balls of whatever gods are listening that Bitcher dies!

A part of her began to mourn the expected loss, but it didn't overcome her hate. A constant war waged within her. She understood Bitcher's anger, given the circumstance, but what she didn't forgive was being left to die. The bodily injuries had healed, but the emotional trauma lingered. She drove herself mad dwelling on it for two days before she forced herself to let it go. Plotting his death without seeming intentional provided the only relief.

It's not murder if I don't drive the sword in his chest, right?

True to his word, Bitcher visited her every day. The first few days he reminded her of the consequences. By the end of the week, when he arrived, she shuffled to the bed without being told and waited. A quicker submission meant the sooner he'd leave. Each compliance brought out his caring gentleness, and she found herself melting into the blissful moments.

Might as well get something out of it.

There were times when the hate died, and she returned his affections. The tenderness made her remember the man he used to be, and not the monster he became. Despite that, she kept a well-stocked supply of moonleaf in the desk drawer. She'd never allow his seed to quicken within her.

A knock on the door drew her attention. If it'd been Bitcher, there wouldn't have been a knock.

"Enter."

Tiny opened the door, ducking his head to keep from hitting the frame. He'd avoided her since the arrival of the new Krey, embarrassed by chasing her around the room. She was too, but in a different way.

Her mischievous grin stopped him in his tracks. She eyed him with a raised brow and waited for him to speak.

"How do you find the new desk?"

"It's nice. Thicker and sturdier than the last."

She shook the table for emphasis.

"Right, sturdy."

Color shaded his face, and she found it amusing. She swiveled in her chair, back and forth, as if it were a toy.

"What's on your mind, Tiny?"

"Well…the uh…that is to say…well—"

"Oh Shades, Tiny, is this about the lusting?"

His face flared crimson.

"That's what I thought."

His eyes found the floor intriguing in that moment.

"Why are you embarrassed? You did as everyone else."

"They didn't chase you around the room."

Rising, she shuffled around the desk. Her small form was dwarfed by the big man. Standing on her toes, her hand caressed his face and tried to make him feel better, but she realized that might've been a mistake, encouraging his feelings.

"Don't be embarrassed. I wasn't there long enough to be caught. Even in the lust, if there's something a person doesn't want strongly enough, they can fight it."

She smiled and turned back to the desk.

Without warning, he grabbed her from behind and hugged her to his body.

Panic exploded in her mind, remembering Bitcher's attack, and she almost lashed out. She clamped down as he brought his mouth to her ear.

"You did fight it."

She forced herself to smile, the fear dwindling, the moment passing.

"The lust receded."

The lie came out smooth, even to her ears.

"Do you want to, then?"

She squirmed out of his arms.

"Maybe," she lied.

She moved away and rounded her desk, sitting again.

He shifted on his feet.

"Really?"

She hesitated.

"I said maybe."

Assuaging his ego was a burden. His eyes glanced away.

"You're not going to profess your love to me, are you? If so, you might have to kill Bitcher first."

"As long as I—" he started before he clamped up.

Xenomene rolled her eyes in disgust. She loved Tiny, but not like that.

"I'm sure there are tavern wenches you could visit. The girls in the new squad—"

"I don't want them."

She pressed her lips together.

"I understand, but I'm with Bitcher. Besides, I've seen your *cudgel*, and that'd hurt more than it would please. It's not how long or broad your sword is, it's how well you use it. The same is said of the bedroom."

She paused long enough to insinuate an intentional subject change.

"So, now with that out of the way, why'd you come?"

"The do-dons of the squads would like to see you. You haven't officially met them. You've been holed up for the past few days."

"The heir left me with a lot to ponder, and to be honest, I'm a bit embarrassed, too."

"For what?"

"You didn't get mounted in front of everyone."

"Well, you weren't the only woman present."

"Valid. Very well, send the do-dons. Return when they're ready. Also, can you bring in some lunch? I'm starving."

He gave a bow before he ducked through the doorway. She rolled her eyes with amusement and pored over the scattered documents on the desk. Maps, letters of authorization, personnel counts, and a letter of declaration from the incoming jynerul cluttered the surface. Before she realized, a rap on the door drew her from convoluted thoughts.

"Enter."

The door opened, and Tiny ushered in two people she vaguely recalled. The big man carried a plate of food, and his frame eclipsed a fourth person, a camp hand, pushing a cart of assorted bottles and a few pewter cups. Once placed inside, the helper took his leave.

The female do-don stood tall and wispy, with a head full of white hair and pale blue eyes that rivaled arctic shallows.

She's far too young for white hair.

The other, a male, had muddied, aristocratic features.

Probably from a minor noble house or a distant relative.

Clean-shaven with long, dark brown hair that touched his shoulders, his features highlighted his near-black eyes.

Xenomene surveyed the plate that Tiny sat down. He brought roasted duck with mashed potatoes and collard greens. A heel of bread sat atop.

"Something to drink?" Tiny inquired.

She nodded, and he poured. While he did, Xenomene studied the two do-dons. Neither twitched under her emerald scrutiny. Xenomene noted the woman was half a head taller than the man. Tiny pressed the cup into her awaiting hand. She took an ample swallow and almost spat it over the desk. At the last possible instant, she turned her head and hit the floor.

"What in the Shades of the Underworld is that shit?"

"Ale."

"It's disgusting! Give me something else."

"What would you like, O' Fair Lady of the Krey?"

She glowered.

"Spiced rum?"

"That we do, O' Mistress of Death and Pain."

"Shut it! If you got lime, give me that, too."

He did as instructed, and she took an appreciative gulp.

"Much better!"

She set the cup down and leaned back in the chair.

"Names?"

"Spectre," the woman replied.

"And I, my lady, am Lyan."

Definitely minor noble.

"At least both of you can talk," she said, remembering the first time Slurp and Smokey made her acquaintance. That brought a chuckle.

The two exchanged glances.

"Who's got all females?"

"That would be me, Ko-don," Spectre answered.

"I don't envy you."

"I don't understand, Ko-don."

"Men are simple. They only care about eating, shitting, fucking, and killing. Women are much more...well, more."

Spectre nodded.

"I believe I understand."

Xeno turned her attention to Lyan.

"What's your story?"

"I'm the firstborn son of the Allison House, my lady."

Xeno stifled a groan.

"I'm Krey; there aren't any ladies here."

"Forgive me, my la—Ko-don."

"Enough chinwag, we've work to do."

She rose and pulled a map close, turning it around for them to see.

"The heir, among others, would like us to take care of some problems. The first is the reserve element at Cape Gythmel. They're taking the town apart so we can't refortify behind them. A vast majority of Xilor's army retreated to the dark reaches of Shadow City. There's nothing we can do but wait. If we attack, we'll be in the open, and they'll hold the fortified position. We'll be decimated. So, one squad will probe the forces at Cape Gythmel. Tiny, that'll be yours."

"You mean *ours*, Ko-don?"

"No, yours. I'm a ko-don without a posse unless the heir decrees otherwise. If that's the case, I have a few select choices in mind, but you're now do-don of the Void Walkers. You may name your squad as you wish. I never got around to changing ours. Who's your second?"

Tiny groaned and crossed his massive arms.

"You mean who's supposed to be or who I want to be?"

"Both."

"Bitcher's supposed to be, but I despise the man. I'd rather kill him than suffer him."

She blurted a flippant response.

"He's just a bed warmer."

A gleam shone in Tiny's eye.

"My choice as my second is Mauler. The superior blade choice, but Bitcher has seniority."

"If we went by seniority rather than skill," Xenomene retorted, "I'd be washing sheets and busting rust on practice armor."

In fact, those in the room were all senior to her.

"True. Mauler's my second."

"Without me in your squad, I leave you one short. I'll write to the heir and send for a replacement."

"As you wish, Ko-don."

"I'll trade you one of my girls," Spectre said, "if the heir sends you a man."

Xenomene stifled a chuckle.

"I'm fine with whichever."

"I don't know," the big man said, slight worry creasing his face. "Without Xeno there to keep her in check, I think Mauler will be all I can handle."

Spectre stared at him, dumbfounded, and Lyan covered his mouth to hide a smirk.

Shades, he completely missed the implied bonus.

She cleared her throat.

"Back to business. There are reports of raiders hitting small communities from Cape Gythmel to Vikal Village. The heir wants them stopped; they're getting too close to Outpost Dire. They've raped women, slain children, and burned crops. One of you will take that. I'll leave it up to you two to decide who goes."

"I will!" Spectre blurted.

She seemed abashed by the impulsive interjection.

"I mean…I didn't leave the Hive to sit behind walls."

"None of us did, but it's part of it. Okay, Lyan, you stay as a reserve element. We received word that a segment of the enemy is marching towards us. It'll be a chance to bloody your virgins. How many have seen battle?"

He looked up towards the ceiling as he thought. It didn't take long.

"Just Omegryk, the goblin."

"Goblin?" Xenomene asked, surprised. "We have a goblin? What the hell's the little guy going to do?"

"I don't know if I would use the word *little*," Tiny spoke up. "He's barely shorter than me, and I'd pause before tangling with him."

"I didn't know the Krey took in goblins."

"We take in anyone who displays the bloodlust," Tiny reminded.

"I want to meet this Omegryk."

"Uh," Lyan started, "I'd suggest you do so only with my Mind present."

"Why?" Spectre asked.

"His magic is strong."

"What magic?" Tiny interjected.

"The lust. He affects the women on a daily basis, and our Mind must compensate when he's around."

Spectre looked at Tiny.

"Keep your male, I'll trade with Lyan. The goblin for his pick of any of my girls."

"Desperate much?" Xenomene chided.

"Randy more like," Tiny chuckled.

"Who cares?" Spectre intoned. "Sex is like air, it doesn't matter unless you're not getting any! We fuck when we aren't fighting or training. Kind of hard without a male."

"True."

Xenomene glanced back to Lyan.

"I'd still like to meet him. Never seen one before."

"As you wish, Ko-don."

Xenomene sat.

"I'll use your Mind, too."

He dipped his head. Xenomene nodded and turned back to the maps.

"Spectre, you'll leave tonight accompanied by a portal master. He'll take you wherever you wish to go. The last town hit lies south of Vikal Village. Begin your search there. Track them, hunt them, and kill all who don't surrender. Those who do will be brought back for questioning and trial."

"Who'll be doing the questioning?" Tiny asked.

"The Krey. After we're done, the army will shackle, try, and execute them under the jynerul's guidance. Whenever his divine ass arrives, that is. He's late."

She turned back to Spectre.

"You'll leave at midnight, as will you, Tiny."

Her voice grew rough while delivering the harsh news.

"Tiny, you're to port in and evaluate their numbers. If you catch them unawares and sleeping, kill as many as you can before returning. I'm not going to lie, this is a dangerous mission, possibly suicidal. If your portal master dies, you'll be stranded, so protect him at all costs. In that unfortunate event, it's every man for himself; fight, evade, escape, and return. If you die, die with a sword in your hand, and a war cry ripping from your throat."

Tiny nodded.

Xenomene regarded Lyan and remembered her cup of spiced rum. She took a hard swallow, wetting her throat.

"Lyan, you'll be the front lines if the enemy attacks here. Last time around, they managed to get through the walls at Cape Gythmel and would've slaughtered the army had we not been there. Kernoyl Tyku thinks it best if we led from the beginning. I agree with the assessment, but it seems to be a one-way trip. The army will back you with archers on the wall, so there'll be many targets for the enemy to choose from. With some skill and luck, you may have yourself a good time. Situation permitting, I may join."

"It'd be our honor, Ko-don," Lyan said with a flourished, noble bow.

"Save it for the courts."

She turned to the only other female in the room.

"Spectre, I'd like to meet your squad before you leave, at least the opportunity to try to learn their names."

"As you wish."

"Yours too, Lyan. Form up this evening."

"It'll be done."

"You may leave and begin preparations. Spectre, see to their armor, and the draycon if you need anything. The heir sent him with regards. The army's apothecary will fill your travel packs. Food and supplies may be drawn from the cook's hall. Questions?"

They shook their heads.

"Dismissed."

All three turned to leave.

"Not you, Tiny, you stay."

The three stopped and exchanged glances before shuffling to the door. Spectre cast one last glimpse before leaving. Xenomene read the expression clear as glass.

She thinks I'm going to fuck him.

The door closed, and Xeno listened for the retreating footsteps before speaking. She pulled the plate close as she waited, cut into the duck, and took a bite. The fowl was moist but cold.

What I wouldn't give for a bit of magic about now.

She took a swig of rum before speaking.

"When I said if you're to die, I meant that, but I'd rather you come back alive."

"Getting fond of me?"

"A bit," she muttered before thinking better of it.

She didn't want to perpetuate the problem by giving him false hope.

"Feelings aside, should the heir make the ko-dons take squads, I'll choose you as my second again. You're loyal and strong and true. You give direct advice and aren't afraid to tell me what I need to hear. I know you'll guard my back no matter what, and I value that more than anything."

"More than Bitcher?"

She didn't hesitate.

"Yes."

Damn, did I just send the wrong message again?

A look of perplexity crossed his face.

"I thought you two were inseparable."

"Only when we share flesh."

A flash of anguish crossed his face at her flippant levity.

"I'm sorry, that was improper. Take this with a dash of sugar: I won't weep if Bitcher dies."

A shadow of animosity and doubt crossed his face.

"What are you saying?"

Tiny never liked Bitcher; even less now that I'm fucking him.

She rubbed her nose and took a bite of potatoes to keep from saying anything stupid. After swallowing, she spoke.

"That I won't weep."

Tiny nodded, confused.

"If that's all, Ko-don?"

"It is. Send the Heart to me, from your squad, then Omegryk."

Tiny left with a weighted, ponderous pace. Xenomene could tell the words turned wheels in his head.

I shouldn't have said anything, but it's done.

She didn't bother with the maps and documents when Tiny left, and with half-hearted diligence, she prodded the food before giving up. She consumed half of the duck and less of the potatoes. The greens escaped unscathed but not the heel of bread. By the time the Heart arrived, she had started a third cup of spiced rum and lime and felt tipsy. She didn't get to drink often since leaving the Hive.

Xeno raised the cup to the Heart.

"Just the southern girl I wanted to see."

"Ko-don."

The Heart had avoided Xenomene since their last argument, and she would've figured the near-death experience would've broken their frosty relationship.

When the Heart used her formal title, her near-jovial nature changed to a sobering melancholy.

"Sit down," Xenomene proffered.

The Heart remained standing.

"Or stand, whatever you want."

She sighed, rubbing her tiny fingers through her dark red hair.

"I wanted to say I'm sorry."

"What?"

"I'm sorry I dragged you into this mess of oath breaking. I didn't know oath breaking included anyone outside the Krey."

"Does it mean so little that you only care if it was a Krey?"

"Of course not!" Xeno protested, heat entering her voice. "Just as the heir won't be dictated to by the Steward of Stratu'Geim, a warlock who isn't Krey won't dictate to me."

A frustrated groan slipped out.

"This isn't why I called you here. I called to let you know I'm working on a way to fix this. I've said nothing because while I don't care what happens to me, I do care what happens to you and the Mind."

"What are you going on about?"

"Swear to me you won't repeat a word of what I'm about to say to anyone."

"Why should I swear an oath to an oath breaker?"

"Because I saved your life!" Xeno screamed, coming to her feet.

The Heart took a step back, startled.

"What are you talking about?"

"Swear it!"

"Alright, if that's what you want. I swear never to repeat anything you say."

"Or act upon it."

"Or act upon it. Now, what are you talking about?"

The impatience left Xenomene, and she slumped in the chair, the energy fleeing.

"Bitcher did it. He's the one who tried to kill me."

The Heart's eyes widened with wrath.

"Bitcher? That son of a bitch, I knew it!"

"There's more—"

"That cunt! I knew from the moment Tiny found you. I couldn't prove his involvement, and Tiny wouldn't act on suspicion alone. He should die for what he did! That smug son of a bitch is still walking around like nothing happened!"

"That's because nothing did happen," Xenomene said.

This drew the Heart up short.

"What?"

"He didn't do it because nothing happened, that's the official story, the way it has to be."

She leaned back, then followed with an addendum.

"For now."

"What do you mean? Why aren't you telling anyone?"

"He's holding it over my head. If I say anything, he'll make sure you get the Mark of the Profane as an accomplice. There's doubt regarding the Mind, and they'll take him, too. I can't have that on my conscience. Just me would be one thing, but with you as an assured accomplice?"

She shook her head and let the question fade.

"Does he leave you alone?"

Xenomene glared at her.

"No. We've continued like nothing happened. My body is keeping you and me from the collar; a small price to pay, don't you think?"

The Heart said nothing, and Xenomene sighed.

"There are times when I'm with him that I almost forget everything he did. It's like there's some part of me that loves him in some perverse way. While I don't want to be with him, I can't break free. His death is the only thing that will unshackle us both. Which brings me back to why I called you here."

"I'm not going to kill him! Well, maybe, but not like you think! That son of a bitch deserves death for all of it, including forcing himself on you every night."

"He doesn't force himself on me. There's a subtle difference. I consent to keep you from an undeserving fate. So, back to why I called for you. What I'm asking is, if Krey should fall in battle, he's the last one you help."

"You want me to choose to let him perish? That's almost asking me to kill him myself."

"No, I'm saying if others should fall, as well as Bitcher, I'm asking you treat him last."

"In the hopes he will succumb from wounds before I can get to him?"

Xenomene didn't respond, letting the Heart draw her own conclusions. The ko-don could see the possibilities flash across the other's face.

"I'll think about what you said," the Heart said. "Gods know other people deserve to live more than him, but I can't commit murder."

"I'm not asking you to. I'm asking you to let him suffer."

A smile blossomed on the Heart's face.

"Oh, I can do that."

"And if a byproduct of that suffering is death, then so be it."

She nodded to Xenomene and turned to leave.

"Not a word!"

"Not a word," the Heart confirmed.

She opened the door to leave, and Xeno spied a massive goblin walking towards her office with an A'uri she couldn't recollect. The mage wasn't remarkable in the slightest. The same couldn't be said for the other. He turned sideways to get through the door, and the A'uri came up beside him.

The ko-don immediately felt what Lyan warned about. The lust was unnaturally strong. She fought the urge to jump him where he stood. Was it the same for Omegryk?

He showed no indication. Xenomene fought for control before the soothing presence of the Mind chased the sensation away.

"Stop it. I want to see if I can resist without your help."

"That wouldn't be wise," the Mind said in a thin voice.

"Are you questioning me?"

She wasn't irritated at the A'uri for questioning her, but because he thought her too weak.

"Get out."

"I don't think that's wise."

He ambled to the door and threw a withering flash back at her.

"Don't blame me if you fuck the animal!"

He stormed out, slamming the door behind him.

Animal? Does he think himself so much better than Omegryk? I'll deal with him later.

With the Mind gone, the lust returned, and Xenomene gripped the arms on the chair until her knuckles turned white. She itched to be free of her clothing and to sheathe him.

Somewhere inside, she resisted the urge. Her eyes danced over his muscled body. He wore no clothing except a loincloth.

I've seen people wear less.

His broad chest was tight and hairless, his skin a color between pale sea green and aquamarine.

It's actually quite beautiful, regardless of how exquisite his body looks.

She clamped down on salacious thoughts as unabated eyes roved his semi-naked body. Eyes closed, she tried to conjure up a sight to take the lust away. A bizarre image of a naked Kernoyl Tyku flashed through her mind. Grateful the image overrode Omegryk, she couldn't help but wonder where it came from.

Opening her eyes, she appraised his facial features this time. The whites of his eyes were black with the pupils matching the color of his skin; they were also wider and taller than wizardkind's. His hair mirrored the obsidian intensity of his gaze.

His facial features were also in near likeness to wizardkind. The tip of his nose was sharp, his ears pointed, like an elyf's but not as extreme. His teeth were small but pointed. Full lips accentuated his large mouth.

Five elongated fingers gave the impression of an extra knuckle, but it wasn't so. His nails were long and pointed, the same hue as his hair. His arms were massive like Tiny's, but as well defined as the rest of his body.

"Is this one not to your liking, little one?" he hissed between small, needle teeth.

"Oh, I like you plenty. I'm fighting to not like you too much."

"So, you like this one?"

His voice was soft and almost raspy, but not quite.

"I like what I see, if that's what you're asking."

She pushed the chair back as if the extra inches difference would lessen the sexual urges.

"Forgive me, I've never seen a goblin before."

"This one isn't like the others."

"How do you mean?"

"This one is neither Leviathan nor Palatine, but different. Magical like Palatine and looks similar, but too big and grotesque. This one was Leviathan and feared. Goblins were glad when this one manifested lust of blood."

"The bloodlust?"

Her hand slipped from the arm of the chair to her thigh, and she consciously crossed her legs. Her insides writhed, and she concentrated on staying seated and clothed.

He wheezed a chuckle.

"Yes, that's what this one means."

"How come I haven't seen you in House Eti?"

"This one's heir thought it best to train away from Krey in the caves until this one could control the lust of blood better. This one wants to eat Krey as well as fight them."

Xenomene gave him a skeptical eye.

"Do you want to eat me?"

He paused for a moment, cocking his head to the side like a bird before he answered. Xenomene grew more worried with each passing moment that he didn't.

"You look delicious, but this one would rather mate first."

A chuckle caught in her throat.

"Then, this one would like to eat you. Wizardkind flesh is good."

"So, as long as I don't fuck you, I'm safe? Why do you have to fight to not eat the Krey?"

"You're never safe. Wizardkind flesh is a delicacy, better than goblin."

"Delicacy? You should eat Bitcher. He's a rare breed from the Forgotten Isles."

"Do you give this one permission to feast on his flesh?"

Xenomene was half tempted to say yes but thought better of it. If he ate Bitcher, it would undoubtedly come back that she approved. She shook her head.

"Does this Bitcher want to mate?"

She burst out laughing. The giddiness made her head swim with lust. She bent forward, face flushed, and the tingling within her intensified. Her sharp breaths didn't help either. His tempting loincloth wavered before her wandering gaze. She could almost mark his bulge. By the gods, she wanted him. The thought of riding him on the desk was overpowering.

Surely it wouldn't be so bad?

Her resolve faltered when a brief thought of his glistening pale blue-green skin thrust into her. She was halfway out of her seat before regaining control. Her white knuckles punched the arm of the chair until the pain made the lust recede.

"You shouldn't fight it."

"Fight what?"

"Your attraction to this one."

"I'm not fighting the attraction, I'm fighting not being eaten. You said you'd eat me after you fucked me. I'll pass on my impulses if it means being a snack."

"This one would not eat you. You are too small. This one would make you a bed slave."

Something close to a purr slithered out of her throat.

"How does that work? Won't goblins think you strange for sleeping outside your race?"

"Goblins have sex with anything they can grab. This one is like Palatine, this one likes goblins more like this one. Wizardkind, too."

"Comforting."

Xenomene considered perching at the front of the desk, to be close enough to touch him.

I shouldn't tempt myself.

She hid her face in her hands, battling against her darker impulses, when his laughter broke the magical hold.

"What?"

"Keep fighting, little one. This one will enjoy it much more when you break. You'll taste much sweeter."

"Alright, enough. I've proven the point to myself. Go to your do-don—with haste," the last was a plea, encroaching on the point of breaking.

He gave another small chuckle and opened the door to leave. Bitcher sauntered down the hall towards her office, and his footsteps faltered when he saw Omegryk. Shock and worry crossed his face as his eyes fell on her. Omegryk gave Bitcher a copious berth without a second glance.

Bitcher entered and barely had the door shut before she was on him. Her lips smashed against his with a hunger that drove her insane. She needed a release.

She broke away long enough to jerk him by the arm, rushing to the bed. Her frantic fingers fumbled for her trousers, jerking them down to her ankles, bending over the mattress. Her slickness accepted Bitcher with ease, primed from Omegryk's aura, and it only took a handful of thrusts for her to climax.

It lasted seconds, really, far shorter than her conversation with the goblin. In truth, she wanted more, but she couldn't waste the precious daylight hours, not without him coming to expect it. Besides, she saw the squads lining up in the road below.

When her body stopped quivering, she dipped to the side, him slipping free, and she hastily fixed her clothes.

"What about me?"

"I have to go. The squads are waiting downstairs. Come back tonight, and I promise to make it up to you."

She slipped out of range of his reaching hands. Making sure she was presentable, she exited before Bitcher could disentangle himself from the bed and his trousers.

I shouldn't have done that to him. He'll make me pay later.

She set out in a light trot, scurrying down four flights of stairs and stumbling out of the front hatch, forgetting the slight drop between the floor and wooden porch outside. It wasn't a graceful recovery.

The squads formed up as she caught her breath. Tiny came up beside her, acting as a second, and grinned. She hoped it didn't imply anything else.

She stepped forward.

"I'm not one for speeches. In fact, I hate them. They're a waste of time, much like meetings, as no one listens after the opening statements. I just want to get to know you before we're separated by war. I want to know your names and something about you."

She nodded to Spectre, signaling the start with her squad.

Xenomene stepped in front of Spectre's second, a woman of unremarkable features and a face not worth noting. In all honesty, they all blurred together. The second straightened, standing almost a full head taller.

"I'm Jynx, the second. People say I'm superstitious, hence the name."

Xenomene smiled and moved down the line.

Next came Summer, who complained about the heat and was born in the dead of winter; Nylla followed, and she traveled with a circus as part of the tumbling act.

Ryver came next, a name bestowed for her love of water and because she always talked of the rivers back home. Vision was by far the most beautiful of the squad, if not of all the Krey; Xenomene felt the sting of jealousy.

Malice was aptly named for her contempt of men. Syn followed, a stark contrast to Malice, and known for sinning against practically every religious view on a daily basis because she couldn't resist the vices and men.

Lastly came Cricket, who rarely talked, in fact, Spectre had to do the introductions.

Xeno finished with Spectre's squad—the Minions—and they filed away. They retreated inside and packed for their mission. She stopped in front of Lyan's second.

Tytan, an enormous man, stood level with Tiny, but the latter squeaked out the victory in height; next came Mouse, a female, whose name derived from a small frame, mousy brown hair, and pinched features. Mouse was shorter than Xenomene, which the ko-don found astonishing.

The men of the Krey named the next female Jugs, merited for an ample bust; Arson followed, a thin man who loved fire. Dyus, another male but Toshii like Mauler, boasted a gambling problem, often taking random bets for asinine occasions.

Atlas, the second to the last female, held a plain appearance with a simplistic cuteness. She always knew the way when others were lost. Harlot, the last woman, rivaled Vision's beauty, but the latter attained a clear victory in the matter. Harlot's namesake emanated from her previous employment as a prostitute, where her first bloodlust arose from a client slapping her around.

Omegryk came last, but she scurried away, not trusting herself.

Xenomene dismissed the second squad—the Demigods—when she finished, and they filed into the barracks. She spoke with each member as they prepared their gear, cleaned swords, or settled matters of personal interest.

When all domesticity was completed, they retreated to the first floor and ate in the common hall. Earlier that morning, before meeting with Tiny, she arranged a small feast since two squads were departing that night.

If they're to die tonight or tomorrow, at least they'll have a good meal.

Her thoughts turned dark as the feast wore on. Some wouldn't make it back, probably Slurp and Smokey, virgins in her old squad. She wished she could've quested Slurp at least once. But her squad was the most battle-tested, since all veterans of the Wizard's War were dead or too old.

If he comes back and Bitcher doesn't, I'll fuck him into delirium.

The heir didn't supply another member by nightfall to augment Tiny's squad, which they called themselves the Xenytes now.

Scrotum of gods, your pining is blatant!

She didn't want to crush his spirit, but she might need to. If need be, she'd arranged to be walked in on while bedding someone else, but who? Omegryk? Slurp?

Still, a squad named in her honor made her chest swell with pride. She missed the meld and longed for battle.

Everything changed that night. The battle, death, my first kill; Raven, and Two-Tons were lost, Jakeb…

A cold emptiness claimed the surging warmth.

They ate, laughed, and cajoled one another, and she took her leave two hours later, her ass numb from the hard, wooden bench. The Krey paused at the sight of her standing. She raised a cup of rum, and they returned the gesture.

"Oblus ina'ti Sepan Eti."

They echoed her words, drinking. She drained the rum and retired for the evening.

The diligent camp hands had delivered bath water, but by now, it cooled to lukewarm. She bathed quickly and dried off, slipping nude beneath the sheets.

She was almost asleep when the door opened, and Bitcher came to claim her one last time before he left.

Chapter 21: The Melodic Mountains

It would've taken Norek another four days to traverse the Valley of the Dead outskirts, but he refused to rest, relying on magic to sustain him.

On the evening of the second day, he reached the entrance beneath the Melodic Mountains. Norek set up camp before continuing his journey through the elevation's dark heart. He tried to sleep, but dreams disturbed him.

He dreamed of the two women in his orb—his mother, Meristal, and the other entity that haunted their steps. The dark woman reached out and struck him down, lifeless before the orb fell from his hand. Several times he woke with a start, until the morbid visions faded and sleep returned.

The sun crept up, blistering the horizon when he awoke for the last time. A woman stood at the edge of his camp, curiously staring at him. The initial panic—the sudden impulse to go on the defensive—percolated through his foggy, semiconscious mind. Her glowing eyes pierced him; he felt vulnerable under her gaze.

Other than the unsettling foreboding of her eyes, which detracted from her simplistic beauty, she wasn't an undiscovered gem.

Her face lacked the sharp, haughty features common to aristocrats and noble families, but a celestial nose graced her features, slightly turned upward. Her long hair was straight and honeyed; thin, arching eyebrows questioned him in silence. Her neck gave an almost delicate look while her cheeks glowed a slight pink.

Norek had never encountered one like her, and he couldn't help but ponder her lineage.

"Good morning," she said. "I didn't mean to startle you. I just arrived, and I saw your fire from the entrance."

Norek sat up and glanced where she was pointed.

"Going in or coming out?"

"Coming out," she answered after a pause. "I don't mean to intrude, but I haven't eaten in days. Do you have any food? I'd gladly pay more than fair…"

Norek scratched his head and rubbed the sleep from his eyes before trying to hide his yawn.

"Nonsense. It won't kill me to share."

"No!"

Her expression and voice softened after a moment.

"No. I don't take. I'll pay or nothing at all."

He held up his hands.

"As you wish."

He reached within to his essence and coaxed it, her outburst at his charity making him anxious. He made a mental note.

"Thank you," she said. "If you'll allow, I'll start the cooking while you rouse."

With a nod and an extended finger, he pointed out the bag with food.

Dressing, he replayed their encounter over in his mind. Unsure if she lied about being hungry, a sense of quiet reservation and caution permeated the air about her. She traveled by herself, brave for someone semi-proficient in magic, foolish for those without.

Moreover, she said she traveled under the mountain and undoubtedly had the ability to ward against hunger. Norek speculated about her magical fortitude.

She's probably hungry, but not near enough to be troubling me. She could reach the next town with ease, so why did she stop?

"What brings you this way?" she inquired as she hoisted the bag of food.

Turning so he could keep her in his peripheral vision yet maintain his privacy, he closed his inner robe. His back might be turned, but unlike with Yugor, the dwaven, he didn't do it as a sign of trust but decency.

"I'm headed to Ralloc for business," he said.

After finishing dressing, he came over to help cook.

She shook her head.

"You've picked the wrong season to go. They're at war, you know?"

"I heard rumors but nothing absolute."

"It's true. My advice, besides not going to Ralloc at all, is to circumvent the Corridor and Dlad City. You need to head Northeast to Vikal Village and then Northwest to Ralloc."

"That's weeks of circuitous travel! I can't afford that; I'm already months behind schedule."

"Why?"

"Damn pirates on the open seas."

"Pirates?"

She raised an eyebrow as she continued preparing breakfast.

"It's a long story, and I've got to get moving. I hear the journey under the mountains is long. Is that true?"

With a movement Norek would almost describe as delicate, she turned her red, softly-glowing eyes to him. After a moment, she turned back to the food.

"Yes."

Norek tried to fight the impulse, but it won out.

"Why do your eyes glow?"

She studied him for a long moment before answering.

"It's a long story, and you need to get moving."

Norek smiled at his reiterated words.

Fair is fair.

Disquiet stole over him, her features, arrival, and taciturn nature providing an early morning conundrum. The question of her lineage came back to him.

"Where are you from?" he asked.

He didn't expect an answer, at least not a direct or truthful one.

Lies often tell you as much as honesty.

"I guess you could say I'm from Ralloc. I don't really know. I can only remember the past nine months or so. That's when I started to remember."

"'When you started?' What does that mean?"

She continued to stir the ingredients over the fire.

"Wait, wait! Let me guess, another long story?"

A small smile broke across her features.

"Perceptive."

Norek abandoned his efforts to dig further into her story. She wasn't going to tell him anything personal.

With the food ready, they ate in near silence. Small talk intermittently disturbed the uncomfortable atmosphere between them but neither shared much. Even their names were withheld. Both attempted an elegant dance of words, but neither yielded to the other's inquiries.

In the end, the young woman paid Norek a silver chip for the food and trouble—well beyond what she should have.

"You never told me your name," he stated, growing bold as she set to depart.

"I wouldn't have given it, and neither would you."

She walked away.

The two parted company, moving in different directions. Indeed, she proved a useful distraction, an enigma to ponder while he traveled. She was charming, engaging, and mysterious.

And she had also lied to him.

By the way she ate, he knew she wasn't ravenous.

Nearing the entrance of the cave, he took out the glass orb. Without using his essence, the dark woman filled the orb, shadowier than before. Her back was to him as if walking away.

He spun around, scouring for the girl, but she vanished without a trace.

Chapter 22: The Valley of The Dead

After Starriace left the man near the entrance to the Melodic Mountains, she called Ava to her side. Diligent to appease, the fairy brought Rusem too, despite her misgivings. Starriace still hadn't revealed his origins, only that she commanded his obedience. Ava's body language and attitude proved what she thought of it.

From the mountains, they teleported a short distance away in case the man tried to follow. She didn't think he would, but it never hurt to be careful. Paranoia and suspicion ruled her actions.

Is that because Judas might be looking for me?

An eerily familiar sight caught her attention.

She'd been here before, back when she trained with Fife Doole. He'd given her a bag of porting stones, and one of them brought her here, a place she could never forget.

"What's over there?" Starriace inquired, pointing with her chin.

"The Valley of the Dead."

Ava's deadpan voice grated on the mage's nerves. Still, the little creature wouldn't diminish her intrigue. Starriace stepped to the ridge, distancing herself from her moody companion. She knew little of this place—one of the many subjects Judas kept from her.

A dark, off-white sand lined the shallow valley. Heading down the slope, the fine, soft powder gave under her weight like ruffles of dust or ash. She hadn't encountered a soil like this before. A muted quality suffused her, an oppressive force against her chest, and it reminded her of the Corridor.

She took a hesitant step. An ominous aura quivered through her.

This place is wrong. I shouldn't be here.

Her essence stretched out, and she tracked the impressions: anguish, hatred, pain, grief, despair, and elation. Her eyes widened, realizing what that meant: the sand exuded the feelings.

It started with the briefest flutters, growing exponentially. Fear, bitterness, and depression rushed forward; ghosts from the past haunted this area. Love, joy, and peace rippled through, an odd texture mingling with her own feelings.

She glanced at the ridge—to Ava.

"This sand has an odd texture."

Her voice sounded flat in her ears.

Ava stirred, a lazy flutter, but her face looked tight, strained.

"This isn't sand. Tread softly; you're on cursed ground. You trample the remains of all slain here."

The realization lanced Starriace's gut, and her breath caught in her throat. She turned toward the ridge, her boot stirring the dirt. By her toes, a skull peeked out from beneath, the forehead and an eye socket were all that was left.

"How did this happen?"

"A great battle, the last official one of the Wizard's War. The armies amassed to make their last stand. But this place was cursed long before those armies engaged here."

"How?"

"Before the Wizard's War, two prosperous cities held each other in contention. One was ruled by an elderly man, ruthless but wise; the other, by a headstrong and ambitious youth. Their long, bloody history hasn't faded with time, and they still hold each other in contempt. The elder ruler ended the conflict under a ruse of truth, then turned his attention to the other lands of this domain.

"Having bloated his military with soldiers, his coffers with gold, and his ego with land, only the young ruler's city remained. But that young king possessed magic, and the way he used those abilities turned him dark and twisted. Not the shadow of evil, but madness. Eventually, it consumed him, but not before he destroyed the elder's forces. The city the young ruler came from was named after him and his ancestors: Stratu'Geim."

Ava's revelation stole Starriace's breath. Her gaze shifted to Rusem. He'd once said his name was Rusem Geim. She never realized Rusem was *that* young ruler. A burning question raced through her: was the ghost she met from before or after the massacre? How many soldiers died here, and for what? Money? Land?

Power.

War inevitably called for death, and from the two cities, wives lost husbands, children their fathers. Xilor's war was similar, but it engulfed two domains. All of Ermaeyth would feel the effects. One man might destroy them all if they didn't fight back. The thought of Rusem's war sickened her. Her anger surged at the thought of the senseless massacre of his citizens.

The cold realization came over her; she stood on the ground in which thousands had died.

She glanced back at Rusem, then to the valley floor. The resentment vanished as she swallowed. She stood on the ground of her future legion, beings who'd already paid the ultimate price. No one else would succumb to Xilor's machinations.

No one else need die.

She'd need a patsy, someone to blame for the army. Starriace scrutinized the powder, thoughts churning in her mind. She'd commit to war against Xilor without sending men to their deaths, not if the soldiers were already dead. The problem was figuring out a way to reanimate them and compel their loyalty to fight against the darkness out there.

Or the darkness within.

Doubt flickered through her.

"What's the real reason you're here?" Ava asked, breaking into her thoughts.

Starriace noted the edge in the creature's voice.

"There are several, all equally important."

"And those are?"

Starriace heard the frustration creeping into her voice, and she regarded the little creature. She debated what she should and shouldn't tell her. At last, she made up her mind to tell the truth.

Well, a twisted truth.

"As I said, I'm here for several reasons. One is to gather powerful, magical stones that a…" she glanced at Rusem, "…man told me about. They're called brimstones. Once these brimstones are gathered, they'll give me enough power to defeat Xilor."

She stopped to observe Ava, her face expressionless except for the tightness around her eyes.

"Also, I've heard of this Valley of the Dead. It's my sincere hope that once I acquire all the stones, I can raise an army to fight Xilor."

Ava's eyes narrowed, and her mouth fell partially open as she thought.

"And how are you going to raise an army when Ralloc can't do that?"

Starriace smiled.

"Imagine a host with one purpose driving them, the complete and utter destruction of Xilor. One mind, one objective. They'll stop at nothing."

"What are you going to do? Bend them to your will? Force them under an enchantment to fight for you? You'd have to be omnipotent."

Starriace shook her head.

"No enchantments, no threats. Imagine an army who can't be hurt, can't die. Can you see it?"

"No," Ava said, the single word a blunt cudgel. "You're insane. No magic can stave off death, especially not for an army. Even the Krey can die. I don't know what you're reading, but the brimstones can't succeed where others have failed."

Starriace gave a single nod.

"And what if the soldiers were already dead?"

A silence filled the space between them, and Starriace watched the creature's eyes dart from her to the valley and back. Right now, Starriace gave Ava a mere glimpse of her plans; it was safer that way, but she needed a confidant.

If Ava rejected the plan, few options remained, and one would be silencing the familiar. If others found out, they'd come for her. The fairies had a direct link and could snuff her out without a second thought.

And Judas? He'd bring his full powers to bear and destroy her. Even now, he probably searched. How close was he?

Starriace regarded the fairy, her eyes narrowing.

I can't believe I'm considering killing her…

Starriace reached out for her essence, feeling the trickle of power welling up in the palm of her hand. She'd act, one way or the other, based on the next few words.

"It can't be done," Ava blurted.

It was the last thing Starriace expected her to say, and ire simmered through her.

"Why not? I've raised someone."

She pointed back at Rusem, revealing more than she planned.

"I've accomplished what you believe is impossible!"

"No, Mistress, you misunderstood me. Yes, it's possible to raise someone, figuratively speaking. It's impossible to return a person unless you went through the Underworld to bring back the soul. What you did has been done before, though not many times. Long ago, one person managed to raise five. More is impossible. It requires a level of power that even someone like Warlock Lakayre couldn't achieve, which is giving him more credit than he deserves."

"Yes, but that's over a period of time, correct? What about all at once?"

"A preposterous notion. It would take hundreds, maybe thousands to pool their collective magical strength together, and that's if the gods or their minions let you."

"The gods? What *gods*? With the power of the brimstones, I'll be unstoppable."

I'd be a god.

The malice of her thoughts surprised her, but once manifested, it felt justified. Xilor was a fanatic. The uncompromising environment he created called for an extreme reaction. He marched to annihilate all he deemed weak. Before he tried to kill her, he attempted to recruit. His plans called for a purge, with only the strong remaining to battle a threat that may never transpire. For Xilor, it was a preemptive measure, a preparatory phase, and his offer revealed the measure of his insanity.

And what does that make me?

But did he have the right of it, if he spoke the truth? Would it be better to do nothing and leave Ermaeyth weak? And what of these other places, these other worlds he spoke of? How would they get here? Traveling beyond their world was a preposterous notion. It couldn't be done.

But I got here from another world.

Ava's words broke into her musings.

"Gods or not, if you don't have the brimstones, it'd take numbers beyond reckoning to achieve your desired results. Furthermore, no one would back your plan."

Starriace's aspirations crumbled. She had soldiers, but not the means to raise them. The pooling power in the palm of her hand itched for release. Each inhale thundered in her ears. She waited for the fairy to declare her intentions.

It'd only take one immense blast.

Starriace eyed her. Judas hounded her steps, and the fairy was being difficult. She didn't need another adversary.

"Unless…" Ava drawled, "…thousands were deceived."

Ava's words stunned her, catching her off guard; within a blink, her pooled energy diminished.

"What do you mean?"

"Well, you could raise an army if thousands were deceived, but with what deception? You can pool magic from countless beings with supplicants and a director. Once the supplicants send their magic, the director can then do whatever he or she wishes."

"That's brilliant!"

Even though the fairy gave the answer she desired, wariness consumed her.

When did she become devious? Does she deal with me in the same manner? I'll have to watch her closely.

"There could be unaccounted side effects," Ava continued, "the first of which is death. That much power...you might simply fade from existence. That'd be the end of the great Starriace."

Ava smirked at her.

"The bigger problem's finding a task to unite that many people."

Starriace gave a noncommittal grunt, and it required further pondering. She lingered for a few moments more before she set out on her first task.

The first brimstone was near, and without it, all her plans were for naught.

"Let's be away."

If she thought to find a reprieve from her familiar while they traveled, she couldn't be more wrong. Ava's tiny voice had whined in an incessant manner since leaving the Valley of the Dead. Enduring the small talk was torturous.

I'd rather suffer a session in Mr. Pleasure's chair than listen to this shit!

Starriace preferred silence to meaningless talk. Since Ava was their primary means of travel, Starriace exerted no small amount of self-control. The mage could teleport and fly, but she'd never teleported more than herself. With her luck, she'd kill them all in a failed attempt.

To lose either would hinder what little progress she'd made.

Ava's magic had to be restored by returning to the Melodic Mountains, and she wished the fairy would leave to do just that. The urge to throttle Ava grew strong.

Rusem didn't talk, which would hinder her unearthing the secrets he held. She'd made an egregious error by destroying the spirit. How had she managed his partial resurrection? An inherited gift?

Don't start speculating.

Did she care if her parents were alive? She couldn't say either way, but she felt contempt for them, for leaving her on another world. Could she forgive them?

She pushed those thoughts away and focused on Rusem and the dilemma of uncovering what slumbered in his mind. She needed his knowledge. Working the mental connection between them remained her only option and a high priority, one they'd start tonight.

Ava's voice drew her attention. When they first met, the fairy had been sweet and gullible, much like her. Circumstance had changed them both, and each summons revealed a new edge in Ava's demeanor. Whatever she'd endured, the result was unsettling—Ava was becoming too much like Starriace.

She'd have to watch her closely.

Apor, the giant blue sun, slinked to the horizon, sending purples, blues, and an assortment of greens through the sky. Starriace called a halt to make camp and connect to Rusem's fractured mind.

With a fire crackling, Starriace sat opposite him, cast wards around their site—a helpful tidbit she'd learned from Harold's books—and focused on her silent companion. She raised her hands to the side of his head and closed her eyes.

Images flashed like lightning strikes; fragments of memories danced through their meld. She tried to grasp each image, but all slipped free.

She imagined his mind like rapids; the images were the water, and the waterfall a symbol of the power and pace. She couldn't grasp the water in her hands any more than the memories unless she learned to slow the water. Each of her varied methods failed, and the futility almost convinced her to give up, but a new thought teased success.

She failed to think in dimensions.

The memories, like the imagined water, held depth, width, and speed. The power rushed them past her. It was then she understood.

This time, she reached out and snatched at it. The memory came to a halt in her mental grasp. She stared ahead, basking in the accomplishment. The frozen moment displayed like a painting, a still image. The remembrance trembled from her exertion, from all the power used to hold it. The quiver became violent, too chaotic to maintain. Blurred colors, figments, and noises overlapped into a cacophony. Before she could release or attempt to exert more control, fire and lightning raced across her mind.

The memory dissipated. The world shattered, and she fell. A scream ripped from her throat. Waves of nausea swept through her. Her lungs burned. She gasped, hand pressed between her bosom to still her frightened heart. She turned to vomit.

Something had happened just after holding Rusem's memory. She'd been torn away by an immense presence, but it'd come from afar. Even now, the sensation was fading like it never existed. But it came when she snagged the memory, and it'd been of a brimstone.

A voice buzzed in her head, not her thoughts, not the darkness, and not Rusem, but the words…she couldn't discern them.

"Empress?" Ava called to her. "Are you alright?"

Starriace's head snapped toward Ava.

"What did you call me?"

"Mistress; why?"

"I thought you said empress."

Starriace closed her eyes against the agony. The pain from holding the memory centered over her left eye, burrowing like hot pins through her flesh and brain. Her eyes ached in the dusky light. In haste, she shut her eyes before fumbling for her cowl, drawing it low.

"The voice," Starriace said, "did you hear it?"

"Voice? What voice?"

Starriace shook her head.

"How long was I unconscious?"

Ava shook her head.

"You weren't. I thought you screamed in frustration at your failure."

Starriace sighed, letting the fairy's insolence slide. She still needed to read Rusem's mind, reclaim his memories for her own. And if she was lucky, that presence might return and reveal something.

Either way, she gained.

Reclaiming her position across from him, she tried again.

Chapter 23: Master Jynerul Reginald Tyku

Master Jynerul Tyku was a walrus of a man, beefy and barrel-chested. His round face was marred by a bushy mustache that swept out to the sides rather than a proper trimming befitting his rank and house. Tyku's looks epitomized the opposite of everything the nobility lauded.

Born into aristocracy, his education and tactician mindset were never doubted throughout his service. Whether by grand design, fate, or sheer dumb luck, he ascended to the highest military rank. None refused him—no one except the consul, and perhaps the grand maghai.

Tyku took a sip of mulled wine and puffed on his dark leaf cigar.

The darker, the better!

Tyku sat in his backyard on an outdoor long chair of thin metal and reeds. He rested the goblet on the wood and glass table beside him. The manicured lawn grew thick but cropped short enough to spy pests crawling along each blade.

He swirled the smoke in his mouth, tasting the flavor before exhaling. His mind drifted over his military career, as his guest had bid him to do.

His *guest* was an emissary of King Godfrey, the king of the Forgotten Isles. According to his emissary—*his herald I believe was the word used*—the man proclaimed his liege was but a week at most from Ralloc.

From the sound of it, the king emptied the Isles to come here in force.

The befuddling question plaguing the aging jynerul was why. What did King Godfrey want?

Tyku sighed and drew on his cigar again. His lustrous career replayed in his mind, a long and prosperous one. He entered service as a serjynt, as did all noble and minor noble houses. Serving beneath common-born was an atrocity ill-afforded for the gentry. Now, he was older, and he didn't agree with the sentiment; the nobility might be served well with a dose of humility.

The baseborn populace could only rise as far as serjynt in the Grand Royal Army. Having noble and minor noblemen enter at the same rank did not give the peasants power over the aristocrats. Tyku entered the service well into the Elyfian and Goblin War.

Wizard's War, Goblin War, Xilor's War, who gives a shit. It was a damn war.

He fought against goblins, trolls, and vampires, but they lacked a unified front. Until Xilor took command. The army amassed resounding victories over the enemy.

Come to think of it, had Xilor marched on Ralloc from the start, we'd all be speaking troll or whatever vile language they utter.

But they took losses, too. Tyku quickly ascended the ranks, from serjynt to master serjynt, and then leftenaut to kaptyn. When it came to promotions, noble houses came before minor nobles. Death and retirement of higher officials had always been the catalyst for his elevations.

At first, the sheer losses in numbers spurred advancements. As the war dragged on, his superiors discovered his merit, and they promoted him over more senior men. By the conclusion of the Wizard's War, he was the most senior kernoyl and poised to take the next slot as jynerul. That promotion came with another death and another retirement. Within a moon turn, he was no longer the most junior of jyneruls.

He took another slow pull of his cigar and let the smoke settle in his mouth.

He saved money throughout his career and came back from the war alive, relatively whole, and rich. True, the nobility were born into wealth, but that was his father's riches. When his father passed, the wealth became his, but he relished in the sense of accomplishment, having achieved his own destiny free of familial handouts. The first thing he did was build a mansion in the innermost walls, nestling near the castle and the seat of government.

Being on the front lines doesn't leave you time for much spending.

He spent three-quarters of his wealth building the house and buying the plot and homes of two other noble families sitting side by side. Once they'd moved, he demolished both, but did so delicately, saving the marble and wood and precious metals and gems within. This became the basis for his own house. With a home and his father's wealth, he looked to settle down.

That proved to be the biggest mistake of his life.

Tyku married in the late summer years of his life. For a woman, that bordered on too old to bear children, so he married a girl two ages his junior. She was of a minor noble house, and though not unheard of, the practice remained uncommon.

The dowry had been immense, nearly bankrupting the father. When Tyku let it be known he searched for a wife, more than doors opened to him. But he yearned for more than binding two houses together. He sought a smart and witty woman, educated but not one who would gloat. He searched for a gentle heart and a friend.

An equal.

She needed to be an appropriate companion to his specific tastes and possess an ample bosom and childbearing hips. He didn't plan to let his lineage die and pass the responsibility to his siblings. And so, he came to his decision on Merida Perry. She met the criteria and surpassed all others, bore him sons and daughters aplenty, and became his companion and friend.

But her taste for luxury grew insatiable over the years.

When newlyweds, he showered lavish gifts of silk, gems, precious metals—anything her heart could want. Their first vacation sailed beyond the Golden Sea, and they made port in Jubaiyin. They spent two moon turns there before returning. At her request, he had bought an estate there.

Another dumb decision.

He never returned.

His family—hers to be precise—enjoyed it over the years. By the time he caught on to the repetitive mistakes, it was too late. His lavish spending included land and houses, horses, bulls, pigs, and more than a smattering of silk, rings, necklaces, furniture, chairs, and beds. Each emerging fashion lured his wife. Instead of selling old possessions or giving to charity as Tyku requested, she gave it to her brothers and sisters, or their sons and daughters. Never did his family receive her generosity with his money.

That, too, held consequences.

His brothers and sisters turned a blind eye to him, informally excommunicating him from the family. One of his nephews—he didn't know which one—was recently promoted to kernoyl by Warlock Lakayre.

At least someone in my family has something going for him.

Years trickled by, and his funds dwindled to dangerous levels. The pay increase for years in service and rank ascension kept the losses at bay. As more money flowed in, the more he lied. He'd fabricated a fictitious salary cap long ago. He then threw around 'preposterous notions' when he mentioned retiring, and she forbade it. He, of course, never thought about retiring.

If I did, I would be selling my house within five seasons.

While his wife's extravagant tastes had receded, he still suffered financial strain.

Which led him to tonight, considering the herald's offer. If he didn't have his wife, he'd never be considering the man's words.

Tyku came out of his revery, the one the herald bade him to seek. His eyes drifted to the four other men with him, personal guards.

Tyku sighed, and when he spoke, it was slow and soft.

"Upon reflection of my life and career, I see a distinguished legacy. Why should I tarnish it for your king, one who isn't part of the Ralloc Domain?"

The herald wore formal robes of a forest green color. His pale hair, a golden hue, and eyes of the lightest shade of blue just shy of gray appraised the jynerul.

"His Eminence means to change that, to join the Ralloc domain, and become part of the government."

Tyku choked on the smoke.

"Your king would lay down his crown? I doubt that."

"Do not doubt, Master Jynerul. He means to join and will be here within the week."

Tyku coughed.

"You're forgetting, just because he wants to join does not mean he *will.* It must be voted on and passed by the Kothlere Council, and only if it reaches them. First, there are the courts."

"It won't be a problem."

"You hold no strategic value," Tyku countered. "Your lands are too small. You want for wood and stone, crops and animals, with little to trade in return. Your exports are unnoticeable. What could you offer upon joining? With what would you entice Ralloc with?"

"We have exports aplenty."

The herald nodded to the cigar.

"You smoke one now. And there are other exports, rums and spear grass, glass and gems, and more to offer than you might expect."

Tyku smoothed his graying mustache.

"Tell your king I said no. I won't support his claim for a petition to become part of the domain. I've yet to hear anything to make me believe you'd be an added value to our sovereignty. Even if accepted and the Isles become part of Ralloc's domain, what good is a crownless and impoverished king?"

Tyku shook his head.

"Good evening to you, sires."

The herald glanced at the men, nodding to them, then back to Tyku.

"We are not sires."

The men moved in unison, lifting a crate by polearms that sat between them. They placed it beside the chairs and opened the container.

"What's this?" Tyku grumbled.

The herald held up a hand to stave off questions until the box was open. Inside were several small chests, each fifteen centimeters long, wide, and tall. Two of the herald's retainers lifted a box to a metal chair which bowed under the weight. The herald inserted a key from around his neck, opened the lid, and exposed the gleaming contents. Tyku leaned forward in his seat, then rose to peer within.

By the gods! Ingots! Lots of ingots!

He noticed each gold bar did not carry the seal of the Treasury, but a simple purity test would determine the value. If pure, they'd melt them and reform into the ingots with the royal seal.

Ingots were the highest currency within the Ralloc domain. Domains to the south had adopted Ralloc's system, too. One ingot equated to six thousand scepters. A bit—a small copper coin with a hole through the middle—equaled one scepter. Tyku himself made just over three ingots a month as the master jynerul, but the vast sums of wealth sitting on the chair made his mouth water.

He looked over the ingots and reached out with a longing hand. The ingots tinkered and chimed as they shifted under his touch.

"It's two hundred and ten ingots, Master Jynerul," the herald said. "Do you know how much that is?"

"A lot."

"Five years' worth of salary. One million two hundred and sixty thousand scepters. Think of what you could do with all that gold."

Tyku's eyes slid out of focus. His hands trembled on the cold metal.

I'd need to hide the funds so Merida can't find them.

He could sort the financial mess his wife had driven them to. The original fault lay with him, but she still burned through his wealth.

She cares more about the gold than me.

Tyku licked his lips.

"And this five years' worth of salary … is what?"

"A gift from His Eminence. One of friendship and loyalty. In return, he only asks for you to do your job should the time ever come."

"What job would that be?"

"His Eminence is worried that if he becomes consul, some might reject his rule. He fears the Krey might rise up and march on Ralloc."

Tyku gave a snort.

"Why would the Krey care? They follow orders better than most in the army."

"His Eminence would like a…revision of command when it comes to the Black Tide."

Tyku scowled.

"Revision of command? What's that supposed to mean?"

"It means he'd like to put someone in charge who'll keep the Krey in line without inciting a riot. He'd prefer a tighter grip on the situation."

"You mean a *puppet*! Is that what I am to you?"

"No, Master Jynerul. You're of the highest caliber the army can offer. That's what you are. As for the Krey, well, see it from our perspective. We've only known stories, never been in a world where stories are as real as the danger. I'm sure you understand and appreciate our position."

Tyku chewed over the words.

They have a point.

The Krey were as alien to them as a navy sitting in Ralloc's port, the latter nonexistent.

"I won't be your puppet."

"Come, Master Jynerul, if we wanted a puppet, we would've killed you and made sure our man got the job, but we're not fools. The army runs better under your rule. We know the difficulties you faced with the politicians and their lunacy. Believe me, sire, it'll change. Imagine—you and the consul will build that world. His Eminence is a fair king, but he's hard and nobody's fool. He understands keeping you in command is in the best interests of all. With you at his side, and with the Krey brought to heel, he plans great reforms. This gift is but a sample."

Tyku's eyes narrowed.

"A sample?"

The other man nodded.

"Of what's to come. There'll be more, I assure you. And when you retire? You'll receive two more chests. I'd say that's more than fair, wouldn't you?"

The herald's words were calm and calculating, a master manipulator of oral diction. Tyku eyed him while considering all avenues. King Godfrey had sent the herald to melt Tyku's resolve against Islander rule, but the monarch made a grievous mistake.

The future they planned was a figment.

First, the Isles had to be accepted, no small feat. Godfrey then assumed he'd win the consul office, but that could be years down the road. In the meantime, Tyku could accept the money and give himself a cushion from his wife's outrageous spending habits.

Or it might embolden me to get rid of the scepter leech.

Tyku's eyes flickered over the herald's face. No doubt the man had a long career dealing with outsiders and politicians. Was Tyku being manipulated now? The master jynerul knew he didn't have any weaknesses to exploit other than his family, and if someone tried to ransom his wife, he just might let them keep her. Merida plagued him and his accounts like a rampant sickness. He had to find a way to cut her off like a gangrenous extremity.

But his children, that was another matter entirely.

"What say you, Master Jynerul? Can King Godfrey count on you?"

Tyku looked back at the ingots. They sparkled in the torchlight. He reached up and shut the lid.

"Aye, I believe he can."

Chapter 24: Xilor

The mouth to the Corridor of Cruelty yawned behind him like a gaping maw, an alluring thrall he couldn't escape. The place affected everyone and in different ways; Xilor and his army were no exception. How long had they been here?

Too long.

Cape Gythmel had fallen, but the Grand Royal Army had weakened him more than he expected. The dragons took the brunt, losing more than he cared to—few as they were. Only ash remained of his hordes of goblins and trolls. The Krey held back the swarms, and his patience thinned like his ranks.

When Xilor had first arrived and seen the fortifications, his initial urge to smite it from existence teased him. But he couldn't, not with Judas present. From their battle long ago, Xilor learned that if he attacked with overwhelming force, he'd be weakened, and Judas would take the opportunity to counter.

As he had the last time.

Coward.

The warlock defeated him when he'd been in an enfeebled state.

Xilor narrowed his eyes as he stared at the Corridor, the call so strong it couldn't be ignored. The pall between the Underworld and this place grew taut and thin, yet able to withstand the onslaught of what tried to escape. Only one other place was similar, or so the stories went: the Melodic Mountains.

At the Corridor, the tethers from beyond could reach through and influence, as they did to him now. The fight to free himself warred longer than first anticipated. He gambled coming through, and he paid the penance.

When no hope for escape suffused him, he reached out to his army, calling upon their essence and draining them of life. In a mighty heave of magic, he tapped into the well of living souls and siphoned the energy to break the Corridor's leash.

The cost had been staggering. More than a third of the remaining army perished, but he was free.

Languishing here burned too much time, and by now, the army had undoubtedly fortified Dlad City. With numbers thinned, attacking would be foolish.

For now.

A shiver of fear crept through him. He feared what else the Corridor may compel. Its secrets eluded him, as had mastery of the place. Judas boasted such a feat, and maybe that helped the warlock defeat him.

But Xilor had learned secrets, too.

Imprisoned in the mirror, he traveled beyond the confines of Ermaeyth. When Xilor finished the war, he planned to find a way back to those other… places. And yet, what lay beyond showed how little he knew. It thrilled and terrified him. There were so many possibilities, so many other places and existing creatures. He had seen them, and had he not, he never would've believed.

But he had.

Many mattered little, but enough of them were a threat. Numerous worlds beyond counting, species evolved into the perfect predators, and some tapping into devastations that annihilated all magical prowess and advantages.

He had to succeed, for Ermaeyth's sake.

And Judas unwittingly created doorways to other places. If we can leave, other people can come in.

A tendril from the Corridor beckoned to him, and he glanced back. The call remained strong, but he resisted its urges, much like he had to resist his urges now.

In the last war, Ralloc was never his target. Some forces were sent, a sign of strength and intention—a distracting strategy and the extent of the plans for the city. And it had worked. They pulled back, recalling legions of troops. This wasted their time and manpower but allowed him to pursue other goals without harassment.

The Corridor loomed as a reminder of his failure, a taunt of what Judas mastered; it burned like a hot knife between the ribs. When Xilor won, he wouldn't kill Judas but enslave him; keeping such a powerful being controlled would be a testament to his divine sovereignty, siphoning Judas's power like poison from a wound. Even the fabled warlock didn't know that trick. To kill Judas outright would make a martyr of him, and Xilor could ill afford an uprising.

Enslaved, tortured, shamed in public, none would dare challenge his dominance again. His old master, Hadius Lacove, had a mantra he drilled into his head over and over.

"Twist a thought to change a man, change a man to sway a city, sway a city to dominate a domain, and rule the world."

Xilor snorted.

The only wise thing that fool ever said.

Hadius had wanted peace. Peace was a lie, an agreed-to chaos. You couldn't have it without bloodshed and violence. Misery yearned for companionship, and hardship bred indestructible will. Iron sharpened iron, chaos birthed order, and tribulations brought peace.

Judas embodied tranquility, no matter how many times Xilor tried to destroy it. He snatched the warlock's brother right in front of him, had his parents murdered, ensured that in defeat, he'd claim a final victory.

All of it strengthened Judas's resolve to fight on.

Only when his faithful minions reported a successful assassination of Judas's infant did Xilor revel.

Xilor turned away from the Corridor, finally mastering his control. He called for a xicx, and when it arrived, he issued his commands.

"Move forward. Let the enemy think we're coming. Destroy Cape Gythmel and move to Cross Roads. Kill everything. I don't care how many die in the process, get it done."

The xicx, a wraith-like creature that resembled its creator, bowed and fled. They, much like the sheol he created, needed his overt direction, and he couldn't stand them for that weakness.

Something sharp and painful stabbed into his mind, a dagger burrowing deep into his skull. He gasped at the onslaught, but he knew what caused it. No, *who* caused it.

Starriace.

He almost laughed, thinking her dead, but the archangels must've spared her. Why would they waste majestic abilities on a pitiful creature? The brilliance of their powers—much like the light of unicorns when amassed—still made him cringe in recollection.

Because of the implant at Far Point, he sensed her essence and mind. Before, he had an open window into her mind; now, that'd hardened to steel and became a maze.

What happened to her?

He reached out to gently probe her mind, but the way slammed shut, and he was certain it was by conscious choice. Though she remained unaware of him testing her boundaries, she blocked him. If he breached her mental barriers, her magic would react like the body does to a bacterial infection.

Her essence would fight to purge him.

She'd become too complex to glean any information. In times past, he'd catch random thoughts, but now she'd become incomprehensible, like water running over a mirror and distorting the image.

Then, the pain erupted like never before, a white-hot bolt of lightning, and a touch of panic flittered through his gut. Something had changed, and he sensed a faint echo from long ago, a ghost of weakness. It was fleeting, barely enough to register.

A past secret he buried stirred within her.

He felt the sliver, that fragment, and he wondered if some part of him rubbed off or transferred to her during their brief and laughable battle. Xilor searched inward, reached for the hidden places deep within. He scoured every vein and cell for a faint taint of her. Further and deeper, into his shattered soul, but the search was in vain.

There was another possibility he hadn't considered, and the longer he ruminated on it, the less he liked the thought. Perhaps she discovered something from his past, and if that was the case, he had to avoid it. If anyone discovered anything about his rise, it'd lead them straight to the brimstones.

The City of Despair.

Where he died and was born again.

Does she know?

Apprehension festered like a gangrenous wound. He checked again for the faint echo and still found it. Had she stumbled onto the brimstones or the path that led to them? If she claimed one, let alone all of them, she could erase him from existence. All the conquests, the Wizard's War, his discoveries, and plans to help Ermaeyth…life would start over, and she'd become him.

He turned back to the army. They milled in front of him, stretching like a horde of angry ants. Within the folds of black robes, he pulled out a fragment of mirror, a piece of the same mirror that imprisoned him for ages.

"Psimond Vlukus."

The mirror swirled green, and the abyssian appeared. The creature bowed, black and reptilian.

"Vlukus, your servitude is needed."

"I'm yours to command, Dark One."

"What of Shadow City? Did the elyves attack as I predicted?"

"Indeed, and we prevailed. We let the commander flee as you wanted, but now have more captives than we know what to do with. What is your bidding?"

"Eat what is necessary to survive. The rest, have them turned with the vampiric caress. We need to increase their numbers. Once administered, decree that all purebloods are to leave Shadow City. The hierarchy must remain alive and intact.

"As for the abyssians, leave a few, less important spawns. They're to remain on guard against another, no doubt imminent, attack. Choose well, Vlukus, you'll never see them again. Take the king and the more notable vampires to the Ruins of Sheol and await further instructions. I know Judas, he'll send another force, and Shadow City's destruction will happen. Get out!"

Vlukus bowed low again.

"It'll be done as you command, my lord."

"There's one more task I will ask, Vlukus. There's a pathway beneath the Melodic Mountains. You and a dozen of your choosing are to take the path and go south, search for the woman I told you about, Starriace. Kill her and bring me her corpse."

"Where do we begin?"

"Stratu'Geim. If she's not there already, she soon will be."

"When do we leave?"

"After you carry out my other orders. The abyssians that aren't going with you or staying in Shadow City are to join me at Cross Roads. I'll march soon. The advanced group should be assaulting them now as we speak."

"As you command, Great One."

Xilor cut the magic and returned the mirror inside the folds of his robes. He allowed himself a small smile of satisfaction. With Vlukus taking care of the noble vampires, their bloodline would continue. The sacrifice of the *scorned* in Shadow City—the lesser vampires—was necessary to make them believe all were wiped out. The abyssians who died would give Ralloc pause. They'd take their time to investigate where they came from and never find out.

A waste of time and resources to keep the enemy busy and off-balance.

Xilor's advance detachments moved north to carry out his will, and now he'd move the main body of the army. And with Vlukus heading south, soon Starriace wouldn't be a problem.

All in all, the future started to brighten.

Chapter 25: Xenomene

A warm, blue-green hand cupped her left breast, the other ran through her dark red hair. His soft lips kissed hers. He shifted above her, his breath tickling her neck. Clawed fingers tugged her undergarments free from her hips and over her raised ankles. Her desire heightened as he spread her legs.

His kisses trailed to her breasts. Needle teeth grazed hardened nipples. His velvet tongue continued past her navel. Heat brushed the crevice where her hip met her groin.

Xenomene's breath quickened with anticipation, the flesh between her legs yearned for attention. His face disappeared from view, and soft, warm tenderness licked her core. Her pale fingers dug through his obsidian black hair. Her body moved in unison with his lapping.

She was glad she stopped fighting what she coveted.

"Fuck me," she panted.

Her breath hitched when his mouth pulled away. Hatred for begging did not outweigh longing.

"Fuck me."

His face swam near, and a whimper of anticipation escaped her mouth. In one fiery moment, he invaded her. Holding her wrists above her head, he pinned her, sliding his entire length inside.

She gasped.

"Oh, gods, yes."

He swelled inside her. She wrapped her legs around his waist as he drove in again, his thrusts quickening. A heady warmth spread through her flushed body.

She peered down her body, writhing as his blue-green length disappeared inside her. His hardness glistened from her arousal.

"Shades, I'm so fucking close."

His face loomed close to hers, and her eyes tracked up as she went to kiss him, but she shrank away from him just as her body was releasing.

His maw opened, no longer strikingly beautiful but animalistic. Mouth wide, teeth gleaming, he struck fast like a viper, a flicker of lightning. His teeth sank into her neck, ripping out her throat before she could cry out. Blood gushed, staining the sheets in liquid rose. Obsidian claws raked her chest, lacerating her breasts, crushing her sternum.

Xenomene bolted upright, throat constricting as if screaming, but no sound came. Panic flooded her, skin drenched in sweat. She panted in gulps.

A dream! Oh, thank the gods, only a dream.

A breeze flickered through the open window. Gooseflesh fluttered across her arms and neck. Both her sheets and shorts were soaked.

Why did I dream of Omegryk? Why am I wearing shorts?

One hand rubbed the sleep from her eyes as she wondered what had awoken her. She didn't remember falling asleep, which would explain being clothed. A rap on the hatch drew her attention.

"Who is it?"

She sprang out of bed and pulled the covers over the wet sheets.

This is embarrassing!

She dashed across the room to the dresser and grabbed the first pair of shorts on top. A deft side-to-side rocking motion freed the soaked garments.

"It's Tiny," he mumbled through the door.

She put on a burst of speed.

"Just a minute—"

"—Is everything…"

Tiny's head popped in and found her half-naked. She stopped, frozen with dread as he entered the room and shut the door. A twist of the mechanism threw the bolt home.

She swallowed, and her voice came out small, betraying what she felt inside.

"What are you doing?"

"Finishing what we started when the squads arrived. It'll be okay."

He smiled and lumbered forward. She shrank away.

"No, I don't want to."

"Sure you do. You did then."

She shook her head.

"Please, don't."

"You'll enjoy it."

His massive hands grabbed hold of her arms, and he kissed her. His lips smashed into hers. She pulled back, heat flushing her cheeks.

Her hand arched out with a crisp slap against his face.

"I said no!"

Tiny touched the stinging sensation, a languid movement before he backhanded her. Spots peppered her vision. The hard blow spun her around. She crashed against the desk. Her knees shook.

A hand shook her shoulder, and her eyes snapped open.

Thank the fucking gods! Another dream.

The Mind of Lyan's squad, Omegryk's handler, bent close.

"What?" she asked groggily, sitting up. The sheet fell away, exposing her breasts. "Are they back?"

"Afraid not. I have something to tell you."

"Am I still asleep?"

"Shit!"

He slapped her.

Angry pins and needles erupted in a plume.

"That fucking hurt, asshole!"

"Yeah, well, thank me later. Right now, I need to tell you something, and I think I might be too late in my discovery."

She moved against the headboard and pulled the sheets up.

"What?"

"It's about Omegryk," he said in a rush. "I've been working with him since he joined us. Each day, I learn more through our constant meld. I found out two things that I don't think he's aware of. Well, one I'm pretty sure, but the other not so much."

"We'll spit it out, some of us would like to go back to sleep!"

"That might not be safe for you. I just learned, because he was sleeping, that he can project himself into your mind while you're unconscious."

Xenomene went still.

"When your mind's unconscious, it's susceptible; during his sleep cycle, if dreaming, he can project into an unwitting mind. He dreamt about you, and I think you were an active party. You were literally part of his illusion. In essence, that Xenomene happened to be the real you."

"How can he do something like that?"

"I don't know. I think it has something to do with his unique magic. I'm not sure he's aware of it."

"Let me get this straight! You're saying the nightmare I just had about him was his?"

"Yes."

She was silent and rolled her eyes.

"Great, so I'm not safe when I'm asleep. What else?"

"The other part is that he can emit pheromones. I'm sure he knows. The other day when you talked with him, I was sure he intended to use them but didn't."

She shook her head.

"How do you know he didn't? The lust hit me incredibly strong. A few more moments…"

The Mind mirrored her movement.

"That's his magic. Trust me."

"But you don't know what I felt! It was so hard not to…"

"Have sex with him?" he finished.

She nodded.

"If he used his pheromones, you would've bedded him."

"Can he change his pheromones? Are only females susceptible, or is everyone in danger?"

"I don't know. Are you suggesting the men need to worry, too?"

Xeno shook her head.

"If he can change the nature of the pheromones, he can make others more agreeable."

A disbelieving expression flickered across his face.

"It's possible," he said.

He's never thought of that scenario.

"He projected into my mind, became something else…"

"I assume that's when I woke him up. The connection between you broke, and from there, whatever you dreamed was your own making. Residual traces may linger once the connection broke."

That explains Tiny then.

Her thoughts churned in a chaotic jumble from arousal to confusion, resignation to irritation. Omegryk. Perhaps it wasn't his fault. Who can control what they dream? Another problem added to the growing mountain, the first of which, Bitcher and the blackmail.

"Thank you for waking him and stopping the…delusion."

The Mind gave a curious glance, not expecting thanks.

"You're welcome."

"If there isn't anything else…?"

"Oh!" he said, remembering she wasn't dressed. "Right."

He left.

A sharp pang formed in her mid-back as she rolled out of bed, a knot of tension. She stretched gently, arms reaching to work out the hardness. It relieved some but not all of the pressure. Dressed, Xeno skipped breakfast and resumed her seat at the desk, a chained prisoner without parole. Eyes roved over the first parchment when she realized Tiny's squad was now hours overdue.

She bolted from the office, down four flights of stairs, and found Lyan in the common room. He broke bread with his members and most composed themselves with gaiety. Others still bore the effects of drink from the night before. She hovered over Lyan's shoulder and blurted before he acknowledged her.

"Any word from Tiny? They should've been back hours ago."

"No, 'fraid not."

Xeno nodded and muttered thanks before trudging back up the stairs in a mindless daze. She didn't remember sitting down behind the desk.

Only a few reasons explained Tiny's absence, most revolved around their death. She knew the outcome may manifest but didn't want to believe it. They were better than that. Perhaps a trap awaited them, or the portal master died, and they made their way back by foot.

Maybe they never arrived.

Did overwhelming numbers encourage a retreat? Too many variables made knowing impossible, but that didn't help the cold fist clenching her stomach. In truth, she only wished for Bitcher's death, to be free of his machinations, but didn't find comfort in that hope.

The thought sickened her.

At this point, she'd gladly stay trapped as his indentured whore if everyone came back unscathed. Minutes trickled by like days. Hours resembled months. By the end of the first day, an epoch had passed in her mind, but so did the vow to wait however long it took.

Captive to anxiety, she neglected herself and her duties, stayed reclusive, and abstained from meals. When Lyan or the Heart of his squad took notice, they took turns bringing food. Most went untouched and some only pecked.

In the stillness of night, when the dark shroud smothered the city and the sea of lanterns glowed softly, she kept vigil, pacing or sitting at the window, waiting, hoping. Religion never tugged at her heartstrings as other Krey, but she considered the vagary.

By the fifth night, her body succumbed to the abuse. Though passing out on the floor, she awoke in bed, the sun bright and hot considering the chilly time of year.

She blinked, eyes focusing on Lyan and his Heart hovering like mother hens.

"What day is it?" Xeno mumbled.

She rose, and a pounding drummed through her head. Lyan reached to push her back down, but she smacked his arms away.

"What day?"

"You've been asleep for a day and a half," the Heart supplied.

"They've been gone for seven days?"

"Yes," Lyan answered.

"Shades! Where the hell are they? Why haven't they returned or made contact? If their portal master died, the Heart can teleport. She can't take anyone but could at least come back herself!"

"Perhaps they're injured, and she's healing them?" Lyan said. "Maybe they never made it. It could be any number of things."

She glared at him.

"No shit, dumbass! That's what's eating me, the not knowing."

She turned to the Heart.

"The Mind and the Hand can heal, can't they? You're all cross-trained, aren't you?"

The Heart remained silent for a moment, then nodded.

"Yes, but we're placed in respective roles for our strength. In a pinch, I could fill a different role, but you wouldn't want me to indefinitely. If the wound is grievous, they'd be of no help, and the Heart would stay."

Xeno sighed and rolled out of bed against their protests and returned to the desk. They continued to pester with advice regarding her health, and no matter how much she screamed or threatened, they wouldn't leave until she ate a *full* meal. Lyan fetched a plate when Xenomene relented. She was halfway finished before remembering Spectre's group went on a mission, too.

"Any word from the Minions?"

"Yes, while you were unconscious," Lyan said. "Their Hand made a report in person. I took it. There isn't much. They didn't come across any outlaws responsible for the raids, but they ran into a small group of goblins. Strange that they'd be out there, don't you think?"

"Define small group."

"Five, I believe."

"Not enough to bloody everyone properly."

Xeno sighed.

"Why would goblins be that far north? If they're with Xilor, they'd be south. If they aren't with him, then why would they be in the wilderness instead of in a city? Something doesn't sit right. I wished they trailed them instead of killing them. If they see anymore, tell them to track them."

Lyan smiled.

"I did. It's nice to know great minds think in unison!"

"Yeah," Xeno added with sardonic tones, "then again, so do the perverted ones, and that doesn't mean every thought is a grand one."

Xenomene showed them the empty plate with grandiose and mocking gestures.

"Satisfied?"

"No, but it's a start," Lyan conceded.

True to their word, they left. The ever-elusive diligence to work failed to arrive and habitual pacing resumed. When that resort neglected to bring a calm, a windowsill vigil invited peace. This continued for another three days, but she ate to keep Lyan out of the office.

On the tenth night, she laid her head on the windowsill and watched Apor and Praema set. Nykron rose alone, sending its harlequin hue over the world. Xenomene, not one for superstitions, took it as a favorable sign. The green tone reminded her of trees and forests and life.

Her eyelids grew heavy.

A noise startled her awake, a continuous noise roiling in waves. The mesmerizing sound encouraged sleep. Her mind fought back, head lurching up. Her eyes searched the darkness beyond and followed the sound. To the right, a small dark form lay. Its tail swished in silence. Leaving the window, Xeno exited the office and entered the next room, lifting the window open.

A black kitten glanced up with a languid and unconcerned movement and meowed. Xeno reached with tentative hands and curled the cat up in her arms. The feline purred louder, giving a content meow. She ran the tip of her nose against its head, the soft fur slick like silk.

Another omen?

She tutted at the ridiculous notion, retreated to the office, placed the cat on the pallet, and resumed pacing. Did the gods not care what the waiting did to her? Either they did, or they weren't real at all. Either way, it came as confirmation to not waste time and energy on something so useless.

If gods didn't care, why should she? Couldn't they send a sign to continue waiting and hoping, or was it all for naught?

Why did she worry so? Being responsible for the lives of others was a lesson yet learned. Having never cared for rank, being the leader provided an outlet to keep foolish people from ascending. The strong of body and mind should lead, but the price for such a levy needed settlement.

Xenomene understood that this was part of it: the apprehension and vexation.

I gave them the most dangerous job hoping Bitcher would die. I deserve this.

She gave up searching for a comforting prospect. If everything went perfectly and Bitcher perished, she didn't know how to feel about his death. There was a side to Bitcher she cared for; the word love would never be uttered, but affection seemed appropriate.

At least until he'd tried to murder her.

She'd never love him now. If only Xenomene and Bitcher were caught in this scheme, she wouldn't hesitate to turn him in. With the Heart involved, all desire for revenge and justice went deferred.

She smirked at her stupidity.

Xenomene, the victim of futile schemes.

Where Bitcher desired her flesh and loved her in some sick, twisted way, she fantasized about killing him. But she'd get the collar for that, unless…

There was a way to settle grievances between Krey, but it was archaic. She wasn't sure the heir would allow the custom. In times past, the nobles settled disputes with combat. With the Krey, the grievance must be severe, and Xenomene's fell in that category. The only problem would be admitting the Heart's involvement during the oath breaking. Tradition wouldn't help in this setting.

Tired of pacing, she sat. The small, black cat hopped down from the pallet and jumped into her lap. It curled and purred. An absentminded hand stroked its fur.

Her predicament did present bonuses, mainly that Bitcher would never stray far, and she could keep him close. At least with her, no other woman would endure his arousal. Before this whole mess, she did choose him out of all others.

That was also before you met Slurp.

Before Bitcher, Xenomene's sex life paralleled the sky's silver lining, rare but spectacular. In truth, she had the same needs as any other. Her inactivity stemmed from a vow to herself, remaining celibate for lengths at a time.

She'd lost her virginity on the anniversary of entering the training program, the day she bested the weapons' master. Born in Ralloc, she'd lived in the Hive since four, the bloodlust manifesting exceptionally early. Adolescent training to become full-fledged Krey began at fourteen, but they started by the season.

The Age of Maturity came and went during initiation, and she waited for the one year mark of entering the program. Most didn't leave that phase until two ages old. Mastering the sword, she challenged the instructor on the anniversary of joining the ranks.

She didn't beat him; she humiliated him.

The current heir graduated her early. That night, the weapon master quested her; the day marked her passage as Krey, but he ushered her into womanhood.

After beating the weapon master, she left all classes, and while in a squad to learn formation and strategy, everyone tried to undermine her in the Pit. They stacked up, and she knocked them down, and most within the first few seconds of the fight. Each victory taught unique lessons and made her better.

Many times the opening volleys destroyed would-be opponents. Half didn't make it to the end of the round, and only five ever made it to the fifth. Of those five, only one went the distance to the ninth.

The gut disemboweled him, had he not dropped his sword and held his stomach. Hearts were on hand to tend to wounds. That night, she awaited his quest, laying naked and ready, and he didn't disappoint. He gained what he called a "sweet victory in defeat."

The memory encouraged a blush.

There was a young man that caught her infatuation for a spell. Perhaps genuine feelings manifested, but the romance wilted. His weak bloodlust ensured dismissal from House Eti. Due to extensive training, none may return to the ordinary life of a citizen. With only a few options available, he took the best alternative and became a sentinel for a religious cult to the south.

She scrunched her brow trying to recall the name.

What the hell's the name of that religion? What's his name?

Silence kept her company and withheld the answers.

They were the Disciples of something…? And his name…?

She couldn't remember, but he was older by an age and a few epochs, too old to still be in the initial stage. By now, he had to be at least four ages old, if not older.

She recalled his boyish features. He flirted and coaxed her from the solitary shell, which led to kissing, but they never copulated during their short-lived romance. He was dismissed before that milestone. He would've been her third lover.

He was bald, I remember that. Bald his whole life.

His dark skin came to mind, a stark contrast to her pale flesh. He hailed from across the Eastern Sea. He wasn't a Toshii like Mauler, but born and raised in…?

What was the name of that city?

It didn't matter, he came from the south, nowhere near the tribal nation.

A flickering light in the room caught her attention as the candle snuffed out, drowned in its wax. The symbolism jarred her memories.

Light. That's it! The Disciples of Light. No. The Disciples of the One!

She wondered what became of that young man. She reached for a new candle in the desk drawer when a commotion from the streets below reached her ears, the sound of running feet.

Several.

Forgetting the cat in her lap, she stood and hurried to the window. From this distance, there was no mistaking Tiny's massive frame. They'd come back! She didn't dare to hope until the big man roared a command for them to…*fall over dead?*

As if on cue, they all collapsed, some to their knees, others to their backs. She turned and almost trampled her furry companion. Scooping up the black cat, she kissed it a half-dozen times.

"You're really an omen, aren't you?"

The cat meowed.

"I dub thee, Arysto Omen."

Placing him on the pallet, she raced down. The four flights of stairs went by in a blur. She burst through the front door and out into the street. She saw Tiny first, still on his knees, and slammed into him with a hugging-chokehold.

"Where the fuck have you been, asshole?"

Their arrival didn't go unnoticed. Soldiers and healers from the army rushed over, carrying supplies, waterskins, and food. Tiny grabbed a woman running by and ripped the waterskin from her grip, chugging down half before daring to speak.

"They were waiting for us," he gasped. "Well, maybe not us, but they were there waiting for something. Tried to sneak around them or through them, but some scouts caught us coming out of the portal. Waited until we were all out and identified the portal master. An arrow through his throat…"

Tiny shook his head.

"When the Heart went to heal him, she caught arrows, too. The Hand took out the scout before he roused the enemy, but the Heart died after a few hours. The Mind and the Hand tried to heal her. The wounds were beyond their limited skill. Shades, we carried her while we retreated. She died about five in the morning on the night we set out."

Tiny drank from the waterskin again.

A pang of sadness lanced her chest. Not five hours after she left, the Heart had perished. Xenomene surveyed the crew, searching, hoping that Tiny pulled a practical joke.

But he didn't.

Her eyes found familiar faces, Patch, Wrath, the Islanders Slurp and Smokey, the fat bodies Drumstick and Keg, Mauler—never happier to see Mauler alive than at this moment—the Mind and the Hand. At last her eyes fell on the one person she wished hadn't survived: Jakeb.

Bitcher.

Though exhausted, he didn't hide his happiness. He offered a warm smile, and for a moment, the man she once felt a twinge for reappeared. She returned the gesture, lost in the confusion of roiling ambivalence, happy to see him, and yet…

Is it possible to want someone dead and alive?

She turned to Tiny.

"Why didn't the Mind or the Hand teleport back and report?"

Tiny gave a confused look.

"Because they can't. I really wished they did, it would've been much easier than running back. Only the Heart could, and barely at that."

"You ran back?"

Soldiers and healers jostled about, tending to weary Krey. Lyan's group came out and worked through their ranks.

"The whole way?"

Tiny nodded.

"Aye. We didn't stop at all, except to refill our waterskins or find some food after we ran out. Hell, I mastered the art of running and pissing. Can't say the same for shitting though."

"How?"

"Cause you gotta squat."

"No, jackass! How'd you run the entire way?"

"Oh, a rejuvenation spell. Apparently, the Hand and the Mind can do that well enough."

Xenomene nodded and inspected the haggard men and women. Now that she knew what they endured, a few appeared gaunter than before. Smokey lost weight from the run.

"Get some rest, all of you. I'm proud and astonished. You did an unimaginable feat, earned what it means to be Krey."

"But we didn't complete the mission or objectives," Smokey huffed.

"True, but don't discredit your resolve to live and evade. It's a tale worthy of the ears of the heir, I promise."

A plan took shape as soon as the words left her mouth.

A war horn peeled through the night and shouts rose in the distance.

"Oh, yeah," Tiny said, as if he forgot. "We were also followed."

Tiny's squad struggled to rise, to answer the call of battle.

"No! Rest. Lyan! Gear up and go."

Lyan smiled.

"Alright kids, you heard Momma. Suit up!"

They rushed to don their armor. The soldiers attending left when the war horn sounded.

"Momma?" Tiny asked.

She rolled her eyes.

"I don't know, but I'll kill him later. I'll rouse the cooks to prepare food. Eat, drink, and sleep. That's all. No one is to be doing battle, understood?"

She left and went to the cooks. It wasn't until she identified herself as Krey did they bolt out of bed. They dressed with alacrity under her withering gaze. She let them believe an imminent slaughter would commence if they didn't comply. They fled to the kitchens and promised food in short order.

Next, she went to the camp helpers, rousing them to boil water and deliver tubs. A good soak would ease aches. They gave less resistance. Following, she searched for Kernoyl Tyku, and found him in the command tent, delivering a preliminary battle assessment.

Xenomene stopped at the edge of the officers surrounding the table and listened.

"A quick survey shows an estimate of ten thousand strong. It's hard to judge at this time of night," Tyku droned. "Just goblins. No trolls, vampires, or dragons sighted yet, but we can't rule them out at this point. Questions?"

"What about siege weapons?" a younger leftenaut asked.

"Again, too dark. Maybe some trebuchets, but if so, they're beyond the range of sight. We'll wait for daylight for confirmation. It's only a few hours away."

"And the warlock? Is he here?" a meyjour to Tyku's left asked.

"I think we can handle this small force without him, wouldn't you agree?"

Tyku rebuked. "Besides, with Jynerul Vikal's men here, we outnumber them. You have your orders men. Jynerul?"

Tyku looked over to Vikal,

"Is there anything else you'd like to add?"

The jynerul shook his head.

"Very well, dismissed."

The officers scurried away, and Xenomene waited for them to clear out, then approached.

"Ah, Ko-don, to what do we owe the pleasure?"

"One of my squads has returned, the one I sent to Cape Gythmel. They sustained a casualty in addition to the portal master."

"How serious is it?" Jynerul Vikal asked.

"Fatal."

"So, you're back to two squads strong now?" Kernoyl Tyku asked. "Terrific! We can use them. Send them to the wall."

"No."

"What?" the jynerul balked.

"I said no. The squad that lounged around here will have to suffice, but not the other. They just ran back for ten days straight. They're exhausted and famished. I'm not sending them out to fight, especially when their healer is dead."

"Oh," Vikal said, almost too quiet to detect.

His face changed to one of understanding and sympathy. Tyku didn't catch the exchange, his face turning red.

"Are you disobeying a direct order?" Tyku asked.

"A direct order would imply that it came from the heir or that you're my superior, neither of which is the case. He wouldn't send them into battle. If he did, I'd ram a sword up his ass to dislodge whatever caused such fetid thoughts. The answer is still no."

Tyku sputtered, then found his words.

"I'm asking politely—"

"And I'm politely telling you to fuck off!"

She leaned in closer.

"Just imagine how it'd be if I were angry."

"The Krey fall under the army!" Tyku began. "If you—"

Vikal cut him off.

"One team is fine, my lady. Thank you for the update. Please, see to your brave men and women."

Tyku bristled but bit back words.

"There are no ladies here, just Krey."

She jerked her head towards Tyku.

"Unless you count him."

She stormed off.

By the time the barracks loomed near, the anger had abated. She didn't want to be irritable around the Krey. The Xenytes burst into laughter and tore into food as she entered. Cooks and servants bustled about, dropping plates of food that were emptied moments later. Livelier than before, Tiny explained that the A'uri of the Demigods used a rejuvenation spell before leaving.

It was a kind gesture, one she wouldn't forget.

A cup of rum found its way into her hand, and they encouraged a chugging competition. She obliged, and the mug was refilled. Toasts went around, and she drank to each of them. By the fourth cup, the effects of the rum tingled. Tiny stood and toasted a solemn oath to the Heart. Each drank until the goblet was empty.

Afterward, rum bottles ran dry, but Xenomene nursed the cup. It'd been hours since the last meal, and the alcohol sat heavy on an empty stomach. As each individual found their limits, each retreated to a tub and bathed. Nudity wasn't uncommon, but bathing adhered to the comports of a semi-private fashion. The late hour and not caring, they washed next to the table with their food. Xenomene understood what the heir meant when he said that some should never be naked in public again.

Though Smokey had lost weight during their run, his loose skin and what remained of his flab made Xenomene's stomach quiver, and not in a right way, either. His back boasted as much hair as his head. Xeno had cute freckles tracing from back to buttocks, but Smokey exhibited moles, large and small, and his pubic hair rivaled the wild unruliness of a sheep's winter coat.

It was a mental image that would never fade.

When Tiny stripped, she averted her eyes, and she made sure he saw the movement. She didn't see him in a romantic way. Attractive perhaps, but personality, interests, and sexual compatibility were more important. Preference also played a part, preferring men closer to her height. She might lack mental depth for deeming him too tall, but women did the same to men but in reverse, disregarding shorter men in favor for taller.

His height only touched the long list of undesirable variables.

Drumstick came next, and by then, she excused herself from the ground floor. She stumbled up the stairs. The thought of donning her armor and joining Lyan's squad crossed her mind, but she wasn't in much better shape than Tiny's team. After days of eating little and fretting, she lacked the strength.

Fuck! I can't believe this! Why did you have to go and die, Heart?

Xenomene let out a small half-sob, half-chuckle, realizing she never knew the Heart's name. When she breached the door to the office, Omen meowed from the pallet. She crossed the room and petted him before turning to the desk. She filled out the report explaining the Heart's demise. Tiny would add his tomorrow.

Done, she filled out a requisition for a replacement A'uri. She was halfway finished when footsteps lumbered down the hall.

Jakeb's coming.

Xeno chastised herself.

Bitcher! His name is Bitcher! Jakeb's gone.

She thought of refusing him, but that would tip her hand prematurely. Giving him what he sought tonight would keep him oblivious. Refraining enticed suspicion.

The door opened.

"Miss me?" he asked, shutting the door behind him.

She swallowed retorts, crass responses, and dark thoughts, and gave him something he wanted to hear without answering.

"I'm glad the squad made it back. It could've been so much worse."

"It's a shame about the Heart. You two were close, weren't you?"

"I worried about everyone, hoping they wouldn't die, and yet all that worry didn't do me a damn bit of good."

Bitcher nodded, then bolted the door.

"A good woman died," she said. "Don't you feel anything?"

Bitcher sighed, rounded the desk, and perched on the nearest corner.

"Perhaps it's because I've been Krey longer than you, or perhaps because I came at an older age, but I've always known we were meant to die. I've never gotten attached to anyone I didn't need to. I grieve that you're sad, and I'm grateful you're now a ko-don and out of harm's way."

"Except the harm you inflict on me."

"I thought…we were past this. I was under the assumption we'd come to an understanding."

Xeno swallowed, watching him, searching for any sign of the man he once was. She glimpsed it in flashes. He reached out and took her hand with tender affection and kissed her on the forehead.

Damn it! Why does he have to be so fucking likable sometimes?

In the turmoil of feelings, she hoped, wished for a sign that he'd changed, that what he did was a one-time event.

A warm smile crossed his lips.

"I missed you," he said. "I couldn't stop thinking of you."

"Neither could I."

That, at least, wasn't a lie.

A flicker of sadness came to his eyes.

"Look," he began. "If you don't want me here tonight, I understand. I'll leave if you want me to."

She had half a mind to run him out, but the other half battled against such action, wanting him.

"Kiss me."

Jakeb pulled her up from the chair and kissed with the passion and fire she remembered. The kiss relayed all the emotions he felt.

At that moment, she knew beyond a shadow of a doubt that he loved her, but the emotion would never be reciprocated from her. She was amazed he could love, but she didn't work that way. The situation couldn't continue.

But it didn't have to stop tonight.

Breaking the embrace, she whispered to him.

"Make love to me. I want to know what it feels like."

Omen, the cat, leapt out of the way as Xeno and Jakeb tumbled to the pallet.

Chapter 26: Stratu'Geim

Grunting with effort, Starriace pulled her consciousness out of Rusem's fractured awareness.

After leaving her own mind for so long, it felt strange to return to her own body. The sickness in her stomach wasn't real, but a byproduct from staying in Rusem's mind—at least, that's what she told herself.

As Fife had taught her, she soothed away the discomfort before returning her attention to the risen. The out-of-body experience made her lightheaded; a sensation of floating, cradled by a gentle wind, rippled through her. She'd felt something similar before with the magelust.

The damage done to the degrading mind was extensive; each attempt to search for memory fragments spurred further deterioration. Repairs at this point seemed moot, but she had to try; otherwise Rusem would be of no use to her. For this formidable task, she practiced finesse using one of Rusem's veins, pushing it back and forth until she'd mastered subtle manipulation.

Molding clay with her mind would help; the more details in the sculpture would measure her success. The vein proved difficult to manipulate, and she floundered for the first half hour. Once proficient, she delved further, past the congealed mass of fleshy granules, until she could count each one. From there, she practiced moving and rearranging each granule individually.

Excruciating work aside, her efforts paid off.

Starriace hoped she'd be able to communicate better afterward, if not vocally, at least telepathically. Now, when she requested, images rushed forward, allowing her to delve deeper. For each portion of the brain she repaired, she strengthened their link by infusing his mind with her essence. In some ways, she tied them together, much like the link she shared with Ava.

As long as she kept the tether, their link would never wane.

Satisfied with her work, she withdrew. It sapped her strength, and she pulled food from her pack, eating to recover. If time allowed, she'd sleep.

In silence, she mulled over what she'd discovered. To repair him, to preserve the majority, she had to destroy other portions. No amount of quick work would save the entirety. When she realized the inevitable outcome, she ensured the survival of his precious recollections.

Sacrifices had to be made, and she purged unrelated knowledge while safeguarding the secrets he hoarded. At the end of it all, dismay rippled through her when she found how little he'd learned. The efforts almost seemed for naught. Rusem didn't know how to use the brimstones, but he did know how to find some.

The brimstones should be in the temple in the City of Despair, where they were last used, but they weren't, and the ramifications troubled her. Perhaps someone had stolen them, or a magical bond on the stones returned them to their original location, or maybe to a new spot altogether. Whoever created the stones most likely put a ward on them, a failsafe to keep them out of aspiring hands.

The quest took Rusem ages, and she didn't have that kind of time. She needed them now. Too much was at stake, and Xilor had to be stopped.

The flashbacks provided information about each stone. They were different shapes, sizes, and colors. Other than the gut feeling she couldn't prove, Starriace believed there was more to it than random characteristics.

There had to be.

Something of immense power couldn't just lie inert without giving off an aura or a presence of some kind. How Rusem was able to find one baffled her, unless he had help, but no memories proved the theory. Either that or when she killed him, it destroyed the memory.

Or worse yet, perhaps when Xilor put the stones together, it erased most.

Most distressing was when she recalled her own flashbacks of Rusem at the temple. He'd said he found one of the brimstones and Xilor had the other six, but no reflection she reviewed showed Xilor among them. Did Rusem lie? Did he work in tandem with Xilor, or was his lackey?

If so, the dark lord purged any memory of himself, the locations, or what happened once they were activated. She had very few clues, and most of the trails seemed cold.

She would've dug deeper into the embedded thoughts of how he found the first brimstone, but she inadvertently expunged the recollection. Those memories cluttered the slow mind, so she savagely erased, scouring his brain clean until nothing but information regarding the brimstones remained.

Oddly enough, several flashes included Judas among them. He was younger and handsome, he held himself in a carefree way. He appeared barely older than a boy entering manhood, younger than she was now. And she had to admit to herself, his younger self free of gray hair or whiskers, shared some facial characteristics with her. How had she never noticed that before?

In the memories, what she saw mystified her, a few scarce moments of Judas in various places, most centered around parties, ladies hanging from his neck, fondling him with wandering hands. At first, Starriace thought she'd mistaken the identity, but the more she witnessed, the more certain she grew. In those moments, he wasn't aloof, holding everyone at a proverbial arm's distance. He charmed and groped the women in return, a stark contrast to the man she remembered.

The youthfulness of his face left more of an impression on her as she internalized, surmising these moments came before the Wizard's War, but the warlock had said that it started before his birth. That only left one option, the events occurred before his joining the fight.

His merriment prior to taking hardships upon his shoulders, the impossible mantle of war, was evident; she focused on that attainment as she ate her stale food. She chewed several times before a thought crossed her mind. She'd made a mistake. Not just some ordinary mistake but catastrophic. The answer as to why Judas was in Rusem's memories.

Emotion clouded her judgement, and she viciously eradicated any memory of him. Only fools were solely ruled by the heart, and she'd been one. Judas had helped Rusem find the brimstones, it was the only explanation that made sense.

The thought sent an ache through her as she let out a groan of desperation.

Damn it! I left Judas in anger and almost killed him in Ralloc. There's no way that I'm going to get his help now! And all those memories I destroyed…

Another legendary blunder. Now, it was all gone, nothing left, unless…

She jumped up, suddenly inspired.

"We've got to go."

"Why? What's wrong?" Ava asked, startled by the explosion of movement.

Starriace was in full stride with renewed energy.

"Ava, I need you to teleport us to Stratu'Geim. Can you do it? Are you recovered enough? That's where Rusem is from, and maybe he left a record of some sort. I need it to continue my search."

"Yes, but my powers are vastly diminished on this side of the mountains. I must return soon. Once recuperated, I can come back."

"Let's go, then."

Ava teleported them just outside the city and bid her farewell. She hadn't lied about her diminished powers, and once there, she lacked her usual brilliance. After her departure, Starriace retreated to a wooded area and followed the gentle, uphill slope leading away.

After a fifteen-minute trek, she reached a hilly area thick with trees, and tucked the risen away in the outcropping and left. Once in sight of the city again, shrubs concealed her as she waited for night to fall.

In the darkness, the hum of nightlife enveloped the countryside, chasing away the commotion in the city. With a stretch to ease her stiffness, Starriace climbed a nearby tree to glimpse over the walls. Her robes snagged, and no amount of coaxing would help. Each jerk ripped the robes; she'd need new ones.

She spied a baronial building with decorative towers and guards posted at the exterior doors of the palace proper.

That has to be the king's home.

She climbed down, hurried along the wall, and followed it until she reached the backside of the palace. She stopped to listen, her ears straining for any signs of movement. With her awareness, in haste, she swept over the cracks and crevices of the wall, through windows and under doors, creeping, hoping she wouldn't find another capable mage within.

Satisfied the immediate area was neglected, she levitated. While she could use displacement like Fife had taught her, she felt it more prudent to practice her power of flight, saving displacement for when she had to manipulate an object.

Like she had in the Corridor of Cruelty, she focused her power in her hand, shaping her intent. With a gentle ease, she lifted, rising in noiseless, measured discipline.

Her feet touched the stone above, and Starriace, at a brisk pace, slipped from the open area. Each door she reached, she checked to make sure no one stirred on the other side. The last one opened into a long passage, and she hunched over, creeping with hurried, quiet steps through the empty halls.

The Palace of Lost Kings was home to the steward of Stratu'Geim.

Inside the walls, an eerie imprint brushed against her, knowing that Rusem once walked these halls. At least, that's what she dismissed it as. The enormous palace held a sense of grandeur, and she idly wondered which boasted the bigger castle: Ralloc or Stratu?

Most buildings she'd seen were either built from wood, stone, or small bricks. The castle consisted of massive slabs similar to bricks, half her height and one and a half that in length. How many men and women found solace here? Stately tapestries stretched from ceiling to floor, a rainbow of colors weaved through the stitching, depicting tales or slivers of history. Busts of heads with strong shoulders graced the empty space between each drapery, and a lonely torch hung above each statue. At a quick glance as she passed, all bore similar resemblance and shared the last name.

Geim.

It mattered little now; only ghosts of the past resided here.

She peered around a corner to find another empty but decorated hall. The Hall of the Kings, the wing in which Rusem used to reside. A hall Judas possibly walked down.

It's odd thinking Judas was here once. Perhaps this was the king he talked about, the one he befriended?

It sparked a buoyancy within her, to think she walked down the same hall as Judas; though he had failed as a teacher, his accomplishments were praiseworthy: stopping Xilor. She intended to finish what he started, and she hoped it began just beyond the doors in front of her, in Rusem's old room.

If anything lay within, she'd find it.

I have to!

A small problem manifested beyond the door: the Steward of Stratu'Geim. The city's custodian took up quarters in the king's old room, and she'd silence him if he weren't asleep. The thought didn't sit well with her. Self-defense was one thing, but to kill an innocent man? Assassination wasn't incomprehensible, but she'd skirt past the task without jeopardizing her objective, giving clemency over bloodshed.

I'm not a monster like Xilor!

She shook the thought away and pressed her hand flat against the door, sensing the room beyond. Quiet held sway. The doorknob turned smooth, the tumbler well maintained. With a steady push, the door glided open.

Rhythmic breathing flitted across the room; the old man slept in an enormous bed. She entered and sealed the door behind her.

When she turned back around, panic filled her. She'd been found! Her magic had failed. Her eyes went wide, her heart hammering, and she crouched into a defensive posture, calling upon her essence. Her hand plunged downward, jerking up her wand.

All around the room, a group of people stood. For a moment, no one stirred or spoke. Her mageshield flared to life, and she remembered to breathe.

With a slow, sinking dread, reality caught up with her. People didn't surround her, statues did. They lined the room's crimson carpet, real and life-like, full bodied and adorned with clothes. Their faces were real and lifelike, painted to look like flesh. Even their stone hair appeared full-bodied in the dim moonlight.

It was unnerving.

Distinctions between them varied wildly, from their look, sex, clothes, to the small placards around their necks. Each represented wizards, kings, noblemen, or gods of each religion; one had the title of apostle, but she dismissed them after her curiosity was satisfied.

They weren't important, and her objective called to her.

Starriace remembered her brief stint with Judas before forging her own destiny. A simple spell came to mind, one he spoke about but she never used, part of the half-dozen frivolous incantations he bestowed before plunging into the Corridor.

Drawing on the memory, she pulled her wand and molded her essence to her will. Hidden rooms and passages overlooked by the naked eye flickered through her second vision. Sweeping the room with her gaze, she wasn't disappointed to find one behind the bookshelf to the left of the bed. She inspected the passage with her double-vision, fingers traced the shelf, searching for a catch to release.

One couldn't be found.

Perplexed, she sat in front of the shelf and meditated, expanding her awareness over, around, and through the bookshelf. Minutes trickled like seconds as she melded with the granules of the bookcase. It happened before she grasped the implication. The bookshelf itself was magical, which was why she could let it meld with her mind.

A smirk came at both the simplicity and multifaceted nature of the conjury.

She stepped forward, magic swirling about her, and willed herself through as if it were no more than a curtain. With a backward glance, the bookshelf still guarded the entrance. Once again, she had learned something not taught by Fife, Judas, or any book at Harold's, though the latter proved periodically useful.

Rusem, or whichever of his ancestors who designed the shelf, constructed it out of magic. To those who lacked power, it would appear as a legitimate bureau. For her, it was a veil.

The hall beyond turned sharply left and dumped out in a small room with a desk, chair, and bookshelves with cabinet tops. The bookshelves were a feint, if she understood Rusem at all. They held valuable, important books, but what she searched for held a treasure of knowledge.

He would've hidden it.

She flipped the top to the desk but knew it wouldn't be that simple. Without disappointment, she lowered the lid and stepped back, casting her magevision again. There was nothing behind the desk or the shelves. The walls and ceiling were solid.

Starriace let out a sigh of frustration and shifted to the left shelf. In mid-stride, she paused. The tile beneath her foot shifted. She peered down with the magevision, finding a hole beneath.

She knelt and worked her fingers until she found purchase and lifted it. Below, the hole was only two feet deep and inside, a dirty old rag covered a small leather-bound book. She picked it up and held it reverently in her hands, caressing the cover.

The smell of old leather and mold filled her nostrils. The first page, stained by time and the environment, sent a thrill through her. As she read, she felt a rush of discovery, as if the cold, dead fingers of Hagen, the Father of Magic, caressed her, finding what she desired. Whatever ancient and forbidden knowledge Rusem sought, he recorded it within, but a leisurely perusal would have to wait.

With a snap, she closed the book and stuffed it in her black robes. Past the ninety-degree turn, she exited the secret passage. On the other side, instant fear gripped her. The steward wasn't in bed anymore, but pacing the room in a slow arc, his back to her. At each statue, he muttered prayers.

In a blind panic, Starriace stepped between the two nearest lifelike statues and stilled. The unreasonable sentiment of going unnoticed filled her. She should've gone back through the passageway, but if he knew about it and entered, there'd be no place to hide.

She reached out to the statue to her left, the one furthest away from the administrator, familiarizing herself with the texture. Her fingers stroked the stone, a plan formulating. Judas and Fife always told her the power of Rumigul resided within the mind and not incantations. She was about to attempt something she'd never dreamed of, and wasn't sure if she would survive, but she'd pulled gold out of solid stone.

Anything was possible.

If caught, she could overpower the old man, perhaps even kill him, but the swarming guards? How many could she take before they succeeded? She'd rather leave the feat untested, and her only option relied on blending in.

She remembered Judas saying how Meristal changed her appearance at will. Armed with the trusted recollection of the rare gift, only a handful throughout history achieved the desired results, and she'd never trained for this type of magic.

What would happen if she tried?

She didn't know, but she didn't have time to debate. The finesse she picked up over the last few days would have to suffice. Essence guiding her, she mimicked the statue's composition and applied it to her skin. It was a slow, painful process, like pulling each individual hair out of her arms and legs.

A quick glance revealed a shuffling steward coming closer.

The change rippled through her feet, crept up her shins, the sensation like dragging the blunt-edged knife across bone. Her thighs burned with thousands of stings. The pain reached a crescendo, and a scream stuck in the back of her throat.

Did it feel like this to Meristal?

She grimaced. This agony reminded her of Mr. Pleasure. She pushed those thoughts away.

The steward stirred again, one statue closer. She stood three away from him. His prayers slowed his progress.

She closed her eyes, gritted her teeth, and urged the magic to move faster.

Again, he moved closer.

Prickling misery rolled across her ribs, and she bit her lip to keep from whimpering aloud. It rolled like fire over her breasts, across her throat like searing coffee, and her eyes watered as it crossed the bridge of her nose as he stepped up to her.

"By the One," he muttered. "Such a beautiful statue. Great beauty, I beseech the god you represent…"

Starriace wanted to kick him; the pain was unbearable.

As he spoke, a premonition permeated her mind. A darkness rushed towards her. The eerie imprint she felt earlier, the one she dismissed as an echo of Rusem, returned. For a brief moment, Xilor filled her mind, but she knew his essence, his aura. Something similar approached, an echo of his core being, but it wasn't him.

The threat brushed the outer parts of her mind. She perceived it—*them.* They crawled through the castle walls like a fog of malevolence. An image of black, rolling smoke filled her inner eye. It was otherworldly, an embodiment tainted by the maliciousness who called it forth.

"… and so, dearest spirits to whomever this child belongs," the steward continued, "I ask for a sign. I ask that you find faith in your servant, who humbly awaits your commands."

He bowed his head, and she couldn't take the pain any longer.

Her hand shot out, snatching him by the throat, releasing the spell about her. It peeled back in the space of two heartbeats, freeing her from the pain.

"Your prayers are answered, Steward."

Fear shot through his eyes. He fell to his knees, mewling like a cur. If he thought her a god or spirit, so much the better.

Zealots…seeing signs in everything.

"The time for deliverance is upon you," she said. "Get up."

He wiped tears away and stood on shaking feet, and his voice quivered.

"What god do I owe the honor of his mighty work?"

She lifted an eyebrow.

"Who said anything about *his* mighty work?"

The steward's face paled.

It was a dangerous gamble, but Starriace wasn't versed in deities, gods, or spirits. Starriace had only heard of one religion, and she didn't know if she was a god or not. The barkeep at Far Point told her about the religion of the Father, the Mother, and the Child. She hoped it'd be enough.

"Are you the work of Soma? The dwaven goddess? I never knew…"

"That she existed?"

Perfect. He can fill in the blanks.

"Please, Soma, I beg forgiveness. I—"

"Silence!"

The shadow in her mind loomed closer, darker. Her eyes itched, and she knew that her eyes glowed. She could see the scarlet highlighting his face.

"There isn't much time. You want forgiveness and deliverance? Here's your first test. You'll help this form escape the coming vileness. She must get out of the palace unseen, unhindered, and unharmed. Do you understand?"

He nodded.

"The next part of the test will come when the wickedness takes hold of your city."

The smoke remained opaque, but the image became resolute. Creatures formed out of the fog, beings with six legs, torsos of a man, massive arms with a face and protruding lower jaw.

"Appalling creatures come to take over the city, waiting for someone or something. Do as they say, or rebel and all will be lost."

"But you will protect us, won't you, Soma? You answered my prayers."

"And so I shall, in the timing of the gods."

Her inner eye spied them as they scaled the walls and broke through gates, killing men mercilessly as they went.

"Help the child I embody now. Do you know of a way out?"

"Yes, yes I do. Follow me, Soma."

True to his word, the old man led her through passages designed to mimic sewers, a facade to hide their true purpose: escape tunnels. Once they reached the end, Praema's bright light graced Ermaeyth with a breathtaking red and violet dawn.

The crisp, morning air greeted her, a welcome charity to the stifling, dark confines of the underpass. Birds twittered in the distant treeline. A gentle breeze washed over her sweaty face, cooling her. Each breath diluted the odor of the musky, stale tunnels.

She climbed out and glanced behind; the city rose up on cliffs. It was several kilometers away. Too far for someone to spot them with an unaided eye.

"Go back," Starriace said. "Be with your people and lead them through their trials. Be strong and persevere. Deliverance will come."

He bowed several times as he stumbled backwards, pulling himself inside.

Alone, Starriace realized she'd come out of the city on the opposite side of Rusem. She wouldn't risk calling to him, not if it meant him being seen. Teleporting was risky; she could overshoot him by hours or days. She didn't have the finesse to command her destination with absolute confidence.

Reluctantly, she set off at a jog.

Once she reached the risen, she'd peruse the treasure she had found, down to the last poignant detail, and unlock the secrets within.

Chapter 27: Mon Kyyr Gr'bakth

Xenomene had an epiphany: Jakeb and Bitcher were not the same. Sure, he went by both, but their personas manifested at opposite ends of the spectrum, and she knew when he slipped into either one now.

When she asked him to make love to her almost a week ago, he did. Afterward, Bitcher came out to play. Jakeb treated her like a woman, a lover, and she lost her mind to their passion. She almost knew what it meant to love somebody.

Xenomene realized where the conflict lay: she loved Jakeb, but detested Bitcher.

It would've been perfect had he stopped after their first encounter. On his second resurgence, he donned Bitcher's persona, one that was vile, cruel, and only cared about himself. With Jakeb, she could do anything and everything he asked, sating and yielding to every whim.

With Bitcher, he just took, turning reprehensible. She did everything to appease both personas, her heart caught in an unforgiving tourniquet.

He'd hurt her again, a rabid animal lost in lust and power. Tied up face-down with her arms and legs anchored to each post, her love of the kinkiness couldn't override his abuse. She didn't care what part he chose to fuck; it was the manner that counted, the lack of care, and she'd never absolve him.

He was dead to her.

Bitcher visited every night, and she discovered the hard way that the man she could've loved was never coming back. On the fourth night, Jakeb returned; the hardening of her heart almost dwindled while he slept, spooning her. She cried half the night, knowing Jakeb would die whenever Bitcher ceased breathing.

Each day mirrored the last, and the first two days were filled with the sounds of battle. Tiny and his squad roused the next day ready for action, but she forbade them to join. After the initial assault, the Krey were not needed. Lyan's team cut a swath through the enemy's ranks. They suffered only minor cuts healed in the heat of battle. They retreated as ordered and experienced the first grievous wound.

Tytan took a stray spear through his leg and shattered his right femur.

The first battle ended with the enemy losing a quarter of their number to the Krey and archers on the walls. The Black Tide evaded relatively unscathed, but the Grand Royal Army didn't, losing a thousand soldiers in the first skirmish.

Once dawn broke, the officers could see the goblin force. It wasn't ten thousand strong as first estimated but eight. With over a quarter now lifeless in the opening volley, victory was assured. Archers picked off the bold few who attacked the wall.

Kernoyl Tyku came up with the idea of having the cavalry flank them by exiting the north gate, hidden by the hills of the surrounding countryside. The maneuver took over a day to get in place, and at dawn of the third day, the horses trampled the goblins. By the close of the fifth night, the enemy fled with less than fifteen hundred remaining.

Spectre returned later that night while Bitcher defiled Xenomene. She used their arrival as her excuse to get away. Spectre's squad was grizzled and tired, their armor spattered with blood, but all made it back alive. The girls' hair looked hideous when they removed their helmets, revealing knotted mops. They smelled worse than a horse stall in summer.

When she heard a commotion below, she pushed Bitcher off and dressed in haste. Greeting the squad took priority over his cock. Alone on the third-floor landing, she collected herself and wiped hot tears of hate away before descending further. By the time she came outside, everyone had arrived to greet them.

Spectre saw Xenomene and shook her head as the ko-don closed the distance.

"They weren't bandits like we thought. They were goblins and lots of them. I swear we picked off half before we openly engaged them. I've never seen so many. They had us surrounded. I don't know how we survived!"

"I'll tell you how," their Heart spoke up. "The gods can attest to my fucking healing abilities, that's how!"

The squad chuckled with mirth. When they subsided, they looked to their ko-don, expecting orders or a word of encouragement. Her inner turmoil kept her from offering praise, but she knew such laurels were called for.

"Job well done," Xenomene said. "You fought hard, honorably, surviving by relying on your training, as all Krey do, as all Krey were born for. I'll convey your success to the heir when I see him tomorrow. We'll feast tonight, and hot baths all around!"

A cheer went up.

"Clean your swords, but the armor can wait. I know you're weary. Eat, drink, bathe, and sleep, that's your orders for tonight."

A girl spoke up from within their squad, but Xeno couldn't catch who spoke.

"Can we fuck?"

All the Krey laughed. Xenomene found it amusing in spite of her situation.

"If you can find a willing partner, fuck until your parts fall off!"

The jest struck the open wound, killing her mood.

As before, she roused the cooks and the camp hands. Food poured in, and scalding water materialized over the next hour. The squads ate together, though Spectre's ate the most.

None skimped on drinking. Ales, meads, wines, and rums of all kinds flowed, and everyone drank with greed, Xeno, too—in the hopes of getting so drunk she wouldn't be able to remember what happened to her later. Pain and violation awaited upon returning to the room, after leaving Bitcher unspent and unsatisfied.

By the time they finished, Xenomene couldn't stand, and Tiny carried her up the four flights of stairs. He opened the door to the office, ducked beneath the frame, and jerked to a stop, jarring Xeno. Tiny locked eyes with Bitcher. The latter rose from the pallet and crossed the room to take Xeno from Tiny. The big man wouldn't let her go.

In a blur, harsh words launched like lethal volleys as the two men bickered. Xenomene drunkenly reached up to hug Tiny's neck, and breathed into his ear.

"Don't worry, it's almost over."

She didn't know if he could comprehend the slurs, she was barely able to form a coherent thought. She could feel Tiny's reluctance to let go, but he did.

The big man left, and Bitcher bolted the door after setting her on the bed. His indistinct form disrobed and stalked forward. His hand fondled her breasts with painful strokes and groped without shame. He ripped her shorts to her ankles and twisted her around.

In the drunken state, she turned a full circle, still facing him. He grabbed a handful of hair and jerked hard.

"Are you fucking with me?"

She tried to focus on his face and only managed a partial image. He kept blurring and moving.

"Not yet. Where do you want to put it? My mouth?"

She opened her mouth wide.

"Put it in. Fuck my mouth."

His angry lips thinned, his teeth peeking through as he debated. Her offer won out. He took another fistful of her hair, and forced himself past her lips. For his efforts, Xeno expended the contents of her stomach all over him. Honestly, she felt better after doing so, and the violation had been worth it.

"What the fuck!" he shrieked.

He jumped back, trying to find something other than his own clothing to wipe away the bile. When none fell in his sight, he left in a hurry, cursing the whole way. That made her smile, and she slid to the floor, sleeping in a bed of her own sick.

Large, gentle hands picked her off the floor. She opened her eyes to find Tiny.

She smiled.

"Hey, you," she slurred.

"Hey, yourself."

He stood her up, and she swayed. He knelt. At that moment she realized how close he was, and how very naked she remained. She placed her hands on his shoulders to keep from falling over. His hands gently pulled her undergarments and shorts up from her ankles without seduction. He came for business, not pleasure; a friend, her second.

"Shades Xeno, if I wasn't half a respectable man…"

She put a hand to her mouth, as if that helped her hold her stomach's contents better.

"If you get my pants up without me throwing up, I'll let you squeeze it."

Or at least that's what she thought she said.

Whatever words passed her lips, it drew a chuckle from him. He finished fixing her garments, then palmed her cheek with an affectionate squeeze, and walked around to fix her blouse.

"You're a mess. He raped you, didn't he?"

"Yup!" she hiccupped. "And for the last time, too, that motherfucker."

She swayed.

"For the last time? He's done this before? I'm going to beat the son of a bitch!"

"Nope. I'm gonna kill him."

"You can't stand, let alone hold a sword. Killing him is murder; even for the Krey, that's taboo."

He glanced down at the floor and stepped back.

"What happened here?"

She glanced down.

"You don't want to know. Get a Heart to fix me, and I'll fix him."

"How?"

"My secret, but if you want, you can watch."

She tittered, then stumbled backward and crashed on the pallet. When she landed, her eye level was even with his groin.

"Your dick is too big."

He snorted.

"Mother of Shades and whores of gods, you definitely need a Heart."

He took a step towards the door.

"Afterward, we're going to have a long talk."

Darkness ensnared her moments later. She didn't see Tiny leave. When she woke again, both Hearts loomed over her, and Tiny paced just beyond. One was Omegryk's handler, and the other was a pale woman with bright eyes and light hair. She noted her clothing had been changed and the sick washed away.

Xeno focused on the woman Heart.

"You're a Forgotten Islander, aren't you?" she asked.

The Heart smiled.

"See? Returned to former glory," the Heart said to Tiny. She turned back to Xenomene, "Yes, I'm from the Isles."

"Scrotum of gods, I'm sick of Islanders."

The Heart's face darkened.

"Present company excluded, of course."

The Heart scoffed but left with the other in tow.

Tiny grabbed a chair, turned it backward and straddled it.

"Talk."

Xeno sat up and rubbed the sleep from her eyes. She felt rested, all traces of alcohol gone.

"Tiny, I don't want to hash this out now when I'm going to do it later. If you want to come, fine, I could use your help. Plus, I need your testimony. Be warned, you're gonna learn things you otherwise wish you hadn't. Under no circumstance are you to lash out in jealousy or anger, is that clear?"

"Jealousy?"

"Yes, I'm not stupid. I know you want to bed me. Hell, probably half the squads do, too. But none of that is happening today."

Why did she keep his hope alive? A flash of self-loathing roiled through her. Perhaps the fear of losing his friendship kept the fire stoked. He seemed an all or nothing kind of man, and if she had to choose between romance or nothing, she'd choose the latter.

"Xeno…I don't—"

"—Look!" she said, rising. "I'm more than a hole to fuck; I'm a person! You don't realize all the shit I've had to do just to keep people alive! I—"

She stopped herself, the tears welling up. She wouldn't go through this now.

"Xeno, I wasn't implying—I was going to say, if you ever need someone to talk to, I'm always your second. That has never changed, no matter what transpires. You give the order, and I'll crush his skull. By your decree, I'll stand by and say nothing, even if the heir is asking. You want my help? You have but to whisper, until death finds me, or old age take me."

Xeno glanced at him, revising her initial assessment of the giant Krey. Her heart lifted at his words. She cried in earnest, like the night she knew Jakeb would die.

Tiny wrapped his massive arms around her petite frame. Ear pressed against his chest, she could hear the comforting beat of his heart. As the tears dried, she pulled away when the weak moment passed.

"Tiny, there are things you're going to hear, and you might think differently afterward. It may turn out that what I say will turn your stomach. Is that something you want to risk?"

He was silent for a time.

"If I don't go, it'll eat at me for the rest of my life. I'm not someone who knows something transpired without the details. I don't care, nothing is inexcusable."

"Nothing?"

"If what you say about Bitcher is true, that might be."

She nodded.

"How do we get him to the Hive? What pretense?"

"Well, you could always say you want to introduce him to the heir, that he should have his own squad."

Xeno shook her head.

"Vanity won't work. He'll detect a trap leagues away."

"Well, you could always say you need his help picking out a replacement for you and the Heart we lost. Add on that you're picking up supplies and need the extra hands. Technically, he's now third in line in my squad and is expected to perform duties beyond the others."

Xeno nodded.

"That might work. Besides, if he can pick out replacements, he might try to find beautiful girls. He may grow tired of me and want a replacement lined up. Make it a command from you. He won't backtalk much."

Tiny smiled.

"Smart girl."

With their plan hatched, Xeno sent Tiny to make his rounds, rousing Spectre and Lyan, grabbing Lyan's Mind, and tracking down Bitcher. She instructed for them to don their dragon-plate armor. This would be a formal visit to House Eti. Xeno donned hers, strapping her blade over her right shoulder. Almost everyone wore theirs on the hip; Xeno proved unique in this regard. She tugged the steel from its sheath. Too many days had passed since she held it, but her lethality never dulled.

From the time she'd been old enough to hold a blade, it had always felt natural, an extension of her body. That became true for all Krey, but hers manifested the first time she touched a training rod. The feeling intensified over time. The last time any edge touched her in combat was during the duel with Mauler, more than two scores ago.

Just after lunch, she met the group in front of the barracks. Bitcher gave a wolfish smile. She knew his mind and his eyes were on her ass, just as she planned. The blindside would destroy him like a city crushed beneath a tidal wave.

The ko-don took the lead, walking across the camp. Everyone fell in step with Tiny bringing up the rear. The command tent marked their first destination. All the officers hurried to step aside once they saw the battle-ready Krey incoming. They were called the Black Tide for a reason, and once you saw their armor coming at you—battle or not—you bowed or you broke.

Jynerul Vikal found the courage to rise albeit slowly. His mouth fell slack and his eyes widened.

"Is there something I should be worried about?" he asked.

He did well to hide the quaver in his voice.

"We're not here for you, if that's what worries you," Xeno assured.

His immediate relief engulfed his features. A smirk flitted across her mouth, knowing how bad his knees shook within his trousers.

In times past, jyneruls would send the Krey to execute officers who were found guilty of grievous insubordination, murder, or known traitors. An archaic and seldom used custom, the retelling of practice still filled a dark corner of the officers' minds. Instead of being called field punishment or field execution, people dubbed it the black death as the Krey arrived in their flat-black dragon-plate armor.

The last instance occurred during the First Wizard's War.

"Thank the gods," Vikal said. "How can we help?"

"We're returning to House Eti, myself and those with me. This is a courtesy. We'll return as early as a few hours or as late as tonight."

Vikal nodded.

"Safe travels."

Xenomene spun on her heel and stalked to the building housing the portal masters. She hadn't made it to the door when one hurried out to greet them. A portal master would send them to House Eti, and one would accompany them so they could return. Mere moments passed before they fulfilled her wish; another mage returned with two porting stones.

The portal opened, and they stepped through, arriving at the base of the steps leading into House Eti. Xenomene ascended, the others nipped at her heels. She opened the front doors, pushing them ajar with a grunt of exertion. Once inside, she turned to catch Tiny removing the knife from his belt and smashing Bitcher in the head with the pommel.

He crumpled to the floor in a heap.

"That's going to hurt," Tiny grinned.

Xeno raised an eyebrow.

"You should've hit him harder."

Either by luck or because a runner had reached the heir before Xenomene and her company entered, the heir watched them from his office balcony.

"What in the Underworld's going on?" he roared.

Xeno glanced up and flashed a smile.

"Hi, Dad; we're home!"

She climbed the stairs, the entourage in tow, with Tiny bringing up the rear and carrying an unconscious Bitcher. They entered the heir's cove, and Tiny dropped Bitcher to the floor. He landed with a thud but otherwise didn't stir.

"Strip him," she snapped with a cold voice.

At once, the others bent to the task, even though they had no idea why, and stripped him to his undergarments.

The heir gave a furtive glance.

"Care to explain?"

The possessions piled in a corner, she ordered for his hands to be bound. Tiny and the others complied in silence.

"Somebody better start talking, or heads are going to roll," the heir warned, color rising in his cheeks.

"Leave us," Xenomene growled.

Everyone moved to leave, including Tiny.

"Not you, big man. You stay."

She stepped over to the heir's desk, leaned close, and talked in a low voice.

"We need someplace private where there's no chance of being overheard."

Daniel's eyes narrowed.

"You better have a damn good excuse, girl."

"I do, I can promise that, or my life's forfeit."

"Damn right it is. You better keep that promise, or it's going to be bad, and I'm not talking death either."

He rose and beckoned them. They followed to the back of his office, and he pulled aside the dust cover, a massive curtain preserving the oil painting of the first heir, Valin of Lor. The eight-foot-tall painting was the closest object to holy texts the Krey owned.

The heir pushed on the left side of the painting's frame. The canvas yawned at a ponderous pace and revealed a door behind. The heir produced a key, inserted it into the locking mechanism coated with dust and grease, and turned the bolt. Xeno held her breath, expecting it to be rusted, but it opened without a sound. Daniel stepped through, ushering them in.

Once again, Tiny lumbered behind carrying Bitcher like a sack of feed over his shoulder.

Daniel lit a torch and closed the door behind them. He took the lead, descending narrow stone stairs. They went deep, much further than the single, extended flight they ascended earlier.

The cold and silent dark loomed unforgivingly.

The stairs finally stopped and opened into a hall. Daniel raised his torch to the right, contemplating for a brief moment before turning left. Another door materialized at the end of the passageway. He produced a different key and unlocked it.

Xenomene entered a room rivaling the size of the entire first floor of House Eti. A massive wood desk with five chairs clustered around it. A couple of beds lay further in the room, no more than thirty paces from the desk. Beyond, in the blackness where torchlight couldn't reach, Xeno made out large shapes resembling wooden crates and other mechanical contraptions.

Tiny put Bitcher down, this time without dropping him. Xenomene sent silent thanks as she wanted time with the heir before he woke. Daniel lit half a dozen more torches along the wall. His movements were halting, bottled rage in each step. He sat at the desk and lit three candles. He placed the last torch in a vacant holder on the wall and plopped in his chair.

"Talk!"

"It's a long story and goes back to Cape Gythmel."

Daniel held up a hand.

"If it's a story, and a long one, you leave nothing out. I'm talking how you felt, what you thought, what happened, down to the last, vivid detail. I don't want a half-truth tale of woe or whatever the fuck you're about to spin. I don't give a damn if it's disgusting, ghastly, crude, or embarrassing for you. Anything less than the complete, unequivocal, and all-inclusive truth will bring about the quick end of your life. Do I make my meaning clear?"

Xenomene nodded.

"The Mark of the Profane."

"The Mark—?" he started, then shook his head and gave a small chuckle. "Oh no, girlie. There are things much, much worse."

Xenomene swallowed.

What the fuck did I just get myself into?

Daniel shifted his eyes to Tiny.

"Why the fuck is your ugly mug here?"

Xeno glanced back in time to see Tiny give a shrug.

"He's a witness, and I'll call on his testimony."

"Are you sure you want him present for the entire proceeding?"

Xeno hesitated.

"Yes."

"Very well. I'll try to refrain from interrupting, but I'll expect answers to my questions."

Daniel sighed.

"Alright, let's hear a tale."

"It started at Cape Gythmel. After the first battle, Bitcher raped me."

"WHAT!" Daniel bellowed, coming to his feet.

He withdrew his sword and cleared the corner of his desk to behead the comatose man. Xeno held up her hands to stop him.

"Please, let me finish!"

Some of the fire died from his eyes, and he slammed the weapon on the table. Resuming his seat, he withdrew parchment, an ink bottle, and a quill from the drawer. He dipped the tip and began writing.

"Continue."

"When I say rape, I mean I neither gave my consent nor resisted his efforts. I was lying naked in my tent—"

"Do you always lounge around nude?" Daniel peered up, waiting for a response.

"When I don't need to be anywhere, and no one's going to interrupt me, yes. I get hot at night."

"Do you sleep naked?"

"What the fuck does anything have to do with that?"

"I'm establishing tendencies, habits, and a baseline of events."

He rose from his seat, his face turning purple.

"I'm already fucking pissed, and this is going to take a lot fucking longer if you fucking question me about my fucking inquiries, you fucking cunt. So, do you fucking sleep naked or not?"

She swallowed.

"Yes," she said in a small voice.

He grunted, sat, and returned to writing. Xeno took that as a cue to continue.

"He came in and stared. I said to him, 'Then do it, if you want to chance the consequences, or get the fuck out of my tent. Your choice.'"

Daniel chuckled but didn't say anything. She continued.

"Instead of leaving, he approached, touched me, and I didn't tell him to stop. He took that as consent, performed oral sex on me and then took me. While at first—"

The heir held up his hand to stop her.

"How did he *take* you?"

"What the hell does that have to do with anything?" Tiny interjected.

Daniel shot him a glare.

"Keep silent, or I'll have your tongue out. May take it myself, boy. If that cunt flap you call a mouth opens again before I address you, I'll make it my cock holder!"

His flinty gaze turned back to Xenomene, and he raised a brow.

"Did he tie you down? Hurt you? Hold a dirk to your throat?"
"He took me in Islander fashion."
The heir tossed the quill on the desk, rubbed his eyes, and spoke with a low and throaty tone.
"I'm losing my fucking patience, bitch. I told you at the beginning, 'down to the last, vivid detail.' What the hell does Islander fashion mean?"
Xenomene stirred, but finally spoke.
"He fucked my ass. Is that what you want to hear?"
The look on the Daniel's face told her that he hadn't expected the statement.
"They do that?"
"You've never heard about it?"
"I thought it was just obtuse bantering, an exaggeration of something else. I never thought it real. Do I look like an Islander, or like I've had a woman from there?"
"It's real. Anyways," she hurried past the detailed information, "once we stopped for breath, I noticed him applying lotion to his…dick. He said it intensifies pleasure during sex and leaves both partners in a drug-induced stupor. Hours later, he left, and the drug's effects faded. I plotted to get justice, and it required me enlisting the help of Warlock Lakayre."
The heir groaned.
"Oh, I wish you wouldn't have. I detest the bastard."
Xenomene felt her heart lift slightly.
If the heir hates the warlock, I might come out of this alive.
"Continue."
She told him everything, the warlock's words, and the promise she made not to maim or slay Bitcher. She struggled over the Heart's portion of the tale, and the whole reveal stung as insults to her memory. Both men winced when Xenomene admitted to severing Bitcher's testicle.
"The Heart was a witness? Why isn't she here?"
"She's dead, Heir. I wrote you a letter explaining it, as well as a letter requesting another person replace me in my old squad. Don't you read them?"
"Fuck no! Do you realize how many pieces of paper I get every damn day? If it doesn't say someone died at the top, I pass over it."
Xeno rolled her eyes and recounted their subsequent fallout and reconciliation, spilling the truth about the Mind and his limited involvement, and the quest at Cape Gythmel. She paused the story when the Mind walked in on her and Bitcher.
Daniel raised an eyebrow.
"Anything else? Did you leave any details out?"
Xeno shook her head, sighed, and cast a glance at Tiny before she spoke.
"I took Bitcher and the Mind together in Dlad City."
"Holy Shades," the heir mumbled. "Why did I never find a girl like you?"
"This happened before the runes were put in place by Warlock Lakayre. He walked in on us…and it just went from there. It's not like we planned the

encounter."

Daniel looked up at the ceiling as if talking to his deity.

"We're going to have a long talk."

Focusing on the ko-don, he spoke.

"Continue."

Recounting the brutal rape, her eyes watered, and the words died in her constricting throat. Dutifully, she trudged on, speaking of all she could remember.

"Is this true?" Daniel asked Tiny.

"Yes, Heir."

"Is that all?"

Xenomene shook her head.

"Continue, lass, if you can."

Her story picked up with Bitcher being present when she awoke, the implied threats, and keeping the Mind and the Heart's lives hanging over her head. Without reservation, she admitted to plotting Bitcher's murder and selecting the hardest mission for Tiny's squad. The plan failed, and the Heart paid for Xenomene's sins. The story finished when she recounted the events of last night.

At this time, Xeno stopped talking, and Tiny recounted his tale of finding her, the extent of her injuries, and the odd but noticeable behavior between Bitcher and Xenomene.

Daniel leaned back in his chair, his fingers steepled. He blew out a breath and scratched his head.

"That's quite a story."

"It's all true."

"Of that, I have no doubt. Even if your side of the story is skewed against him, he's going to die. The question is what to do with you."

"With her?" Tiny spoke aghast. "Hasn't she suffered enough? To give her the Mark—"

"Shut your fucking mouth, boy, before I throat-fuck you!" Daniel thundered.

His voice softened as he turned back to Xeno.

"He's right, of course, you've suffered enough. And as far as breaking your oath with Lakayre, well, I never liked the snooty son of a bitch. All his superior and judgmental shit. To top it off, Meristal has to be so cock-eyed and sappy over that pretentious cunt. Gods, I can fuck better than that bastard, and the redhead knows it—"

He stopped, looking at the two Krey.

"Shall we take his head now?"

"No," Xeno said. "I have noticed something about Bitcher. His real name is Jakeb, and two very different personalities fill his head. There's the side I almost fell in love with—Jakeb, the kind, caring, and gentle person. Then, there's Bitcher, his other personality. Before I punished him, he coexisted as a perfect harmony of the two. I think since that day, something happened inside of him, and he went crazy. I don't think it's right to kill him."

"Ha!" the heir barked a laugh. "I don't give a good god damn. As for your misdeeds, you're absolved of breaking your oath to Warlock Lakayre. You're right, you hold no allegiance to him. You're Krey, he isn't. End of story."

"Bitcher said the last—"

"—The last heir changed it? Yeah, I changed it back in the first month I took over. Ain't no way I'll let my Krey be beholden to some sorry excuse for…yeah, fuck him!"

"He lied to me? He lied!" she screamed.

She spun around and kicked Bitcher in the gut.

"You son of a bitch!"

She kicked him again.

"You asshole!"

Another kick. Each scream elicited another kick.

"Good for nothing lying cunt! I should have! Cut! Your! Dick! Off! YOU FUCK!"

By that time, Tiny grabbed her, pulling her away. Bitcher curled in a ball, doubled over in pain, and coughed a storm. After a few moments, Bitcher stirred to his knees, noticing his bound wrists and bare self.

"What's going on?" he gasped. Daniel ignored him. Tiny moved her far enough away that no one could eavesdrop on their words.

"I'm sorry, Tiny. I'm sorry you were an audience to all those terrible details. I'm sorry I'm an oath breaker, and you had to listen to everything—"

He silenced her with massive arms wrapped around her. His muscles were taut and tense, like a predator waiting to explode into action against an unwary prey. Xeno pulled away quickly, not wanting to linger and send the wrong message, and returned to Daniel's desk.

Her hands trembled.

"Well," Daniel said, "let's drag him back topside. It's been a long time since we've had an execution."

He stood.

Everyone shouted at once, all except for Xenomene. Bitcher cried for clemency and screamed that she'd told nothing but lies. Tiny whooped and hollered like an adolescent, asking if he could behead him, and Daniel shouted back at Bitcher.

"No!" Xeno broke in.

Everyone quieted. She shook her head.

"No, there'll be no execution. I declare Mon Kyyr Gr'bakth!"

"What the fuck is that?" Bitcher and Tiny asked in unison.

"That son," Daniel said as he perched on the front of the desk, "means you're totally fucked. Mon Kyyr Gr'bakth is from the shared language of the trolls and dwaven—well, their former dwaven tongue—which loosely translates to 'settle all debts.' It means it's just you, her, and two swords."

His attention went to her.

"How in the name of the gods do you know about the ancient tradition?

Shit that started back with the fourth heir, the first dwaven heir of House Eti."

He cocked his head.

"I'm surprised you're aware of it, let alone can pronounce it, and rather well I might add. It's been a long time since I've heard my native tongue spoken."

"You're wizardkind," Tiny blurted.

"Half," Daniel corrected. "Very well, Xeno, if anyone deserves Mon Kyyr Gr'bakth, it's you."

"Can I watch?" Tiny asked.

"If she wishes it," Daniel said.

"No."

"Xeno—" Tiny started.

"No."

"I just—"

She turned to face him.

"If you want to have a friendship with me past today, you won't say another word and leave now."

Tiny paused for a moment, searching her face and the severity of the scowl. He nodded and left.

Daniel cut Bitcher loose and tossed the condemned a sword from the rack as Xeno undressed. She staged her armor and clothes until she had nothing on but undergarments, the way Mon Kyyr Gr'bakth was intended. She unsheathed her steel and closed on Bitcher.

"What the fuck are you doing, bitch?"

"I want you to hurt."

Bitcher lunged, and she riposted with ease, pivoted her blade, and sliced a shallow cut on his fighting arm.

"Drawing blood so soon?" Daniel heckled. "Not good for you."

Xeno stopped and turned to him, pointing her weapon.

"Keep silent. This is my Mon Kyyr Gr'bakth, and it'll be as I wish it."

While distracted, Bitcher swung overhead, hoping to end the fight at once. She snapped her head back and stepped into the attack, driving the flat of the sword's guard into his face, shattering his nose.

He stumbled back as blood gushed.

"Did you think it was going to be easy?" she goaded.

"Fucking whore! You broke my nose!"

"This isn't a game, Bitcher. This is the end for you. I've planned this for a long time, waiting for the perfect moment."

He swung again, from his right shoulder down. She met his blade, testing her strength against his, but as a man, he proved much stronger. He tried to lock up their steel, but she spun past him, hitting the back of his head with her pommel.

Bitcher staggered, caught himself, and turned.

"Do you know when the last time I was cut, Bitcher? Two scores ago. Forty years!"

"Then, it's past time you bled, bitch."

She feigned a high strike, changing direction in mid stroke, the tip of the blade whistling past his gut, rendering another shallow cut. Blood beaded a thin, red line.

He gave in to his rage and charged.

His blows rained down like a blacksmith hammering iron. In the bloodlust, he was faster and stronger, but Xeno refrained from entering herself, wanting to savor this moment.

She matched each blow, blocking, parrying, riposting, and chipping away at him when he left himself open. She yearned to remember this moment, every exquisite cut, the sweet satisfaction of her steel passing through flesh. Never once did she sever muscle.

His body wept like a mutilated tomato. Even in the bloodlust, he still couldn't match her. As he drove her back, she dodged, juked, and spun away. The longer this went, the slower he moved.

Blades whistled, but she materialized like a ghost, shifting before he registered the movement. She laughed as the dance continued, taunting him. With each missed blow, she cackled, something high and bright. Xeno refrained from landing strikes with all her strength. Her counters were just enough to turn his steel aside. She could've ended the facade long ago, but she played a different game.

Before long, she danced circles around him, riddling his body with wounds. Sidestepping a giant swing, she closed, driving the sword's guard and pommel into his face, nose, jaw, and throat. He lunged in desperation. She sidestepped to his right, latched onto his sword's wrist, and drove her left palm through his elbow, shattering the joint.

A scream pealed through the air as bone jutted through skin. His sword dropped uselessly to the ground. She swept his leg out from under him.

Picking up his weapon, she twirled both in her hands like toys. Bitcher rolled to climb to his feet, planting his left hand on the floor to push himself up. She drove his blade through the hand, pinning him to the floor. He screamed so loud her ears rang.

Xeno circled behind him.

With Bitcher on his knees and helpless, she drove the other through his right foot. Steel entered at the arch of his foot and exited at the top. He was beyond screams now, he just grunted and groaned, his veins bulging in his throat. Blood wept from his body, and the red glow faded from his eyes.

Walking to the front, she jerked the steel from his hand. Moving behind him again, she slid the sword in his undergarments, severing the last scrap of concealment.

She pulled the sword out of his foot, and he crumbled to the floor. The weapon rack caught her gaze. She dropped the two she held and removed several more blades from the rack as Bitcher rolled to his back. By the time he achieved this, she'd returned. She drove a sword through his left forearm, missing the vein as intended, pinning him to the floor. She kicked his right arm, the broken one, away and drove steel through the hand, giving him matching scars.

"In more uncivilized areas," she spoke, "they crucify murderers and rapists. Alas, I don't have a cross, but…" she lifted another saber and drove it through his right shin.

He screamed again, jerking against the blades that held him down.

"…I can make do without."

She plucked another sword and drove it through his other shin.

In all truth, she didn't put him in a typical crucifixion pose, but spread-eagled. She picked up her blade again and began cutting small, shallow cuts all up and down his legs, on the insides of his thighs, over his kneecaps, and on his feet. She continued, working up his belly, chest, and arms.

Satisfied, she dropped the weapon and straddled him. He flinched in pain. She took the meaty portion of a closed fist and hammered his cheek until she heard a satisfying crunch, breaking the bone and eye socket.

"Just like you did to me," she said, leaning back and admiring her work.

Standing, she picked her blade up again and stood between his legs, looking down at his manhood.

"A lesser person would rob you of it, but I'm better than that."

She reached down and pulled the stretchy flesh of his scrotum, then slid the edge through the tissue between his testicles, cutting a gash.

Blood flowed bright, gleaming like rubies. His screams turned to grunts, then sobs. She worked his flesh over until cuts covered every inch of his body except the face.

"I'm leaving your face, so if you ever look in a mirror again, you'll see what once was. As for the rest of you, now you're just as ugly on the outside as the inside."

She straddled him again and leaned over his face. Her lips were mere inches from his ears.

"I only took one testicle, Bitcher. If you ever find redemption, I've not robbed you of a worthy future."

A smile flitted across her face. This was justice; he earned every cut.

She removed the swords from his limbs, jerking them up without grace. Her fingers dug into his hair, and she pulled him up to his knees. Tip of her blade planted in the dirt, she stood facing the heir. He looked comical with his mouth hanging open.

He swallowed a few times.

"Finish him."

She shook her head.

"No."

"Finish him. That's not a suggestion, girl, but a command."

"No!"

"Cunt, by the gods, I swear, you'll die beside him!"

"This is my Mon Kyyr Gr'bakth! Not yours! I decide. Your rank has no meaning here!"

Her hand tightened on her hilt. The tip left the ground, but she didn't raise the weapon. Not yet.

Not if she didn't have to.

"He dies! After everything you told me, he dies!"

Daniel snatched up his sword from the desk and stormed forward.

"So help me, I'll do it myself. Stand aside!"

"No! He lives with this. That's worse than death!"

She stood in his way and lifted the steel point up to a middle guard. The heir paused and evaluated the movement.

"You'd dare raise your weapon against me? Your heir?"

His face flushed red with rage, and his eyes burned scarlet. Xeno noted his bloodlust but refrained.

"Withdraw, or I'll remove you!" Spittle splashed her face. When she didn't move, he grabbed her and threw her to the floor, raising his sword at her before coming to his senses.

Xeno had never crossed blades with the heir. Two ages his junior, if not more, she'd received training with the elyfian outside House Eti. She claimed the honor alone, one that everyone envied. She knew Daniel was aware that she toyed with Bitcher, never exerting herself. The question that undoubtedly rolled through his mind was whether he stood a chance either.

I could destroy you so easily!

"I'm the heir, not you," he breathed. "My word is law, my commands absolute! He dies."

He circled around to Bitcher's back, to drive the saber straight down his spine. Even a grand maghai of healing couldn't undo that.

"Stop!" she cried. "Don't! I want him alive! He must suffer! I'll do anything if you spare him! He needs to live with this pain!"

When Daniel didn't stop, her desperation rose.

The sword tip rested on the base of Bitcher's spine.

Daniel took a deep breath.

The blade rose, loomed for a second before the fatal plunge.

A stray thought entered her mind, Daniel's random rambling. He said something about a redhead and Warlock Lakayre. He hated Lakayre because of a woman he desired. No...Daniel had fucked her, and Xenomene was a redhead.

It was a long shot. The thought sparked a possible venue for a refrain. She rose to her knees and shouted.

"I'll fuck you!"

Daniel stopped, pausing.

"What?"

Xeno picked herself up off the floor. Tears streamed down her face. She glanced at Bitcher, the broken man, and swallowed. Thank the gods she paid attention to the heir when he went on tangents. If she ever found this redhead he spoke of, she'd thank her in person.

"If you spare him, you can bed me."

"Why?" he asked, voice filled with perplexity. "And your cunt ain't that holy."

"Because if it's the only way I can keep you from killing him, so be it."

Daniel lowered his saber.

"No, not that."

His eyes shifted, the scarlet fading.

"Why do you want him to live?"

She swallowed hard, faced with the rawness of emotions and the weight of truth.

"Somewhere inside him is Jakeb, a man I could've loved, and I can't kill him, but I can punish Bitcher until he dies. That's what he deserves."

The heir paused, sighed, then nodded.

"Your Mon Kyyr Gr'bakth, your rules."

She dipped her head.

"Send for a Heart and make sure they bring a collar."

"I'll have Tiny do it. I bet he's only halfway up the stairs, waiting, no doubt. Er—"

"Business first," she reproved. "I'm a woman of my word, regardless of my testimony. The details can wait."

Daniel nodded and left.

"Kill me," Jakeb whispered.

Xeno knelt beside him. "I can't, for the sake of the part that is buried deep within."

"Please?"

"Jakeb, given time, you could've had my love. Hell, maybe you would've sired my children, if I was to have any."

She kissed him one last time.

"You fucked it all up the day you left me for dead."

"I'll find a way to kill you, bitch!"

He spat, and blood speckled her pixie features. She made no move to wipe it.

"Ah, I was wondering when you would be joining us, Bitcher."

She wiped the phlegm away, flinging it off her fingers. He chuckled.

"That wasn't so bad; you've put worse things on my face."

She leaned in closer.

"What's the saying? 'No wrath of the gods compares to a woman who nurtures scorn?' Looks like you just discovered it."

"I'll find a way, I swear! If you think what I did was bad before, you best kill me now!"

She shook her head.

"No, I don't think so. I want you to live and plot your revenge and every time you're ready to carry it out, just look into the mirror and remember what I did to you. I want you to live with physical and mental pain, knowing I toyed with you and could've ended your life. As far as emotional anguish, well…"

She leaned in, whispering in his ear.

"I'm going to fuck every Krey in Dlad City, the goblin, too, but I'm starting with the heir. I want you to think about all those men inside me, enjoying what you'll never have again."

She pulled back and relished the torment on his face, then leaned closer.

"And I'm going to enjoy it more than I ever did with you."

In breathy words, she told him every dirty and salacious thought that came to mind, painting a vivid and erotic scene for him to obsess over. She spared no detail in the acts, positions, or the number of partners she'd take. It brought a smile to her face knowing the distress she caused him.

She stood as the realization sank in, and she gave a malicious smile. He believed the evil glimmering in her eye. The desolation on his face was more than she had hoped for.

"Thank you for this," she said. "I'll cherish it forever."

She took a step back and kicked him in the face, putting all her weight, strength, and fury into the blow. He fell back, cracking his head against the floor, and oblivion took him.

Chapter 28: Disciples of The One

Glato smoothed the front of his red silk robes, garments befitting his rank. He plastered on a smile for those present—the peasants, vagabonds, sinners, the lazy, and inept—and tried to deescalate the moment.

They're all disgusting and not worthy of the One.

If it were his decision, he'd drive them all from the city.

His dark hair lay combed to the side, and his dark brown eyes sparkled. The immaculate goatee was twisted, bundled together, and coated in an oily sheen. Maybe he should trim it? It might make him look more dapper than an ancient clergyman.

The woman standing before him cursed at him, and he kept his disdain hidden, but only just. She had no idea who she yelled at, no idea what he was capable of, or the power he wielded, both within the Order and without.

The woman's anger smothered her voice, and panic shone in her bulging eyes. Neck veins throbbed in cadence with the verbal lashing. Her hand gripped her son's shoulder, and she backed away from him like Glato was diseased.

If anything, she's the one carrying the filth in her blood.

"Why do you fear for the boy's future?" Glato asked.

He truly didn't understand. Most leapt at the opportunity he was giving her. A well-practiced smile hid his confusion and contempt.

"Why do you fear the glory of the Light, the works of the One? Yes, his life will be of devotion, a duty for the One's children, but it's a life of righteousness."

"I don't care about righteousness!"

Spittle flew from the gaps in her teeth. Her rancid breath rivaled her body odor.

"My son won't be joining your cause."

"It's irrevocable; it's the law—do you oppose the sanctions of the land?"

He wanted to blast the woman to the Underworld rather than put on a facade.

The woman shook her head as tears rolled down her dirty features. Streaks smudged her face. Most parents didn't need to be reminded of the law; they gave their kids over willingly. The wealthy offered enormous contributions that went in the child's stead.

The lower and middle classes leapt at the chance to give their kids a better life. They'd still be allowed to see their children from time to time, but once they became a disciple, they discouraged family ties until they reached the age of maturity. By then, they were so brainwashed with propaganda that they didn't want to return to their families.

Most folks didn't understand that, or they did, and they kept quiet about it...for control.

Children could be twisted, influenced; they were malleable. If they were told something was natural, they'd believe and accept it, all stemming from the trust they put in the adult. And that's how Glato and the Disciples operated.

Adults were harder to mold.

Her resolve melted under Glato's gaze.

"Why my son? Look at him! He's poor, a nobody! He's dumb to boot."

"He'll be given an education—"

"—Not stupid! Dumb! He can't speak!"

"That doesn't matter. He was tested, and the Disciples of the One will see him remanded in our care—for the work and glory of the One."

Glato's patience frayed, and his temper boiled to the surface; soon, he'd lose control in view of everyone. No disciple could afford to let the public know they were only human in the end. As living visionaries of the One, they had to appear…more.

He nodded to the guards standing with him. They stepped forward and separated the boy from the screaming mother. Rage flickered in her eyes, and obscenities spewed from her mouth. The guards dragged the voiceless boy away.

Once out of sight, the mother crumpled to the ground, sobbing. Glato glanced down in disgust and pity. He hid both beneath a practiced mask.

He knelt in front of her.

"The One will forgive your remarks, and I absolve your sins. In the name of the One, I pray blessings upon this unfortunate child."

He placed a hand softly on her head. She hit it away.

"Don't touch me, you vile creature!"

She spat in his face.

Glato gathered himself, wiping his face with a red handkerchief and a trembling hand. From his belt, he pulled a small leather pouch of coins. He dumped half into his waiting palm and weighed the coins for a few heartbeats.

"The One has shown you kindness and mercy today, and you spit in the face of a holy follower. You were to be rewarded for the sacrifice of your son to the One's service, but in light of your inappropriate behavior, you'll only receive half."

He threw the coins down in the muck, then waved at the gathered people before he turned and left.

"Damn you!" she screamed. "Damn you and whatever One you serve! If he was such a caring and compassionate god, he wouldn't allow you to take my son from me!"

Glato rounded the corner of a building and let the mask drop, his face contorting with the rage he felt on the inside. He clenched his fists and took a deep breath, paused for a count of five, then exhaled. He walked on, heels striking hard on the dirt road.

Bloody ungrateful cur!

He did his job, as instructed by the archbishop and their laws. His robes billowed in a quick gust of wind. He folded his hands behind his back and put his head down, oblivious to the surroundings.

The Disciples of the One had grown stronger for over a legend. They were the prominent religion in the south and had migrated north over the years. The last few domains lay within reach, but the Marcoalyn and Ralloc domains were less apt to adopt.

Agnostic heathens.

The further north they traveled, the more unyielding the cultures became. Even the people of the Geim domain were tame compared to the lands farther south—Elysys or Heaven's Spire. If there was a center of Ermaeyth for sin, it was Heaven's Spire.

Well, it used to be.

Heaven's Spire had been purged of vagrants, riffraff, and dregs, and became a capital of the One. All who didn't repent or convert were cast out. The woes that once plagued Heaven's Spire migrated to Elysys and beyond. Many fled Merlul across the Golden Sea, another nexus of sin, greed, and carnal lust.

In Merlul, depending on the hour and location within the city, people walked the streets naked. There was public intoxication, murderers and cutpurses, thieves, public sex, even the sanctity of marriage was laughable as everyone shared spouses—a sexual ritual disguised as a holy rite. They worshiped heathen gods.

In the Kran Empire, just south of Merlul, they held gladiatorial games, with slavery, drugs, and gluttony—some sunk so low they partook of bestiality. Sometimes, such capital punishments were reserved for women.

The same could be found in Elysys and more. It wasn't uncommon to hear about the raping of men and women, pedophiles walked openly, and homosexuality was rampant.

The One should smite those cities, but he must have reasons to abstain.

But Glato didn't believe that. He followed another path. The migration of Glato's Order played right into his master's plans. Pinnacles of sin were needed, even treasured, and it obfuscated his darker purpose.

His steps finally led him to the stone stairs that ascended to the front doors of the citadel. Two young pages opened them as he drew near. Glato didn't acknowledge them as his feet left the exterior stone for the marble interior. From here, he took off his shoes, as was the custom. Shoeless, he grabbed slippers and continued deeper inside.

As he entered the main chamber where the congregation sat, he walked up to the white marble basin and washed his hands with Purified Water, signifying the washing of sins away. He placed a dab of water to the forehead and one over the heart.

The simple ritual complete, he made his way to a side door, one closed off to the public. The door led to a small, empty room. Once shut behind him, he pressed his hands against the back wall and it slid away, revealing another hallway and ascending stairs. He pushed the false wall back in place and continued up the stairs.

Today was their gathering, and if he didn't hurry, he'd be late.

Well, not late, but not first!

Glato was always first. He liked to get the best seat, the furthest from the door, and his back to the smallest part of the room, so he could watch everyone and everything. The younger disciples would run in right before the start, but the older the disciples advanced, the earlier they arrived. Perhaps age and pace had something to do with it.

Glato entered the room, the first to arrive, and found his choice seat. The elders arrived in short order, filing in at a ponderous rate, like a turtle watching a stalk of corn grow. More trickled in, younger but not young. Finally, the chairs were nearly full.

Glato surveyed the people gathered. Large, plush chairs with thick, soft padding covered in dyed leather matched the robes of the disciples. The room smelled musky, but something else lingered beneath, and for some reason, it reminded him of impending death.

This meeting wasn't for the countless, meddlesome worries, but the true business of the Order. Here, they'd decide actions to further their cause—salvation in the Light or some such nonsense. Glato spied a deep blue—almost purple—chair in the midst.

The bishop's chair?

It was just as well. He needed to hear what Glato discovered.

A disciple cleared his throat as he moved close. Glato turned to see the man, Osco.

"Disciple Osco."

He gave him a bow of humbleness he didn't feel. The gesture was returned.

"Disciple Glato."

Glato saw the nervousness in the man's darting eyes.

"The bishop's presence is a rare treat for us lowly disciples. I wonder what divine words he'll bring forth."

Probably utter bull shit!

Still, Glato played his part as expected, sycophantic and awed.

"Indeed. What words?"

The bishop's presence would steal his moment, but the words would reach him regardless if he attended or not. Glato yearned for the accolades for what he'd done for the Order. He'd been studying the prophecies of the One almost since he came into the service. None knew more or better than Glato, other than the One who wrote them.

If he wrote them. If the god even existed.

In hushed tones, the decrepit men mingled, awaiting the chime to begin. As he thought it, the small bell was picked up by the bishop's aide and rung. As the sound died in the stone, circular room, the disciples moved to their assigned chairs and sat. As soon as they did, the bishop entered, and they all rose again.

Glato was the first to rise. The bishop's eyes found him, and a small smile touched his lips.

The bishop was a tall man, taller than most, but still came a half head shorter than Glato. The man's hair had once been a full, magnificent blond, but was now thinned and silvered. The top of the bishop's head was devoid of hair, and the sides clung to the last remnants. His light blue eyes had lost their dazzle, and his face clutched deep lines from the long years of servitude.

If I have to look like that in four ages, I might want to pass on the job.

"Be seated," the bishop said as he sat.

The others returned to their seats as the bishop leaned forward.

"What news of the One's work?"

The others launched into tales and deeds they'd done, people they'd saved, their charitable work, and the outreach program to Ruhkhi. The latter was a week's travel on foot or three days by horseback from Crystal Falls, their headquarters in the Geim domain.

After each finished their tales, all seeking the bishop's favor, the treasury aide spoke of funds, used for the order and for the less fortunate. Glato didn't envy the job, counting all that money, documenting everything coin and reason for coming in and out of the vault.

Glato wouldn't have minded bathing in those endless piles. Money bought power. Their liberal, altruistic use for temple upkeep, food and supplies, clothing, and giving to the impoverished never allowed the vault to encroach barrenness. Like a dammed river, the vault pooled the wealth, the coins always trickling back in.

"Very well," the bishop spoke in his soft, old voice. "There's one more matter before we adjourn. I've long advocated for the prophecies. I knew that one day, those prophecies would come to fruition. I study to this day."

The bishop paused; his eyes locked on to Glato's.

"Much like you, young Glato."

Astonishment ran to Glato's core. He sat riveted. To be singled out by the bishop was, by all accounts, a great thing. Glato's unease sharpened, wary of the old man. He believed the bishop to be a mockery, one who professed the will of the One himself. Glato never believed the One would lower himself to speak to a mere mortal, and a sinful one at that. They were all sinners, doomed to an eternity without the One's grace.

"Thank you, Bishop," Glato managed with a bow of the head. He feigned embarrassment and humility.

"Don't thank me, young Glato. Thank the One for divine influence…" the bishop trailed off. "Before we delve into that, there's a bit of sad news. The archbishop has ascended to be with the One. He walked the hallowed halls of the dead. He passed in his sleep, and it was peaceful, so fret not."

Each one of them bowed their heads for a moment, saddened by the news.

"Since passing, his last testament has been read, and he named me the next archbishop."

Everyone flung themselves to the floor and bowed in reverence, uttering oaths of fealty to him and the One and some other such nonsense.

"Rise, children. Rise."

They found their seats, tears of joy and adoration streaming, everyone except Glato. He was in too much shock.

The archbishop dead?

The archbishop had been in the role since Glato's induction to the Order. It was baffling, one that Glato's mind couldn't begin to comprehend. He had plans to remove the man, secretive and underhanded, but now…

"Glato?" the archbishop called.

He snapped from the reverie and back to the aging man.

"Yes, Archbishop? What command do you have for me?"

"Tell everyone about the revelations that will now be fulfilled because of you."

Glato's mind reeled. How did the archbishop know what he'd found? Was he a *real* vessel of the One? How else could he have known about the boy?

"There's a revelation," Glato began. "The One will deliver us from damnation. The time will come when the Order of the One will rise up and take hold of the land from its early seedlings. A silent child will be the vessel of the One, coming from the world of men, and hold both the life of the One and death of the grave. The child shall be named ruler. A devout guardian will die, a lord of darkness destroyed, and the mountain that weeps a song shall go silent."

He glanced at the others around the room.

"That's the first part."

"Go on, tell them the rest," the archbishop encouraged.

"The land promised to the loyal followers shall be the seat of power, taken from the clutches of vile and sinful at the foot of the mountain. Forever against the rises, their reign shall be absolute in the service of the One, and lead by the silent ruler that holds sway over life and death for all of time. All shall be saved by either Salvation or Judgment, for they are a blade forged to do the bidding of the One."

"Very good."

The archbishop smiled, his joy evident. He eyed the circled chairs.

"Who can tell me if that revelation is coming to pass?"

"I can," Glato spoke before anyone stepped in.

This was his moment.

"Continue."

"The revelation is coming to pass. Revelations, like prophecies, tell you what will happen, but not necessarily in order or direct interpretations. Any one thing can happen before the other, not the how or why, but that they will."

"Yes. Good."

"The lord of darkness has already been destroyed: Hagen."

"But what of the dying guardian?" Osco blurted.

"He's already dead," Glato said. "This is a double-edged revelation. Hagen was also the guardian. Before he became the lord of darkness, he woke the magic in the world. From that power, he became mad. The man he once was died as he sequestered himself in darkness, thus the double-edge."

"Excellent," the archbishop said. "I'm truly overjoyed your studies made you so sharp, young Glato. This is pleasing."

Glato swallowed, still talking.

"Now that we've found the child who can't speak," Glato continued, "he must be raised and groomed to become the ruler for the One."

Glato shook his head, letting insincere wonderment cover his face.

"I never thought I'd live to see this day."

"Neither did I," the archbishop said. "Now, all that remains is what?"

"The mountain that weeps a sad song shall go silent." Glato finished.

"Yes, good. I've great faith in you, *Bishop* Glato," the archbishop declared.

Immediately everyone threw themselves from their chairs, and they fell to the ground praying and swearing oaths much like before. The archbishop rose and crossed to Glato. The archbishop held Glato's shoulders and embraced him in a hug.

"You do me proud, son of the One."

Glato bowed his head, unable to speak.

"Thank you, Archbishop."

He was too dumbfounded by the turn of events. He'd just been promoted, an honor for one so young. Glato couldn't believe his luck, and he didn't have to scheme for it.

He wondered silently how his master would take the news. Surely it'd be welcomed, but somewhere deep inside, he was afraid to find out.

Chapter 29: Ralloc

Meristal schooled her features and stifled a yawn. Her backside had gone numb, and the Islander king had yet to make his appearance.

Pompous bastard! Making us wait.

She knew it didn't take *this* long to get here from the main gate. But she sat, waiting, like a proper consul. After three hours, patience evaporated like the feeling in her lower extremities.

The king had arrived at their walls just before dawn. Ten thousand men stood at his back, a laughable amount compared to the army stationed in Ralloc. They outnumbered them five to one, coupled with the advantage of high walls, but the king didn't come for war, or so he proclaimed.

The banner signified peace, white with a green and brown olive branch embroidered in the center. He sent his commanding officer to negotiate a truce for them to enter the city. Meristal herself wanted to go down and meet them, but the War Council forbade the action, telling her it would reflect poorly if she did.

"In the eyes of the king, it'd be as if you're less than his commanding officer," Tyku advised. "I'll deal with the parlay."

And so he went.

Now, boredom had set in. She spied Judas in the crowd, and he looked as brooding as ever. She also spied Toddison—Todd Wynters—and he fidgeted with excitement. Each passing week, she saw him more often and did her best to avoid the endless, incessant questions. He roamed freely, talking with many, asking questions, taking notes, then publishing in that riffraff of a column at the *New Suns Times.*

She liked him, his personality, his hunger, despite his annoyance. She'd been similar when younger, the whole of Ermaeyth unfurling before her. As time wore on, the newness vanished. His wide blue eyes roamed the room, his hand scratching in haste, washed anew with pent-up energy.

Good for you, Todd. Write until your damn hand falls off, and you'll ask less tomorrow.

She stifled another yawn and squirmed in her seat.

Meristal debated on leaving the council chambers and returning once he'd officially entered, but it'd add to her current political disaster. The elyfian had been routed at Shadow City. Scodd Yullus managed to escape with a small contingent. Now, they'd have to wait to see if the unicorns held true to their pledge. If they did, the genocide would hang around her neck like a weighted noose.

One political disaster at a time.

The chamber doors opened, and she half expected the Islander king to waltz through. The first few moments would set the tone. Meristal had never met him, and as far as she knew, no one else had either.

What's he doing off his islands anyway?

Forgotten Islanders were notorious for shunning outsiders and their isolationist policy. With all the rumors coming out of there, the Isles were a place of enigmas, intrigue, and taboos.

The royal guards took position at the doors, and the king's procession filed in.

About damn time.

A man walked to the center of the room just below the council's bench. He planted his wooden staff on the floor, thumping it three times. As he spoke, he spread his arms to encompass all attendees.

"All hail, His Eminence, the wise and benevolent Callum Godfrey, second son of Edmund Godfrey, King of the Forgotten Isles, Master and Commander of the Forgotten, Raging, and Storming Fleets, Lord of the Golden Sea and beyond."

There were no hails.

Three fleets? Didn't realize they had so many ships.

For a moment, Meristal thought he expected them to applaud, cheer, or even bow. His face announced that he didn't receive the welcome he thought they deserved. He turned, glancing at the door.

A hard, austere man entered with the bearing of unyielding iron. A burr-cut of strawberry blond hair shot with grey and a matching, cropped beard framed his features. His pale blue eyes glittered not with joy or malevolence, but with lifelessness.

"All hail, King Godfrey," the herald cried again.

Again, no one hailed.

Upon Godfrey's head sat a crown of bent and twisted gold adorned with rubies; to call such a thing a beauty would've been a travesty. His rigid bearing reminded Meristal of a military man, his steps measured. His white silk under-robe stood out against the ebony inner layer; forest green marked both his outer robe and traveling cloak. Each garment was gilded with gold thread, the traveler's cloak more so.

The king stopped at the bottom of the sloping floor next to his herald. His blank gaze swept the council in one languid movement. It wasn't until his eyes locked with hers that she knew they weren't empty but calculating.

"Introducing the king's wife," the herald spoke again, "her Majesty, Mercy Godfrey, third Queen of the Forgotten Isles."

The husband and wife manifested as opposites in appearance and demeanor. Where the king stood unforgiving, the queen's movements were filled with grace, supple and fluid. Her hair, a light red shade with hints of blonde, accentuated her hazel eyes. A radiating smile and a lovely face drew muted mutterings from the crowd. She appeared decorous, friendly, almost as if attempting to catch each individual's eye and grin.

Her gown of near-sheer gossamer emphasized her voluptuous physique. Had it been only one or two layers, Meristal and everyone in the room could've glimpsed the queen's nether regions, but as it was, just the faintest trace of her legs could be seen.

Meristal glanced around the room and noticed every man scrutinizing the foreign royalty.

The herald spoke again, drawing her eyes. "Introducing the king's eleven sons and daughters."

Eleven! Shades!

"Marshall, Marc, Mabel, Macy, Maddox, Madisyn, Mara, Malcolm, Merryn, Morgan, and Mercy, the second of her name."

The children lined up beside the queen, and all were behind the king. The kids resembled a living rainbow. Some bore similar features; no one child had the same hair or eye color. Their hair ranged from platinum blonde to a light red like the queen's. Eye color covered the gamut of blue, hazel, gray, and green, each in different shades. All in all, they resembled typical Forgotten Islanders except their clothes and bearing.

Meristal observed the sons standing with unmoving intensity like their father while the girls carried the near-grace of the queen. Meristal peered closer at the children, noting slight differences.

Madisyn, Mara, and Malcolm had platinum blonde hair and different facial features than the older five or the younger three. The longer she looked, the more she could discern their different elements. Each set of kids must've had a different mother.

When the procession ended, at least the herald's part, Meristal realized Islander officers filed into the chambers without introduction.

She waited.

Daylynn Reese stood and spoke.

Meristal held her breath.

Don't overdo it. Just like I told you.

"On behalf of the Kothlere Council, as the governing body of the Ralloc and Marcoalyn domains, we welcome you into our city."

You overdid it, twit!

Meristal's face made no expression, nor did she turn her gaze.

Instead of the king speaking, the queen stepped forward, coming one stride shy of abreast.

"We thank you for the warm welcome. Indeed, it's as we've heard: Ralloc is divine, and we thank you for your hospitality."

So, a dance, then.

"Of course," Daylynn said, "we'd welcome you as all who come under the banner of peace."

Reminding everyone of their method of approach, under a banner of peace, went a long way in assurance.

Meristal had to concede the brilliance of Daylynn's maneuver.

"As our banner assures our peaceful intentions," the queen said, "let me reassure you that we come not as enemies but as emissaries."

Daylynn sat down and Lagelm, the goblin with black eyes like wells of eternity, stood. Meristal suppressed a shiver.

"Greetings. On behalf of the council, I wish to inquire about your honorable volition."

Oh, he's superb. Better at his second language of Myshku than most wizardkind.

The queen smiled.

"We wish to join the sovereignty of Ralloc."

Muted mutters rippled through the crowd and turned to full-blown conversations; the noise level escalated to the atmosphere of a tavern during dinner.

Kellis banged the magical gavel against its platform, sending echoing knocks through the room. Vamor Poplu, one of Kayis's old supporters on the council and a thorn in her backside, stood.

It wasn't something planned.

Sit down you imbecile before you ruin everything.

"If indeed that's true," he said, "should we not hear this from the king? Or is the Isles run by a matron?"

Jeers and taunts came from the crowd.

Damn it! His head will grace a platter later.

The king took a slow, menacing step forward. His lifeless eyes grew frostier, and he spoke in a quiet, clipped tone.

"Your ignorance is an insult to the ears of the cultured. Your very presence defiles the sanctity of law and order. Had you been one of my men, I'd remove your tongue for insolence."

During his entire monologue, his face remained expressionless. His blinks were few, and his breath never elevated. Meristal was pretty sure his heart rate didn't even tick upward.

Knowing this would elevate beyond control, Meristal stood. Her violet eyes locked on Godfrey, who still faced Poplu, and matched the king's demeanor.

"Is this true, King Godfrey? You wish to join the Ralloc domain?"

"Ah, she speaks," he said.

He turned.

"Indeed. Shall we retire to a private setting where we won't be interrupted by the quips of fools and the semi-literate?"

His words were more cultured than she was accustomed to. His voice had a quiet harshness. He didn't mince his words, and some would call him crass, an accurate if not poetic description, but he didn't have foolish people like Poplu around him.

Must be nice to be a king and rule with utter conviction.

"I think that's best. Would you accompany me to my chambers?"

For the first time, an emotion flickered across his face, and Meristal knew he'd perceived the wrong impression. She didn't see lust but repulsion.

I'm not going to bed you, twit.

She gestured with her hand.

"My office chambers would be better suited for working out unification details, wouldn't you agree?"

He schooled his features again, but not before he recognized his mistake.

"Agreed. If it's acceptable to you, two others accompany me, my fleet admyryl, and my herald. Perhaps you would care for two others to confer with?"

Meristal smiled.

"Wise and gracious of you, King Godfrey."

She caught Judas's eye and gave him a look that left nothing to interpretation.

To her right, the same way as her office, she made eye contact with Master Jynerul Tyku, and gave him the same regard.

He nodded and rose.

With all eyes on them, the six made their way to a side door. That door went to several places, the kitchens, a stairway to the dungeons, and even to the Mirror of Imaesion, if one knew where to search. Meristal opened the door and walked down the hall, the king on her heels. At the other end, she opened the door and ushered the procession in.

She reached the chair at her desk but decided at the last minute not to sit to avoid any misconceptions. Instead, she dragged the chair around the desk, sitting opposite the long chair. Judas and Tyku slid their chairs into flanking positions; the king and his two advisers mirrored them.

Meristal watched Tyku smooth his pants as he sat and observed his dress uniform. His coat was made of beautiful wool, the insides lined in supple leather, giving the coat both a rigid form yet soft enough to bend and fold. The coat was a deep phthalo blue, the same used in the guards' uniform, but with gold piping and buttons.

She noted the gold bands around the cuffs, signifying his time in service. Wide bands represented an age, while thin ones represented an era. They alternated, starting with a thin, then a wide. This pattern continued, culminating into four and a half ages of service.

His pants were made of the same type of wool minus the leather lining, and black instead of phthalo. Medals and awards decorated his chest, campaign ribbons, and badges of proficiency with the sword and bow. He was an impressive image to behold.

On his shoulders rested his rank, one giant gold star. The other jyneruls wore silver stars, befitting their seniority. The most senior of the jyneruls wore four silver stars, while the least senior wore one. When Tyku retired, everyone would advance by one.

Judas, by contrast, wore simple clothing, formal robes all made of silk; his under, inner, and outer robes ranged in hues of white, scarlet, and black respectively. Obsidian shades covered his traveler's cloak with red piping. Tyku looked smart in his dress uniform, but Judas embodied splendor fit for royalty.

At last, all were seated.

"Perhaps you'd like to begin?" Meristal offered.

"Introductions would be for the civilized, wouldn't you agree, Consul?" Godfrey asked with the faintest smirk.

He indicated to his left.

"My Fleet Admyryl, Klevyn Arco. This young man to my right is Hynry Zahn."

Meristal nodded to each in turn.

"This is Master Jynerul Tyku, Commander of the Grand Royal Army. To my right is my advisor, Judas Lakayre."

The king's gaze snapped to Judas, and his eyes narrowed, almost too minute to tell.

"The exile? I find it impressive that an outcast ensnared the ear of the consul, let alone be in her…chambers."

Judas leaned forward, but Meristal cut him off.

"He's impressive in many ways, not the least of which is magic. Have you come to discuss terms of unification or the people whom I associate with?"

Godfrey stared back with pale blue eyes, this time they glittered as if she had struck a nerve.

"Direct and to the point; perhaps this will be less painful than anticipated. I appreciate directness without descending into the realm of discourtesy."

"I, too, like directness. Politics is a lot of double talk and half-hidden messages."

She leaned back, giving the impression of being relaxed, but her insides were far from it.

"Very well; let's be direct. The Forgotten Isles would join with the Ralloc Domain if we can come to terms."

She paused for a moment, giving the impression of deep thought.

"I find it hard to believe that after so long as isolationist, the Isles would suddenly wish to join. Why the sudden change in policy? Some hidden agenda?"

She crossed her legs, her hands folded in her lap.

The king leaned forward.

"If there were a hidden agenda, it wouldn't stay hidden if I told you."

He gave a small, tight smile. Meristal noted his amusement, a smile so small that his lips twitched just above horizontal.

"No hidden agendas, but I don't expect you to believe that. The policy changed because I rule. Had my brother been king, you would've never been approached."

"Why isn't your brother king?" Judas inquired.

Meristal couldn't read Judas's face from the side. Had she taken the time, it would arouse suspicion.

"He's dead," the king said. "Unification is beneficial."

"Beneficial for whom?" Tyku challenged. "For you? For your people? Or for everyone?"

"For all."

Meristal rejoined the conversation.

"And what exactly is the Ralloc domain getting out of this? From where I sit, the Forgotten Isles is making off better for the unification and Ralloc will be left holding the bill of sale."

The king stood and began pacing to the side of the couch, making everyone shift in their seats.

"Taxes," he said. "Generally speaking, it all comes down to money. As part of the domain, there's an influx of taxes and coin into your treasury. Also, no more tariffs in either direction. Further, it drops the cost from the merchants who must raise prices to pay such. The Isles have long been a generous customer of wood. We'll continue to be so. Ralloc is also building a canal from the Golden City to Ralloc. This will be a long and expensive process. I'm willing to designate a significant portion of my fleet to aid in this endeavor."

"What's a significant portion?" Meristal asked.

"One-third of my standing fleet."

"That doesn't sound like much," Judas commented.

"You insult me," Godfrey said in mock-chiding tones. "As it stands, your navy is stationed at the Golden City. When we docked, I blinked and it was gone, that's how small your fleet is. How many ships do you have? Forty? Admirable, but a jest. Forty ships isn't a fifth of my fleet."

Tyku's lips opened, but he said nothing. Judas leaned back in his chair, his hand pulled on his goatee.

"And how are we to pay these new employees?" Tyku asked.

The king flickered his gaze to him for a moment before returning to the consul.

"We'll pay their wages for the first half-score of years. By then, you'll make enough from taxes Islanders will pay to induct them to your payroll."

"A generous offer," Meristal commented. "But with the protection we'll provide you, the standing army and active conscripts, no doubt an increase of migration of your people, I still don't see how it evens out."

"Ralloc will also be given command of my ships as part of the Royal Fleet. Couple that with the canal, you'll never worry about sieges."

"And what of the Isles? Will they be left undefended?" Judas inquired.

"No, for the relinquishment of my ships, I want, in writing, that twenty percent will be used in defense around the Isles or patrolling the sea between the Isles and the Golden City, leaving no less than five percent in the dock at the Forgotten Isles at any time."

"Twenty percent? What value do you possess that needs so much protecting?" Judas asked.

"You mean besides my people?" Godfrey countered.

"It'll be our people," Meristal corrected.

"That'll also be expensive," Tyku reasoned, "not only for Ralloc but you as well. You must house and feed sailors sitting in the docks."

"The sailors will reside with their families, who will feed them. As for anyone not from the Isles, accommodations can be made."

"I think we can come to an agreement on that part," Meristal said.

She leaned forward.

"But there's the issue of debt."

"I assure you, the Isles owes no one."

"No, not your debt, ours. Ralloc is drawing heavily upon our treasury. Soon, it'll be empty, between the canal and the sewers."

"Then, they were poor choices, weren't they?" Godfrey retorted.

"I walked into this. The previous consul started these projects and spent funds like a fool. Since I took over, I've cut back on unnecessary expenditures, but the damage is done. It'll take time to recover."

The king was silent for a moment. He ambled to the window and looked at the city, taking in the tall towers on the walls, the spires of the university and the religious temples in the distant Sinner's Court, and the clay shingled roofs of houses.

Godfrey turned back.

"Then, we'll renegotiate our deal. I'll give two-thirds of my fleet to the building of the canal and pay their wages. For the first five years, the men they relieved will return to Ralloc to finish the sewers. At the end of five years, whether completed or not, they'll return to the canal and work alongside my own men until finished or a score of years have passed, whichever comes first."

"And how can the Isles pay for all this?" Judas asked.

Meristal cast a glance his way and understood the expression on his face. Mildly put, he was skeptical.

"Our mines go deep."

The king didn't elaborate.

"What else do you want?" Meristal asked.

She hoped Judas would take over the questioning as he searched for whatever he sought, but he fell silent, and she continued.

"My fleet admyryl. Just as if any one of my men would join the Grand Royal Army and be subjugated to the leaders appointed over them, so too would anyone who joined the fleet be under Klevyn Arco. He's to remain the fleet admyryl until he retires."

"I think that is more than fair," Tyku spoke up.

The king gave him a nod of appreciation.

"So, that's why you want so much wood," Judas mused aloud. "You've been building a massive fleet as a bartering chip when you came to the table."

"Perceptive man," the king said in warmer tones. "Yes, as you've guessed. My fleet is the largest in Ermaeyth. Add yours to mine, and you'll rule the largest fleet and one of the largest armies in all of the world. In essence, you'll be untouchable, especially behind the high walls."

He cast a quick glance back out the window before turning back.

"If you ever finish them."

Judas took a breath.

"So, the ships, the canal, and the workforce along with their payment. What else?"

"The families of my islands, the ones we consider noble and minor noble. They're to be transplanted to the same standard as your people."

"That won't be too hard," Meristal agreed after a moment of deliberation.

"Additionally, we're standing by to recast seventy-five percent of our currency into yours. We've already started with the ingots, the only thing we lack is the treasury seal. Of course, we'll provide you with samples from each batch to be tested for purity, and once you do, you'll gain an influx of one billion scepters in ingots."

"A billion?" Tyku gawked, his eyebrows shot up.

"Impossible!" Meristal blurted.

"How can you afford that?" Judas asked, scrutinizing the king. "Where did you get the gold?"

"As I said, our mines go deep. Do we have an accord?"

"The foundation for one, anyway," Meristal declared. "Granted, this decision isn't mine to make alone. With these preliminaries being the major points of the unification, we can delegate all minor matters to panels of representatives. Once finalized in writing, the council will look over the unification petition. If everything is in order, I believe a vote will be called. Does that satisfy you, King Godfrey?"

"It's sound in theory, but it must be written."

He smiled again, and she almost missed it.

"Very well, I'll have someone show you to rooms here in the castle."

She stood and shook his hand.

"Master Jynerul, would you be so kind as to notify the guards to send for a guide?"

He clicked his heels in response and carried out her request.

Once the king and his entourage left, the doors were shut again, and she spoke to the two men that remained with her.

"What do you think?"

"A solid offer," Tyku conceded.

He voiced what she dreaded but didn't know why. Perhaps because they were always isolationist. Maybe it had to do with the king's countenance, a hard man with hidden agendas lurking in the corner of his soulless eyes?

Tyku broke into her thoughts.

"We're making out rather well."

"Too good, if you ask me," Judas retorted. "The only reason we're considering this is because of his fleet and gold. How do they have so much?"

"'Our mines go deep,'" Meristal mocked in a Godfrey-likeness.

The men chuckled.

Tyku took a deep breath, hesitated, then trudged on.

"Looking from a military standpoint, we're far better with them than without."

"Militarily maybe," Judas said, "but what about cultural differences, the small things we're not looking at?"

"What do you mean?" Meristal asked.

She was almost sure of where this was going, but she didn't want to jump to conclusions.

"They're closer to us than any domain south of Marcoalyn."

"They have different customs, different ways," Judas stammered. "Their noble families aren't considered minor nobles here. And now, he wants them transplanted. Sounds to me like they are making off with the better end of the deal."

"Since when do you care about nobility?" she scoffed.

"I don't, but is it right or fair to others?"

"Nothing is ever fair in life," Tyku voiced.

Meristal seconded that.

"If you doubt that Judas, take a long examination of your own."

"They're crass and vulgar," Judas said. "It'd be as bad as letting the Krey live here minus the bloodlust. The only thing the Krey do besides train and kill is drink, sleep, curse, and fornicate whenever and wherever they can."

Meristal's mouth fell open.

"That's what *this* is all about? Rumors of sexual proclivities?"

Judas winced.

"Not entirely."

"Not civilized enough for you?" she continued.

She found it humorous to watch Judas blush like a noblewoman; she'd never shared his level of closed-mindedness.

"Come, Warlock Lakayre," Tyku chided, "we're all adults here."

"Master Jynerul," Meristal started, "you've been from one side of Ermaeyth to the other. Is there anything you've seen that would make the Forgotten Islanders seem paltry?"

"Aye," he said, nodding. "Ever hear of a place called Elysys? They do crazy things that'd make you sick. I'll never forget the place. And should we ever send the fleet that far south again, I strongly advise you make the city off limits."

"Come now, Jynerul. You must give an example to Judas, or he'll turn his nose up to the Islanders forever."

He blew out a breath.

"Men get raped in the streets in broad daylight, interspecies breeding, acts of bestiality as punishment for women…"

He went quiet after that, and Meristal and Judas remained that way, too.

When Meristal swallowed, it was so loud in the silence.

"Thank you, Jynerul; you may return to your duties."

Tyku clicked his heels and left.

"Okay," Judas said once the doors shut. "The Islanders aren't as bad as Elysysians, but—"

Meristal rolled her eyes and hugged him.

"You're hopeless, you know?"

When he didn't say anything in return, she broke the embrace.

"You're too restrictive for me, Judas."

"In what regard?"

She shook her head, not understanding how he could be so dimwitted sometimes.

"Everything. If it doesn't fit in your little box of comfort, you look down on it. You segregate everything, labeling it this or classifying that, whether it's great for someone else or not. If it doesn't conform, you vilify. The Krey is one area where you could use a lot of help. They're people just like you and me, but the difference is they know they were born to die. They have no inhibitions. Sure, they're crass, drunkards, but they feel and love the same as everyone else."

She paused a moment, growing pensive.

"I find them quite refreshing. You have no excitement in your life, just you and your books in your manor. And the Forgotten Islanders? They're just another example of you being closed off. There's more to life than sticking your nose up at everything."

She leaned into his ear and whispered.

"You've squandered numerous years, and you should live a little before you die. Try it."

She pulled away, kissing him on the end of his nose, then traversed to the door.

"Try what?" he asked.

Meristal rolled her eyes as she placed her hand on the doorknob.

"Living a little."

With that, she left the room, abandoning Judas to reflect on her words.

Chapter 30: Norek

Korlin's Cove came as a beautiful and welcome sight. The absence of light under the mountain produced a physical and mental strain on Norek.

Man was not intended to live in the absence of light.

In dawn's pale glow, he exited the labyrinth into blinding brilliance. A cool morning mist blanketed the air, and in the distance, families milled about, driving their carts, tending their fields and livestock. At the nearest farm, Norek spied a boy returning home with two milk buckets. The boy's father readied draft horses, affixing a plow.

A deep breath of crisp air reinvigorated the mage. Winter neared its end. Spring was associated with the beginnings of life, and Norek loved the season for its literal and metaphorical meaning.

He felt more alive.

The town appeared to be waking; shop owners, merchants, and customers flitted through the streets in slow, steady trickles. Children ran, playing in muted tones, coming from their homes and yards. Their choppy, quick footsteps thundered up and down the sidewalk of wood slats.

How can anyone possess so much energy at this time of day?

He sighed and started down the hillside, his legs stiff. Pebbles and stones shifted beneath his boots, each step precarious. He almost lost his footing half a dozen times. His staff kept him upright, leaning on his trusted companion. In the obscure landscape beneath the mountain, the staff saved his life more times than he could recall.

Strolling past the nearest farmhouse, the road opened, an invitation to enter their fair town. The street led a straight path to the center. No one cast a glance his way, too enamored in their business and bore him no heed. It seemed odd that no one cared. He doubted many people traveled to or beyond Korlin's Cove that often. Perhaps that's why they never gave it much thought?

Shouldn't the opposite prove true? Shouldn't a stranger draw the eye?

Rebelling legs kept him upright; momentum and will propelled him forward. Each torpid foot dragged, weighed down by an unseen compulsion. His head throbbed from lack of food, water, and proper sleep. He needed a bed and a stream to drown himself in. After slumbering for two days, he'd need to find a woman. Then, he could continue his journey north.

Ralloc. Why does it have to be so far away? Why couldn't I debark in the Golden City?

His tongue swelled, and his throat itched. Desperation compelled him onward. His distended feet shuffled him through the gates, where a guard blocked his way, parchment and quill cradled in his arms.

"Name?"

"Norek."

"Family name?"

"I don't have a family name."

The guard's bored eyes shot up.

"What? How can you not?"

"I'm an orphan. Is that adequate enough?"

Too tired to bicker, his current state set him in a foul mood. The sentry glowered, his hand resting on the hilt of his sword as he worked his jaw.

The soldier turned his attention back to his notes.

"Final destination?"

"Here in the city, or where I'm going eventually?"

The stack of papers fluttered to the ground.

"Look here, jackass! Don't get smart with me. I have half a mind to let my men whip you for insolence, break that wild-horse spirit. It's by our grace that we allow you entry at all. One more smart remark, and you'll wish you were traveling 'neath the Melodic Mountains."

The guard glared for a moment longer before bending to retrieve his belongings.

"So, final destination?"

"Ralloc."

"Business in Korlin's Cove?"

"A place to sleep for a few days."

"Profession?"

An apt question, indeed. How best to answer without drawing ire? He held so many occupations yet no career. Norek embodied several aspects, and most should remain unspoken.

And some things were better left unthought.

Unless pivotal, he didn't see the need for the soldier to know he possessed magical abilities. More trouble than it was worth. The last problem he needed right now was fixing people's issues or having a man trying to marry his daughter off.

"Profession?"

"Scholar, specifically, a traveling scholar who writes about events and cultures, publishing throughout the realm. I just finished with the Forgotten Isles."

The guard's face changed from cold scrutiny to thoughtful contemplation.

"Very well, Scholar Norek. I'm sure the governor would be honored to have you as a guest at his table. Perhaps you'd entertain him with a few tales. We don't get many visitors coming through."

Yeah, no doubt, if you're here greeting them.

"It'd be my honor," Norek lied.

He didn't care for a semi-formal event.

"First, I must rest. I've traveled many days without a proper meal or sleep."

"Say no more!" the watchman clapped him on the right shoulder. "That building."

He pointed to a three-story, white stone building.

Close, thank the gods, only five buildings up and to the left.

"That's our finest inn. I'm sure you'll find the accommodations most adequate. Shall I tell the governor of your visit?"

"Yes. That'd be great."

With a few more short exchanges, the guard directed him to a business for laundry and supplies.

The soldier called after him.

"Anything you require," the guard shouted after him, "the innkeeper will take care of it. On the word of the kaptyn of the Cove's guard!"

"What's your name again?" Norek called, peering back.

"Kaptyn Hiba, at your service."

"Thank you, Kaptyn Hiba. I'm sure the governor will reward you helping others in his name."

Norek turned back to the open road and trudged on.

He half-walked, half-crashed through the inn's door. The pain in his feet caused him to limp. He leaned against the counter out of necessity. Norek ignored the decor. The lodgings could adjoin an outhouse, and as long as it had food and a bed, he'd gladly pay.

The keeper wore cotton and wool robes, keeping him warm in the colder parts of the year. His face remained free of wrinkles despite his advancing age. A full, white, bushy beard and matching mustache covered the majority of his face. He was taller than Norek and just as thin. Spectacles attached to a chain hung around his neck.

"Need a room?" the keeper asked.

"Yes, and water and food."

Norek spilled his coin purse on the counter. Several silver chips spilled out along with a bright eye, the latter rolled across the countertop toward the manager.

The barkeep snatched it up and turned the coin over a few times, not believing his eyes.

"Want a whore, too?" he asked, handing the coin back.

Norek nodded, his desires making him ache.

"If I had the energy."

"Right then, we'll fix you up. I'll send someone to draw you a bath in your room. Need any clothes washed?"

"Yes, yes to everything, just wake me before supper. I'm to be with the governor to dine."

The barkeep laughed, shook his head, and whistled; a girl with butterscotch-colored hair appeared. She was shorter than Norek, but not by much, a curvy woman with a small waist, most likely indicating she hadn't borne children.

"Ah, Jessica, show this young man to his room. I'll bring water up for his bath and bring whatever clothes he requires to be cleaned down. Take good care of him."

She slipped her arm through Norek's.

"Come," she beaconed.

Only forward momentum kept Norek from falling asleep on his feet. After entering his room, she shut the door and helped him with his pack and staff. With languid movements, the mage peeled off his outer robe while Jessica pulled the tub from the corner to the center of the room.

When she finished, the innkeeper plus two other ladies brought in two buckets apiece filled with steaming water, pouring it into the tub. They left without comment, but Jessica stayed.

"Want me to help ya out of ya clothes?" she offered.

Norek nodded weakly.

"Yes, but not for the reasons I'd hope for."

This drew a smile from the woman as she moved closer. The moment she peeled another layer away, he started shivering. She placed a small, warm hand on his forehead.

"Shades, ya burnin' hot! Ya got yaself a bit o' fever, ain't ya?"

She hurried to get him out of the rest of his clothes and into the tub. He meant to sink in, but instead, he plopped. Waves encroached the edges. Jessica washed him, and with the aid of a cup, she poured water through his lengthening hair.

"Bit shaggy, ain't it?"

Jessica hummed a soft melody as she soaped her hands with shampoo and scrubbed his scalp and hair. She rinsed him with the cup and soaped up a cloth. Helping him stand, though he held on to her as his legs shook, she scrubbed his body with vigorous diligence.

A knock at the door ended his bath, and Jessica threw a towel around him. The manager brought another tub, and the two girls brought more water. After they had left, Jessica removed the towel and helped him out of the dirty tub and into the clean water.

She resumed her tune after the others had left.

The melody soothed him and sent him to the cusp of sleep. She snaked fingers through his hair and a new noise, almost inaudible, snagged his attention. His eyes fluttered open, but she soothed him.

"Don' mind me, sire, jus' trimmin' ya' hair is all. Make ya' look dashin'."

She continued to hum and trim, and Norek couldn't remember falling asleep. When she woke him, the water was cooler, and a hot meal of sausages, eggs, with biscuits and gravy sat on the nightstand. She pulled him out of the tub, dried him off, and helped him dress in provided sleeping clothes.

She combed his hair dry while he ate like a starving wolf. When his stomach felt engorged, he lay on the bed and couldn't recall her leaving or falling asleep.

The mage bolted upright, roused by his foot being shaken. He squinted and scrunched his eyes at the light pouring into his room. The elderly man left, satisfied his duty was discharged.

After a few moments, Norek's eyes adjusted to the late evening light. With a yawn, he rolled out of bed and washed his face in the basin. The door opened. Jessica returned with his clean clothes folded. She gave him a coy smile.

"I mended ya robes, some need replacin'. Best ones on top."

A weak smile came to his face.

"Thank you."

With a curt nod of her head, she placed the robes on the edge of the bed and moved with slow steps towards the door. He caught the glances over her shoulder. Norek wanted to ask her to stay. Like an alcoholic unable to say no to the drink, unspoken desire filled his face. He'd have her stay all night without his prior engagement.

Damn that bureaucrat!

"I'll be back later tonight," he muttered.

"Then, ya be seein' mo' of me."

"Preferably all of you."

He smiled, and she blushed. She gave a single nod and left, and he dressed in his best robes, many notches below formal wear. He'd use the same story he told the sentry, a traveling scholar and one who hadn't packed for a formal event.

Surely he'd understand. But then again, nobles and people of importance are often fools and jackasses.

Upon leaving, he inquired about the location of the governor's house. Simple instructions followed, given in a single breath. The small community held a certain appeal, the stillness with the promise of wilderness just beyond.

It was safe.

I could live my latter years in a place like this. Shades, even raise my kids here, if I ever had any.

Norek wasn't sure marriage loomed in his future. Whether greedy or vain, he didn't think one woman forever would suit him or his desires.

He eyed the town with an appreciative sweep. Still, it lacked the opportunities of the city, and Norek doubted the small town catered to his vices of women.

The trip took a few minutes, even at his leisurely stroll. When he arrived, a butler opened the door before he knocked.

"Welcome!" the official boomed from within, spreading his arms as Norek entered the sitting room.

The home was a nice two-story building made of dark, grayish-turquoise brick and oak paneling with tall, gray stone pillars holding the second story balcony. The administrator was middle-aged, the first traces of gray hair showing at his temples.

"Governor," Norek greeted with a curt bow.

Despite the dull ache throbbing through his body, he'd try to put on a show. Perhaps his discomfort would change with some food in his stomach. Jessica came to mind, and it lifted the mage's spirits, knowing he'd be in a better mood after the dinner.

"Come in, my boy, come in! I'm so glad you decided to grace us with your presence. The Cove doesn't receive many visitors, and I'm more than eager to learn about your tales."

The governor grasped Norek's hand.

"I thank you for your hospitality, and for the chance to dine with you and your family."

Norek was no stranger to verbal jousting, political or otherwise. He knew proper etiquette for more races and cultures than he cared to remember. Wizardkind etiquette was by far the easiest to remember but the hardest to conduct. For most races, words and meanings never changed, but for wizardkind and Myshku, an ever-evolving dialect woven with body language and voice inflection plagued him.

Either a culture spoke with conviction of their feelings, or they conveyed without them, but not wizardkind.

The far-flung race could change from positive or negative emotional deliveries by altering the pitch and harmony of conversation. Elyves spoke without emotion unless pranking others. Dwavens spoke with emotion and directness alike. And as Norek noted with firsthand experience, it was rude to use flowery language.

"You're too kind with your words, traveler. It's you who honors me."

"Nonsense. You've invited me into your home. Should I, a traveler in tattered rags, dine with the Cove's finest?"

"You," the elder spoke, then paused, a thoughtful expression on his face. "You're very careful with your words, traveler."

Norek didn't say what he truly felt but let a smile touch his lips.

"My guard tells me you're a scholar. I'm not such a neophyte myself, and I realize every race has a different type of social register. Do you know any?"

Norek nodded, treading on safer ground.

"Yes, several in fact."

"Good!"

The governor beamed.

"Let us use the last culture you encountered that wasn't wizardkind. Agreed? I find the experience refreshing."

"That could be entertaining. I just spent time with some dwaven not long ago. If you have no objections, we'll use theirs. Do you know it?"

"Can't say I do."

"Don't worry, you'll catch on fast."

Norek cleared his throat and took a steady breath.

"Your home's beautiful. Something smells wonderful. I'm hungry. Let's eat so I can get back to my room and to the company of a woman."

The governor burst into a thick, full-bodied laugh as he clasped Norek on the shoulder. The mage let himself be dragged from the foyer into the dining room, laughter echoing through the halls and announcing their arrival far in advance.

They dined and chuckled heartily as humorous stories were exchanged, the odd happenings of his town, and Norek recounted embarrassing incidents with other cultures. The host's wife made it difficult for Norek to focus; she was as beautiful as engaging. The sight of her made him realize how long he'd gone without a woman—well over a moon turn, and perhaps three to four fortnights.

They drank plenty, first an imported tea from the Forgotten Islands. He had much to say about the Isles, how he liked their imports but puzzled over the lack of land for farming. While each import came in small amounts, they imported exponentially more than previous years.

Norek noted the stories relayed by the bureaucrat, deciphering the boredom with his life, living vicariously through others. Over the course of the meal, the dignitary introduced himself and his family. They dined until they had their fill, their plates removed by the hired help.

"That meal was the best I've had in a long time," Norek said, still carrying the dwaven custom.

Norek noticed the gleam in the eyes of the governor's wife. She was both pleased and distraught over the use of such blatant speech, pleased with showered compliments, but uncomfortable when words turned to touchy subjects such as cultures, politics, and beliefs.

But the compliments were justified.

The governor snagged a prize in his wife, beautiful, intellectually stimulating, and a dark sense of humor that Norek enjoyed.

"Indeed. Quite fitting for a guest of honor. Perhaps you'd care to join me in the sitting room, where we may discuss your journeys and the places you've visited."

"I'd be honored to share my travels," Norek said, dropping the dwaven pretense.

Norek offered to share his tales with the civil servant's family and hired help, but the other refused citing impropriety. The man thought lowly of servants, viewing them as little more than slaves with an allowance.

The host claimed his chair in the sitting room, but Norek didn't relinquish his quest, hoping to change the governor's mind.

He asked again.

"You ask a lot for a guest," the other's tone grew quiet.

Norek began to speak, but the official held up a hand to stop him.

"You're a traveler from another land, so you don't know our customs. Our servants are of the working class. What you are asking is unheard of."

"I realize that; however, in doing so, it'll allow a great many things. First, I can impart my experience to everyone's benefit. They'll go home and tell their family of the traveler who came to eat at your table. Secondly, it'll show your kindness and compassion."

"How so?"

"Your compassion for them and their learning. You'll be the empathizing master who encouraged his workers, and they'll gain understanding about the world around them. They'll be grateful. A great master elevates himself by elevating others."

Norek swallowed.

"Lastly, no one should be denied knowledge."

Silence settled as the host mulled over the words. Norek watched his eyes as he worked out the problem. Finally, the other nodded in the end.

It was Grace, the governor's wife who spoke.

"You speak with elegance and fluidity few of my husband's guests possess."

Both men turned to regard her standing in the doorway of the study. She entered and stood by Norek, snaking her arm through his. The governor looked shocked, more at his wife disobeying his wishes.

"It comes with the trade," Norek said.

"And what trade would that be, Traveler Norek?" she inquired.

"Many, traveling and documenting what I find is but one of them. I help draft laws back home, but those moments are few and fleeting. There are other trivial but equally indulgent activities I do in my spare time."

She gave him a look, and he couldn't begin to figure out what it meant before she turned to her husband.

"You see, Sebastian? We're blessed that Norek has come to us. Perhaps the Father, Mother, and the Child, sent him here to help guide you."

The governor's face brightened.

Clever woman, tying it back to religion.

"Indeed! I'd be honored if you'd stay for an extended visit," the governor invited. "Take a rest from your travels in our fair town. I could use your help."

"I'd be honored—" was all that Norek could get out before the governor began celebrating prematurely.

"That's outstanding! Really! Good form, man."

"Alas, I'm afraid I can't."

The host wasn't the only one disappointed by the news. Grace made a small frown but otherwise showed no outward appearance.

"Why not?"

"I have to get to Ralloc as fast as possible. I need to leave tomorrow; the journey is long, and I can't delay."

"The call of Ralloc is strong," Sebastian agreed. "The journey to the Corridor is a moon turn at minimum, and that's if you rode day and night, changing horses at every town."

Norek nodded his agreement with the assessment. A daunting task lay ahead.

Sebastian continued on, thinking aloud.

"However, if you give me three weeks, I'll personally hire someone to teleport you to the mouth of the Corridor. You'll be there a week earlier than expected. Is that agreeable?"

The thought of not having to travel four more weeks made Norek breathe easier. He was already so tired from his Eastern City trip. Sebastian was willing to pay the exorbitant fee to teleport Norek, a bargain too agreeable to pass up.

"You've given me an offer I can't refuse," Norek said with a smile.

"Excellent! Really, excellent. Good form!"

Sebastian stood.

"Grace, dear, would you be so kind to gather up the staff in the sitting room? We may reconvene with Master Norek and hear the wonders of his travels."

The hour was late when his tales drew to a close. With careful consideration, he omitted the inappropriate parts for the children's sake. Grace kept his wine cup full after each tale, even more so for her husband. Norek noted his slurred speech, his blurred vision. If he was tipsy, Sebastian was a befuddled lush.

The stories ran their course, and Norek stayed after the help left, sitting with the official. Sebastian lit his pipe and drank a pale wine shipped from the Golden City. A bottle later and unable to walk straight, Norek recalled the girl he met on the beach in the Isles. Riveted, Sebastian sat in awed silence.

Norek took his leave afterward and stumbled drunkenly through the streets. The return journey took him five times as long as his first.

When Norek opened the door to his room and stumbled in, he found Grace waiting for him without a stitch of clothing. His insides fluttered, and his heart quickened at the sight of her.

"Where's the other girl?" he slurred.

"I sent her away," she said. "It's just me tonight. There will be plenty of time for both of us in the coming weeks."

With a smile, he closed the door behind him.

Chapter 31: Starriace

Starriace lounged against her pack, poring over the contents of Rusem's journal.

My frustrations grow by the day, as my search for the seven brimstones leads nowhere new.

She'd escaped the city, retrieving Rusem as night fell in earnest, panting and drenched in sweat. With her essence pulled tight around her, she masked her presence from those creatures who took Stratu'Geim. The small, portioned meal did little to help her stomach or mood.

Only Rusem's journal sated her appetite.

Reading his words, she discovered that Rusem—as the ghost in the temple—had lied to her. She should've expected as much; he wasn't the first to do so. The presence she'd felt while fiddling with Rusem's mind still lingered.

Pulling the journal near, she continued reading.

I possess four of the seven brimstones and time is running short. I can only hope to please my master, because the consequences will be dire. I find my failures less fulfilling even though every defeat forges understanding. Frustrated, my master's lash rankles me as a constant reminder for the price of success, long delinquent. I know he only wants the brimstones for himself, claiming knowledge of what will happen when united, but I foster doubts. My powers have grown exponentially since my servitude. One day, I'll destroy him.

After reading the passage, it occurred to Starriace that it detailed his journey, not a journal of crucial facts. At the mention of a master, she flipped through the earlier passages to see if she missed the crucial detail, but Rusem carefully omitted the information.

I begin to understand the meaning behind the brimstones. You were right; they're the attributes of Hagen, the Father of Magic, perhaps attributes of creation itself. They differ from our initial speculation.

She frowned, wondering who Rusem was writing to, as if it were a letter rather than a journal.

It wasn't just his lust and greed, but his love and compassion, all are filled with thoughts and feelings I can't describe. I'm sorry, should you ever read these words, the words of one you once considered your friend. I'm not as altruistic as you tend to think. You were always my friend and accepted me for who I was. I pray you find forgiveness in your heart, and accept me, Judas.

Shades of the Underworld! Judas!

The revelation rocked her. Did Judas have a copy, or did Rusem never reveal this to him?

A wave of undefined emotions washed over her. Confusion and anger clouded her mind, repulsed by the very notion of Judas being friends with a man like Rusem. Once vile, cunning, and perhaps evil, the risen endured as a slave to do her bidding.

But Judas? What was his excuse for tangling in Rusem's threads?

How did they meet? When? What caused these two diametrically opposite men to bond in friendship?

Starriace tucked these thoughts to the dark recesses of her mind, her gaze turning back to the small pages. She noticed the passage had ended and flipped to the end, reading the last entry.

It's been two seasons since my last entry, and I can't wait any longer. I won't suffer under my master any longer. I realize you're on your way to see me now, even as I write, but the chances that I'll be alive when you arrive are dim. This is my last testament. I can't give anything from my kingdom because you're not a descendant of my bloodline. No matter. I've rewarded you beyond measure for what you've done for me. Should I fail, or die, or even succeed, this will guide you in my footsteps. The steward, since my health is failing, promised to give this book to you upon your arrival.

Health?

Starriace pondered what Rusem meant. Any number of things might cause health issues, but why was he sick? From the brimstones or something unrelated? Maybe a misdirect, like at the temple and the brimstones?

She read on.

I hold faith you'll follow, and should I fail, you'll succeed where I couldn't. You're brilliant and cautionary where I'm too headstrong, as you've noted countless times. I now go to fulfill my destiny, whatever that has for me. So you may learn the truth, I shall tell you where I found the first four brimstones. I can't guess what will happen to them when I'm done, but I assume they'll return to their point of origin where I found them.

The first three are, ironically, the closest. The first in a small town called Ruhkhi, northeast of my city. A man within, John, collects a vast number of ancient artifacts, such as the Sword of Judgment. Regrettably, he didn't own the matching blade, the Sword of Salvation. He said those accursed Disciples of the One took it, something about a blade of cleansing. I sometimes wonder if they even grasp how much 'cleansing' the blade really did. I spent half the money in my kingdom for the brimstone and was almost tempted to buy the Sword of Judgment instead, but without the matching blade, the Sword of Salvation, it's next to worthless.

The Sword of Judgment stirred something within Starriace, the name authoritative and mystical. As she read the words, she envisioned the longing in Rusem's voice, even if the weapon was next to worthless without its matching blade, the Sword of Salvation.

Starriace wondered what the name implied. Would the steel save the wielder or have properties of the divine? Letting the whimsical fantasies fade, she focused again.

The first brimstone comes out of an act of greed, like Hagen. My act was using half my fortune. My greed was all I had, to gain it for myself and no one else, and it came willingly. Be warned, if you don't use the proper emotions to trigger the stone, it'll destroy you when you attempt to use it.

Starriace blinked.

Proper emotions to trigger the brimstone?

Starriace had never heard of a sentient stone. A sentient anything, other than people and creatures. How could a stone be sentient?

The second is in the destroyed Chissu'Nanuci outpost, not far from the place where we first met. The ground collapsed, and underneath lies a crypt, a place that scared the hell out of me. The emotion to trigger this stone is malice, also like Hagen. All the stones are like Hagen, always remember that! My malice destroyed my enemy.

The third took a long time to locate; did you know Hagen built the school for mages? Divinity Enigumas? It's rumored that Hagen hid the third stone within the walls, and he was buried there. Something terrible lurked in the darkness, something like death itself, perhaps a remnant of him or the stone, and I truly believe this is what's killing me. The price or trigger for the brimstone is death. You'll find a way to defeat this obstacle. If anyone could, it's you.

Starriace rubbed the soreness out of the back of her neck.

So, that's what was killing Rusem.

He never mentioned it back at the temple. He also made it sound like he had found only one brimstone and not four. How did the brimstones kill him? Would she make the same mistake?

The fourth is similar, yet distinct. If I can speculate correctly, the brimstones are divided three, three, and one. The first three I found are on one side of the proverbial veil, the darker emotions, the evil in Hagen. It's simple, if you think about it: greed, malice, and death. I believe the other set of three are exact opposites. Temperance, control, or restraint is the opposite of greed; I believe these emotions trigger one of the others. Kindness, sympathy, or compassion might trigger one of the other ones. Life would be the direct opposite of death, but how to use that one? Perhaps someone who is alive need only touch it. I don't have the answer.

As for the fourth one, I think of it as a neutral stone. Located in my palace, I'm unfamiliar with the original location. If I use it, it might revert somewhere unbeknownst to me. You must be prepared for this. The brimstone was an heirloom of my house for generations, and no one ever suspected anything other than a beautiful, timeless stone of incalculable value.

One last thing. I think the first three, the three I found, are bound to the wizardkind. Long ago, during Hagen's time, nephiliam lived. I think the other three are bound to them. They are an extinct race. The only other immortals I'm aware of are elyves, descendants of the nephiliam, but they aren't pure offspring. Will any of this help you enough?

Thank you for your kindness and indulgence. You've been like the son I never had, and a friend I was lucky to be blessed with. I wish we had more time together. You were a tremendous influence, and it's been my privilege and honor being your friend. Thank you for everything.

Your Dearest Friend, King of Stratu'Geim, Lord of the Valley of Stones Domain,
Rusem.

Starriace's eyes tracked back to a single word.

Nephiliam.

The word made Starriace's mind buzz.

Where did I first hear the word?

A hiss filled her mind, a sound from memory. The hiss slithered through her dark recesses, untouched and veiled. She couldn't recollect at the moment. Something about the name nephiliam called to her. With so many things pulling her, it was hard to focus.

"Ava?"

"Yes, Empress?"

There's that word again. Just like Fife.

This response was becoming more common. Why did she behave like this? She needed to find the underlying cause, but now wasn't the time, more important matters needed attending.

"On the morrow, I need to go to Ruhkhi."

"What's there?"

Starriace stared off into the darkness.

"The Sword of Judgment, and the first brimstone."

The next morning, Ava teleported them, and she returned to the Melodic Mountains afterward. Starriace's heart leaped with elation when the fairy departed. This marked the second time Ava returned to the mountains.

Ava had waned throughout the night; her inner light diminished with every hour that passed. Her death would create more problems than solve, and the mage relied on her too much. Despite the attitude as of late, a part of Starriace yearned for her company in short spurts. She'd spent more time with Ava than anyone else, excluding Fife. Ava was a part of her, albeit an annoying one.

Starriace eyed the town. She was here, alone, with a single clue to aid her search: John.

Ruhkhi was small but elegant.

It's either a small city or a growing town.

Two walls surrounded the city with a deep trough between them. The outer wall was made of white stone, and the inner doubled the height due to the slope of the ground and the dug-away earth between them.

The town's architecture was different than any she'd seen before. All structures in the Ralloc and Marcoalyn domains had similarities, either tall, square, and resilient-looking, or shorter with rounder dimensions.

In Ruhkhi, angles and shapes prevailed. Triangles, octagons, any shape, all seemed acceptable except the plain and ordinary. The stark wall colors belied the guts of the city. As eccentric as the structures, so, too, were the colors. Vivid jade and amethyst, silver and earthy brown, royal purple and orange, the clash of colors merged into a headache. After the initial shock passed, there was something peaceful about the quiet place.

Starriace hadn't come for the architecture, but for a purpose. The first brimstone would soon be in her clutches, but she needed to trigger it with greed.

Rusem's journal gave explicit instructions; his own trigger was also greed, giving away half of his kingdom's treasure. It was odd that Rusem would trouble himself with the purchase when he could take it by force—also an act of greed. But not all lands in this domain yielded to the throne.

The name rolled through her mind. Rusem almost gave up the search for Judgement. It held undeniable value. Was the sword key to getting the first brimstone? She coveted the blade for its power, but not as much as the brimstone. Maybe it was more than just a piece of steel?

As she advanced, the sentries eyed her from the open gates. Almost everywhere else she visited, the watch would ask her name and why she came. She entered the city unmolested and strolled through the first street, quickly overwhelmed by the number of buildings.

A man trotted in front of her, close enough to be touched. Her gentle hand on his arm pulled him to a stop. He gave her a flash of belligerence before it softened, taking in her face and features, and hid the dead chicken clutched in his hand behind his back.

"Help ya?"

She smiled.

"Yes, please? I'm looking for a certain place, but unsure of the name. A place of odd trinkets and old relics of a time long gone? Do you know the place I'm talking about?"

"Yeah, Old John's. You can't miss it. It's the dullest building here. A two-story of brown rock, sitting near the outskirts on the western side. Rectangular with the dome roof. Can't miss it."

He shuffled off, pulling free.

Starriace progressed to the west side of town, lurking near the wall. She passed milling people looking at wares, buying vegetables, selling jewelry and cloth. Lace, silk, and other fine products were on display, and vendors tried to garner her business, but she remained focused.

After pushing by filthy beggars, ale-soaked men, and manure-sodden workers, she traversed down the street and stumbled upon Old John's building. She noted its plain structure and odd roof compared to the surrounding buildings. A darker building than most, a deep brown with subtle hints of gray. The roof was a deep shade of crimson, darker than blood.

She ascended the small steps. Bells at the top of the doorframe chimed a cheery tone as she pushed the hatch open. Her initial impression was that she was in the wrong place, but after sending out the tendrils of her magevision, she distinguished otherwise.

A tailor's shop filled her view upon entry with bulky machines spaced throughout, for either spinning cloth, sewing, or making lace. Where they sat didn't impede customer traffic. Racks of clothes filled the broad room with three long rows. Pants, shirts, robes, vests, undershirts, everything someone would need was right here.

The store was bigger than the one Lily took her to in Far Point, or the one she visited in Ralloc, but not by much.

"Welcome stranger," an old man's voice rang out.

Whoever called to her was hidden amidst the rows of clothes. The slight rustling of cloth and hangers grating against the metal rod reached her ears.

"Oh, and a lovely stranger you are. You're not from these parts. What're you looking for today?"

The elder exited the row, and he appraised her for a moment with a small smile on his lips.

"Well then, I can see why you're here. You need new clothes. How can you let yourself be seen like that in public?"

Starriace glanced at her robes. She planned on acquiring new ones when she visited Harold, but her studies had distracted her. Now, necessities clouded her desire. With her reclaimed money, she could afford to buy new ones.

Or steal them.

If she were going to pilfer the old man for a priceless artifact like the brimstone, the least she could do was buy the robes.

She returned his smile.

"Yes, new robes. That's one of the reasons why I'm here. The other is a rumor that you carry certain, shall we say, artifacts?"

"Of course, I do. In this town, none know what I have hidden between my walls except for a select few who work for me. The man with the chicken? He works for me. Anyone new eventually talks to him."

He held out an old, frail hand.

"Old John is what they call me."

"Well, what do you call you?"

"Just John, then."

"Well, John, I need new clothes. After we've settled that, I'd very much like to see your back rooms."

His smile faltered, and his face twitched before he recovered. He chuckled, but his voice came out somber.

"Well, well, another mage in the town, eh? It's been some time since I've talked to one of my own."

"I'm not a mage, not like you think; I don't know what I am."

"You're a mage; you possess the affinity to wield magic."

For a moment, the two stared at each, John plumbing her enigma, and Starriace trying to expose any deceit.

"Robes?" she prompted.

John was quick to assess the length of her arms and legs, waist, bosom, and buttocks. An uncomfortable feeling crawled inside of her throat as the man neared the more private areas. The cold claws of remembrance squeezed her heart, and she fought against the anxiety. The fault didn't rest on his shoulders or hers; John was guiltless of any transgression.

The banished memories threatened to haunt her. John garnered no pleasure from the task of ensuring a proper fitting. His touch reminded her of a delicate breeze, free of the ill fondling she feared.

Finished, he scratched his wispy white hair and ambled to a row of clothing. He fiddled, examining each and discarding until he crossed a light orange and deep pink set. He held it with admiration before glancing over his shoulder.

"Absolutely not!" she admonished.

"What color and cut do you seek?"

"Black. Oh! I almost forgot. I love silver, do you have anything like that?"

A faint memory tickled her, remembering the black leather pants Lily wore, hugging every contour. The garment had an effect on Kam. She wanted to inquire about a pair for herself but abstained.

"To sneak about at night or to portray someone in mourning? A new-found widow, perhaps?"

"Unmarried, but black will help me be unseen at night and discourage others during the day. If possible, I'd like a reversible cloak, black on the outside, silver or gray on the inside. To help break up the monotony, of course."

"As you wish. I'll have my workers make them now, and you and I can venture to unseen places."

"Why not hand me something off the row?"

"Because, my young mage, your measurements aren't...the medium in these parts. You're far skinnier, shorter, and bear more backside than the women here, but you're not as endowed in the bust as women here. With those measurements, I'd say you're from up north, Rallocan domain. So, I must tailor the robes to fit you; hemmed for height, taken in at the sides, and the gods didn't grace the local women here with a divine seat like yours, so, we've got to amend the cloth. Not to mention your waist—"

"I understand," Starriace interrupted, her face turning crimson.

While he described with methodical detail, she couldn't help the embarrassment radiating in her chest, but he spoke in educational tones rather than longing.

"When will they be ready, John?"

"You'll have them before you leave. Let's explore the real reason you came."

He waved his hand to the back, picked up his cane leaning against the rack, and led her deeper into the shop.

In the back, he produced a key on a silver chain around his neck, which sparkled in the muted sunlight, and opened a door in the wall. He thrust it open and bade her entry.

The cluttered room was a chaotic assortment of books, scrolls, weapons, potion bottles, jewelry, armor, paintings, and more. The room scarcely contained the collection. Swords hung on the walls, their blades pointing to the floor. Some were of high polished steel, a silvery glare, but not all.

Only one wasn't.

The blade was black, as dark as the shadows that hid Xilor's face.

"That one there, why's it black?"

"Ah, caught your eye, did it?"

John moved beside it.

"This beauty captures everyone's eye. That's a weapon of lust to the right people. Certain circles would kill to own it, for others it is merely an alluring oddity, only coveted for its difference. They don't realize how right they are."

"A weapon of lust? Then, why do you have it?"

Starriace held his gaze for a moment before returning her attention back to the black steel. She drew close, admiring the detail. The hilt was gold with spiraling black leather accentuating a thin glimmer peeking from underneath where the leather did not overlap. Closer inspection revealed the decorative state was intentional. The pommel and guard were gold. Even without touching, she sensed the magical properties, a faint buzz in her head.

The large, black pearl centered the guard, the width of its circumference peeking out on both sides.

"For safe keeping, as a collector of such things. The Sword of Judgment isn't to be wielded lightly and incurs a terrible price for those without its twin: Salvation."

She made sure not to react, still acting out the part of inspection while waiting for him to continue.

"Where's the other?" she prompted.

"Alas, not here. I had it for many years before the Disciples of the One set up camp in our town. The archbishop saw the holy steel and took it, declaring that 'someone who isn't pure shouldn't possess a blade of the One's glory.' He didn't even pay, just took the damn thing like he owned it. I find that odd, a disciple stealing? Isn't that against their beliefs?"

He sighed, and Starriace waited, questions poised at the tip of her tongue.

"I believe the new archbishop inherited my property when he assumed the post. There's a ruckus at the Halls of the One, buzzing like flies on horseshit. Something's got them all stirred up. Maybe nothing, but I doubt it. Perhaps the archbishop died, he's been at that post for as long as anyone can remember."

"Where do the disciples stay?"

With a disgruntled flick of his wrist, he pointed in the general direction.

"Their hall is outside town."

Starriace mulled over his words. Judgment could be the trigger, but she didn't yearn for it the ways she hungered for the brimstone. How could she covet the blade when she yearned for the other?

"May I?" Starriace asked, pointing to it.

"Yes, please."

John's brows narrowed in concentration.

"Be careful, it's still very dangerous."

Her cautious fingers inched forward. In the blade's gleam, she caught her reflection, and that of John behind her. Something moved beneath the glossy surface, drawing her attention. A wisp she couldn't quite discern. In the breath of a few moments, more images came floating out of the dark pitch, forming blurred vapors.

Starriace had never seen spirits or believed they existed…until now. Wraith-like bodies floated over one another; the longer she stared, the more they swarmed like a school of fish. Some spirits were missing arms and legs but carried them in their remaining hand. Some lugged their heads like lanterns to light the way on a moonless night. Phantom whispers teased her. A hum of moans droned while screams of agony tolled in the distance. She couldn't discern what the whispers said, but they spoke something maddening.

Tearing her eyes away, she reached up tentatively and grasped the hilt. As her fingers wrapped around the haft, she let out a breath of relief.

Nothing happened.

The blade came free of its bracket, and she held it in the guard position, the blade weightless like an extension of air. Her grip tightened until her knuckles turned white. The power within it awoke and sent jolts of painless energy up her arm and furrowing into her mind.

The steel weighed but a sliver of light. A dark glimmer came to her eyes, one that John would understand. The call awakened between her breasts.

At this moment, she understood the sword and why Rusem coveted the blade. With this weapon, the wielder became unstoppable, able to deliver terror in battle. The steel was true to its aim, its sole purpose was to kill, and it chafed with disuse. In the hands of a true wielder, it'd cut down anyone nearby, foes, friends, or loved ones. In time, it'd consume and destroy the wielder.

Armed with the insight, Starriace pulled herself—her mind and soul—free of the sword's clutches. She loosened her fingers, and the imploring hunger receded. She returned the onyx weapon to the bracket. She shivered as she backed away and regarded the old man.

"You're right. It's dangerous."

Old John nodded agreement.

"What other artifacts do you have?"

He frowned, thought for a moment, then took her on a tour, revealing the treasure he hoarded, and concluded roughly an hour after she arrived.

"You have quite the collection, John."

He showed her everything, save one object: the brimstone. What was the best way to broach the subject? No matter how subtle she attempted, she'd have to ask. The only alternative was directness.

"What do you know about brimstones?"

"Brimstones?"

His mouth quirked as he scratched the stubble on his chin.

"Don't know anything about brimstones. But …" he added, his eyes glittered with recognition, "I believe I know what you're referring to. This way."

They shuffled through the room, and he pulled a grand portrait of a mountain aside. Behind the massive painting was revealed a safe inset in the wall. He dialed it left and right a few times each, stopping briefly on a designated tick and threw open a lever.

"This artifact has the strangest story," he said.

He reached within and withdrew his hand a moment later, turning toward her. The stone was a touch smaller than the width and length of his hand, but at least three hands thick. The red light within glittered, dancing across the walls.

"May I?" Starriace asked.

"Sure."

A sense of awe filled his voice.

"An odd story, that stone. I found it a long time ago—can't rightly remember where, I wanna say it is a family heirloom—anyway, a man came to see me about it. A king, if you can believe that. He was very taken with the Sword of Judgment, but when he saw this hellstone, well, he just had to have it. Insisted on buying it. He told me to name a price, but I told him no amount of money would make me part with this treasure. When he named his price, he proved me wrong."

John sighed.

"Then, those blasted Disciples of the One came and took my money and Salvation, all for the noble deeds of the One, of course. Damn bastards! I want to strangle each one."

The fire in his eyes subsided, and he went on.

"Can't remember how much time had passed, but one day, I found my hellstone in my vault. No one returned it to me or broke in. It was just there. Peculiar, isn't it?"

"Yes, odd indeed."

Starriace turned her gaze to the hellstone, unsure of everything except that it was a rock. A hellstone wasn't what she was looking for, but maybe they were one and the same.

"Tell me, John, why did you recognize the word brimstone when you said you don't know anything about it?"

She watched him, her eyes hard.

Is he like everyone else? Always lying?

"I—what? What are you talking about?"

"Earlier, I asked you if you knew anything about brimstones, and you had a distant look in your eye. Then, suddenly you remembered this hellstone sitting in your safe."

A look of recognition washed over him.

"Because that's what the king called it. He was eager to hold it and had an awful glitter in his eyes."

John looked thoughtfully at the hellstone before his worried gaze slid to Starriace's eyes.

"Much like yours do now."

Starriace peered deeper into the rock with the aid of magic. She sifted through layers of swirling vortexes, a faint trace of magic lingering, undeniable but dim. For this hellstone to be what she sought, it'd need to radiate more than a faint aura, but she detected the touch of Rusem within.

She followed the semblance, tracing as it swirled away, evading her touch. When the aura's movements became erratic, sensing no way to escape, it turned and attacked her. In that infinitesimal moment that stretched for an eternity, Starriace felt the echo of pain and horrors.

Agony exploded in her mind; her insides convulsed, wanting to implode. Her body trembled from so much pain, but she fought to keep from lashing out. Like a flickering finger of lightning, it started and faded.

The hellstone had been with Rusem in his last moments. To the end.

She withdrew from the hellstone and handed it back to John.

"Thank you," she struggled to say, still rattled, her face feeling cold.

She used to think of Rusem as a slave and not a person, but now, after witnessing his final moments filled with agony…

John laid the prized possession in the safe and shut the door, spinning the dial and covering it with the enormous painting.

"I believe," he said, "your clothes should be ready by now. Shall we go take a look and settle the bill?"

She charmed him with a smile, but she needed more than that. She embodied a duality, and it was vital to express those characteristics, to grab a man's attention, and to hold it for as long as she desired. For the converse, she needed to melt in the crowds, another face in the masses.

"About that," she said, as they worked their way through the room. "I have a new clothing request, one I'm sure you'll be eager to handle."

Chapter 32: Xenomene

Xenomene delivered her edict to the heir—what would become Bitcher's fate. His eyes widened at the demand. He grumbled about ill luck and misfortune.

"You're going to owe me much more for this!" he warned, his voice dark.

"Name your price, and it'll be paid. I don't care, as long as this happens. I've heard stories…"

"Yeah, and they're all true! I've got a bad feeling about this. I don't think any Krey deserves that fate, maybe not him either. If you're sure, you'll stay at the Hive until this whole ordeal is done."

She hesitated for a moment.

How long would this take? She could end up staying for a moon turn, a season, or longer, and she didn't want to abandon her duties, but it was the price. There could be worse fates.

There's always a price, like paying for this service with my body as currency. Makes me a damn good customer.

"Agreed," she said.

Daniel stormed away to make the preparations.

While gone, she reflected on the things said to Bitcher in anger. When making those threats, she'd meant every word; in a frothing wrath, she would've committed those acts in front of him just to break his spirit. Her bravado faded with her agitation.

She couldn't become the squad's personal whore, no matter how the majority comported themselves in House Eti. Here, sex was as frequent as bathing, but she was more Rallocan in nature.

Now that she was free, what would she do? It wasn't as if she could quit the Krey and start life over, taking a new name and identity with the past erased. She was Krey in her blood and a ko-don in her bones. There were only two ways she could go: up or dead.

She considered taking another vow of celibacy. The distractions of the flesh could wait until she conquered everything, including the title of heir; there'd never been a woman in the role, and if the men had their way, there never would be.

When the time came, she had a plan to ensure her succession.

Bedding Daniel troubled her. The rumors would start, and all would assume it was to receive the title of heir next. If trying to sleep to the top, she'd need to bed the ko-dons first, even the married ones. Being a married Krey differed from most marriages. Krey marriage, in most cases, signified that you would only bear children with your domesticated partner, but were free to pursue frivolities as both parties wished.

There were, of course, a few members who followed the old ways.

An A'uri Heart arrived, and he blanched at the sight of Bitcher. The Heart handed her the black collar, the Mark of the Profane. She regarded the mage entirely for the first time, realizing three distinctive things. One, he was handsome, born of good genes from noble blood. Two, he was a Heart and not a woman. No rule existed that men couldn't be Hearts, but it was rarely seen. The third was that his green eyes were a shade lighter than hers, and dirty blonde hair.

"Fucking Lord of the Underworld, another one?"

He paused, confused.

"Another one what?"

"You're an Islander. Did you guys have breeding contests in caves and decided to invade the rest of Ermaeyth? I swear by the gods, your lot is like a venereal disease, and you just crop up fucking everywhere!"

The Heart gave a quizzical glance.

"I'm from Chissu'Nanuci."

"Oh."

The embarrassment rippled through her.

"I like you more now."

"Thanks, I think. You wanted me to heal him?"

She looked down at Bitcher and back to the Heart.

"No. You're to heal his bones and the wounds of his feet, hands, and forearms, but leave all scars. Am I clear?"

He nodded.

"Yeah, but I don't understand why."

"You don't need to; just do as you're fucking told."

He knelt and set to work. She knelt as well, snapping the collar around Bitcher's neck. If the Heart was at all worried about seeing someone receive the Mark, he didn't express it. She retrieved the knife from her belt and returned to Bitcher, eyes glittering with mischief as she unsheathed it.

The Krey kept every blade razor-sharp as part of their daily routine. Now, it would serve another purpose. Knife to scalp, she shaved his head. By the time she was done, the Heart was, too.

"Collect your things and get out. Not a word of what transpired, or you'll answer to me, understood?"

The Heart's eyes widened, and he nodded, then scurried away. Bitcher roused not long after, noticed his 'healed' wounds, the collar, and his bald head. The reality set in then, and he rocked himself on the floor. He didn't speak or cry; his shattered spirit didn't possess the energy.

Daniel returned an hour after his departure. He glanced at Bitcher and couldn't help but laugh.

The heir regarded her.

"You're in luck. They've got a man close by in the Golden City. It'll take time to get word to him, and it's over a week's ride on horseback, if he rides hard. You're probably looking at eight to ten days. The man you requested…I don't know if they'll send him, but Bitcher will be taken."

Xenomene nodded and knelt in front of Bitcher.

"This is your punishment. You'll wear the collar forever. A man's coming to collect you; he's from the Disciples of the One. You'll become a servant to those zealots."

She stood and regarded Daniel.

"Take him to your quarters."

"He ain't fucking sleeping there! He can rot in this dungeon. I got a nice cage for him just down the hall. The goblins can keep him company."

"He's not sleeping. Take him to your room and bind him to a chair. Then, take a bath. I will, too."

"Why the fuck do I want him in my room, especially if I'm bathing? And what the fuck am I bathing for?"

"Because," Xeno rolled her eyes in exasperation, "you're not fucking me until you do, and I want him to watch."

The heir blinked a few times, too floored to speak. He jerked Bitcher to his feet and guided him to the staircase. She followed on his heels.

After they ascended the stairs to the heir's office, Xenomene greeted Tiny with a nod. They made eye contact and held it until the heir left with Bitcher.

"What's the plan?" Tiny prompted.

"You're returning to Dlad City and will assume command until I return."

"When are you returning?"

"In about ten days."

"Why in ten days?"

"You don't want to know."

"I'm a big boy, I can take it."

She shook her head.

"What if I don't want you to know?"

"Well, I'm aware of half of it."

He crossed his arms.

"What? You yell really loud, and I was only halfway up the stairs when you did."

She blushed.

"Yeah … I'm sorry you had to hear that."

Tiny's swallow was audible.

"Do what you need to do."

"Do you believe that, or are you just saying it because you want me?"

His lips drew together in a tight line.

"Why can't it ever be one and the same? I'd do whatever I must to get revenge. I wouldn't have spared him, and I ain't going to ask why you did, but if you want to talk…So, why ten days?"

"I need to see this through, and I have a debt to pay."

His brow lifted in disbelief.

"For ten days?"

She nodded.

He rolled his eyes.

"The heir's a lucky man."

"It's turning me into a whore."

Tiny shrugged.

"You sound too Rallocan."

"Well, I was born there. He'll be the seventh, and that might not be—"

"—Shades! Only seven?"

Tiny's eyes widened, and he shook his head.

"Most folks here average around forty, and I'm well over that."

She cocked an eyebrow.

"Who's the whore now?"

He smiled and turned his body, readying to leave.

"I would say, 'live and die by the sword,' but I don't think the heir intends to kill you. Save some for me."

He winked and lumbered away.

She swallowed. Why didn't she kill it in the cradle? He still wanted her, and now would've been the perfect opportunity, especially since Tiny knew she'd be with the heir.

Damn it. One of these days, I just need to do it.

She left and went to Daniel's chambers where she had a bath waiting for her in the adjoining, private room. The steaming water loosened the knots in her back and shoulders. After a lather from head to toe, ensuring to scrub her feet in case he had a thing for her toes, she exited the tub, toweling herself dry and donning fresh undergarments.

Gazing into the mirror, she readied herself, steadying her breathing. When she entered the main chamber, she caught Bitcher bound to his chair, facing the corner like a child in timeout. Daniel, in a night robe, stood from the bed. She crossed the room with halting steps.

His eager hands gripped her shoulders as he pulled her close and kissed her. Though pleased by his desire, it felt too close to the torment already endured.

He broke away first, a wolfish grin on his face.

"Treat me like a lady," she said. "Remember, I'm not your prostitute. I can be your darkest desires for as long as you want, but you'll treat me well."

He nodded, licking his lips.

She gave a single dip of her head.

"Good."

She moved to Bitcher and turned the chair around to face the heir's bed. She held his gaze for a long moment, seeing him break, the stinging glitter in his eyes.

Yes, that's what I want.

She walked away, returning to the heir's side.

"How do you know he'll watch?"

She smirked.

"He can't help but watch. It'll eat him up inside."

And Xenomene had been right. Bitcher couldn't look away. He shouted through his gag, screamed muffled obscenities, and the hope faded from his eyes by the end.

Retreating to the adjoining bathroom afterward, two novices came to remove Bitcher. When she returned, he was gone. Daniel laid in his bed, and she slid up beside him, her naked flesh pressed against his.

"You were terrific," she confessed in surprise. "I would've never guessed."

"And you're a beautiful woman. That was amazing. Never let anyone tell you different."

She kissed him, expressing gratitude, then nestled beside him, planning to stay that night, and thought he'd gone to sleep when he spoke again.

"I release you from your oath of the ten days. If I died tomorrow, I'd die content."

She smiled at that, that someone found her so pleasing they'd die happy. She sat up.

"Even though I'm not her?"

"Who?"

"The redhead you spoke of?"

He shook his head.

"That's from days of antiquity."

She put her head back down on his chest.

"I want to stay," she said at last. "This is an oath I won't break."

"Is that truly your wish?"

She nodded and shivered.

"The last night we're together," she said, "don't hold back. Not like you did tonight. I can tell."

She felt him nod behind her, but he didn't say anything.

He was quiet for a time, but she heard his deep inhale as he readied himself to speak.

"Why go through all this trouble?"

She paused, considering what to say. Would he even understand?

"I want to destroy any hope he might foster, and I want to poison his soul."

"Shades, I'm beginning to think you didn't come away unscathed."

"You're right, I didn't. He fucked me up, peeling everything away until only ruthlessness remains."

"That's what we call psychotic."

She gave a single chuckle.

"I was always that way, just more so now."

Xeno slept in his bed that night, waking to find his arms wrapped around her, his stiff prick resting against her backside. She yawned and rolled out from under his embrace, stretched for the ceiling, then bent to collect her clothes and dressed in silence. She'd make a point to sleep in her own room from now on. Overnight stays sent the wrong message.

If stuck in House Eti, she'd spend it wisely. Before Mon Kyyr Gr'bakth, she hadn't used a blade since Cape Gythmel. She traipsed down to the Pit where she worked on her swordplay, switching between strikes and forms far beyond the knowledge of ordinary Krey.

In House Eti, they instructed that there were eight sword forms, but few progressed past the second. All through initial training, they drilled Form I, known as the novice. It was just swordplay, learning to defend and attack. Once they graduated from raw recruits, they were introduced to Form II, the guardian, and they incorporated the shield and working within a unit.

A few people—like Smokey with his hammer—learned Form VII, just a variant of II but for mallets and axes.

If fighting alone, Xenomene preferred the eighth form. The Zealot matched her speed and agility, not to mention the more acrobatic nature of her fighting style.

Exceptional at a young age, she'd mastered the traditional styles years before her peers. An elyf selected her for training at the Enclave. There, she learned under a new teacher, one that she grudgingly called Master. Being his inferior fueled the fire to become better, to hone her skill.

At first, she didn't appreciate the new assignment, ripped from the comfort of the place she knew as home. Once settled, defeat became a constant companion, and long-lost friends of humiliation and bitterness visited frequently. Shame and ire burned bright and hot from the resounding blow to her pride, and toward the heir for sending her there.

Her new masters beat her until her spirit broke. Upon shattering, the elyf told her they'd mold her into a Jaikari. That first morning, she learned the history of the Jaikari, and by surprise, the Krey. Valin of Lor, the first heir of the Black Tide, was a Jaikari. No other Krey had been one since.

Xeno had become the second.

The Jaikari were seldom spoken of, with each subsequent heir learning of them. If a Krey showed exceptional skill, they were remanded to the elyves. She fit that description, but she wasn't among them long.

To become a full-fledged Jaikari, it'd take more ages than she had to live. By the time she had learned two of their forms, she'd have staked the site of her grave, if not already taking residence.

When she returned from the brief sojourn, she had to temper her fighting skills lest she leave her squad far behind.

After working up a good sweat dancing in front of the wooden dummy, many of the younger recruits came to observe. She scrutinized them, and upon closer inspection, many emotions rolled across their faces, awe, inspiration, lust, envy, brooding.

Why do I always assume people are thinking negatively about me?

It was ironic; she was the best of the Krey, and she expected them to think less of her.

A younger man came forward, challenging her in front of the spectators.

She laughed.

"Do you know who I am, boy? You'd have a better chance fucking me than besting me. Come back when you're older or with five friends."

She didn't actually expect him to come back, let alone with friends, which numbered seven. Upon seeing them, she laughed, accepted the challenge, and exchanged her sword for a practice one. She entered the Pit, took the center, and waited.

Blades rose and fell but not a single one reached her. She never lifted her sword to block, only using the pommel to smash them on the head and face. When she walked out of the Pit, seven hurting bodies littered the floor. She wouldn't be surprised if one tried to quest her that night, but she'd be with the heir until she returned to her room.

Would they still be awake by then?

Xeno spent the rest of the day running through drills outside House Eti in the 'killing field.' She ate a moderate dinner and soaked her tired muscles. It'd been a long time since she had to exert herself in training.

She finished her business later that night with Daniel, and recruits came and removed Bitcher. Xenomene hid in the adjacent privy room. Each of the following days passed much in the same manner. Wake, eat, train, push the limits, humiliate someone, eat, bathe, and spend time with the heir.

Who would've thought a man I've never given a second thought to would turn out to be the best?

He wasn't attractive, just middle of the road and much older, but Daniel made up for it. Though, when it came to physical beauty, it mattered little in the end. Looks faded, but the core of a person, one who resonated with her, that would last.

And she hadn't found that person.

Looks and sex mattered only at first, but without compatibility, which mattered most, boredom became the common enemy. All of her partners had lacked cognitive depth. She'd yet to stay with a man longer than a season. By then, the passion had fizzled. For her, the vitality of a relationship hinged on two fronts: keeping her intellectually invested and sex.

On the eighth night, she intended to break Bitcher. Over the last week, Xenomene carefully identified several Islanders. One woman worked in the apothecary.

Xenomene entered and browsed the extensive shelves until only she and the worker remained. The woman identified herself as Karis. She was a short woman, though taller than Xenomene by a little. Her platinum blonde hair and bright blue eyes marked her as one such descendant.

"Ko-don! Anything I can help you with?" Karis inquired when Xenomene approached.

"I'm looking for something specific and obscure."

"I can help you there."

"When I say obscure, I mean to most, but not all."

"Okay."

"Something indigenous to the Isles but not Ralloc's domain."

"We carry several herbs from the Isles. If unsure of the name, perhaps you could tell me the desired results. I can narrow it down from there."

Xeno stopped her false perusing of shelves and eyed her.

"Something intoxicating and used between lovers."

Karis nodded but said nothing. She left Xeno for a few moments, retreating behind the counter and through a door. When she returned, the ko-don immediately identified the bottle in her hand.

"Thank you," she said with a curt nod.

Karis called to her as she left.

"If you run out, come to me."

In Daniel's room, she pushed the bottle into his hands, an evil glint sparkling in her eyes, and she let Daniel have his way with her. She gushed when Bitcher howled in rage through his gag. He screamed so much he busted blood vessels in his eyes. With the deed done, she stood, glowering down at the shell of a man.

"I never want to see this mother fucker again."

She returned to her room and sagged against the closed door, unable to help feeling elation and a sense of accomplishment for eradicating any shred of dignity within Bitcher. Was it justice? It felt like it.

Would it have been better to kill him? She didn't think so. He should live with the pain like she had to.

But were her acts driven by justice or revenge?

Sometimes they are the same.

On the ninth day, a full day sooner than expected, the man Xenomene had been waiting on, arrived.

It wasn't the man per se, but what he represented. He stood in the heir's office, flanked by two Krey. His black robes covered him from head to toe, even his hands were gloved; a hood drawn up over his head hid the mask that resembled a skull in shadows. Only the skin of his chin showed beneath the lower edge of the mask. The heir entered with Xenomene following on his heels.

Daniel took a seat behind his desk.

"Heir," he said in a deep voice.

His voice brought Xenomene up short, and she did a double take, unsure if the man before her was the boy she once held affections for.

"Whom do I address?" Daniel asked.

"You may call me Summoner. I take it you've had dealings with my kind before?"

Daniel nodded.

"The terms of our arrangement need to be settled, then you can be on your way."

"I assure you, my order will meet any terms you demand, within reason. It's not every day that we're offered a Krey."

Xenomene stared hard at the Summoner as if doing so would allow her to peer beyond the mask.

The heir nodded curtly.

"The collar is to remain until the day he dies. If it's removed by magic, he'll control his bloodlust again, and then he'll kill you all."

"Agreed."

"He's to never set foot north of the Corridor of Cruelty. In fact, the further away, the better."

"Agreed."

"You'll take him as is, and he'll never be altered."

"Disagree. We'll not take a maimed and broken man."

"He's not broken," Xenomene interjected.

The Summoner regarded her, longer than necessary to tell who spoke. His attention went back to the heir.

"She speaks the truth," Daniel said. "He's a functioning man, but he bears the marks of punishment, and he's to live with it for the rest of his life."

The man in black nodded.

"Then, we agree."

"If any of our terms are ever broken, and we find out, his life is automatically forfeit, and your order will pay two hundred and fifty ingots to this woman," he said, pointing to Xenomene, "for pain and suffering as recompense."

Xeno balked and shot the heir a shocked expression. He hadn't told her this part of the deal.

"Agreed, on one condition," the Summoner said, looking at Xeno.

"What?"

"You'll tell me his crime, and why my order has agreed to pay one and a half million scepters to you. I had no knowledge of this deal before I was contacted, nor was I told anything other than the one term that was not negotiable: this payment, if we breached the contract."

"Alright, but alone."

The Summoner turned back to the commanding officer.

"If there are no other conditions, that concludes our business. I would have my man."

"Aye," the heir said, rising. "We're done."

He motioned for the Krey to leave their post. When gone, Daniel regarded Xeno.

"Would you like to be here when he leaves?"

She shook her head.

"No, the last time he saw me, that's what I want him to remember."

He nodded and left.

The Summoner turned toward her and spread his hands.

"This person you're taking is a vile man. He tried to kill me, and when that failed, he blackmailed me and raped me beyond counting. How is it that your order wants a man like this?"

"All are sinners in the eyes of the One. All transgressors can be forgiven."

"If your god can forgive this man, then that's no god to me."

The Summoner nodded and took a step back to leave.

"Are you not going to say hello, Dane?" she asked, her voice soft.

He stopped in mid-step.

"Who?"

She crossed over to him, standing less than a pace away.

"You can't tell me you don't remember me. I remember you very well, sometimes even in dreams."

"I don't know who you are referring to."

She nodded, understanding that he wasn't going to talk, or he'd been brainwashed into silence.

"If you see him, tell him I wished I could've said goodbye. I wish…for a lot of things."

She walked past him.

"This Dane you speak of is dead," the Summoner called.

It stopped Xenomene in her tracks, but she didn't turn around.

"Then, I'll mourn the young man he was before he left, a Krey."

She left without another word.

By the time she reached the fourth deck, Bitcher was brought out. He was dressed in black with a black hood and shackled. She didn't want him to lay eyes on her.

They left the heir's office. Each step lifted her spirits. The doors rumbled shut behind the figures, and her heart soared as if a tremendous weight lifted.

She felt alive and vibrant with the whole world ahead.

The dark chapter was left behind.

Today was a fresh start; tomorrow would begin one full of hope.

Chapter 33: Starriace

Old John had filled Starriace's order, and she purchased a larger backpack with her new garments. Her old one was torn, frayed, and cramped with all the knickknacks she toted.

Now, all she had to do was wait, but she lacked patience, as evidenced by her training under Judas. His pace had been excruciating for lack of exposition. The difference between the warlock and the gnomling was that Fife had never cared to get to know her, only train. Judas mentored.

If I ever have my own apprentice, I should be a combination of both of them. They did have their qualities.

She waited for darkness, then descended upon the vibrant-hued village. The suns slipped beneath the horizon hours ago, and she settled in until the moon reached its peak. Upon its pinnacle, she stirred.

A brittle cold snapped, dispelling the sweltering weather south of the Melodic Mountains. She pulled the traveler's cloak tighter, grateful for the garment.

Stars glittered like diminutive gems in the cloudless sky; Auqyn, the pearl-colored moon, rose full—too bright for comfort—but delaying any longer would jeopardize the mission. Until she learned to shroud herself in darkness or obscure her figure, clothing was her only ally. Was such a thing possible?

Still, she found the pearl orb comforting. Something about it seemed familiar, like she should know it.

Turmoil boiled within her over the hellstone and the small amount of magic within. What troubled her most was that the stone had somehow captured Rusem's essence in his final moments, which was nothing short of depraved torture. Did it last a heartbeat or minutes? Her stomach churned at the thought. Mr. Pleasure's booming laughter echoed in the back of her mind, his face leering near.

Quick and silent, she descended the hillside next to the eastern edge of the city. Her thoughts drifted to the new clothes she wore. The tailored robes hugged her form, and her special order exceeded expectations. She solicited him to make her pants of black leather like Lily's.

She appreciated the flawless appearance, how they hugged her hips and clung to her legs. She wondered how Kam would react. To accompany her pants, she asked for a matching, sleeveless, black vest with black buttons fastening in the front. Her short top allowed her stomach and lower back to peek between the two garments.

She planned to wear it the next time she visited Kam.

If I ever get the chance.

Once Kam and Lily's child came…

She pushed the thought away.

More than an outfit to entice her lovers, it served a dual purpose: to captivate an audience if need be, worn when she needed undivided attention. Sexual overtones could help in the right setting. Fawning men tend to be less circumspect and bound to make mistakes.

A prideful gleam had come to Old John's eyes as he appreciated his work.

For her mission tonight, she wore a dark blue inner robe, a black outer robe, and a matching traveler's cloak. If the need arose, she could disappear into the darkness. Black cloak tight around her, she darted toward the tall walls.

She stretched out with her essence, but the area was devoid of sentries. Magic carried her up and over, landing without a sound. A small plume of dirt kicked up as her robe swished.

In the distance, the soft crunch of feet ambled in her general direction. A pair of men conversed, their voices reaching her but not the words.

Probably guards making their rounds.

The shadows between the nearest two buildings welcomed her. She had three items to acquire this night, the hellstone, and the swords of Judgement and Salvation, the latter appropriated by the archbishop from the Disciples of the One.

Old John's establishment wouldn't be a problem, not with magic, but the archbishop? Reconnaissance of the Halls of the One had been fruitless, not with security so tight. For one reason or another, they barred entry to everyone today, even those seeking atonement.

She saw the disciples, of course, clothed in robes of red, blue, green, and purple, and one donned white vestments. More curious was the few she spotted in black attire, like the Summoner from the Embrace who visited her. The chapel dwarfed any structure in the multicolored city, but it fell short of the grandeur of Stratu'Geim.

Starriace imagined the innards abuzz with devoted followers walking their hallowed halls like self-proclaimed monarchs. One day, they'd learn their place. The disciples would fester and overstep too many bounds, drawing ire. They were nothing more than a flea on a wolf's back. Eventually, the wolf would purge his coat of pests.

The guards passed, never noticing her, and their voices and footfalls faded in the night. Starriace dashed from the safety of one building's alley to another, bounding in this manner until she reached Old John's. Checking one last time, she stretched out with her senses and neared the front door.

Intention formed in her mind, and she waved her wand. The locks slid free, the sound thunderous in the stillness. A gentle nudge urged the creaking hinges to announce her arrival. Remembering the chimes, she buffered the air around each chime, then displaced it, lifting it clear of the door.

Upon entry, she closed the door, lowered the chimes, and withdrew her conjury. Her magevision flickered to life, illuminating the dark room. Had her intrusion gone unnoticed?

When no one stirred, she went to the hidden entrance and slipped through with no difficulty. On the other side, she beheld the wonders of ancient artifacts. Most were nothing, just odd trinkets and keepsakes, nothing of great value except what the owner invested. Few artifacts in the room held any kind of magical trace, but her eyes were drawn to the strongest magical presence in the room.

The Sword of Judgment.

The pitch-black blade made the room seem bright by comparison. The magically-aided gold twined around the hilt, and the gold guard shone like a beacon. With careful fingers, she plucked the sword from the bracket. The will of the blade rose within, calling to her, screaming to be released. Hunger ached inside of her, for the blood of foes or innocent alike. The blade, she'd come to realize, represented death, no matter the cost or who got in the way. When the last foe fell, the blade would yearn for a new target.

Death, like the blade, was absolute and all-consuming.

I swear this blade was forged in the heart of the Underworld. It should've stayed there.

The sword's hunger would never be quenched, no matter how often gorged.

Starriace retrieved the scabbard below the bracket. The sheath mirrored the weapon, gilded tips at both ends and an obsidian sheen between. A thin gold vine snaked the length like the hilt, connecting the two ends.

Starriace sent the blade home, and an arcing cold from the steel made her shiver. With one object claimed, she turned to the safe. She reached up and opened the portrait, waved her hand over the lockbox, but it held fast.

The second attempt ended the same.

Perhaps she had not concentrated enough?

Desperation made her heart flutter. How could she open the locked safe? Her thoughts whirled through countless tactics but dismissed them out of hand, each more absurd than the last.

The last and most preposterous notion involved breaking down the granules of metal to a finite level, rearranging the matter to gain access. The feat would be complex and difficult, not counting the time constraint and general lack of knowledge.

While training with Fife, he instructed her to siphon gold from a cave wall, pulling ore through stone. But that was different. Then, she pulled something through another object; now, she was rearranging matter to allow her admission.

The safe filled her vision. She drank in every detail, the hinges, the door frame, and the lock. The subtle variations in the metal, hairline fractures, fissures too small to detect with her naked eye availed themselves to her. Need spurred her, and desire drove her, clearing the pathway for what she wanted.

Despite the vastness of her attempt, even on something small like the safe's door, Judas's words resurfaced, simplified: if it can be dreamed, it can be achieved.

The problem lay with finding the limits of reality, dreams, and ability.

Her eyes bore straight ahead, looking at, in, and through the safe's hatch. She applied intent and focused her will through the tip of her wand. How long she waited, she couldn't say, but the breath in her lungs burned as the solid matter stirred under her influence. The metal granules swarmed like angry hornets.

At the center, the surface peeled back, and a small hole appeared. Her focus hardened as an opposite force resisted her magic. The moment she let her grasp slip, the metal would reform. An angry red edged the opening, heat caressed her face. The warmth slickened her wand hand with sweat. An acrid scent coiled through the air. With one final push, she forced the opening larger, and the resistance doubled.

The hellstone lay within, naked and attainable. Her hand darted in, found purchase, and pulled it free. The large gem glittered red with her sudden touch. She could still feel the faint trace of Rusem's death in the stone. The small amount of magic within swirled at her touch but otherwise remained inert.

And now, she had what she came for.

The metal trembled at the edges of her consciousness, and she released her hold. The hole disappeared like waves crashing over jutting rock, but the metal did not ripple. Her tentative fingers touched the door. Other than the tepid surface, nothing seemed amiss.

Satisfied, she worked her way to the door and caught her reflection in a mirror. The faint scarlet glow of her eyes disturbed her. With her body covered in black robes, and the deeds she just committed, shame roused within her. In many ways, she stared at a reflection that screamed despised villain. She was Xilor, minus the towering height and hidden face.

Her gaze flickered back to her eyes. Rusem's tale of how she unleashed a magic too powerful to control came back to haunt her. Her eyes would glow for the rest of her life.

Is this what I have become? Some kind of monster?

As she mused on her reflection, her mind drifted, and she realized that her eyes hadn't burned with irritation in a while, nothing like they did that night she received the Embrace's offer. She'd almost lost control then, wanting to kill him for daring to insinuate her helplessness and that she was a monster like him, like the men she killed.

Her gaze flickered to the sword and the hellstone.

Guilt crashed over her. She stole from an old man, a fellow mage, and a kind person. There was no way she could ever repay him for the priceless artifacts. Did that make her like Xilor—taking these treasures? Rusem had paid half of his kingdom just to get the hellstone.

She reached into her coin purse and pulled out three bright eyes, the golden coin of the Ralloc and Marcoalyn domains, and placed them on the counter, a paltry gift, but it helped soothe her disquiet.

She glanced back at the mirror, but this time, instead of seeing a malefactor, the beautiful woman that Old John raved about appeared, the lover of Kam manifested. When was the last time she glimpsed her reflection?

An appreciative hand smoothed the front of her robes, and she admired the way they hugged every contour despite her not being as voluptuous as Lily. Starriace was pleased with John's tailoring.

She exited in the same manner she entered, threw the bolt, and secured the door. The lock clanged louder than she would've liked, but she couldn't change what was done. Her aura expanded, and she hastened to the nearest alleyway that held the promise of shadows and slipped into the night, seeking her last destination.

Sentries garbed in black stood by the front doors to the Halls of the One. Through a window, the interior glowed with faint candlelight, and the outside was poorly lit with torches spaced too far apart, offering her shadows between each bracket.

She gathered herself to dart to another spot when bells tolled in the city behind her.

She glanced in the direction of old John's place. When she locked the bolt back, it must've awakened him. He no doubt inspected his shop and found himself robbed. The bells were certainly for the city guards, putting them on alert. They'd search to find the thief. Only another distraction would help her now, a diversion to pull citizens and patrols away from the search.

Leaving her spot, she worked her way down the slope from the religious castle, keeping to the shadows. In the town, the first building she reached offered little concealment, but the alley across the street teased a deeper obscurity. Crossing the street, she flattened herself against the wall, the gloom offering a reprieve to think.

Not for the first time, she wished for a spell to conceal herself, but if such magic were possible, it'd require a subtlety she didn't possess or the time for methodical practice. Subtlety wasn't her way, and perhaps that'd be her downfall, but not tonight.

She was too close to her goal to be denied.

After a quick assessment of the buildings, she found a suitable target. One hundred meters down the main road and across, she saw the local blacksmith and a stable. Inside, hay, feed, and other flammable objects would catch fire, but not before she released the animals.

She may be cruel, burning down a stable, but not a monster.

A fire could be doused, but rounding up scared horses would buy her more time. She darted between alleys until she reached the stable. In the distance, she heard the voices of several people, guards most likely. The jingle of chain mail and the sound of swords leaping from their sheaths confirmed her suspicions.

Arriving without incident, she steeled herself, pointed her wand and watched as a fire engulfed the hay and wood within. Wand stowed, she concentrated on the latches and urged them to unfasten. In the panic, she overexerted. Gates exploded from hinges, ripped away by an unseen force or caved in, shattering into fragments.

The pandemonium spurred the animals to bolt.

The structure was engulfed by the time she made it back to the Halls of the One. Silence no longer mattered next to the effulgent glow and roaring flames. At the crest of the hill next to the chapel, she noted that the guards had moved closer to town, observing the peril from a distance. They chortled, and Starriace glanced back at the city. The whole town seemed to have shown up for the chaos.

A sentinel came running from the settlement, materializing from the darkness. He was doubled over in exhaustion, catching his breath. The armor and weapons didn't help.

"What is it? Speak quickly," one sentry said.

The running soldier pointed back toward the city.

"There's a fire."

"Yeah, we can see that. So?"

"We need more men to help. If we don't get more men, the flames will catch neighboring buildings, too."

"We were told not to leave the disciples."

"Damned be the disciples! Who cares if they go back to the One early, it'd be a great day for us. The request comes from the kaptyn of the watch, not me."

"Very well, we'll send more men."

Starriace watched the messenger scurry back down, but the two guards and the Halls of the One missed his departure. The first guard turned to his fellow sentry.

"Gather all the men and help. When they're done, do anything they require, then return."

"But what about the disciples?"

"I'm sure they'll be fine, but you won't unless you move your ass!"

The sentry scurried off. The first looked back to the messenger but only found Starriace standing in his place.

"Good evening," she said.

Her arrival flustered him for a moment, but he recovered.

"Be welcomed, lass!"

A smile crept on his startled face as his appraising eyes roved over her.

Well, at least John's clothes are doing what they're supposed to.

"What are you doing here, especially at this hour? Come to confess? Need help with your Enlightenment?"

He seemed to remember his duty faintly, his hand resting on the pommel of his sword.

"None are supposed to be here. We have orders."

His eyes alone tell me he's not truly devout.

He closed the distance between them, his head swiveling as if expecting to see someone or a trap. When she didn't answer right away, he gave her an expectant look.

"Have you come alone?"

"Yes, and I'm not sure what Enlightenment is, but—"

He snatched her by the throat, his grip cutting off the rest of her sentence.

"Only the heathens prowl the night," he said, as if quoting sacred texts. "The vagabond, the harlot, and those with the seed of murder in their heart welcome the shadows of night just as their soul is tainted by their deeds."

He jerked her hard, pulling her to the shadows of the wall. She clutched his hand around her throat, just to keep from being dragged. The lone sentry manhandled her without compassion or remorse, flinging her against the wall. The blow knocked the wind from her lungs.

Starriace tried to pull away, but his strength in one arm overpowered all exertions. When she dug her heels into the ground, he laughed at her pitiful attempt and wrenched her around like a child. She tried to mouth a scream, to demand release, but no sound escaped other than struggling breath.

"We've known your kind before. How many times do you wicked wretches think you can steal from the One and not be punished?"

What? He thinks I'm someone else!

He leered close. His callous hands tightened. His breath smelled like rotten fruit and a touch of decayed flesh. She tried to dart away, but he shook her.

"None of that, now, or you won't be able to walk away."

She didn't know if he meant to kill her if she resisted, or if he planned to ravage her so hard she could only crawl.

He released her throat, and she slumped against the wall, coughing. With a rough jerk, he grabbed her by the arm and hauled her up.

"Come on, lass. The disciples will want to question you."

He started dragging her forward. She dug in her heels. With a heave, she pulled free.

"Oi!" he snapped, reaching out again, his fist closing around the cloth by her breasts. They opened with the sudden movement, partially exposing her.

"None of that!"

The memories came back, the ones she buried and locked away. She swore to forget them, but the moment brought them to the forefront. Anxiety rocked her. Her insides turned cold, his words reverberated through her ears. The panic was all too familiar. The jumbled memories came rushing back, forcing her to relive those moments in the hovel with the three men.

He's going to rape me!

A laugh escaped the guard, and in retrospect, it was one of disbelief. In the moment, it seemed leering.

His laughter jarred her out of the disturbing moment. The repressed memories flooded through her mind. The laugh, the smell, the jeering face, the three men, and Mr. Pleasure.

Rage made her eyes burn, a pain unlike anything since her encounter with the sheol that nearly took her life. Wrath filled her, hot and agonizing. The need for release washed over her. Animosity lashed out, its heat melting the ice around her insides.

Her essence welled up.

Acrimony devoured all pity and remorse, guilt and sadness. Without hesitation, her hands lashed out, touching the guard's face. His eyes went wide as if witnessing a ghost. Horror riddled each feature, and he dropped to the ground.

Dead.

She gazed down at her hands in a mixture of horror and awe.

How in the Shades of the Underworld did I do that?

She eyed the man. His pale face made him appear as if he'd died hours or days ago rather than seconds. Her frantic mind tried to piece it all together, but rage kept coherent thoughts from forming.

She'd…siphoned all the life from him. More than that, it was the horror that throbbed through her. She hadn't meant to kill the man, and what if she did the same to Kam or Lily on accident. A jolt of trepidation shot through her.

She stumbled away, shaken, straightening her disheveled robes to keep her hands busy, her mind from fixating. Shouts in the distance reminded her of the fire and the necessity of time. Without wasting any more, she made her legs move, entering the building, and casting aside any discretion she once held.

Inside, she paused, contemplating where to start.

The archbishop is an important man, so where would he reside?

In the Ralloc and Marcoalyn domains, patrons of importance would reside in the levels closest to the ground, but she didn't know about here. Haste quickened her actions; the fire would burn out or be dowsed soon. She lacked the understanding of the religious order and altered her approach.

The male wizardkind, religious or not, would flaunt himself in vanity whenever he had the chance, though there were exceptions. Here, where everyone was supposed to be equal, she could think of nothing that might set him apart but his elevated status.

Elevated status…

She cast an eye up, letting her magevision flicker. A honeycomb of stairs, doors, and rooms filled her sight.

Of course! He'd be in the highest reaches of the chapel, the best view and the furthest away from everyone.

Using her enhanced vision, she spied the hidden door in the wall to her left and opened it. She bounded up the first staircase she stumbled upon and started her ascent, taking two steps at a time. Beads of sweat flecked her hairline as she progressed in squared circles, climbing higher.

The stairs ended in a long hallway lined with crimson carpet edged with gold tassels. The door at the end, and presumably to the archbishop's room, was silver, gold, and wood.

She crept towards the hatch, pressing her ear against it. The cold sent goosebumps down her neck, but no sound stirred beyond.

Stepping through the door, she expected to search for the concealed prizes, but Salvation sat on the archbishop's desk. The ornate display stand rivaled the weapon's beauty.

This is way too easy.

A voice taking Rusem's form entered her mind as she reached for the hilt, reminding her of Hagen's greed and malice. Starriace shook the voice clear; she didn't have time for that now. She did, however, use malice to kill that guard.

Would it be enough?

Still, the recollection brought up a good point, one that illuminated the flaws in Rusem's quest for the stones. Starriace retained her own theories as to why they didn't work for Rusem.

The answer was simple: he didn't have the real brimstones.

He thought he possessed four when he only had one, Death's brimstone. It was why he never wrote in the journal afterward or wasn't friends with Judas, or the fact that the warlock never mentioned Rusem.

He died.

When she first met his spirit in the City of Despair's temple, Rusem told her he couldn't remember what had happened to him.

Death is what happened. And Xilor...

Starriace had her own thoughts on the actual brimstones and she was fairly certain the hellstone wasn't one. Erring on the side of caution, she took it. Judgment called to her, pulled her into its grasp of greed. Once she held the blade in her hands, she knew beyond all doubt that the weapon would be hers.

The first brimstone only will come to you out of an act of greed.

Rusem fought the urge to not take the Sword of Judgment. How he resisted its call, she'd never know, but was convinced that Rusem made a fatal flaw, and doomed himself.

She presumed why Judgment had called to her and Rusem. Taking the sword off her back, she scrutinized it in the pale candlelight. Her thoughts floated back to the room of artifacts with Old John. Starriace had been thinking in the wrong definitions of the brimstone. She thought it would be red and filled with magic, almost like John's hellstone. The brimstone was devious, hiding in plain sight...like the black pearl within Judgement's guard.

The brimstone was in the Sword of Judgment, which was why Rusem felt the pull of greed, the calling mirroring the intent of his heart. But he rejected it to his doom, and Starriace almost made the same mistake.

Starriace reached out and touched the white steel on display. If Judgment was beautiful, the nearest description of Salvation was breathtaking. Silver where Judgement was gold, ivory-white where the other had been black. In the guard, a large white pearl gleamed.

The second brimstone? Could it be that simple?

She plucked it from its stand and ran her fingers lovingly across the surface before placing it in the scabbard and shouldering it. The twin blades mirrored each other, forming an 'X' across her back. Once secure, she turned to leave but jolted to a stop.

A man stood behind her.

Age riddled his face; she guessed he was in the autumn years of his life. Older than Judas, but not by more than an age. He still had hair on the sides of his head, but the top was gleaming in the faint light, portraying his baldness like a crown of splendor.

"That doesn't belong to you," he said.

"It does now."

Starriace strolled to the door, but he moved to block her way.

"You'll not leave with that! It belongs to the Disciples!"

The rage she felt earlier returned, her eyes festering with irritation. She blinked several times, resisting the urge to scratch. A haunting voice filled her head.

Remove him from your path.

"Move."

"You can still leave without harsh ramifications. A pretty girl like you? Your atonement could be in service to the One, and bringing others to the thrall of Enlightenment. Your actions are sacrilegious, but you can find redemption and forgiveness. This will only be offered once."

Starriace noted his slow, casual movements as his hand slipped down towards something in his robes. Was it a wand? A dagger? In a blur, he reached, muttering an incantation before his wand cleared.

Ferocity gave rise to savagery. Her hand thrust out, launching him back. He hurtled towards the wall that tore itself apart under her influence. As if an arrow released from a taut string, he flew, then plummeted to the ground far below.

The wall rippled, rebuilding itself the moment he passed through.

Anger fueled her potency, her magic.

And by the gods, she felt unstoppable.

Once more, she noticed the correlation between her and Xilor, more alike than she cared to admit. Her eyes burned hot, bringing forth cleansing tears. Agitation always festered beneath, and when the old man drew on her, the rage took over.

There were times when she had thought she'd reached the pinnacle of her abilities, only to be surprised the next time she called upon them. The library in Ralloc came to mind, as did her battle with Judas. This marked another, as did the man whom she killed outside.

The old man's death triggered the second brimstone: malice.

She picked her way back down the stairs when bells in the Halls of the One tolled out their distress.

Chapter 34: Dlad City

On the tenth night, Daniel led Xenomene down to the room where she'd dueled Bitcher.

Toyed with, more like.

When she arrived, she noted a bed and several other recent additions to the room, too many to take in with a glance. They puzzled her more than anything. She peered back at him, arching an eyebrow.

"You said you wanted the real me, to hold nothing back. Is that still your offer?"

She cast a wary glance at the newest additions.

"Should I be worried?"

He chuckled.

"Not really."

"Then, the offer stands."

She didn't regret the decision, though couldn't say with certainty she enjoyed its entirety. Daniel proved to be in his element, which fueled the flames of her arousal. He played with her, inflicting small amounts of pain. In short, he was a sadist.

She didn't balk, but it would've been better for a true masochist, which she wasn't. She enjoyed submitting to his petty tortures, but her heart lay within the domination rather than the pain. The man could make her body sing, whether tied up, her ass blistered scarlet, or being choked, he took advantage of holding nothing back.

With modesty abandoned, he left nothing of her untouched. Many times, she almost asked him to stop, but pride kept her from giving in, and by the end, Daniel probably knew her body better than Bitcher ever did.

His appetite sated, she rolled to her side facing him, sore all over. She lay there, hair sweaty and disheveled, face glistening with sweat, and panted. Glancing down her body, red welts marred her alabaster skin.

"Are you satisfied?" she asked.

"You're angry."

"No, I'm asking if you're satisfied. Did I uphold my end of the deal?"

"Are you saying I can do more?"

She nodded.

"If you're not done, then finish. This will be the last time."

"Why?"

Even to her ears, his voice sounded wounded.

"Don't be petulant."

She wiped wet hair from her face.

"Our ten days are up. I don't want people—"

She stopped, considered her words, and started again.

"Some will say I'm fucking you to become the next heir. I don't want to perpetuate the rumor. After this, I'm staying far away from you to dispel the myth. If I'm to be heir after you, it's by my own blood, sweat, and tears."

He nodded. She could tell he tried to understand but took it as a personal refusal.

"You're the best I've ever had," she said, and she meant it. "If it came down to a choice of who I fucked the day before I died, you'd be first on the list. Please, try to understand."

"I do, but it doesn't lessen the blow."

"I know, and I'm sorry. So, are you finished?"

"Yes," he intoned with heavy finality.

When they were dressed, her shirt falling into place, her demeanor changed to business.

"I need one Heart and one Krey to replace me in Tiny's squad. Oh, and a replacement for Bitcher, too. If you have a suggestion for the Krey, then I've already made my choice for the Heart."

"Take your pick. Tiny left with Bitcher's replacement already. I'll send someone to fetch a portal master for you."

"With your permission, I'd like to change some personnel of the squads, shuffle them some."

"Xeno," Daniel sighed, and she heard the frustration.

He finished slipping his foot into his boot.

"I'll forgive your ignorance, since no one taught you better, but you are a ko-don. You do what you want, as long as you have justification. You speak with my voice, and you carry the authority of my office, as all the ko-dons do."

She crossed her arms.

"About fucking time someone gave me some real power. Now, shit's gonna happen."

He chuckled and led the way back to his office. From there, she returned to her room with quick steps and avoided all contact with waking Krey. She may no longer care if they judged, but walking around in garments bearing all the red marks wasn't the greatest decision. She changed into black pants and put on a long-sleeved shirt.

It was cool enough to warrant the change.

Dressed in her armor, she packed a bag, grabbed her sword, and returned to the heir's office. When she entered, Daniel instructed her to drop her things and follow. In the Pit, the most senior of Krey stood in formation—that only meant they weren't raw recruits—but still virgins yet bloodied in battle. A few were veterans, of course, but they were old and decrepit by comparison.

All could help whatever squad she decided to put them in, but she'd end up replacing the veterans in short order. She'd rather not take them, leaving them to be teachers rather than ushering them to their imminent deaths.

She walked through the lines, scrutinized their facial features and demeanor. The last thing she needed was another mean-spirited person. Health, height, weight, and weapon of choice, played a part in deciding. From their stance and making sure they had all their teeth, no detail was deemed too trivial.

Squads didn't need a Krey with a mouth infection. It'd put them out of service, kill him, or the disease could spread if careless enough.

She settled on a Krey of average height and build; he wasn't dashing and kingly nor a mutt, but he had brown hair and eyes which made him distinctive from Islanders. There were too many of them running around anyways. She told him to collect his things, dress in his armor, and meet them in the heir's office.

When they returned upstairs, Daniel sat down behind his desk.

"Who's this Heart you want?"

"I want the man who healed Bitcher. Having him near me will ensure he keeps quiet. And since I've never worked with a male Heart, other than the one with Omegryk, I'm curious."

Daniel grunted and signed some papers in front of him, cursing.

"What?" she prompted.

"Fucking Ralloc. The lot of them have their head up a unicorn's ass. They're thinking about letting the Forgotten Isles become part of the domain. Apparently, they can bring a lot to the table; that's why they are considering it."

"And a lot to the bedroom."

She shrugged.

"It makes sense, we're already overrun with fucking Islanders. They fuck like dogs over there and birth litters like cats."

The word cat made her remember her little Omen back at the barracks in Dlad City.

Shit! I forgot about him! I hope he's not starving or dead.

Daniel whistled at his guard, a man posted at the door. He sent him to fetch the A'uri Xenomene requested. By the time the A'uri entered, the Krey she'd chosen was back with his gear.

"We're leaving the Hive. You're now part of my units down at Dlad City," she said without preamble. "Any questions?"

When they didn't answer, she nodded and shooed them out the door. She turned to the heir.

"Any last words?"

He shook his head.

"Just remember what I said: I'd die content."

She basked in his gratification and favored him with a smile.

"Well, I can say the last nine days have been fun, and last night was… interesting. I think I might've picked up a few tricks from an old dog."

He chuckled.

"Got more, too!"

"I'm sure, but I'll never know."

Xenomene turned, leaving the Hive again.

Outside, the two newest members were waiting with the portal master. She nodded to the third man who began casting his portal. It would take a little while to activate the rune. She turned to the Krey.

"What's your name?"
"Rabbit."
"Are you fast, Rabbit?"
"Depends on if you like it that way."
Her lips pulled into a grin.
"You'll fit right in, but I'd change your name to Slave or Meat."
"Why's that?"
"You're a lucky man. You're going to a team full of girls. You'll live like a king there, I imagine."
"Then, I better just stick to Rabbit and only hope I'm fast enough to satisfy them all."
She rolled her eyes and looked at the Heart.
"You're going to my former squad. The last Heart died, so you'll take her place."
He nodded but didn't reply. By then, the portal was opened, and they stepped through and into a world of carnage.
A massive boulder crushed a half dozen men right beside them, showering the emerging group with dirt, blood splatter, and flecks of rock. The stone rolled and shattered a building, where it finally came to rest.
Fires erupted all over the camp. Resounding roars jarred her to the bone. A massive shadow passed overhead; the beating wings reached her ears before she spied the dragon. With an open mouth, a pillar of molten fire rained down and blazed a trail through the middle of the camp.
She dodged before being consumed by the inferno.
"To me!" she yelled to the Heart and Rabbit.
She sprinted away from the battle to their barracks.
"Drop your shit!" she shouted over the noise. "This is your chance to get bloodied, virgin!"
Rabbit tossed his stuff aside and slid on his helmet. She did the same, and they darted forward, toward the carnage. Rabbit and Heart trailed behind her as she ran for the south wall, outdistancing them, and ascending the ramp. From atop, she looked over the engagement.
It wasn't a massive force like she expected. There were, perhaps, twenty thousand goblins and trolls, and though large, they had at least four times the soldiers and three squads of Krey. The victory was almost assured, but the dragons might turn the crux of the battle.
There were only two.
After the Cape Gythmel assault and Warlock Lakayre dwindling their numbers, perhaps Xilor decided on discretion.
She glanced down.
The Krey fighting just outside the wall and a hundred meters to the right of her. She spied the Minds of the squads on the parapets and worked her way over to them. Spectre's Mind caught sight of her as she closed the distance, and the meld overcame her.
Xenomene!

Hey girl, where ya been hiding?

This is so much fun—

I'm glad you're not dead—

Look out for that troll—

Come to my blade, you pretty—

I have a new Krey, Rabbit; he'll be joining you, as well as a new Heart—

Good, cause I'm getting tired of pulling double duty. Next person that gets cut, doesn't get healed—

I thought Krey were supposed to be good—

Cut down on the banter.

Aye, aye, big man—

Watch it, arrows incoming—

Move left, now, reform!—

Wedge left, go.

I have the lead.

That fucking cunt shot me. Coward!

That's because you're so ugly—

I can't concentrate with all this useless banter—

Listen here, my little bitches! Tiny's in charge, obey him as you would me—

Oh, I'd obey your every whim—

Rabbit, go, jump down the wall, you too, Heart—

More arrows incoming, move—

Incoming soldiers, making a beeline for us—

Open ranks, wedge front—

Wedge front, aye—

I have the lead—

Big man has point—

Alright cunts, next person that talks and it isn't fight related, they're going to get it—

Rabbit coming into wedge—

In the back, Peewee—

Xeno, see to those dragons, would you?

On it.

She withdrew from the meld and searched for the dragons. One swooped mere meters overhead, a boulder clutched in its claws. It released the rock before climbing and turning. She followed the rock with her eyes, watching it crush soldiers as they put out fires.

Xenomene turned back as the other dragon landed atop the wall, settling a dozen meters away. Goblins and trolls covered its back. Letting go of their restraints, they dropped into the inner courtyard.

Leaping into action, she pulled her steel and charged the dragon, the bloodlust taking her. Without a unit, she could fight to her full potential, but without a Mind, if anyone got in the way, they'd perish.

In a few quick steps, she launched herself, blade raised overhead, coming down like a dagger. The point pierced one of the few vulnerable spots.

Its left eye.

The dragon thrashed as she hoisted herself onto the beast. Her fingers clutched scales with her left hand; her right gripped the sword hilt.

The dragon swung in the other direction, throwing her atop its head. She yanked her sword free. Half of the molten-colored eye came out with the blade. She swung the saber down on its head, and it ricocheted off, almost rattled out of her hands.

She twirled the steel, pointing down. The tip slipped between scales. She pushed with all her might. The sword slid in a few inches, but it didn't penetrate to the crystallized bone within. She pulled it out, reared back, and drove down in the same spot.

The weapon snapped.

Half remained with the hilt; the other half stayed planted in the skull.

She rolled off the left side, slamming the broken blade deep into the wounded eye, then dropped to the wall, landing on her feet. She ran to the nearest archer, snatched the sword from his sheath, and turned back to the dragon.

The man reached for his taken weapon; she spun back, and he lost an arm for his trouble. Warm, spurting blood soaked her face.

Turning back, goblins and trolls swarmed her position and blocked her path. They fell on her, and she cut a swath through them. The press of bodies fell away, no more than saplings bending in the wind.

She traversed as a black blur, death incarnate. Green-black blood covered the sword. Entrails highlighted her path. The thrashing dragon lay before her, struggling to retrieve the blade from its eye and skull.

Limbs, heads, and weapons fell as her steel whistled through the air. Before she'd drawn a dozen breaths, fifteen bodies lay in her wake.

She reached the dragon, leaping for its eye. Her left hand gripped the eyelid. The new steel plunged deep a half dozen times before the dragon managed to fling her loose.

The backs of unsuspecting trolls broke her fall in the interior far below. Before her momentum stopped, she rolled away but struggled to suck in a breath. The trolls found their feet again and attacked.

She ducked between them, dragged the saber across the belly of one and swept the keen edge through the leg of the other. Both crashed to the ground, and she impaled both with a single blow.

Another troll loomed close by. Her blade flickered, and the creature fell, beheaded.

Most trolls and goblins failed to notice her arrival. She ran through the ranks from behind, plunging through backs, legs, and throats. She paused, gasping for breath as red filled her vision.

Someone approached, and she pivoted, striking him down. The horrified expression registered as a wizardkind soldier, but it was an enemy coming for her.

Out of the corner of her eyes, soldiers turned their attention to her. Unintelligible shouts rang out, but they didn't pierce the bloodlust. Two more came forward, yelling and pointing. One got too close and lost his hand and half of his forearm.

The other charged. Her leg snapped up, catching him in the groin. With a twirl, the steel breached the top of his skull. The sword held his mouth agape. His tongue fell out when she jerked the blade free.

More soldiers closed in.

She bent and picked up a second sword, one for each hand.

An arrow slammed into her chest, where the right shoulder connected to her torso. She broke the shaft. The bloodlust screamed for carnage, for satiation. She rushed them, answering the call.

Their mail and armor helped little against her fury. Screams filled the air, matching her bellows of primal rage, and she survived the windmill of steel.

Someone shouted above the commotion.

"Shoot her, bring her down, shoot the bitch!"

The who didn't register, but the threat did. Someone of authority, a rallying point.

She pivoted, changing course, working to the new threat. Swords and spears struck at her as fast as angry serpents trampled underfoot. She caught, trapped, and rolled the incoming weapons out of play. Each attacker was mercilessly gutted, maimed, or killed. When the last two that blocked the way fell, she sprinted at the man.

"Kill the bitch! Kill 'er. Somebody fucking stop her!"

She leapt and drove both blades through his chest. Wrenching them free, she swung in a crisscross pattern, quartering the man.

The bloodlust cooed with praise.

And she wanted more.

She turned around, and the sharp edge of a sword nicked her left arm, missing her back. She slapped the attacker with the flat of the blade and lunged low, the other sword stabbing up through his manhood, the saber exiting through his lower back.

Dragging the steel and pivoting, an arrow whistled past, so close the wind from its wake tickled her nose. The archer drew another arrow.

She ran, dodging, juking, and hopping over attacks, paying them no heed, focusing on the archer.

He had to die.

He let loose, and she batted the arrow with a flash of steel. He nocked the third. With a deft pivot, she spun past him, cleaving him at the waist. His torso thudded at her feet, his legs sputtered, danced, then fell.

The soldiers closed in on her. She lifted the blades, the battle stance of the Jaikari, forward saber low, rear one high.

Before she could blink, A'uri surrounded her, and a hand snagged her by the shoulder, projecting thoughts into her mind, melding, bringing the bloodlust under control.

Her mind fought it, but more A'uri reached out, joining the meld. All the A'uri surrounded her, the Hands and Hearts facing out to keep the advancing soldiers at bay. The red fell from her vision, and she saw them. Most wore faces of contorted rage and malevolence; they wanted blood, revenge for the bodies left in her wake.

The soldiers drew their circle tighter.

"Get back," a Hand warned.

"Fuck that! She's to die, she is!" one soldier cried out.

"Cut the wench's head off!" said another.

"Stay back, you've been warned," the newest Heart echoed.

"Like hell! Turn her over, or you'll all die!" someone else shouted.

The crowd chanted for her head. The Hands drew on their magic with incantations, their hands erupting in green-blue fire.

"Next one who takes a step forward is going to fry like bacon."

"Oi! Move!" Tiny roared.

The soldiers spun around. He scared one soldier so bad, he jumped and dropped his spear. The angry crowd poised to riot quelled, seeing a small sea of flat black wading among them. Yells turned muted, and silence descended in hushed waiting.

The appearance of the Krey reminded the soldiers that if one could be an unstoppable force, twenty-seven Krey and nine A'uri would be impossible to stand against. The Krey trounced opponents ten to twenty times their number.

Removed from the bloodlust, Xenomene wiped the gore from her eyes. She looked down, finding her alabaster skin covered with sanguine fluid, armor drenched, and two swords clutched in her hands.

"What happened?" she asked, still breathing hard.

"You don't remember?" Tiny's Mind queried.

She shook her head.

"You entered the bloodlust. When you finished with the goblins, trolls, and the dragon, you turned on the soldiers."

"Did I win?"

The Mind jerked a thumb over his shoulder, and she had to stand on her toes to see beyond. On the parapets lay a dragon, its head hanging, nearly touching the ground. A massive pool of blood lay underneath.

"How is it you don't remember?" the Mind posed, perplexed.

An uncontrolled Krey generally remembered portions of what happened, despite being unable to stop themselves.

"I don't know. How bad is it?"

"Bad. You killed or maimed all the goblins and trolls, then you cut down a shit-ton of soldiers, including Jynerul Vikal."

"Will he survive?"

The Mind shook his head, his face grim.

"He's in four pieces."

The Krey surrounded the A'uri, their weapons ready. As a cohesive unit, they moved from the courtyard and toward their barracks. Soldiers followed but gave a wide berth. They trailed them halfway through the city until Kernoyl Tyku came out and ordered them to stand down.

They reluctantly obeyed.

Once in the barracks, the Krey removed their armor in silence.

"When you're done seeing to your armor and weapons," Xeno called out, "the do-dons are to report to my office. You too, Rabbit."

She asked the A'uri, who didn't have armor to attend, to have the camp hands fetch water for bathing. She and the do-dons were to be the first in line. The A'uri set off with a nod, and she ascended the stairs alone.

She'd just reached her office and started to strip out of the mired armor when steaming water arrived. She inquired as to how they were so quick to respond. One helper, a man, said they began preparations at the start of the conflict.

With a nod, she pulled off the rest of the armor, stripped out of her blood-soaked clothes, and sat on a stool, waiting for the tub to fill. Dried rivulets of blood caked her ivory skin. Gore, flesh, and other unidentifiable elements had snuck through the crevices of the dragon-plate armor.

When the camp hands finished, she sank into the tub and lathered up. The warm water helped her back to the present, breaking her stupor.

Finished washing, she toweled herself dry and dressed. The hot water hid all of Daniel's red welts. A plate of food materialized as the female camp hands returned to empty the tub. The men returned with buckets, disappointed to find her dressed.

She wolfed down the meal like a famished saricrocian. Before long, everyone retreated, taking the empty plate, too. As the last one left, the do-dons and Rabbit entered.

"I'll be brief," she said without preamble. "Spectre, meet the newest member of your squad. You now owe Tiny a member."

Spectre grinned.

"Take your pick, big boy, they'll all fuck, I assure you."

"No doubt," he commented.

"Syn's always had a problem saying no. She isn't Harlot, but she'll do just as good."

"Fine, Syn, it is," he said curtly.

Xenomene watched the exchange, noting Tiny's defensive posture, his arms crossed.

"Right," Xenomene said. "Rabbit, Spectre's your do-don. Leave, go play. Tell the girls that you're part of their squad. It sucks to be you."

"Are you kidding?" Lyan blurted. "That's a lucky man!"

"Yeah, until his dick falls off," Tiny countered.

Lyan made a painful face.

"Hadn't thought about that part."

"Ever seen a bull in a pen of heifers in heat?" Tiny continued. "He'll breed himself to death. That's Rabbit's fate."

"We'll take good care of him," Spectre said with a mischievous smile.

Rabbit left, his hurried footsteps echoing down the hall.

"Where's Bitcher?" Spectre asked.

"Not with us any longer," Xenomene said. "Tiny, the new Heart is yours. Will it be a problem?"

Tiny unfolded his arms.

"No, I don't foresee any."

"Good. Anything for me?"

She looked at each in turn.

"Where have you been?" Lyan inquired.

"Taking care of business."

"Would that business include Bitcher?" Spectre asked.

She gave her a cold look.

"Yes. Anything else?"

"Yeah, when are we getting out of here?" Lyan asked. "I feel like we're wasting our time by not being where the fighting is. The groups coming against us are too small to be considered a true battle."

"Like a feint?" Tiny supplied.

"Yeah," Spectre agreed.

"I don't know. I'll attend the meetings again if they don't take my head when I go."

"They're going to want to know about that," Tiny mumbled.

"They aren't the only one. Anything else?"

They shook their heads.

"Go, eat, take care of your Krey."

They turned to go when she spoke again.

"Not you, Tiny."

A look passed between Lyan and Tiny, and Spectre gave him a smug grin. The door shut behind them, and Tiny faced her.

"Is there a problem with you and Spectre?"

"No."

"Okay, what about you and Syn?"

He shook his head.

"If anything's going on, I'm going to find out, so I'd rather hear it from you first."

"I fucked them," he said in a rush.

"Both?"

"Yeah, sorry."

She laughed, and to be honest, it was what she needed to hear.

"You don't sound sorry."

"Yeah, well…you don't sound sorry, either!"

Her laughter died.

"Oh, so this is about the heir."

"Damn right, it is! You shouldn't have done that!"

Agitation darkened his features, and his eyes blazed with indignation.

Xenomene let her voice drop.

"You should never assume to tell me what to do with my life. You don't see me having a problem with you fucking Syn and Spectre, do you?"

"But you were just a hole for him to fuck. He has no feelings for you!"

"And what were Syn and Spectre, if not a hole to fuck?"

"That was me …"

"Getting revenge?"

"I was going to say, being stupid, but yes."

"Well, I hope it was a good revenge."

"I—" he stopped.

"Yes?"

"They weren't the only ones."

"So? Who cares? Do you think I care, Tiny? We're not together and have no obligations to each other. You're free to do whatever with whoever."

There, she'd said it, and it was now in the open and lying between them.

His head jerked up, eyes blazing, but he held his tongue.

"You're not beholden to me, nor I to you. What the heir and I did is none of your business."

"I hope it was good and worth it," he said, voice dripping with bitterness.

Xenomene took a moment before responding. She'd let Tiny foster a hope between them for too long, and she was to blame for the current predicament.

"The best I've ever had."

Tiny spun on his heel and stormed out, slamming the door so hard it broke. He didn't bother to look back or apologize.

Fuck, everything I say makes shit worse! Where the hell is he getting this attitude from? And now, I've got to replace that fucking door. What a whiner!

She sat on the bed in a huff. Omen came up from behind, crawling out of his hiding spot near her pillow. He meowed and purred as she petted and hugged him.

"I'm glad you're happy to see me."

She glanced around the room and spotted a food and water bowl and a litter box against the back wall on the far side of her room. The desk hid it from view.

"Someone took care of you, but who?"

Tiny. He's the only one that would.

With her head nestling the pillow, she pulled the cat into her chest and curled up with it. An unfamiliar odor laced the cushion. Nose to the pillowcase, a suggestion of Tiny's scent hit her nostrils.

Fuck, he even slept in here. Is he just another man with a fixation?

The longer she thought about him sleeping in her bed, the angrier she became. He, like Bitcher, invaded her space.

With a sigh of frustration, she got up. Too many things required her attention to wallow in irritation. She was a ko-don, and as Daniel stated, she spoke with his voice, and her actions carried the weight of his office.

Her gaze swept to the two swords she used in battle. She grabbed a rag and wiped them down. Cleaned but without sheaths, she used a belt to hold them in place. She left the barracks and went to see the camp hands, reporting the broken door. They dithered, saying it would take time.

"Now! Get it done before I get back. And change my fucking sheets, too!"

From there, she visited the blacksmith, a young man apprenticed to some kaptyn still stationed in Ralloc. She gave him specifications for a new blade to be forged, replacing the one she'd lost. The last stop, the command tent, welcomed her with open hostility.

The officers were up in arms. They swore with colorful iterations about the anatomy between her legs, what to stuff between them, and where and how she could sit. When the original, spiteful quips ran their course, she silenced them with a menacing glance.

"I'm sorry about your men. You all know what happens when a Krey enters the bloodlust. You've all been told and warned, and now you pay the price for your arrogance. You know it has to be controlled; you've heard the stories at your military schools. Don't you dare place all the blame on my shoulders. Had I not felt threatened, had someone not been too close to me, I wouldn't have attacked. Someone, somewhere, knows the truth because they saw it."

She straightened, her spine stiffening.

"The next time I come into your presence to attend the meetings, you'll treat me with the cordial respect you would give a noblewoman or any officer befitting my rank. I'm a ko-don, equivalent to that of a kernoyl. I speak with the heir's voice, and it carries the weight of a jynerul."

"But you're no lady nor a noble," a kaptyn grumbled.

"You're damn fucking right! And I can descend upon you in a hail of steel and fury without a moment of hesitation. I'll probably feel better about it afterward, too."

A heavy silence fell on them, and she smiled at them.

"I think this has been a productive meeting. We'll try again tomorrow."

She turned and left, storming back to the barracks. The meeting didn't go as planned and it soured her mood. Tiny's whining returned in full strength, and she grew angrier with each step towards their residence. Remembering one last thing she wanted to do, she made a slight alteration.

Traversing around their barracks once, she searched for specific markings, the sigils or runes the warlock placed to keep the Krey from entering the lust. She found twelve. On the second time around, she destroyed eight. She was of the mind to obliterate them all, but reason stayed her hand.

It won't do to have all the Krey fucking during a battle.

By the time she entered, a roiling sea of emotion had constricted her throat and knotted her muscles. Her composure clung by a single cobweb strain. She tried to escape up the flight of stairs, but Tiny grabbed her arm.

"Xeno—"

"Don't!"

She jerked free, retreating up the stairs, and at the fourth floor, she noticed the replaced door.

At least one fucking thing went right!

She entered and found someone waiting within. She turned to the occupant.

"What in the Shades of the Underworld are you doing in here?"

Omegryk frowned.

"This one has come to talk about your slaughtering of the soldiers. This one saw and liked it very much."

He hissed a chuckle. His magic, and his pheromones, mutated her fury. Still, her ire at Tiny hadn't simmered long enough to cool.

That fucking asshole thinks he can grab me!

The officer's remarks made her irrational and foul, and coupled with Tiny's tantrum, she was in no mood for any more bullshit. At least Omegryk related with her on the killings. The fleeting remembrance of the sensation buzzed like Omegryk's magic.

She was physically tired, mentally and emotionally exhausted, and Tiny's sulking behavior and scything judgement brought everything to a sharp, fine point.

Omegryk's pheromones swirled about her, driving her into a frenzy.

"Fuck me," she blurted.

The goblin's mouth fell open, his black eyes widening.

"What?"

"You must have come here hoping things ended like your dream."

She pulled off her shirt.

"Hit me with your strongest pheromones and fuck me."

Chapter 35: Emissaries

Judas Lakayre eyed the newly-decorated chambers of the Kothlere Council. The old consul's—Kayis Dathyr's—decorations remained under Meristal; the new regime insisted otherwise.

There are more important things right now.

The chamber seemed warmer and more inviting than the dark and brooding hues of the former administration. Still, Judas shivered despite the improvement. He hadn't seen Meristal since Godfrey made his grand entrance. She worked tirelessly to finalize the unification declaration. No sooner than it was ratified by the courts and passed by vote did the king make his true intentions known.

An ancient law triggered once they signed the pact. Any new territory joining Ralloc's sovereignty constituted a vote for a new consul with a two-year time frame.

Before the ink dried, Godfrey pushed.

The matter divided the council evenly. Vamor Poplu and Piero Capraro voted for Godfrey. No surprise there. The final vote was split three-to-three, and Meristal couldn't break it. Following the law, the army's commanding officer, Master Jynerul Tyku, broke the tie.

In a stunning turn, he voted for Godfrey.

And so, Meristal had two weeks to complete any tasks she started before Godfrey took office. The reality tasted bitter in Judas's mouth.

He wanted to alter the outcome, but his morality made him refrain. He glanced about the chamber as workers hurried around. Today marked the last time Meristal would be the most influential person in the domain.

Much had changed since his last visit. Godfrey's personality oozed from the new colors of forest green, tan, and gold. It illuminated the chambers compared to the old consul's black and purple with gold linings. Remembering his late student, Kayis Dathyr, sent a pang of sadness through him. He was Judas's last pupil until he met Julie.

Starriace, not Julie.

Starriace had cast aside the last remains of her former life and claimed her heritage. Once accepted, her true name snapped taut with thrumming certainty.

Did it have something to do with the book I gave her?

His daughter was gone now. She plunged down a wayward, blind path of darkness. Even he wasn't immune to its pull. While younger, he dabbled in things he didn't comprehend...until he did, and it scared him back on the path of integrity. Age and distance granted him wisdom and siphoned away his recklessness.

Almost a year had passed since Judas last saw Starriace, except for those few brief moments in the streets of Ralloc. She sought something in the library. They hadn't been able to find out what she sought. Asking the old man wouldn't be possible, he died from a seizing heart during the carnage.

Other died while she tried to escape.

Judas closed his mind and focused on Starriace. He hoped she was alive, safe, and happy wherever she may find it. He plunged deeper into the faint link between them. A vast wave of power rebuffed him, and the force seemed more potent. He doubted he or Xilor would survive her unleashed ire.

Whatever she took from the library made her more dangerous. Judas couldn't imagine what kind of destruction she'd be able to call on a mere whim. If that happened, Judas would have to hunt down his own daughter, and he didn't know if he could.

Her essence, what he sensed from her now, swelled. Just when he thought she couldn't pull any more magic to herself, she pulled harder. The tension built in size and strength. The sheer power left him panting for breath.

She's so overwhelming now. If I can feel her power, so can Xilor. Who is she directing magic against?

Xilor.

Judas swallowed. If Xilor got his hands on her, he'd recruit her.

Or kill her.

Judas almost didn't care who or what she directed her magic against, but then he remembered the three thieves she dispatched, and that made him change his mind. He had yet to determine the why, only that she did.

The pent-up energy released in a fatal blast. Whatever stood between her goal and her power would be wiped from existence.

Sweat beaded on Judas's brow and ran down the sides of his face. Everything went suddenly still on her end, the link lost.

Shades!

Opening his eyes, Judas blinked away the sudden brightness of the council chambers. A thread of worry snaked his heart, fearing for his daughter. Carrying the burden of knowledge, knowing she survived but Meristal's child didn't, weighed on him.

His thoughts lingered on the power, recalling Kayis's same desire.

The consul's office never appealed to Judas, the choice between war and words, peace and politics. But if war came, he'd answer like his daughter: swift, decisive, and direct. There were times for subtlety, and that wasn't one.

Now, Godfrey *ruled*; the militant man would no doubt crush Ralloc's enemies. Where Godfrey destroyed enemies, Judas would turn allies. He still couldn't believe the master jynerul voted against Meristal, but Tyku was a military man, and he and Godfrey were more alike than not.

Too many changes too quickly.

Someone moved in the distance, and Judas's eyes shifted to the man.

Vamor Poplu.

How is it that Poplu survived another consul? What is this? The third?

Vamor clung like a shadow in the darkness.

"Warlock Lakayre," Meristal called to him, breaking into his musings. He glanced behind, seeing her coming down the sloping floor.

He bowed his head.

"Consul."

"I've summoned you for a subtle mission."

She closed the gap between them. A flicker of giddiness tickled Judas.

"This delicate matter need not burden the rest of the council?" Judas prodded.

Meristal's lips thinned, holding back her smirk. A betrayer sat amongst them still, but winnowing the suspect out proved difficult. The public display was for their benefit. But all that would soon be Godfrey's problem. And, the front lines harkened to him. He heard the reports of probing attacks at Dlad City, but no main force besieged them as of yet, so he stayed near Ralloc and Meristal until called.

"No. They know I'm reinstating your citizenship. You're no longer an outcast, but not that I'm giving you an assignment."

"What do you require?"

"Go to the Elyfian Enclave. We need their help and support if we are to survive."

Judas blinked.

That wasn't part of the plan. What's she talking about?

He frowned, trying to piece it together. Then, it hit him. Meristal intended to go over the Supreme War Commander's head and ask the elyfian king directly.

Judas opened his mouth, but she cut him off.

"Please, Judas, I'd go myself, but I must remain here. I wouldn't ask, if it wasn't important."

He closed his mouth and swallowed with a shallow nod.

She indicated with her head toward the chamber doors.

"Walk with me."

He fell in step with her.

She was still upset with him regarding the Islanders, but now it seemed warranted. He'd not wanted to trust them, regardless of what caused his judgement.

Now that they were walking, he hoped they were getting back to their rehearsal in earnest. As people redecorated the chamber, there was no telling who listened.

"The Supreme War Commander, Scodd Yullus, escaped the slaughter of Shadow City," she said. "Since I've refused to send a rescue mission, he's taken what remains of his forces and returned home. You need to speak with him."

Judas's lips thinned.

"And the traitor? Is anyone close to discovering the identity?"

She shook her head.

"No one has come close to discovering who he is—if it's a *he*."

Staging this conversation in the open felt weird, but it was his idea. He was confident that if the betrayer overheard how far they were from finding him or her, they'd be emboldened.

"There's one other small task I'd ask of you."

Judas's gaze snapped to hers, realizing she deviated from the script.

"What?"

"Take Vamor with you, monitor his behavior, and report back to me on both the situation of the Enclave and him."

That was definitely not part of the conversation they agreed upon.

"As you wish."

His narrowed eyes roamed her face.

"I'll leave at once."

She gave a curt nod.

"Thank you. If you could, send Staell in as you leave?"

Meristal turned away and retreated to the council bench.

I'm going to give you a piece of my mind the next time we're alone.

He stormed out and into the main passageway. He rounded the corner and saw Staell coming. The Clydesdale-sized unicorn dipped his head, the crystalline horn gleaming in the torch and magelight. Staell's translucent skin radiated his inner brilliance like constellations in the cosmos.

Judas jerked a thumb over his shoulder.

"Meristal wanted—"

Staell, without breaking stride, spoke.

What you fear will see the inner light and guide them in the end. For within the heart of darkness, only light can escape.

Judas stopped, head snapping toward Staell as he passed, but the unicorn didn't stop. Once more, Judas was left with troubled thoughts.

Snow capped the mountains in the elyfian territory. Vamor Poplu, disgruntled at being carried along with Judas during the teleport, emerged with a scowl on his face. Judas chose not to teleport within the elyfian city; the act might be considered hostile, making them more unwilling to cooperate.

Elyves were fickle folk.

The glacial air rebuffed them with sharp gusts, and the duo bundled their robes. The furs did nothing against the onslaught of winter. Snow-laden trees resembled festival decorations, the ground covered with the pearly powder, laying claim to the ancient woods like a cake's frosting.

Judas took in the sights with a deep breath of thin, mountain-fresh air, one that ignited memories of times ventured here.

The first excursion came right after the Wizard's War, their territory covered by observation posts reaching the edge of their borders. As the years progressed, their circumference of influence shrank until only a twenty-minute hike separated the boundaries to the outskirts of their city.

Peace lulled one into laxaty.

As Judas walked, he mused over Staell's words.

What you fear will see the inner light and guide them in the end. For within the heart of darkness, only light can escape.

Did the unicorn refer to Starriace or something else?

Staell spoke in riddles, never giving more than disjointed ramblings. The unicorn reminded Judas of reading prophecies. Prophecies were riddles, puzzles of the mind; both in written form and when they came to pass, and hardly the way they were read. Predictions could be altered by choice and free will.

Judas had his own beliefs about such nonsense, namely that he didn't believe in prophetic destiny. Prophecies needed someone or something to enable them, such as a reader. Destiny would manifest regardless of what one read or wrote. To him, the two walked hand in hand.

Judas had been tempted by the darker aspects of magic.

Well, it's only darker because we tell ourselves that for morality's sake.

Following the desires of the flesh and mind seemed easy in this aspect, but he warred with only thinking of himself, regardless of the cost to others. Every choice creates a ripple effect. He found his proverbial line and crossed it only once, though he toed it a handful of times. Judas practiced every known magic, the incantations of wizardkind, chanting arts of the elyves, wild magic of the dwaven and dwandur, but nothing compared to Rumigul.

His power lay in his mind, not in words, scrolls, songs, or dances. Those novice techniques helped people center their mind and focus, but such incantations proved distracting for him. Words were a waste of energy, and Ralloc exiled him out of fear and lack of conformity.

Thoughts twisted away from the past and turned to his daughter.

Concern didn't begin to describe the war raging within. Her location and wellbeing eluded him, and he continued to worry in silence without the aid of friends to share in his burden. Though her father by blood, he hadn't filled the role when they traveled together. How could he? He thought her dead.

How did she escape as a newborn? Who took her and protected her? And more importantly, why don't I have any memory of it?

He had memories of her death.

Could the same be true for Meristal?

Did someone protect her…son? A thought flitted through his mind, and he gave chase, but as his mental fingers caressed the elusive ideation, it vanished without a trace.

"So," Poplu said into the silence, breaking into Judas's thoughts, "a new consul. Who would've thought?"

Did Poplu really think to goad him? To the question, the elder said nothing.

"It'll be a good change, even if he's an outsider."

"Not anymore."

"Pardon?"

"He's no longer a foreigner, but a citizen, and tomorrow, he'll be your boss."

"Ah, yes. I bet that burns you up, to see it all fall apart just when things were coming together for you and Meristal. How are things…coming now?"

Judas gave him a sidelong glare, but his desire to shut the younger man up arose within him.

"I bet it burns that you're still not consul after all this time, especially when that outsider led the coup."

Poplu smirked.

"I'll make sure Godfrey overturns your reinstatement of citizenship. It's about time we righted some of the wrongs that bitch of yours foiled."

Judas shrugged.

"That won't bother me. Speaking of, how's your sister?"

Poplu's eyes went wide, his face flushing crimson, lips thinning.

"Fuck you."

Poplu teleported away.

Judas allowed himself a chuckle.

Poplu long suspected the warlock of deflowering his oldest sister in their youth, but no one could prove it. Judas never bothered to confirm or deny the allegations, but the story did fit his younger self.

With Poplu gone, Judas realized how deep the quiet stretched. He took note of the trail and how far along he was.

Where are the sentries?

They should've stopped him and Vamor long ago. Something wasn't right. Forgetting all formalities, Judas called his power and teleported to the Enclave.

Fires raged about him as he exited. Buildings crumbled and bodies lay dead. Judas slipped and lost his balance. He almost fell face-first onto the soggy ground. Rainwater didn't create the mud, only blood. Body parts lay strewn, intestines strung about like red rope. Flayed, rubicund faces wept sanguine fluid; bones jutted out of skin and sinew.

The carnage unfolded like a nightmare. War had come to the Enclave.

A kneeling man in the center of town wept over a fallen comrade. Judas's eyes went wide with recognition.

Yullus.

Judas approached and waited, letting the Supreme War Commander grieve in peace, but as the moments stretched, Judas found his patience wearing. He had to know what happened so Ralloc could prepare.

"Who did this?" Judas asked.

Yullus answered without looking up.

"Dragons."

"Xilor's?"

"I don't know." Another sob escaped him. "This one shouldn't have died today."

He ran his hand over the battle leathers of the fallen one.

"Who is she?"

"My daughter," Yullus choked, "She looks so much like her mother, like Ama Ka."

"Where's her mother?"

"Dead, gone, what does it matter now?"

Standing, he turned to Judas. A mask hid what the elyf thought and felt, though it couldn't obscure the redness of his eyes.

"We need to organize a counterstrike."

"No! You can organize all you want; we're staying out of your affairs. Look at what happened when the younger warrior caste joined the battle, captured like amateurs, the veterans obliterated. We won't fight your war."

"And what will you do when Xilor defeats us? Run for the hills? Hide? Escape to your Virgin Lands? Your people have fallen far from your origins."

"I won't be goaded into declaring a war that'll wipe out my people."

"Look around you! You're already being wiped out!" Judas's voice softened. "I wasn't trying to goad you, Yullus. I think you've underestimated the enemy. He doesn't want to destroy Ralloc; he wants to bring the world to its knees. He'll destroy us, and he won't stop there. And when his horde has won him a resounding victory, he'll turn on what he considers lesser races, destroying every creature within our world. The time for folly is over. If you don't fight, then all will be lost."

"Then it's lost!" Yullus shouted.

He backed away from the warlock, shaking his head in disgust. Yullus didn't stop when Judas called after him.

"The unicorns will free your people in Shadow City," Judas called, but Yullus didn't hear.

Flickering flames caught Judas's eye, and he turned to the right. Just beyond the fire stood Vamor Poplu, his face ashen. When their eyes met, the younger wizard teleported away. Meristal had to know about this; Godfrey needed the warning.

Judas's essence surged, and he teleported back to Ralloc, leaving the chaos behind.

Chapter 36: Halls of The One

Power surged through Starriace. The twin blades on her back flooded her with their energies. Judgement sang with an urgency of death.

Starriace flung the door open, wand clenched tight in her hand, and broke into a brisk jog. The bells tolled loud overhead.

Nothing can ever be easy.

A man ran into her as she reached the stairs. They both fell. Quick reflexes readied her to strike. Her wand flickered out. He raised his hands, eyes wide, and he leaned away from her.

"Wait!" he shouted.

She had expected a plea, for him to beg, even a quivering in his voice, but he offered none.

"What?"

"The archbishop?" he asked. His eyes skipped to the room over her shoulder.

"Dead."

His eyes slid to hers. "And you are?"

She jabbed her wand under his chin to direct his movements.

"Your executioner, if you don't get out of my way."

He stepped aside, his hands still raised. A smile crept over his face.

"By your leave, my lady."

Something about the man riled her, perhaps the haughtiness of his eyes. From the brief contact, he left an imprint on her, enough to warrant a secondary inspection. As she neared, he backed against the wall. Every fiber of her being screamed to kill him. Something malevolent coiled off him like acrid smoke.

The grip on her wand tightened.

The urge to dispatch him intensified, but reason finagled through and held sway. She couldn't kill on suspicion alone.

I'm not a monster like Xilor. The archbishop was different. I acted in self-defense.

Starriace pulled away and descended the stairs.

One final glance over her shoulder revealed his jovial state, a malicious grin, and the wave of his hand. He yelled something at her, but with the expanding distance between, she couldn't hear.

"Thank you!" Glato called after the fleeing woman.

He couldn't hide the smug smile as his insides glowed with relief. The woman was, though sacrilegious to say, a godsend. He couldn't believe his luck, his new appointment by the archbishop couldn't have come at a more opportune time. All his early staged schemes could be scrapped. Ascending to the office of bishop, he initiated his next round of well-formulated schemes to be rid of the archbishop by accidental means.

The lovely young woman on the stairwell completed the deed for him, a gratifying act for a glorious day. Nothing stood in his way to ascend to the highest rank of the Disciples of the One. He alone controlled the disciples now, and his master would be pleased.

Pride rippled through him.

His first order would be to initiate changes, from titles to religious decrees. He hated the stupid title of bishop and archbishop. Apostle was more to his liking. His fellow disciples were occupied with the foretold prophecy. Let them worry about the boy, his puppet while he pulled invisible strings.

Appearances must be kept, of course, but otherwise, he faced limitless possibilities.

Apostle, that's more suiting to the office.

He watched the young woman descend to the ground level, but her glowing eyes sent a shiver up his spine. They were unnatural, and he didn't know what could've caused it. He'd never forget her eyes, just like he'd never forget his master's.

Far below on the ground floor, the woman engaged personnel beyond his sight. Light flashed off the walls, an array of spells as she stormed out. Whether she escaped or not was of little concern. She'd weed out his ranks, and that would tighten his control.

She'll be captured and killed. A pity and waste. She's a beautiful girl, a fine gift for my master and his minions of darkness. No matter, any flesh of wizardkind will do. There are whores aplenty.

He turned from the battle to lay claim to his new chambers.

Guards spilled out of every doorway between her and the exit. Her wand moved in a blur, sending sentries flying through splintering doors and fireballs consuming all in her path. Conflicting wills clashed, those trying to contain her, and her need for escape.

She lashed out, free of pity and remorse. Those who raised a hand against her fell, some screaming while they burned, others with shattered bodies. She didn't discriminate.

The last guard within the castle fell, his final gurgle smothered by the rattle of his armor striking the wall. Over the smoke-curled husks, frozen forms, and fractured bodies, she stepped through the tangle and threw open the doors to the cool night, but she was not alone.

Dozens of armored men arrayed in a semicircle formation pressed in, her flanks and front covered. Many had bows drawn, quivering in anticipation. At this distance, she'd have time to react, but she couldn't stop, deflect, or dodge that many arrows.

There has to be at least fifty of them.

"It's over," a guard shouted.

Starriace couldn't discern their features in the gloom, but his voice seemed similar to the guard who rounded up the others to deal with the fire. He wore black robes, same as the one who grabbed her, the same as the summoner.

The men stirred a cautious, forward step. Mail jingled. Anticipation tightened its grip around her heart. A paralyzing fear seized her, more potent than when she faced Judas in Ralloc. With any threat she faced, when her fear rose, so did her anger.

And it wouldn't fail her now.

"Nothing's over," she answered. "No one behind me is alive. Forsake this place, or suffer their fate."

A ripple of laughter peeled through the night, and some whistled lewdly. One man hooted that she could kill him by riding him to death.

Their catty remarks enraged her, not for what they said, but that they didn't take her as a threat. Their obscene comments and dress reminded her of the Summoner's offer. If the Embrace was affiliated with this collective, she didn't want anything to do with them.

Worn resignation snaked through her, realizing they'd never take her in earnest.

"Then, you've chosen death," she whispered to herself.

The men continued, their voices a background bed to the thrum of blood rushing through her throat. They'd never let her go, and if taken into custody, they'd do all they promised, and worse.

She couldn't allow that.

Magic and fury entwined through her trembling body. A guard shouted, a sudden yelp, but the words remained indistinct. It didn't matter, it was too late for him.

For all of them.

Her head snapped up, eyes shimmering scarlet. Her aura expanded, tracing every released arrow. A cold presence washed over her, an acquainted spirit taking control. An all too familiar voice filled her head, admonishing her.

You should've never sent me away.

The arrows quivered in midflight, stopped by an unseen barrier mere feet from her face. The night illuminated through her shifting vision, one of conjury and wrath. Her magical essence danced out in a roiling plume, the arrows and elements under her sway.

Arms wide, fingers splayed, she drew them inward, a slow pull as the power welled up. As she molded the mystic energy, an external force that she could only describe as nature fought against her sorcery. Her arms inched closer together, like being pulled through thick honey. The force that fought her did so in both the physical realm and the arcane.

Her back hunched the closer her hands drew to her chest. The ground trembled as she coiled, subtle at first, then grew into a tremor.

Panicking cries clamored and ringing swords rose in the night. The quake built. The suspended arrows snapped, shattered by invisible power. A small, pale blue, almost-white light emanated from her core, not from her abdomen, but within her curling fingers.

Rocks rolled toward her as if summoned.

Her arms drew closer.

The castle walls behind her quivered from the strain, bricks and stones ripped away by an imposing gravity. All drew in, but nothing touched her.

The force jerked the guards from their feet, clawing at their armor and weapons alike. Screams filled the night as sentries were wrenched away. Grasping hands searched for anything to halt their headlong plunge toward her.

Another volley of arrows soared, but they never reached her, disintegrating when they passed through her expanding sphere of essence. One man screamed as he rushed headlong toward her, only to disappear in a bloody, pulpy mist.

A tree ripped from the earth, knocking down several defenders, and both tumbled towards her. Drawing near, the tree splintered and disintegrated; the soldiers were crushed just the same, folding in on themselves with snapping bones and wet crunches.

Only a fine spray of blood managed to escape the purge, slickening the ground.

The pale light brightened, her hands and arms nearly touching. The external force shivered through her body with a fierceness that caused her teeth to chatter. In startled fright, another volley arched but turned to granules like the previous barrage.

What few sentries remained turned to flee, only to be snatched up and drawn into the same void. The bell in the tower above broke free and plummeted, but it never touched her, disappearing into the void like so many before it.

The light intensified, spreading through her arms and hands.

The wall behind her shook its last defiant stand before crumbling.

Then, the night went quiet, the ground stilled, a hushed silence that echoed for a long heartbeat, the eye of the storm.

She threw her arms out, away from her body, fingers splayed. The sheer might of the blast obliterated all in her path. Nothing survived. The guards, trees, and rocks were incinerated, eradicated by the magnitude of energy she released.

In the span of an inhale, she destroyed everything, leaving all in her path barren.

She swayed on her feet, feeling all that energy leech from her body in a single moment. Her eyes rolled back in her skull, and fatigue seduced her, but she couldn't give in to exhaustion.

Not yet.

A glance behind revealed the remains of the religious center. The front half of the building was gone, and the back half threatened to topple from a strong gust of wind.

In the remains, she could see stirrings of survivors amongst the rubble.

Most bled from wounds inflicted by flying debris.

You see? the voice asked. *Anything is possible. Now you know, which is why I'm never leaving again.*

Her legs trembled, and her breath hitched. She staggered to her knees. One last time, she sent her aura out and found a faint, familiar presence.

Honing in, she winked out of existence.

When her feet touched the ground again, a massive figure rose and eclipsed the fire's soft glow. Dead fingers reached out for her, and Rusem caught her before she fell unconscious.

Chapter 37: Xenomene

Xenomene had to admit that her latest idea wasn't the greatest. Impulsive thoughts rarely were, and those based on emotions alone led to catastrophes. It wasn't her norm.

When it came to men, no matter the race, they were an enigma, for the most part.

Omegryk hit her with his most potent pheromones, and it made her sick.

Not at first.

The initial blast lit every pore with bliss, and she yearned to bask in them forever. Nothing quite compared, except for the Islander lotion. She'd heard of drugs like oblivion and underworld's gate but had never partaken. She imagined the pheromones being similar.

There were certain things in life that Xenomene sought to try, maybe even attempt a second time, but letting a goblin fuck her wasn't one of them. The next morning after bedding Omegryk, the sickness remained, and she knew she would never, for the rest of this life and any other reincarnation after, ask for Omegryk's pheromones.

Once is enough.

From the moment they hit, rapture took her. Coupled with Omegryk's powerful magic, the destroyed runes around their barracks, and her ire, overwhelmed didn't begin to describe it. Omegryk made sure she couldn't walk straight the next day. And he ravaged her long after she was spent and deep into the night.

By the end, she lay motionless beneath him as he rutted her.

The soreness paled next to the withdrawal she suffered. The goblin sex was what she expected: fast, furious, and primal. The duration was unplanned, like a never-ending thunderstorm that lasted uncountable hours.

Too many hours.

The nape of her neck ached where he bit her.

The memory flashed through her mind, and it brought both a smile and a pang of agony. When he drove her to climax, he sank his teeth into her, drawing blood, then proceeded to lick the wound.

The next day, after emptying her stomach, she couldn't stop eating, trying to replenish the spent energy. The sustenance came up a few hours later, and she acquiesced to being bed-bound.

She ached all over, her sore jaw and swollen lips, her thighs when she hobbled to the privy, the bite and claw marks. He made it near-impossible to sit. Unless she stayed in bed, pain haunted her every waking moment.

He ruined the sheets, ripping them with his razor-sharp claws, but it was better than her face. For that, she was grateful but otherwise remained perturbed.

Xeno spent two days in bed, drinking water, throwing up, and shivering with fever. Her head spun with almost every movement.

By the third day, she felt almost herself. She'd forgotten why she chose Omegryk, but all that came back once she bounded down the steps to find Jynx straddling Tiny's lap. They melded together in a heated lip lock. She rolled her eyes and grunted in disgust, going about her duties as far from the barracks as possible.

Why should she care what Tiny did? But flaunting that shit in front of everyone smacked of disrespect. She didn't want to see it, no one else would either, but she hoped they were fucking. It'd help put distance between her and Tiny. She could always just tell him she let a goblin destroy her, but even she was prudent enough to keep that to herself.

To her relief, Omegryk used discretion and didn't reveal their escapade. He was more of a gentleman than the rest of the Krey. For that, the goblin endeared himself to her.

As promised, she returned to the command tent. Without the weight of a sword at her hip, the vulnerability made her hyper-aware, but knives would suffice. No doubt the officers saw them, too. They planned and talked, changed everything half a dozen times again before settling on a course of action. Three hours of wasted time, most spent talking what-if scenarios instead of actual battle plans.

She stormed off, visiting the smithery next, and her mood didn't improve. The blacksmith hadn't begun on a sword, and she might've lost her composure when she started screaming at him.

"I could've walked to the fucking Hive and back before you even get started!"

The ko-don left with a storm billowing in her wake. Most fled from the Krey as if plagued, but she noticed the extra-wide margin. A cursory glance at their frightened, angry faces reminded her of the lynching they yearned for. The jynerul's death and massacre of soldiers didn't make her popular.

Xenomene went to the only place where she didn't have to be herself: Lord Yeates's current residence. She met the ancient man at Cape Gythmel, and he evacuated to Dlad City. He was a stubborn codger but full of stories and humor. Once the army took up residence in Dlad City, they evacuated all non-essential personnel to Ralloc, but he refused to go.

Some called him a fool, but she couldn't question his bravery and loyalty. The retired kernoyl took up quarters with the rest of the officers and took over Warlock Lakayre's room once he left Dlad City.

His wife stayed with him for a time, but after the first attack, she opted to wait for him in Ralloc. Xenomene spent the rest of the day with Lord Yeates, listening to stories and forgetting her woes; he was quite verbose when he wanted to be. Late in the evening, as he handed her a goblet of wine, he fell over dead without warning.

She launched out of the seat, opened the door, and screamed for help.

She returned to the fallen man, but he was cold like winter's deep chill. He showed no signs of pain or heart problems. He wasn't dizzy, pale, or nauseous; he just simply died. It was so sudden and jarring, Xenomene didn't realize what she'd witnessed.

The pharmacon mage arrived a few moments after she yelled for help, and the battlemage checked for signs of life, which Xeno considered pointless. Grumblings arose that she killed the retired kernoyl, but the mage came to her defense.

"There are no inflicted wounds. Magic took him. Krey don't possess magic like this. This is the work of someone with exceptional power. If the warlock were here, I'd almost point my finger at him. The only other person I can think of would be Xilor, but he isn't here either. I have no theories to offer."

"Who would want to kill an old man?" Tyku demanded.

"I don't know, but the question you should ask is *how*."

For two hours, they interrogated her before everyone seemed satisfied she wasn't the culprit. They tried hard to pin her with blame. The warlock's absence made the whole ordeal difficult—he had the final say in magical matters. Instead, they went on the word of the pharmacon mage.

Without establishing guilt, they released her, and she returned to the barracks.

She entered and only saw three Krey on the first floor—their chow hall. She was about to ask where everyone else had slinked off to when the moans of Krey reached her ears.

At least destroying the runes worked.

She may have fixed that problem for the Krey, but she found herself without a dance partner. Before she even considered Omegryk, she dismissed it.

Never again!

Just an accidental slip of thinking about his pheromones made her nauseous. She didn't spy Tiny either, a plus, but she knew where to locate him, not that she would.

Why didn't I kill his hope when I had the chance?

On the second landing, she paused before ascending to the fourth floor. She knew the best thing would be to keep going, but curiosity coveted answers. She needed to know.

She pushed open the door just as a dressed Tytan stumbled through. She couldn't say the same for almost everyone else in the room. If they weren't naked and participating, they watched and awaited their turn.

"Looking for someone?" Tytan teased with a smirk.

She almost responded when she caught sight of Harlot's head bobbing in Tiny's lap, his trousers around his ankles. She pulled out of the door to avoid being seen.

"Yes," she answered Tytan. "Don't worry about it."

She retreated upstairs, stripped, and crawled into bed, too exhausted by the long day and by dealing with so many people.

Her door burst open the next morning, and the do-dons filed into the office for their meeting. She bolted upright. A haze suffused her, the panic of forgetting.

"Are we the only ones having fun?" Spectre teased.

Lyan appeared amused whereas Tiny wore his fury for everyone to see.

"Would you like us to leave so you can change?" she asked.

"What are we? Rallocans? Don't bother."

Xenomene dressed in haste. Tiny averted his eyes, but Lyan didn't, and watched with rapt attention. Even the twine he fiddled with rested forgotten in his hand. She caught Spectre looking, too, but not as Lyan, more judging the competition than anything.

She's better at hiding things.

Their meeting went smoothly, if one discarded the undertones of open hostility and a proverbial white saricrocian in the room. Everyone except Tiny danced with grace. The meeting concluded, and Tiny stormed out before the others had risen from their chairs.

"What's his problem?" Lyan asked.

"He's pissed 'cause I won't fuck him."

Lyan looped his long piece of twine, then pulled it straight.

"Well, I can see being crestfallen, but angry?"

Spectre cocked an eyebrow.

"Seriously? I thought you and Tiny have been fucking all along."

Xeno shook her head.

A knock on the door interrupted their conversation. It wasn't timid, but one of authority. Perplexed, Lyan tossed his twine aside and answered it.

Kernoyl Tyku entered and asked the other two Krey to leave. After they departed, he and Xenomene sat with the desk between them. His eyes flickered to the unmade bed and stayed for a moment before returning.

"What?" she demanded.

"Nothing."

The defensiveness in his voice warmed her soul. Now, if only she could bask in his tears…Lyan's twine caught her eye, and she picked it up, looping it around her fingers.

"Does my unmade bed unnerve you?"

"No, I'm fine."

"Ever fucked a Krey woman?"

She enjoyed needling him, making him uneasy. She remembered doing the same to Warlock Lakayre, asking him if he knew how to handle his sword.

"No."

A glimmer of amusement coursed through her, but she kept it hidden.

"Do you want to?"

The way he shifted in his seat, the sheen of sweat on his forehead, revealed how much he was flustered.

"Perhaps another time. I have orders for you."

That made her frown, forgetting all about teasing him.

"Orders? Whose orders?"

He held up a scroll.

"They come from the consul."

"What does that woman want now?" Xenomene asked, holding out her hand for the official scroll. "I was just starting to like her."

"No. He," Tyku corrected.

He handed the decree over.

"Yesterday, the Forgotten Isles were accepted as an annex of the Ralloc domain during the Unification Declaration. A vote was called for a new consul. The former king of the Isles is our new leader."

Xenomene groaned and placed her head down on the desk.

"Oh, you like them as much as I do, huh?"

She sighed, speaking her words into the desk.

"They're like a venereal disease, once you got them, you can never get rid of them!"

"Well, technically—"

Her head snapped up.

"Just shut up. I know, magic…I'm trying to make a point. What does he want?"

She broke the seal and unrolled the scroll.

"He wants you and the Krey to return to the Hive within a day, and given that he penned the orders this morning, I'd say no later than tomorrow morning."

"Majestic timing."

"Look, I don't agree with these orders, but we obey. I don't blame you for the jynerul, but given the circumstances, this might be best."

She almost retorted something flippant but thought better of it.

"You're right, of course."

Tyku stood, giving her bed a quick glance before reaching out to shake her hand.

"It was an honor to witness the Krey in battle."

"You sure you won't relent?" Xeno teased, jerking her head towards the bed.

She arched her eyebrows.

Tyku shook his head, chuckling.

He started to turn away when her soft voice made him stop.

"You can do whatever you want to me."

Something—words, a gasp, a cry—died in his throat, and she noted his shaky breath and the glimmer in his eye.

She held up the twine, one end bound around her wrist.

"I'll let you tie me up, too."

She could've sworn he stopped breathing.

"Or do you want to bend me over the desk?"

He gave a single harrumph, shook his head, and left. His legs were stiff, unwilling to cooperate.

Xeno waited a few moments, smiling. She swore she almost had him, but what would she have done if he said yes? The thought didn't cross her mind, and she'd need to think about such things before teasing someone else.

Enough time had passed that when she exited her office, the kernoyl wouldn't think she was following him. She reached the first floor as he exited the building. She turned to the nearest Krey, Mauler, the dark-skinned Toshii.

"Get everyone out of their cots and down here. I've got word to pass."

Mauler set off, and Xenomene didn't have to wait long for them to assemble.

"Pack your shit; we're going home tomorrow morning."

Most let up a whoop of joy and laughed, but Xeno didn't: She liked being in the field, not in the confines of the Hive. House Eti would always be home, but freedom tasted too damn good. When they first started their forced march to Cape Gythmel, she hated every minute, but the new scenery and independence changed her mind.

"What time are we leaving?" Spectre inquired.

"I want to be up and outside by dawn," she yelled over the celebrations. She turned to Spectre. "Wake me up in the morning."

"Okay."

Xeno left the barracks and spent the rest of the day exploring the city. She had no battle plans to prepare, no gear to maintain, no requisitions to complete. With the whole day to herself, she returned late, long after dinner. She grabbed a plate and picked over the remains.

The only people on the first floor were Smokey, whose head lay on the table, passed out drunk, and Slurp, who played a card game by himself. Drumstick, who bravely trusted the strength of his chair, dozed, his snores rivaling the distant echo of thunder. Was it her, or did he get fatter since the war started?

Between the two, Smokey and Drumstick, a close race ensued to claim the coveted prize of biggest gut. She considered Slurp, crossed the room, and sat opposite of him.

"What are you playing?"

He gazed up and returned to the cards.

"King's Run; an Islander game."

She gave a half-wince, half-smile.

"I almost forgot you were from there."

She didn't forget—a gander at his eyes and hair was a reminder—but he wasn't an asshole like Bitcher, or as blunt and crass as Smokey. He seemed more refined than most in the Hive.

"What are y'all doing down here? I'm surprised you guys aren't up on the second deck having fun."

Slurp snorted, still doling out the deck. He jerked his head to the two fat Krey.

"They're here because they love to drink and eat, and no one would fuck them."

"There are enough girls…"

"Aye, but would you fuck them?"

She shook her head, conceding his point.

"And why are you here, Slurp?"

"Same reason why I play this game and you don't: I'm an Islander."

"What does that have to do with anything?"

"Islander girls are unique, other girls are curious, most are intolerant. Get my meaning?"

"Yeah," she said, looking around to see if she'd missed anyone in the common room. "You could just make love to a woman the normal way."

"Never done it. Almost seems forbidden, taboo. Just seems wrong."

"Because you're not married and trying to make a baby?"

Slurp nodded.

Her lips thinned, and she took a breath, hesitated, then danced past it.

"You going to be up for a spell?"

He nodded.

"Yeah, gonna drink some, too. This game goes on forever."

He sighed in frustration as he flipped another card.

"Fucking damn it."

He glanced up.

"Why?"

"Come on," she said with a casual voice, standing.

"Where are we going?"

"I want to make a proper man out of you. And then, we can do it your way afterward."

She arched an eyebrow. He left his chair in a hurry, the cards forgotten.

It wasn't Spectre who woke her in the morning but Tiny. Xenomene expected as much. There was no way Tiny missed Slurp's naked, unconscious form lying next to her. Tiny's angry breathing thundered in the early morning silence. His whispers came in low and menacing.

"What are you doing?"

"What does it look like? Sleeping."

"Why him?"

Xeno heard the unasked question: "Why not me?"

She regarded Slurp. If she was ever going to break free of Tiny's pining, she needed to be firm, almost vicious. Once made clear, she hoped he'd back off. The conundrum lay in not pissing him off too much that she lost a friend.

But what could she say? You're too tall? Your dick is too big? I don't like you that way? I'm not attracted to you? No right answer came to mind.

She focused on Tiny's glowering face, his anger, his judgmental eyes, and she yearned to slay his obsession.

"Because he's refined, a gentleman, and he's an Islander."

After uttering it aloud, she found there was more truth to the revelation than she realized. The Islander oil was what she craved. In some ways, she acknowledged that she might be an addict in the making.

Fury radiated from Tiny, but he didn't make a sound. He stormed out and didn't bother to close the door. She pulled the sheets down, exposing Slurp's bare backside, and rapped a quick drumbeat.

"Time to wake up."

She stood and dressed as Slurp crawled out of bed. She kissed him and teased his cock with a fondling hand, then smacked his buttocks.

"Can I see you again?" he said, stifling a yawn.

She shrugged.

"Sure."

She hoped her response wasn't too blasé, but she didn't want to appear eager either. He nodded and left with his clothes bundled around his groin.

She slung a pack over her shoulders and grabbed the knapsack with all their documents. Downstairs, Rallocan mages had portals awaiting them when she came outside. Leading the exodus, she walked through with the Krey on her heels.

The opened doors of House Eti greeted them on the other side. Filing in, Xenomene directed the squads to line up in the Pit, much as they did when they first left the Hive. The heir came to the rail, peering down from the balcony.

"Welcome home," he drawled, stifling a yawn. "I know these turn of events are sudden, but the climate has changed in Ralloc."

Somewhere in the pit of her stomach, Xeno's insides turned to ice. She didn't like Ralloc, and liked its culture even less, but if something changed in the megalopolis, the Krey would feel the effects, both good and bad.

The heir continued.

"We'll be having an official visit from the new consul in three weeks. He wants every Krey to be at Outpost Dire. He wishes to address us."

The knot in her belly turned into an anvil.

This is becoming less agreeable by the word.

Never, in all her time with the Krey, had she seen anyone official or otherwise from Ralloc, unless you counted the battlemages who came in to teach the A'uri. In fact, to her recollection, she had never known of anyone coming from Ralloc. Her stomach dropped out.

"We have some cleaning to do," the heir continued. "We're getting our house in order. We'll also need to build a stage for him to speak from since we can't all fit into the Pit. Relax, go back to sleep. After midday, we can start preparations. Ko-dons will be expected to attend the meeting at noon in my office."

His eyes found her.

"Get some shut-eye."

Tiny approached Xeno from behind, and she noted the lack of hostility in his voice and found herself relieved.

"What the Shades of the Underworld is going on?" he asked.

The trepidation didn't ease. She shook her head.

"I have no fucking clue, but that new consul reeks like an overused, disease-ridden whore."

Chapter 38: Crystal Falls

"Shades of the Underworld! Are you going to sleep all day?"

Starriace awoke with a start, recognizing Ava's familiar, whiny voice. Her words lacked the accustomed kindness. Ava's tone conveyed a frostiness Starriace hadn't yet heard. The shift in temperament couldn't be ignored anymore.

"What?" Starriace snapped, bolting upright, a throb lingered in her head.

"You've slept for three days! Every time I show up, you're on your back and lifeless! If you want to eat and change, you'll do it yourself. I'm your familiar, not your slave."

"Your tasteless bile has become irksome!"

"Tasteless bile?"

Ava crossed her arms.

"The dark thoughts flitting through your head are troublesome enough without shifting blame."

"Underworld take you! What are you prattling about?"

"My attitude is a direct reflection of you, dotard! Whatever you are, I am! Your personality and traits bleed through our link. You've changed, and therefore tailored me to suit you. Nobody asked me if I wanted this! Who are you to change me? Did you ever think about that? No! You didn't. You just thought, 'Oh, here is a cute little fluttery thing that I can command. Oh, little slave, teleport me here, clean up my piss-coated feet, fetch my friend.' You disgust me!"

Starriace held the little creature's gaze for a moment before standing. She fought the urge to look away as her eyes burned with anger and shame, the words sinking in, not the venom behind them.

Was Ava right? Were her thoughts and attitude responsible for changing the fairy? If so, everything she had done, did, or thought, wasn't a secret.

If it's true.

"You know it is," Ava confirmed.

Wide-eyed, Starriace stared at her familiar, trying to recall the exact time the changes started to occur, about the time she returned from the Melodic Mountains and her tutelage under Fife Doole. She'd come back a different person, and it had a profound impact on her familiar.

"Ava," she started, all the heat left her. "I'm sorry. I didn't realize we're linked that way."

"Didn't they tell you? Didn't they tell you that when you were made Head of Creatures?"

"No! Judas didn't tell me anything."

"Yes, he did, maybe not everything, but he told you about the link."

"I don't recall."

"I remember, even if you don't."

"How can you remember? You weren't even there."

"Anything you hear and see, smell, touch, and remember is shared. Your turmoil and anger? The destruction you wielded? It awoke me from slumber."

"Your slumber? My memories?"

Horror reached Starriace's eyes, realizing the best and worst of her recollections were like an unrestricted scroll of text.

"I haven't told anyone," Ava assured quickly. "Not a soul, I swear! I'll never, even to save myself."

Starriace knew what she spoke of; her most terrible memory flashed through her mind, and Ava had been privy to it.

Starriace nodded, letting her eyes fall.

"Thank you."

Ava unfolded her arms.

"Judas told you about the link; I'll show you."

In the silence, Ava shared the memory.

A chagrin smile crept across the mage's face, unable to believe her naivety. An early morning yawn escaped her lips, and a stretch relieved the tension in her muscles.

"Since I'm privy about what you're doing and looking for," Ava said, "let me state the obvious: you can't go back to Ruhkhi; they'll be looking for you there. Stratu'Geim is no doubt still under Xilor's control with his vile creatures. Crystal Falls is close though, and we could restock supplies there, collect our thoughts, and plan the next move."

A sound thought, better than any Starriace could offer at the moment, and Ava was right.

"Alright, let's pack up, and then I'll teleport us there."

Ava gave her an incredulous expression. It was Starriace's first attempt to teleport them all, but after her last feat of strength, she didn't doubt her abilities.

Erring on the side of caution, they came in sight of Crystal Falls after a half dozen short jumps that burned through the remainder of the day. Starriace commanded Rusem to keep hidden, and Ava stayed with him. On the seventh jump, Starriace stopped a dozen paces shy of the town and entered. The low, pitiful walls lacked guards. One thunderous blast of magic would breach the stone. Did they not fear aggressors here?

Crystal Falls lay in a clearing of woods surrounded by cliffs and overhangs with several waterfalls stretched sparsely between the north and west. Frothy, white cascades pooled in dark blue hollows, the overflow slipping out in percolating streams.

Gentle, rolling hills stretched through the town like ripples in a pond; steep slopes and foliage obscured the game trails and sporadic trees weaved through a serpentine road. The village was made more of wood than mortar and stone, but she found the latter peppered throughout.

Starriace's mind shifted to her quest and the numerous possible locations of brimstones. She'd never admit it aloud, but she needed help. She couldn't search for every potential clue alone. Followers would alleviate the burden, beings capable of independent thought, but who'd do her bidding? Rusem couldn't. He only took orders.

Ghosts inhabited Crystal Falls, judging by the deserted streets, but the faint merriment of evening nightlife tickled her ears. She followed the sound, her footfalls silent on the stone road. She expected dirt this far from a large populace, but she was pleasantly surprised by the cobblestone-like surface built of flat rocks and mortar.

The buildings stood with weathered wood, almost a pale ash color. Most had knots, holes, and splits, making her question the structure's integrity. One place looked promising, a pub, which probably had the kinds of people she needed, so she chose the establishment.

Upon entering, none gave her any notice except the barkeep. Goblins and wizardkind filled the tavern, and the tables lay about the room in a hazardous manner. Starriace had seen a goblin before, but never from this close. Despite its docile state, these creatures crawled out of nightmares with their multiple limbs of all different sizes and shapes, facial features, and numerous eyes.

There were others, too.

One man kept to the shadows of a dark corner with glittering black eyes and pale gray skin. His hair hung down over his face, obscuring his more animalistic features.

A vampire? I didn't know they made it this far south.

Starriace picked an isolated table, away from the crowd but close enough to overhear with her magical abilities. A barkeep came over and took her order; she decided on something new instead of her usual, going with a drink called koja rum from the Forgotten Isles.

Kam's home.

Upon his return, she grabbed his wrist as he went to leave, and he bent down.

"What's that elyf over there next to the fireplace?" she asked. "The one playing cards?"

His skin held a pale amethyst tone with hazel eyes.

The barkeep glanced over.

"A dark elyf. They keep to 'emselves and don't start trouble, but they seem to finish that which finds 'em. I'd suggest you not tarry with 'em, m'lady."

He left.

Starriace surveilled the gathered crowd. Would she find followers here? She took a pull of her nip; the drink was smooth, sweet, and left warm trails down her gullet.

A movement caught her eye not five tables down.

A goblin hunched forward and harshly-whispered phrases passed between a cloaked figure and the little beastie. The cloaked individual had their hood drawn, concealing their identity.

Starriace concentrated, willing enhanced hearing into manifestation. She needed to practice, yet another feat that required finesse, but the more she practiced the subtle skills, the more she added to her repertoire.

A cacophony poured into her ears, the scraping of coin across the table, laughter, belches, and idle conversation exploded through her head. Lower lip between her teeth, she weeded them out in sequence until only what she sought hummed in her mind.

"… can't be said for sure, but we do know Divinity Enigumas is here."

Divinity Enigumas?

Where had she gleaned that before? A school, wasn't it?

"All rumors carry the same little seed," the goblin crowed, "follow the river of Emaas. When it meets with Vergence, you'll be close. I need not remind you it's hidden, and those who intrude perish."

"Thank you, Satsgul," said the woman's voice from beneath the hood. "You've been most helpful."

She laid out a handful of silver coins.

Satsgul snatched at the coins when a pale, amethyst hand grabbed his wrist.

"And I need not remind you what the penalty is should you entertain fickle notions of crossing me, do I?"

The goblin shook his head.

"The punishment would be…most severe."

She released his wrist and stood in a fluid motion. The concealed figure turned and paused for a moment in the direction of the dark elyf Starriace had noted earlier before leaving. Starriace glanced back to the card-playing elyf. Everyone at the table laid their cards down, and the elyfian gave a smug look as he reached for the pot.

"Wait a minute, boy," grumbled the man opposite of him. "No one loses that many times in a row an' suddenly wins big. I recall ya sayin' this be your last hand? Ironic ya should win right afore ya leave, doncha think?"

"I've played fairly, and it was inevitable I win eventually."

The man opposite stood and leaned across the table.

"What reserves be tuck't up your sleeve, daf?"

Daf?

Starriace repeated the word a few times to herself, trying to remember if she'd ever heard it before. She found the word odd, the term unbeknownst to her. Perhaps it was his name, but surely not, considering how the other's face turned hard. The elyf stood, crimson hair fell from his shoulders and covered his face.

"Don't test me, homugon spawn."

The man's eyes went dead at the insult. In the time it took her to blink, the initial scuffle was over. The man lunged across the table, dagger in hand. Twin blades rang, drawn from sheaths. In a spray of red and a curling scream, the elyf severed the man's hand. Blood squirted as the man's two companions kicked their chairs backward and lunged.

The elyf spun, hilt cracking against the base of a man's skull, rendering him unconscious. The other companion drew a dagger and threw it. A sword batted the flying dirk aside, sending it plunging into the wall.

The elyf charged.

Another knife materialized. The flat of a sword blocked the stab, and the elyf's other elbow broke the man's jaw. The man howled in pain and crumpled to the floor. The elyf stood over him and glowered at the crowd.

"Anyone else?"

When no one stepped forward, the elyf collected his earnings and tossed the barkeep a few coins.

"For clean up."

I need this man's talents!

She threw down a single copper bit for her drink and hastened to follow.

Outside, she caught him ducking into an adjacent alleyway to the left of the bar. As alacritous as she could without running, she pursued. She made the alley, and a shadow dropped down from the rooftop and blocked her path. She drew up short.

The vampire from the bar loomed in front of her.

"I've been waiting for you," he grated.

His black eyes were filled with frustration. This close, she could see his animalistic features, long canine fangs, the angular nose with diamond-shaped nostrils. He wasn't hiding it well. Perhaps he wasn't one of the upper echelons who could pass for wizardkind with ease.

"It's not wise to keep the Embrace waiting."

"The Embrace?"

Starriace remembered the dark-skinned man and his offer.

"Ah, yes," she said. "Not interested."

Not after the Halls of the One.

The vampire snatched her by the arm. Long, black claws pierced her skin.

"Not interested?"

"Let me go!"

"I don't think you understand."

Irritation made her eyes burn.

"I understand quite well. Unhand me, before you get hurt."

The vampire smiled and removed his hand, a chuckle filling his throat. A blinding pain flared across her cheek, and she staggered against the wall. His hand poised for another blow; the smile gone from his lips.

"You'd threaten me? A brother of the Embrace? Foolish wench!"

Stars swam in her vision. A cold, hard hand snatched her by the throat, pinning her to the wall. A sudden jerk and her feet dangled above the ground. She tried to rasp something.

"What? The whore wishes to speak?"

He took a step forward, a sneer spread across his features.

"No one declines the Embrace."

Her lips moved, and he leaned in close, his strange ear so close to her lips.

"I warned you," she managed.

The glow of her eyes intensified, illuminating his face in subtle highlights. Red-purple energy arched out from her fingertips. The hand released her as he collapsed and writhed in agony. His body shuddered and convulsed, unable to scream.

The power subsided, replaced by the familiar glow of his life essence being ripped away. His black eyes glazed over when the last of his life slipped away.

She should've been repulsed, but no pity mired her soul. It'd been the same with the sentry and archbishop. The last time she attempted this particular magic, it almost killed her, but after escaping the religious fanatics, she had better control and confidence.

Without looking back, Starriace staggered forward in search of the elyf. She followed the freshest boot prints down alleys and around corners.

Hope kept her moving forward.

As she ducked into the next alleyway, she caught a figure disappearing around a building not far from the outskirts of town. Knowing that she was losing her quarry, she redoubled her efforts, but the elyf was nowhere in sight once she reached the same location.

"Damn," she muttered.

Crestfallen, she turned back the way she came. Maybe she misread the tracks?

The elyf materialized behind her, his blade drawn, the edge resting against her neck.

"Why are you following me?" he barked.

It was hard to be certain, but his face tickled something in her mind, as if she had met him before. He seemed familiar.

"With a talent like that, I'm surprised you'd ask."

"I should've suspected. The answer is no. I don't work for anyone, especially wizardkind. I won't slave for your kind again."

"Who said anything about being a slave?"

"There's nothing you can offer me that I don't already have."

That stopped her short.

Starriace bit back a reflexive response. Her mind fluttered back to when she searched Rusem's mind. She had never tried the trick on someone alive, would it work?

He leaned closer, wariness filling his eyes.

In a surge, she invaded his mind so quickly that she wasn't sure of its success at first. A light touch against the contours of his thoughts, she probed in a frantic rush, searching for a way to connect with him. The meld lasted for an instantaneous moment, within a pulse of her heart, and she pulled out as lightly as she had entered.

Her endeavor ended with fragments and broken ideas. Again, she possessed prowess but not precision or subtlety.

"There are more of you," she stated.

"Of course. You think I was the only one of my kind?"

"How did this happen?"

A dark flicker crossed his face, and she returned the gaze unblinking. With every ounce of strength and control, she manipulated her aura, projecting a sense of charisma and trustworthiness while attempting to shroud his better judgment.

The elyf deliberated.

Starriace stretched out with her essence and imposed her will, influencing him.

"I was deceived by a lie," he said. "We all were."

A flicker of disbelief crossed his face, and he blinked several times.

"Eight legends ago we went into service for a ruler. He, in the end, turned and cursed us, betrayed us in his final hour because he thought we had failed him."

Again, she wove conjury with her words.

"Where did he rule?"

"In the land to the west of the Valley of Stones, in the Infernal Wilderness. A wasteland now."

"Who was he?"

Sweat trickled down her temple while she maintained her hold on his mind.

"A powerful sorcerer in the Derengi arts."

Her grip over her aura and the influence faltered. She wiped the sweat from her brow. He blinked several times as if coming out of a trance.

"Perhaps, I can help find a cure for you and your people?" she offered.

"My people? A cure? What are we? Diseased?"

"That's not what I meant."

"Of course, you didn't."

He took a single step back, lowering the sword. His tone turned waspish.

"We've been cast out from our people, and now I'm to take ridicule from a mere apprentice?"

"Be certain, friend, I'm no apprentice."

"A novice, then, and I'm not your friend."

He sheathed the blade in one fluid motion.

"It matters not. There's no cure."

Starriace kept the smile from reaching her face as Harold's warning floated through her mind.

Only Rumigul can undo Derengi magic.

"A warlock could."

He smirked.

"And what experience would a young girl have with Rumigul?"

"A lot. It's my specialty."

He was silent for a long moment, his eyes distant, but when his gaze flickered to hers, she noticed the skepticism on his face.

"What do you propose?"

"Let me talk to you and your people. If you don't like what I say, we can part ways."

From Rusem's teaching, before she corrupted him, he taught her how to sense the truth of someone's words. She used the technique now.

"Your presence is an invasion."

That much was truth. He grew pensive, but his gaze never faltered.

"You're different than what I expected."

The truth of his words radiated out to her, but something else lingered beneath. He said it as if he'd known her, or at least her from before all the horrible things that happened to her.

He sighed.

"Very well, let us go and heed your words."

"Before we do, shouldn't we introduce ourselves?"

His reluctance hung heavy between them.

"You may call me Iddrial."

Iddrial. I remember that name. Shades! It's the same elyf I met at the creek outside Far Point!

Chapter 39: Starriace and the Nine

Iddrial led her deep into the dense forest northwest of Crystal Falls. Dense was a relative term, nothing like the forest she witnessed while using the porting stones during Fife Doole's tutelage. They traveled for what seemed like hours. Iddrial tried to confuse her, but his ploy didn't work.

She tried to put him at ease and divulged some truths about herself. Since it could potentially alter her dealings with Iddrial and his group, she revealed her origin from the *Other Side* of the Mirror of Imaesion. Iddrial found this fascinating and probed her with questions about a place she couldn't remember. Despite this, he remained tight-lipped about himself or his people. After a short introduction, she fell silent and followed in his wake.

Starriace hungered for power, a craving that drove her to commit near-atrocities like the archbishop and the guards. The vampire that cornered her? He didn't leave her much choice either. In those moments, something took over, like she wasn't in control.

Maybe she wasn't?

The satisfaction of their demise bothered her. The power terrified her, and the claimed victims consumed a part of her. Those faces plagued her waking mind.

As embarrassing as it sounded, she wished for a master to guide her. Each instance she sought a brimstone or fought for survival furnished another chance to fine-tune her gifts. Learning new feats became a daily occurrence rather than a weekly or even monthly ordeal.

Without direction, her experimentation resulted in cultivated subtleties; her newest self-taught exercise required attunement with her surroundings. Nature communed with a hushed whisper of grass, a quiet groan of an oak tree, all teeming with life and secrets.

It was very much like her experience at Harold's the first time she met him.

Each essence in the immediate vicinity tickled her senses. In time, she'd practice expanding the sphere of influence.

The twin blades crisscrossing her back presented another enigma. The sword of Judgment on the right shoulder, Salvation on the left. She couldn't explain the odd sensation of having Judgment be near her dominant hand, ready to spring forth should the need arise.

Magic should be her first answer.

The sword wouldn't do her much good. She lacked training. All the lives the blade took rose up in her when she drew the steel, sensed the cold, calculated death waiting to unleash. Physically, a frigid shudder crawled up her arm each time she held the blade.

Salvation, by contrast, radiated warmth when drawn, and a sense of security suffused her. That she could detect, only a handful of lives were extinguished with Salvation. She needed more time to ponder their mysteries.

"We're here," Iddrial announced as they came into a clearing, pulling her out of her thoughts.

Seated in a semi-circle around a small fire were seven other dark elyfs. Each jerked their eyes to her, the intruder in their midst. Though seated, Starriace sensed their tenseness, readying for a confrontation at the slightest provocation. She returned their wary gazes with a steady, glowing stare.

Their clothes, she noted, were simplistic. Leather appeared the dominant material while some sported silk, cotton, wool, or light furs. The men wore loose-fitting material over their legs with leather around their waist. The women wore leather pants and a halter bodice. Most of the females wrapped themselves with a shawl of fur. All had thick cloaks that shrouded the figures.

Starriace also noted their jewelry.

The females wore bracelets and earrings, most studded but some dangled. They dressed for fighting or traveling at a moment's notice, not fashion. Some men wore an earring, others two. Each wore necklaces, but all were different and made of leather and stone or bone.

Another startling fact she hadn't realized the last time she met them was their facial structure. During their prior meeting, she had been too terrified to take in the details. Their cheekbones were more prominent, as were the sockets around their eyes. At the corner of their foreheads where the brow arched, the structure beneath gave their faces a more defined aesthetic. A strong, sharp jawline added an angular appearance. The extra features made their faces seem more definitive. Elongated ears poked through hair of varying lengths.

They gazed at her with an unwavering stare.

Their eyes snapped to Iddrial when he spoke in their native language. His words came at a rapid pace, and a woman with a choker with an oval stone of jade barked a response.

Iddrial responded and gestured to Starriace.

"So," the female elyf with a choker said, "you have an offer?"

"Yes. I'm here to offer you a chance to become yourselves again, to be like the other elyves: normal."

As soon as she said it, she knew it didn't come out as intended, but she couldn't retreat.

"Normal?" another male elyf said. "We've been cast out of our society only to put up with this?"

"Patience, Fir Ki. She didn't mean it that way," Iddrial said, stepping in to rescue her. "She isn't a normal wizard and is unaccustomed to the ways of our people."

That much is terribly obvious.

Another woman spoke, her tone harsh and her eyes scathing.

"Has she been in a dungeon her whole life? Everyone from their pretentious school should be acquainted with other races."

"Still your tongue," Iddrial chastised. "Many of our kind passed through those hallowed halls. Arrogance blinds you and exasperation festers on your tongue. She wasn't raised here."

He turned to Starriace.

"Were you?"

"No. I was born here, but when I first arrived, I was referred to as a Wcic."

"Perfect," muttered the first woman, "just what we need."

Starriace's anger grew taut, and she snapped before she could stop herself.

"Are you just going to bicker, or be silent long enough to know why I came?"

The group grew still. An unspoken deadliness quivered through them.

"We'll be silent," Iddrial said.

"You know Xilor has declared war again?"

Some stirred while others cast glances at their comrades. Starriace noted that something passed between them.

"Yes, we've heard," the first woman said.

"Well, I battled him myself."

"And you survived? What lies!" someone spat.

"Peace, Ahn," Iddrial said.

"Yes, I survived, and survive was the only thing I did. He was more powerful than I anticipated."

A taste of bitterness formed in her mouth from admitting failure.

"Xilor obliterated me, but I was saved, rescued. It wasn't my former master, nor was it a legion of troops, but an archangel."

A small scattering of conversation flitted through the elyves in their native tongue: Thymulous. Didn't they realize how rude it was to speak in a language she couldn't understand?

"Why would archangels save you?" the woman with a choker asked.

"Because, I think I may be one of them."

She caught all their glances at each other, but one woman, the one with the jade choker, locked eyes with Iddrial, and something passed between them. If she had to call it anything, Starriace would've said it was understanding, but perhaps she mischaracterized the expression.

They were of a different race, after all.

"Outrageous!" one man said.

"Can you prove any of this?" Iddrial asked.

Since her flight from the Corridor, and the night at the Halls of the One, her abilities came easier. A moment of hesitation trembled through her. She hadn't flown in a long time. Would her power fail her now?

She reached for her essence, and it responded, floating her above the ground. A hush came over the elyfian. With her point made, she descended.

"Here's my proposition: I want to bring Xilor to an end, but I can't alone. I need help. If you help me, I'll do my best to restore you for your service."

"What? We're supposed to be your slave?" a woman interjected.

"Peace, Fir Fera," Iddrial said.

"No. You'll be my inner circle, my trusted advisors and confidants, my hands when I can't reach out myself. In return, I'll help restore you so that you may go home."

They cast silent, skeptical glances at each other. The absence of sound filled the void between them. The woman with the choker spoke first, a long sentence in Thymulous.

"Well said," Iddrial remarked.

"What?"

"Ama Ka quoted an ancient proverb: 'When someone offers you hope, look at what your counselor has reserved for themselves.' I find her words true, and yet, what do we have to lose?"

Ama Ka stepped close to Iddrial and whispered something. He shook his head and stepped away, putting space between them. The elyves turned their backs, retreating to their earlier activities, and they huddled in quiet conversation. Iddrial gave a weak smile and moved to join them.

Her offer took a great deal of convincing. Iddrial seemed to be the de facto leader, and Ama Ka, to her surprise, warmed others to the idea. After deliberations, Iddrial declared they were in agreement.

While accepting of her presence, they weren't eager to engage. Starriace took this initial awkwardness in stride and called Ava to her side. When Ava appeared, she ordered her to bring Rusem. When the fairy left, Starriace tried to become acquainted with the elyves, who weren't too keen.

After a few unsuccessful attempts at conversation, Iddrial came and spoke with her for a long while. The others took heed and, in turn, approached her for short discourses.

Night had fallen, and two moons rose before one approached in earnest, the woman with the choker, Ama Ka, and only when Starriace was alone. The elyves never slept simultaneously. One always stood vigil. On Ama's watch, she came.

Starriace noted the woman carried a wooden staff, a smooth and flawless piece except the top which splayed out like a reaching hand. The elyf perched beside her on the fallen tree.

"I apologize for my earlier words," she said. "We don't take to outsiders well. Most fib and attempt to cheat us, or use us in a manner unbecoming. They think we've fallen and will do anything because of it."

"I understand."

"Do you?"

Ama Ka gave a pointed look, her eyebrows rising.

"Do you really know what it's like to be an outcast? I think not. Magic you possess can be hidden. Mine, and that of my brethren, is our skin."

Starriace's gaze roamed over the woman, hearing the bitterness in her voice, seeing the sadness in her eyes, and sensing her muscles knotting in frustration. Not knowing what to say, Starriace kept silent.

"I'm Ama Ka," she said, holding out her hand. Starriace reached out to shake it, but the elyf grabbed her elbow and planted a kiss on the forehead.

Ama Ka smiled at her confusion.

"It's our greeting."

"I'm Starriace."

"What kind of name is that?"
"I'm not sure. I believe druid."
"Did you choose it?"
"No, my parents gave it to me. Why? What kind of name is Ama Ka?"
The other woman gave a slight laugh.
"It's the name given at the Coming of Age ceremony. Every elyfian child is referred to as a girl or boy, son or daughter of their father's name. When of age, our parents give us names that fit our strengths, characteristics, and personalities."
"Sounds unique."
The oddities of other cultures and customs excited Starriace, experiencing something new and strange.
"It makes the most sense," the woman said. "I don't understand how wizardkind could name their child at birth. They don't even know what skills they possess. How could they possibly fashion a name from nothing?"
Starriace shrugged.
"I can see the logic of your custom."
"Perhaps. To answer your question, though, Ama Ka means Dragon Charmer or Charmer of the Wild."
Starriace smiled.
"Slay any dragons as of late?"
"Slay them? Spirits, no!"
The elyf regarded her for a few moments.
"Befriend them, yes. I'd never harm creatures of such strength and beauty. I'm blessed with a strong connection to them. They're shunned and often times misunderstood, like me. I guess that's why I feel so strongly for them."
"So, you just study them?"
Starriace had never seen dragons, but from what she knew, they were creatures of strength and terror. Where beauty fit in, she couldn't guess.
"No. I sometimes commune with them, and other times, if they're willing, I request their assistance."
"That could be helpful."
Ama Ka gave a single, slow nod.
"Dragons have a mind of their own and a complex society. Their will to survive is unparalleled."
Though the subject infatuated Starriace, she needed something more tangible. She regarded the camp and the sleeping bodies. Wanting to know more about her new companions. She used her essence to prod Ama Ka into talking.
"So, who's everyone?"
"Over there," Ama Ka said, pointing, "is Ahn Bael, the Defiant Protector, and the woman laying with him tonight is Ari Sha, which means Shrouded Thoughts. You have Fir Ki, and Ru Sol lays with him. Their names mean Lonely Warrior and Ambassador of Minds."
She shrugged and glanced at Starriace.

"At least, as close as we can say in translation. Over there, that's Cal Cas, the Voice of the Ancient, and Fir Fera, the Shadowed Heart. Mia Ther means Celestial Force."

"Wait, why does Fir Fera and Fir Ki share the same name, yet they don't mean anything similar?"

"They're siblings. As with anything in our language, the meaning of a word changes based upon the word used before or after. Also, the glyphs of our language require many strokes. A glyph may possess the same sound, change one stroke, and it'll change the meaning."

"Sounds complicated."

Ama gave a single nod.

"It is. There are over ten thousand glyphs in our language."

Starriace paused, trying to imagine a language so complex.

"Why are your names short and choppy and Iddrial's isn't?"

"Elyfian names change trends periodically. Sometimes they're like ours in the old tongue with meanings, others are longer combinations making a name more like wizardkind's. Iddrial is the oldest, and during his time, they fashioned similar names, a style out of fashion."

"You also said, 'laying with him tonight.' What do you mean?"

A small quirk flitted across the elyf's lips, and she drew a deep breath.

"Two answers. The first, for body warmth and connection. The second, none within the group is bound to another, so we lay with who we want. No one forms stronger attachment, which keeps us focused in battle. No one person will grieve more than another."

"Do you mean sex, too?"

Ama Ka smiled, and let out a soft chuckle.

"Wizardkind burn out so quick with your short lives, and your race focuses on what doesn't matter, like violence, which your kind glorifies. I say lie with, and you hear sex. Why is your kind so adverse to life's natural facets, like love, nudity, and sex?"

Ama Ka paused, glancing up at the stars.

"You were conceived because your parents were once nude. You were born the same way and take baths naked. Yet, for all your nakedness, you hide the most basic desires in the deep shadows of a bedchamber."

She has a point there, but it's different. Our lives are short.

Ama Ka shook her head and rolled her eyes. Her tone carried soothing overtures of reason, but Starriace caught the faintest whispers of chiding and mockery.

"Your race will never outgrow its greed or possessiveness."

"I haven't seen that!" Starriace protested.

"Wait until you have beheld the vastness of Ermaeyth, child. Take Ralloc for instance. You'll scarcely find a more civilized city, but not all borne carry the same morality. Other places enforce slavery for wealth and power. There's the gladai games across the Eastern Sea in the Kran Empire and Cronele. And you bind others to you with antiquated customs and call it marriage."

Ama Ka glanced at her then and took a deep breath.

"So, yes, we lay with each other to fulfill the desires of our flesh—if we choose. The only thing that separates us from animals is our ability of speech."

She paused and regarded Starriace closely.

"Don't be so judgmental of our ways."

"I'm not judging," Starriace said, "it's just a lot to take in."

"It is," Ama agreed with a nod. "Others adopted the elyfian way, the Krey for example. I discovered in our travels abroad that our way of life lives on throughout almost every culture in one manifestation or another. The further from Ralloc you go, the more you see."

"Who are the Krey?"

Ama Ka smiled.

"A story for another time. Too much truth would besot your fragile, wizardkind heart."

Starriace let her eyes roam over the sleeping forms. Their way of life was an extreme variance to anything she had witnessed. The only exception would be Kam and Lily. They were similar, sharing their bed with whom they pleased. A guarded gleam came to the mage's eye as she inspected her narrator's sleeping blankets.

No man twined within the covers.

"Why doesn't anyone lay with you?"

Ama Ka hesitated, her voice a whisper.

"I had a husband before I was cast out, and I loved him. I love someone else now, but once married by our customs, I can't lay with my beloved until my husband is dead. We are, of course, allowed to divorce, but only after a legend. Finding another mate breaks the tedium of life, but both must consent and be present before our royalty. Death only comes in war, and the elyves avoid it when possible. I'm without a mate and a burning, silent love."

Ama averted her eyes, hiding something.

Starriace laid a comforting hand on her shoulder and gently squeezed, offering her a heartfelt smile. She knew what it was like to truly enjoy companionship and not be around them. She was fond of Kam, perhaps too much since he was a married man.

Thinking of him stirred a thirst within her, a tinge of the magelust.

It was then Starriace saw something in the woman's eyes. Ama Ka didn't share her full story. Perhaps patience would reveal the entirety?

Starriace's eyes flitted over the group again, and she remembered there were two elyfian in the town earlier. When she voiced it to Ama Ka, the other nodded.

"Ari Sha. She's very good at persuasions and influence, detecting treachery with ease. She brought the others around to accepting you into the group. The business in town earlier…we use her as our voice."

"I saw her talking with a goblin about Divinity Enigumas."

"Did you, now?"

For the first time, Ama Ka turned her gaze fully toward her. Starriace noted the wariness creeping through her eyes, her muscles tensed. Starriace siphoned a small trickle of her aura and built a mageshield between them in the event the elyf attacked.

"Yes, I overheard them in the tavern."

"I find that unlikely."

Ama Ka turned her gaze back to the sleeping group.

"So," Starriace said, "you speak to dragons, and Ari Sha is good with persuasion. Anyone else have a gift?"

Ama Ka was silent for a time before she spoke.

"Ahn Bael is a steadfast warrior; his defense is impeccable, but his attacks are horrid. Ru Sol lacks skills of battle but is a mastermind at strategy. From observation alone, she can deduce how a person or race will act or react, be it clothing or architecture, and she's yet to be wrong. Mai Ther can converse with every creature that inhabits the sky, but dragons refuse communion. Cal Cas is a messenger with telepathic ability at short distances and possesses other means of sending us messages over greater distances. When we travel, we let him fall to the rear to observe for scouts."

"What other ways to communicate?"

"You must be seasoned slowly, mage. Not all secrets are revealed at first glance. Fir Fera is a tracker, and her target never slips away. She prefers the night to conduct her business and enjoys the enviable ability to blend into her surroundings."

That could be useful. I need to see if I can learn it.

"And you talk to dragons?"

"Yes, I talk to dragons, among other things."

"Like what?"

Ama Ka stood.

"Later. My watch is up, and I'm tired. You should get some sleep, too. With an open mind and the ability to take direction, I could impart some knowledge, but you don't give the impression of one who yields to authority. We shall see."

She shrugged.

"It's Ahn's watch. If your intentions are true, I hope you open yourself to our way of life and find happiness. We've welcomed you, and while that may take more time for others to acquiesce, you should know, once acknowledged, you're a part of us."

Ama Ka went to wake Ahn, and Starriace retreated to the sleeping furs they provided and rolled on her side. With the knowledge Ama Ka imparted, endless scenarios stormed through her mind. Perhaps these acquaintances would become genuine friends.

If she truly wanted their loyalty, she'd attend Ama's direction, opening herself up to their way of life. Most of what the elyf imparted made sense, but bedding someone at random didn't sit well with her. It also felt like a betrayal to Kam.

True, once their child arrived, she'd be without. Perhaps it was time to start thinking about her future without them?

The elyves were gorgeous, some the epitome of perfection.

They're tools and disposable, the voice spat from its dark recess. *Don't become attached to those meant to serve you.*

Even so, a carpenter replaced broken or lost tools, and that could prove costly.

She struggled against the voice until she fell into a fitful sleep, maintaining her belief that they could be friends and more than tools.

Other than Lily, Kam, and Ava, Starriace was in short supply of both.

Chapter 40: A King's Master

Niam, the vampire clan king, bowed low. The image of his master, his maker, loomed before him. Niam's master served the vampires' cause far greater than he or Xilor, to whom Niam had pledged himself over a year ago. Xilor was their best hope, but things had changed.

The maker had returned and revealed himself.

"What news?" the raspy croak came from the shrouded form.

"The war proceeds as you predicted, Glorious Blight."

The other flicked his fingers and tsked through his teeth.

"You're above flattery. Your honorific titles, Great Taint and Glorious Blight, sicken me."

"But you are worthy."

"Master will do."

Niam lowered his head as the other stepped forward.

"And, of course, it happened as I predicted. Only an incompetent fool wouldn't be able to foresee it. Without me, you would've been routed by the elyfian."

Niam kept his head down.

"Then, you free us from our pledge to Xilor?"

The master went silent for a moment; Niam glanced up, seeing those black orbs studying him, burrowing deep into his soul.

"Not anytime soon. I have uses for the affiliation. Continue to serve him as you would me."

Niam felt his master's fingers on his chin, so cold, so clammy. Niam stared at his master's refined features.

"Manipulations take time to yield fruit, but they're often the sweetest. Trouble has arisen in Ralloc, something I didn't predict. This king from the Isles has twisted my set plans."

"I'll do as you command and remain tethered to Xilor's whims. Have your powers been restored? Is it safe for you in Ralloc?"

"Yes, and it is."

"How do you know?"

"I tested Warlock Lakayre. I presented myself as his dearest friend, Meristal, and he was none the wiser, even in that place he calls home. I don't see why everyone fears him. He's but a shadow of the power wielded long ago. If I can hide from him, no one will discover me. I can change at will."

The fingers let go of Niam's chin, and he dropped his gaze back to the floor.

The master continued speaking as he moved away, his voice turning wet, giving him more of a sneering rasp.

"This war will continue until a weakened victor prevails, then I'll obliterate the champion. But we must be quick and ruthless. Did you find out who Xilor's apprentice is in Ralloc?"

"Yes, my master. His name is Krurik."

"What does he look like?"

"Xilor protects his identity like his own. I'm not privy to such information. Forgive my failure."

"The fault lies not with you. This Krurik is still in Ralloc?"

"To my knowledge. The only other thing I know is that he's wizardkind."

Niam watched a contemptuous smirk come across his master's face. No, not master. His god.

"Why not end our allegiance with Xilor now?" Niam asked.

He shrank away after asking, a quiver of fear threading him. He was too accustomed to Xilor, a madman with unrivaled power.

"Don't fear to think, little Niam. I value a follower capable of competent thought."

Niam raised his face, daring to glance up. Though Niam had felt his master's hand on his chin earlier, and though the sounds of his movement filled the room and the resonance of his voice lingered, the man wasn't present at all.

He never was.

"Where are you, Master?"

"Where the fools will never find me. In their midst: Ralloc. It's far different than I remember, bigger, busy, but that was legends ago. When I claim victory, Ralloc will be reborn into what Shadow City once embodied. And then, I will slip among the Krey and sow seeds of discord."

"What can I do to further your plans, Master?"

"Do you know the history of the vampires?"

"Yes, we're your creation, spawned from your mind."

"No. Vampires were selected, turned—the purest of blood—able to live in a perpetual state of the wizardkind image. Those precious few are the ones who can transform or morph into their animalistic state, feeding their desires should they so choose. The scorned, more beasts than not, were spawned, created for a specific purpose: to guard the hierarchy. To serve, to protect. That's why we have the beasts among us."

Those black orbs burned into Niam, pinning him to the ground.

"Use these beasts, now that you know their true purpose. How you let them breed in hysteria, turn every beating heart into one of those monstrosities is almost unforgivable, but you may find redemption yet."

"Tell me, Master."

"The purebloods can't die. Take them and the best of your beasts and flee Shadow City. Leave soon. I hear whispers within the walls of Ralloc; they'll unleash the unicorns. We can start anew. True to the original purpose of what you were created for."

"Where shall we go?"

"The Ruins of Sheol. Await there for further instructions."

"As you command. Xilor already ordered as such. We leave in three days."

"Perhaps," the Glorious Blight said as he faded away, "Xilor isn't as foolish as I believed."

Chapter 41: Lakayre Manor

It'd been almost a moon turn since Judas returned from the Elyfian Enclave. He reported the devastation to Meristal, and they grieved in silence before making it official to the council. The near-complete destruction crippled the resistance to Xilor's march, and now time and lack of defenses were against them.

All preparation in Dlad City was for naught. Scouts reported movement in Xilor's masses, and he circumvented Dlad City and continued to Ralloc. The probing attacks were a misdirection. Instead of attacking Dlad City from the south as anticipated, half of Xilor's army peeled off and struck from the north. Two hundred thousand goblins and trolls decimated the city. Judas helped fortify the defenses but focused the efforts on the south and west. Xilor went east, then cut north. In this direction, for a time, it seemed Vikal Village and the Krey above would be his next victims.

Has someone else become Xilor's strategist, or am I losing my touch?

With the fall of the Enclave, the withdrawal of elyfian troops from Ralloc, the loss at Dlad City, and the death of Jynerul Vikal at the hands of a lone Krey lost in bloodlust, things fell apart faster than Judas could conjure solutions. Every morning he woke with the hope of good news, and every day passed without it.

Meristal losing the consul office stung her, but sat ill with Judas. Immediate changes followed after Godfrey took over. He reorganized the army, shifting men and commands, giving several to Islanders. That was expected; he looked after his people, the new minority. Still, it irked Judas to no end. Godfrey snaked his way into their midst. Now, he flaunted the abuse of powers for Islanders everywhere.

Meristal had said as much during their last conversation in her office. Other truths were revealed in that day, too. She'd been upset, and when Judas admitted that she'd been right, she reached her breaking point.

"I'm sorry, you're right," he said.

"Of course, I'm right! I've followed you around since we met, and what did I get for it? Headaches and heartbreak."

"I never meant—"

"But you did and never realized. Or you did and just didn't care; which one?"

When he didn't answer right away, she scoffed and turned back to packing.

"What do you want from me?" he asked.

"I want you, Judas. It's always been you, but you shunned me after Daylynn and never let me back in. I forgave you, but you punished me. I stuck by your side, through the worst, but was never as close as I was once."

"I'm sorry."

"Sorry doesn't get us the time lost. We're not too old. I still want children with you."

Judas scrunched his lips at her words.

She huffed.

"I guess that's too much to ask, huh?"

She went back to slamming things in her box.

"Maybe you should just leave. Since it's so hard for you to loosen up and actually live, just go. And I'll go, too, but this time," she looked back at him, "I won't be coming back. I've wasted enough years on you."

Those words cut him deep, lacerating further than he thought possible. Meristal had always been here. True, she served posts in other towns, but she'd always come back. Now, it sounded as if whatever good grace she clung to had reached its coda.

To keep her, to show remorse, he did whatever she asked. He couldn't lose her. A new color of blush rose in his cheeks in remembrance.

"You know what I'd like?" she asked.

He shook his head.

"Sex; it's been a long time."

Judas glanced around the office, making sure no one was present.

"Meristal!"

She shook her head.

"You're hopeless! What's the big deal? Everyone does it. We've done it."

"Yeah, but they don't talk about such things in public."

"You should go live with the Krey for a season, maybe then you wouldn't be so...uptight. You can't tell me you don't want to, too."

"I do. It's just been a long time."

From that day, things were different. He and Meristal were a couple again. He'd waited ages; she was his last and his first again. Everything about her, mannerisms, peeves, the curves of her body, came back just as he remembered. He couldn't say the same for himself, drooping where he shouldn't, and plenty of extra padding. Partnered again, he took better care of himself, but mainly because Meristal pointed it out, and offered copious compliments of budding approval.

He smiled to himself, took a sip of his coffee, and watched the twin sunrise from the front porch rocking chair. Life was great, except for the war. Judas hoped Xilor would grow distracted with Dlad City and halt, giving them more time to solidify defenses in Ralloc.

A fool's hope.

The psychological spirit of the army reached its nadir when reports trickled in about Dlad City.

Xilor spared no expense when he attacked. The dragons came. From the tales Judas heard, the smoke and fire they rained down blotted out the suns.

Goblins and trolls smashed the walls with trebuchets and battering rams and poured over the rubble in the thousands. The army's commanding officer, Kernoyl Tyku, engaged them at the breach to bottleneck them, but sheer numbers overran them not long after.

Tyku kept him informed. Judas wasn't privy anymore, not since the fateful but legal coup against Meristal. Others whispered to him. Todd, the young man who harried Judas for an interview, reported everything coming out of the castle. Todd wrote a piece on the Unification Declaration, calling it 'the greatest, debatable twist in political history.'

He wasn't far off the mark.

The journalist supplied Judas with a constant stream of castle gossip. Todd hadn't met with the new, ever-reclusive consul, but did finagle council members and Godfrey's herald for quotes.

It was the best Judas could expect.

Meristal had offered to stay and advise, but Godfrey gave her one of his polite yet patronizing smiles before refusing. Since then, neither Judas nor Meristal had set foot in Ralloc.

"Let the people see what kind of man he is for themselves," Meristal had said. *"With some luck, they'll call for his head before Xilor arrives at the gates!"*

Judas couldn't help but agree.

That had yet to happen, and Xilor drew ever closer to Ralloc. What kind of man would the consul be when he faced war? Godfrey proved to be an enigma, and Judas only glimpsed what he sensed at the first meeting.

Judas fought the urge to perform an illegal coup, but morality stayed his hand—even if it was for the good of the people. Judas could lead the fight against Xilor; it had to be enough. The sword of virtue cut both ways; some would say he overstepped his bounds.

But how many would thank him? How many would call for his head?

Either way, he'd be wrong. How many innocents would die while he stood by and did nothing?

The door opened, and Meristal walked out, a cup of coffee in hand.

Judas did a double take.

Her disheveled hair and sleepy eyes didn't diminish her radiance. Since moving in, the two of them worked in harmony to broaden each other's horizons, though Judas needed work. One of those aspects was coffee for Meristal. She'd whined, but after a month of drinking it, she had come to… accept it. When she cooked, she made Judas eat things he always turned his nose up to: carrots, raw fish, and hard-boiled eggs.

"Beautiful morning," she commented, as she sat beside him.

"It is now."

"You? Flirting? Already? Are you not satisfied after last night?"

"Well, I have a reason to flirt now."

She rolled her eyes.

"Anything new?"

Judas knew what she asked, news coming from the council.

He shook his head.

She snorted.

"Well, I hope it's going terrible!"

"Give it time, be patient."

She shot him a glance.

"Do I look patient to you?"

"You waited on me…"

"Don't push it."

Judas took a sip.

The creak of the iron gate opening caught his attention. Judas glanced in that direction. He set his coffee mug down and moved his hand closer to his wand.

Lagelm, one of the goblins on the council, ambled down the stone path, hobbling on his short, stunted legs. He mounted the deck, scrambling up the two steps, and stopped a few paces away.

"Lagelm," Judas greeted.

"Good morning," Meristal said.

She took another cautious sip of her mug.

The goblin nodded to each in turn.

"Judas, Meristal."

"What brings you out here?" Judas asked.

His insides fluttered with excitement. Lagelm's presence brought forth feelings he repressed, news that may prove ill for Ralloc, but good for them.

"Who says I'm here?" Lagelm countered. "I don't remember going to the Lakayre manor and catching Judas and Meristal drinking coffee after a night of —" He sniffed the air. "—Mating."

Meristal snorted her coffee, laughing as Judas turned bright red.

"No, I distinctly remember walking the woods and lamenting about the woes of the council."

"By all means," Meristal encouraged, "lament away."

The goblin sighed and scratched his pale chin.

"Shades, why was Meristal voted out?"

Judas gave Meristal a sidelong look and raised a brow.

"I never thought I'd live to see the Islanders leave their rocks, nor an ancient law invoked. Why, that was terribly crafty."

Judas noted Meristal's narrowed eyes.

"What was even craftier was how Godfrey secured the votes. Of course, it was obvious that Poplu and Capraro would vote for him; they hated the wonderful, beautiful Meristal for stepping over Kayis."

Meristal rolled her eyes, but a smile graced her lips.

Judas shifted in his rocking chair which creaked in protest.

"But maybe there's a way to prove he cheated? I wonder how much that information would be worth?"

Lagelm scratched his chin, making a show of mock contemplation.

In unison, Meristal and Judas leaned forward.

"What if I found evidence that hints to meddling? If only someone connected the logic behind the theory. Someone with a lot of time on their hands."

Judas sighed and almost spoke, but Meristal laid a hand on his arm.

"I find it odd that the master jynerul, a man known for financial trouble, bought a mansion in the Golden City, a shipping company that services the

Golden City, the Isles, the Eastern City, and cities far to the south like Vas Grath, Maelstrom Shores, Elysys, and Celestial Reach. With a company, he'd never need to work a day in his life if he nipped his wife's spending habits."

Judas took a cautious sip of his coffee, and Meristal fidgeted.

Lagelm's black eyes grew pensive.

"But where did money like that come from? It wasn't from his accounts at the Royal Treasury. I wonder what his wife would say. Perhaps she's unaware, just as I'm sure she's unaware of the master jynerul filing for divorce two weeks ago."

Judas and Meristal started, nearly coming out of their seats.

Divorce was uncommon in Ralloc but wasn't unheard of, and even less likely the longer two people had been married. The master jynerul had been married long and fathered many children.

Why would Tyku be filing for divorce now?

"I wonder what would happen if Judas and Meristal found out about Godfrey passing and enacting strange, new laws. Domain laws require council approval, but for the city, well, his wishes become edicts. All he'd need is a Rallocan judge, one that was born and raised Islander. Perhaps ethnic camaraderie played its part?"

Meristal stood and paced. She went from hugging her arms around herself to wringing her hands.

Judas crossed his right leg over the left and leaned back.

Lagelm posed many theories that Judas had been mulling over.

"So many laws," the goblin continued. "He set up a personal guard and gave them autonomy from the constable, the courts, the royal guard, or the army. Are these the first steps of a tyrant? Perhaps I'm paranoid, but then, I heard rumors of his plans for the Krey."

Judas's spine went rigid. He was acquainted with a few Krey, especially Xenomene. Idly, he hoped she was alright.

"I've never seen the council so divided. It seems only myself, Sedrus, and Daylynn have any sanity."

He sighed.

"It reminds me of this last vote, the one involving the Krey, giving the consul jurisdiction and direct dominion over their affairs. They've always been a part of our army but left to their own devices, answering the call of war when summoned. Now, the consul plans to reorganize the Krey, removing the heir from power."

Meristal muttered Daniel's name, causing Judas to gander up at her. Those two were far friendlier than Judas ever liked. He didn't know what Meristal saw in the short, Krey leader, but he never hindered their friendship.

His attention turned back to Lagelm.

"I shudder to think what Godfrey is up to, but with all those Islanders in the Krey ranks, nothing good. Why, if there were any doubts how devious and cruel the Islanders can be, one would only need to visit the heir and listen to the tale of Xenomene and the Islander named Bitcher."

Meristal stopped pacing and glowered at the goblin.

For the first time since arriving, the little creature acknowledged their presence, noting Meristal's flushed face.

"But that's not the biggest discovery. I think I may have stumbled on to something monumental, something that Judas and Meristal have sought forever: the Betrayer."

"WHAT?" they both yelled at the same time.

Chapter 42: Vlukus

Stratu'Geim, a once great city, reached for the ideal of pinnacle civilization. It held vast riches of precious stones, thousands of leagues in rolling plains, mesas, and farmland, and an education system that shamed Ralloc's scholars. No city came close, not even Chissu'Nanuci.

But that had been before the abdication of the throne by the lost line of kings.

The people and all they strived for meant nothing now. Stratu had lost its luster with the fall. With the depleted bloodline and no true heir to the throne, the city shimmered with the glimmer of the lost. Still, Stratu took your breath away when beheld.

But Vlukus didn't see it. He didn't see many things these solid creatures idolized.

He and his most trusted abyssians walked the halls of the palace. They didn't know the city's history other than what Xilor imparted, that a powerful young ruler dwelled here, young when he ascended the throne at age nine. The boy-king's hunger for power grew unmatched, and he sought to increase dominance by any means necessary. The city carried the name of his bloodline.

The young ruler was Rusem Geim.

Vlukus understood that Xilor withheld information, like he did now. He appreciated Xilor's ability to manipulate those around him with misdirection and twisting of knowledge. But Vlukus hated when Xilor didn't reveal everything before ordering the abyssian to invoke his will.

Vlukus watched those around him, Xilor, the lord of the xicx, Niam, and he noted their flaws, ensuring not to be like them. They all had something in common: blindness, either by obedience or desire. If one support structure were removed, they'd all topple, and Vlukus wanted to be far away when it happened.

It was just a matter of when.

Xilor kept his own counsel for the war, blinded by the shadows he cast. Vlukus would've marched straight to Dlad City and razed it, smashing it with the might of legions. Xilor remained content to dither and squander resources to exact vengeance against a petty band of elyves who defied him. He wasted assets hunting this woman wizard who'd survived an encounter with him.

Pathetic.

Vlukus held nothing but disgust for Xilor, though he owed him gratitude. Xilor granted them physical form. This bought the dark lord borrowed allegiance, and it quickly slipped away. If Xilor dithered much longer, Vlukus would take his kin and never look back.

And yet, here he wasted away, waiting on someone who hadn't shown up. Or maybe they missed her? Magic wasn't precise, and the power eluded him; he had no contextual reference but feared Xilor had lost mastery. Xilor loved to boast of power and knowledge, having cheated death, but he'd been helped along the way.

The abyssians prowled the city day and night, searching every crevice and questioning citizens, sometimes torturing for information. Either the person Xilor awaited had come and left, or she hadn't shown up at all.

Vlukus's razor-sharp claws dug into the rail of mortar. The citizens went about their business as if nothing was amiss, besides having monsters in their midst. The citizenry, of course, had mounted a resistance, but they crumbled in the first bout of combat.

They're pathetic and weak, just like the one we seek, just like the citizens of Ralloc... like Xilor?

Vlukus couldn't deny his power; he'd seen it first-hand.

The people of this city were once warriors, but he couldn't tell from the resistance they mustered. Either Vlukus and his kin were good fighters, or the people were contemptible. They lived on the laurels of their reputation now. Indolent with disuse, they grew weak. And the gene pool of potential magic wielders was small in Stratu, or so the steward had professed.

Magic meant nothing to Vlukus, both literally and figuratively. Whatever damage dealt, only half struck with the intended force. The other half became absorbed and rejuvenated them, healing them as the battle wore on.

Vlukus didn't know if Xilor planned it or not. He didn't want to give Xilor that much credit.

Still, Vlukus detested magic and couldn't trust what he couldn't see or control. Though he had traits to negate its influence, magic still affected him in one way or another. More than ever, he wanted to end magic. Anyone who wielded it was a potential threat and enemy, including Xilor. As much as he didn't trust magic, he trusted Xilor less. Until a solution presented itself, he bided his time.

The elyves proved to be a devastating force at Shadow City. Most interestingly, the elyves hadn't waged war in ages, and the best way to eliminate them would be in a fell stroke before they called to arms. And while he thought Xilor an inept strategist, a fool attracted to folly, he hoped sending dragons to the Enclave would succeed.

A preemptive strike could wipe out the threat.

Vlukus stepped away from the railing and walked through the halls to the throne room. His six spider-like legs clacked on the floor in an eerie echo. His thoughts drifted to the future as he stroked his long, raptor snout, the bottom jaw jutting out further than the top, creating an under-bite appearance.

He pushed the double doors open and entered the throne chamber. The torchlight gleamed off the polished dome that flared behind his head and protected his neck from swords.

The shard of glass Xilor gave him grew warm in the leather pouch on his body. Vlukus thought about ignoring it. He didn't want to answer the summons.

"Vlukus," Xilor called from within the pouch.

Vlukus reached for the shard, extracted it, and bowed his head in acknowledgment.

"Your skills are needed," Xilor said.

"What do you require?"

"I still sense the woman; why haven't you killed her?"

Vlukus grew quiet for a moment.

"She wasn't here like you said."

A strain came into Xilor's voice.

"She's nearby. I can feel her, to the east. I've been meditating to pinpoint her location. She nears the Valley of Stones."

"It will be done."

Xilor's image swirled and faded.

Vlukus would do this, Xilor's last request. He'd hunt this mage and kill her. Xilor feared her, feared her abilities. If Vlukus and his brethren could destroy her, Xilor could fall, too. Depending on how Xilor's next few actions in the war played out, he may very well be in his final days, one way or another.

Vlukus glanced at the abyssians around him, those crouching in the shadows.

"It's time for a hunt."

Chapter 43: Starriace

Starriace pored over Rusem's journal. She'd studied with diligence since becoming part of the elyfian group. That, coupled with what she overheard about Divinity Enigumas, meant she had the location of another brimstone narrowed down.

A smile flitted across her lips.

Cal Cas bolted upright, abandoning his lounging position against the fallen tree. Starriace's head snapped in his direction. All the elyves stopped, a sudden stillness in the camp, their armor maintenance forgotten.

The gentle breeze faded and shifted from another direction like a forming cold front without the chill. Bright, quick chirps from birds altered to longer, somber tones. Starriace's aura quivered as the grass rippled with a mind of its own.

Nature spoke.

"What is it?" Iddrial whispered.

Cal's brow frowned in concentration. He turned his head as if listening to someone speaking in the distance. Starriace only detected their immediate surroundings.

Cal glanced up at Apor, the giant blue sphere scarcely peeking over the treetops.

"If I'm not back in two hours," Cal said, "head east as planned. I'll meet you there."

"What is it?" Iddrial asked again.

"There's a malevolence to the air; I can almost feel it, hear it, taste it. I must get closer."

"Go," Iddrial said.

Cal disappeared through the trees with a silent, swift, and graceful departure.

"What's going on?" Starriace asked Ama Ka.

Over the past month, the two had grown close, enough to call her friend, but not to the measure of Lily. The mage closed the journal and stuffed it in her pack.

"Remember me telling you he was a faithful messenger? Nature speaks to him."

Starriace nodded, thinking about the statement's implications. She was jolted out of her silent reverie when Ahn Bael stepped close, and she turned her scrutiny upward.

His green gaze bore into her through the curtains of his long, red hair. He was the last of the nine to warm to her, speaking directly to her for the first time a week ago, which came brusque and crass.

Why does he despise me?

"That blade," he said pointing to the black and gold hilt, "where'd you get it?"

"I found it in Ruhkhi at a tailor's shop."

"His name?"

"Old John. Why?"

"That's an ancient sword, and an heirloom of the elyfian kingdom."

"You sure?" Ama Ka asked. Incredulity filled her voice.

"Yes, any defender of the crown would know the blade. The Sword of Judgment wielded by Valin Lor, the greatest of the Jaikari."

A rich laughter filled the air after his words. Ama Ka stopped cleaning her own sword.

"Yeah, right! That's fantastical! You almost managed to pull the veil over my eyes."

Ahn Bael's face hardened, eyes glaring. Ama quieted, realizing he wasn't joking.

"The Sword of Judgment is part of Valin Lor's armor, lost since the day of his death."

"Wait a minute," Starriace interjected. "I thought Valin Lor was wizardkind, and aren't elyves immortal? How'd he die?"

"No," Ahn said. "He didn't die a warrior's death, nor did he die from battle wounds, but poisoned and passed in a plush bed. His loved ones surrounded him throughout the ordeal, but so did his students, other masters, and acquaintances; all hoped he'd bestow them the right to carry his swords and don his armor. He never anointed a successor and died in the night, a quiet end. The next morning, his loved ones found him dead; the others found that someone had taken elements of his armor."

"So, did you ever find out who took it?"

Ahn sat opposite her.

"No, the elyves never did, but I think Valin knew, died with a smile on his face."

"What's the Sword of Judgment in relation to your lore?"

"The Sword of Judgment is part of Valin's armor. Judgment is a blade of death and punishment, an adjudicator for the guilty. The blade feeds on the minds and thoughts, the hearts and emotions of anyone who'd potentially fall under its edge. The blade can think for itself, following the will of the wielder, but can ignore the call of anyone not its master. Judgment has harvested countless souls, and everything that was once them are now part of the weapon. The blade determines right and wrong and judges all guilty."

"You're telling me this sword can detect what's in someone's heart without even touching them? How?"

"Imagine, you can understand, see, hear, and feel everything at once. Now imagine when you're inside a cave, you can't perceive any of those things. That is the way the sword is. When sheathed, it's nothing but a piece of inert steel. When drawn in battle, it's pulled from its cave, and can perceive everything."

"So, then, what is it precisely?"

"An executioner. Malice forged."

The second brimstone will only respond to the trigger of malice.

"And Salvation?"

"Is trickier," Ahn Bael mused aloud, his eyes drifted over the white and silver hilt.

He scratched his chin and took a deep breath.

"Salvation is Judgment's key. Both form a symbiosis. If Judgment was your executioner, Salvation is your defense."

"That doesn't make any sense."

Ahn shrugged.

"I never said it did. You asked what I knew, which isn't much. Stories stipulate that Valin Lor never wielded one without the other, and when he did, it was to wipe the blood off."

"Strange that he'd wield both at once."

"Yes and no. I've seen those who wield a metal staff in battle. Deadly, but no match for two swords."

"Why not?"

He smiled, and she felt like it was more at her stupidity.

"When the staff strikes, you don't have to worry immediately about the other end because it's in the exact opposite direction. Two swords can strike in tangent, from any angle, and at different speeds. The staff is flashier, but the life-ender is the man who holds two swords."

"Was Valin the only one to ever wield two swords?"

Ahn shook his head.

"No; he was simply the best. No one came close, except his student, but wisdom won that bout, and Valin defeated him in the combatant circle."

"The combatant circle?"

"For simulated training where warriors test their skills. An apprentice's final opponent is a grand master. If the student can touch his opponent, they're allowed to progress to the ranks of the king and queen's special guard. If they can't, they're stripped of prestige and must start over."

"Sounds harsh. So, who was the grand master? Was it Valin?"

"No," Ama spoke up, "it wasn't."

Doubt crossed the mage's face.

"No?"

"No," Iddrial confirmed from across the camp.

"You can hear us from over there?" Starriace whispered.

Iddrial had to be at least ten full strides away, possibly more.

He smiled.

"Yes."

That's just perfect.

"So, who was the grand master?"

"The grand master was a novice of the Jaikari," Ahn explained. "The worst of the Jaikari could defeat any great elyf."

"How does one become so good?"

"Thousands of years of patience and perfect practice," Iddrial said.

He came closer, but his gaze lingered on where Cal Cas had disappeared.

"Ages," Ama muttered.

Starriace pointed out the obvious.

"Isn't an age the same as a thousand years?"

"Yes," Ama said, looking up from her steel, "but the grandeur loses its luster when you just say a thousand years. A mere blink for elyves. To wizardkind, well that's a tenth of their life gone, like the humans and their—"

She trailed off abruptly, her face turning scarlet.

Iddrial jerked, his body taut, and shot her a venomous glance.

"What's a who-man?" Ahn Bael remarked.

"She meant homugon," Iddrial supplied.

"What's a homugon?" Starriace asked.

"Don't worry, you'll never meet one. Mythical creatures, demons of the Underworld."

Ahn shuddered at Iddrial's explanation.

"Anyways," Ama continued, "the point I'm trying to make is: by the time one wizardkind could become a Jaikari, they'd be long past dead."

Starriace pondered everything they imparted: the Jaikari, homugons, the swords, Valin Lor, and the grand master within the combatant circle.

"Any tips for me when it comes to fighting?" she asked Ahn.

"Yeah, stick to magic."

"No, I meant in sword fighting."

"Don't ever pull Judgment or Salvation at any cost, even for your life."

Starriace paused, contemplating. Resolved, she spoke.

"I'll return the swords to you after I'm done. If they're an heirloom of the elyves, then you're the rightful owners."

"We can't take the swords," Iddrial said. "You're their rightful owner now and wouldn't have been able to pick them up otherwise."

Ahn nodded and snapped his fingers.

"Yeah, I forgot about that."

"What?" Starriace asked.

Iddrial took a deep breath.

"There are few times when a person can pick up the swords. One, when they're the rightful wielder. Two, when someone's the rightful holder. And three, when the blade wills it."

"I don't understand what you mean between the first and second exemptions."

"Valin Lor," Iddrial began, "was the rightful wielder of the swords, he could pick them up. The difference between the first and second reason is closely related to the third, when the sword discerns that allowing a person to pick up the blade will make them cross paths with the rightful wielder."

Starriace glanced between the two elyves.

"The swords have a mind of their own?"

"In essence, yes," Iddrial intoned.

"Lunacy."

"Perhaps to one who doesn't understand. The magic you wield seems madness to us, almost mystical and extraordinary."

"Come."

Ahn Bael held out his hand. She took it with reservations.

"I'll teach you how to use a blade to get your mind off this rubbish."

He led her away to a clearing still within sight of their camp. They used wooden sticks for swords as his lessons commenced, and the beating she took felt premeditated.

Two hours had almost passed since Cal Cas had left, and Starriace dripped with sweat, exhausted from fighting. Iddrial, moving near, spoke.

"Roundup. We head out in five minutes."

Starriace glanced around the campsite. With all their gear strung out, their fire, bed rolls, and gear unpacked, there was no way they'd move out in five minutes. She cast about and noticed they were a few elyves short.

"Where's Fir Ki and Ari Sha?"

"They went for a walk about an hour ago," Iddrial said. "They'll be back soon, don't worry."

"Fine time for a walk."

Ama Ka walked by her and leaned in close.

"They're pulling petals off flowers."

"What?"

"Rutting," Ahn gibed, shuffling past her, his gear in his hands.

Starriace felt her face turn a shade of red.

There's no need to blush.

After a month of living in the open without privacy, she had seen them naked more than once, and they her. While all did possess some magic to a small degree, it wasn't enough to make Starriace enter her lust, another entity she yet controlled, but she noted the way they responded to her presence.

She affected *them.*

Her passion was easy to control, a twinge of minor annoyance until she went to the river about a week after joining them. Cal Cas stood nude on the bank. Her lust manifested, and she tackled him into the water, but the frigid temperature broke her out of carnal lunacy.

Much to her surprise, the elyves maneuvered with grace and speed twice that of any wizardkind. The impossible five-minute deadline proved ample, and they set out.

"Ama, if you'd do the honors and cover our trail," Iddrial called out.

Ama turned back to the campsite, muttered, and shifted her hand from left to right. The wind picked up in a gentle gust and the earth churned, burying any signs of their presence. The fire dwindled and died, the ground beneath swallowed it. Ama Ka and Starriace with Rusem formed the tail.

"That was a neat trick," Starriace commented. "I've seen something similar before, just not the same way."

"Much can be learned from subtlety."

The words haunted Starriace, remembering how she ridiculed herself for not being more subtle in her arts. She had fallen out of the habit and needed to reaffirm her practice.

"Very true."

They marched east, never stopping for rest or meals. The distance they covered impressed Starriace, especially by foot and without the aid of magic to alleviate fatigue. They had quicker means by teleportation, but she couldn't be sure where they'd end up, or if she'd make it back for the next trip.

It's a shame they can't teleport.

Cal Cas emerged from a clearing behind them, and the elyves turned in unison and waited. His body gleamed with sweat but he didn't appear tired. Something deep inside stirred and squirmed at the sight of his gleaming flesh, and she was grateful to be in the rear with Ama Ka and not amongst an audience.

"What news?" Iddrial inquired.

"He's after her," Cal said, dipping his head at Starriace.

"Xilor?"

Cal nodded.

"He's sending a small unit after her. Either he underestimates you, or you're not powerful enough to be considered a true threat."

"How small of a force are we talking about here?" Iddrial asked.

"A dozen plus creatures of unknown origins."

"You call that small?" Starriace asked.

Cal cocked an eyebrow.

"We can stand against an army of one hundred strong. A dozen is small."

"Where are they?" Iddrial asked.

"Near. No more than half an hour by foot, and they travel fast."

Iddrial nodded and looked at Ama.

"If you would please, Ama?"

Ama Ka took a few steps away from Starriace and produced a sound from her mouth, like that of an animal. The elyves stood still, waiting, and the mage decided to follow their lead. Five minutes passed, and a noise rose up behind Starriace. She turned, expecting the enemy, and pulled her wand, but a hostile force didn't materialize. Wild horses burst into the clearing, trotting over to them. Each dipped their head and brayed.

Charmer of the wild, indeed.

Mounted, Iddrial guided them through the forest. Starriace and Ama Ka hurried to catch up. She couldn't mount the creature as gracefully, and Ama had to help. The horse sprang after the elyves with Starriace gripping tight to its mane, but the mounts waned before long.

They had ridden their horses to death, and no magic Starriace could muster rejuvenated them. The wild mounts had saved them and paid for the safe passage with their lives. The group continued on foot, and she drew on magic to keep going. She wasn't an athlete, and tired out long before the others.

The elyves, by contrast, didn't appear winded.

Rusem stumbled behind, trying to keep up, hitting everything along the way, snapping branches, crushing twigs, and bumbling over rocks in the process. Ahead, she caught sight of the elyves.

Usually, Cal tailed the group, but today, Iddrial sent him ahead to find the best and quickest paths. Starriace didn't know how Cal had marked the trail, but the others intuited which way to take.

A small disquiet formed in the pit of her stomach. It had been hours since they'd seen him. The mage imagined something terrible had befallen him, or their pursuers had flanked him.

Starriace cleared the forest with a sudden nothingness beneath her feet, and she tumbled down a sharp slope into a rocky valley below. The sudden change in landscape seemed improbable, but the agony of hitting jutting rocks reminded her of the reality.

Landing in a heap at the bottom, she glanced up, a noise coming down the slope. Ironically, Rusem kept his feet and ran down the hill, the most gracious of the bunch. In a heap of tangled arms and legs, the elyves rolled off each other, crawling on the ground.

A plume of dust kicked up, casting everything in an opaque screen, making it difficult to breathe. Their ragged gasps heightened the discomfort, dirt flooding their nostrils from exertion. Only Ru Sol broke bones in her left arm.

Starriace sprang into action, holding the arm gently.

She closed her eyes and reached out with her essence, delving into the granules of flesh and bone and blood. Ru Sol's mind released a chemical that dampened the pain, and the mage grabbed hold, tasting it with her essence before altering it, doubling the potency.

The immediate effect manifested in slurred speech and drooping eyes. Starriace surmised she'd over-exerted. Ru Sol's lips parted, drool dribbling from slack lips.

The mage's essence drifted from her mind to the arm.

Exerting her will, she jerked it back into place, the bone receding beneath the skin. Soft manipulation of magic compelled the bone to knit together faster than naturally possible. She pulled her aura back to the flesh, drawing fresh blood to the open wound as she mended the skin.

"Done, but you'll have to carry her until that wears off," she said. "And her arm is going to be tender a while yet."

Ahn and Iddrial pulled her to her feet, looping each arm over their shoulder and carrying her between them.

Starriace searched for a way out of the steep ravine. The cliff they'd fallen down was too sheer. The top of the rocky slope encroached the forest's edge, casting dark shadows through the gully.

It was too dark for mid-afternoon.

The cliff faces and the soaring, massive stone slabs bulged out of the rock face above like interlocking fingers. The incline they had tumbled down was much higher than initially thought. They were lucky to be alive, let alone without serious injury.

"The air is very still here," Iddrial commented, "yet the dirt stirs as if something moves beyond our vision."

"I sensed that, too," Ama Ka said.

The dirt clung to the air like a thick fog.

"Listen," Starriace said.

The sound of stones tumbling from a cliff face to the ground crackled in the distance. The eerie, hollow echoes sent chills down her spine. The sound reverberated in the valley.

"Many stories grow from this place," Ari Sha said, "of stones with minds and souls."

As soon as the words left her mouth, the world exploded around them like a brontide thunderclap.

Starriace's teeth jarred from the unexpected sound. A new rolling cloud of dust expanded out as the ground trembled, knocking them from their feet. Pebbles and sharp fragments pelted them, stinging like invisible hornets, tearing superficial wounds and drawing fresh blood.

Starriace regained her feet first, expanding a mageshield around herself.

Fear thrummed through her veins; her eyes burned as her hands began to glow with the familiar red-purple radiance. She didn't know if Iddrial and the others took notice, but they said nothing as they drew weapons.

Something stirred again, *out there.*

Starriace hurled the deadly energy in the direction of the movement.

Before she could cut off the volley, a huge boulder, twice her height, soared from the sky and landed amidst their semicircle. The impact rattled their bones, the painful, concussive blast buckled their knees. The air was wielded like a secondary weapon, buffering against her body.

I should've displaced the rock.

But she didn't have time to react. None of them did.

Where the group found the strength to return to their feet, Starriace couldn't fathom, but this time it was much slower. The elyves cast wary glances at each other. The boulder had vanished in the commotion, but its crater remained. Upon closer inspection, Starriace noticed drag marks and followed it with her eyes until the trail abruptly ended, as if someone had lifted it into the air and absconded with it.

A deep, slow voice resonated out.

"Who invades our sanctum?"

The elyves glanced at each other before turning to her. She rolled her eyes and muttered a curse for their cowardice and stepped forward.

"I do. I'm Warlock Starriace."

She paused, considering her words. They sounded empty and impotent, and she chastened herself for worrying about it in a time like this.

"Titles mean nothing," barked the deep, echoing voice.

The bass resonated all around, making it difficult to pinpoint the place of origin.

"What does the warlock want?"

"Safe passage and haven for me and my companions."

Starriace waited with bated breath, hoping that was enough.

"You must be powerful to compel others to follow you to certain death."

Starriace glanced at Rusem. He was more slave than a companion.

A deep rumble resonated from beyond the wall of opaque fog. Whatever stood on the other side sounded massive, both in voice and movement.

The elyves, as if communicating by telepathy, scattered like cockroaches in the light. She followed suit, but wasn't quick enough.

Another boulder flew out of the sky, crushing the hard-packed earth she'd just vacated. She dove, her whole body shuddering from the impact. Fear flared into anger, pins and needles of hot pain riddled her body. The fragments stung worse as they peppered her flesh anew.

Another plume kicked up.

This time, Starriace watched the retreating rock, lifting away as if by magic, but the boulder was attached to another, which was bigger and longer than the first.

No wonder it hurts so bad; it's more than one hitting the ground!

Starriace summoned all her strength and leapt. Displacing herself, she used the momentum to carry her.

She landed atop the massive stone in a crouch, then ran the moving length, following it up to the origin as it rose. The dust thinned as the boulder moved higher. She welcomed the unfiltered sunlight, fighting the impulse to bask in the clean, clear air.

The boulder drifted close to an enormous round cliff face which…moved?

Shades of the Underworld! Is that—?

The rock noticed her and shuddered, and she splayed her arms out to keep her balance. She noted the weathered erosions on the rock face and swallowed, realizing what stared back.

"Interesting," the dark, slow inflection echoed.

Closer, its voice boomed, and she had to cover her ears from the deafening sound. She gazed into the eroded eye sockets.

"You lasted longer than previous trespassers."

This time Starriace knew an attack was coming from the right, could feel the creature's weight shift. She leaped again, toward the face and over.

And for the first time, her gift of flight came without the struggle to focus, the fight to concentrate on her intent and will. The vast well of magic flowed through her as she opened herself. She soared past the head at a blinding speed.

But this flight was different than before. It wasn't a glide down a mountainside as she fled Fife's cottage, it wasn't a softer landing as she fell from a tree in the swamp, or the chaotic, headlong rush to leave the Corridor.

This was real flight, bound to her will, a clear connection manifested.

She hadn't perceived it until recently, ever since she killed that guard at the Halls of the One. There was a different magic within her. It was faint, subtle, and alien; it whispered to her, almost drowned out by her Rumigul abilities, but it was there, and it was hers.

She knew beyond all doubt.

That essence she used for flight, that same gift she used to suck the life out of that guard, differed from Rumigul magic. But now that she could detect its presence, it was a wonder how she missed it all along. And the more she used these gifts, the easier they came to draw upon.

What in the Shades of the Underworld am I? What is this power?

She used her arms and head to steer and change course, rolling her body to bank. The speed flickered like lightning. The wind cut like a knife's edge, peeling her skin from her face. Her eyes watered and dried and watered again in the span of a few breaths.

An idea flitted through her head, and before it took shape, a thick barrier of air welled up around her face, protecting her from the elements as she cut a swath through the sky.

She rolled and dived at random, making herself an impossible target. Nimble and quick, each hail of rocks missed her darting form. Focusing on speed, she dipped, a smattering of stones passing overhead. She dove until she skimmed the valley floor. Dust and rocks kicked up in her wake, creating a cloud of obscurity between her and the stone giant.

A wall rose up in front of her as she escaped, another giant emerging from it, and she landed in a clearing two hundred meters away.

The ground shook as the giant pursued her. The one at her back stirred but kept its distance, its job to only keep her from escaping. Starriace fought to keep her balance with each tremor. Reaching for power, she splayed her fingers wide, grabbing hold of the rocks and stones and boulders around her. She drew them to her, creating a protective cocoon.

Both giants roared.

The mage looked up as the last rocks slipped into place, as the creature's arm raised to smash her, but it pulled up short.

"Who would dare?" the first said haltingly. "Use one's children?"

His children, what's he talking about?

"Come out, and we'll not harm you."

She noted the pleading, the sincerity in its voice.

Cautiously, Starriace used her magic to peel away her protective cage. With the dust descending, the cloud settling, she could see the giant in its entirety.

I've never heard of a stone giant. What else don't I know?

With the most basic and crudest resemblance of a man, she craned her neck to see it in its entirety. It towered over ten meters, probably closer to twelve; it was entirely possible that two saricrocians could stand on top of each other and come close to even. Its face was weather worn, but she could detect the shadowed impressions where eyes would be.

"Promise me. Harm not my children, and what you ask will be," the giant vowed.

The one behind her stirred but made no forward movement. A quick glance told her that the second one was far smaller. A younger stone giant?

Dumbfounded, Starriace managed to find her voice.

"I won't harm your children," she said, finding her voice, "for your service."

"A slave?"

"Not a slave, but as a rescuer, a friend, and a defender of the realm."

"Titles mean nothing."

Well, he's got a point.

She reached out with her magic and rose, hovering near his face. The depressions for his eyes were taller than her.

"There's an evil stirring, drawing near. It hunts me, but if it finds you, it'll destroy you and your children. They're minions of Xilor, the dark lord. Will you help me?"

"A nephiliam?" he grumbled. "Your race is gone, long dead. Where have you come from?"

"A nephiliam?"

She'd been called that before, but no one ever elaborated.

"Druids became wizards and elyves. Archangels bred with them, and your kind emerged. You're nephiliam."

As his words reverberated through her chest, all the garbled memories tumbled into place. Her mind flashed with all the times the nephiliam were mentioned, even in passing, and hit her with a torrential downpour of understanding.

Judas spoke, "The first race to walk Ermaeyth was the druids. The archangels fell in love and began to breed with them, giving birth to the first new race, the nephiliam. From their descendants came two dominant races, wizardkind and the elyves."

The memory shifted to the nest with the Ancients, the saricrocians in the swamp.

Yes, the left Ancient thought aloud. *She's strong with passion, desire. There's something odd about her, though.*

She's something more than that, the Ancient in the middle spoke. *Something I've not felt in a long time, not since…*

The nephiliam.

The passage from Rusem's journal sprang to the forefront of her mind.

There are no more nephiliam left; they're an extinct race.

While Judas might be too young to know the difference, to have the right details, the ancient races knew. The saricrocians knew, and the stone giant confirmed it.

But such thoughts would have to wait; a threat still lingered.

"Are you going to help me? Your life and that of your children are at risk. They'll kill anyone, it doesn't matter who."

"I think not. No one survives in here. No one knows."

"The master they serve does," Starriace pleaded.

Why didn't this creature know? Was he ignorant of Xilor and the affairs of wizardkind, or did he just not care? She changed tactics.

"He's destroyed many lives and will come after you when he finishes. You said you didn't want me to harm your children. He has slain many men, women, and children, and he won't stop until he accomplishes what he seeks."

The giant remained still, and she couldn't sense its emotions, or read its expressionless face.

Finally, he spoke.

"There's only one like him. He's dead."

"No, I've battled him myself. He has returned."

"The sorcerer, Xilor, was killed by Judas, the warlock. We know. We were there. We are everywhere."

"Then, if you've helped before, you must help again."

"You mistake me. We didn't help, we saw."

"If you stand aside, he'll come after all you hold dear. He'll see you as weak, and he wants a world where only the strong survive. You said I was different, a nephiliam, that should prove my worth. If you don't help me, there'll be none left."

"No. Leave."

Her hopes crumbled, the rock-creature staring her down. An epiphany struck her, realizing what the stone giant meant by children. Stretching out with her aura, she plucked a smaller stone from the ground, letting it hover between them.

"What're you doing?"

She swallowed, hated what she was about to say, but she was desperate, and this creature was a key to survival, not only for her, but many others.

"Believe me when I say I need your help. Turning away now will ensure others die, but we don't have to wait for Xilor to come, we can find that conclusion now. I'll crush your children to ash, then turn my powers on you, unless you help me."

"He'll kill my children if we act!"

"No, that future isn't set, and he won't harm anyone if you stop him first!"

She took a breath.

"Besides, Xilor's arrogant. To him, you're a lesser race and beneath him. Fight with me; help me end him once and for all."

The massive being was quiet for a moment then spoke.

"We'll help. You speak like the nephiliam before. What's the first task?"

She suppressed the frown on her face, wondering what he meant by that, that she spoke like the nephiliam from before. Instead, she took a breath of relief.

"There's a group of creatures following us; they'll be here any minute. Destroy them to prove your allegiance. After that, we'll talk."

"It will be done."

The creature shifted, as if its form melted away, and sunk back into the earth below.

The way ahead lay quiet, too quiet. Vlukus hated silence.

A forest held animals, and they flitted about, but not in the stretch of land ahead. No crickets chirped, no birds sang, even the wind kept still. This place ached like a void in the world, hollow of life and nature though trees and dirt manifested all around him.

Vlukus suspected another factor to account for the stillness: his presence. Still, a pattern emerged. Vampires shied from him, the people of Stratu'Geim kept their distance, and now the sounds of the forest hid.

Only the sheol were drawn to his presence.

Another possibility formed in his mind. Vlukus knew an ambush when he saw one, or when he didn't. Heart hammering, he exuded pheromones into the air to cover his excreting apprehension. Beyond the ridgeline and down the steep slope, death awaited.

"Groups two and four, check the ridgeline and below," he ordered.

His orders weren't interpreted as strange, nor the fact that he didn't go first. Most of the time, he led, but sometimes he'd fall back and let the others take the point position.

Let them go to their death.

The six-legged abyssians moved forward and down the slope. It didn't take long to find out he was right. The earth shook, and dust billowed in the air. The sound of an avalanche crushing their bodies filled his ears.

Then, all went quiet.

He hissed between his needle-sharp teeth.

"We're leaving," Vlukus ordered.

He didn't care about the dark lord and his failure. He wasn't going to die for Xilor or for a cause not his own.

Starriace stood facing the smooth cliff face.

The gore of broken and twisted black creatures lay at her feet. The elyves walked amongst the corpses, studying their anatomy, discovering strengths and weaknesses to avoid or exploit during an actual confrontation. They played with the limbs like puppets, manipulating, twisting, and contorting them, finding how they moved and bent.

A partial shell or neck protector was found and pulled out among the devastation. Swords could nick it, but the shallow gouge would not sever through in one stroke.

The elyves, with Iddrial and Ru Sol leading, studied the odd points of their figure and found their blood corrosive. Ahn's toe sizzled when he probed with the tip of his boot. Ru Sol orated while Iddrial made notes. The others combed through the remains until they constructed a full creature, cobbled together from the remains.

"See here?" Ru Sol said.

Her red hair glistened in the retreating sun.

"Their scales change from the back and sides to the underbelly? They're a different shade of black, almost gray. Here, they'd be vulnerable to a spear, but not a sword. None could close the distance enough due to height, reach, and formidable legs."

Ru continued on, but Starriace didn't pay heed. She wouldn't engage them in combat unless with magic. The elyves proved far more sagacious than she realized, scrutinizing their defeated enemies. Even in death, their adversaries helped their cause.

I bet Xilor didn't predict that!

After today's unusual events, Starriace acknowledged she couldn't predict all outcomes either. It was impossible to discern what lay within the Valley of Stones, but now that she'd come, a far better plan took form. She'd gained a grudging ally whose full potential remained undisclosed.

The task ahead appeared simple enough. Xilor had created a new breed of creature. Ralloc needed a warning. Who knew the creature's full capabilities?

By alerting Ralloc, she extended a peace offering to Judas and Meristal, a paltry compunction for the physical damage she'd caused. Perhaps with time, they could meet face to face without worrying about killing each other. Notifying Ralloc forced her to face the demons that compelled her down the dark path on which she trod.

Would she ever find her way back?

I'm not Xilor. I'm not a monster.

But that line was getting harder to tell.

How could she hail Ralloc and face all she forsook? Leaving Judas equated to spiting in his face. In their duel, she came close to killing him, and that hadn't been intentional. How could she face the warlock now, especially knowing all that she did? How would she explain herself and her actions?

You don't have to, the voice said.

And what about those three thieves she killed? Was there enough justification for their deaths?

You don't need to justify your actions to him or anyone.

Would she have the chance to plead her case, or would they shackle her in irons and throw her in the stockade?

Then, there was the guard she killed before slaying the Disciples of the One's archbishop. How many countless others were crushed beneath her pull of that strange magic?

In seconds, they went from living beings to granules smaller than air.

Granules.

The word granules reminded her too much of her time spent with Fife Doole.

And what of Meristal? Starriace almost neglected Judas's long-time companion. Her kindness couldn't be forgotten. How might Starriace face her after she'd nearly killed Meristal's best friend?

Something dark and secretive whispered in her mind. There was more to Meristal than what she seemed, some untold story that gnawed at her insides.

She hungered to discover the truth.

In an idle thought, Starriace wondered what happened to Meristal, and where she was now.

Probably far from Ralloc, or with Judas somewhere.

The manifested notion faded into oblivion. Most likely they stayed at his manor or in the city.

An image of Judas filled her mind, one with a knowing gleam in his eye. Before she drew breath or uttered why she had come, the older warlock would divine everything.

Though kind and compassionate, morally right and lawfully obedient, she feared he wouldn't forgive her. She prayed his morality and lawfulness stayed his hand from destroying her outright.

You imbecile. You're stronger than he is!

Did she dare to look him in the eye after killing so many people? Despite being for the greater good, judgment lay in the perception of those who considered the implications.

Perhaps they'd understand, but chances are, they wouldn't.

Starriace took a deep breath and swallowed hard.

Ease wouldn't come to those who wait. The inner demons she feared whittled away at her resolve.

Staring into the muddy puddle at her feet, she sent her essence forth and called to Ralloc.

Chapter 44: Daylynn Reese

Daylynn rose early each morning, as was her custom since coming *here.*

Her long, shapely legs slipped free of the sheets.

Ralloc had been her home for a long time now, but it still felt strange compared to her previous home, one she couldn't return to, not yet. Not until she fulfilled a promise, one that hadn't been collected since she struck the deal.

Daylynn had come to like Ralloc, a quaint place compared to where she hailed from. She found it humorous how every Rallocan thought themselves as the center of Ermaeyth, and that everyone yearned to follow in their *inspiring* footsteps. She wondered how the general population of Ralloc would respond if they learned the truth.

The ignorant live in bliss.

No one knew where Daylynn called home. People asked, even her one-time fiancé, but she kept as tight-lipped as she had with her secret.

She held many close to the chest.

When anyone pried into her life, she played coy, teased, and changed the subject. One time, the late Kayis Dathyr cornered her until she relented and told him. When she revealed Celestial Reach as her origin, she had been partially truthful. In fact, that was the closest to the truth she'd ever gotten.

With her hair and eyes, many mistook her for an Islander or Rallocan, but when they judged her height, they changed their assumption. As a principle, Islanders weren't tall, their tallest reaching the average of the Ralloc domain. There were exceptions, of course. Islanders were a head taller than dwaven at best, and if lucky, a head and a half. Daylynn stood equal to most men in Ralloc, sometimes taller.

She stretched as she rose and ran her fingers through her honey-colored hair. The short locks didn't quite reach her shoulders. She went to the basin on the dresser and washed her face with water heated with a flicker of magic.

That was another secret, her superior magical abilities.

Judas might be the only person to know, and he never said anything. She expected as much. He minded his own business, a redeeming quality, but he had too few of them. To Daylynn, he seemed too…tightly-wound, too stubborn to change, to realize not everything, including Apor and Praema, revolved around him, his ideals, and moral acceptance.

If only she'd realized that sooner.

Judas liked to preach, to make others see things his way. The unredeemable quality was one of the first things she noticed. She'd experienced people like him before, both from Ralloc and before. Those types always preached their way as right, and any other method became a grievous infraction on your part.

In short, Judas.

He made all others petty by comparison. She couldn't recollect, for the life of her, why she'd once been infatuated with him. She was enamored before but couldn't understand why Meristal—of all people—threw her life away to be with a self-absorbed idiot.

Meristal, who had everything she ever desired at her beck and call, chose the warlock over a lavish life. Meristal could've had anyone, and she decided him.

Wisdom may be a boon to the old, but youth and love is squandered on the young.

Had Daylynn the foresight, she would've never dared to weave her life into Judas's. Youth was the age of mistakes, and it'd been a big one.

She toweled her face and glanced in the mirror. She looked the same as when she first arrived so long ago. Meristal remained ageless, too. In some ways, it seemed a lifetime ago Daylynn had arrived in Ralloc, and at other times, a mere blink had passed.

She'd heard of the people who lived on the *Other Side* of the Mirror of Imaesion, the mirror Judas used to travel to the discovered world. Judas gave an oral dissertation about it when the Mirror first came to Ralloc. She didn't believe it until she saw it with her own eyes. The people on the other side grew fast and died exceptionally young.

Life on the *Other Side* drew her interest, an experience without the aid of magic or longevity made her feel depressed. Judas surmised that wizardkind's life spanned ten times longer than the exiles.

It's sad, having to live a life so brutally short. You barely have time to discover who you are.

But her life was much longer, more so than wizardkind's. In fact, she wouldn't die.

Ever.

Death would be held at bay unless she chose, a type of sacrifice she'd have to make if she wanted to return home. Once dead, she'd be welcomed back. Death was part of the journey, the end of her sojourn to the mortal world.

Daylynn, despite walking among wizardkind, wasn't one.

She was an archangel.

Secrets kept Ralloc moving. If there weren't any to be had, Ermaeyth may very well stop spinning and head straight for the suns to end its miserable existence. Everybody held secrets. Hers were just better.

She went to the closet and pulled out a set of formal robes. She chose to wear pink today. The under robe was white linen of fine thread, the inner robe held a pale pink hue with a white silk stitching, a mural of elyfian glyphs. The outer robe, a dark shade of pink, resembled someone's cheeks in winter.

Once dressed, she appraised herself in the mirror before brushing her hair and grabbing a quick bite of warmed oats and fried bacon. She washed down the quick meal with goat's milk. Her teeth cleaned, she left the house, locking it with magic rather than with a key.

Unlike all the other members—all had homes—Daylynn lived in the castle. Kayis's idea. The late consul made arrangements for his concubine when he stayed late or came in early in instead of traipsing halfway across town to crawl into her bed.

He always came early.

The thought made her smirk, and not about his punctuality.

She reached the end of her hallway and descended the stairs.

Sex was one thing she enjoyed the most about wizardkind, but not the act itself. Archangels had sex. Life as an archangel was spent in perpetual bliss. As a mortal, the only time she ever experienced anything remotely close was during intercourse. The lack of an elevated state made fornication thrilling now that she became desensitized.

And it felt wonderful, too.

Depends on the partner.

Daylynn was a creature of unfathomable power where she came from, and as a mortal, the most powerful people drew her like a magnet. That's how she met Judas, but Meristal held the warlock in her thrall by the time Daylynn stumbled on the scene, and none neared his potency.

Daylynn, like Meristal, could change her features at will. Since she couldn't have him as Daylynn, she took Judas in Meristal's form, duping him.

She had to admit the thrill of getting away with it, but the lure of trying again became too strong to resist. Daylynn had lost count of how many times she'd lain with him, but of all the men she'd bedded before him, only Judas had gifted her with a child until that point.

But Meristal caught them, walking in on them during their passion. Daylynn let her *Meristal* mirage fall away, revealing herself. But Daylynn wasn't completely heartless. She could've shattered both of their worlds by confessing the truth. Judas had been screwing both her and Meristal for four months.

Instead, she lied, saying it occurred only once.

She hoped they didn't compare notes after she left the tent. Both were so anguished they probably didn't talk about it, and still don't, to keep the painful chapter in their life buried in the past.

Thus began her feud with Meristal.

In Meristal's defense, Daylynn was wrong, even she could admit that, and would be as angry as Meristal, but Daylynn didn't prolong the resentment. For the brief time, Meristal served as consul, and Daylynn found she liked the woman.

The former consul had a different approach than most, often times outside the established perimeter. Daylynn found it easy to support some of her ideas and plans; most formed from logic which won the men over, and she couldn't help but nod in approval when Meristal broke through the men-only club when it came to the consul's appointments. Had Daylynn not been caught making love to Meristal's intended, she and her could've been friends.

At the bottom of the fourth flight of stairs, she reached the second floor and headed to the council chambers. She left the residential wing of the castle and passed through the gardens, the entertainment wing, the Halls of Religion, the Halls of Law and Justice before nearing the council's wing.

The council: filled with fools and power-crazed narcissists; hopelessness resided in the body of leaders.

Ever since Meristal's removal, life took a quick turn for the worst, more so than during Kayis's reign. The difference between Kayis and Godfrey was that the former catered to the will of the masses, trying to appease them by giving them whatever they desired. This move, though disastrous in closed sessions, kept him in the seat of consul for nearly an age and an epoch.

Most consuls were elected or deposed by the people during the election each epoch. For a vote to be held, the people must petition; none would dare ignore or refuse such a request. The petition triumphed over all. One hundred citizens could sign a petition, and a judge would invoke a cessation of all government decisions before the council until the election finished.

Since no one petitioned at the end of each epoch, Kayis stayed in power.

There were exceptions, too. If a consul was found guilty of innuendoes or illegality, they'd be removed by the council. From the collective, the next consul is picked, or in the event like Meristal, a majority vote can be established for someone who isn't currently residing as a member.

Most votes must pass four to two with six members plus a consul. Lately, every tally came to a deadlock of three and three with the consul—Godfrey being the one who proposed the new law or proposition of funds—breaking the tie. Capraro and Poplu sat smugly as if the good old days with Kayis were back.

Why Kellis supported the king, she couldn't guess. All three wouldn't be swayed to oust one of their own colleagues. In truth, she, Lagelm, and Sedrus had to be careful or suffer expulsion before being able to beg for mercy.

Something had to change.

Lost in thoughts, the trip went far faster than she remembered.

A change was needed, but not a shift Godfrey wanted. They needed Meristal back, or have Judas remove Godfrey. She knew he'd never do that, went against his image as a law-abiding, morally righteous man. And because of that, she, the council, and Ralloc, was fucked.

She rolled her eyes in disgust.

Maybe Xilor has the right of it despite being a madman.

Godfrey, like Xilor, set himself up as a tyrant. All the signs were evident. The subtle changes to the military, the royal guard, the treasury, the laws. Every time Godfrey brought something new to the table, Daylynn's opposition didn't bother to read whatever they cast for.

Poplu often ranted how the Islander king proved better than Meristal.

"Godfrey's a hell of a lot better than that wench we had. He knows what's best, anything's better than the whore!"

Poplu often expounded about what he thought of Meristal, or what she could do with various body parts. The same sentiments came from Capraro, but with slight variations and less colorful or vindictive words.

Capraro, much to Daylynn's surprise, remained much more courteous than expected as if he quivered on the edge of uncertainty. Kellis differed from them, and if any of them turned on the other, it'd be the goblin.

Kellis's logic was sound on principle.

"We need change, change is marvelous, and with this war going on, Godfrey has more of a military mindset than Meristal. She's a sweet lady, but she can't lead during a time of war."

Daylynn almost agreed except for the difference between the two consuls.

Meristal used the people in the position to direct the war, like Judas and the jyneruls. Godfrey didn't employ anyone. He shared counsel with a handful of close people, the master jynerul, the fleet admyryl, and the herald, Hynry.

The doors to the chambers were closed, but the guards opened them as she neared.

Even the guards have changed.

She broke the threshold and walked down the phthalo colored carpet to the council's bench.

Godfrey had his own unique entourage of guards, wearing the same armor as the ceremonial dress but forest green instead of black. It was an insult continuing the colors of his house.

He isn't king here! He'll be worse than that if someone doesn't stop him.

Daylynn made the mistake of going to Godfrey, the newest man in power, a compulsion like an oblivion addict; she had to conquer the most influential. She availed herself to him, and he took full advantage.

Godfrey assumed, incorrectly, that her coming to him allied them. That wasn't the case at all. No, she wanted to steal from the Islander's former queen, Mercy, bedding her husband behind closed doors like a hushed secret. There might be power in holding the highest post in all of Ralloc, but there was untold power in fucking him, too.

Enough to sway him from his gorgeous wife and forget his vows, but somehow, she doubted it was Godfrey's first time.

Her personal achievement aside, she spent day and night looking for a loophole or some obscure law to thwart him like the one he used against Meristal, but she found nothing. She needed Meristal's expertise and was confident she wouldn't get it. Meristal had vanished after her last day of work.

Probably off screwing Judas.

When she dropped her robes for Godfrey, like Kayis had done before him, he'd abused her. After sating her initial impulses, she tried to break away, but Godfrey wouldn't let go.

He was a twisted man.

He hurt her during sex, and his poor wife, he reveled in the mental and emotional damage he inflicted upon her. Had Daylynn known their secret would be used like daggers against the former queen, she would've abstained.

Daylynn wondered what Poplu and Capraro would say about their newfound leader if aware of what happened in secret. Godfrey embodied cruelty, and that was before making his wife watch as he sodomized Daylynn in front of her. Even when she ducked out at the end of the day, guards in green would pound on her door and escort her to the consul's chambers.

Moving in town became a must now.

Maybe moving isn't enough; perhaps it's time for me to go?

She'd never once contemplated her end, but now, it seemed more like the right choice every day. Daylynn didn't know how much longer she could gaze into the former queen's eyes while Godfrey did as he pleased. Sometimes, he'd make them watch each other, other times he'd have Daylynn face away.

Islanders are sick people.

She came to the conclusion not minutes after the first time Mercy watched Callum take her. Though a sweeping generalization, not all were this way. Perhaps he was used to it because he was king and had absolute power?

The Ralloc domain would be better off if Islanders returned to their rocks in the sea.

She mounted the steps and took her seat. Members shuffled in to start the day's work. She noted her group—she, Lagelm, and Sedrus, always arrived first; the others waited until the final moment. She fostered a small fear that Godfrey's supporters might speak ill and scheme to remove her if she didn't arrive early.

At last, Godfrey filed into the room, coming from the door leading from his office to the chambers. He took his seat without a word and kept his gaze on the herald. Hynry always read off the changes Godfrey wanted while presenting the documentation.

The herald announced an amendment and the highlights before the others pressed for a vote, passing it while Daylynn and the others just watched. What she wouldn't give for a distraction, a reprieve. Someone needed to put this man in his place, somewhere far from Ralloc, back on the throne of the Isles.

She needed to turn one of the others, any one of them, to give them pause and think about what they committed to. They needed to *read* the damn amendment before voting. Poplu had been dumb enough to actually tell her that they needed to pass the amendment so they could know what's in it.

What a bunch of dumbasses.

Not only read what was thrown in front of them, but scrutinize the ambivalent meanings and fine print. If she could plant a hiccup in their unrelenting stream of blindly passing laws, she'd seize it.

Godfrey nodded to the herald, who spoke from the floor below the council's bench.

"Greetings members. This session is called to order. The first part of today will be utilized for the passing of legislature, both amendments and new bills for approval. The first order of business is the Segregation and Isolationist Act of Aggressor and Adversary Parties."

Daylynn opened the folder he handed out, thumbing past the first five pages which he'd summarize. The first handful of pages were used for an overview and the titles and credentials of every person who warranted gazing upon the document.

It also showed in great detail—if an amendment to existing law—what law volume, section, chapter, page, paragraph, and sub-section of each altercation, or if a new charter or decree, its placement, and why it'd be better.

Whoever drafted the documents had an excessively tedious job and undoubtedly were meticulous beyond reproach. Apparently, this particular law was monumental because the overview lasted nine pages rather than the typical five.

On the tenth page, Daylynn skimmed, searching for flowery political double talk or jargon to convolute the meaning. It wasn't until she reached the thirteenth page that her heart lurched in her throat. She realized what Godfrey intended with his Segregation and Isolationist Act.

By the time she looked up, Capraro was already speaking.

"I think it is a great idea. Anyone who becomes an enemy of the sovereignty should be considered a threat, and anyone tied to them should also be regarded as a potential hazard. I move to accept this notion."

"I agree," Kellis began, but was interrupted.

"Really, Kellis?" Daylynn asked. "You?"

"Yes, why does it matter how I feel? It's exceptional."

"In theory, you'd be correct, except under the current circumstances."

She held up the papers, emphasizing with her movements.

"With this passed into law, you and Lagelm would be considered accessory to the aggressor and adversary parties since most goblins support Xilor. A significant portion of the Leviathan caste makes up eighty percent of his army. That's if I am reading this correctly."

Her eyes darted to Lagelm's folder, then to Capraro's and Poplu's. None of them had opened it.

Lagelm's eyes narrowed, scrutinizing her, but said nothing. He opened the folder and began thumbing through at a boorish, perusing pace.

Daylynn turned in her seat towards Sedrus.

"And the centaurs? Their lack of presence on the battlefield could be misinterpreted as support of Xilor rather than Ralloc's sovereignty. You, too, could be considered an Adversary Party. Do any of you know what that means?"

"I do," Lagelm said.

Godfrey turned his pale blue eyes to Daylynn, schooling his face to show no emotion. She suppressed a shudder beneath his withering glower. Lagelm didn't miss any of it.

"It's a means to segregate, enslave, or exile undesirables from Ralloc, the council, the realm, or domain. We'd have to go south of the Corridor to be out of violation of the terms, but with Marcoalyn a neighboring and friendly sovereignty, everyone would have to go south of the Melodic Mountains. Isn't that right, Consul Godfrey?"

Godfrey's face held no emotion or gave any inkling to his thoughts.

"It's true," he said at last.

His voice mirrored his face: unreadable.

"Our enemies can be anywhere. Our ability to deal with them is child's play. They can twist and devalue our way of life. Given time, they'll overrun us. Even now, we may have enemies within our walls, plotting and waiting until Xilor draws near and then cut our throats in our sleep."

He shook his head.

"I'll not sit by as this poison festers in the lifeblood of our city."

"Except this also festers like a poison against…well anyone," Daylynn retorted. "Used to expel unicorns, goblins, dwarves, centaurs, Islanders, Rallocans, the list is endless. It's whatever you want to deem an enemy. Is this the tone we want to set for this administration? Is that power we want to give to one person? What if you're no longer the consul, Godfrey? What if the next person is a madman who abuses power and declares himself a dictator? He can expel on a whim! If anyone has forgotten, expel means exiled like a warlock. Does any of this sound familiar?"

She was careful not to call Godfrey mad or a dictator or trace anything back to him, but she planted not too subtle seeds for her bedfellows, especially the exile part, reminding them of Judas.

So, Judas is an exceptional example of reminding everyone what a crappy life it'd be to have.

For the first time since he assumed the role of consul, Godfrey's exterior cracked, and she saw his rage and disgust. She changed tactics, talking straight to Kellis who'd been a Godfrey supporter since day one.

"Is this what you want for your people? What about the Palatine caste? Many of them live here. Soon, if this is passed, they'll be back in the Goblin Forest. What happens if Xilor calls for your heads? The only thing keeping the Leviathan in check is your ability to use magic and their lack of it. With Xilor, they won't be afraid for long. Then what? You'll be dead."

"That is, of course," Lagelm spoke up, directed at Kellis, "you don't care for our people? I will have to notify the prelate of your actions, and he'll have no choice but to replace you."

Kellis clenched his jaw.

Godfrey turned his guarded gaze back to his herald who took the cue.

"Let's call for a vote," Hynry said.

"Yes, let's," Daylynn muttered. "I'm not in favor."

She looked down the line to Capraro and Poplu, who elected the opposite, but she'd expected that. Sedrus and Lagelm voted against as she knew they would.

Now, it came down to Kellis.

If he motioned for, the group would be deadlocked, and the tie-break would go, by default, to Godfrey. If Kellis moved against, the bill would be shuffled to the bottom of a very long stack of bills and petitions that hadn't been seen in almost an age.

Kayis was the last consul to sift through them, and he hadn't done it in at least an era.

Kellis mulled it over and flexed his lips as if tasting something bitter.

"I move against," he said at last.

Godfrey schooled his features. Expression unchanging like a statue, he nodded to Hynry.

Daylynn smiled inwardly, achieving the hiccup she sought, but doubted if it'd be enough. Ever since Meristal stepped in as consul, Daylynn saw how a real politician should work. Kayis never pondered the long-term issues or consequences. Meristal moved with precision during the moment and to lasting effects. She couldn't appease the masses.

Not everyone agreed on every issue, so she struck to find a middle ground, working on compromises on both ends of the spectrum and all people between, as a leader should. Daylynn had always been a follower, even as an archangel, but she saw admirable qualities in Meristal and realized what it meant to be a leader.

She could only try to emulate Meristal and hope it worked.

"The next order of business," Hynry spoke, "is the Redistribution and Reacquisition of Funds, Titles, and Lands of Adversary Parties. We shall call for a vote."

"Wait a minute," Lagelm spoke up. "You haven't read the overview. By law, if it's a new bill, you have to read the overview to give us an idea of what it entails."

Godfrey nodded to Hynry, who swallowed hard.

The herald began reading the overview, but at a much quicker pace than the first. Together, Sedrus, Lagelm, and Daylynn turned through the folder he handed them and began to dissect the proposition. Kellis inspected it. Poplu and Capraro didn't bother to open theirs, but stared at the herald as he read or shit her glares.

Daylynn flipped through pages, the race having begun. If Hynry finished before they found the fine print, he could force the motion, and she realized Poplu and Capraro would go along just to be done with the tedious paperwork. She could cast against, but without a substantial reason such as pulling out a segment of writing, she'd be asked why. With no valid reason, she'd lose her vote, as would the others.

This amendment to the passing of laws was enacted long before Kayis Dathyr took office, to keep people who had personal issues with other party members from stalling or tabling fair proposals for the betterment of all. Luckily for her, Sedrus happened on a page she wasn't reading.

"I find this abhorrent," he interrupted.

"Please, do tell," Poplu snarled. He rolled his eyes.

"This proposal," Sedrus said, "was to be ran in conjunction with the Segregation and Isolationist Act of Aggressor and Adversary Parties bill. Since the last one failed to pass, I move to strike this as well. Obviously, if we struck down the Segregation and Isolationist Act, and this Redistribution and Reacquisition was supposed to work in tandem."

During his ramble, Daylynn continued searching for something more concrete. His stall tactic wouldn't delay them for long, and he stretched the boundaries of calling in disfavor.

"I don't see anything wrong with it," Capraro said.

"You would if you bothered to open up your folder," Lagelm countered.

"Look here, goblin," Poplu started, but Daylynn cut him off.

"Actually, I second Sedrus's motion."

"On what grounds?" Poplu snapped.

"On the grounds that soon you may no longer be considered of noble birth but a peasant."

Poplu sneered at her like she was an imbecile.

"What are you talking about?"

Daylynn eyed Capraro, whose face dropped.

Hit them where it hurts, in their coin purse and on their lineage standing.

"According to this," she said, "it states if any person or species is found guilty, guilty by association, or has been conveyed into any acts considered barbarous, illegal, or otherwise ill-conducive propaganda or statements to the domain, realm, city, or ruling body, said parties will be stripped of birth status, titles, lands, and monetary wealth and regelated to the status of the common masses. In addendum to said segment, any party seen as cooperating, or in association through goodwill and manner with the ruling body of Ralloc will be given an elevated status as payment for their assistance. All lands, titles, housing, and money shall be regulated to the sovereignty and redistributed as the ruling body deems worthy."

Poplu scrunched his face up as if trying to understand what she said. At least he started to think; Capraro thumbed through the folder, a worried expression on his face.

"Let us vote," Hynry called.

"Wait!" Capraro said.

Daylynn took this as her opportunity to continue speaking.

"Vamor, this is saying if you fall into disfavor, your noble status as House Poplu is gone, and they'll give it to someone else. Your home, money, everything. Perhaps it'll be given to someone of common birth, a fellow Rallocan, or a dwaven far away, or an old friend of the consul from the Isles."

At this, the venom in Godfrey's eyes almost charred her soul.

He must realize I'm onto him. I won't be here much longer. He'll do everything in his power to send me off, or kill me.

Poplu peered at his folder in horror before tearing it open and skimming through the pages.

Since her intentions were made clear, she continued. She had nothing to lose now.

"You know what else I find odd? It never says council on it, as in us, it just says, 'ruling body.' We aren't mentioned in here, and I confess it may be a simple mistake. I'd agree except it's done more than once. In fact, there are quite a few times in here where we aren't mentioned, almost as if there won't be a council to enact these laws. Does anyone else find this strange?"

"I do," Kellis said, rising to her defense.

He gave Godfrey a hateful stare, but the consul continued facing forward, tight-lipped, and expressionless.

"I call to dismiss this proposal," Daylynn said, raising her hand. Lagelm and Sedrus followed suit. Kellis refrained from voting at the moment, watching Poplu. Vamor closed his folder and blinked a few times before turning and locking eyes with Daylynn.

"I favor...dismissal."

The visage on his face said it all. He was unaware of the fine print, or what all the other recently-passed laws said. Daylynn fought the urge to rejoice. He'd finally realized what an ass he'd been, but now wasn't the time for divisiveness.

Again, Godfrey said nothing, but his eyes narrowed at Hynry. It must have been a prearranged signal, or Hynry just knew his king so well.

"I call for a recess of deliberations."

"Actually," Daylynn said, raising her hand to stop the dismissal. "I have a motion I'd like to bring up. I move that all new laws must be brought to the council's attention a fortnight in advance, that way there's no misuse of power or fine print we're unaware of. I vote in favor."

She raised her hand.

"You can't call for a vote," Hynry sputtered.

"She can," Capraro said. "Motions are verbal, not textual, they're not laws but rules for us to abide by. Once passed, they're written, and I second the motion."

After Capraro gave his support, all the members raised their hand in favor except Poplu. Capraro had to nudge him, but he still didn't vote. With a five to one, it didn't matter anyway, they had the majority.

Godfrey rose in deliberate slowness.

Hynry spoke up immediately,

"Council's adjourned until after lunch."

Godfrey kept his silence as he closed the distance to the consul's door. He said nothing, but Daylynn noted the strides of contained rage. She allowed herself a small, victorious smile, but found it short-lived.

Hynry glanced her way and shook his head. Dread etched his features with a tinge of pity.

His message was clear: she'd pay dearly for her defiance.

Chapter 45: Council Chambers

Meristal attended the council meeting from the back of the chambers as Daylynn dissected Godfrey's schemes.

So, this is what Lagelm was talking about. Now, I understand why he's so worried.

If Godfrey had managed to pass anything into law remotely as deviant and sinister as these two, Rallocans and everybody else were headed for a bleak future. She worried over the segment that referred to the ruling body rather than the council, almost as if Godfrey planned to be rid of them.

From a legal standpoint, he couldn't unless he'd already passed the law since Poplu, Capraro, and Kellis hadn't cared for the specifics. Meristal was glad—and that indeed came as a shock—that Daylynn remained on the council.

Maybe being around me did some good?

Somehow she doubted it.

Meristal spied Todd Wynters, the reporter, who scratched with a zealous hand; a small table accommodated the few possessions he brought, strung across the surface. His dark hair bobbed up and down as his arm jerked in erratic strokes. She almost imagined hearing his quill fly across the parchment.

Meristal turned her eyes back to Daylynn.

Daylynn's smile fell as Godfrey made his exit, and Meristal caught Hynry shaking his head at her before following his master as if his leash grew taut. Daylynn turned forlorn for a moment, but that changed when Meristal caught her gaze. The former consul gave a small nod, signifying a job well done. Daylynn allowed herself a hesitant grin before turning to speak with Lagelm and Capraro.

Even if her current acts didn't bring any goodwill between the two, Meristal genuinely hoped that Daylynn bought goodwill with Capraro who needed to sway Poplu, and end Godfrey's rise to…well, an emperor.

Meristal hoped it was enough.

Once the political wagon rolled, it was hard to control. If Godfrey had a slight breeze in the sails, there'd be no stopping him.

The scribes broke from their small tables, collecting their squiggled notes from the brief session. With the council officially on break, there was no need for their presence. Meristal was about to leave when a scream from the scribe's table pulled her attention. A woman was pointing at the massive glass window directly behind the council's bench. Meristal's breath caught in her throat.

A face loomed there.

Honeyed hair and a celestial nose marked her attractiveness, but her eyes clashed against the simplistic features. They burned, a shimmering red filled with hostility.

By the gods! Something foul has marked her, but what? How?

Even though an image, the aura she exuded radiated power and a commanding presence. A shudder ran up Meristal's spine. She shook her head, not believing the image before her.

There's no way this person is the little girl I saved in Cape Gythmel. It's impossible! She's…evil incarnate!

Meristal hadn't seen young Julie for almost a year.

What could've gone so wrong that she became this creature?

Meristal tried to swallow, but her throat had gone dry. Since her appearance and the first initial scream, the room grew still. A creeping hush clawed at the collective throats of those present. All eyes turned, transfixed on the back wall. Daylynn, and the others, stepped away from the bench to get a better view.

The ghostly image shocked them, Meristal most of all; Julie had been touched by formidable magic. The signs were evident. At least, that's what all the tales said. Whatever this magic was, it nearly killed her; how did she manage to stay alive? Most would assume the visible signs of vile magic—her glowing eyes and crackling aura—and from the collective gasps, Meristal surmised everyone believed it.

Poplu puffed up his chest, as if he were someone important.

Don't be a blowhard.

"Who dares invades the privacy and sanctity of the Kothlere Council?" Poplu barked.

"Silence, fool!" Judas snapped, manifesting in the room. Judas had been searching the castle for the master jynerul while Meristal sat in on the meeting. Either he hadn't found him, or the commotion or sudden surge of essence brought him.

He took a few cautious steps forward, centering himself in the room. His eyes never left the girl he'd awakened, but what became of her, that had to be hard to accept.

Meristal studied his face, which showed a mixture of surprise and guilt. While Meristal knew they'd parted ways, Judas never elaborated on the tale.

She made a note to press him later.

All eyes watched the exchange. Meristal didn't see anyone move. It was almost as if they weren't breathing.

"Julie," Judas said, "what an unexpected surprise."

As Judas's voice faded, a skitter of hurried and breathy conversations rippled through the crowd, little more than background noise.

"Master Judas," she said with a quick dip of her head.

Though less than cordial, both acted terse and wary. The fact that she called Judas *master* was a favorable portent.

"I hoped you'd be here. Is Meristal around?"

"She…" Judas started. The shock on his face spoke volumes. He was surprised that Julie remembered her. Meristal was about to step forward, closing the distance to Judas when the warlock spoke.

"She's on her way and will arrive shortly."

Meristal stopped.

Judas lied! Why would he? Either he lied deliberately for time, or he didn't see me standing here. Is this all part of a plan?

Meristal made a note to tease Judas later about lying.

Maybe I'm starting to erode those pious morals.

"Then, I'll await her arrival," the young woman countered.

The mutterings rose higher as Julie pulled back, waiting in silence. Her enormous visage cast glittering eyes at everyone who dared look up and judge her. Meristal ducked behind a pew, playing to give Judas time. Some of the mutterings reached her ears, words like 'archangels', 'Xilor's spawn', and 'homugon'.

Meristal hoped he would try to stifle such ramblings with a stern expression. If he did, he failed miserably.

"How have you been since you departed?" Judas asked. "Are you well?"

"Do you mean since the first time or the last time?"

Her voice was a mixture of surprise and contempt.

"If it's the last time you're referring to, I almost killed you, or do you not remember?"

Meristal swallowed hard.

So, she knows how close she came.

Meristal hoped that Julie didn't know, that she'd be too scared to try again. Now that she knew, if another confrontation occurred, the knowledge may embolden her.

Meristal peered over the pew, glimpsing Julie's face. Instead of fury, she spied relief, as if the knowledge burdened her shoulders with an enormous, unseen weight.

It must have gnawed on her soul ever since.

Meristal took this glance in the span of two heartbeats. In that time, Julie's face twisted with regret, not of the deed, but of the words she disclosed.

"Too many things have happened to tell and not enough time," Julie said, her voice flippant.

Meristal didn't know what Judas's intention was, but she decided to end the charade. She crept to the edge of the row and walked down the aisle to stand beside Judas.

"Meristal," Julie said with a bowed head.

Is that a sign of respect?

"Now, I may begin."

"Julie?" Meristal breathed, baffled by the image. Having drawn closer, she didn't want to believe her eyes.

The young woman's brow frowned.

"Julie?" the youth echoed.

Did the last tethers of a previous life fade with the passage of time? Does she not remember her name?

The youth leaned forward, her face growing larger on the window.

"That's the second time someone has called me that. My name is *Starriace*."

Meristal sucked in a sharp breath, and out of Meristal's peripheral, Daylynn Reese turned her gaze to Judas.

"Very well, Starriace," Judas said, spreading his arms wide. "What do you wish to speak with us about?"

"Xilor is undoubtedly marching to destroy Ralloc. You're going to need help to survive. I'm arranging that help now."

"Are you now?" Daylynn Reese asked.

Meristal noted the edge in her voice.

Shades Daylynn, keep your mouth shut before you make it worse!

"What help could an apprentice bring?" Daylynn queried. Meristal and Judas glared at her in unison. Did Daylynn not realize she would ruin this chance to speak with her?

"You'll know."

Starriace's eyes slid over to the woman, her gaze lingered. Something passed over the young woman's features, almost like recognition.

"*They'll* help fortify the city."

She turned her attention back to Judas and Meristal.

"Starriace?" Judas called.

He must have sensed her readying to end the transmission.

"Are you okay?"

A puzzled expression clouded her features, and she scrutinized Judas. Meristal shifted on her feet, leaned away to get a better look at his face and stance.

"Is there something you wish to say to me, Master Judas?"

The words rolled out at a languid pace.

"No, nothing...I merely wish to know you're well."

"Yes, I am. Your help makes all haste for Ralloc, but it's coming from afar."

The dismissal in her voice was hard to miss. She stepped back to end the transmission, but the door to the consul's chambers burst open, and Godfrey marched in with his heels clicking smartly against the floor.

A storm swept in his wake.

"And who might you be?" Godfrey demanded, his cold blue eyes glittering up at her.

Starriace leaned in for a closer look. All considered, her face remained neutral throughout the transmission. Now, her face darkened.

"The one who's going to save you," Starriace said. "I suggest you remember that when you address me."

"You mistake my question. Who are you to me? Last I checked, you're no emissary from some foreign dignitary, nor a queen, but a mere child who meddled with things she doesn't understand. I don't recall asking you or anyone else for help. So, again, who might you be?"

Starriace's image leaned in until her eyes filled the entire window.

Meristal shivered.

Starriace's eyes burned with rage at Godfrey's insolence.

"Master Judas, tell this little madman who I am."

Judas stepped forward, but Godfrey rebuked him with a sharp wave of his hand.

His shell is really cracking today. Daylynn really got him in a foul mood.

"I asked her, not you," Godfrey growled.

"I'll show you who I am!" Starriace said.

The words came out almost as a hiss, and Meristal's skin crawled.

Godfrey let out a demonic scream before falling to his knees. His white fingers splayed over his scalp. He screamed until the veins bulged in his neck. Meristal thought they'd burst through his skin. His hands clutching his head shook back and forth as if to rip off his own head.

And then, all went quiet. Those few moments, mere heartbeats, seemed like hours.

His screaming stopped, and he lay still. Hynry rushed forward, but Godfrey teetered over and face-planted on the floor. No one else stirred, frozen in place but what they witnessed.

Even Judas appeared at a loss for words.

But Starriace wasn't done. Godfrey twisted and flopped on the floor like a fish. Meristal focused on Starriace, the youth's face contorted with fury. Then, concurrently, became serene, showing no outward concentration. Godfrey stopped twitching, foamed at the mouth, and his face turned blue.

A little more, and she'll kill him.

It was the first time Meristal could recall where she was faced with an evil and felt compelled to let it happen.

If she kills Godfrey, she can save many lives, especially when and if Xilor falls. If he lives, the future will be worse. Which is the lesser of the two evils?

But no, she couldn't let Starriace kill Godfrey. Godfrey's future was little more than speculative, a potential possibility rather than actionable fact. Just as she stepped forward, Judas moved, too, as if he'd had the same internal battle and conclusion.

Before either could do anything, Godfrey's body went slack.

The faint smell of urine lingered in the air.

Drool poured out of his mouth as his trembling limbs stirred to pick himself up. When he made it to his knees, Hynry and a few of his new guards in forest green rushed to help.

Starriace's voice came in low and dark, filling the chamber.

"Now, do you know who I am?"

Blood trickled down Godfrey's nose and ears.

He nodded.

"Aye, you're a dead woman."

Meristal's brows shot up.

The son of a bitch has nerve, I'll give him that!

"You can try; there's a queue," Starriace retorted. "What chance do you think you have? Who'll save you from me if I decide to end your life? From the looks of everyone in that room, you have no friends, and none to come to your aid."

"There are powerful wizards here! Battlemages of the aegis caste. The warlock."

Godfrey turned and pointed at Judas.

"And his ever-faithful sidekick. They'll stop you!"

Starriace's mirth burst out like bright wind chimes. Her voice ascended several octaves. The laugh reminded Meristal of hysteria and belonged to a troubled soul.

Meristal's soul sunk with foreboding.

That's a laughter that belongs to madness.

Starriace's laugh ceased, and she leaned forward, face looming again.

"Judas came within a breath of dying. He doesn't appear too eager to test himself again, you pitiful man."

"I'm the consul—"

"Godfrey!" Judas shouted, but the former king took no heed.

Starriace's brow quirked up.

"Consul Godfrey?"

She peered down at him.

"The next time I call, don't be there."

"You—" he began, but Starriace cut him off.

"Godfrey, I'm nephiliam."

Meristal's eyes went wide at the proclamation, and she felt her stomach drop out.

Oh shit, but that means—

"I can teleport, fly, and kill a man with a single touch. I've destroyed buildings, grinding them into particles smaller than the dirt beneath your fingernails. What chance do you have?"

Godfrey's mouth twitched with a retort, but nothing came.

A genuine smile crossed Starriace's face.

"Well, you've been quite entertaining. Go change your pants. Urinating yourself is unbecoming of a consul."

She cackled again, her voice high, filling the chamber.

Before Godfrey retorted, the transmission ended, the laughter terminated, leaving the echo curling through the tomb-quiet assembly hall.

Godfrey made it to his feet and rounded on Judas and Meristal. He glowered, his lips twisting as if he wanted to rebuke them but thought better of it and left in a hurry. Hynry and his guards followed on his heels as doors slammed in his wake.

That poor girl, she's lost it. What happened to her to make her so...

What word would be correct, fitting?

Chaotic? Evil? Mad?

Meristal's thoughts couldn't decipher the enigma of Starriace, or what foul circumstances befell her. Could she not see it herself? Or was it just the perspective of one who had not seen her in over a year? Before she could ask Judas, the room erupted in raised voices.

And she and Judas had a lot to talk about.

Starriace was the name he'd chosen for—

The thought flitted away, as if it was never there, and the onlookers surged forward, pressing them on all sides, and the questions came tumbling out like a waterfall.

Chapter 46: Divinity Enigumas

Starriace slept in the Valley of Stones with her elyfian companions. That night, Fir Ki kept her warm.

The glimmering coals cast an eerie glow. The remains of Cal's and Ahn's deer lay in thin strips over the spit, drying. She would've preferred beans or corn or some other kind of vegetable with the meal.

With their bellies full and the Hour of Challenging set, which Starriace wouldn't have, she crawled under the pelts with Fir Ki. A night that granted a full sleep was a rare occasion indeed.

Early on, when they told her to sleep naked with whomever she bedded down with, either male or female, she was appalled, but they spoke the truth. It kept her warm. She watched them strip down every night. Sometimes this led to nocturnal activities around the camp, but most of the time, it didn't.

She never partook.

After a week of freezing and having the most terrible sleep she could recall, she followed their example. By the third week, it almost seemed like second nature.

The past few weeks felt like a nonstop, cross-country race. Sometimes, they paused long enough to refill their water skins and grab something to eat. But the running was over.

The last two days were the worst.

Exhausted, Starriace fell asleep, wrapped in Fir Ki's arms. She rarely had troubled sleep—except for the week she refused their advice—but tonight dreams haunted her. She dismissed dreams as they held no truth, but tonight, this dream terrified her.

She looked on as Xilor battled a shadow. Destruction rained down. Ralloc trembled in the distance. Armies amassed as far as the eye could see. Darkness and light blurred, and the dark figure struck Xilor down. His body lay lifeless. The dark figure turned towards her. Was it a woman?

And beyond her, she saw a mass move, faintly the outline of a man, with glowing, golden eyes.

Starriace rushed this dark figure. The shadowy woman reached for the heavens and rent the sky. Pulled energies from the cosmos and tore the world asunder. Starriace marveled and trembled at all she beheld. In a blink, all had vanished, and only a mountain of skulls and rivers of blood remained.

Ermaeyth turned to ash, a barren wasteland of lifelessness.

Was this a nightmare, or a shadowcast of the future?

While sleeping?

The surroundings rippled and changed. Darkness invaded like a pestilence. An eerie disquiet flickered up her spine. The atmosphere radiated an urgency, something more immediate. Her skin prickled.

A vivacious man danced before her, the song merry. A crowd rose up around her, seated at tables for a feast. Others laughed and cheered him on, nobles and attendees of a court.

She almost joined their merriment, the ripple of emotions echoing through her.

The dancing man was dressed in a gaudy fashion; his unnatural cherry-red hair graced his jawline, obscuring the green with black designs on his face. It was meant to give a comical appearance, but apprehension gnawed at her insides, growing with intensity each time she gazed upon him.

His silver and white eyes gleamed in the light, freezing her with terror. He entertained, parading around as a court jester, and the crowd loved him, pleased with his antics and sleight of hand.

Men and women laughed at his jokes and charades, his slips, trips, and falls. He juggled knives, but he missed, and a knife furrowed deep in his hand. The hilt kissed the flesh of his palm. He danced a jig, acting like the unbearable pain spurred him.

The onlookers laughed all the harder.

The jester picked a lord from the crowd to help pull the knife out but to no avail. He waved the fellow off and tugged on the knife. He turned, squirming. The nobleman laughed all the harder, watching the jester prying the knife. The buffoon gave a sharp tug, the blade coming free, but it flew from his hands and through the lord's mouth, impaling him against the chair's back.

"Oops," the jester said, laughing.

His smile sent shivers down Starriace's spine. The once-cheerful grin turned sinister.

"Kill them all."

His voice was raspy, like tearing parchment.

With rapt fascination, he attended his obedient entourage, two men and a woman. They stormed the room and butchered the bystanders, and most seemed docile, content to let it happen.

The jester's face shifted from jolly and cheer to demonic and malevolent. His laugh, a sick and twisted coughing, echoed through the halls. With blood pooling on the floor, he rolled through the slick sanguine fluid, coating his clothes and face. He even cupped his hands and drank, then ran his fingers through his hair.

His eyes rolled back into his head as he laughed.

On his hands and knees, he drew symbols on the floor, cutting swaths through the blood. He tilted back, looking up and through the ceiling, that manic grin never leaving his lips. Seeing her own name scrawled across the floor sent a tremor of fear through her.

Starriace followed his gaze up, but she didn't see anything.

"You're next, my sweet."

She lowered her gaze in time to see him turn toward her. A smile of depravity split his lips.

"Let's be naughty."

He cackled-coughed again before lunging at her.

She woke with a start before his hand closed around her throat. She gasped as the dawn's early light paled the sky, and the troubling vision didn't fade as she hoped it would.

The residual, nightmare images plagued her. Xilor's battle, the dark figure. She understood the symbolism, but was she the shadowy figure? Did she glimpse the future?

The second dream made her soul cringe and her stomach turn. Who could be so sick to bathe and drink the victim's blood, then to play with their fluids by drawing symbols on the floor?

The jester courted madness.

He was demonic; no other word conveyed the severity. He stood and heckled like a hyena, his strange eyes glittered with hysteria, and he enjoyed it.

She'd never let herself forget those eyes, the silver with white pupils.

His antics had lulled the people, and then he murdered everyone. No witnesses, all victims. Only theories, speculation, and rumors would be left in the wake.

Why would anyone do this besides evident sickness? His silver eyes flashed through her head. No, he was something else, not a man. But what? Some ancient race returned? Some scion of darkness?

"Kill them all," he'd said.

Was that literal for the people present, or did it have a deeper meaning she couldn't see?

The symbols drawn in blood peppered her vision, and her stomach threatened to turn. Why did he draw them? What did they mean? More important, was it part of his psychotic fantasy or something else she couldn't see? Many etchings littered the floor, but she'd seen her name clearly.

What were the other ones?

Bile threatened to erupt from her throat. She turned and stormed off, driving her heels as she walked. The movement helped chase the sick dreams away. She snatched up her pack and headed away from the sleeping group.

If the dreams troubled her, so did her recent displays of strength. The ability of flight both thrilled and terrified her for its unnatural elements. The guard at the Halls of the One, the lone sentry she touched and granted instant death to, still rattled her.

She doubted the man deserved the fate.

She was at fault, mistaking what he intended. Once he grabbed hold and her robes parted, the faces of those three men filled her vision, and she lashed out.

She shook her head to chase the memory away.

The self-discovery of her nephiliam heritage accounted for a good portion of unexplained powers, but without confirmation by another, it proved nothing. She needed help, answers. She dropped the pack and took a deep, steadying breath before plopping down.

But didn't she already have confirmation? The stone giants and the saricrocians? It didn't help that no one had the same answer besides that the nephiliam were all extinct.

Starriace rummaged through her bag, moving her new clothes aside until she found the book Judas had given her before she'd left him. With legs crossed, her fingers traced the outer edges of the book.

A vibration thrummed in her chest as her essence responded. She stretched out, exerting her will on the book. The binding trembled within her thoughts, and she felt its own power rise within. In her mind's eye, webs of energy coursed through the book, holding the secrets at bay. Through a fissure, she spied the vast force at the book's disposal and shivered.

She'd seen and felt a similar potency once in her life. Fife emanated this type of presence, which made her question his origin and the book. All said, she had to marvel at Fife's temperance. He could've killed her many times over but refrained.

Even if she wanted to force the book to bend to her will, she wouldn't win. She caressed the cover and cleared her mind.

"I'm the Bearer of Secrets."

The book's blinding light—metaphorical—radiated from the inner spine and burst open. As the voice spoke to her alone, the light dimmed.

"Speak."

"Can you tell me where Divinity Enigumas is?"

"Follow the river of Emaas, where it meets with the Vergence. There it shall be revealed. Don't be tempted by the madness that claimed him."

"Him, who?"

The book answered as if it hadn't heard.

"The time draws near for when you'll unlock the past, Secret Bearer. Trials lay ahead, and many will test everything you think you know. The harbinger of the Underworld draws nigh."

"What do you mean? Is Xilor the harbinger?"

The book remained silent to her question. She'd come with questions about her past, the nephiliam, but they seemed to fade with the book's opening declaration.

"You follow false information, Secret Bearer. Rusem was wrong about the brimstones."

A cold lump formed in her chest, and this drew her up short. The questions that she yearned to ask fell away.

"What do you mean?"

"Follow his advice to your peril."

"Will they kill me like they did Rusem?"

The book remained silent and she shifted tact.

"How do I kill Xilor?"

"What little of him clings to life does so with great greed. He transformed and became Xilor. Any trace of essence or personal soul that was once him is eradicated and bound to another. There are many ways to kill him, but only one can truly end his existence. Unbind that which is bound."

She drew in a sharp, exacerbated breath.

"What is he bound to, and how do I unbind him?"

Just when she thought the book wouldn't answer, it spoke one last time.

"Behold, the Time Warden approaches. Do not run."

And then the book fell silent, the light receding.

"Fucking useless thing," she groaned, snapping it shut, and chucking it away.

When the book landed, a jumble of images flashed through her mind. Like a stabbing pain, it came and left in an instant. None of it made sense, and the imagery had been fleeting.

In truth, she couldn't discern what she saw.

She let out a frustrated sigh. That had been a waste of time. Or had it? The riddles and jumbled half-truths did impart some information. She once suspected that Rusem had been wrong about the brimstones, and now the book confirmed it. But one other bit of information the book revealed, the only answer to one of her questions, she had the location to Divinity Enigumas.

Her thoughts flitted back to Rusem's journal.

He found a brimstone there, and something else, a manifestation of death. Rusem had thought whatever it was beneath the school is what was killing him. And the rumor of Hagen's final resting place stirred something within her. If what she thought was true, that Rusem once held the brimstone of death, it had to be there. Too many coincidences lined up to be anything else.

In haste, she lurched to her feet, retrieved the discarded book, and returned to the elyves.

They watched her with curiosity, seeing her bustle about. Usually, she was the last to rise.

"Shades, what's wrong?" Ama asked.

"Hagen."

Iddrial's face wore his naked skepticism.

"You know of him?"

"I know where to find him, his rumored remains at least."

Jumbles from Judas's book came to her, something half-remembered from a fevered dream.

He awoke the trees from slumber, the water springs began to speak, and the stones themselves breathed life.

Starriace worked her way over to the motionless stone giant. She stared up at him. Unmoving, he resembled a natural formation.

Did Hagen make the stone giants?

She pushed that thought to the wayside.

"Are you ready to serve me?" she asked it.

His head lumbered in her direction, and he stared for a moment.

"I serve."

She nodded, motioning him close. He lowered his hand, and she stepped up and sat down. He brought her close to his face.

"I have something further to ask of you..."

Starriace followed the book's instructions. She and the elyves traced the river until it went underground. The nine waited, expecting something magical. When nothing transpired, she ambled away, searching for any sign. She sensed their frustration, their accusatory glances, but they followed without a comment.

The suns dipped in the south. Dusk encroached on what precious light remained.

Like my hope.

The water bubbled, splashing the stony shore. The rolling hills and deep ravines twined through dense vegetation, adding to the deepening darkness. Just when her hope threatened to break, her essence rippled. A soft-glow luminance coalesced in the distance. The treetops helped obscure it, but certainty gripped her.

"Do you see that?" she asked.

"What?" Cal Cas queried.

"That light above the treetops in the forest."

She glanced at her companions, then back.

"Do you see it?"

Cal came up beside her and scrutinized the way ahead.

"No."

"I think that's the way to the school."

"Alright," Iddrial said walking to her, "we'll join you."

Starriace turned to him.

"That won't be necessary. Cal will do; he can guide me and watch where I enter. Should I run into any trouble, you all can find me."

Iddrial was silent for a moment but nodded.

"Very well."

She hoped he understood. This dealt with magic, something he knew little about, at least wizardkind magic. He had gifts like the rest of the exiles, but this magic went far beyond his control.

Starriace set off with Cal Cas following. The suns dipped below the horizon, and the sky's dark velvet claimed dominance over the fading rays. She crept towards the faint haze, yet Cal remained oblivious. After a few minutes, they broke through the forest at the top of a short hill.

A castle lit with torches lay below.

She couldn't make out every detail in the darkness, but it boasted a grand size. Still, the castle in Stratu'Geim outstripped it in size. The stones came in all sizes and shades, all arranged in a random geometrical pattern that was both abstract and eloquent. The trail before them disappeared down the slope, no more than another hundred meters, and she'd make the front doors.

A moat lay around the castle, and the drawbridge was down, welcoming visitors.

"Why have we stopped?" Cal inquired from behind her.

"Beautiful," Starriace whispered, a smile spreading across her face. "Can you not see?"

He moved up to her side.

She pointed.

"Divinity Enigumas. It's right there, can't you see it?"

His eyes followed her finger.

"No, I don't."

Flustered, she reached out and touched Cal's shoulder. When she did, she saw his eyes widen in wonderment.

"By the gods, suns, and stars," he rasped.

Starriace smiled at his reaction and pecked him on the cheek.

"You're like a child full of wonder sometimes."

She glanced back at the castle.

"Now, you know where to come, if I don't come out."

Without waiting for a response, she trotted down the hill and closed on the lowered bridge. Judging by his lack of exclamation, the school still filled his sight after she let go.

Her smile broadened, a glimmer of dark want writhing through her.

Now, to make this quick.

Cal Cas gazed after the mage as she ambled down the hillside. He stared in wonderment and chastised himself for every foul thought he'd sent her way. For a long time, Ahn Bael proclaimed that she'd lost touch with reality, but she proved herself many times over.

So far.

Cal still waited for her to fulfill her promise, but first, they must attend to Xilor, and they wouldn't do it while digging through sarcophaguses and hunting ancient ruins. What buried totem would aid her journey?

Starriace's form grew smaller.

In a brief flicker of pale light, she disappeared from view. He blinked, unsure of what he witnessed. The school still stood before him, but she had vanished. Within that glimmering moment, he sensed something malevolent, a vile scavenger of the Underworld.

An aura of evil clung to the air. His flesh rippled in discomfort. Death radiated out.

But Starriace was gone. She walked to her death. He had to warn the others. If he didn't hurry, she'd fall victim to a terrible fate.

Turning on his heel, he sprinted away.

Ama Ka stepped closer to Iddrial.

She hoped the others were far enough away that they couldn't eavesdrop.

"Something's not right with her," she whispered.

Though Iddrial had unshakable faith, Ama didn't, and he never entirely convinced her. The times that he had been wrong in the past could be counted on one hand. She hoped this didn't add to the list. Guilt wracked her for questioning him after everything they'd survived, what they'd done.

"She's different," he conceded.

She narrowed her eyes at him.

"An astute observation!"

She winced on the inside, the words coming out far louder than she wanted, but she kept it from her face.

"I don't think she's so bad," Fir Ki chimed in as he walked by.

While joining their conversation, he remained oblivious to the depth, and Ama breathed a sigh of relief. He hadn't even scratched the surface. If any of the others had an inkling, they'd think she and Iddrial mad.

"We all grasp what you think," Ama snapped at him, "and only when her clothes come off."

Iddrial chuckled.

Ama glanced behind her, making sure no one lurked nearby, watching Fir Ki continue on his path.

"Perhaps it's been too long," Ama said in a low voice, "but I don't recall this madness."

Iddrial nodded.

"You're right, it has been a long time. Perhaps we didn't see it then, and time away has given us perspective."

Ama's lips thinned.

"Was she always touched by madness?

He shook his head.

"No, there's a marked difference."

"What are you two whispering about?" Ahn Bael called from behind them.

Ama grimaced, but he wouldn't see. They both turned to face the group.

"Starriace," Iddrial confessed, which shocked Ama.

"What about her?" Ahn asked.

"I like her," Fir Ki said. "She knows what she wants and how to get it. I find her decisiveness rather refreshing."

Ahn Bael shifted, his lips twisted.

"She runs without a cause or an end. I can't be the only one who senses it."

Ama suppressed a sigh. She didn't want the others involved in their conversation, but the fault was hers. If only she had been quieter. It was hard to have a conversation when others had exceptional hearing.

Ahn glanced about, and Ama wondered what kind of discord he'd sow with his next few words. Ahn lacked the grace or patience to think beyond the surface of a subject, which made him stalwart for swinging a sword or axe. His lack of acumen notwithstanding, the others listened when he spoke his troubles.

"What are we doing with a woman like her? We've lived longer with our affliction than without it. Why change now? What does it matter?"

"Yes, we have," Ama said.

Just agreeing with him sent a wave of melancholy through her. Had it really been that long? She dared to speak for both she and Iddrial.

"We've noticed her lack of a cause."

Iddrial crossed his arms.

"We gave our word, just as we did so long ago, and it's binding."

"Long ago, the cost was great," Ru Sol commented. "I don't want to see the same thing happen again."

The weight of her words settled between the members. A reminder of the past did little to quell present worries. A brittle silence stretched.

Ava's abrupt appearance fractured the reticence. The tiny creature winked into existence in their midst. Ama flinched at her sudden appearance.

"You must go to Starriace!" Ava pleaded.

Desperation and urgency filled her voice.

Iddrial motioned with his hand.

"Pray tell. What troubles you?"

"She's in mortal danger! She'll die!"

"I've seen her magic," Ahn said. "She'll be fine."

"If she wanted our help," Fir added, "she would've asked us to accompany her."

Ama's eyes flickered through the group. The fairy's warning didn't bode well.

"This is urgent!" Ava pleaded. "She's going to fucking die!"

Ama scrutinized the others. They didn't seem eager to help their newest member, and that troubled Ama. Regardless, as Iddrial pointed out, their word kept them pledged.

She beckoned to Ava.

"Tell me."

The little creature floated forward, worry and frustration etched on her face. Ama held out a hand, her palm up, and the fairy landed.

"Will it ease your mind if I go?"

The fairy nodded.

"Yes. Please, save her. And when you see her, tell her that I have her thousands. She'll understand. Go!"

The words scarcely left her lips, and she vanished.

Ama glanced at the others.

"What was all that about?" Fir Fera inquired.

Ama glanced at the woman.

"Starriace will be fine," Ahn Bael assured.

"Strange, is it not?" Iddrial commented. "Why would a fairy worry over a single wizard? Why would she care whether the tether between life and death is severed from this particular one?"

Cal Cas burst from the forest. Ama leapt out of her skin, reaching for her staff before she realized who it was.

Cal looked pale, and a light sheen of sweat coated his arms and peppered his face. For such a short time to be gone, he perspired too much.

Dread formed in the pit of her stomach.

"We must go after Starriace. She's in danger," Cal Cas said, "She vanished from sight, but not before I felt the impression within me."

"So, she's not crazy like we thought?" Ahn Bael snarked, referring to Divinity Enigumas.

"No, it's worse."

"What could be worse than pledging ourselves to one who's lost her sanity?"

"She didn't go mad," Ari Sha broke in. "She's been mad all along."

Iddrial ignored them all.

"Speak, Cal."

"Something of the Underworld has slipped through. I felt it. She walks to her death, and maybe the death of us all."

The castle didn't hold the opulence Starriace imagined she'd find in Ralloc, nor the heritage of Stratu'Geim, but she did tremble in its majestic aura.

Magic permeated the air. It was tangible. Her body thrummed with the energy emanating from within its hallowed halls. Starriace reached out for the magic, a glutton for its intoxicating effects.

The pull called out, writhed like a lover, but swirled with the gusting speeds of a cyclone. How many ages, eras, or legends had passed with magic coursing through its foundations? The vast energy swept out, impossible to fathom its furthest reaches. She could never obtain this potential, not in her life, not in a hundred lifetimes. Her abilities were a mere speck, a single flake in a blizzard.

It felt as if the school had gorged itself off every person that ever passed through the doors.

A terrible thought flickered through her. Ermaeyth would shatter if all the energy were released in one blast. The theory made her skin crawl. The desire to wield such mastery sent a furious itch through her eyes.

Would it be possible to command such power?

After basking in the presence of such prominence, she forced her legs to move. Starriace entered the mouth of the castle. The interior lacked signs of occupants, but she knew better. The suns had set, and evening fell in full. People would be retreating to a mess hall to have dinner.

Her ravenous stomach grumbled at the thought of food. She soothed the hunger pangs away. Eating would come after success. Enchanting aromas reached out, the scents guiding her steps. Her mouth watered and again her stomach groaned. She siphoned more magic, delaying the hunger.

Her concentration wavered as the tang of sweets tickled her nostrils.

Broad, white marble stairs stretched out before her, and a buzz of conversation reached her ears once she blocked out the distractions of food. The mess hall was near, possibly at the top of the stairs. Ascending, her steps reminded her of a prowl, a predator waiting for the perfect opening. She couldn't be inattentive. Hagen's tomb was here, and by what the book said, maybe even a brimstone.

Or was she misinterpreting what it said, too?

At the top of the stairs, the dining chamber opened to the right. As she entered, a hush rippled through the crowd of students and teachers. All eyes turned to her, an intruder in their midst. Starriace's glittering red eyes bored into each in turn. She stretched out with her essence, sensing the rise and ebb of emotions. Fear rippled through the student body, and resolve solidified in the cluster of scholars.

She shifted her gaze to the disciplinarians and laid down a silent challenge. One approached with reserved steps. He hid his uncertainty well, but not enough to go undetected.

"I mean you no harm," Starriace said, her voice soft but holding an edge of caution.

She appreciated that her tones wouldn't carry across the great dining hall. She glanced at the man.

"But I'd advise you not to take another step."

The man stopped, waiting for her. Starriace could sense his resolve fluctuating. If it hardened anymore, she'd have to draw her wand.

"I need to speak to someone in charge."

To her left, a woman rose from her seat.

"What can I do for you, traveler?"

Starriace turned to her and ambled forward. She dropped her voice so that only the woman could hear her words.

"I'm looking for something."

"I'd say so. It's no easy task finding this place." She paused. "How *did* you find this place?"

Starriace ignored the question.

"I need the passage that leads to the furthest point under the castle."

"Is that all?" the woman scoffed. "What do you expect to find? Secrets that evaded you during your stay here? Like we tell all students, there isn't an arcane and mystical stash of ancient scrolls to unlock powers we aren't teaching."

"Take a good look at me," Starriace said, her words spitting out through clenched teeth.

Did this woman mock her?

The red of the mage's eyes glittered a shade brighter.

"Do I look like someone who went to school here? I've never set foot in this place before today. For your sake and that of your students, answer my question before you irritate me further."

"Your threats are meaningless, stranger. My primary concern is for the students alone. You'll not find what you're looking for. You waste your time and mine with this folly. Only a fool ignores wisdom."

"Tell me what I wish, and I'll be on my way. Don't, and I'll leave a trail of dead bodies in my wake, children or not."

The woman's face contorted, and her hand plunged into the pocket of her robe. As her hand cleared, the polished gleam of her wand caught Starriace's eye. The tip never manifested. The weapon grew slack in her hand.

Starriace reached out with her essence. An invisible force grabbed the teacher by the throat. A strangled gasp escaped her. This woman dared to attack her?

"All you had to do was answer my question!" Starriace screamed.

An itch festered in her eyes. The urge to claw them out arced through her like the searing pain of a knife through skin. She remembered that feeling well, when Mr. Pleasure toyed with her and flayed her arms. The pain yearned to be quenched. Without volition, her hand reached out, glowing with the familiar red-purple of the life drain, and siphoned the essence from the scholar.

She wondered if this power was related to her use of killing that guard with a single touch.

Starriace brought her would-be attacker to the cusp of death. She sensed more than perceived a movement behind her. Her head snapped in that direction. The man she halted early faltered in mid-stride, his eyes going wide.

"If you value your life, don't," Starriace warned.

"Let her go," the man pleaded.

Starriace's red eyes turned outward, glancing at the children and the staff, the latter coming forward, stepping out from the far corners of the dining hall.

With a twitch of her fingers, the woman who hung suspended in air, flew across the room, knocking down several teachers who broke her fall. She lay limp but still alive.

"Now," Starriace said in hushed tones, "I'm only going to say this once more. Someone point me to the passage that leads deep underground."

Children backed away at her words, and the teachers looked torn between acquiescence and protecting those in their charge. Some of the youngest children whimpered, their eyes on the teacher she threw. A young girl with blonde hair stepped forward.

She had to be no older than ten.

"Please, my lady. I know the way."

"Then take me there, and you'll live to see your parents."

She glanced up, more in warning than anything.

"All of you will."

Because I'm not a monster.

Chapter 47: Starriace and the Nine

The little girl led Starriace away from the mess hall.

Children rushed forward, leaving the safety of their chairs to watch them disappear below. Teachers protested, but none dared to follow. Through empty and twisting halls, beyond the opulent, then later, rotten doors, past dim wings and darker corridors, they made it to the bowels of the castle.

Marble stairs transitioned to stone steps, and then to half-rotted wood slats. The halls, which constricted to tunnels at this point, reeked of mold and dirt; the farthest reaches dank and inky. Classrooms, dorms, kitchens, and common areas fell away like distant memories.

Their progression slowed to a crawl as passageways turned into narrow crevices, and any new forward progression came from holes in the wall. The man-made enclosures changed to natural, coarse rock.

Down, down, down, deeper into the beast's belly.

The floor's moisture and the smell of mold filled the air, unmolested by the cleaning staff. The winding path ended with one last staircase made of stone crumbling from age. The torch clutched in the little girl's hand did little to keep the consuming darkness at bay.

Drenched in a profuse sweat, they reached the bottom, and the girl pointed forward.

"This is as far as I've gone, my lady. The end is ahead."

"Thank you," Starriace said, placing a hand on her shoulder. "You've been brave. You may go."

Starriace tore her eyes from the girl and glanced to where she pointed. Though her methods were questionable, coercion and manipulation, she wasn't Xilor.

You just keep telling yourself that.

The young pupil turned back, taking the lone torch with her. Starriace peered deeper within, but her limited sight revealed nothing. She took a hesitant step forward and stumbled over a rock that slumbered in the shadows. She knelt and plucked it up before throwing it in frustration. A satisfying crackle echoed off the wall as it skidded to a stop.

Closing her fist, she splayed her fingers, willing a globe of magelight into existence. The small sphere cast its luminance wider the higher she lifted it. Hand on the wet wall for balance, she continued forward.

The enormous cavern stretched out like an endless pit. Trepidation of plummeting to her death flickered through her mind. How long she spent searching each passageway, she couldn't guess, but she followed the faintest trickles of power.

Tugs more like gut instincts than actual magic eventually led to a small room. Inside and to the left were dusty, nearly rotted shelves with a few scrolls sitting next to a metal box. To the right, a small, wooden, decomposed desk that promised to buckle from the slightest pressure.

At the back, a brick wall blocked her way.

The magelight swept forward, washing the dead end with luminance. Starriace stepped close and examined the wall. Faint fissures and hairline cracks trickled throughout the wall like endless forks of lightning. A tentative touch with her essence confirmed the weak foundation. In another age or so, the wall would crumble away. It still served its purpose for the moment, to block any advancement.

She glanced over, and the desk filled her gaze.

A gentle nudge of her essence lifted the desk from the floor. No secrets hid beneath. She put the desk back down, afraid any jostling would shatter the decrepit furnishing.

Her eyes swept over the shelves. Her tentative hands reached out to gather the yellowed scrolls and the metal box, and she stuffed both in her backpack. The documents didn't crumble, which implied magic had sustained them.

Like the desk, she tried to levitate the shelves, but they were bolted into the rock. She could've torn them from the wall, but that'd accomplish nothing besides a mess. Besides, if not gentle, the whole place might come down. She didn't like the calculations of survival, but she had to take risks.

Fist raised, she crushed the shelves with delicate precision. Thousands of pieces rippled out with the smallest touch of energy. After the dust settled and the splinters fell away, her efforts proved futile, revealing nothing more.

The dead end irritated her, yet the challenge intrigued other parts of her mind. It appeared the teacher upstairs was right. There was nothing, no hidden rooms of knowledge, no ancient tomb of a forgotten sorcerer.

Nothing.

The book had either misled her or was mistaken.

A stray thought entered her mind, her eyes flicked back to the brick wall. She released a held breath and stretched out with her mind. The magesight fell over her eyes, spying a smaller, arc-shaped tunnel behind the wall. She blinked and the second vision faded.

With splayed fingers, she reached out. The wall trembled. An ancient magic strained against her. The wall fought back, fortified by enchantments placed in a time long gone. Its energy sapped, the wall gave way, crushing inward. As the dust settled, Starriace culled through the last few moments before the wall collapsed. For a brief moment, it almost seemed like the wall fed off her power.

Strange magic.

Undaunted by the thick darkness lurking behind the new opening, she stepped through and strode down the ancient tunnel.

The magelight raced ahead, illuminating the way. The passage didn't snake back very far, another hundred meters from the entrance, but the cave opened up into a domed room. With limited light, she almost missed the solitary structure ahead.

A small, solid stone table no more than a meter high and a meter wide lay in the center of the room. She approached with caution, fighting giddiness. Her eyes danced out to the darkness, searching for any signs of danger. As she did, the wind whispered, tickled her ears.

Starriace turned, and her heart drummed in her chest.

"Who's there?"

The only answer, another wisp from the other direction.

She pivoted to catch a glimpse. The uninviting obscurity played tricks with her mind. The darkness reminded her of the arduous journey beneath the Melodic Mountains.

The memory made her shiver.

In the distance, dripping water echoed with a faint splash. Had the rains worked through the soil and limestone before seeping through the ceiling?

Searching without finding the cause of the breeze, she turned her attention back to the table-like structure. Stepping close, she tried to decipher the language etched upon it. The symbols reminded her of the Corridor of Cruelty, where someone had carved 'Here Madness Dwells' into the root. The markings changed before her eyes, and she recognized the Ucoric. The letters shifted into Myshku, and she read aloud.

"Only death awaits."

It came out of the table, whatever it was, fast like a darting shadow. It reached with long, skeletal arms. At first, she thought of Xilor. How did he find her? How did he get here? She desired a confrontation, but not here, not now.

She almost seized up in terror.

A sharp inhale jarred her into action. Her heart gave a strong kick, and she blinked, and her mind scrambled. In haste, she backed away.

The creature spilled out and took form. She couldn't believe her mistake. It was so much bigger than Xilor, and it glided rather than walked. Her eyes darted back to the box-like structure and realized it wasn't a table but a sarcophagus.

Eyes back on the behemoth, she drank in the details.

This massive horror held vague similarities to the dark lord as it rose into the air. And kept rising, pooling out. Its staggering reach had to stretch at least half the room, maybe more. The shadow solidified, and the stench of death and decay washed over her.

She had to get away, run, or fight! But how? A vague remembrance of the sheol outside the Melodic Mountains came to mind. Her muscles tensed, ready to run. An enormous hand reached out and snatched her up. Its cold, skeletal fingers wrapped around her throat and chest.

The creature loomed closer.

Panic gripped her. Energy leeched from her body, siphoned by the living shadow. Somewhere in the back of her mind, she recognized the power. She had the ability, too. Starriace had used the life drain before. Now, this shadow, this phantom, did so.

As her vigor left, so too, did the heat. Cold ached through her, and she shivered. Opaque obscurity filled her head, making concentration impossible.

It was strange to feel herself dying, to understand the nuance. The wraith pulled on her essence, drawing on her life force. In a desperate effort, she reached into the wraith and funneled its essence into her, draining it as the phantom drained her.

A shriek of pain bellowed from the phantasm. A rebuffing surge shot out from the apparition, throwing Starriace to the ground. She crashed into the sarcophagus. Before she could recover, the phantasm swooped down again.

Instinct took over.

She threw up a wave of energy. The invisible gale hurled the creature against the wall. Starriace kept the phantom pinned. She hadn't encountered anything like this except the sheol. The sheol clung to some form of life; this phantasm exuded death.

Something large caught her eye. She turned her head and saw a huge boulder. With a grim line on her lips, she pulled her wand, grabbed hold of the rock, and hurled it towards the dark specter. The rock shattered and the wraith reformed, solidifying on the other side.

What in the Underworld was that? A morphing technique?

Temporarily free of her hold, the phantom lurched forward, arms outstretched. As quick as her reflex, she reached out with her essence, bringing the ceiling down.

The cavern walls trembled, and the ceiling broke apart. Huge chunks of stone fell from the rock-enclosed sky. One section crushed the sarcophagus. The wraith gave a horrible, ear-splitting shriek, and a bright luminance tore through its tenebrous form. She reinforced her efforts to hold the creature against the wall. In its death throes, its strength amplified. It yearned to reach out and touch her.

Splitting her concentration, she sent energy into the ceiling. This time, she wanted the entire roof to come down. Risky, but at least she'd have a chance to survive. If the wraith broke free, she wouldn't live through a second bout.

With abilities diverted, the phantom surged forward, breaking free. She jerked on the ceiling, then pushed against the specter. Above them, it cracked with a loud split, the only warning she received.

Letting go of her concentration, she dove clear as another colossal segment smashed into the ground.

The dying phantom, pushing against her now-absent resistance, stormed forward. The last tethers reached out, clung to the nape of her neck, and oozed into her body.

A frantic hand tried to wipe it away, but her fingers came back clean. The faintest notion of something crawling inside her stirred the manic side of her psyche. The sensation prickled like a spider crawling inside her skin. She shuddered and inspected her fingers again.

They were clean.

Was it her imagination? A last baffling notion from a dying entity?

Drained, she climbed to her feet. The battle left her fatigued, not the use of magic, but the phantom's siphon. After a few careful steps through the rubble, she detected the aftereffects. Her depleted energy plummeted. Each step made her weaker, the life leeching from her.

How could that be? I killed it, didn't I?

The ceiling trembled again. Her head snapped up as more gave way.

Iddrial and the group sprinted through the woods. They broke the ridge and hurried down into the valley where Starriace had disappeared. Cal took the lead and hurtled through the area where she vanished.

He burst through the invisible barrier. The others followed without hesitation but were jostled on the other side. A mob of teachers and students fled the building. The nine drew their weapons. Swords unsheathed, bows made ready, and Ama Ka's staff glowed a pale blue as she called upon her magic. Panicked screams, gasps, and cries filled the air.

A fearful stampede.

The crowd slowed at the sight of the armed elyves. Iddrial noticed the throng of children ranging all ages, sizes, and species. His heart swelled at the sight of a few elyfian. He hadn't seen another of his species in countless eras. Goblins and centaurs peppered the mix. Abashed, he lowered his weapons, and the others followed suit.

"What did she do?" Ama whispered.

The crowd stopped, and a hush came over them.

"What're you running from?" Iddrial asked.

A boy near the Age of Maturity stepped forward, his face pale with fright.

"A woman came in and demanded entrance to the catacombs. After she went in, we heard a great howling, and the school shook."

Starriace.

He turned to his brethren.

"She needs our help."

He bolted forward, and the crowd parted.

After breaching the front steps, Ama overtook Iddrial and led them down the halls. Doors stood open, but they couldn't be sure which was left by Starriace or the children. They hurtled along the corridor and almost passed another door on the right, but a blonde-haired girl burst out and stumbled into Ama.

Terror etched the young lass's face. She tried to flee, but Ahn grabbed her by the robes and jerked her back.

"Which way did the stranger go?" Ahn demanded.

The child, too frightened to speak, pointed a shaking finger at the door she'd exited. Ama tore through the hatch and Iddrial followed.

The large passageway quickly narrowed, the construction turning to stone the deeper they descended. Dirt and mold filled their nostrils, and darkness swallowed them whole as they raced down the narrow crevices.

"Wait," Ama said a little later as she stumbled over a rock. Iddrial watched as she plucked it up and placed it within the clutch-like grip of her staff. She tapped the rod twice on the ground, and the stone shone brightly from the muttered incantation.

"What do you sense ahead, Cal?" Iddrial asked.

"Nothing but a void, death."

"At least we're headed in the right direction…" Ahn muttered.

They stumbled through dark, twisting passages and ran all out down sloped floors, through a small office and beyond, where they found her body amidst broken rocks and boulders.

"Should we move her?" Iddrial asked.

Ama knelt beside Starriace's broken body.

"No!"

She glanced up apologetically at her sharp reply. Shaking her head, she spoke while examining Starriace.

"Her wounds are more than physical. I don't know how, but she's dying."

She shook her head.

"I can save her physical body, but this is something more."

"How can this be?" Ru Sol asked.

"No willpower," Fir Ki commented.

Only Ahn edged out his antagonism in the group, but not by much.

Ama cleared her throat.

"Thankfully, we didn't ask for your opinion."

"How can this be?" Iddrial echoed Ru Sol.

"I don't know, I've never encountered anything like this. My best guess would be speculation."

"Then, speculate!"

"Maybe it's this place, or the aura Cal told us about, or that she's wizardkind. I couldn't tell you."

"Maybe it's simpler than that," Ahn Bael spoke up.

Ama spared him a glance.

"How do you mean?"

"Perhaps the aura accomplished what it wanted, draining her life."

"She wouldn't be alive," Ama countered.

"Perchance," Iddrial spoke up, "maybe this aura manifested."

"Like a phantom?" Cal asked.

Iddrial nodded.

"If she touched it, and this phantom stuck with her, perhaps that's the cause? I don't know any tales about people escaping phantoms."

As the words left his mouth, Starriace jerked awake. Her eyes were wide, her breathing erratic.

"Don't move, Starriace," Ama blurted. "Something's killing you."

"The phantom," Starriace breathed, "it's inside me."

"Don't talk, conserve your strength," Iddrial said.

"Oh," Ahn said, interjecting.

He shuffled closer.

"Ava came to us and said she has your thousands."

Iddrial was about to chastise Ahn, but much to Iddrial's surprise, Starriace managed a weak smile. Whatever the cryptic message meant, it brought hope and let her cling to life.

"Thank you," she managed.

Heartbeats later, she fell unconscious again.

"What in the Underworld was that?" Ama said, glaring at Ahn.

"What?" Ahn murmured.

Fir Fera smacked him on the back of his head.

"You want the last words she may hear to be 'Ava has your thousands?'"

"Try encouragement next time," Cal added. "Like you love her, or that you're here for her."

"Yeah," Fir Fera chuckled, "but that wouldn't be a lie. Ahn's smitten."

"Shut your mouth before my fist does!" Ahn snapped.

"He courts madness because she won't share furs with him," Ari Sha spoke up.

"I'm warning you all," Ahn said.

"Ahn must be intimidated," Ru said. "As I understand, wizardkind males are more endowed than the elyves."

Ama's head jerked up.

"Really?" she asked.

"Enough!" Iddrial yelled. "She's dying, and the only thing you can talk about is *this*?"

He eyed those around him and most had the decency to look embarrassed. Ahn's lips twisted and his shoulders squared. Whatever nerve he sought, Ahn found it.

"People have died with us before, what makes her any different?"

"She isn't one of us," Iddrial said. "We're the ones tainted, not her. Yet, she offered us friendship and aid to lift the curse wrongly placed."

"You see, that's the difference between us," Ahn said, his voice cold and flat. "I've made peace with what I am. You never did. We're not going home. They don't want us. If she could've cured us, she would've done it already. I didn't let my hopes soar; you shouldn't have either."

Ahn shrugged.

"Let her die."

Ama and Ru gasped.

Iddrial stared at Ahn.

He was such a different person, had always been so. But this? At the edges of his vision, the others stirred, taking small steps away from Ahn.

At least they see the madness of his words.

"You'll owe her if she pulls through. I swear it!"

Ahn shrugged.

"Just another young, wizard pup. A good cuffing around the ears is what she needed."

Iddrial glanced at the others. Mixed emotions rippled across their faces.

How did it come to this?

Through gritted teeth, he spoke.

"Name one who asked to help us? How many remember our names? Did anyone care for us when we were cast out?"

He gazed at Ama, who still attended Starriace. She glanced up and gave him a single, solemn nod.

He knew what she meant. It was risky. Both of them played their parts well, and the rest of the group was none the wiser. If they ask questions, delved too deep, they'd discover all.

He couldn't allow that.

Resolved, he turned to the others.

"Ama and I swore the blood oath to her. We'll be a part of her life until she dies, and our families will be twined until the end of time. She's family to us, now. What's she to you?"

He didn't expect an answer, but Ahn broke the ambiance.

"You swore the blood oath to her? She's not even an elyf!"

"There's more to people than their species and physical features," Ama retorted.

"But she isn't even…" Ahn began.

The frustration and disgust rippled across his face. He raged against a war of emotions. The haunt of betrayal, confusion, and disdain. If left unchecked, his heart would succumb to the poison of discontent.

"When did you do this? I don't remember seeing this!"

Iddrial shook his head, buying time to scramble for an answer. This was a question he wished to avoid.

"Does it matter when? It's done."

"And if she survives," Ama joined with an edge in her voice, "you will, too. She'll prove herself to each of you in her own way and time."

"And you'll still owe her," Iddrial finished. "Leave me, all of you. Who knows how long we'll be here. Set up a camp, fetch wood and water."

The seven rebuked elyves slipped quietly away, expressing their sorrows in mumbled words. Iddrial's eyes flickered over to Rusem, the silent risen standing vigil on the far side of the cave. Iddrial hated the thing, but as long as it didn't attack, he'd let Starriace keep her pet.

When they were far enough away, Ama spoke, but not in Myshku like the wizardkind, and not Thymulous like the elyfian.

"Do you speak with truth?"

He turned to her.

"I speak with truth."

"Then live in peace."

A small, sad smile spread across her lips. She no longer tended to Starriace but sat nearby. Her eyes fell on the mage.

"I'm worried now. I fear the longer she's gone, the weaker she'll become."

"She'll pull through. There's strength left."

"Where does she get it from?"

"Probably hate," Iddrial answered honestly.

"Who wronged her enough to warrant such wrath?"

He shrugged.

"Hate has its uses. The question is: what's the root, the seed that makes her so? Surely not us?"

"No!" Ama gasped, horrified. "She doesn't even…"

Ama let her comment die.

Iddrial noted that something still bothered her, but he didn't press. Ama would talk when ready.

She took a deep breath.

"If she survives—"

"She will."

"If she survives, we must break her of the crutch. Hate can drain a soul."

"So can love, Ama."

But she was right, of course. He wouldn't avow it aloud. Hate consumed, but anger had purpose. Those emotions weren't something to shy from. Only a coward would.

Iddrial squatted, reached out, and gave Ama's hand a gentle squeeze.

She stopped to eye him.

"Please, don't."

"Do you not still love me?"

"I do," Ama admitted.

She glanced about the darkness, but the other elyves had left with their tasks.

"I can't. I can't be like the rest and throw out my vows during exile. Not until I'm certain, one way or another."

"I understand."

"And you shouldn't either. Though never married, you let them lie beside you at night."

"Yes, but I give not my body. That's for you alone. I give warmth and companionship, nothing more."

Ama kept her eyes on Starriace.

"We've been over this."

"Just tell me …" Iddrial started.

"Yes, I still do."

Her words were good enough.

He stood and left, leaving Ama to work whatever magic she could.

Chapter 48: Xilor

Instantly, the pain in Xilor's skull went away.

Starriace.

His thoughts warmed at the notion of her demise, and he smiled.

His abyssians had completed their mission, and she was no more. A pity she didn't join him. She could've been a potent ally. Either way, she would've been too hard to control, much like Judas. He couldn't afford the luxury.

Starriace would never take Olga's place, even had she joined him. Starriace would serve until an opportunity presented itself to destroy him, and most likely, before he completed his work.

He'd expect nothing less.

Only the strong should survive to perpetuate bloodlines, as he did now with Ermaeyth. This world, whether they realized it or not, needed him. Let them label him the villain. Besides, there were more threats than the other places he'd seen in the mirror, and he didn't have to go to another world to see them.

Not when they were right here on Ermaeyth, so to speak.

Most assumed he sought to rule, a half-truth. Once his business was complete and Ermaeyth grew stronger under his direction, he'd slink back and let a new world take hold, but not before he purged the weakness. Then, he'd turn his focus back to those other realms, slipping in and ripping them apart like he'd done so many times before. When Ralloc fell, the rest of the domains and sovereignties would fall in line.

If they didn't, he'd crush them, too.

A pang of sorrow ripped through him. Starriace, a powerful being, was gone, and in many ways, that was a tragedy. He could've used her had she only listened, but she wasn't submissive and would've created problems. Even if he broke her daily, she'd never remain so.

The pleasure he'd take from the spectacle would keep him sharp, too.

The duty to put Ermaeyth right before the threat came hung heavy about his neck. Formidable adversaries kept you sharp. Starriace would've done so, as Judas had. One day soon, they'd face each other, and only one would emerge from the carnage.

Judas had been lucky last time; this time, he'd be ready for the warlock's tricks.

Those who weren't allies became tools, used until broken, then discarded. The Betrayer came to mind: he and the sisters, Olga and Miza. Once victory was assured, Xilor planned to take Olga for his own and dispatch the other two. They'd outlived their usefulness once the war came to a close. Despite the Betrayer's work to incite the trolls into action, they proved fruitless with his hordes of goblins at Dlad City.

Xilor had learned the Krey sent three squads to Dlad City, a prospect unforeseen and which boded ill. After losing thirty thousand to Dlad City and the Krey, Xilor decided to attack from the opposite direction. First, he'd moved his army as if to circumvent Dlad, turned back from the north, and attacked. The resounding victory came sweet after so many setbacks.

He slaughtered many of the Grand Royal Army. Some escaped through portals, but not enough to make a sizable difference to Ralloc's total tally.

Let them retreat to Ralloc and spread fear among the ranks.

The notion pleased him. The anxiety of the unstoppable would steep before he reached their walls.

Despite the number of obstacles, the war turned in his favor now. A fortuitous event occurred; the Krey had left Dlad City by the time he attacked in earnest. Whatever fool decided that just handed him a great victory, and now he'd have more in his hordes to throw against the walls of the capital.

They closed in on Ralloc, had overrun Dlad, won at Shadow City, and smashed the elyves at the Enclave. Their subsequent withdrawal from the war weakened his opponents further. Xilor would've thrown five times the numbers he had to ensure the same results.

He'd stolen a prize at a fraction of the bargain.

A warm vibration from within the folds of his robes brought him out of his musings. He pulled the shard of glass.

"Yes?" he hissed.

"My lord," Vlukus said.

"You've done well, Vlukus," Xilor interrupted.

"My lord?"

"You've ended Starriace. You'll be rewarded for your faithful diligence."

The creature shook his head.

"I don't know of what you speak. We were ambushed. She survived, and half of my men were destroyed."

"Really?"

Xilor pulled away from the shard, expecting some kind of trick or ploy.

"Strange, her presence has faded."

"If she's dead, we're not responsible."

"It matters not how; the deed is done."

Xilor began to break the connection, but a thought rippled through him.

"Where'd you end up catching her at?"

"The Valley of Stones, my lord."

Xilor clenched his fist around the shard of glass, shattering it. It mattered not; he'd renew it, making it whole again. The Valley of Stones concerned him. He knew little about the place other than rumors. If true, it'd get a whole lot more complicated.

Xilor didn't like surprises, and a sense of foreboding came from news of that place. There were always tales, but nothing he believed. Xilor dealt in facts, not fiction, but one point remained.

Those who entered never returned.

Assured that Starriace met her end, he turned back to the war at hand.

Chapter 49: The Betrayer

Deep in the bowels of Xilor's long-hidden fortress, Gryzlaud, whispered conspiracies, half-truths, and outright lies ran rampant, and if you wanted to survive, you played the game, too. The irony made the Betrayer chuckle now. He'd long conspired against his own kind, his own flesh, but now, he did so against the perceived loyalty he fostered for so long.

The Betrayer hated Xilor, always had. He'd never trusted him and tried to stay away, willing himself smaller in the hopes he'd be forgotten.

It worked for a time.

Xilor loved to toy with him, to make him squirm. The Betrayer never deceived those who mattered to him. He lacked the inherent evil Xilor prized. Had he not coerced the Betrayer, threatened the lives of those two girls…their blood would've been on his hands.

He sighed.

No sense dwelling on the past you can't change.

The war kept Xilor away for some time, and the Betrayer doubted he'd be returning anytime soon. At least, that's what he hoped. He steeled himself, exuding calm through his near-panicked heart. This was a calculated risk, both on Xilor's absence and the gamble with Miza.

Xilor had let slip they entered the last push to Ralloc. With him preoccupied, the Betrayer hoped it'd give him enough time to enact his last desperate measure. He risked all under the diligent and watchful eyes of Xilor's minions. He didn't care what happened to himself, only that someone else would survive.

That was all he *ever* cared for.

His usefulness neared its end, a disquiet in his gut. Xilor hadn't summoned him, and once the war concluded and Xilor became the victor, the Betrayer was a loose end in need of severing. But before that happened, Xilor couldn't risk his face being seen.

Further, the dark lord thought him weak.

"The weak serve the strong, and then are culled from existence," Xilor once said.

The Betrayer had strength but of character, all things considered. He didn't hold a magical candle to Xilor or the legendary warlock. It mattered not; he held his own if necessary. Should Xilor turn on him, he might keep him at bay long enough to flee. He could certainly hold his own against Sidjuous.

Nothing mattered except the safety and security of the sacrifice, as Xilor and Olga put it once before. Right before Xilor retook form, Olga, Xilor's future wife, promised to make him a blood sacrifice. That sacrifice would be her own sister, Miza.

A knife of sadness ached through the Betrayer; how could flesh turn upon flesh? He once did, but the circumstances were hardly the same. He did so to save the girls.

Olga would do so out of sheer wickedness.

Or maybe she was turned long ago. Living in this place, the walls reeked of malevolence. Perhaps that had some how changed her, altered her mind until it no longer was her own, but a shell for Xilor to inhabit.

What if Olga broke free of this place? Would all that was done to her change her back?

If there was only a way to go back and change one little thing. How different my life would be.

He reached Miza's chamber doors. He knocked sharply twice, checked to make sure he wasn't followed, and entered. She rolled over in bed and glanced at him, rubbing her sleepy eyes.

"I must get you out of here while we still can," he said in a hurried whisper.

She frowned at him, either because she was sleepy and didn't understand, or because he misjudged her.

"What do you mean?"

The unasked questions etched her face.

She yawned.

"Your sister has a dark plan for you."

He rushed to her walk-in closet, pulled robes out, and stuffed them into a bag.

"What?"

"She's to wed Xilor when he claims victory."

"Yes, and he wants to kill my uncle, Judas Lakayre."

The Betrayer paused, a shudder going through him.

"Exactly."

He reshuffled the garments so they'd fit better.

"Your sister promised him a blood sacrifice. Do you remember when I started to spend a lot of time with you about six months ago?"

"Yes, of course, I always enjoy your company."

She smiled at the fond memories.

"Well, that's when your sister made the promise to Xilor. I thought you were about to be killed, and I wanted to spend as much time with you as I could before you were gone."

Saying the words aloud made the bile rise in his throat.

"And you're just now telling me?"

Her anger no doubt rose like the volume of her voice.

He shushed her.

"Yes, there wasn't a need to upset you."

"So, it's okay now?"

He stopped packing and came out of the closet, hurried to her bed, and took her by the shoulders in his hands.

"Listen to me," he said.

He paused, listening for any soft footfalls in the hallway outside. Then, he turned back to her.

"Xilor's been gone for a long time, and I don't think he'll come back anytime soon. They're nearing the most crucial point of the war. I must get you out of here and to safety."

"Why don't I confront her? I'm stronger in magic. Surely, I can take her."

"And slay your own blood?" the Betrayer said, his voice strained with revulsion. "Even I wouldn't slay my own blood when I betrayed them. It's one thing to betray in the open, but a deceitful betrayal like mine…"

He shook his head.

"To carry a secret is too hard."

He let go of her shoulders and sat on the bed. She scooted closer.

"But you've told me."

Her voice was warm, as was the embrace she offered. For the first time, he knew what it felt like to be a proper father.

"Doesn't that make it easier?" she asked.

He hesitated before he spoke.

"Yes and no. Though I spoke of my betrayal, I didn't reveal everything, and you don't need to understand, so please don't ask."

He pulled away and went back to packing.

"Tell me one thing: did it involve my family, my uncle?"

From within the walk-in closet, he stopped and glanced in her direction. She couldn't see him. He hung his head.

"It involved everyone, so yes, your uncle, too."

He closed the bag he'd packed for her.

"Now, we must make haste. You must leave tonight and never come back."

"Where will I go? There's nowhere he won't come after me, nowhere my sister won't tread."

"Ah, but in the thousands of years, one learns a thing or two in the absence of pain."

He gave a subtle smile as he slung the pack over his shoulder.

"Do you remember when you were little? You'd hide, and I would come to find you?"

"Of course. What does that have to do with anything?"

"Do you remember how I'd move to rooms faster than you two?"

"Yeah, you'd use magic."

"Alas, no, I wasn't powerful enough in my youth. There are secret passageways. I used them to chase after you both. Xilor, if he even knows about them, doesn't use them and never told anyone."

"How'd you find them?"

"I, my young lady, happen to have an uncanny ability to find secret passageways. It's one of the only gifts I possess."

She didn't say anything, only cast him a glance of uncertainty.

"I'll show you. There's one that connects from here to my room. We'll take that one. Once there, I'll tell you where to go."

He walked back into the closet, and she followed. With careful movements to not make noise, he slid the shelf of shoes to the far right side.

"I knew it could do that," she said, rolling her eyes.

"Yeah, but what about this?"

He squatted, his fingers clutching for the large tile on the floor. The half-meter by half-meter square came up. Beneath, a winding stone staircase spiraled in the dark. Shock riddled her face. He stood, snatching a robe from a hanger and tossing it to her.

"Dress, then get inside."

He hurried out into the main chamber, closing the closet doors behind him. She changed and reopened them.

The Betrayer ushered her to the hole, directing her to climb in. She did, and he pulled himself in behind her, replacing the tile square above him, leaving a crack in the direction of the shoe shelf. Once ready, he withdrew his wand and pointed it at the shelf, and it began to slide back into place. He lowered the tile, and a soft grinding noise came from above, settling everything as it once was.

He lit the tip of his wand in soft light and took the lead. At the bottom of the stairs, he set off on an easy jog as he led the way from the dead end. Under Olga's room, they slowed to pass without noise. They didn't start running again until far enough away to not be heard.

They reached the end at another winding staircase, and he led the way back up. Behind a movable bookshelf, they emerged in his study. The Betrayer used his wand to move it back into place. They stood panting, catching their breath.

A sprawling crimson rug covered the majority of his floor, its border etched in gold tassels. The faint scent of familiar vanilla hit his nostrils, and he found comfort being back in his suite.

"So, that's how you always got us," she said with a twist of her lips.

"Yes. Come, we must hurry."

But she didn't move, which stopped him short.

"Come with me," she pleaded.

He shook his head and waded deeper into the room.

"I can't."

"Why?"

"Because, from here, I can serve you better, know what he's going to do in retaliation, and warn you of potential danger."

Though she didn't speak, she followed. A myriad of emotions rippled across her features. He understood what she thought—this would be goodbye and probably the last time she'd ever see him.

Worry and sadness marred her young face.

"Where can I go?" she asked. "He'll find me wherever I hide."

He stopped and held her arms, almost as if he was about to hug her.

"Oh, he'll find you, but he'll do nothing to reclaim you once you reach your destination. You're strong; I've trained you since a child. I recognized the temptations and desires of your sister's heart since your youth. Ambition and vindictiveness have always driven her, so I trained you twice as hard should you need to defend yourself against her."

"Why?"

He let go of her, his hands dropping, but she clasped them in hers.

"Don't worry about the why, child. Just know I did my best. Perhaps, I thought I could wash some of the taint and blood from my hands by doing something good, helping a relative of Judas Lakayre."

As he said his name, his face quirked as bitterness filled his mouth.

"Where must I go?"

"I've taught you about the domains and the realm. Do you remember the tale of the wars between the two cities Chissu'Nanuci and Stratu'Geim?"

She squeezed his hands.

"Yes, of course."

A flicker of perplexity flashed across her face at the odd reference.

"A border dispute because the Chissu'Nanuci wanted to build an outpost closer to their enemies on the river of Emaas."

"Yes. Well, Xilor won't set foot in those two cities. Maybe he fears them or doesn't care. I know not, but you'd be safe there."

"What if he sends Vlukus after me?"

He could tell by her voice that she feared this almost to the point of irrationality.

"You're strong, smart, and resilient, all will serve you in the end. You'll be okay. Should all else fail, contact your uncle, but only as a last resort! He doesn't realize you're alive, and it'll raise many questions. It'll be a hard time for you. Everyone will question your credibility; you'll be cast in doubt by the Kothlere Council."

He paused, considering his next words carefully.

"If they find out about you, they'll find out about your sister, and she's a lost cause."

"How can you say such a thing?" Miza hissed.

She let go of his hands, taking a step back.

"She's my sister!"

He reached out with his right hand, cupping the side of her face. It hurt him to say, but she needed to hear.

"We all see what we wish in those we love. And in those we hate, we find nothing but darkness."

He grabbed her hand and pulled her along. She came, following him into the bathing chambers.

"This is your way out."

He lifted the grate in the center of the room. Miza peered into the dim depths.

He glanced down, seeing the long drop of four meters. The sides of the hole were covered in slick, green fungi.

She wrinkled her nose in disgust.

"You're joking, right?"

"Afraid not. There are holds along the sides. I cleared them for you. Follow the sewers down; it opens up to the lake. There'll be a boat and an additional pack with food, water, and a few supplies. Don't come back for me or any other reason. You must do this! You must be strong."

She took a moment, and he noted the steel resolve in her eyes.

"I understand."

She swallowed hard.

"I wish you'd reconsider."

"I know, child."

The sting of emerging tears twinkled in his eyes.

"Perhaps in time, I can erase the wrong I've done."

He embraced her in a hug as if it were the last time he ever would.

"You were always my favorite, but that's our secret."

She gave a chuckle, but it was stifled quickly. No doubt, emotions raged within her. They rose up in him, too.

He took her face in his hands and planted a kiss on her forehead. He lingered, feeling her warmth, and noting her fragrance, burning it into his memories. It'd be the last he ever had of her. He'd never see her again, if all went according to plan. He'd be dead, but she'd be free.

He pulled away, for fear he'd never let go, and she looked back up into his eyes.

"You were always like a father to me."

A tear rolled down his cheek, and he nodded understanding.

"I tried to be. You deserved one, one far better than me."

He cut off, not trusting his voice. He took her hand and helped her into the hole, then lowered the grate. She reached the bottom and glanced back up. He stared down at her and could barely make out her frightened face.

"Thank you for making my life worthwhile," he said.

She nodded.

"No matter what you've done in the past, you're a good man. I'll be sure my uncle knows when this is all over."

He smiled and wiped a stray tear.

"I love you, Miza."

It seemed easier to reveal this truth with the distance separating them.

She smiled at this.

"I love you, too."

He nodded.

"Run, and don't look back."

She paused for a moment, gazing up at him. He'd remember it for all eternity.

And then she was gone.

A shuddering breath escaped him as his heart ripped in half, leaving him hollow. He ached for her to return, but her fleeing would ensure she lived, and that was far more important.

A part of him burned with shame. He hadn't been completely honest. He remained behind so he, too, could escape. But his escape was a ruse to draw attention from her.

In truth, there was no escape. His actions would be a mask, a sacrifice to ensure she survived. His death would prolong the search for Miza, and he found that he could live with that, while it lasted.

My last great deed. I'm allotted one per lifetime.

Chapter 50: The Apostle's Master

Glato's mouth twisted in disdain as he came out to see the ruins of the Hall of the One. Their Ruhkhi building was in shambles, and it'd be two seasons before they fixed everything.

That damn bitch. She ruined the empire for my master.

She'd have to be dealt with. It wouldn't be hard to track down a woman with glowing red eyes. No one crossed him and lived to brag, not when his master would be displeased with any delay.

I'll send the Embrace after her. After all, what else are they doing?

The Embrace served the needs of the One in a manner ill befitting the proper disciples. They were necessary, an unholiness absolved in their mission to rid the world of other sacrilegious teachings. But they, like the Disciples of the One, had evolved.

The woman who nearly destroyed everything actually helped him. Twice now, Glato had ascended to the next rank without having to scheme or kill anyone, and untimely deaths were highly scrutinized. It was an odd feeling and not one of satisfaction.

Since coming into service of the One, and his master afterward, his bare hands pulled him from the lower rungs. Now, a bittersweet sentiment filled him, knowing the simple wheels of fate spurred his ascension.

"How long to rebuild?" Glato asked the men standing with him.

As the appointed archbishop, he changed the title to the apostle. Glato's first official decree after his followers mourned the loss of the last archbishop was to retire the title. In its place, he assumed the title apostle, a ruse fostered by false aspirations to be close to the Creator's magnificent hand, and as a way to honor the archbishop that was taken from them.

"Only an act of the One could've caused me to rise so fast to the top," he had told them. "Preordained. Who're we to doubt the will of the One?"

An engineer spoke up beside him, breaking into the memory.

"It'll be many years. The damage is more extensive than anything I've ever seen."

Shit, there goes my two seasons timeline.

"The fact that it's still standing is an act of the One. Perhaps you should consider tearing down the whole thing and start over?"

"Start over?" Glato echoed.

He had to put on a show for his followers.

"Have you taken leave of your wit? Tear down the home of the One? I think not!"

He shook his head, his eyes going back to the remains. In truth, it would be better.

"No, we'll just have to mesh your task with the ancient and blessed works of those before you. Continue to rebuild as planned."

Someone called out to him.

"Apostle Glato?"

Glato turned to see a younger disciple running up to him.

"Yes, what is it?"

"The disciples are all gathered as you asked. They await you in the welcome chambers."

Glato nodded and patted his shoulder.

"Thank you. You've done well. I'll be there shortly."

The boy scurried off, and Glato headed after him at a slower pace. He allowed his thoughts to drift from each current event.

It was time for them to move forward with the plan his master had given. They were to take over Ralloc and secure it for his master's arrival. It was only a matter of time before he came to rule the world.

One problem endured: the release of his master from confinement. Only one step remained; the mountain that weeps a sad song shall go silent. That was the key to many things. The prophecy of the One was the roadmap for the disciples to go to Ralloc, or so they thought.

That weeping mountain held the containment of his master. He awaited the day when he'd walk alongside the great being upon the ashes of Ermaeyth.

It'll be glorious.

Glato entered the area where the disciples awaited him. He didn't waste time; he never liked those who prattled. He hoped his followers enjoyed that about him and returned the gesture.

They turned to face him as he entered. Numerous faces greeted him, old and young, and in between. Some held looks of wonder, others furrowed concern. Most clasped their hands in front, while others found the opposite sleeves and slid their arms across each.

"Okay," he said as he came to a halt before them, "we've got a lot to do and not much time. I can feel the hand of the One upon me, and the time is coming soon for the prophecy to be fulfilled. The last part will fall into place, and the mountain that weeps shall go silent. I was just told the repairs will take years. In the meantime, we'll move forward and begin an outreach program as intended. No longer will we hide in the same old halls in our ancient cities.

"I'm moving us forward with new plans. We'll place two more halls, one in Stratu'Geim, and one beside the Valley of the Dead. People may come for a grand monument, but all will leave knowing the power of the One, how he smote those who did not heed his warnings."

This caused a smattering of murmurs, but none too loud. A few older disciples crossed their arms.

"I believe within a season the mountain shall go silent. The time for the One to reveal himself is upon us. Now, we must divvy the ranks of who will go where, and what they'll be doing. I shall stay here for a time, but I'll travel to other sites. I want half of the disciples to pack for a journey north, pushing into the Marcoalyn domain. After we have a foothold, we'll divide again and move north again. Don't worry about our ranks growing thin, we'll have many new fresh recruits from growing congregations. Are there any questions?"

"How are we going to pay for this?" someone in the back spoke up.

"We'll pull the funds from our coffers."

A collective gasp rose up from the disciples at his revelation.

"Preposterous!" someone shouted.

"You'll do as I say, for I'm guided by the voice of the One. Do you choose to be ignorant of his wishes?"

He fought the growing smirk on his face. He eyed them for a few more moments, then left the baffling idiots to mull over his words. Arguing over who'd go or who'd stay would make them soon forget.

Later, he took his evening meal in his study. He didn't want to listen to the squalling followers, no doubt coming to snivel and interrupt his meal if he ate among them. Instead, he kept to himself in his private chambers, contemplating what his master would say about the setback.

He thought to put it off but dared not.

Hatching a scheme to mollify his lord and deflect ire, a plan formed, one that would sate both his and his master's appetite. He'd need a woman of the cloth.

When night had fallen upon the wrecked Hall of the One, and a thick silence lay upon the face of Ermaeyth, he set to the task of seeking a harlot. Once finding one to his liking, he secreted her away back to his chambers. The hefty bag of coins he'd given persuaded her to 'live out' a fetish.

For the glint of gold, the foolish believe anything.

In his room, he set to work, readying for the night. He'd cast the correct spells and said all the right incantations. The room was soundproof. Everyone within the ruined remains fell under a spell of influence.

All slumbered deep.

Only the rising sun on the morrow would break the conjury. There would've been ringing in Glato's ears had it not been for the heavy breathing of the girl. Being a cautious man when contacting his master's minions, he also used spellcraft on the room, the door, and the chains that held the prostitute.

He had manacled her to the stone table he dragged from his closet. Once bound, he expended his pent up energy on her until he sated his primal needs. When he released his seed in her, she'd still thought it part of their game, for which she received handsome pay.

But he disillusioned her with the promise that his master would also partake.

She laughed.

"Who's your master?" she asked with a high, sing-song voice. "It'll cost you extra. Are you sure he can handle me?"

"You'll see," he said.

He rendered her unconscious after that.

Let her wake in terror, with my master inside her.

Glato set to work preparing for his master's arrival. When the small details had been readied, he retreated from the room to adjoining chambers, leading a lamb back to the bedroom. He tied it to the black slab, then knelt in the middle of his new room, the old archbishop's, with books and candles all about him. Incense burned as cauldrons bubbled with an odd assortment of herbs, plants, and animal parts.

The lamb bleated its distress.

Glato began his chant, strange words resounding like a cleansing mantra, filling him with a sole purpose: to commune with his master. To do that, sacrifices must be made, praises offered in the demonic, homugon tongue, and gifts presented.

The homugon were demons, living incarnations of people's worst fears. Still, to Glato, they were beautiful creatures of vileness, and they enjoyed the flesh of mortals, specifically wizardkind for their magic.

The creeping sensations that crawled on his flesh and tickled his brain in their mere presence made him writhe in pleasure. It was one of the most significant moments of his life, like an addict as the opiates entered their blood for the first time after many days.

Sheer ecstasy.

The homugons were his drug, and he was addicted to the thrall. His body's elated terror reached a crescendo in their presence. It was a shame they didn't walk Ermaeyth, but he'd soon change that.

Finally, Glato stopped chanting and bent down to slit the lamb's throat. Warm blood spilled on the floor, and Glato used magic to spread the fluid in a circle, so his master would come.

The process for allowing the homugon to breach the pall between worlds was complicated, done with the utmost care. He glanced back at the naked girl and dragged her, table and all, into the casting circle. The usually small circle expanded many times larger, to offer her flesh to whoever came.

No homugon walked in the world of the living unless intentionally set free. Prophecies and folklore about the end times remained—when the Underworld took hold. Glato basked in the thought that he'd help pave the way. He'd be his master's pet, more than he'd ever hope for.

The blood closed its circle, and Glato knelt like a faithful servant. Normally, no master would ever come to a servant, but in the case of the homugon, they'd come for a glimpse, a small taste of the living world.

The room flickered darker in the waning candlelight. A blast of scalding air rebuffed against him as a figure emerged from the ripples of heat and darkness. Its demonic form and power sent Glato into convulsions on the floor.

The bull hooves came first, touched the ground as massive legs helped it stand erect.

The face of the creature jumbled in a conglomeration of many animals, both odd and natural to Glato. He gazed up to his *god*, as the shivers came under control. From his back, the demon loomed large. The beast-like figure was massive, nearing twelve feet in height. Its thick neck and shoulders stretched out like a mountain standing on the pillars of Ermaeyth.

The glittering yellow eyes found him, the one responsible for calling. The summons of a mere mortal was a ghastly sin, but he was special. The homugon stretched from head to tail tip and scratched his ram horns.

"Come," it encouraged, its voice deep and inviting, barely above a whisper.

Glato crawled forward on his belly. The large, scaly body squatted. Deep yellow eyes pierced him. The gaze gave Glato nightmares, and he was grateful. The eyes are what did it most for the apostle, not just the sheer size or terrible appearance of the homugon, but the actual visage.

The eyes were difficult to comprehend, three sets inside a single pair. The homugon had the same shape as Glato's did, but the orbs were that of a serpent, vertical diamonds that would change in size and dilate like a cat in proper circumstances. Three in one. Right now, they bored into him as the face loomed near. The homugon flicked out its forked tongue, tickling Glato's face, tasting his sweat.

"You're terrified," it said in its deep voice, one so deep that it felt more like a vibration than that of a sound. "And yet happy."

The face drew near, the yellow eyes looming large.

"You're an interesting specimen. Do I please you, Glato?"

"Y-you know my name?"

A sneer curled on the face of the demon. Its massive arms, which looked like wizardkind's, bulged with muscle and veins. Long claws extended from its fingertips, black like event horizons. An enormous hand reached out and grabbed Glato by the face, palming his head and lifted him from the floor to his feet.

"Gaze upon me, Glato. Do I not seem different to you, different than the ones before?"

It folded its massive, tattooed arms. Its red body gleamed in the faint light where the darkness receded. The black lines scrambled over its body, up its arms, and across its bare chest. Glato appraised the demon with wary eyes from head to hoof, this time noticing its black, bat-like fleshy wings. No answer came come forth, and the homugon continued.

"The others, the ones that you communed with before, are servants of mine; I am the master."

A long dark claw pointed in his direction.

"You groveled to them like they were gods of the Underworld, as you should, as all mortals will. But the way you praised them is the way they worship me. I am their god, the Lord of the Underworld, the master of Hell. I am Apocalypse."

His deep voice boomed with a seduction Glato had never known. His body convulsed as the massive figure's eyes bored into the weak, mortal flesh with a penetrating gaze. The homugon's pheromones permeated the air, and it became too much for him.

When the convulsing subsided, Glato positioned himself before the Lord of the Underworld and came to his knees.

"My master—"

"Why have you called? Being here gives me great pleasure, but you called me from the dark pits of fire and death, from the ghosts and their echoes, from the endless void. What do you want from me?"

"Your guidance, Master, and your blessing."

Then, he remembered, waving a hand behind him to the harlot.

"I've brought you a gift."

Apocalypse's eyes drifted over to the naked woman, then back to Glato.

"The last time you asked for an audience, you asked for the release of a soul, Vlad Vikal, the first vampire. Yet nothing has been done about the gateway barring our entry to your world. Tell me, what's so important about releasing that soul, Glato?"

The apostle was at a loss for words in the presence of the mighty homugon. What could he say to make the Lord of the Underworld understand?

"There are many things in particular about that soul, Great One. The first and foremost is that he was the first true follower of the homugon teachings," Glato said.

"I know him not."

"Not in the sense I am, but he embraced the ideals of the theology. He believed tampering with what the One gave was the only way to achieve greatness, completeness. Like wizardkind's mekkaniques evolve, the farmer and his plow evolve into something better, he too wanted to change the body and soul."

"Prattle not," the homugon snapped. "What's your point?"

"I've no doubt he'll again try to make what he created better, and by doing so, will draw Ralloc's attention and all those who'd fight to keep you imprisoned. If they knew I intended to release you, they'd stop at nothing to ensure it doesn't happen, my lord."

"So, he's a distraction."

Apocalypse mulled over his words, and Glato looked up at his master.

"When Ralloc's in the fervor of chaos, I can move in and begin working on releasing you. If you shall grant, in your divine wisdom and mercy, one last boon, I can assure your freedom."

"And if I'm not free? What then, little mortal? I'd still be banished."

"Please, master, I know I won't fail."

"What do you ask?"

Glato licked his lips, knowing that this moment would be the greatest boon, or seal his fate.

"Please, give me the Jackal, my lord. Give me the Jackal and his Shades."

Glato bowed low, resting his head on the floor at the hooves of the demon. The deep resonating laugh came from the belly of the beast, and the room trembled as it echoed out.

"The Jackal of Shades? Most amusing, Glato. You shall have it, the Jackal and his Shades."

The homugon's eyes flickered to the naked woman.

"Bring her closer that I may partake of her flesh."

Glato dragged her closer. The Lord of the Underworld moved between her legs, leaning over her, leering. Her eyes snapped open at that moment and filled with horror.

She screamed and screamed, but no one would hear her.

She looked to Glato, pleading, but he smiled, watching the homugon ravish her. Eventually, her screams were replaced by the groans of the homugon.

When he finished, he devoured her flesh before returning to the Underworld to torture her soul.

Chapter 51: Daniel Laket

Xenomene paced like a caged animal, cutting a rut in the floor of Daniel's office. His eyes followed every movement. Well, they followed her ass.

The other ko-dons ogled her swaying hips, her ever-too-small shorts, and the tease of her heart-shaped ass. Some found the pacing amusing while others enjoyed the sight of her passing. Every few moments, she picked at the long-healed scar on her right cheek.

While physically present, her mind remained aloof.

Daniel didn't bother to make her sit, she'd just fidget. Besides, watching her pace made him pay more attention to the proceedings.

If she doesn't stop walking around, she's going to give me a swollen scrotum.

"I don't understand," Panther said.

The ko-don was usually the quietest of the group. Daniel flitted his gaze to him as he continued speaking.

"What does the new consul want with us?"

Daniel didn't respond immediately. He appraised his ko-dons again, noting their hair and eye color and affirming that none were, indeed, Forgotten Islanders. As for Xenomene, he wasn't sure, but if she was, she never said nor remembered, having come to Outpost Dire so young.

Daniel recalled the day with clarity. She was so tiny, so young. She couldn't have been older than five.

"I don't know," Daniel confessed, though the admission didn't sit well with him.

"Perhaps," Chimera broke in, "he's coming to familiarize himself. We are, shall we say, an enigma to those of the Isles."

Xenomene stopped pacing, looking at the older ko-don.

"Shades, you're the stupidest cunt," she spat, then resumed trail blazing.

The other ko-dons balked before returning their gaze to her.

"Care to comment?" Daniel asked, but she waved him away with a grimace. When evident she wouldn't elaborate, the heir returned his attention to the others.

"I've no clue either, Heir," Adder said. "This doesn't sit well with me, either."

"It can only be bad," Craiboar added.

Daniel sighed, climbed out of his chair, retrieved a poured drink, and returned to his desk with the bottle and glass. He set the glass down but raised the bottle to his lips, drinking from it.

Xenomene stopped pacing long enough to snatch up his glass, downed the contents in one swallow, and slammed the cup back down. With a muttered thanks, she continued pacing.

Daniel pulled the bottle away from his lips and barked at her.

"That wasn't for you."

"Mhmm."

Daniel took another long pull, then set the bottle towards the front of the desk. Chimera leaned in and took the bottle. He drank as Daniel had before, then he, too, passed the bottle to the next in line.

Daniel's eyes found Xeno's backside.

If you weren't so fun in bed, you'd be scrubbing floors until you were gray.

Her back and forth both amused and agitated him, and the rum he just drank emboldened him to speak.

"No good will come from this visit; I feel it in my bones."

No good ever came from politicians.

"That's the alcohol talking," Stallion said.

Xenomene stopped pacing and stared at Stallion.

"Disregard my last, *you're* the stupidest cunt," she snapped.

She resumed pacing.

"Shades of a dead pig's ass, spit it out woman!" Chimera thundered.

Xenomene stopped and stared at him, her emerald eyes narrowed to slits of fury the gods would fear.

Chimera glanced to the others.

"This is why we don't have kids be ko-dons or let women be heirs. You need more than your body to be worth a damn in this position."

She moved almost too fast for Daniel to register. Her arm flashed out. A knife materialized between Chimera's legs, missing his scrotum by mere inches.

"Say that again. Go on. I'll turn you into a woman faster than you can scream."

Daniel stood, his fist pounding the desk, and roared.

"Two shits of a fucking prostitute! You two knock it off. Xenomene, put your fucking knife away. Chimera, that's exactly the kind of thinking that'll keep you from becoming heir! Xenomene, sit the fuck down, stop fidgeting, and tell me what the fuck's on your mind!"

The red-haired woman gave both a glare from the depths of the Underworld before complying. She collected the knife and sat, arranging herself like a noble woman, sitting prim and proper. Her antics drew a chuckle from Daniel.

"You're no arysta, Xenomene, so drop the act."

Her demeanor melted, and she slouched in her chair.

"That's more like it. Now, what the fuck are you going on about?"

"Let's think about this logically."

She leaned forward.

"I know that's what you men like to do, but honestly, you're about as bad as a mother hen."

She sighed and scratched her forehead.

"I can't believe you guys haven't figured this out yet, or at least see it this way. The king of the Forgotten Isles abdicated his throne when he sought unification, but instead of receiving a new ally, Ralloc received a monarch as their consul. If anything can be believed about what's coming out of Ralloc, he's changing laws to his liking with most—if not all—of the council's backing. He's making the country as he likes. He even has a private protection detail now…what're they called?"

"The Iron Will," Adder supplied.

"Yeah, the stupidest fucking name I've ever heard, if not a bit foreshadowing," Xenomene said. "Iron Will? What part of that says freedom or republic? Peace or democracy? Nothing. If anything, it sounds like the absolute totalitarian control of an emperor. He may not be it yet, but if things don't change, we could be looking at a king who left his small throne for a much bigger one. And now, he wants to come here, to see the Krey? If I was him, I'd be coming here for two things: devotion and regime change, placing someone loyal in charge. But, he can't. The position of heir's only relinquished upon death. He can't remove you."

"How do you figure that one, replacing the heir?" Stallion asked.

"Well, when he gets here, we're all supposed to be unarmed, our weapons locked away by a group of his Iron Will until he leaves."

"Maybe he just doesn't want to take any chances," Craiboar supplied.

"Yeah, at us revolting," she retorted.

Daniel smiled at her sarcasm. It'd been too long since he'd heard her usual inflections. It gladdened his heart to see her returning to her former state with the whole bloody mess with Bitcher left far behind. He still didn't agree with sparing the former Krey, but it wasn't his call.

Bitcher probably wished he was dead by now, if he wasn't already.

"Okay," Daniel spoke up. "So, he wants to remove me from power. We need to decide who my replacement will be, that way we hold an element of control."

Silence descended upon the seven. The ko-dons fidgeted and cast apprehensive glances at each other, wary to profess their desire to ascend. Stallion and Panther, the oldest of the ko-dons, seemed bemused while Adder and Craiboar stewed over the words.

Chimera appeared thoughtful, on the verge of speaking, while Xenomene looked indifferent.

"Don't be shy," Daniel antagonized. "I won't think any less of anyone who shows initiative."

This ought to be entertaining at least.

He smiled at the thought.

"Then, I'd suggest Stallion or Panther," Chimera spoke up, "seeing as they're older and have seniority."

"Yeah, but I don't have the mind for it," Panther admitted.

Stallion's brow rose in thought.

"I can honestly say I've hungered for the title when younger, but now that I'm older, I wouldn't last long, nor want to put up with all the shit the role entails."

"We could go younger," Panther said, looking at Craiboar, Chimera, and Adder.

"I agree, younger," Stallion said. "I move for Chimera's nomination."

"You know, Daniel," Xenomene said, interrupting them, "you don't have to step down."

Daniel's chest swelled with warmth and pride with her support. The men seemed startled that she spoke, as if they'd forgotten her presence.

"What do you mean?" Stallion asked.

"The Krey have always operated outside the jurisdiction of Ralloc. We're outcasts, in essence, warlocks. We fall under the rule of the army's highest members but are set apart."

"Aye, that's true," Craiboar seconded. "They can't tell us what to do in House Eti. Let them try! We'd destroy them all."

"Hence why the consul wants us disarmed before he arrives," Xenomene reiterated.

Stallion shifted in his seat.

"We don't need weapons."

"What's an old man like you going to do?" Xenomene retorted. "Piss all over them with your malfunctioning bladder?"

"How—?" Stallion began, but Craiboar cut him off.

"Old man, the walls are thin. We hear everything in the dead of night, every time you hit the chamber pot."

"You curse when you miss," Panther added.

"And we can all tell when Panther takes a shit," Adder said. "Nothing's secret around here."

"Yeah, and we can hear when the heir is fucking Xenomene," Chimera spat with vehemence.

His narrowed eyes glittered with enmity. A sharp inhale from the other ko-dons punctuated the icy stillness. Their eyes darted to him in agitation.

"What? Think we wouldn't know? Did you think it was coincidence when we didn't mention you as a possible successor? Thought to fuck your way into the title?"

Daniel groaned internally.

Fuck, this isn't going to be good. It's bad enough they know, something she wanted to avoid, but they actually think it was for the title? We should tell them the truth.

His eyes darted to Xenomene whose face remained composed, neutral, but her eyes bore into Chimera.

"Little girl," Chimera snarled, "drop the stare before I rip out your eyes and fuck your mouth until my cock comes out the back of your skull."

"Chimera," Daniel rumbled a warning, but stopped when Xenomene lurched to her feet.

"First of all," she said, her voice harsh and raspy, "if I meant to fuck my way to the top, I would've fucked all of you to ensure I was awarded the rank. By *fucking* the heir, I've placed myself at odds with the ko-dons, which was partly the reason I did it. So, when I take the mantle of heir, it's either because you granted it or I ripped it from your cold, dead fingers. You won't be able to whine and say I cheated my way to it."

"You actually think—?" Chimera started.

"I'm not finished, cunt," she snapped.

She radiated malice, and the hairs on Daniel's arms stood on end.

"Secondly, who I fuck is none of your business."

"You may be Krey by day, but you're whore by night." Chimera said.

A blur of black moved through the semicircle of chairs surrounding Daniel's desk. The echo of the chair slamming against the floor drowned out the grunt that followed. Xenomene sat, straddling Chimera, the knife's edge pricking the flesh of his jugular.

"Call me a whore again, and I'll make what I did to Bitcher seem mild in comparison."

Daniel eyed the others in the wake of her words. The ko-dons knew what happened to Bitcher, but not the why. It wasn't everyday a Krey was banished and taken away in chains. They were privy to the knowledge of what ensued in the dungeon below, the Mon Kyyr Gr'bakth, the broken bones, and his riddled flesh.

Chimera paled as he stared up into her eyes.

"Do you understand?" she demanded, the pressure drawing a bead of blood.

With fluttering breath, he nodded. She dismounted and faced the other ko-dons.

"I'm going be the next heir," she said.

Daniel's brows rose in surprise.

Fucking bitch has got bigger balls than all these men combined.

The ko-dons leapt to their feet with shouts and curses. Arguing ensued with Daniel watching the debacle unfold. The ko-dons were nearly at blows over her declaration. Some fools were either brave enough or foolish enough to get up in Xenomene's face. Spittle flew and arms flailed with each lambasted obscenity thrown before Daniel took control and called for silence.

"What claim do you have to be heir, Xenomene?" Daniel asked.

He dared to let a chuckle bubble out.

If anything, it'll be original, if not humorous.

"Superiority."

His breath caught in his throat.

Well, I didn't expect that one.

The ko-dons blanched, some hissed swears while others mocked with scorn, but Daniel held up his hand.

"Superiority at what?"

"With the sword. Any weapon, choose one, it won't matter."

She looked from the heir to the ko-dons.

"I challenge you, all of you, as the old ways before the heir was voted in by peers. We'll settle this in the Pit for the title. To the death, if you wish to perish needlessly. I can take you one at a time, or all at once, but you'll fucking die regardless."

She went quiet for a moment, giving each a pointed look.

"I *will* be the next heir, so you better get used to the fucking idea."

"I accept your challenge," Panther acknowledged with a dip of his head.

He stood.

"No, you don't," Daniel said. "Sit your ass back down. None of you accept. She's right."

"Why, because she fucked you?" Chimera asked, his incredulous eyes narrowing. "Was she truly the greatest cock purse you've ever had?"

He turned his eyes to Xenomene.

"Did he squirt his seed in your jelly bag, and now you're pregnant with his bastard?"

Daniel moved to rebuke the man when Xenomene spoke.

"I doubt I was his best," she confessed, "but I'm sure I was the funnest."

Daniel blinked.

How can she be so nonchalant?

But he couldn't play in line with her humor. He was too angry.

"She's right. If she lays down the challenge, then by all accounts, you'll have to best her in the Pit. Raven, her old do-don, told me she was undefeated. I went over the records. He was right. No one has bested her. You all would take a brutal beating in the presence of witnesses. Do you really want to look like idiots in front of the Krey? And if it's to the death, well, hug your loved ones goodbye."

A heavy silence hung in the gulf between the ko-dons and Daniel's desk.

"I take it from your silence that you're amenable."

One by one, they nodded acceptance.

"Good."

He stood.

"There's one more possibility," Xenomene said, her eyes on the floor. "For why Godfrey's coming here."

Shades, what now?

"Yes?"

She glanced at him.

"He could be coming here to kill us all."

"Fucking spectacular," Daniel muttered.

"And you draw this conclusion from…?" Adder inquired.

"Weapons locked up, arriving in force with his special group. He could bring an army with him, and we'd be fucked."

"Well, that's comforting," Daniel said, "and a great note to end this meeting on."

Daniel sighed.

"Hit the rack, it's late."

The men shuffled out, retiring to their rooms, but Xenomene stayed behind.

"Something I can help you with?"

"I'm not sorry," she said, "but I hope you didn't find me out of line about being the next heir."

He crossed his arms.

"No, I didn't. If you're next, I have nothing to worry about. Except…"

She arched an eyebrow.

"Yes?"

"Well, you once said if you knew you were going to die…"

She smiled, rolled her eyes, and finished it for him.

"…that you'd be the person I'd want to fuck."

"And as you aptly put," he added, "it may be on the morrow."

Her smile broadened, almost bashful. He could tell she didn't believe it, their imminent death, but she colored all the same, glowed knowing he yearned for her.

"Nice try."

Her smile remained tight.

"Good night, Heir."

She turned to leave, and Daniel drank in every detail, her swaying hips, toned legs, and firm buttocks.

He called to her one last time as she reached the door.

"Xeno? Do you really think we're going to die tomorrow?"

She paused, thoughtful. Then, with a shake of her head, she answered with a grin.

"You might, but I'm invincible."

She left him with aching loins, and a pang of regret.

Chapter 52: Xenomene

Though she declined the heir's offers, Xenomene didn't spend the night alone. On the way to her quarters, she spotted Slurp and invited him in. The Islander agreed, a grin spreading across his face.

"No sex tonight."

His lips pressed into an incredulous line.

"What's the point in coming in?"

She shrugged at that. What would be a good enough answer?

"I just want to sleep next to someone."

He shrugged, and his smile returned.

"If you want me to hold you, just say so. There's no shame in it."

She rolled her eyes.

"Fine, I want you to hold me, but if you tell anyone, I'll cut your balls off."

He nodded somberly.

"I believe you."

Once he graced her bed though, she couldn't keep desire at bay. She rolled to her back and kissed him with tender affection. With that little encouragement, he climbed on top, slipped between her legs, and entered her. Had it been any other night, she would've rolled to her stomach and offered him her ass, as she'd done many times with him, but tonight, she didn't want her back to him.

She wanted to see his face and feel him in her core.

She held him close the entire time, legs wrapped around him, holding his chest against hers, arms locked around his neck. Their rhythm stayed gentle and slow. His kisses came plentiful, and a part of her soul wept that she found him too late. It was the most intimate she'd been with any man, and she was glad she chose him.

And when he reached the apex, he released inside her, and for once, the moment felt right.

She kissed with a soft passion, letting her lips express every word never uttered. Sated, she rolled to her side, pulling him close, his arm draped about her. In his arms, she felt safe. Her soul quivered with an adoration she'd never felt. The way he comported himself, heeding her direction, he made her feel whole rather than a harlot to rut.

But on occasions, that wasn't bad either.

The night passed without incident. The warmth of his body put her at ease, finding a deep sleep for the first time since Cape Gythmel. The morning came too soon in the few scant hours of sleep. It passed in a blur, and before she knew it, all stood outside House Eti, staring at a magical portal. The portal stayed open much longer than usual. Battlemages of the aegis, pharmacon, and barrage caste, had already filed through and taken positions around the stage and the gathered masses.

She glanced around, and seeing eyes snap in her direction she lowered her head, and that's when she saw it. The ground, it almost looked normal except a vague impression running beneath the soil. In fact, she couldn't be sure if what she saw was real or her overactive imagination.

Better safe than sorry.

With slow movements to not draw attention, she dug the ball of her boot into the soil, rubbing it left and right, breaking what she thought might be a rune beneath. She was probably being stupid, imagining things, but what if…?

When the last of the personal guard—the Iron Will—stepped through, Xeno noted the spears gripped in their hands, the swords hanging from their hips, and the shields they toted. Impenetrable masks covered their faces, their gazes pale, cold, and distant.

When the last settled into position to protect the consul, Godfrey arrived through the shimmering pall.

Generally, portals closed after the last person went through, but this one didn't, another thing Xenomene noted as odd.

Maybe thinking there was a run beneath our feet was so crazy after all?

Instead of greeting their consul in their dragon-plate armor, they wore bare essentials and usual garb, flat-black, coarse wool. She shivered upon seeing Godfrey, but she didn't know if it came from his visage or the weather. The Vikal Mountains were always cold year-round.

Godfrey's pale blue eyes glittered perniciously as he took the stage. The only people permitted with him were the guards and the heir, the latter weaponless. The consul gave Daniel an appraising look before he turned to the sea of bodies before him. Xeno cringed as his eyes swept over her. It was hard to miss her and the other ko-dons, who stood directly in front of the stage, a place of honor in the shameful venue.

Xeno watched every move, every detail, the creases of his face, searched for clues as to what he intended. He stood with a rigid, military manner. His strawberry blonde hair was cropped close like his beard, both shot through with gray. Godfrey's face, a chiseled perfection of composure, was the antithesis of liveliness.

He revealed nothing.

Wide, powerful shoulders and a tapered waist honed the impenetrable appearance. Xenomene had heard the expression of people wearing their heart on their sleeve; she doubted Godfrey had one.

His movements were methodical but assured. Godfrey was enshrouded with an aura of the divine as if the actions were ordained by the gods themselves. He stepped to the edge of the platform and clasped his arms behind his back. When the lifeless eyes stilled, he smiled. The smile itself was big, full of white teeth and glowing. Cold washed through Xenomene, seeing it more as a sneer.

He's goading us, lording over us as if we're nothing more than sheep fattened for slaughter. It's contempt.

"And so, the Black Tide at last," his voice boomed.

He projected for all five thousand in attendance. Xenomene couldn't help but think he used magic to amplify his voice. But he didn't. It was as if he held contempt for magic as he did for the Krey.

"I've always heard the tales, but I've never seen one in person. Truly, a magnificent sight. As I'm sure you know, I'm Callum Godfrey, former king of the Forgotten Isles and consul to the Ralloc domain. I've come to see you for myself, to hear of your fealty and allegiance."

He turned to Daniel and stepped toward him.

"Do I have the Krey's allegiance and fealty?"

Daniel nodded but didn't bow or stoop. He stood as militarily-straight as Godfrey, but his gut bulged where Godfrey's did not.

"Aye, Consul. You have our faith, fealty, and loyalty. We're patriots of Ralloc's domain."

Godfrey nodded.

"Swear it."

Daniel's eyes widened a touch, his jaw set, but the words came smooth.

"I swear by the sword; you have our faith, fealty, and loyalty."

"On a knee," Godfrey insisted.

He turned to the audience.

"All of the Krey."

Daniel seemed to want to object. Instead, he swallowed pride, nodded, and went to a knee. The Krey followed the heir's example. Xenomene took the time to drag her foot harder across the dirt, then with her knee in place, ground into it all the more.

If Daniel can fucking do it, so can we.

"I swear to live and die by the sword in faith, fealty, loyalty, and in service of Ralloc's domain."

Godfrey nodded and eyed the kneeling Krey.

"You as well."

The words went up from thousands of voices in unison. Godfrey's eyes watched the masses, overlooking Xeno, who didn't utter the words. A warning resounded in her head. Never had a consul felt the need to visit the Krey for an oath. Godfrey nodded and beamed a tight smile.

"Rise," the consul bade, and the Krey obeyed. "Now, with that bit of unpleasantness out of the way," he said with a flourished smile, "I hear some Krey who defended Cape Gythmel and Dlad City were Islanders," he said to everyone, but the question was directed at Daniel.

"Aye, there were."

"Well," Godfrey said with a wave of his arms. "Bring them forth."

"Aye."

Daniel looked at Stallion, the eldest of the ko-dons since Bear's death. Stallion, center in the ko-don row, stepped forward towards the stage. At one pace shy, he did a military about-face and stood at attention.

"Ko-don Xenomene," he called.

Fuck!

She grimaced.

With precision, she marched to the front, stopping a pace shy of him. Normally, in a ceremony, she would've pulled her blade and saluted with it before planting the tip in the ground. Without, she just stood.

"Call forth the Islanders of the Cape Gythmel and Dlad City defense campaign," he ordered.

She, too, did an about-face.

"Squad Xenytes!" she bellowed, much louder than everyone would've given her credit for. "Slurp! Smokey! To the front! Report to the consul."

When finished, Stallion dismissed her, who, in turn, Daniel dismissed. By the time both ko-dons returned to their respective spots, Slurp and Smokey stumbled up the steps of the stage.

Smokey's face was an impenetrable mask, but anxiety-riddled Slurp's face, almost as if he didn't want to be there. They came to a stop before Godfrey and stood at attention. The consul bade them stand at ease.

"It's great that Islanders are still serving the good of all through their affliction," he said, patting both on the shoulder.

Xenomene bit back the urge to scream at him and opted for her venomous thoughts instead.

Affliction? We're not diseased, you asshole!

Godfrey turned to Daniel.

"I heard of three Islanders."

It was a statement, not a question; she couldn't glimpse his face but guessed he scowled. His tone mimicked displeasure.

Daniel cleared his throat.

"Aye."

"Well, where's the third?"

Without lying, Daniel answered.

"There *were* three, Consul."

Godfrey nodded, a solemn movement.

"I see. I regret I'm unable to commend him. If you'll permit me, I'd like to conduct a small ceremony?"

Daniel's brow frowned.

"We're at the Consul's disposal. You're the final word here."

Xenomene smiled to herself. Daniel danced around what he wanted to say, or at least, what she wanted to say.

Hell no, you can't! Go back to your fucking office. Better yet, go back to your fucking rocks!

Godfrey gave a small, close-lipped smile.

"It was a courtesy."

He nodded to the guards behind him. One stepped forward with something laying in his arms, a forest green silk cloth draped over whatever lay beneath. With a flourish, Godfrey pulled the silk free, revealing three finely crafted swords. While beautiful enough to grace a wealthy nobleman's collection, the swords were built for purpose as well. He pulled the first one out and walked to Slurp.

"Kneel," he commanded.

Slurp complied.

"Do you know who I am?"

"Yes, Consul. You're my commander, and the king of the Forgotten Isles."

Godfrey nodded.

"In the tradition of kings who've come before, and for the service of extraordinary men, I dub thee, Defender of the King's Guard with all appropriate titles and lands of the Isles that accompany such a prestigious barony."

He touched each of Slurp's shoulders before he rose. Godfrey handed the sword, hilt first, to the Krey, who took it with a humble bow.

What the fuck's that bastard doing? What's the point? He can't leave the outpost, even if he wanted to.

She hated ceremonies and all the petty nobles and lords that accompanied. King or consul, she made no exception.

Fuck this pomp and circumstance!

Godfrey repeated the procedure with Smokey, who also rose and accepted the blade. They bowed again and took position behind the consul, standing at attention, the tip of the blade down, right arms locked out with their palms resting on the pommel.

Godfrey picked up the third blade and raised it high.

"For a fallen brother, his sword shall always adorn my office for as long as I have it. May he never be forgotten."

He looped it through his belt.

"One last thing, and then I'll leave you," Godfrey promised.

Her chest tightened with apprehension.

Choking on a donkey's ball sack for dinner is better than this shit!

"Heir, if you please?" Godfrey said, indicating for Daniel to come beside him. He complied, looking out over the Krey with Godfrey. From where Slurp stood, Xenomene could just see him between the heads of Godfrey and Daniel. She tried not to smile, remembering the night before.

But she couldn't see Smokey anymore, hidden from sight when Daniel stepped up, and she was glad for that.

He's an ugly son of a bitch.

"Let's hear it for the heir!" Godfrey cried.

A roar of approval ripped through the air. Had Godfrey not called for silence, Xeno was pretty sure it would've droned on for minutes.

"You've been the leader a great many years. It's a service to the people and a position of honor. You've done a splendid job."

Another small ripple of approval cascaded before dying out.

"So, accept this as a reward. I hereby relieve you of command and grant you a commendation for your years of service. There are two estates we bestow upon you, one in Ralloc, where you'll be part of a special council, and one in the Golden City for you to spend the summer months in lavish comfort."

A surprising cheer went up from the Krey, louder than the first, but she didn't. Were they stupid? Godfrey couldn't do that, and Daniel couldn't accept.

What's he trying to do? Buy popularity?

When the cheering died, Daniel nodded and spoke.

"I thank you, Consul, for a most generous gift, but it's a gift I can't accept. I'm Krey, bound by law to Outpost Dire. I can't leave."

"Ah, but you're forgetting," Godfrey said. "I'm consul, and laws can be rewritten or amended. I'm sure the council will accept this as a sign to progress out of the old ways."

Another round of crowd rousing came, but more subdued than the first. Maybe by now, they were starting to ask the right questions in their heads.

"Aye, but even amended, the post is for life. I can't leave my Krey. This is my home, Consul, and I can't abandon them for comforts."

Godfrey's grin faltered.

"Is this truly your wish?"

Daniel gave a single nod, glancing out at his brethren.

"Aye, it is. They're my people."

Some applause came, a smattering, but by now, the excitement of the moment wore off.

Take it, you fool. If he's offering you a way out, get out of here while you can.

It might be a ruse, but it was better than their outpost.

Godfrey nodded.

"I understand the call of your people. I do. It's commendable. Loyal to a fault."

"Aye. All Krey are loyal to their oaths!"

He pumped his fist in the air, and the Krey cheered louder, pride rippling through the ranks. Xenomene smiled at that. It was nice to see him remain true to their people. He had an escape, and no one would blame him, and he chose to remain.

Godfrey nodded in approval and addressed Daniel again.

"Then, it'll be as you wish."

He patted Daniel's shoulder. The crowd cheered, and the heir pumped a fist again. In a blur of movement, the point of a sword exited his chest, piercing his heart.

Daniel sputtered, blood spilling out of his mouth.

In the time it took for the crowd to fall silent, Daniel turned pale as he stared at the blade in awe. Gasps echoed out.

"No!" a voice cried out, Slurp's, his eyes riddled with shock.

The heir locked eyes with Xenomene, and she felt her heart lurch in her throat. Daniel smiled as best as he could, considering.

"Two shits of a—,"

Daniel slammed face down on the stage.

Dead. Lifeless. Murdered.

Smokey towered where Daniel once stood, and he was weaponless.

As one, the Krey surged toward the stage.

"Stay where you are!" Godfrey shouted.

Instantaneous, all the Krey stopped. Xeno hadn't even moved, still in shock.

"Kneel!" Godfrey screamed.

Again, against volition, the Krey kneeled, and Xenomene only did so that she wasn't the only one standing. She stared at Daniel and the bloody steel.

"Do you take me for a fool?" Godfrey asked. "You've sworn an oath! Loyal, obedient! You swore an oath on a rune drawn beneath your very feet! My battlemages made sure to draw it before you swore! You can't come against me! The rune prevents you from disobeying!"

By the Shades of the fucking Underworld, I was right!

She was glad she did all she could to break the rune with her boot.

Godfrey composed himself back into the same emotionless man upon arrival.

"Edmund," Godfrey called.

Smokey walked to Godfrey. The consul smiled and placed his head against the Krey's.

"Brother."

He smiled and embraced Smokey as if they hadn't seen each other in years. Godfrey pulled back and knelt in front of Smokey.

"I abdicated the throne of the Isles to you, my brother. It's yours as it should be, as planned."

Godfrey stood and clasped his brother's shoulder and spoke to the kneeling Krey.

"This is my brother, first son of King Edmund, the fifth. I present Edmund the Sixth, rightful ruler and king of the Forgotten Isles. I present to you," he pointed to the Krey, "your new heir."

They took the news in silence, but Xeno looked on with venom. The rise of anger swirled around her from the others, almost palpable.

A weight settled on Xenomene's chest, slowly being crushed. Her eyes never left Daniel's lifeless form. Guilt wracked her. She denied him the night before, a dying man's last wish, and she'd chosen Slurp.

A fucking Islander! Like Godfrey, like Smokey, the betrayer.

Her misting eyes found the Islander she bedded the night before. Slurp's face was slack, eyes watery, disbelief and abhorrence alight on his face.

His eyes found hers.

He didn't know. He's blameless.

"My last order to the Krey," the consul said in a strident voice. "You'll not harm my brother and obey him as you would your previous heir. This is my command!"

The consul hugged Smokey again before spitting on Daniel's body and crossing the stage, disappearing through the glowing portal, retreating behind the high walls of Ralloc.

Xenomene shot the portal a venomous gaze, hoping Godfrey suffered her caustic stare.

They may have to obey, but I didn't swear to follow your orders!

Chapter 53: The Time Warden

A long, cruel week trickled by and faded from memory for the nine. At least, it felt like a week. It was hard to tell while in the cavern.

With scant hours of sleep, they took turns watching over the warlock who wasted away before their eyes. Considering how much longer their lives were compared to wizardkind, her death became more apparent with each blink. Conversations withered and restlessness fostered doubt.

During their downtime, they maintained their armor, changing out worn leather, or reinforcing it with small spells. Elyves struggled with bold displays of magic, but they weren't without. Their mysticism differed from wizardkind, who never acknowledged the gifts of other races.

Weapon preservation punctuated the monotony of armor upkeep. Oiling blades, honing edges, and cleaning every crevice devoured vast amounts of time. Those who carried shields like Ahn spent many hours buffing out every scuff. Pommel grips were rewound with new, pristine leather. Some were forced to rewrap using the same hide as supplies dwindled. When such mundane tasks reached their end, the elyves moved to practicing their battle forms and sparing.

Elyves had two pursuits in life, beautifying themselves and the world, and war. Their culture, born from habit and art, pursued war as another form, and they perfected it like any other. No nation, race, or army could claim victory over them.

Iddrial wasn't as sure anymore. He'd heard whispers an elyfian army suffered a defeat at Shadow City.

Iddrial's life before banishment revolved around war. He once commanded the Enclave's army and found himself doubting the resounding massacre.

It had to be magic.

None matched the elyves in blade combat—except perhaps a few Krey; wizards wielded magic and held the upper hand. Powers of that magnitude made elyves jittery. Iddrial turned his eyes toward Starriace. She and one other made Iddrial wary.

She flew without wings.

That troubled Iddrial. He'd never encountered a tale of anyone who could fly. He'd witnessed the rise and fall of countless powerful men and women. The tales of Hagen, the Father of Magic, still gave him chills, but Hagen couldn't fly. And his demise was rather quick and violent, or so the tales went.

The elyfian group had once witnessed the world turning black, not just their sight, but the *entire* world. From that day, he awaited another day when darkness covered Ermaeyth.

It hadn't yet.

The unnatural event left a profound mark on Iddrial, more so than the rest of the elyves in company. True, they were but children at the time. The complete and utter darkness was a sign to all, something unnatural brewed among the gods.

He gazed down at Starriace.

She coveted power she shouldn't, and it terrified him. One wrong move, ill word, or unspoken deed would send the young warlock to a dark place. If she chose to pursue that path, she'd become something Xilor couldn't compare to. She might topple the myth of Hagen, forever erasing his legacy by supplanting him with unfathomable deeds.

Iddrial's vigilance never wavered.

The rest of the group didn't know much about Starriace, not like Iddrial and Ama Ka did, but they knew defending Ralloc and defeating Xilor remained her priority. Once done, she'd turn her focus to finding a cure for their affliction.

If there's even a cure. We've been told that once before.

Ru Sol, the strategist of the group, devised schematics to strengthen Ralloc while she worked on designs to assassinate Xilor with Fir Fera. The group's assassin would almost certainly fail against a magical being armed with only a blade, but she practiced anyway. Cal Cas and Mia Ther ventured to the surface often, Cal to commune with nature, and Mia to converse with the beasts of the air.

Ama Ka spent her time with Starriace, attempting to use her meager skills to heal the mage. At most, she slowed the affliction. When she wasn't treating Starriace, she ate, slept, or delved into her latent gifts with nature. Everyone tried to aid her, but only managed to feed the mage water and wipe down her extremities with a wet cloth.

The mood grew foul and brooding, like an ill omen. Silence and darkness became a constant antithesis of the companionable body warmth and fire. Sex among the group had lost its appeal in the forlorn waiting.

Iddrial prowled through the cavern, tiptoeing between sleeping forms. Snores rose up from the group. After endless hours in the dark, a lack of normalcy coupled with fatigue from idleness, the band fell into a deep sleep. Ama sat on her haunches, feet curled underneath and meditated. Iddrial padded in slow circles around her and Starriace.

The sense of eyes upon him grew taut, and he stopped. Peering into the darkness away from the camp, he stood still.

Without a sound, a figure appeared.

Startled, he reached for his weapons, a shout leaping from his throat, but no sound came. A pressure came over Iddrial, and he was unable to move. He could only assume that the same had happened to Ama. An invisible force plucked him from his battle stance and drew him towards the figure. Whoever it was turned on their heel and walked further into the cave, away from the group and dying mage.

When the figure stopped and faced them, a wave of unease washed over Iddrial in recognition. He knew that woman, her stance, her cloak, the dark cowl. Shadows covered her face except for the tip of her nose and the lips beneath.

"You!" Iddrial whispered.

He noted his voice and free will had returned.

"I remember you," he said.

He looked back at Starriace lying on the ground, helpless, making sure she was alright.

It's been so long!

"As do I," Ama said. "It's been a long time."

"Indeed, my friends. I must say, you still look the same," the shadowy figure said.

Her black robes coiled about like writhing shadows, shrouding herself in obscuring darkness.

"And you're only vaguely familiar," Iddrial said.

"I've another task for you."

"No," Ama blurted. "We've done as you asked and have yet to receive your promises."

Both elyves stared into the woman's cowl. Iddrial felt his chest tighten.

"Everything I said transpired, she sought you out, didn't she? And I've fulfilled my end of the original bargain, haven't I? You're with your people, and none are the wiser. Wouldn't that make us, at the very least, friends?"

"Friends? Friends don't abandon."

"No, Iddrial," the woman said. "I never abandoned you."

Iddrial sensed Ama's hesitation, but she nodded in agreement.

"What you imparted came true," Ama admitted. "How do we know what you say is true now?"

The shadowy woman shifted her gaze to the campsite and back to her two companions.

"With this."

She pulled out a sword from within her robes, its scabbard white and silver. She handed it to Iddrial.

"Pull the blade and see for yourself."

Iddrial scrutinized the weapon, then pulled the blade halfway from the sheath. There was no mistaking the sword.

"By the gods," he whispered as his eyes widened. "The Sword of Salvation?"

He turned and glanced at Starriace.

"Yes, her sword. There's only one Salvation, and she still possesses hers. How's that possible?"

Iddrial held his words, daring a glance at Ama. Remembering the sword, he sheathed it. He shook his head, refusing to believe the words that came.

"All of this is making sense now."

He saw her head tilt up toward him.

"Go on," she said, and he caught the intrigue in her voice.

"That place you took us to, the things you said that didn't make sense at the time, but they do now. You're a Time Warden."

He saw a small smile spread on her lips.

"No. *The* Time Warden," she corrected.

"What's a Time Warden?" Ama asked.

"It's an entity of immense power who can manipulate time and events," Iddrial said.

His eyes roamed over the woman. Shadows hugged her like a lover, keeping her identity secret.

"And apparently, she's the only one left. Time Wardens keep others from abusing and tampering with time. Why are you here, then? Did we not do as you asked?"

"Yes, you did. But I'm here to make sure things happen as they should, and to help. Things are about to happen, terrible things. Ermaeyth will grow dark three times, and the pall between the Underworld will be weakened. Gods will wake, and pestilence will rise up."

"Help?" Ama asked. "How are you going to help with that?"

The woman of shadow ignored the inquiry.

"Are we wasting our time with this one?" Iddrial inquired.

He jerked a thumb towards their campsite, indicating Starriace.

"Did we waste all our time before? I want to believe we aren't, but I can't help but feel—"

"—that she's as lost as you?"

"Yes."

"It'll take years for her to discover herself, but there's more to her story than she told, more than she knows. What has and will transpire, try not to be so judgmental. She's suffered, and she'll suffer more, far more than you or her could ever realize."

Iddrial noted the shadow lady's voice. She spoke with emotional undertones as if she empathized with Starriace's pain. Perhaps she did. Time Wardens knew everyone's endings and beginnings. They lived a thousand lifetimes, a million, infinite. Each person's life was a story.

What I wouldn't give to see her face.

The Time Warden dipped her head to them.

"Thank you for all you've done and will do in the future."

"In the future?" Ama asked, her voice incredulous. "We dance to your fiddle with no end in sight. What makes you think we'll continue to subject ourselves to indentured servitude?"

The Time Warden apprised her for a few moments.

"Ama, you're so different than I remember. You've changed so much, and yet you're nothing like what you will be. You're going to suffer, too."

Iddrial rolled his eyes.

Well, that's terrific. Sounds like a bleak future.

"Very well," the Time Warden said, "continue following her, for now. She'll be your...salvation. She'll lift the affliction you've carried for so long, but it will be years yet. A cleansing is coming, I can promise you that, along with much more."

"I heard her say," Iddrial spoke up, "that she's nephiliam. Is that true?"

The Time Warden paused, hesitated.

"Tell her nothing, assume nothing, and let her walk the future unhindered with foreknowledge."

"If she isn't nephiliam," he pressed, "what is she?"

"Are you asking for your own curiosity, or because you want to tell her?"

"Curiosity."

He saw the dark woman give a small dip of her head.

"She's to be something so much more. I'm not saying she isn't, nor am I saying she is."

Iddrial held the woman's gaze—at least, he assumed so since he couldn't see her eyes—for a long while.

Ama Ka broke into the conversation.

"You said you came to help?"

"Yes, Ama, my task is for you. You must go and meditate beside her, use the same ability you use to commune with dragons."

"How did you—?" she started.

"I know many things. You can commune with her and bring her out of her unconscious state. Project yourself as a dragon within her mind. As the fire stokes in the belly of the beast, stoke her embers of rage. Once you have, she'll do the rest."

"What do I do?" Ama queried.

"Whatever she tells you to do."

"That's pretty broad…" Iddrial spoke.

"If I told you everything, there wouldn't be any magic left to live."

"What *can* you tell us?" Ama asked.

The woman's lips drew into a line.

"Be ready to mourn."

The words hit him like a mace in the gut. Iddrial glanced at Ama, and for the first time, doubt took root. Would Starriace die? Is that what the Time Warden meant?

"Go Ama," she said. "Do as I say."

Ama turned away with reluctance, but her steps quickened back to the mage's side.

When Ama was far enough away, Iddrial turned back to the Time Warden.

"There's a darkness in Starriace's heart."

"There's darkness in everyone's heart, and it calls to her. Sometimes we must stumble to walk, and sometimes the baser side of ourselves nurture monsters, but not every monster is evil."

She took a step back. No, that wasn't the right word. She floated backward.

Iddrial placed a hand on her arm to keep her from leaving. Agonizing heat and a searing cold shot through his fingers. He jerked back as if bitten by a venomous creature.

"Yes?"

"Call me selfish—" he began.

"You are, but everyone is."

His brow flickered, and a touch of ire rolled through him.

"Is Ama Ka's husband still alive?"

"Ah, you wish to mate."

The lady of shadows reached out and touched Iddrial's face; this time, the touch was warm and soothing.

"I've told you before, Iddrial, son of Yanriel, 'All good things…'"

With that, she faded as if never there. A lone tear blazed a glistening trail down his cheek, but he smothered it. He finished the saying in his mind.

All good things are seeds planted long ago.

He returned to Ama's side, but when he arrived, Starriace started to stir. After all this time, she awoke. He glanced an unspoken question to Ama, who nodded.

So, the Time Warden had been right. Just as she'd been right so long ago.

His heart lightened, but the mage's red eyes glowed brightly. Had Ama stoked her rage too much?

He shook the question away and hurried off to rouse the others.

Chapter 54: Starriace

Starriace climbed to her feet just as the world shook and plunged into darkness. Everything fell away, the fire, Ama, the elyves. Heat rolled over her in mighty waves, like quick gusts of wind across a bed of coals. The oppression flowed and ebbed like a living, breathing entity. An agonizing, charring heat singed their skin. Gasps escaped them all. A whimper reached her ears.

Was that mine?

The absolute darkness made Starriace's first thought amble down a bizarre path. She thought she'd died. Her second notion bordered on the residual effects from the phantom. Was it responsible?

The dark pooled about them with an indescribable thickness, almost tangible. A wet oiliness clung to her reaching fingers, attempting to find a way in the dark. The tenebrous, asphyxiating shroud sent shivers down her spine. Tinges of the conjury reminded her of the time she claimed the life of the guard, and the sorcery used to destroy the Halls of the One.

All are connected, but how?

Her panicking thoughts stilled as she heard the elyves murmuring. They didn't seem keen on the darkness. How long until they panicked?

And then, a flicker, and all returned. The cave's darkness seemed bright in comparison.

Did that happen everywhere around the world, or was it only here?

"What in the Shades of the Underworld was that?" Ahn Bael shuddered.

His pale face relayed how little control he clung to and gave the impression of a man ready to lose his bowels and stomach all in one go.

Starriace sympathized.

"I haven't the faintest," Cal whispered.

He was shaken but remained composed.

"It was like death," Ru Sol said. "Part of the Underworld."

"I hope to hell I don't have to go through that again," Ahn said. "I'd probably die if it came back."

"Then, let's hope for a swift return," Starriace said, a frail grin on her lips.

A nervous titter weaved through the group, and in slow order, they regained their composure—their sense of humor returning first. Ahn remained the butt of jests, but the teasing stayed mild.

How can they recover so quickly?

She surmised their long lives strengthened their psyche. What just transpired may not register as more than a moment.

She rose, and the elyves seemed to remember her then. They hurried to the camp and scrounged up a quick meal for her. Ravenous didn't begin to describe the ache in her stomach. She wolfed down the food, and they produced a second helping without encouragement. She didn't bother to ask what they served. Judas's slop in the Corridor of Cruelty would rival a gourmet meal at this point.

That had been before her visit with Mr. Pleasure. Before he broke, molded, and changed her with mental, physical, and emotional torture.

Something in the pit of her stomach stirred, an inky blackness. She dismissed it as a reaction to the dark memories she tried to forget.

"How long was I out?" Starriace asked.

"A week," Ama answered. "At least, that's what it felt like. Could've been less."

"That's a lot of lost time. We'll have to be quick and make up what we can."

"Yes, but not much of a setback," Iddrial said, "considering all that can be lost."

"True."

Starriace let her mind drift. A war still waged out there, and she still needed an army.

"What?" Ama asked when Starriace fell silent.

The mage glanced at her and shook her head.

"There are things I must do."

Ama nodded.

"There's something in this cave I need to find, and I need to raise an army."

"Army?" Ari Sha laughed. "Haven't we told you? You don't need an army with us at your side."

"I'm aware."

Starriace paused and debated on how much she should divulge. She tried honesty for a change.

"The point is, you and Iddrial and the rest of you can fall, die in battle. I don't want good people to die. I don't want anyone to die. I need an unkillable army."

"Noble sentiment," Ama said.

Starriace caught the flicker across the elyf's eyes. Ama looked to Iddrial and back to her.

"What you plan could be fouler than the creature you fight."

"I've thought of that, too. What I fight is unadulterated malice. Xilor's nihilism must be stopped, and sometimes that means showing him the mercy he'd mete out: none. What's more evil? To let a madman strip Ermaeyth of life and remold it in his image, or fight him by any decisive means? In this case, the end is just and right, and that can't be heinous."

The group fell quiet at her words. Iddrial broke the silence.

"The decision is yours, as is the battle to come. Just know that every choice has unforeseen consequences."

She nodded.

"What were you doing here, anyway?"

"I came to collect a..." she almost said brimstone, "...totem, but now it's buried under a mountain of rock."

"What does this totem do?" Mia Ther asked.

"The exact abilities remain unknown to me, but I was led to believe it'd help me in some way."

"We'll pack while you search," Iddrial suggested.

The mage dipped her head and rose.

The others set to cleaning their belongings, and she returned to the sarcophagus. She didn't doubt that it lay broken and beyond repair, but did anything survive? Did the rock pulverize all within? Reaching out with her essence, she sifted through the boulders. In ones and twos, she lifted them clear until she unearthed the crushed grave beneath.

To her surprise, only the tabletop portion lay broken. The rest stood strong and unwavering. She approached and peered inside. Decayed and unrecognizable remains lay within. Her eyes scanned the Ucoric glyphs. The etchings lined every inch of the rock.

The passage warned that Hagen's remains lay within.

Dust filled the bottom. Various containers lined the edges, each filled with the last possessions he wore—rings, necklaces, amulets, and other such trinkets. She sifted through the personal effects with methodical care. She tested each against her essence and discarded all in turn. A sliver of horror fluttered within, knowing she desecrated the deceased's remains.

Still, Hagen did far worse when living, or so the stories went.

Each item frustrated her more as they turned out to be simple jewelry. She knew before searching that the tomb didn't contain what she sought: a brimstone. When she opened the third to the last container, a golden necklace with a small figure eight symbol, lay within.

She hesitated for a brief moment, then plucked it. Energy resonated from the necklace, something strange, yet in tune with her essence.

Starriace gazed at the jewelry for a moment. Other than its gold, it remained unremarkable. She opened the loop to put the chain around her neck.

"Whoa, wait a minute," Iddrial interjected. He stood close, having slipped up on her while she plundered. "What if it's something bad like the phantom? I mean, you're young. What if it kills you?"

Starriace held his gaze for a moment, contemplating. He had a valid point.

"I doubt Hagen would put something lethal around his own neck."

"True, but are you sure you want to take that chance? There's still much to live for: Xilor's defeat, the army you wish to raise."

He had another valid point, and he reminded her of Ava. The elyves said she came to them.

Ava? she sent out the mental call.

Remembering the fairy preferred to be called once, she let it fade without beckoning again. Agony slithered through her abdomen, writhed like slimy eels squirming and a flicker of pain arched through. She closed her eyes, focusing inward. The movement stopped, the pain receded. She imagined the discomfort forming a gaseous cloud and dissipating.

Shades, what's wrong with me?

But she knew what ailed her. Some part of the phantom lived inside of her.

I've to get this out or it'll kill me!

The fairy materialized.

"You called, Mistress?"

Starriace smiled.

"You said you have my thousands?"

"I do."

The fairy beamed, pleased with herself. Starriace was glad to see her attitude had mellowed. Perhaps her time with the elyves had soothed them both?

"It was quite simple, Mistress. I didn't ask a single mage either."

"Who are they?"

"You already command them."

The fairies! Of course, why didn't I think of that?

She didn't know how many fairies there were, but their numbers must be numerous if Ava claimed to have their thousands. Could it really be that simple? As their Head of Creatures, she could ask them to pool their magic and raise the army.

It's amazing how brilliant the most straightforward notions are.

"You've done well, Ava."

Starriace glanced at Iddrial.

"We've got a monumental task ahead, and the way lies in the Valley of the Dead."

Iddrial nodded.

"We're ready when you are."

"I'll be another moment or two."

Iddrial left, and Starriace glanced back down at the chain. Power trickled from it. The longer she stared, the more mesmerizing it became. The energy rose up in her mind, and she let the necklace fall to the ground.

Perhaps Iddrial's right. It might be foolish to wear such things. And just because it didn't kill Hagen doesn't mean it won't kill me.

But something so powerful shouldn't be left behind nor easy to find. Perhaps, in time, she may have a use for it. Reaching into the sarcophagus, she grabbed a container.

Her legs shook, and her stomach fluttered. Whoever buried Hagen had the right idea. She thought to destroy the necklace but had a feeling someone might've already tried.

The phantom came to mind.

Her cautious fingers scooped up the chain and she dumped it into the container. If she found this place, who knows who else might. A teacher? A child?

The jewelry was safer in her care.

Tucking the jar into the crook of her arm, a figure caught her gaze. Rusem stood nearby.

"You'll have brethren soon," she told him.
He didn't respond, as she expected.
"Come," she called to him, and they joined the nine.

Chapter 55: The Siege of Ralloc

Crossroads would've been nothing of a challenge against Xilor's army, but he circumvented with hardly a glance. He let the rear element take care of it, just like Dlad City. The survivors who managed to escape his onslaught at Dlad City were sent to augment Crossroads. The city was minuscule, barely more than a few stores and inns, farms and herds, with an old, dilapidated castle.

Ralloc lay ahead, the last jewel of this domain, one of many capitals in Ermaeyth, but the most prestigious. If he controlled Ralloc, all would fall to him. One last item remained to complete his task: the Mirror of Imaesion. Once in possession, he'd reach back out to the other realms with better control.

Perhaps, with mastery, the threat beyond Ermaeyth would never manifest.

With the loss of time sitting in the thrall of the Corridor, impatience spurred him with reckless abandon. Instead of crushing enemies at each turn, he skipped to the prize. He'd let nothing stand in his way, not when so close to achieving his goal. None challenged him, and the only one that could hadn't been seen since Cape Gythmel. Age would cripple Judas, and soon his power would fail. People revered the warlock, but veneration only went so far. Between that and outright fear, dread would win every time.

With victory certain, doubt festered. Only a fool lived worry-free. Had Starriace not died, he'd be less assured. She haunted his dreams, he felt a tremor of fear when he surrendered to sleep, knowing she'd come to him, a pestilence to terrorize his soul. Perhaps he underestimated her, and she still lived?

He doubted it.

Xilor had underestimated things only twice in his life, and only once paid dearly.

It was a damned thing what Judas and the Kothlere Council did to his followers. Stripping them of powers and imprisoning them on another world like savages. He could've used their help now. Did they live still, or had they become part of the threat he sensed?

They'd soon be within striking range of Ralloc. He'd let his vast numbers tear down the walls. It remained imperative to conserve his energy for the confrontation to come. Xilor called his army to a halt. The flag bearer waved the appropriate banner, and all stopped.

"What're your orders, my lord?" a goblin at his side asked.

"Send in the dragons first. Crush them from above, burn them out, and when they come running, crush them. No one lives unless they've pledged loyalty. Bring me Judas, unmarked. I'll destroy him, an example for all who dare defy me."

The goblin blew the appropriate horns, and the sounds of war began as they swept across the rolling grassland to the city walls. The guards shouted orders, and archers took their posts along the watchtowers. The dragons gave their wings a stretch as they bounded for the sky, their roar tearing into the air. The dragons' higher king hesitated before taking flight.

Xilor watched him go, knowing that soon, he'd have to deal with him.

They followed Xilor for the taste and spoils of war, but their fealty lay with their leader. If he chose to leave, the bound dragons would obey.

The dragons swooped in vertical dives, spewing blasts of liquid fire at the walls. The higher king roared overhead, orders for his followers, and the few who ventured further into the city pulled back to the outer wall.

What in the Underworld is he doing? Those weren't his orders.

Xilor's ire rose. The higher king didn't yield. Would Xilor need to replace him? Guthric, the lower king of the dragons, the second in command, openly opposed Diebach, the higher king.

Dragons gathered low, their beating wings sending gale winds in front of them. Molten fire liquefied the stone, and the outer wall crumbled away. Xilor's legions poured forth. With another roar, Diebach ordered a retreat.

Xilor flexed his hands in agitation.

A few of the airborne beasts drove hard towards the city, those who followed Guthric, their gaping maws filled with gigantic, razor-sharp diamond teeth. Within their bellies, the fire churned and came forth, destroying structures. The falling debris crushed the ant-sized occupants below.

From this distance and the gaping hole in the wall, Xilor watched as tiny figures jumped from the burning buildings, leaping to their death in the hopes of survival. Xilor enjoyed the view of carnage from a hilltop among the rolling grasslands leading up to Ralloc.

After he laid waste to the city, he'd take the council chambers by storm.

Diebach roared again overhead, a primal bellow, and eventually, the rest turned away from the city.

Xilor whirled on the goblin next to him.

"Call the dragons back. Bring me Diebach."

The goblin waved the flags, carrying out his orders. Horns rose up in the distance.

Diebach landed gently for such a mammoth creature, almost soundless. Diebach was originally a reddish-brown, and a few scales remained with his coloring. When he challenged for the higher king, Diebach emerged the victor, but his scales were forever burnt black by his opponent's fire breath.

The higher king turned his long neck towards Xilor.

"You need something?" Diebach hissed through giant teeth.

"Why did you call your dragons back from attacking the city? I need the fortifications destroyed. I want the men, women, and children to be charred ash!"

Diebach lowered his face level with Xilor's. Up close, Xilor was taken aback at how massive his head was. His maw alone was wider than Xilor was tall.

Diebach gazed at him with red eyes.

"You don't answer for the lives we take. I do. You won't be hunted to extinction should you lose; we will. If you lose, you're dead, but us? We'll be hated forever. You play your war the way you want, dark one, but leave my kind and how I run things to me."

"Careful, Diebach. In the end, whether I win or lose, you may not be around to see either."

"A sorcerer such as you can't stand against the nation of dragons. I doubt you can hold your own against me. If you don't like our assistance, perhaps we'll take our leave."

"That won't be necessary."

"Good. Know your place, for I assure you, I know mine."

Diebach leapt into the air before flapping his vast wings. He rocketed fifty meters into the air. The power sent Xilor and all within ten meters to the ground.

Xilor picked himself up. It was time to rid himself of Diebach. Perhaps Guthric would be more amenable.

Xilor turned his attention back to the burning shambles.

Suddenly, the ground trembled, the earth shaking in its foundations. Goblins toppled over around him, and the sea of bodies swayed. Once again, Xilor found himself sprawled on the ground.

Ermaeyth threatened to shatter.

Rock spewed from the earth outside the walls, rising up, up, and further still. Just when it appeared the rock walls would fall and crush Ralloc, they stopped. Xilor couldn't tell, but it seemed there was an opening at the top to let sunlight in.

Or dragons.

Guthric, in disobedience of his higher king, attacked the dome surrounding the city, but his breath had no effect. Before long, his group retreated to the back of the army.

What in the Underworld was that?

He stared at the towering walls. What started out as an assured victory turned swiftly into a prolonged siege.

"We are under attack!" shouted a guard who burst into the council chambers.

"Who is it?" Godfrey asked, rising to his feet. "Xilor?"

"Yes, and he's brought dragons!"

In the faint distance, they heard screams, explosions, and buildings crumbling. Against the dragons, they didn't have much in the way of defense besides magical attacks.

"Run," Godfrey ordered. "Get archers on the walls, close the gate, call all barrage, aegis, and pharmacon battlemages to the walls!"

"Archers are already on the walls, Consul," Master Jynerul Tyku reported as he walked through the doors. "The gate's been sealed and secured. We're moving the children to the caves as we speak."

"The women and children into the caves? What caves?" Godfrey asked. "Don't waste manpower on a helpless cause."

"Consul," Tyku said, closing the distance and leaning forward, "if we survive, do you want to be remembered as Godfrey the bold and brave who saved the helpless, or Godfrey the vile and cruel who let the helpless become a target?"

Godfrey ground his teeth and set his jaw as he considered the jynerul's words.

"Get them to the caves."

"Good," Tyku said, turning towards the doors.

He bellowed out to the officers clustering around him.

"Get all battlemages out on the wall. Make ready the trebuchets."

The rest of his orders were drowned out by distance, the roar of dragons, and the carnage of the city.

Meristal couldn't believe her eyes when she burst through the doors of the castle and into the courtyard. She stood in awe as the last bit of rock formation enveloped the city. Despite the trembling ground, none of the buildings suffered any structural damage besides the ones the dragons attacked.

Running steps sounded behind her, and she turned. Resentment rose up in her, seeing Tyku coming out of the front doors, but she cast those foolish emotions away.

Now wasn't the time for petty squabbles.

"What happened?" Meristal asked Tyku as he drew close.

He shook his head.

"I don't have the faintest notion, Meristal."

The rock formation in front of them moved, and from within came another, several stones moving together. It lumbered near, and they began backing up.

"Good evening," a deep, slow, echoing voice said.

Meristal, unsure of what to do, took a few hesitant steps closer.

"Good evening," she said back.

"I've come from far with my companions. I'm Rawk."

"Rock?" Meristal echoed, ensuring she heard him right.

"Yes, Rawk. I was sent to provide protection."

"By whom?"

"A little nephiliam called Starriace."

Chapter 56: Valley of The Dead

Inescapable nightmares still plagued Starriace whenever she slept.

They had evolved, too.

The lunatic with a painted face and scars all over his skin, haunted her in a way that marred her soul. Without the paint to make him seem comical, his image would be abhorrent to behold. The jester cackled and danced about as he pulled a knife from his flamboyant harlequin suit.

His eyes hid behind a veil of a cherry-stained mane. He mounted a fallen victim but looked up to Starriace. His lifeless eyes, filled with madness, bored into hers, and he smiled a most charming grin.

"Wake up, little homugon, wake up," he sneered in his nasal voice.

The nefarious leer widened as he slid the blade into a victim's throat. Blood spilled from the incision, and the court jester coated himself in the still-warm fluid while drawing glyphs on the floors. As he caroused, Starriace observed his three companions, ones she hadn't seen before—not in their entirety.

There was a lithe woman with sorrow etched on her beautiful face, but even her attractiveness couldn't smooth her hideously bent nose. Next to her, an enormous man stood a few heads taller than the court jester. His massive, crossed arms, thick chest, and broad back accented his physically dominating presence. Beside him, a pathetic man with gaunt features stood in the shadow of his towering bulk. His frail frame with lanky limbs displayed a weakness that Starriace couldn't find in his cold, calculating eyes.

He was a man who contemplated the mysteries of the universe.

Finished with the symbols, the clown and his three companions drew together in a tight semicircle and stalked towards Starriace. As they closed the distance, the court jester cackled and warned through the laughter.

"You'll not stop me. Your world will end in chaos. No one can stop the Jackal."

Her eyes snapped open.

She blinked a few times, adjusting to the pale light, and glanced to Cal who lay beside her. He didn't stir. Rolling from the covers, she stood and lowered them over his sleeping form. She glanced at the swords, Judgement and Salvation, and decided to leave them where they lay.

With careful steps, she tiptoed through the cluster of bodies and worked her way to the valley.

The journey here had been long and arduous. Their fast pace and heavy reliance on magic to sustain them left them all fatigued and exhausted. After eating, they drew lots for the watch and slept even though the suns wouldn't set for hours.

Now, twilight encroached.

She stopped on the cusp of the Valley of the Dead. Seemed like a lifetime ago when she came here. The fine, powder-ash stretched out to the horizon.

She sent tendrils of her essence out behind her. Her elyf companions slept in fitful bursts.

Funny, they used to be tools and nothing more. Now, they're almost friends.

Their efforts kept them from death.

Starriace's eyes swept out to the distance. A gentle gust of wind rippled across her face, teasing a stray strand out of place.

"The Jackal," she whispered to herself.

The name sent shivers down her spine. Now, she wished she would've grabbed the blades, for comfort more than anything. It almost felt unnatural to not be carrying them.

"Can't sleep?" Ama Ka's voice called.

The mage jerked, startled.

"No," Starriace said. "It's not that. It's the dreams about what's coming. It's almost like…shadowcasting."

"Shadowcasting?"

Ama's eyes swept the dark horizon.

"What's coming?"

Starriace cocked her head, pursing her lips, trying to figure out the best way to explain it. How could she take a high concept that she barely understood and give her the laymen terms?

"Shadowcasting is seeing a possible future but altering it at the same time. As far as what's coming, I don't know. How do I stop something if I can't stand against Xilor?"

The words tasted bitter in her mouth. Somewhere in the back of her mind, the dark voice sneered at her weakness.

At the utterance of her deficiency, the world turned dark, the same smothering darkness that had enveloped the world before. An intense heat rippled across them. The ground shook with tremendous force, threatening to tear everything asunder.

Starriace fell to the ground. She heard movement from Ama, but couldn't see her. Like before, as soon as it began, the darkness, heat, and shaking faded.

The sleeping elyves shot to their feet as the last of the tremors dissipated.

A faint, nasally voice lingered in Starriace's mind.

"I'm coming."

Not for the first time, she wondered if she was the only one who could sense the world turning dark, as if it was localized to her, and the elyfian saw due to their proximity. She couldn't imagine how everyone else would react if it went dark for everyone.

"Damn the Underworld!" Ahn Bael grunted.

Cal muttered something about it not being the Underworld, but Ahn's mother and father having a tumble in the sheets. A groggy titter rose from the group, but Ahn turned red, his fists clenching at his sides.

"Quiet!" Iddrial said.

Starriace noticed the dynamic that formed in the group between her and Iddrial. She led them, but Iddrial commanded them.

Starriace turned her eyes back to Ama. She swallowed.

"The darkness? What I've been dreaming? They're connected. Something's coming, but I don't know what."

Ama nodded and helped her stand. The group waded closer to the two women.

"We need to find out what's causing this and stop it from happening again," Ama Ka said.

"Yeah, but what is it?" Fir Fera asked.

"Haven't the foggiest," Ru Sol said with a yawn.

"Wait, you mean this hasn't ever happened before?"

"No, not in our time, never," Ru said. "Why?"

"I don't know," Starriace conceded. "But I've got a bad feeling about this."

"Yeah, well, if we had an army …" Ahn muttered.

"I don't think an army would help us," Iddrial said. "Nothing that I know of, other than some majestic being or myth, can cause the world to shake with darkness."

"What do the myths say?" Starriace queried.

Iddrial shrugged and shook his head.

"Well, the elyves believe in vile creatures trapped in the Underworld, homugons, the opposite of archangels. Instead of wisdom and benevolence, you have depravity, malevolence, and chaos."

Chaos.

The single word exploded into Starriace's mind, triggering the dream, the Jackal's warning.

Her resolve hardened, aware of what she must do. With her thousands, she could save so many lives. A risen army might be vile, but the alternative of Xilor's dominance wouldn't bode well for the people of Ermaeyth. The dark lord wouldn't stop at Ralloc or the continent of Ernrul.

His next victim would be Ermaeyth, and he'd said as much.

Starriace turned her back on the elyves and stepped into the valley as the sunlight's last whispers glowed on the southern horizon.

"Ava?" she called to her familiar.

"Here, Mistress," came the near-immediate response.

It's almost as if she can read my thoughts.

A ripple of embarrassment shot through the mage as she remembered that Ava *could* read her innermost musings.

"Bring them."

"As you command, but we must hurry, I have news."

No sooner than Ava finished the words, the sky littered with hundreds of new stars—no, thousands!—all listing above her. She could almost hear the hushed wind as thousands of wings beat rapidly. Their small movements made music on the wind.

"Thank you for coming," Starriace addressed. "I'm eternally grateful you've chosen to come and help."

"My lady," one fairy spoke, "what matter are we attending?"

The lie almost caught in her throat, but the deception was paramount. If she told them the truth, they'd refuse, but once she had their magic, she could do with it as she pleased.

"The end goal is fortifying the defenses of Divinity Enigumas. The war has sent Ralloc reeling. Xilor may claim victory. That is an outcome we must acknowledge and accept as forgone. When he does, what will happen? Many will die in a great purge. I know; he told me when he tried to recruit me."

Her eyes swept the vast swarm of fairies.

"Xilor may find entertainment in the slaughter of what he calls the impure, but eventually he'll turn his attention to the young. In his clutches, they can be brainwashed through lies and propaganda. Children believe wholeheartedly because they trust to easily. We must do whatever necessary to ensure the safety of our future. We must secure the school. If I can find it having never been there, what about Xilor?"

Her audience kept silent, their unwavering gaze on her.

"When he finds it, he'll slaughter every teacher, student, mother, and father he can find. He won't stop there, razing any knowledge that could dethrone him. He'll have legions of children to raise in his likeness, slaves that bolster his power, purging the unworthy."

She swallowed.

"I'm pleading with you to help me protect our future."

Silence ensued, and she wasn't sure she'd won them over. She hoped she'd chosen the right words, the proper emotions to pull off the deception. The dreams of the Jackal floated forward in her mind. Should she relay that as well?

Just as she opened her mouth to speak, the silent fairies glowed brighter.

"What does this mean?" Starriace asked Ava.

"It means get ready. They're channeling their essence to you."

At first, Starriace couldn't detect any difference. The subtle sensation grew until it was undeniable. Her essence had grown exponentially, but now a vastness crashed into her like ocean waves against rock. With all their energies coursing through her, something new arose within.

The energy churned hot like a furnace. Something dark and sinister squirmed in the pit of her stomach, writhing in agony, yet not fading. The phantom was still inside her.

She glanced up. Half of the fairies had yet to contribute. Did they start in sequence? Was it to make sure they didn't overwhelm her?

Her skin tightened over her entire body. The sensation of scalding sewing needles pierced from hairline to toes. Her vision fluttered, drunk from the endlessness pouring into her.

With this power, she was a god, and they had still so many more to go.

Xilor, who seemed all-powerful, was now insignificant against her might. The slightest twitch could send him into eternal damnation. The Jackal from her dreams quivered in a laughable memory. As her powers grew, she realized her limitations, knew the bounds she'd yet to discover for herself.

And she'd perish if she clung on for too long.

A bright hope died within her. She had seconds, not hours or days.

Power seeped from her pores. Sweat streamed out, her body heat rising. Her essence drifted, clinging by the faintest of tethers. Physical boundaries meant nothing now. Radiance glowed from her hands. Her body fought to keep from being ripped apart. The magic almost overtook her.

She yearned to give in; how weak had she become? Succumbing to the *energy* didn't seem like a terrible way to go.

She once understood what Xilor must've felt like, and now she didn't want to relinquish this power. The temptations were too great, too strong to control. The gratification rivaled and toppled urges of the flesh.

In this joining with the fairies, she understood her faults in refusing to collaborate with Xilor.

She should've accepted.

He wanted to protect the world, and she could've been hailed a hero at his side. But that time had passed, without the possibility of turning back.

Starriace could destroy Xilor right now in one swift stroke, utilizing the thousands that channeled their energy into her. The irritation in her eyes rose to a crescendo. The refulgent crimson shined, bathing the ground in rose tones.

Bright shining beings as luminous as stars filled the sky. All channeled their power now.

She turned her gaze to the ashes of the dead, and she'd be one of them if she didn't release the power. She had heartbeats.

In a surge, she flung the sorcery forward. Bright tendrils of energy ripped through the earth, the ash plumed in its wake. The crackle of mysticism forked out like lightning.

The channeled magic erupted in a violent explosion as it saturated the once-bloodied battlefield. The graveyard quickened beneath her feet. The ash coiled, stirred by otherworldly winds, and encouraged long-forgotten remains to return. Residue reformed into bones and sinew, the bodies reconstituting from the decomposed.

She laughed in fascination, enthralled by her accomplishment.

The energy ran its course, rushing out of her body, and rippled through the valley with arcing waves. The vale bubbled and roiled as dead creatures rose from their slumber. They were soldiers, her soldiers, infantrymen immune to pain and death.

She turned to face the elyves.

"Isn't it wonderful?"

But it wasn't awe she found on their faces, but horror. Did they not see? Did they doubt her? Why didn't they see this as a resolute and imminent victory?

The light from above faded with the suddenness of a snuffed candle.

She spun, looking up to the fairies, but the sky lay devoid of the small creatures. A movement caught her eye, something dark and small fell to the earth below.

She glanced at the valley floor.

In faint moonlight, she caught the glimmer of diamond wings as their small bodies impacted in plumes. The fairies had come to help and drained their magic. They died to fulfill a wish based on lies, to create an army of risen.

Without a thought to consequences, she sacrificed the winged creatures for personal gain, and the cost was too high.

She rushed forward, no longer thinking about her growing army. At the nearest fairy, she fell to her knees and picked up the limp, cold body. A sob escaped her, quiet at first, but then she couldn't hold back the grief.

Her anguish echoed out.

She clutched the body to her. She sent her essence into the fairy, hoping to spark the life in her.

"Starriace," Ama Ka breathed, her hand touching her back.

After a while, Ama quit calling her name, and just sat there and held Starriace while she cried. How much time passed, she couldn't say, but the darkness had deepened and left no trace of the suns.

What'll Judas think of me now? Would he see me as no better than Xilor? What would Meristal think? And poor, Ava, I've killed her, too!

"Don't weep," Ava's voice drifted to her. "I'm still alive."

Starriace searched for the familiar and found her hovering behind. A sad smile etched her tiny face.

Starriace rubbed the tears from her face.

"How's that possible?"

"I'm your familiar; I'm bound to you when outside the Melodic Mountains. Within them, I'm bound to them. I was quite safe. As long as you live, I can't die. We're tethered."

Starriace nodded, choking on the miracle. Without Ava, she'd be lost.

"I never realized…I'm so sorry, Ava. I killed so many. I never meant to. I didn't know this would happen."

A fresh wave of anguish washed over her, and she wept anew.

I'll never forgive myself. Nothing can make up for what I've done.

"You didn't kill them," Ava soothed, "they gave their lives. They chose their involvement. They knew the price and had no reservations."

"But so many died. Can you or the other fairies forgive my transgression?"

Ava grew quiet for a moment.

"Other fairies?"

"The ones that didn't come tonight."

Ava's response was a long time in coming.

"There are no other fairies. I'm the last song."

A wave of nausea ripped through Starriace, and she retched the bile rushing from her stomach. She'd killed them, to the very last. She emptied her stomach again. The contents splashed her boots.

I was so wrong. I'm a monster, just like Xilor.

She had no idea that her actions would cause consequences of this magnitude. In a single stroke, she'd committed genocide, snuffed them out like they never existed. She did what Xilor had never accomplished, passing the threshold from mass murder to genocide.

"How's that possible?" Starriace asked when she wrangled control of her body. "How're all of them dead? There were only hundreds, maybe a thousand here?"

"Two thousand, and yes, that's all there is."

Ava sighed, floating closer.

"We're a dying race, been dying for a long time."

Ava came forward and touched Starriace's face.

"There wasn't much hope. We were but a temporary solution to a much larger problem. Now, that larger problem is in your hands, Starriace. You must find a way to right this."

That was the first time, as far as Starriace could remember, that Ava had called her by name.

Ama Ka, who was still stroking Starriace's back, spoke up.

"What's this much larger problem?"

Ava shook her head.

"I'll tell her, and only her, when the time is right."

Ava's gaze drifted to the growing mass of risen, and Starriace did, too. They were still coming out of the ground. The little creature sighed.

"You need to do something about them, and you need to get to Ralloc."

"Why?" Iddrial asked. "What's wrong with Ralloc?"

"Please, don't ask questions, you're wasting time."

Starriace remembered the familiar saying something about news.

"You," Ava said, pointing to Iddrial, "get to the Enclave. It may be too late to save anyone."

"The Enclave?" Ru Sol asked, her voice filled with worry.

"Yes, Xilor has sent orders for the dragons to attack the Enclave again."

"Again?" Ama Ka leapt to her feet. "We have to go!"

"How do you know so much, bright one?" Iddrial asked Ava.

"I was told."

"By whom?" Iddrial inquired.

"By a lady of shadows," Ava said.

Starriace glanced up at this, watching the exchange. Whatever the lady of shadows was, the elyves seemed to understand.

"The lady—" Ama started.

Iddrial held up his hand to stop her.

"We have to go, now," Fir Ki said, "before we lose everyone and everything!"

Iddrial turned his eyes to Starriace, and he knelt in front of her. His warm fingers touched her face, wiping tears away.

"Only if you say it's okay."

Starriace swallowed. She didn't want them to leave, not like this, seeing her at her lowest point, not without fulfilling a promise she had no right to make.

But she couldn't hold them, not when their people, their entire way of life was being crushed.

"Go."

Before she gained her feet, they were gone, moving faster than she'd ever seen.

We've been going slow this whole time because I couldn't keep up!

Starriace glanced to Ava, then to the risen.

"What're we going to do with them?"

Ava floated forward, peering at them, and crossing her arms.

"You don't wish to use them against Xilor?"

Starriace shook her head.

"I can't stand to look at them. I can't see them without remembering the cost."

"I can think of a quiet, desolate place to put them, but you must issue the command."

Starriace took a deep, weary breath.

"I still need to deal with Xilor."

"If you break a plow, you send it to a blacksmith. Destroy the blacksmith, the tool stays broken."

Ava had a point. Xilor had to be destroyed to dissipate his legions.

"Go on," Ava urged, "Give the command and send them to the Desert of the Forsaken. No one goes out there. The risen will be out of the way."

Starriace swallowed.

"They're linked to me through Rusem. I must see them away, and I never want to lay eyes on them again."

"If that's the case, you could destroy them, but it'd mean my people died for nothing. Send the risen away, but don't destroy them."

Starriace nodded.

In her mind, through her connection with Ava—the little creature had always been aware of the union, but now that Starriace knew of the link, she could feel the connection as well—she saw Ava's determination and resilience.

"Rusem?" Starriace called, and the lumbering risen came forward. "Rusem, take your risen, and go where Ava tells you. Stay away until I call."

Whether he understood why remained unclear, but he heeded the command. He paused for a moment, sending one last tug between their connection, then she turned away.

"Hurry," Ava urged. "Time's running out."

Ava's mental voice filled her head.

There'll be time to mourn later.

The little creature's resolve to stay strong took the mage's breath away. How could she stand unwavering in light of being the last of her kind?

Starriace took a few steps back from Ava, giving her a small, watery smile and sending her thanks through their link. She hurried over to her possessions, slung the swords on her back, then the backpack. Once her gear was donned, she reached deep, past the familiar Rumigul to the strange magic within her.

The power could sweep past existing boundaries, had the potency to destroy buildings, and kill with the slightest touch.

The familiar blue-mist enveloped her, and she teleported through the Melodic Mountains to the mouth of the Corridor of Cruelty.

Chapter 57: Ralloc Domain

Xilor was cunning, Meristal had to give him that.

The uneasy pact with the elyves didn't last, not with the outright destruction of the Enclave and the blunder at Shadow City. Xilor had driven a wedge in Ralloc's forces, sequestering a portion of the elyfian army and driving the remains from the walls of Ralloc and back into their homeland.

But Staell would come to her aid, fulfilling a promise he made before she'd been removed as consul. Xilor fought on their doorstep, but the unicorns moved to free the elyves at Shadow City. She'd kept the information from Godfrey during his hostile takeover.

A part of her cringed, knowing whatever vampires were still within would die. It'd be a massacre, a genocide. She should feel terrible, but when diplomacy and rescue had failed, they were left with no recourse.

The Krey had been removed from the frontlines as well, and whispers about them reached her ears. They'd been recalled to the Hive and placed under someone else's authority. Whoever the someone else was, she hadn't a clue. They could use the Krey now.

The danger of them loose in the city paled next to the hordes Xilor amassed.

Todd, the young journalist, blundered into her view, but he didn't catch sight of her. He was in too much of a hurry, running off to chase a story.

Probably off to rub elbows with the newest regime. Have we fallen so far, Todd, that we're no longer worthy?

He moved deeper into the castle, and she sighed.

Lagelm had told her and Judas to scrutinize the council. Lagelm narrowed the list of the suspected betrayer to three individuals: Poplu, Kellis, and Capraro.

Ironic, with him coming to us, Judas and I never thought to question Lagelm.

While she doubted Kellis was capable of such treachery, she'd do her due diligence. He'd always been a staunch supporter of Judas's. Lagelm, however, she never doubted. Those black eyes of his, pools like event horizons bore into her every time, sending ice and terror down her spine.

She hated his eyes.

So, she'd study him, too, just in case.

But Poplu and Capraro, she had no doubts. They were slime, their families morally reprehensible, House Poplu more so than the weak-willed and easily-led House Capraro. But she was content to wait, and when suspicions solidified into proof, she'd strike fast, forcefully, and fatally.

The suns dipped below the southern horizon, and Xilor's hordes stirred restlessly. The sudden appearance of the massive rock wall made the camp uneasy.

Xilor more so.

He paced in his massive pavilion, his generals standing, watching him move like an enormous raptor searching for prey. Why did they cling to the useless notion of hope? Did they not see his logic or how pitiful it was to fight the inevitable?

He couldn't blame them. They didn't realize the threat they faced. Logic dictated resistance, and Xilor would've done the same in their situation. He wouldn't roll over and die, not for anyone. He suffered a setback with the wall, but the momentary pause made him stronger.

The world had gone dark twice now, and with each episode, Xilor grew in strength. He could see it; of course, why wouldn't he be able to, not that he was so much…more.

Something otherworldly was happening in Ermaeyth. Powers were at play, awakened since the time before remembering. With each turn of darkness, another part of himself awakened. That, coupled with the cataclysmic event he just sensed involving the Melodic Mountains, meant his body gorged itself on power.

But could others sense it? Would their abilities be altered?

The fairies and the Melodic Mountain. Whatever happened, it was devastating and massive. And something else had happened that he did not expect, the stirring from a time long ago.

The brimstones were in play again, and that meant Starriace had discovered them. Xilor reached out, searching for Judas, and found him within the city. That left only one option: Starriace.

She'd survived.

He reached out, trying to find her faint trace far to the south. It moved just as he saw her, a small flicker. Then, nothing. He couldn't find her despite how much he searched.

Was she coming here? Surely not.

But he remembered what he felt within her presence, the *stones*. They were with her, but she didn't know what they were truly meant for. And it'd all be for naught. She followed the same lie he had, and it'd be to her ruin.

It wasn't until after he…created himself that he discovered the truth. Everything had been off, all his calculations, his count, even their very nature.

He'd been a fool then, and he'd only scratched the surface of what they were: the building blocks of creation itself. In his folly, he walked with one foot in the Underworld and one in the living world.

You can't kill what's already dead.

He needed to finish that quest, but with the knowledge of the threats out there, culling the weakness became the priority. The brimstone quest would take years to complete, and the wasted time would doom Ermaeyth, especially if left unfinished.

He turned back to his lackeys, speaking as he paced.

"Find a way to breach that rock."

"Our battering rams have no effect," one troll spoke up.

"Burn it," Xilor commanded.

"The rock mends itself," another said.

"Send the dragons!" Xilor roared.

"Their fire doesn't penetrate deep enough, and they can't fly through the top without being smashed by the forces inside," another muttered.

Xilor turned, grabbed him by the throat, and dug his skeletal fingers through soft flesh. A sickening squish punctuated the silence, and the goblin fell away.

"I don't want excuses. Find a way, or I'll find successors for you."

A tremor of magic manifested behind Xilor, and he turned as the mirror inside his tent glowed green.

"My lord," a goblin said with a bow. "There's news of Shadow City."

"Speak."

The goblin quivered with fear.

"It's fallen, my lord."

The words rang through his head. His rage came full force. How had Ralloc managed to put so many roadblocks in his path so quickly?

"How?"

The goblin hurried through an explanation. The unicorns had amassed and overrun the vampire's holdfast. Unicorns, when gathered, generate unfathomable light, the vampire's weakness. Against a wall of something so pure and effulgent, they withered away. At night, even though many leagues away, you could see the unicorn valley from afar, a soft glow radiating from their area.

The city was gone, the vampires dead, and the elyves free.

Xilor clenched his fists, feeling the anger course through him. It built, spurring him to action. He exited the tent, and his minions followed on his heels. Each step compounded the fury. Ralloc loomed before him, the rock walls encompassed the city and filled his vision.

With a mighty heave, he poured his anger into his essence. He lashed out. His power ripped through his camp, incinerating all in its path. The conjury hit the wall, the stone fragmenting. He reached out with curled hands and pulled. The rock groaned. With a crushing motion of his fists, the rock splintered, fissures running up and down its length. In one last desperate measure, he flung his arms wide, and the foundation gave way, showering out into thousands of pieces.

A wide gap lay before them. Wide enough for hordes to pour through and gain a foothold.

Xilor heaved from the exertion. His body trembled beneath his robes. He couldn't let his followers detect how much energy he'd used. They couldn't think him weak.

And he felt so very weak in that moment.

He turned his shadowed hood to them.

"There's your opening. Wipe them out. All of them."

His officers nodded and hurried off to follow his orders.

He glanced back at the opening. A finger of worry wormed through him. He shouldn't have done that. He had been conserving his strength for the inevitable confrontation with Judas. If the warlock attacked now, Xilor would perish.

He needed rest.

A dragon landed softly off to the right. Xilor turned and eyed Guthric, the lower king of the dragons.

"Do you want us to move in, my lord?" Guthric's voice hissed.

He could sense his hope, see the quiver of rippling muscles beneath the scales.

"No. Let the army sweep over the city like a plague. I have another task for you. I want the elyves to hurt. Go back to the Enclave and eradicate all those who'd still oppose. Wipe them from the face of Ermaeyth."

Guthric hissed, and a ripple of pleasure came from him.

"All who'd oppose?"

Xilor gave him a single nod.

"All."

Guthric bounded for the air and bellowed out a command. Xilor watched as other dragons rose into the air to follow. He swept his gaze over the camp until he saw Diebach, the higher king. The beast eyed his dragons taking to the sky and bounded after them.

With his army advancing, the dragons going to the Enclave, he needed to recuperate. If he used the rejuvenation spell, he'd feel better, but it'd drain his overall stores.

He required a genuine rest.

Satisfied by the turn of events, he retreated to his tent.

The dragons swooped down from the peaks of the mountains. Xilor had made it clear to Guthric what he wanted: complete annihilation. Many times on the flight over, Diebach tried to call a halt to their headlong rush to the Enclave, but Guthric paid no heed.

He had a mission from his lord.

Xilor made his wishes known, and Guthric would take his shot, his chance at the mantle of higher king. He had to play this smart.

Being the lower king, Guthric allowed Diebach to lead in the destruction. Flames spewed from the higher king's mouth as he swept in. The slaughter commenced, buildings incinerated, the forest burning, and people running, alight in flame.

Guthric waited as the carnage unfolded, conserving his strength. He landed on the edge of the settlement and watched the events unfold. He studied Diebach as the higher king wasted his energy.

The slaughter carried on for a time, and Diebach landed next to Guthric when he finished, tired and weary from the battle and flight.

"What's the matter with you?" Diebach hissed. "I thought you wanted this? A chance for destruction."

"I do," Guthric said. "I just want something else more."

As quick as a viper, he lashed out, and his teeth sank into Diebach's neck.

Chapter 58: The Corridor of Cruelty

The mouth of the Corridor loomed ahead.

Trepidation lanced through her chest. Her lungs burned with anticipation, breath held. Ava urged haste. Would Ralloc fall if she dawdled? She shook aside the fear and anxiety. The last time she intentionally set foot within was in Judas's care.

That seems forever ago.

She heaved, the exertion of the teleport taking its toll on her body. Pins and needles flashed across her skin. What little contents were in her stomach didn't remain there for long. Her head swam, and she fell to all-fours.

Ermaeyth gave an unforgiving tilt. Deep in the pit of her stomach, the dark, inky blackness of the phantom slithered up from the base of her spine.

It's moving!

She realized too late that the teleport exertion didn't weaken her, but the wraith that crawled within her body. It fed on her magic and life. With resigned dignity, she intuited her fate.

If it reaches my heart, I'll die! If it lingers, I'll die.

She didn't have much longer. Would she reach Ralloc before succumbing? Would her presence hinder the war effort? With each use of magic, death slipped closer.

I need to purge it!

The last vestige of fear abated. Why would she dread the Corridor when death, the ultimate cruelty, could be only hours away? She looked to the lightened, southern horizon. Ermaeyth had given way to night while in the Valley of the Dead, but now the suns slinked in the south?

Her journey implied instantaneous travel, but somehow, more than mere moments had passed. Had she spent a day in travel?

How's that possible?

She had no way of knowing, and Judas never mentioned such a possibility. Something was wrong with her magic. Was it the phantom, the fairies' death, guilt, the world going dark twice? There was just no way to tell.

Resolute, she stood and marched into the yawning mouth of the Corridor.

Like the first time she entered, the atmosphere changed, but not as dramatic as before. The muted twilight, the suppressed sounds, everything seemed similar except the oppressiveness. That sense had almost vanished. Sunlight was practically nonexistent during the daytime, but not as bad as traveling in the unbearable pitch of the night. The dusk-like ambiance, the temperature drop, and the mind-dulling yet silent thrum didn't help as she stumbled along the uphill path.

At the top, she came across her first irritant. The Corridor placed a small wooden sign in her path, and like before, a riddle was scrawled across the surface. It read:

Look into the mirror and find what dominates your heart. The problem is doing what you don't see.

The odd puzzle didn't rhyme or make sense. If anything, it was more cerebral than all the others. The sign rippled like heatwaves, and a mirror took its place. She stared into the mirror, transfixed upon her dark countenance.

The recessed area of her eyes was deepened. A glint of deep crimson glittered from within. Her eyes were red, not just the whites, not the iris, the whole thing. Even her pupils were smothered in the hue.

Her skin's pigment grayed to ash tones and neared the pale amethyst of the dark elyves.

She turned away. Despair flickered in her heart. Was this path set? Would she be the next dark lord? She spent her entire journey keeping clear of decisive actions that Xilor would pursue, but there'd been casualties along the way. She didn't have any delusions; her hands and soul weren't pure.

And now, with the dead fairies…she owed Ava so much.

She'd never be done repenting for the atrocity she'd committed, never be finished of the work to repair the damage that had been done, undoing the monster she'd become.

The despair turned to anger and self-loathing. Spinning around, she pulled her wand and lashed out at the mirror. The furnishing shattered into a hundred pieces.

When the light faded, a man stood on the other side. His sudden appearance startled her, and the wand tip flickered to him.

"Who are you?"

He looked almost as spooked as she felt. He dipped his head in haste.

"I, my lady, am Norek."

"What are you doing here?"

"I'm a wanderer of these parts and parts afar, and who might I have the pleasure of addressing?"

He flashed her a smile. She noted that his eyes flickered to the swords jutting over her shoulders.

"Starriace," she said.

Norek bowed low.

"I'm very obliged to meet you. Do you know the way out of this strange place?"

He shivered.

"It's quite disconcerting."

"It's also the fucking creepiest and vilest place on Ermaeyth."

She paused, considering his words, and her eyes narrowed.

"I thought you said you were a wanderer of these parts?"

Where had she seen him before? She had, hadn't she?

"No, my lady, I said 'I'm a wanderer of these parts and parts afar.' I must confess, I'm new to this area, I'm usually far to the south."

"You mean the Melodic Mountains?" Starriace clarified.

"No, the Melodic Mountains are far to the north where I'm from."

Norek regained some of his composure.

"Starriace, right? Would you be agreeable with showing me the way through?"

She paused to consider his dilemma and empathized with him. Not too long ago, she traveled through and was stuck. Judas's intervention made escape possible.

Why did he look familiar?

Still, he was a stranger, and the history between her and men remained riddled with bloodied blemishes. He wasn't Harold, Judas, or even Fife. He'd never measure against Kam. The last time she had been around strange men, it'd cost her dearly. The apprehension tightened in her throat. But he didn't seem to be a threat, and she felt confident she could annihilate him without dilemma.

"I don't know you well enough," she said after her assessment. "I sure as hell don't trust you. I can't say with certainty that helping you would serve my best interests."

"Acquaintance aside, why would you be any more worthy of my trust?"

She snorted.

"Good. As long as we are in accord on that front, and you don't hold me up, I'll help."

"Most agreeable."

She shouldered past him, then once past him, glanced back.

"I've seen you before."

"Yes, at the opening of the Melodic Mountains."

She nodded and turned away, stretching out with her essence. In a perpetual state of panic, Starriace crept through the Corridor, but found it vastly different than the previous encounter, which terrified her all the more.

What evil lurked out there?

When would she stumble upon the twisted doorframe made of root? The words 'Here Madness Dwells' filled her mind, and her soul trembled in remembrance.

This time, the Corridor stretched as grassy hills and rocky ravines with jutting limestone breaking through the vibrant green. This was such a stark contrast from before, but many things had changed since then: the fairies, Xilor, the swallowing darkness...did they affect this twisted place?

On the first visit, the strip of land appeared devoid of life, and only muted and unreal sounds filled the silence. Now, crisp, clean, and almost-cheerful sounds swarmed about her. The mental game protracted the longer she traversed, and the Corridor was winning.

Jittery, she eyed each blade of grass, afraid that over each rock rise the person she feared most would find her. She yearned to battle Xilor, more so than confronting the man who broke her.

Not long after setting off, she had to admit it was too dark to travel anymore. Defeated, she called a halt. Her traveling companion prattled on. His careless and uninterrupted stream-of-consciousness talking made her weary.

She couldn't tell if it stemmed from his tone, his voice, or his excitement for something new.

Maybe he didn't realize what awaited them.

Starriace built a fire, remembering how Judas did it the last time. Afterwards, they sat around the glowing flames, and she basked in Norek's nervous silence, grateful for the absence of his droning. He sat, his back against a log, brooding. Every eerie sound made her twitch in terror.

Was he out there? Mr. Pleasure? Would he come for her again?

While Norek brooded, she contemplated the mystery of the Corridor. Last time, this place tormented her mentally, physically, and emotionally. If she had to guess, only the mental part of it remained. The emotion had yet to cause distress, other than just being here. The elements making up the physical aspects faded as well.

She closed her eyes and willed herself to forget the surroundings for but a moment.

Kam filled her mind. He and his wife, Lily. Her belly would be swollen large by now. How long until Lily gave birth? Starriace went to Ralloc not long ago, and Lily had appeared normal, and that meant she wasn't far along. How long had Starriace been gone? A moon turn? Two?

Her gaze tracked to her new associate, and she scrutinized him. As part of her calming technique, she took great care in analyzing and learning anything about him. He wore a light cloth fabric for his inner robes and a dark brown outer robe. At his waist, a brown leather belt hung snug. A worn traveling cloak —patched in several places—settled over his garments. When new, it must have cost a handful of chips.

Most notably, he didn't possess a wand.

The only other thing of note besides the pack he carried lay not far from him. A long wooden staff rested within arm's reach. The rod was straight, slim at the bottom, and grew fatter at the top. The smooth staff, sanded with care and stained, boasted intricate carvings of swirling patterns along the length. The foreign engravings eluded her knowledge as to their origins.

Perhaps it was a language?

He dug through his pack and pulled out a glass orb. His eyes flickered to her, noticing but paid no heed, and stared into the sphere.

The stranger's eyes widened at what he saw within. Another quick glance in her direction. His brown eyes were calculating, measuring her with more than the briefest sense of worry. He continued to flick his eyes between the two.

"What's that?" Starriace asked, indicating the orb.

She plucked a stick from the fire and stirred the coals with it.

"My orb. It tells time."

She caught the slight quiver in his voice, his hesitation. He'd just lied to her. She decided to play along. For now.

"The hour of the day?"

"Yes and no."

"Okay, then what does it do?"

"It shows me things, from the fog of things to come, or the things that were. Moments of time."

Starriace frowned. She tried to hide her skepticism but failed. Why didn't she believe him? Harold had taught her shadowcasting. Was this another form?

"It shows the future?"

His head bobbled from side to side.

"The orb is beyond your understanding."

Did he imply her ignorance?

"Try me!"

He gave a tight smile, and then a quick and noisy breath. He climbed to his feet and plopped down beside her. She noted that he left the staff behind.

"This orb," he started, "holds no knowledge or truth or secrets, nor what *is* to come."

"Then, why waste your time?"

"Because it does show you what may happen in the time to come."

Shades, he's talking about Shadowcasting.

He brought the sphere closer.

"This shows you what you *want* to see and what you *fear*. In a sense, you glimpse a future truth of what you wish, almost as if willing it into existence. Understand?"

"So, this shows your desires and fears?"

Starriace reached for the orb.

"But not that it'll happen?"

He let her take the sphere.

"As a rule, yes. Try, and tell me what you witness."

She held the glass ball close to her face, and the clearness turned to a milky-white fog. She sat still, gazing, hoping for a manifestation. The opaque cloud gave way as Ralloc—what may have been Ralloc—took its place. She couldn't tell, she only had descriptions from Judas to recount.

Her one-time, ill-advised incursion didn't count.

Wherever it was, once a beautiful and massive city rose to impressive heights. Now, the shambles of established desolation stood, ruins as far as the eye could see. How? Did an enormous battle take place and everyone died in an instant? An unexplained phenomenon? Smoke rose from crumbling, charred spires. Trees and grass gave way to coarse sands as black as the abyss.

Everything, everyone…gone.

The image fell away and reformed. A lone figure stood wrapped in heavy black robes. The silhouette turned, and Xilor stared back.

Did he have anything to do with the destruction?

The image drew closer until only the upper half of his body showed. He reached up to pull back the hood and reveal his face.

I'm finally going to be able to glimpse him!

The hands wrapped around the edges and threw back the hood in one swift motion. Instead of Xilor, Starriace stared at her own reflection, a face distorted by rage, pain, and anguish. The entirety of her eyes glowed red, and her skin cracked in ashen fissures. Scars stretched across her face, racing down her neck and under the folds of her robes.

In her hands, she twirled Judas's wand. A souvenir? Trophy?

Next to her, the new consul of Ralloc, Godfrey, stood with a military rigidness. A twisted and blackened crown of forged thorns sat aloft on his head. A gold chain clung tightly around his neck.

On Starriace's shoulder, Ava perched, as dark and twisted as her master. The bodies of the elyfian lay around her feet.

The vision gave way to the milky white fog, and nothing came again.

She blinked a few times, realizing she hadn't in a long time, and shuddered. A sickness crept over her, dread, recognizing that a part of her—the portion she kept denying existed—wanted the conception to come true.

The other half was repulsed.

"What did you discover?" Norek asked.

She swallowed, and her eyes widened when a voice spoke in her mind.

To be the Bearer of Secrets is to be alone.

The book spoke a warning. Did it not want her to say anything? To keep silent? Did she witness something Norek shouldn't? Or did she shadowcast like Harold had taught, and the orb only allowed her a mechanism in which to see.

"Nothing," she said.

"Odd."

She couldn't tell if he believed her or not, but she didn't risk looking at his face.

"So, the gazing," she said, changing the subject, "you said it shows desires and fears?"

"Yes, quite."

He took his prized object back.

"Like reading a mind, it can be misleading and perilous."

"I can read minds, sort of."

She noticed his lingering gaze. Rusem had begun teaching her, and when she attempted to repair his memories, she gleaned a better understanding.

"I haven't had much practice. Probably not that great…"

"Shall we test your claim?"

A hollow and nervous laugh escaped him. He stood and returned to his previous seat near his staff. The distance gave him bravado.

"You probably want to know some things about me. Let's test how good you are."

The corner of her mouth twitched in a smile. She settled her mind. Unblinking, her breath came slow and calm like her strokes at the edges of his mind. His mental shield vibrated with strength.

Circularly, she probed random spots along that route. The ironclad shimmer keeping her out trembled. She worked to the back of his mind and down the backside. A little more than halfway down, Starriace found an entry. An unguarded door, an unbeknownst passage.

She entered tentatively.

"You're a traveler?"

"Yes, I told you that."

"But you lied," she whispered the accusation. "You're not a traveler at all, but you are seeking something. A path of discovery."

His dark brown eyes dropped to his orb as if it provided refuge. She braced for his defensive measures. His shields thrummed with redoubled strength. Random thoughts flashed between them.

A distraction, nothing more.

She dug her claws into the original idea she'd first gleamed. Memories of his childhood flashed, the vigorous way he took a naked woman on a beach, a wedding feast he attended and became intoxicated, two different women he made love to in an inn, a horse gone lame, the sails of a ship—all these and more flashed through to keep a memory out of reach.

The harder he tried to hide, the more he dwelled on it. Unwittingly, he illuminated the trail. A few times he attempted to shock her with memories of sex, but her promiscuity with Kam and Lily dulled her to such tactics.

His walls redoubled around the probe, but it didn't affect her. She was already inside.

"You're searching for…a *woman?*" said Starriace, perplexed.

He tried to refortify the walls.

"Yes."

"If you don't want me to continue …"

He didn't respond, but she felt the wariness. She closed her eyes and probed deeper. His complex mind reminded her of a labyrinth, of the Corridor. Interlacing thoughts crisscrossed in every direction, but she picked up on the original reflection and continued.

How far could she follow it?

"She was taken from you?"

"Yes."

"That's why you search for her."

"Yes, that's right."

"But why?"

She was asking herself more than him. He didn't answer, so she continued.

"Many of your thoughts dwell on her. One would almost call it love, but…"

She probed deeper, pushing past his perceived mental barriers. The deeper she plunged, the more resistant his subconscious became. She was an invader, a pathogen that didn't belong. Her brow frowned as she strained to find the woman in his memories.

"Strange."

"What is?" he asked with a shaky breath.

She could hear the strain in his voice and reassessed him with her inner eye. He shook as if chilled and paled from fever. A sheen broke across his forehead. Her mental probe had consequences.

In a breathy revelation, she told him.

"I can find no trace of this woman."

"I know."

"How can that be?"

"It's a long story, and I don't wish to share," he grunted and shook harder. "Please, release your hold."

She complied with immediacy and let the last traces fade.

He gasped, taking a deep breath, and when he had a few moments, she probed him again but with words.

"Why do you look for her?"

"I have a desire to. I just *need* to look for her."

Starriace noted his voice and body language. Admitting the truth aloud had cost him, but he concealed something, too.

"What happens when you find her?"

"I've never thought that far ahead."

He gave a bark of a laugh.

"I haven't allowed myself the delusion of possible joy. That'd be too hard for me to handle, if I never found her."

"Your drive and ambition to find her is admirable," Starriace admitted after a few moments.

She appreciated her newest acquaintance in a different light, stood in awe of faithfulness to the quest, to a woman he'd never laid eyes on. She hoped to one day find a man that'd do the same for her, if there'd even be time for that.

"Admiration and ambition can be just as bad as good," Norek said. "It's about the desire behind the decisions we make. If too much grabs hold of you, well, folly has led to darker places than wisdom. I pray to the spirits it isn't so with me."

"Darker places?" Starriace repeated, thrown by the sudden correlation between the two.

She swallowed hard, realizing how close his arrow came to inflicting a wound.

"How so?"

"Ambition isn't evil, but ambition without restraint can be."

"I disagree. You'd link ambition to corruption? It's more complicated than that. Nothing's ever that simple."

"But isn't it? What's ambition?"

"A determination."

"Yes. You can have a determination to do well, but I've never met a soul driven to do good. It's a choice, not an impulse."

"Yes, a choice to be ambitious, not vile."

She tried to comprehend his philosophical stance. She wasn't evil, was she?

How can I be evil when I've always had the best intentions at heart?

You had the best intentions for those three men, didn't you? the voice sneered back.

"What makes a person ambitious?" he asked.

"Power. Most sentient beings are ambitious about power, through which they gain knowledge."

"Keep going."

"Does it not stop there?"

"No. Keep going."

She sighed.

"Must I?"

He gave a small smile.

"I suppose not. I'm sorry. I rarely get to talk with someone on a philosophical level."

She nodded but didn't say anything.

"Traveling the world gives you a different perspective," he said. "Makes you realize how ignorant you are."

"I guess it doesn't make you more in touch with rudeness."

He smiled.

"I didn't mean you. I meant me. And truth is often a rude inconvenience."

She set aside her irritation to focus on what he said. Was she ignorant and couldn't tell? Norek's musings brought Judas to mind. Both even carried similar physical traits. Norek seemed odd, eccentric. Perhaps Starriace never realized Judas's oddity, having been exposed to him first. When Norek spoke, she heard Judas's voice. The younger man's views were based on logic, his meaning wise beyond his years.

He and Judas would have a lot to discuss, and she found that she could, too.

"Perhaps," she admitted. "For now, I'll retire. Tomorrow's going to be a long day."

Especially if you're going to talk the entire time.

Dawn came too early for both travelers. Starriace stood and stretched and chased away the early morning chill. Her movements arced with energy, and they shouldn't. In the heart of the Corridor, nothing was invigorating. Anger, anxiety, or depression should've impacted their movements. Waking in a good mood made her cautious.

Their morning trek passed in silence with little more than grunts and groans and aimless ambling, and by the gods, Norek kept quiet. Thankfully, he, like her, lacked the appropriate cognitive functions in the early morning hours.

"Are you an arysto where you're from?" she inquired half an hour later.

"No. Not a sire or arysto. Where I'm from, those aren't our titles."

She glanced back, watching him work his way up the trail. He used his staff to forge the path. The environment hadn't changed overnight, which she expected. The Corridor stretched a mere two leagues in length, but with all the backtracking and twists and turns, the end hardly came in a straight line.

The morning journey defied time and her internal clock. Since invading his mind the night before, Norek kept to himself, although he did mutter to his palmed orb throughout the day.

Starriace's mind drifted to Ava. The mage had killed every fairy. The weighty burden hung heavy and rent her heart open; each reflection bled the wound anew, a fateful decision that eradicated the collective instantaneously.

All were gone.

Starriace marveled how Ava clung to life by their bond. When Norek spoke, it snapped her back to the moment.

"Who's that?" he asked.

She spun and caught him nodding up the trail. Starriace turned and ice formed in her heart. Panic constricted her throat. A flush of heat and frothy rage washed over her.

Ahead, a massive man, both in height and thickness, stood blocking their way. His shaved head gleamed, and his shirtless chest glistened with sweat. His tight pants were barely fastened around his bulk. A pale white scar just below his left eye shined. The discoloration extended to his jawline; his face glowed with menace.

Shades of the Underworld!

Her eyes went wide at the sight of him, her nostrils flared.

No fucking way!

"My name's Mr. Pleasure," he called in a booming voice. "You shall call me by no other name than Mr. Pleasure."

Waddling forward, he reached across his body and drew a long, curved knife. The wicked steel cleared its sheath. Another ponderous step.

"Should you call me anything but my name, I'll knock out your teeth with the hilt of my blade."

"Who's Mr. Pleasure?" Norek asked.

From the moment Starriace laid eyes on him, she relived every endured nightmare. The flash of his hands on her, each kiss of steel, every atrocity, all the tortures, humiliations, and the vile deaths suffered by his hands. Though the events transpired in her mind, the inflicted scars left a lifetime of affliction.

Rage—pure, unequivocal, and fulsome—rose within her. The pressure built and the animosity surged like a geyser. A red shade fell over her vision. The blood rage painted the world in scarlet flame.

The initial terror triggered in her silence, and she tingled with magic and fury. She let it build. When it threatened to plateau, repressed memories fueled it further.

He lumbered forward, so close.

The power swelled, trembling to be released. He was just a few strides away.

"I've seen your pretty face before, haven't I?" he leered.

Just the sound of his voice, the smell of his nasty, disgusting body unraveled her soul.

"I believe the last time you managed to escape. We can arrange a little visit for you and the boys…"

She let out a scream of pain, of acrimony, and released the devastating magic within. The powerful blast scorched the dirt where Mr. Pleasure stood. One massive volley that sent echoes and subsequent shocks through the landscape in rippling waves.

At the edge of her awareness, she noted Norek. The outburst flung him backward, the concussion throwing him to the ground. He managed to climb to his knees but no further. Her power hammered down on him as it obliterated Mr. Pleasure.

The magical blast subsided, but the rage didn't fade so quickly.

Uprooted, twisted trees lay strewn. The earth churned with broad swaths of obliterated grass. Boulders still floated in the air, orbiting above in a circular motion, while others crumbled from the inside out. She felt the madness festering in her mind, and she had no doubt it shined in her eyes.

Raising her hand over her head, she drove it down, sending the massive projectile crushing his limp, rotund form. The rock shattered at the impact, and she hurled another. Cracking open, she dashed another, and another, and another.

Five shattered boulders later, Starriace stumbled, drained of rage and magic. A slick and bloodied gloss covered the ground. Not a solitary piece of her antagonist remained. Free of her hold, Norek stumbled and fell forward before rushing to her side.

He dropped beside her as the world shook.

Norek screamed at her, trying to break through to her.

"Starriace! He's dead and gone!"

And the world still shook.

"That's not me!"

A sizzling blackness devoured the planet in the absolute night. A deep, throaty rumble that sounded both like thunder and laughter echoed out. In an abrupt reversion, the heat dissipated, and the treacherous shadow receded.

"What in the spirits was that?"

"I'm going to be sick," Starriace warned right before she heaved. Wiping the last vestige of sick away, the phantom stirred, shuffling up her spine and slipping between the ribs.

I have to get this out! There must be some way to purge it.

Something else stirred within her, beyond the phantom's irk. She sent her essence inward, trying to ascertain the alien sensation.

Her eyes snapped open upon discovery.

"What?" Norek asked. Worry filled his voice.

She glanced at him and shook her head. She couldn't tell him. It's not like he could do anything, and he was a stranger after all.

"It's nothing. Sorry."

She bottled the rising emotions, wouldn't weep in front of a stranger. Starriace had chosen to forget Mr. Pleasure, to shutter him in the darkest nook of her mind. Repression worked thus far, coming to terms with the time spent in his dungeon.

She could hold it together for a little while longer.

She struggled to her feet.

"My friends say they've never seen that happen before," she answered his earlier question. "It troubles them as it does me."

A troubled expression crossed his face, and he repeated her words in a slow, questioning draw.

"Your friends?"

She smirked at his worried expression.

"They're elyfian, and obviously, they aren't here with us now."

Norek nodded, relieved, then looked out at the remains of her destruction.

"Who was that guy?"

"Someone I don't like to talk about. Let's just say he made me suffer."

She turned to what remained of Mr. Pleasure, but he'd vanished. The blood and gore had disappeared. A flicker of uncertainty rose within, but Norek had seen him. Mr. Pleasure had been here. The ground, trees, and surroundings were ravaged by her magic and rage, but he was gone.

"I've got a bad feeling about this," she said.

"What?" Norek stepped closer. "Oh, shit."

"Yeah."

"Why's he gone?"

"I don't know."

"Could it be the darkness? He was here before, then it came, and now he's gone."

Starriace stretched out with her essence, but the peculiar sensation associated with the Corridor had vanished. In fact, she couldn't feel anything.

The Corridor was dead.

"I don't know," she conceded.

Norek arched a brow.

Her legs trembled, and she reached down to stifle the shaking.

"You're lucky," he said. "If you deplete your essence, you'll die. It's almost impossible to expend it all, I know, but it has happened. Perhaps a touch of restraint in the future?"

Her brow frowned. She had never heard of that. If true, why didn't Fife or Judas ever say anything? Her legs trembled again.

Norek stepped closer.

"Let me help you."

The old mantra flared in her mind.

I'll never be weak or helpless again.

He threw her arm around her shoulder and helped her walk. Over the next rise, Cape Gythmel, or what was left of it, stretched out to greet them. The horrific and charred ruins sprawled on the horizon. She knew a war waged on but had never seen the devastation firsthand.

"By unholy spirits!" Norek gasped.

Xilor will atone for this atrocity with his life. I swear!

After her moment of silence, Starriace teleported them to Ralloc, leaving behind the inner demons she'd slain, and searching for one more.

Chapter 59: Xenomene

Xenomene untied the drawstring of her shorts, pulled them down, and sat on the chamber pot.

She tried not to breathe in the lovely aroma of her fellow Krey. Now, she'd wait.

Stealth and subtlety were never a strong suit for Xenomene. In fact, she detested those traits. Born in the month of the Inferno, her ardent and excessive philosophy remained: do it right, be grand, or not at all. To survive, to exact revenge, she'd work within the confines she'd been given just this once. More than her life was on the line, again, and she wouldn't risk them in a cavalier way.

But their new heir? He had to die.

The ko-dons sought Smokey's death for the murder of Daniel, their true heir, and for usurpation, placed in power by Godfrey. Xeno agreed despite their fixation on flawed priorities, and her motives differed.

Smokey sat in *her* chair.

She was the rightful heir now, not some fat fucking slob from the Isles with sausage fingers and moles resembling engorged ticks. No, he was grotesque and horrid. The son of a bitch was *farting* in her chair. Now that he'd desecrated the would-be throne, it'd need replacing. First order of business after removing him would be to burn the fucking thing.

Fucking politicians!

Smokey assumed command, but the Krey didn't answer to politicians before, and she'd be damned if they'd start now.

She yearned for his death for murdering Daniel. In that regard, she was in accord with her fellow ko-dons. The truest sin remained unacknowledged, weeding out a man of exceptional skills, both with the sword and in bed. Lastly, and almost inconsequentially, she hadn't forgiven the slob for his transgression during their first meeting.

After Daniel's death, his advances and overtures became more aggressive. She wouldn't put it past him to order her to his bed. It'd happen, and sooner rather than later.

And for that, he had to die.

In agony.

What's it with guys and my ass?

Perhaps they were right, and it was her best feature.

It certainly isn't my face or tits.

If she ever did have a baby, it'd probably starve, poor thing.

By now, word had spread of her indiscretions with the late heir, or her spending time with Slurp, and for the first time, she didn't care. She enjoyed the attention, seeing as men ignored her in the past—for the most part. Now, she was coveted, but other women gazed upon her with scorn.

For fun, and to twist the knife in Tiny, she played it up, often speaking with random men, attractive or otherwise. The last thing she wanted was to become predictable. Though they engaged with enthusiasm, she never let it carry on for more than a few sentences before sauntering off.

No matter where she moved, heads turned. It was an enjoyable game of cat and mouse, and the men didn't realize she stalked them like prey.

Omen resided in her quarters. Every night, he curled up alongside, purring as they fell asleep. His presence put a smile on her face, both going to sleep and upon waking, regardless of their current predicament. The situation was much worse than an ordinary usurper.

Smokey kept all weapons sequestered and guarded. This wouldn't stop them for long but acted as a deterrent. An uprising could be quelled in quick order by a few loyal Islander Krey under his sway. Such actions needed careful and precise timing. At this point, she was glad Bitcher was gone. It'd be a gamble on where his loyalties lay. Jakeb was devoted to her but Bitcher? He served only himself.

Smokey also didn't allow the ko-dons to gather in groups of two or more. They were always watched, segregated unless in a meeting with their usurping, murderous heir.

Hence where the stealth and subtlety came in.

Grumbles trickled in, and it began the day of the murder, but as time passed and restrictions piled up, they came flooding.

Whenever they could, the ko-dons met in secret. Most of the time, this meant the communal lavatory like now. It offered little privacy. Small, half-walls presented some concealment, but she could turn and see the food stuck in the teeth of the person next to her. A simple lean in, and you could examine someone's glory. To the regret of the ko-dons, this offered the only place with ample opportunity to meet.

Xeno sighed in annoyance, her legs numb and tingling from sitting on the cold chamber pot. She glanced down at the bunched shorts around her ankles. Stallion saw her go into the lavatory. The sliver of patience she clung to strained. Each knew to never enter unless they needed the facilities. The men were cruder than she, defecating while they whispered, but she had more class, and waited until they left before concluding business.

Today, she couldn't.

Perturbed, but unable to fight nature, she gave into her bodily functions. As she did, Adder walked through the door, spotted her, and took the adjoining chamber pot.

He sat down, and she couldn't stop. Flatulence escaped her as he situated himself.

"You're shitting now?" he asked. "Spirits, that's disgusting! Girls don't shit!"

"Listen, asshole, if you hurried the fuck up, I wouldn't have waited so fucking long. Now, you're just going suffer as I suffered through you all."

Adder chuckled.

"God, I can see why the—er—Daniel liked you so much. Aside from fucking you, I mean."

She rolled her eyes.

"He liked me before we fucked, and I guarantee I liked him more afterward. What's the word from Stallion?"

Adder didn't say anything for a moment, and she grew impatient.

"Well?"

The question was punctuated by Adder moving his bowels.

"Invisible gods, you couldn't wait?."

"Hey, everyone has to at some point!"

"Except girls?"

"Except girls," he confirmed with a nod. "We're meeting tonight, all of us."

"How are we managing that?"

"We're not, you are."

"How do you figure?"

"Tonight, in the common room, you're getting stupid drunk. And then, you're going to ask the Mind and Tiny to take you upstairs to fuck. Make sure it's loud, and everyone sees you."

She narrowed her eyes. The urge to scream obscenities at him almost passed her lips when he held up a finger.

"Wait."

His bowels released again and Xeno turned away in revulsion. She knew everyone had to, but it was another thing to sit next to a person defecating. If she was going to suffer through theirs, they could suffer through hers.

"The louder you make it," he said, "the better. We need everyone watching you."

"Loud in saying that I'm fucking, or loud while fucking? And why the fuck would I do this?"

"Are you daft? We know about the men taking bids now that you've come out of your celibacy stint. Do you not realize how many waited for you? Shades, you *are* daft. Since you were with Bitcher and Slurp, more men want you now, though, after today, you can scratch me off the list."

"What list?"

He reached for the paper, disinclined to comment further on the subject, and continued.

"Once everyone's watching you, they won't be looking at us getting into place. This is a massive operation we're undertaking. There are more conspirators in movement for this than you realize."

"You don't expect me to actually—?"

"Would that be a problem?"

"Yes! Tiny isn't for me. Neither is the Mind, though he's better than Tiny. I didn't realize the ko-dons wanted to whore me out."

"Don't worry, it's taken care of."

He concluded his business and stood, pulling up his trousers.

"One more thing," he said, leaning over the low wall. His hand darted in, grabbed the paper, then he bolted for the door.

"You fucking shit, I'm going to kill you!" she hissed at his retreating form.

Remembering he had paper, she stood, leaned into the next stall, and grabbed his. Finished, she left in a sour mood and fought the urge to laugh at his antic. She might've done the same had she thought of it first. It was the small things, the little laughs that mattered now that Daniel was taken and the future seemed bleak.

She was about to enter her room when Smokey spotted her and called out.

"Where are you off to in a hurry? Now would be a good time to—"

"Nope," she interrupted, "just got back from the privy."

She slammed the door to her room. Throwing the bolt, she moved away and laid face down on the bed. Omen jumped up and poked his cold, wet nose on her neck and purred. She smiled. He curled up and warmed her bare arm.

The other ko-dons only fixated on the short-term goal to their predicament. She thought long term. There was more than just killing Smokey and removing the shackles Ralloc had bound them with. Once the consul found out, he'd return in force for revenge.

The Krey occupying the Hive had the advantage. At House Eti, they could determine how and when to engage their enemy. Godfrey could deposit legions on their doorstep, and the Krey could decimate them. But Godfrey would be aware of their vulnerability to magic.

She arched a brow and stared up at the ceiling.

It's probably too much to ask for the consul to remain oblivious to the fact, isn't it?

If he was, the master jynerul wasn't. With battlemages in the mix, the losses would be substantial. The killing field and the narrow stairs would choke their numbers to where the Krey could cut them down in droves.

But before that, they needed armor and weapons, which meant taking the keys and firing up the forges. No matter if they worked through all hours without stopping, it still wouldn't be enough time. At this point, they only had enough to armor a mere third of their numbers. Even with minimal losses, they'd lose weapons and armor faster than they could replace them.

Once Xenomene took over, they'd need a massive influx of Krey. Having fresh recruits show up whilst at odds with Ralloc lacked feasibility.

We have all the new recruits we'd need right here.

The idea built slow but developed with gradual certainty. She'd take a leaf out of her own book and do what she did in Dlad City, seek out and destroy the runes that kept their lust in check. With more Krey having sex, the possibility they'd birth bloodlust children multiplied.

She could breed their army.

Bloodlust wasn't considered hereditary, but the odds were greater if one parent was a Krey. With two, it was almost a sure thing.

She couldn't order a few men to take what few women they had; the gene pool needed diversity. Some women had to take multiple men. It wasn't fair that some would get to partake and others didn't. But then again, it wouldn't be fair for the women to take so many men.

We're fucking Krey, they'll take as many as necessary. It's not like we keep count. Besides me.

Breeding an army meant she'd need to do her duty, too. Sex was one thing, but none of the men in the Krey was someone she'd want to have a child with.

Except Slurp.

None appeared overtly terrible, at least the ones she wouldn't mind enjoying, but they weren't the kind of men she yearned to spawn a little version of herself with. It was an enormous step. She'd need to figure out who she'd take for a mate.

She sighed.

The ko-dons thought themselves smart, coming up with a scheme to whore her out, but a gaping hole glittered madly. People would be listening for moans, imagining themselves as the one making her pant. How was she going to meet with the other ko-dons and pull off a convincing sex escapade?

If she was going to fuck, she wished to pick the potential mates, but Adder had spoken. The Mind and Tiny. The latter filled her mind, and the thought was revolting, and it started with his personality. After Bitcher, she didn't want anything remotely similar. She'd tangled with the Mind before, questing him at Cape Gythmel and in Dlad City.

Tiny was a different story.

Before his pouty behavior, she could admit to tension between them, but she couldn't deny what festered within. At Dlad City, he chased her around the room as the three squads gyrated in an uncontrollable lust. She almost gave in, and that ignited his fire.

But she'd denied him several times, and now, she wasn't sure if he still had her back. A comely face aside, the urge to mount him failed to manifest; he was too tall, lacked the mentality to keep her engaged, and his pouting ruined any strain of hope he might nurse.

Jakeb awakened her in more than one way. To the outside world, Xenomene knocked down everything in her way, wouldn't take no for an answer. If she didn't command respect, she demanded attention. She found comfort in leading from the front, the focus on her. Later, Daniel stoked the fires Jakeb had ignited.

When she submitted to Daniel, it wasn't his depravity she enjoyed but the complete dominance, giving up and letting go. She controlled her world beyond the walls of her bedroom, but within those confines, she just wanted to give it up, to be unburdened by the shackles of control.

Now that Daniel was gone, she found herself missing him in more than one way.

But he wasn't here, and it was time to move forward, time for revenge, justice, and to claim her right.

It was time to ascend.

She'd be the first ever woman heir, and it all started with one simple step: fucking.

Her stomach quivered at the revolting thought.

She still didn't see how they planned to pull this off, but if it brought the end of Smokey, then she'd fuck whoever she had to and make it happen. She bathed and groomed and dressed while drinking a lot of water. If she was to be stupid drunk, tomorrow's dehydration would be all the more painful.

She left Omen sleeping on the bed and made her way down to the dining hall. When she entered, many cast glances her way.

She stopped in the doorway, and the longer she stayed, the more the men scrutinized.

"Tonight, one of you is going to be lucky," she announced to the room.

A moment of stunned silence was destroyed by the cacophony of voices. Men rose to their feet, clambering for attention. She held up a hand to silence them.

"That's after I eat and drink and who knows? I may just pick two."

Nervous chuckles rippled through the room. She picked up a tray where the line of cooks served. She ate and drank with a false mirth, but her mind burned and tumbled around the ko-don's conundrum. A meeting without her.

Who the fuck planned this shit? They don't want me there, because they want to cut me out of being heir. If they're the heroes, who'd dare back me?

Her dark mood turned toward the mission. She hoped to be so deep in her cups she couldn't remember it.

The men kept filling her mug with rum, her choice drink. She tried so many types: spiced, sweet, aged; towards the end, it all tasted the same. But early on, she decided on koja rum from the Isles.

Her cup never went empty as men hoped to be the fortunate bastard to sheathe their sword in her. Not long after the second cup, the discussion switched from the mundane to perverted japes. They were funny, and most never heard before, but the conversation turned from innuendo to blatant, graphic, and provocative.

Her mood went from sour to yearning within a few hours.

The last time she got up to relieve herself, she barely managed to find the lavatory or walk straight. Mauler came out of nowhere, and half-carried, half-guided her to the chamberpot.

"Now's the time for your declaration," Mauler said in hurried but hushed tones. "Do you understand me?"

Mauler snapped her fingers a few times then slapped her.

"Ouch, hey, bitch, that hurt!

"Your declaration, do you know what I'm talking about?"

"Yup, you want to fuck me."

"No, stupid."

Mauler's slap stung her face again, but it didn't hurt as bad as anticipated.

"Go out there and say you want Tiny and the Mind."

When Xeno finished, Mauler carried her to the mess hall where a full cup awaited.

"Who wants to fuck?" Xenomene yelled.

Ogles and whistles accompanied by tankards thundering on the tabletops swelled in response.

"Well, I don't feel like fucking all of you, so, I'll only take two. I want..." she looked through the crowd.

Faces swam in and out of focus, but she glimpsed the Mind.

"You," she said, pointing.

Half a dozen Krey lurched out of their seats, all screaming that they were the one she picked.

"No, you fucks, the A'uri, right there," she said pointing.

The Mind sidled up to her, a massive grin on his face. He pulled Xeno close, throwing her arm over his shoulder. His hand snaked down and cupped her ass.

The next part of the plan almost made her hurl. She didn't want to do this but remembered the goal: Smokey's death.

"Where's Tiny? I want Tiny, too. Is that okay?" she asked the Mind.

He nodded, and Tiny came lumbering into view, taking place on Xeno's other side, slinging her other arm over his shoulders. The two men stood with Xeno hanging between them, feet dangling off the floor.

"Let's go," the Mind said.

"Wait!" she slurred. "I haven't tried three men."

Men leapt from their seats, screaming for attention.

"Stick to the plan, damn it!" Tiny cursed in her ear.

"Just kidding, two's enough."

The two carried her from the mess hall.

She almost nodded off before they ascended the first flight of stairs. Her head lolled by the time they reached her quarters. She eyed the men far below. They watched until the last possible instant, as she disappeared behind a closed and locked door.

The duo dumped her unceremoniously on the floor, jarring her to full alert. She sat up against her protesting body. The world spun as she came to her knees.

"What happened? Did we fuck already?"

She glanced at the big man.

"Tiny, this is the best time to get what you want."

She held up a hand and waved it in front of her.

"I'm not going to feel a thing."

She let out a giggle.

"Alright, whose dick am I sucking first?"

"Shades of the Underworld," Tiny barked, "will you fix her?"

"Fix me?" Xeno asked. "Fix me some dick, right?"

She hiccupped.

The Heart of Lyan's squad knelt beside her.

"What the fuck are you doing here?"

He didn't answer. He closed his eyes and held her hand. A few moments passed and sweat drenched her.

"What are you doing?"

She wasn't feeling as terrible as before.

"He's nullifying the alcohol," the Mind answered.

The process didn't take long, and she went from unable to stand to buzzed. From the floor, Xeno glanced at the bed looking for Omen, but found Harlot instead. The former prostitute of Spectre's squad sprawled across her covers without a stitch of clothing.

"What's she doing here? And on my fucking bed! Where's my cat?"

Harlot chuckled and pointed to Omen. The Heart spoke.

"Someone's got to have sex so you can make your meeting."

Xeno glanced at the two and the full plan unfurled. The ko-dons never intended for her to have sex, just Harlot.

Oh, thank the scrotum of gods, I'm not going to bed Tiny.

"Who's going to do the deed?"

"That would be our duty," the Mind said. "We can't just go waltzing out of your room now, can we?"

He and Tiny started to remove their clothes.

"Besides, if someone burst in, they need to glimpse one girl and two men."

Xeno appraised Harlot and swallowed.

"Thank you."

She meant it, more than Harlot realized, not just for helping the ko-don, but saving her from something she saw as revolting: Tiny.

Harlot nodded and smiled.

"Don't worry, I'll break them off before they break me."

"I doubt it," Xeno chuckled, pointing in Tiny's direction.

Harlot smiled.

"Oh, I'm well-acquainted, why do you think I agreed?"

Xeno glanced at Tiny's manhood before gazing up at his face. She climbed to her feet.

"Have fun."

"Not as much fun as I'd have with you."

For a moment, the tension was back, and she hated it and the awkwardness.

"Eh, maybe later."

Son of a bitch, why the fuck did I say that? Gods, strike me down with the plague.

"No," he said, letting it hang for a few moments. "No maybes, only definitely."

She suppressed a grimace.

Then, definitely not

The Heart cleared his throat.

"There's no time for this. Xeno, we need to go, and they Krey below need to hear Harlot moaning before they think something is up."

"Yeah," Harlot seconded. "Who's first?" Tiny laid on Xeno's bed, and Harlot straddled him while the Mind edged closer. It seemed like a lifetime ago that Xeno had her own threesome in Dlad City. For a moment she almost envied Harlot, but a quick glance at the partners changed that in a heartbeat.

The Heart led her to the privy. He shut the door behind them and stepped to the washtub. The wall on the far side slid as he pushed hard against it. Shock rippled through her.

"What in the Underworld?" she whispered.

Had there always been a sliding wall? Was it something new? Could people gawk through the wall? Through the small opening, she spied a narrow passageway between the walls. With a frown, she advanced.

Once inside, she stepped to the side so the Heart could enter. With the wall back in place, the Heart shuffled down the narrow passage. Xeno managed to walk straight given her petite frame, but the Mind turned to the left and ambled forward at an angle, making his gait awkward. They hadn't taken a half-dozen steps when Harlot's moan reached their ears. No doubt the Krey below could hear.

I'm glad I don't moan that loud. Damn, now I'm gonna have to clean the sheets.

Along the way, she heard water running through parts of the wall. In another section, heat suffused them, coming from the ventilation system and carried by pipes from the furnaces far below in the basement. They followed the narrow walkway until it dumped out into a small room, an alcove slightly wider than the passageway.

The narrowness made them stand shoulder to shoulder. Xeno could reach across the small circle they formed and touch the person opposite. The intimate proximity didn't escape her, and her companions weren't the first choice of company for such confines.

"Nice job, Xeno," Stallion commented with a smile. "I didn't think you'd do it. We told Adder not to tell you the second part of our plan to see how you'd react. You did well. Had you proved uncooperative, he would've divulged the truth."

"Underworld take you, old man!"

"Had I found you in a drunken state," Chimera said, "I wouldn't have been so gentlemanly…on numerous occasions."

"Yeah, and then I would've cut your balls off on numerous occasions. Just ask Bitcher."

A tense but short silence followed.

"Time's of the essence," Stallion said, breaking the brittle moment. "Down to business."

While she was heir-apparent, she deferred to the elder on many occasions. His plan worked out better than expected, and she reevaluated him in the new light.

"Anyone bringing any new ideas on how to kill the son of a bitch?"

"Well," Panther started, "other than dropping him off the side of the mountain or trying to jump across the desk to strangle him, I haven't anything new."

Xeno suppressed a groan. They didn't have anything new, and they wasted a perfect opportunity to solidify the final touches on a sound plan.

"We need a weapon," Stallion said.

"There aren't any available," Chimera said. "The only one that isn't locked up is the one on his hip."

"No," Xenomene interjected, remembering. "There's another. The blade his brother gave him and Slurp. Slurp's is in his room but under lock as well. The one in Smokey's room is hanging on a display rack above his bed. We could use it."

"I forgot about that one!" Stallion said. "How do we get it?"

Adder scratched his chin.

"We could storm the room, or be sneaky."

"The room is guarded day and night," Chimera said. "Though Islanders, I'm loathed to slaughter my misguided brothers in arms."

"Agreed," Stallion seconded. "Still, do their loyalties lie with the Krey, or with the megalomaniac? If we succeed, not all need die."

Xenomene glanced down both ends of the small passageway.

"Does this tunnel dump out into the heir's chambers?"

Craiboar shook his head.

"That's a different system, and we don't know where it dumps out at or if it's accessible through the other side."

Adder sighed.

"So, that leaves us the direct approach."

"Or an indirect approach."

Everyone turned to her.

"Go on," Stallion encouraged.

"I could get it."

"How?" Chimera demanded.

"I give him what he wants. I fuck him."

The ko-dons were quiet for a moment. Panther spoke as he picked his nose to dislodge the newest resident.

"That's gross. Islanders are disgusting vermin, him more so."

"That won't work," Chimera agreed. "You've turned him down how many times. He'll know you're up to something."

"Normally, yes, but if we do it now, he won't."

"How do you figure?" Adder asked.

"The perfect cover is now. All the guards are unarmed. People are turning in for the night. Everyone knows that I'm 'stupid drunk.' The gods couldn't divine a better time to act."

Craiboar shifted his feet.

"It's too risky. I wouldn't wish the man on my worst enemy, and you overvalue yourself in this situation."

"There's always the chance he'd turn you down," Stallion added.

Adder gave a raspy chuckle.

"Doubtful. Even now, knowing she's with two men, people would still line up."

Xeno's eyes darted around, looking between all the ko-dons.

"He won't turn her down," Chimera said, appraising Xenomene with a gleam in his eye. "That's if you're brave enough to suffer what might be the worst night of your life."

Chimera's words almost mirror my own the night Jakeb came to my tent in Cape Gythmel.

"Worst night?" Stallion inquired.

"He's saying," Xeno clarified, "I should offer him the one thing he or any other Islander won't turn down."

"I don't get it."

Panther cuffed Chimera.

"That's a discussion for another time, then."

Stallion turned his full attention to her.

"Xeno, you might have to go through with the deed."

"There's always a price."

Stallion chewed the end of his fingernail. He was nervousness, and it warmed her to know his concern.

"It's up to you. Your plan, your call."

"My title, my kill," she corrected.

"I hope you can still act drunk," Adder added.

"That's the simple part. We need to wake the loyal armors and weapon masters and be ready to help break open the swords. The A'uri, too, in case there's any magic spells on the locks."

"We can do that," Chimera assured.

"Good luck," Stallion offered.

"Thanks."

They broke apart, the Heart leading back to her chambers. Still drenched in sweat, she wasn't sure if she was sweaty enough given how much Harlot moaned. She entered the bathroom again, and the Heart closed the panel, but this time, he stayed in the tunnel. Xeno went to the doorframe leading to the main chamber and stopped.

A living, graphic art unfurled before her, and an itch tugged in all the right spots. Watching the scene of flesh stirred something within her.

Why couldn't Slurp be waiting for me in my bathroom?

But she knew why. He was an Islander, and his loyalties were unknown at this time.

With a pitcher of water by the wash basin, she filled the bowl. She sprinkled water over her body and through her hair to simulate sweat. Finished, she disheveled her clothing to make it appear she dressed in an alacritous fashion. She almost felt sorry for interrupting the enraptured bodies in the moment of passion, but the mission called. In a few moments, it may be Smokey mounting her.

"You need to finish, posthaste," she muttered.

The three of them were so lost in their pleasure, they didn't hear her reenter the room.

"Already?" the Mind asked.

"Yes, and we're moving now. The plan involves me, so finish or get off. There's work to do."

She stepped away and grabbed a bottle of rum she kept on the dresser. Sitting in her chair, she drank and viewed the affair. It was exotic and arousing. She chugged a few large gulps of rum before filling her mouth, letting the liquid part her lips and trickling down her chin, soaking the cloth and skin between her breasts. She'd come away reeking of alcohol.

They finished with Harlot hitting a high pitched crescendo.

Panting, Tiny paraded away from the bed with his drooping, expended flesh.

Does he really think I'm going to want to jump him more?

"How'd the meeting go?"

"How'd the sex go?"

"Fantastic. Harlot knows what she's doing."

"Well, I'm just happy for you."

"Why don't you fuck me, and you can be happy, too?"

"I'm saving myself for the usurper."

His face contorted with a dark fury, but he held his tongue. When all parties were dressed, she walked to the door, double checked that everyone was in place, and Harlot was out of view. She opened the door and stumbled through, walking drunkenly down the hall, bumping into the wall as she went. She didn't go far before one of the Islander guards grabbed her by the arm and escorted her to Smokey's office. They threw her to the floor, and to sell the act of being drunk, she exaggerated the landing.

"Well, if it isn't Xeno," Smokey said, anger brimming in his voice. "Had a lovely time?"

She glanced up at him.

That's my chair your disgusting ass is sitting in, you bastard.

She clamped down the anger and focused on slurring her speech.

"Got a drink?"

He smirked.

"There's koja rum. I hear you like it. That's not the only thing you like from the Isles, is it?"

"Got anything else?"

With languid movements, she picked herself off the floor and leaned against the desk. Her loose shirt gave him a flash of skin beneath.

"Like what?" he asked, leaning forward, his gaze darting between her eyes and breasts.

"Something robust maybe? Something to work for?"

His glare grew cold and distant, and he leaned back in the chair.

"Well, that's quite a different tune than you sang this afternoon, or all along for that matter."

Shit!

He scrutinized her.

"Why the sudden reversal? Last I heard, fairly recently too, you don't need me for a good time. Were the A'uri and Tiny not enough for you?"

She leaned in further, half crawling atop the desk. She gave her best drunk-mischievous grin and whispered.

"They weren't Islanders."

His eyes twinkled in amusement.

Or is that arousal? Gods, I'm disgusted. If I had a dick and he a woman, I'd be flaccid for the rest of my life.

Some of the frost left his cautious voice.

"Why the turnabout?"

"Can't a girl have needs?"

She let her stare slip out of focus and placed her head on the desk.

"Wake up!"

Smokey leaned in close and grabbed her chin, searching for deceit.

"So, you want Islander cock?"

"Yes. Want to help me?"

"Oh, I think that can be arranged," he said with a jovial voice.

The hairs on the back of her neck stood on end.

"Pint!" he called.

One of the guards shuffled around the desk to where Xeno could see him. He stood next to Smokey. She exaggerated her movements to see him.

"This is Pint; Xeno, say hello."

"Hello."

"Check for weapons, Pint."

Pint pulled her from the desk. He lifted her arms up, locking them together at the top of her head. He wasn't rough, just a boy following orders. He patted with quick efficiency, and then stood back. Smokey eyed Pint for a few moments before letting his gaze slip back to her.

"You didn't check under her shirt. Search her bosom wrap."

For a few heartbeats, Xeno found herself worrying, but the flatness of his voice made her reevaluate the scene. Smokey tested her as much as Pint. The way he glowered at the diminutive boy gave her hope.

Pint stepped forward to obey and groped. She risked finding his gaze and saw the discomfort. He followed commands he disagreed with.

I promise I won't kill you if I don't have to.

A lazy grin spread across her face as she played the part of a horny drunk.

"You can put your hand inside my shirt if you want? Play with my nipples."

The words startled Pint, and he stepped back once he finished.

Smokey's mouth twitched as if he chewed his gums.

"You didn't check her shorts."

He leaned forward, his scrutiny never leaving Xenomene.

"You don't mind me being cautious, do you?"

She shook her head, her dark red hair leaving strains in her face.

This time, the hesitation was more evident. Pint's footstep faltered for half a step as he closed the distance between them again. With timid fingers, he pulled at the waistband and reached within.

Xeno widened her stance.

To distract Smokey and Pint, she took Pint with a passionate kiss. She noted the fingers stopped well shy of the ordered destination. She pulled away, breathy.

"You want to fuck me?"

She kissed him again.

"Well?" Smokey barked.

Pint pulled away with an abruptness.

"She's clean."

"Happy?" she goaded.

"Not yet. Bend her over the desk."

Her eyes narrowed, but she played it off with a languid blink.

"I know where this is going, and there better be dick afterward," she taunted Pint.

Pint was younger than her, and she wasn't by any means old. He seemed almost a child by his youthful appearance, barely past the Age of Maturity. Xeno hadn't reached two and a half ages, and she judged him less than two ages.

She understood why Smokey had chosen Pint. It was an initiation of sorts, to test obedience and loyalty. She only hoped Pint obeyed and avoid a swift death for defiance.

She bent over the desk, her hands resting on the edge. She looked back as Pint stopped behind her.

"Lick your fingers," she purred.

She turned her gaze back to Smokey and watched him.

It was an act, that's all it was. If this made Smokey feel more secure, she'd do it. She could endure a little humiliation for the goal. Smokey longed for a show, and she'd oblige.

Pint moved in close, a hand touching her. He pulled on the waistband, and his hand entered her shorts, but not the undergarments. His hand dipped in, fingers nearing her crevice, hand obscured from the view of Smokey and the others.

She almost forgot to act, noting a decent man defied orders. Her lips parted, a moan slipped out, and she rolled her eyes in mock-pleasure. As quickly as he started, Pint pulled away.

"She's clean," he stated again.

Smokey stood and leaned over the desk toward her.

"So, you want some Islander cock, huh?"

"Yes, are you going to help me?"

"How bad do you want it?"

She writhed before him, like an addict going through withdrawal.

"Bad," she slurred.

"Okay, I can help you out. Pint, take her to my chambers and fuck her."

"What?"

This came both from Xeno and Pint at the same time. Pint just stood there shocked. Xeno recovered quicker.

"No," she cooed, "I want *your* cock."

Smokey shook his head, his scrutiny cold and calculating.

"I just…don't believe you. Your change of heart is too quick to not be suspicious. If something is too good, then it is. So, here's what I'm going to do…"

Xeno let her eyes flutter as if heavy with sleep. He reached out and shook her face.

"Maybe it's because you're drunk that you're relenting. But if you're lying, then you'll back out now. Cock is cock, right?"

"There's cock, and then there's cock from the most powerful man in Outpost Dire."

She hiccupped.

"I fucked the last heir, did you know?"

His face grew slack at the declaration and leaned back in his chair.

"No, I didn't."

"I let him do whatever he wanted to me."

She almost missed the flicker of his reaction.

"I let him tie me up, too. And I know what you want. You told me the first time I met you."

A cruel smile flitted across his face.

"What I want is for Pint to carry out my orders. So, what's it going to be Xeno? Yes or no?"

"I guess as long as it's on the heir's bed…"

Smokey scowled at Pint, a cross between hate and disgust.

"Go!" he growled. "If you disobey me again, you're finished, as is your family in the Isles, you hear me? You better be fucking this bitch when I get there. Go!"

Half petrified, half reluctant, Pint dragged Xeno off.

Fucking Shades and minuscule, invisible, irritant gods! What the fuck was that about? How the fuck am I going to get out of this one now?

She knew that answer. She wasn't.

Everything has a price.

Pint opened the door to the heir's chambers and shuffled them through. He struggled to the bed and let her go. She fell face-first on Smokey's mattress.

Daniel's bed.

Fingers curled around the sheets, remembering the last time she was here. Pint's panicking voice tore her from the memories. The fear was real and paralyzing, and she sympathized with him.

"What the fuck am I going to do? Shades! He'll kill me, but I can't just rape you. And my family?"

Xenomene empathized. Not long ago, she laced the same boots, blackmailed with the lives of people hanging over her head. Pity swelled within her, and she remembered the vow about not killing him for following orders.

How many others were stuck following edicts they didn't believe in? How many of them were genuinely loyal to the Godfrey regime? Pint disobeyed Smokey once. He defied him tonight when he didn't violate Xeno's sanctity, and that had been twice.

When they took the Hive back over, she was going to have to find a way to test all the Islanders. Some would argue for safety and put them all to the blade. In good conscience, she couldn't.

She sat up, her emerald eyes watching him pace back and forth.

"Why can't he just choke and die?"

He stopped, his panicked visage finding her.

"I've got to get out of here."

As he searched for a way to escape, she knew the boy sought no part of Smokey's reign.

"And what of your family?" she asked, dropping the drunk act. "If you leave, he'll butcher them."

He stopped and gawked.

She gave him a grim grin.

"Do you want to get out of this alive?"

He swallowed hard and nodded.

"Yes. He's going to kill me if I disobey again."

"What did you disobey him on?"

"He ordered me to murder the ko-dons except you, and to start with Stallion. I couldn't—they're innocent."

Her grin widened into a genuine smile.

"I'd hardly call those old, decrepit men innocent."

She sat up straighter, taking in the room. On the wall above Smokey's bed, lay the presentation sword in its display rack. She glanced back at Pint and stood.

"Do you want him dead?"

"It's him or my family, he made that abundantly clear."

"Do you want to live?"

The panic left his face.

"What kind of question is that? Of course, I want to live!"

"Then, I need you to follow orders."

"Follow—" he scoffed. "You want me to—"

"He said he'd kill you if you are not fucking me when he arrives. So fuck me, and I'll take care of the rest."

He made no move to comply, and she stepped closer, and slapped him.

"It's simple, Pint. Fuck or die. I'd choose to fuck every time; why do you think I am here now?"

She waited a few moments and recognition dawned on his features.

"You're gonna—"

She nodded.

"Yeah, I'm going to kill him, tonight."

She let her voice drop, so Pint had to step closer.

"We're in the same predicament together."

His eyes lifted, and she knew he found the blade on the rack. He pointed.

"Take it. Execute him!"

She nodded.

"I thought about it, but there are a few problems. If he opens the door and sees you not obeying, he'll do what?"

"Call the guards."

She nodded.

"And that'll ruin any chance to take him out. If I'm not on the bed, he'll be suspicious and not enter. Again, he'll call for guards. His death must be done in secrecy so we may take the others by surprise. If he shouts, it's over."

She turned away and tugged her shorts down but left her shirt in place. Then, sitting on the bed, she glanced at him.

"You might want to hurry," she reminded him.

It spurred him to disrobe.

As he came forward, she shifted, sliding on the bed, and laid on her back. Pint climbed up, his movements timid, afraid to touch her. She reached for his hands and pulled him closer. His small body pressed against hers as they lay face to face, and she found they were nearly the same size. There wasn't an awkwardness with a massive height difference.

She hooked an arm around his neck as if a lover.

"Go slow," she said. "This is your first time?"

His body melted against her, but other than that, he hadn't moved at all. He nodded vigorously, afraid to speak.

"It's okay."

Her words breathed into his mouth. His body trembled. She leaned closer and kissed him. The effects were immediate. He went still, focused.

"Now," she said, "I want you to put yourself inside me."

He started to, but she clenched down on him.

"Your first reaction is going to be natural, but I need you to fight it. Smokey said he had to witness it. Try not to move until he opens the door, or I tell you. When he does, you can start in earnest, got it?"

He nodded, and she kissed him again.

"It's going to be fine. Now, do as I asked."

He situated himself, quivering with anticipation, and slipped inside. His mouth opened in a gasp, his face slack, his breath hitched.

"By all that is holy," he panted.

Her arms tightened around him again.

"Yes, I know, I'm that damn good."

She smiled.

"It's like the gods have awakened inside of you, isn't it?"

Another kiss, diverting attention from his swelling member and the pent-up need to release. Virgins had a tendency to not last more than a few seconds. She lifted her lips near his ear.

"I won't get another chance at this. Don't fuck this up."

He shifted only a little, taking her advice to heart, but he teetered on the edge of giving into the overwhelming sensations. Though technically sex, she didn't count it as such. Sex involved orgasms and actual movement. Pint just laid on top, contouring the shape of her body and shifting when the need arose.

Footsteps outside the door grew louder. She kissed him again, this time with tongue to excite him.

"Start; he's coming."

Pint obliged with eagerness.

The door opened. She hugged Pint to her body, gave a moan, and let her gaze fall to Smokey's silhouette.

Pint's eagerness ended a dozen thrusts later. His body shivered in ecstasy, and a moan escaped him. Her chest warmed from the moment. She'd brought a young man to climax, his first, and he hadn't lasted long.

His breath turned sharp in her ear, and his body shuddered and jerked. This time, he kissed her, his tongue exploring her mouth. Her eyes widened at the passion, but she returned it, vowing to remember this moment.

Smokey called from the doorway.

"I was worried you didn't possess what it takes."

The usurper came to the bed. Pint's weight shifted, and he slipped free from her core. She remembered to act drunk.

"Happy? I made a man out of him."

She sat up and reached for Smokey's manhood, massaging him through his trousers.

"Can I get what I want now?"

"Oh, yes. I'm going to make it come out your throat."

He turned to Pint.

"Clean her up and leave us."

Smokey stood and undressed just out of reach. Pint came forward with a wet towel. She spread her legs, and he gently wiped. His gaze darted between her flesh and eyes. She noted his anxiety.

Pint left moments later, and Smokey stood in the nude. He was covered from head to toe with dark, curly, sheep's wool. The massive moles riddling his body proclaimed she stared at the final layer. A few encircled the base of his shaft like a ring. He slid on the bed with fat jiggling.

There's no way I'm letting him inside me.

"You know what I want?" she asked.

"What?"

She leaned forward and kissed him, and tried not to throw up in his mouth.

"Something that Slurp does with me, and it drives me wild."

"What?"

"Put your tongue in my ass."

She stood, turned, and placed her hands on the wall at the head of the bed, bending at the waist, giving him unimpeded view and access.

A grin split his face. He slid forward, a hand reaching, groping, spreading her.

"I can help you there."

He rose to his knees, and his warm, wet tongue invaded. She shuddered in revulsion, but Smokey took it as pleasure. Encouraged, he pressed deeper.

"Oh, right there," she said, gasping.

She glanced back at him, curled her fingers through his hair, and pulled him hard against her body, making sure he couldn't squirm away while he explored. Without looking, her right hand snaked blindly up the wall and reached for the sword. She plucked it from the wall, moving slow as Smokey moaned into her flesh.

In a sudden movement, he pulled free of her hand holding him there, and he smacked her ass hard.

She yelped.

"Gods, I love your ass."

His eyes flitted up to her, then beyond. His mouth fell open as his eyes widened.

She turned, striking before he could raise the alarm.

The steel drove down his throat, the hilt stopped by his lips.

To be extra sure she struck true, she twisted the blade before pulling it free. Smokey toppled off the bed, blood flowing from his mouth and back where the sword exited.

She stepped off the bed, standing naked over the corpse. She rose the blade overhead.

"Time for a family reunion with your baby brother."

The sword fell.

Chapter 60: The Council Chambers

Starriace and Norek dropped out of teleport inside the rock dome. Their appearance went unnoticed.

She doubled over in pain as the phantom stirred. It closed in on her heart. How long did she have? Hours? A day? A few more teleports or excessive use of magic, and she'd die.

She straightened before Norek saw.

His gaze had been roaming over the buildings, the massive stone walls, his eyes filled with wonderment. She took a moment, too. It was the first time she truly beheld the city, and she half-wished it was under better circumstances.

Soldiers bustled through the streets, their armor jingling as they trotted by. Some archers hurried after the group passed, their mail tinkling in their wake. She glimpsed mages among the people and rubble, identified by their color-coded robes—or so she assumed.

Her eyes turned upward, past the curved monolith and to the hole above. It was dark outside. Again, the teleportation had taken much longer than the near-instantaneous blip. How it felt, and the reality differed. With a furtive glance, and the knowledge she had from Judas's transference, she ambled off in the direction of the castle.

The council chambers awaited.

It seemed an era since she'd been here, but the last trip ended in a duel with Judas. Would this time be the same? She nearly killed him and the guards who tried to stop her. She barely managed an escape.

On the way up the path, Ava appeared.

"Mistress," she breathed. "You must come, Lily's calling for you."

"Who's Lily?" Norek asked as he stepped up beside her. "Who's this?"

Starriace waved his questions away. Duty and loyalty to a friend tore through her. Something stirred within at the thought of seeing Kam. Part of her yearned to run to Lily, the other reminding her of duty and the vow to honor the fairies' sacrifice.

But Lily wouldn't have called unless necessary. Starriace had made a bargain with Ava. If Lily called the fairy, she'd go. Perhaps she needed help, or the situation had turned dire. Surely it wasn't because she missed her?

An ache resonated within her.

What's more important? One person, or the two million inhabitants of the city?

With reluctance, she spoke terrible words.

"Ava, I'll come as soon as I'm able, but I can't right this second. Go to her, be with her, let her know I intend to keep my promise. I'll be along shortly."

"As you wish," the fairy said, and she disappeared.

Starriace paused for a moment, wondering if she'd made the right decision. Assured, she wove between houses, through alleyways, and sidestepped the harassed pedestrians until she met the main road.

Norek kept up with the breakneck pace.

She weaved through the semi-crowded streets. She didn't know the time of night but assumed it wasn't too late due to the amount of traffic. Perhaps the council was still in session, devising a plan to counter whatever Xilor would throw at them. She hoped someone in charge would be there.

If it's Godfrey…

She shook her head at the dark thought and entered the circular courtyard. The gates were open, much to her surprise. With the rock dome covering the city, it made some sense. At the entrance of the ancient castle, guards stood posted on each side of the door. Their faces were taut with tension.

The guards looked down their noses, their gazes wandering over her before fixing on her glowing eyes. They hardened their grips on their pikes, ready for hostilities.

"Name?" one asked.

"I have an audience with Warlock Judas Lakayre, and the former consul, Meristal Raviils."

She focused her essence on them much the way she had the steward in Stratu'Geim, bending their will to hers.

"They're expecting me."

The guard's glazed expression slackened with understanding.

"Sure, love. Here you go."

He opened the door and smiled like a fool.

Perhaps I exerted too hard?

She smiled and walked through and into the arching halls beyond. The lavish castle stretched out in opulent decorations. Rugs, tables, vases, paintings, and tapestries, each giving hints to their origins, troll, dwaven, elyfian, and vampire. By comparison to every other place she'd visited below the Melodic Mountains, Ralloc gleamed with grand and elaborate trappings but came across as dull in ingenuity.

She missed the busts of statues of Stratu, the outlandish designs of buildings littering the cities of Ruhkhi, even the quaint Crystal Falls.

She noted the religious references in the artworks and décor along the spacious hall. Specific colors were meant for carpets or curtains, others for upholstery. Her steps slowed in the headlong rush to reach the council chambers, spying the royal guards who wore forest green. Even some of the carpet had been replaced with the new color.

Aren't they supposed to be wearing phthalo-blue?

Starriace's black boots clicked sharply against the massive stones as she ascended. She rounded a corner and slowed as she reached the antechamber. A few people milled about with papers, dressed in fancy robes that dignified their stature. The guards snapped to attention, flashing their pikes to block the entrance.

"You may not enter," the first guard said, eyeing the swords. "You haven't been recognized by the council and aren't permitted at this time. Also, you'll need to surrender your weapons."

A quick flash of anger rose within Starriace, and her eyes burned. She clenched her fist and took a staggering step towards him. Norek cut her off, planting himself between them, and conferred with the sentry.

I could destroy this little cockroach.

She half-wished to for the inconvenience. But that was the old way. She had to be different, not the monster she'd become. Now was the time to repent for the atrocity she'd committed.

While Norek spoke to the guard, she manipulated her essence and made the guard more pliant to let her enter with the swords. She wouldn't part with them at any cost.

Norek spoke just above a whisper, and she couldn't hear them. Moments later, the guard spoke.

"Very well."

The sentry disappeared through the door.

Norek turned to her.

"Not everything should be resolved with violence," he admonished with a grin.

Starriace let out a huff that blew a few strains of hair out of her face. Did Norek have the ability to sense thoughts like Judas, or did he guess?

Perhaps it's because of what I did to Mr. Pleasure?

Before she traced the idea further, the soldier returned and motioned for them to pass.

Starriace strolled forward; Norek followed in her shadow.

From the steps above, she took in the scene. The council chamber was shaped like a large, half bowl, the council's bench at the bottom and centered. The place for aides and scribes stretched across the floor, and the council members arrayed like a panel behind them. People filled the stadium seating around the room, able to hear the council from pure acoustics.

Starriace continued down the steps to the council's area. Somewhere in the back of her mind, she sensed that Norek hung back. She stopped mere feet from their tall bench.

"Where's Meristal?" she asked.

"With the consul," a goblin answered.

His gaze flickered to the swords.

"They'll be along soon, child."

His black eyes bored into her, eternally deep, like the darkness that had descended on the world three times. They pierced her, searched for answers.

She held his gaze.

Those dark pools stirred memories of vile things. The urge to lash out came forth, and she fought the impulse.

She glanced at the small placard in front of him: Lagelm.

Her attention roamed down the bench and spied another goblin. By comparison, he seemed warm and inviting. She caught sight of his placard: Kellis.

As her concentration pulled away, the doors to the far left opened. Meristal and Judas walked in with Godfrey on their heels. Starriace observed how close Judas and Meristal stood together, their suggestive body language, and the way they composed themselves near one another.

They'd always proclaimed they were friends, but this revealed more. Seeing them again, and in such a fashion, she wondered if they'd always kept their distance from one another while she was in their presence.

Gazing upon them was also something of heartbreak; the two of them were both tragic parents of lost children. Their attraction after all they'd been through spoke volumes and warmed her heart.

They both deserve happiness after all they've been through.

The couple hurried over, and Meristal embraced her in a hug, then Judas. It was the oddest welcome Starriace hadn't expected. His eyes flickered to the swords, but he didn't ask where she got them.

That surprised her.

"It's so good to see you again," Judas said, his voice filled with relief.

She sensed the emotions rolling off him, but she didn't have time to contemplate the meanings. Starriace took in Judas with a furtive glance; his essence felt as different as his physical appearance. And he was slimmer than she remembered.

"It's agreeable to see you both," Starriace said with a dip of her head.

"Well, isn't this touching," Godfrey's voice called from behind them.

He stepped around Judas and Meristal, and his cold regard fixed her with a blank expression.

"Come to die with us?"

Her eyes narrowed.

"I don't plan on it."

"Then, why come to Ralloc?"

Starriace glanced at Judas and knew he burst to ask the same, where she'd been, and what she was doing.

"To fight."

"I see."

Starriace caught a flicker of Judas's well-hidden disappointment.

The warlock stirred.

"Since you're here, let me thank you for your aid. I don't know how you managed to get the stone giants to help us. I'm intrigued by the story you'll no doubt share. Stone giants have always been rumored but never proven."

"That's because no one's ever survived. I wasn't sure I'd make it either."

"But you did," Godfrey said, the disinterest molding his face for a brief moment. "Luck, a means for the foolish to explain their superiority. What exactly do you propose to do about the war? If the warlock is of no use, what good are you?"

Starriace's regard flickered over to Judas, then back to the consul.

"I've unfinished business with Xilor. It's time I repaid the favor of humiliation."

"Perhaps," Meristal interjected, "now isn't the best of circumstances."

"In war or in a single battle," Starriace countered, "there are never best of circumstances. Sometimes you've got to make choices and sacrifices."

She glanced at the consul.

I'm willing, are you?"

Godfrey stared at her for a few moments, his face placid, but his eyes shined with malevolence at the challenge.

Judas took the opportunity to speak.

"No. Who am I to say who lives and dies? That isn't my decision."

"But it's mine," Godfrey said.

Starriace ignored him and spoke to Judas.

"I understand, but people die in war. Many more will perish if Xilor isn't stopped here and now."

"By law, Ralloc's stand on this subject matter," Meristal interrupted again, "is that we won't sacrifice the few to save the many. Once you take a step on that slippery slope, the rest will become easier."

"I dictate what Ralloc's stance is," Godfrey said. "Not you. You're no longer consul."

"Yes, we know, you remind us every chance you get," Meristal replied.

"Nor are you an advocate of law anymore. You retired, remember?"

Meristal rolled her eyes, but her voice came out sharp and a touch strident.

"Just because I retired doesn't mean I forgot the law. Let the grownups talk."

The chamber went quiet as Godfrey bristled. He was on the cusp of saying something when someone ran up and whispered into his ear.

Starriace glanced between Judas and Meristal, and the latter answered.

"His herald, Hynry."

Starriace nodded.

For the first time, Godfrey's face went into a state of emotional flux. She saw the anguish in his eyes as they glittered with held tears. Fear swept over his features for a brief flash before he solidified on anger.

"Master Jynerul, to my chambers! We've some Krey to cull."

Godfrey stormed out with his minions and the master jynerul in tow.

Once gone, Starriace continued the conversation with Meristal.

"By doing nothing, you're sacrificing the people of the city. Every man, woman, and child will die because you're unwilling to make the hard choices. Either way, there's a cost. What are you going to be responsible for?"

Judas stood straighter. Both adults exchanged glances.

"Your thoughts are confused," a new voice spoke up, making Meristal and Judas jump.

Norek closed the few feet between them to join their conversation.

"It matters not which way you look at it. Sacrifice is sacrifice, and evil is evil."

Meristal and Judas exchanged glances, but they didn't greet him.

"Yes," Starriace said, "but what may be evil to you is good to someone else."

"Starriace?" Judas queried.

She noted the defensiveness in his voice.

"Who's your new *friend*?"

"I'm known as Norek in my travels, sire. I'm a wanderer and explorer of these parts and parts afar."

Starriace cringed internally as Norek recited his lines again. He tried hard with charisma and charm, but it came out thick and lacking authenticity.

Judas's brows twitched in a scowl.

"I met Starriace in a most peculiar place."

"The Corridor," Starriace offered.

She gave Norek a don't-screw-with-me-now look.

"And what is *your* business here?" Judas asked, crossing his arms.

Starriace balked at the warlock.

"Are you alright?"

Judas's voice and expression softened.

"Yes, why?"

"You're acting...odd."

His mouth opened and closed a few times, and when his words came at last, he stumbled at first.

"I—I uh—I don't like meeting new people unexpectedly, that's all."

He thinks that I am involved with Norek. Shades! He can never know about Kam, then.

Meristal picked up the conversation to save him.

"You said you're called Norek in your travels. What are you at home?"

Norek paused and locked gazes with her.

Starriace stretched her senses. Norek's elation was almost more than she could bear. He was ecstatic, and that put it mildly. Starriace pulled back the sphere of influence and shut herself down.

The emotion was too strong.

"You're the first person to ever catch that sleight of words," Norek beamed.

Meristal took it as a compliment, but his smile had nothing to do with Meristal's cleverness.

Norek watched Meristal intently now.

"Ethanyul."

Meristal's brows shot up, and she turned a shade or two paler. She took a step back, glancing to Starriace, then to Judas.

"Excuse me."

She hurried out the chambers. Judas rushed after her, calling back over his shoulder to Starriace.

"Sorry, Starriace...nice to meet you, Norek."

In another few moments, they were both gone.

"I wonder what all that was about," Starriace said.

She turned to Norek.

"You better stay here."

"Why?"

"Because I'm sure they can help you when they return."

"But you can help me. You've been here before."

"No. I've got something else to do."

"Oh?"

Starriace debated on what to say, so she decided on nothing.

"Stay out of trouble."

She turned on her heel and hurried up the sloping floor.

"Thanks for your help in the Corridor," Norek called. "I'm sure we'll see each other soon."

She rounded the nearest corner, nearly knocking over guards in the process. The halls passed in a hastened blur. A couple of servants stood just ahead. Their conversation caught her attention as they stood in a closet off the main hall with the door open.

"Take these cloaks down to the laundry and have them washed," the first said.

"That's going to take a long time because there are so many, I'll need some help."

"Fine, just make sure it's done today, or there'll be hell to pay from the guards."

Starriace stopped a dozen paces shy, turned to a statue bust, and put on a show of studying it.

A thought came to her, remembering the steward in Stratu'Geim, ludicrous had it not been so brilliant. She dared to hope for a brief moment, then acted.

The servants closed the door, cast a glance in her direction, wrote on their parchment, and moved on. Once out of sight, Starriace crossed to the closet and flung it open. Cloaks and guard robes hung in the deep room, hundreds of them. Starriace scanned the hall to make sure no one saw her, stepped in, and closed the door softly like a thief in the night.

Chapter 61: The Duel of Fates

Xilor paced near the front lines of his army, waiting, watching, praying for a chance to exact revenge on Judas, who cowered within the city. The warlock was responsible for this damn rock formation.

Thousands of torches glowed at his back, holding the night at bay.

Xilor's black robes billowed behind him like a plague of demonic spirits. He stalked like a predator, searching for helpless prey to devour. His anger built, and he'd slaughtered hundreds of his own to satiate his rage after learning of the defeat at the Enclave.

True, the dragons decimated the place, but the elyves mustered a defense and slaughtered seven of his dragons.

How's that even possible?

He'd lost a sixteenth of the entire population in one fight with the elyves.

There was a rumble from his followers, a touch of agitation, and Xilor turned to face Ralloc.

A figure walked through a gap in the stone surrounding the ancient city, the light beyond illuminating the figure in silhouette. The wall sealed itself behind the approaching figure.

Xilor allowed himself a smile. Judas had finally mustered the courage to face him. It'd be a duel of destinies, violent, swift, and poetic. People would sing of Xilor's victory for generations to come, and he'd still be there to hear it.

Troubling emotions lingered within him. Xilor both respected and hated Judas. He hated the warlock for nearly destroying him, for the imprisonment that lasted nearly three ages, for tearing his soul away, draining his blood, and burying his body.

His admiration stemmed from the young boy who sought him out, bringing the war to its end. The warlock had earned his respect.

But Judas had escaped his fury for too long, and today, his blood would taste all the sweeter.

The figure was still some distance away, but Xilor's goading would carry in the night.

"I knew you'd come," he said. "I'm surprised you have the courage. I almost suspected you'd cower until I came for you."

The hooded figure stopped roughly five meters from him, keeping his face concealed.

Xilor turned to the army around them.

"Back away. He's mine. None interfere."

The ranks started moving back, a roiling commotion as the press of bodies obeyed.

Xilor turned back to the lone figure.

"Really, Judas?"

He cackled.

"Surely you haven't lost your witty tongue in old age? Or are you silent in fear of what's to come?"

Xilor waited for an answer, waited for the warlock to twitch, and let the battle begin in earnest. He cocked his head, trying to pierce the shadows. Despite the numerous torches lighting the area, he couldn't see beyond the cowl.

"Are you so unnerved you can't even show the fear in your eyes?"

The hooded figure didn't move, didn't speak. In fact, it was awkwardly still, almost like a statue. Judas's unwillingness to humor him turned to frustration and made him wary.

It could be a trap.

During their first battle, Judas had fooled him into action, and it almost proved disastrous. Xilor pulled his metallic wand from within the fold of his robes and advanced.

Judas didn't stir.

Xilor reached a large hand out to unmask the hooded figure, ripping the cloak away.

Rage shook him.

A statue stood beneath, a perfect replica of Starriace with two swords crisscrossed over her back. He recoiled at the sight, startled. He'd never heard of animating stone. He took a step away, unnerved by the unknown magic.

Fury shot through him. He'd been duped. He spun to his army, searching for a victim to release upon.

A hand clamped down on his arm. He jerked back around. Starriace stood before him.

"Got you, you son of a bitch!"

A sensation shot up through his left arm. Pins and needles crawled across, his hand, robes, and skin, turning to stone. Before he could gasp, it reached his elbow.

Starriace coiled and lashed out. A blast of energy hit him. His arm shattered, and the stump remained clutched in her hand.

Horror and pain rolled through him.

The mage tossed his arm away.

A swell of energy boiled up, and he threw up his mageshield. The blast rocked across him, but his barrier held.

He righted himself just as she started conjuring again.

Starriace reached out, calling on the power lying within.

She grabbed hold of Xilor's essence, his life, and began the life drain. Xilor roared in pain and lashed out, a wave of energy. She stumbled back, but her mageshield didn't waver.

In his right hand, his wand sputtered to life with a swirling, green blade of acidic sorcery.

A wizard's sword?

She had read about them but never attempted one herself. Even if possible, her feeble skills were no match. Ahn said as much.

A tremor of her strange magic whispered through her, but she ignored it.

He swung wildly, all primal and wrath and no finesse. His army cheered.

She ducked and hit him again with another siphon.

He staggered under the blow, but still came on. Another cut, this one over the top.

She leapt to the side, rolled up to her feet, and siphoned again. The energy crackled against the barrier he kept.

Again, the strange essence called. She pushed it aside.

The wizard's sword died, the wand point centered on her, and a wave of conjury flew out, unseen but felt. The energy picked her up and slammed her to the ground. Xilor glided forward like a wraith. The green, swirling spiral came to life again and he drew it high.

Without conscious thought, she reacted. Her left hand reached over her shoulder and snatched up Salvation. The white saber came free and blocked Xilor's blow. The impact reverberated through them. Both stared in shock. Power radiated in her hand. She trembled in its might.

Xilor recovered after a heartbeat. He kicked her square in the chest. She reeled and rolled up to her feet. Xilor advanced. With her right hand, the siphon shot out again. His defenses crackled as he closed in. Another mighty swing. The sword blocked, knowing where to be.

This time, she blasted him with a wave of energy. He staggered, and she lashed out again with the life drain. The strange essence still screamed, begging to be released, but she smothered the call.

Shades, how strong is his shield?

A needle of worry furrowed through her. She expected the shock of her initial attack to do more damage. Despite missing half an arm, Xilor seemed more dangerous. Rage and pain no doubt fueled his attacks, but Judas once said emotions would drain you quicker.

How was Xilor still standing?

The first sign of weakness came. His barrier flickered, wavered, but remained. The purple-red energy washed over him in a torrent, but he still came forward.

Again, the essence begged to be wielded.

I don't know how much longer I can survive.

The notion of hitting him with everything wormed its way through her. She could, and might be victorious, but she'd die. The phantom neared her heart. Without holding back, her death would come quicker. But who'd die first? Her or Xilor?

Either way, death was inevitable.

The sizzling blade arced through the air, and with reflexes faster than she thought possible, Salvation blocked and shifted the blow away. She stepped through, the movements Ahn had shown her, and swung with all her might.

Salvation passed by Xilor without touching. The momentum carried her beyond, and she stumbled.

Salvation had moved away. The sword had a mind of its own.

Agony ripped through her body with her back to Xilor. His legion of soldiers hooted in admiration. An unseen force constricted, holding her still.

He'd done that before in their first fight, holding fast as he tried to recruit her.

She traced the sensation, finding the tether to his essence, and followed it back. In a mighty shove, she lashed out. A bellow of agony came from the dark lord, and the hold released.

Able to move again, she stumbled, catching her balance. She spun around as Xilor, his feet off the ground, descending like a giant bat snatching prey.

The essence welled up in her, lashing out without restraint, and it wracked and momentarily blinded her. She shook it away, finally understanding what was howling at her.

She struck again with the life drain to lull him in. As he neared, she cut off suddenly. His blade rose high. Her right hand jerked to Judgement and pulled. The steel screamed as it came free. Xilor's wizard's sword came down. She blinked, disappearing.

And materialized behind him.

She drove Judgement through his back and out his chest, driving to the hilt. Xilor arched and bellowed.

An explosion cleaved the air, catching her unprepared. Both swords were torn from her grip. She tumbled away and landed on her back. The air rushed from her lungs, and she blinked stars away. Beneath, the wraith slivered closer to her heart. She staggered up, trying to catch her breath.

By the time her gaze tracked to Xilor, he'd pulled the weapon free of his back, no doubt with magic. His right hand touched his chest, and when he pulled away, Starriace noticed blood.

By all that is holy, Judgement went through his shield.

A sliver of hope settled in her gut. A black ink-like substance dripped out of him, blood like tar.

She smirked.

"Oh? So, the mighty can be killed?"

His hood tracked to her, and though she couldn't see his face, she felt his fear and loathing.

With her essence stretched out, she awaited the first sign of an attack. A flicker of uncertainty flashed through her right before Xilor moved. No words came, only spellcraft.

Pure, unrelenting magic.

Each spell powerful in its own right was fueled by fury. Starriace didn't know how she managed to dodge, block, or defend against the vicious onslaught, but she did, and only just. The assault scored, grazed, or reflected off the mageshield. Each impact crumpled the barrier inward but it didn't dissipate.

Without a doubt, Fife's training saved her life.

Xilor marched forward, his wand weaving too quick for the eye to track. Starriace couldn't counter. She jumped and dived like she had during her last duel at Fife's, making a hard target to hit.

In a sudden lull, she countered.

The curses flew toward him, harking back to the brief duel she had with her old master. Xilor, weak with wounds and fatigue, was too slow to block the ferocious volley. By the time she ended the sequence, she'd ripped through his shield. He staggered but kept his feet.

His robes smoldered from where the blast struck.

He straightened, coming to his full height. His mageshield flickered back to life.

Fuck! Isn't he dead yet? How much more can he take?

"You didn't think it'd be that easy, did you?"

He's too strong. I can't get through the barrier without wasting valuable energy.

He let out a volley of power, a sweeping arc in all directions. She bolstered her mageshield, knowing she couldn't dodge. Her feet left the ground. In the air, the energy coiled around and held her, and the rest swept back to assail. Each blow made her magic waver.

She reached deep, strengthening the cocoon around her. The phantom within slid ever closer to her heart the more she drew. Concentrating on the deep well of power, she held out for as long as possible. Like all muscles fatigued from constant stimulation, her grip eventually faltered.

The last blast hit her; icy sensations chilled her to the bone, slowing reflexes and giving an instant case of hypothermia. She fell to the ground and curled up for warmth. Her teeth chattered as her body shivered.

A shadow loomed overhead.

The thought of dying at Xilor's hands made her cling on through sheer will. She remembered fighting Fife and the wall of fire. She let the memory fill her, molding her essence, and let go. An inferno rose up, protecting her, and keeping Xilor at bay.

The chill left as she basked in the heat.

Clarity suffused her and she readied herself for the next round of volleys. Her eyes festered, the irritation crawling through her skull. Direct attacks weren't working.

Her hand waved out, influencing the fire, and she pushed. The flames leapt at the command and encircled him. She allowed herself to dip into her untapped rage, and it wasn't hard. She had a lot to spare.

The flames rose high, latching on to him and his robes. In a single moment, he was engulfed. He shrieked with an otherworldly voice. A gust ripped through, and the flames dissipated. The ground beneath him had charred.

Panic washed through her.

I'll never be helpless again.

The mantra brought back images of Mr. Pleasure. She remembered what it felt like seeing him again in the Corridor. Like this. Throwing caution aside, she gave in.

The ground churned behind him, and he turned. A boulder tore from the earth, coming up through the flesh of dirt, and crashed down on him.

With a sickening crunch, he crumbled.

She didn't see Xilor on the ground, but Mr. Pleasure. She raised it high and brought it down again with all her might. It ricocheted off his mageshield. She reached deep and broke another rock away. It came crashing down like a meteor. This, too, was partially turned, both by his barrier and feeble casting.

Sensing his weakness, she dropped her wand and used both hands. Half a dozen massive slabs of limestone erupted from the ground, and she sent them plummeting. The first three were still cast aside, the third one only just. The fourth, fifth, and sixth crushed him.

Drained, she dropped to her knees. Her wand lay within reach. With trembling hands, she snatched it up. The phantom coiled and slithered. She hitched, and the sharp affliction snaked past her heaving lungs, encircled her heart, and constricted.

By the phantom or by Xilor. Either way, I die today.

She accepted that fate. The prophecy of the fairies said as much. She remembered back to when Judas first spoke of the prophecy.

"… a powerful mage coming from beyond the realm of magic. It's said this mage will be a perfect balance of light and dark."

In the moment of clarity, she was content. She'd lived and experienced new things, new friends in Iddrial and the other elyfian. She came to appreciate the unique relationship with Ava. Harold. She adored and would miss the old hermit.

And she had known love. She loved Kam and Lily, and now they'd have a family together.

If there ever was a man… I'm sorry I couldn't come to you when you called, Lily. Forgive me.

A hand lurched up, reaching for her. She tried to jerk away but only swayed. It was black, skeletal, and darkness misted about it. She tried to find the energy to stand, to fight back, to kill Xilor, but couldn't. Before long, he'd pulled himself to his feet.

Knowing he still lived gave her strength. Trembling legs protested as she rose. Within, she strained against the wraith, biding a few more moments to finish Xilor.

I've got to get this thing out of me!

"You've grown," he said, almost sounding amused. "I can confess I may have been too hasty in trying to eliminate you."

He took a step forward. Starriace's eyes flickered over to the stump of his left arm. At least she had that. She'd marked him in a way no one else had.

It would stand as a testament for all time.

But shock coiled through her. His stump appeared to grow back. She wasn't sure, but where she had sheared the flesh seemed longer than before.

Can he rejuvenate? Regrow limbs? Can he truly not die?

"During our first fight, I toyed with you. I'm surprised you're still alive now, which attests to your skills. I won't make the same mistake again."

He took another step as she tried to find her feet. Exhaustion washed over her. She placed a hand on the ground to steady herself.

"You've managed to hold your own, and that brings me great joy. I need you. Ermaeyth needs you."

Another step closer.

"Don't throw your life away. Help me strengthen Ermaeyth for what's to come. There are dangers out there you couldn't possibly comprehend."

"I don't yield."

He gave a harrumph.

"I take no pleasure in ending your life, but I'll take joy in laying your broken, lifeless body at Judas's feet. After I've feasted on his agony, I'll lay his body next to yours. A quick death."

He paused.

"And they say I'm not kind."

She found her resolve, her feet, and her essence came back, renewing her limbs and shield with vigor.

"This fight will be different from the last."

A slight chuckle escaped him.

"Don't delude yourself, child. You'd be dead if not for interference in our last encounter."

As he spoke, Starriace's mind raced through the possibilities for the next attack. She discarded them. None of them would work. Then, she remembered the way she entered Norek's mind in the Corridor. She reached out softly and touched his mind with all the finesse she could muster.

"Amazing!" he said. "Your probe was almost undetectable. A soft touch. Reminds me of Judas."

Her mind almost latched on to his words, that her probe was like Judas's, but she dismissed it.

Xilor redoubled his efforts to fortify his mind. Iron walls swallowed him up and barred her entry.

Starriace shifted, found the back door, and slipped through.

And gasped.

She'd always assumed someone like him had a complex mind, layers upon layers of intricate secrets and mysteries. But it wasn't. Simple, yet savage and deadly, driven by one desire: survival.

And what was more, he was honest.

Everything he'd ever said, needing her help, strengthening Ermaeyth, mourning her passing, the threat from beyond. It was all true. He really did see himself as a tragic hero branded a villain. He realized everyone viewed him as a monster, something vile and profane, and how everyone would see his conquest as a blighted mark on the world.

Every threat he saw, every civilization, those who looked much like wizardkind, and those born out of nightmares. There were too many to count, too many to remember, but malice dripped from the vast majority she'd witnessed.

She almost wept at the truth.

Yes, what he did was evil, shameful, a sacrifice he made to save his world. He offered up his soul, his tarnished name, and his life to ensure Ermaeyth survived.

His thoughts rolled through her mind.

There's a monster in everyone; I embraced mine to save us all.

The voice echoed in her head, a mantra he'd told himself as he stared at his reflection.

She shivered.

There was a monster within her, too. A darkness so deep, it terrified her. And she'd shied away, pulled back from the brink when faced with a situation where she could no longer deny it.

Xilor had plunged headfirst.

And still, the probe slipped deeper. It was dangerous to lurk inside the monster's mind, but she searched for something more and found it.

Brimstones.

She pushed, skimming the surface of those particular thoughts as quickly as she could. She found hints to locations, jumbled and written like poetry or riddles. And with each revealed secret, his emotions roiled through her: dismay, agitation, and weariness.

But one question remained: how did he know of them? Perhaps that would lead to the truth. Xilor clamped down on his thoughts, and she pulled free.

All passed within three breaths.

"You're right," she said.

The horrors of the revelations, of the truth, swept through her.

"There are dangers out there, and we need to be prepared."

"You'll join me?"

He stood, his army at his back. In truth, they were an impressive and terrifying sight to behold. She wondered if anyone from Ralloc—behind her—could see them, if anyone witnessed the battle, the sparkles of lights in the night.

She let her eyes drop from the army of goblins, trolls, and various creatures throughout. When would he turn and slaughter them?

She shook her head.

"But there's a danger here, now, and must be stopped."

He seemed to sigh at this—if he could. His cowl moved slowly, his head bobbing.

"You've chosen death…again."

The end of his wand lit with the acidic fire. The swirling, green wizard's sword sputtered to life.

Starriace reached out a hand, calling Judgement and Salvation, but they didn't stir. Fear pummeled her, and she searched for them. She spied Judgement, the black blade gleaming from the torchlight a dozen paces off. She reached out, focusing, and the steel only shivered.

"It's a shame your power has failed."

The phantom wormed through her failing hold and closed around her heart. In a single stroke, it squeezed.

"I rather hoped you'd die fighting."

He raised his blade.

She gave one last effort, but lunged at him at the last moment, closing the distance. Both went sprawling to the ground. She landed on top, and the wraith jerked inside.

This close to Xilor, it felt the call, the pull.

Her body convulsed as if to yack. In one swift moment, the phantom let go and left willingly. What remained of it passed from her mouth and into Xilor's chest wound where Judgement pierced him.

Did he even realize what happened? She wasn't entirely sure she did.

When the last of the inky blackness was expelled, she heaved a deep breath.

Xilor twitched on the ground, and the vapor entered him. It reacted with his magic, and the blast knocked her clear from him.

In a rush, her power returned, like seeing for the first time, or noticing colors that were never there. Her body thrummed.

She turned to Xilor, and pity swelled. She understood him now, empathized with his plight.

He'd become a monster to save them, but he'd gone about it the wrong way. He culled the weak from them, killing thousands, and eventually millions. But there was another way to save them. She was already on the path.

The brimstones.

Somewhere along the way, both Xilor and Rusem had stumbled and hadn't completed the quest. Maybe they were never on the right path to begin with?

But she would find them.

She gazed down at Xilor as he thrashed, wracked with pain. She'd only been a host for the entity, and it fed on magic. From the sounds, it devoured Xilor from the inside out. She was half-tempted to leave him to that fate, but if she walked away without finishing him, he could rise again.

And that was something she couldn't abide.

"I'll finish what you started," she promised.

Energy crackled between her fingers.

"I'll make sure Ermaeyth survives."

And the energy tore from her, screaming from her body into his. The familiar tingling sensation erupted from her fingertips as the familiar red-purple lightning lurched out, enveloping Xilor in a cocoon of energy.

He withered and shrieked under the bombardment.

Fear poured into her channeling. Despite understanding him, empathizing with him, he was still a monster. Trepidation, hate, and all the pent-up acrimony burrowed along his body as the arcs rippled across his convulsing form. She'd never been so afraid as when she faced him, never been so horrified as when she realized she became him; Mr. Pleasure broke her in ways Xilor never would, but he crumbled at a distant second.

The energy, driven by emotions, became unbearable.

And then, the life drain lightning stopped.

She swayed, reached the limit of pouring into him. Her hands ached like a deep cut itches when it heals. She was drained, completely exhausted, knowing she could go no further.

She had expended herself.

And he was *still* alive.

Her eyes roamed over the hordes in front of her. All stood still, their eyes locked on the action. She could've sworn, at the back of the army, she saw hundreds lumbering off as if they sensed the end. Starriace had to admire their discipline to not attack, or was it fear?

His charred husk smoldered, and the scent burned her nostrils with something thick and acrid. The black mass lay within the swaths of curling smoke.

He has to be drained, barely clinging to life.

Xilor twitched, then stirred, and found some unknown strength to keep going. He came to his feet and swayed.

His voice came out weak and thready.

"You can't kill what's already dead."

He coughed.

"That's the closest I've ever come. Perhaps, I've underestimated you again."

He stooped and plucked up his metallic wand. Starriace eyed him as he did. They'd fought to a standstill, and it was a matter of who'd recover first.

As she thought about the grueling battle continuing, she sensed it.

Danger. An imminent threat. A swell of intensity.

She reached out to Xilor with her essence, discerning if his power returned.

It hadn't.

She traced the essence and cast her eyes in the direction of the building strength, back towards Ralloc. In the torchlight, a man stood in the distance, his staff planted on the ground beside him, his arms weaving.

"Oh shit," she blurted.

Xilor glanced at her.

With the last bit of energy, she gave her all and shoved the looming shadow as far as possible. Xilor went tumbling, landing deep in the ranks of his army.

And then the world erupted in blinding light and fire.

Chapter 62: Gryzlaud Palace

In the darkness of his chambers, Xilor clung to life. A hushed stillness permeated the incensed air. His sweeping frame lay sprawled on the bed.

Smoke coiled in the stench of earth and decay.

The door to his chambers opened, and Xilor's gaze fell to the door. Krurik stood within the frame, silhouetted by the light outside.

"Come," Xilor rasped.

Krurik stepped inside, shut the door, and came to the bedside.

"You're actually dying."

"Yes."

His wheezing rasps sounded like a death rattle. No doubt he was moments away from the final one.

"How may I serve you one last time, Master?"

The emotion of an ironic grin flickered through Xilor.

"I have last commands."

"Speak, and all will be done."

Xilor had to be careful. If Krurik realized what he was about to do, he'd rebel in the final moments. Xilor could trust Sidjuous, but after Xilor perished, he couldn't trust Krurik not to kill him.

Then, his plans would fail.

"My time has come to an end. You must carry on my legacy."

Xilor coughed, feeling that thing Starriace put inside him. It ate at him, his magic and physical body, but his soul was forever beyond reach. The *thing* inside was killing him, as was the wound from the black blade.

"You must prepare Ermaeyth. The threat may not manifest for ages or legends, but it will happen."

"I will."

"As I've prepared you, you must prepare another. As I've culled the weak from Ermaeyth, you must cull the weak from within."

"What are you saying, Master?"

"All of my apprentices, all of my minions, must be destroyed. Kill them all and start again."

Krurik bowed low.

"If that is your wish, it shall be done. Is there no one you'd have me spare?"

"Yes," Xilor said softly.

Another wracking cough took him, and the entity within slithered.

"Derms, my goblin slave. He's served me well, and he'll serve you. And Sidjuous. There are many uses for those who are faithful. Show him your command and clemency, and he'll show you loyalty."

Xilor watched as Krurik's face twitched with disgust. His lips narrowed.

"You know how I see him."

"You've trusted me in life, trust me in death."

Krurik dipped his head, his dark hair obscuring his face for a moment.

"And the Betrayer? Olga and Miza?"

Xilor took a deep breath.

"He dies. Do what you will with the girls."

A glimmer came to Krurik's eyes.

Xilor took a few breaths.

"Let me bestow my blessing upon you. Help me rise."

Krurik came forward and positioned Xilor on the edge of the bed. He coughed again and felt his body sway.

"Kneel."

Krurik obeyed.

It all comes down to this, these final moments.

Xilor placed his palm on Krurik's forehead.

"As I die, I ensure our survival. Within you, I live on. With my fall, you rise. In your death, I shall live on."

Xilor sent out the last tendrils of his magics, binding him and the apprentice to the ritual.

"You're now the protector of Ermaeyth, may it endure."

"May it endure," the apprentice echoed. "Thank you, Master."

The apprentice rose.

"Now, I'm the dark lord?"

Xilor gave a single chuckle.

"I never liked that title. Ralloc dubbed me such, not me."

He coughed again, his body shivering.

"One last thing," Xilor said.

He pulled his wand out and thrust it to Krurik. The student took the metal object with reverent hands.

"Destroy it and reforge yourself a wand from the shards, as I have done."

"I will, Master."

Xilor shook his head.

"No, now. Break it, release me, and seal our fates together."

Krurik laid the wand on the floor and pulled his own. He held it for a moment, his eyes flickering to Xilor.

"Thus begins my reign," Krurik said.

A flash of magic washed out. Xilor's wand sheared, and agony ripped through him. Magical fire engulfed his body, and for a moment after, he realized he was no more.

Panic filled the Betrayer. He hurried through the deserted, secret corridors below Gryzlaud Palace. Not so long ago, he'd helped Miza escape through these very tunnels.

Xilor had returned in a weakened state a few hours ago, and there wasn't any doubt he'd dub Krurik as his successor. Only the tradition of the wands exchanging hands remained, and once complete, the Betrayer was a dead man.

The ceremony wasn't concluded until the new lord forged a wand out of the remains of the old. Once finished, the new reign would begin. Usually, the apprentice took the master's wand by force, slaying the teacher once he'd garnered enough power and followers.

Had Xilor not been unfortunate, Krurik would've eventually attempted a coup.

This is my one chance to escape, while they're busy.

He considered going to Olga's room and pleading her to flee with him, but he knew how that'd play out. He worried for her wellbeing despite how she turned out. What he feared throughout her life came true. Olga turned out like her father, a black, cast-iron heart, her parents' evil seed, filled with anger, bitterness, and jealousy. Clearly, more than her father's heart had passed to her.

But one good thing came from all of this. Miza was gone, escaped. He took comfort that he hadn't heard anything. Either it was still undetected, or she'd found safety.

He hurtled down the cramped tunnel, nearing the end. The opening to the river was dead ahead.

And then, he felt the blast of power, rushing out from within the castle. Dark and cold, searing and bright. It washed over him in waves like ripples in a pond.

After the power faded, the Betrayer turned in the direction of the blast.

Whether Ralloc realized it or not, they traded one monster for a bigger one.

Once Krurik solidified his hold, he'd begin a purge, but not structured like Xilor's. No, Krurik would sweep through and butcher families as they ate, towns as they slept. It wouldn't be strategic but a slaughter.

I've got to delay that from happening.

But Krurik was single-minded. He wouldn't begin until he wiped out all of Xilor's followers and started over. And that meant the Betrayer.

I can delay him if he never finds me. But where will I go?

He didn't have the slightest notion, only that Krurik would hunt him without end. It didn't matter now, surviving did.

With a renewed sense of urgency, he made his escape.

Chapter 63: Ralloc

A familiar figure breached the threshold, and Starriace glanced up.

Judas spied her and hurried over.

Though she couldn't explain what precisely, he had a constrained look, as if he wanted to say something paramount but feared to. Something warred within her, a conflict. Did she really want to visit now? As he drew closer, she detected a restrained fury in his eyes.

Probably because I confronted Xilor without him.

Had it not been for Norek's intervention, he might be attending her at a funeral rather than the pharmacon's wing. Was his ire about her actions, or because she didn't tell him? She expected a lecture.

Instead, she received praise.

"Your display was extraordinary," Judas said.

Pharmacon mages bustled about, tending her wounds. Now that the phantom had abdicated her body, the healers tended the inflicted damage. The discovery of such corruption required a maghai's touch.

"I'm very proud of you."

She gave a weak smile but remained guarded.

"Thanks. Xilor's army?"

His brows twitched up, and he glanced in the direction of the battlefield far off.

"Fled the moment he teleported away."

He gave a sigh of relief and shook his head.

"You're my only apprentice to face Xilor and live. A dignified feat."

He cleared his throat, his brows drawing down, his lips moving like he chewed on something bitter.

"The council would like to debrief you once you're…on your feet."

She kept silent. She wasn't about to tell a panel of politicians anything. She eyed Judas. His tight voice hinted at holding back despite the jovial exterior; his eyes were reserved with perhaps a touch of fear.

For one dubious moment, she thought about entering his mind, sifting through the layers of enigmas, and tearing out his secrets. Restraint kept her from violating his sanctity. Privacy remained her prerogative; she had to respect his. The touch of trepidation radiating from him also stayed her hand.

But there wasn't any harm in hovering near and seeing if she *heard* anything. Taking deliberate care, she moved her senses to the back door to his mind, much like she'd done with Xilor, but she hovered away. Xilor had said her gift was much like Judas's, and the loud thoughts flowing out of him, the panic, the tightness of his distress, she understood what he wanted to say.

She let her hovering essence fall away before he realized she was there.

"What are your plans now?"

His voice quivered, but was it in mutual apprehension of each other, or what he was bursting to talk about?

"A bit of soul searching," she answered.

It tasted bitter in her mouth, but she needed to.

"There are things I need to discover."

Though vague, it was the truth, not only of herself but of the brimstones and continuing Xilor's work. The dark lord, if he deserved such a title after what she discovered, had recruited her to the cause but not to his side.

Judas wouldn't accept her explorations and experimentation. He'd balk at her relationship with Kam and Lily if he found out. She couldn't stomach his revulsion if he discovered her most intimate secrets, and she wasn't referring to affiliations.

Especially if what she sensed just now was the truth, but she had no reason to doubt it.

With Xilor dead or dying, she could seek the brimstones in peace, and find out their real purpose. Traveling excited her, but friends had earned devotion, and promises had to be kept. But studying endured as the priority, and Harold proved an apt teacher. The elyfian curse still lingered. With Ava the only fairy alive, the pixie deserved a faithful companion. She had her whole life ahead.

"I was wondering," Judas began, "if you considered completing your training with me?"

Starriace glanced at him, the brimstones and all else swept away by the profound sorrow and hope in his voice.

Shades, he missed me.

She shook her head, and she made sure her voice was just as gentle.

"Not at this time. When I'm ready, I'll come. You have my word."

She didn't reject him out of disrespect, or to shun and hurt him. Despite their rocky relationship, his flaws, she acknowledged he was a great man.

In the past, anger blinded her, blaming him and Fife Doole for every misdeed that came her way. She didn't want that life anymore, besides, how could she resent her father?

That's why he's so reserved now. Why he was protective around Norek. But is he going to tell me he knows the truth?

His eyes and voice betrayed the hurt, but her answer didn't crush his spirit as she feared.

"When you're ready, I'll be waiting. Besides, you need more of a guide than a master."

His acknowledgment of her prowess brought a genuine smile to her face.

"Thank you, Judas. Just give me time."

In an alarming moment, he leaned forward and hugged her. His embrace was warm, his scent carried subtle spiciness and cloves. Confusion, acceptance, and a yearning to belong ran through her, and it felt odd hugging both her former master and the man who sired her.

A stray thought came to her during the embrace.

When will I find a man for myself?

Kam came to mind, but he was Lily's husband. Did Kam have any friends?

How comfortable would that friend be, knowing she and Kam slept together?

Harold's prophecy came to mind, the line about her finding the arms of a lover. She hoped it was sooner rather than later. She was tired of being alone. Even though surrounded by the elyfian, Kam and Lily, even Harold, she was alone.

She could give up Kam. It's not like she had a claim to him, anyway. But trying to imagine her life without her Rallocan friends was too painful. Surely, they'd still be friends?

With a light kiss on her forehead, Judas broke the embrace and retreated without a word.

A knock came on the door as Judas reached it. Norek poked his head inside and smiled.

"You're awake!"

His arrival stamped out her wandering thoughts. Judas gave one last smile and left.

"Hey, there," Norek said, approaching her bedside.

She kept the same reserve with the new visitor.

"Norek."

"Why are you here? You only have a couple of bumps and bruises, right?"

"Thanks to you. You tend to show up when least expected but most needed."

"Well, I'm not going to be around forever, so don't get used to it."

"Oh? Got plans?"

A smile lit his features.

"Personal things. Someone to talk to."

Starriace deliberated for a moment, remembering Meristal's strange behavior when she left the council chambers, then decided to pursue the notion.

"You're talking about your mother, aren't you?"

His eyes widened a fraction, and he seemed to hold his breath.

"I hope you meet her."

She changed the subject to give him privacy. She had all the answers she needed. Between Judas, Meristal, and now, Norek, the puzzle took shape.

"As for me, I won't be staying much longer."

He gave a wooden nod.

"Then, I'll take my leave and let you rest. See you around."

He stepped away.

"Are you sure?"

He turned back and gave a smile.

"You're forgetting, I've got my orb. I've seen it."

That made her smile. The brimstones came to mind. She needed help and couldn't go to Judas. Could he help her on the quest with his Owlen magic?

"Why don't you come with me?" she asked. "I could always use an intellect. Maybe even someone to save me?"

He stopped and turned, grinning.

"An intriguing offer, but I'll skip the perilous, full-time job. There's no money in saving you every day. A man's got to eat, right?"

She laughed without mirth.

"Seriously, why not come?"

"Starriace," he said hesitantly.

He started back to her bed, speaking as he closed the distance.

"Power will come when it will. Searching is spurred by ambition, and you know where the trail leads."

She closed her eyes and shook her head.

"You sound like Judas."

She focused on his face and cocked her head.

"You even kind of look like him, too."

And now that puzzle that took shape became all the more clear.

Norek made a noise in his throat.

"If the warlock couldn't bring you around, need I say more?"

"I've only thought of survival," she blurted. "To never be helpless or weak. The strong live without shackles, and the weak cling to them as saviors. If we're strong, don't we have an obligation to do something with our gifts?"

The statement rang with truth, and it did hedge the promise she made to herself and Xilor.

"That sentiment, young lady, is a slant of Xilor's beliefs. You've become what you hated."

Without another word, he departed.

His words were a splash of cold water, followed by a slap to the face. She remembered when Xilor first offered her a place at his side.

She'd refused.

Now, she knew he spoke the truth. Were they so different? Were they identical?

No. We're not the same.

Their general ideals were compatible, but she did what she must to survive. Xilor purged the world of perceived weakness. To him, the inept were a disease, a plague bleeding the world dry. Her plans were to become all-powerful and to save the world without the loss of life.

Satisfied with her conclusion, she laid back down and let the fatigue sweep her away.

In the afternoon of the day following her fight with Xilor, the maghai declared her fit enough to leave. Others needed the bed more than she. Soldiers with missing limbs, civilians burned by dragon fire. She left the castle as discreetly as she could, hoping none recognized or stopped her.

In the courtyard, she called the stone giant who helped her.

"Rawk?"

The mounds of rock slid and morphed, the creature reforming out of the greater mass.

"Ah, you've come, little nephiliam," he said with that deep, resounding voice.

"Yes. Thank you for doing what I've asked. You're free to return home with my most humble gratitude."

The stone giant studied her for a moment.

"Are you certain?"

"Yes."

"We've been of service to you, nephiliam. We shall be so again."

She was puzzled by his words but thought it nothing more than a parting pleasantry.

He stepped away, reforming in the wall, and then the entire dome began to sink back into the ground. The courtyard shook as the mammoth slabs receded. Frightened people came running out of the castle. The earth churned beneath him as he sunk down, the dirt swallowing them whole.

His words reached her as they slipped below the walls.

"Until you require us, we'll be waiting."

Not likely. Xilor's dead.

Apor, the giant blue sun, which had only been up for a few hours at most, blinded the idle watchers. The common people, the council, and other essential delegates watched as the stone giants slid back to the earth.

When the last bit of rock vanished, a movement at ground level caught everyone's eye. A young girl about Starriace's age stumbled forward and collapsed in a heap. For a moment, no one moved, but then everyone exploded into action.

Starriace almost rushed forward, but Judas beat her. Guards formed a ring around the young woman, and Starriace slipped back, content to watch. Someone thrust a waterskin forward, and Judas accepted it gratefully.

The warlock cupped the back of the young woman's head and lifted her off the ground. He poured the water in her mouth. She responded with groggy movements at first but drank with greed after a few moments.

Judas glanced up at the guards.

"It's fine, you can move away."

They did, and he turned his attention back to the young woman. Starriace came closer to eavesdrop.

"There, there, child. It looks like you've had a long journey."

She pulled her parched lips away from the waterskin.

"Y-yes."

She coughed and reached for the water again. Once she had her fill, she asked.

"Is—food?"

"Someone fetch food," Judas called out.

One guard broke off to the castle, and another spoke up.

"Why don't you use a rejuvenation spell on her?"

"She's barely alive. If I did a spell of that magnitude on her, the shock would make her worse rather than better."

By this time, Norek had come out to see what the commotion was. He didn't notice Starriace hovering near the edges. He gazed down on the young woman who was sitting up now.

"You look like you haven't eaten in days."

"I haven't," she said.

"Where'd you come from?" Judas asked.

"The dark lord's tower."

It wasn't the answer Starriace expected, nor did anyone else. The girl's eyes slid out of focus, and she trembled. Murmurs broke out among the throng of people. Starriace scrutinized them all as they conversed. She noted Meristal had arrived, and she made her way closer to the circle.

"Xilor's fortress?" Judas asked. "How long have you been there?"

"As long as I can remember. I may have been born there, I don't know."

"How'd you escape?" a guard asked.

"A kind man helped me."

"Why are you here?" another guard asked.

Judas glanced up at them and waved them to keep silent.

"I'm here to see my uncle."

"Tell me about this kind man." Judas said. "What's his name?"

"I don't know, he was always referred to as the Betrayer."

"The Betrayer?" Meristal asked.

Starriace noted Judas and Meristal exchanged glances.

"What did he look like?" Meristal asked.

"He was old, not real old—" the girl glanced at Judas, "—about your age, if I had to guess."

Meristal and Judas exchanged looks again.

What are they thinking? What are they not saying aloud?

"Come on," Judas said. "Let's get you inside, some food in your belly, and you can tell us all about it."

"No," the woman said with a shake of her head. "Not everyone, just you. The Betrayer said my uncle had enemies."

Judas nodded.

"Okay, only me. You have my word."

Starriace eyed the group as they helped the young woman up. She almost went with them, to hear the secrets of Xilor and his fortress, but decided not to.

With Judas occupied, it's the perfect time to leave.

As the group ushered the traveler inside, Starriace slipped away.

Behind closed doors, the council deliberated the traveler's tale, how she managed to escape, the kind man who helped her, and her declaration of an uncle.

Judas and Meristal remained behind, too.

Vamor spoke first.

"Why should we trust her? It might be a trick or a trap."

"I can detect no deceit in her," Daylynn rebutted.

Lagelm, the black-eyed goblin, cleared his throat and leaned forward.

"She speaks the truth, as far as she's aware."

"At this point in time," Kellis, the other goblin, said, "we've no reason to doubt her. Does she belong to any family among us?"

"Do we even have her name?" Godfrey asked in his flat voice.

"Not at this time," Meristal said.

Godfrey's cheek twitched at her words, and if possible, his eyes grew colder.

"Until we can determine the proper course of action," Sedrus said, "we should place her in the care of someone capable as we seek out relatives."

"I agree," Daylynn said.

"So do I," Vamor concurred, then offered, "She could stay with me. I have that large manor to myself. She'd have plenty of room."

"If that is the case," Lagelm spoke, "she should go with Starriace or Norek. They did defeat Xilor, after all."

"I'd agree, Councilman Lagelm," Vamor replied smoothly, "but Madam Starriace has no home. She's a vagabond at best. As for this newcomer, Norek, no one's ferreted out his true purposes here."

"We're not here to discuss Starriace and Norek but the girl," Daylynn spoke up. "She still needs a place to stay."

Kellis glanced down the panel at Vamor.

"Placing her in the care of a male close to her age may cause problems."

"I agree," Meristal spoke, "she should also be placed with a capable master. If the council should decide, I volunteer my house and my tutelage."

"I find that agreeable," Lagelm said.

"As do I," Kellis said.

"Aye," Sedrus said.

"Aye, as well," Daylynn said. "Very well, Meristal, she'll be transferred to you pending when we can find her family."

"I haven't agreed," Godfrey said suddenly. "And I'm almost certain Poplu and Capraro don't either. In fact—"

"Let me save you the trouble, Consul," Lagelm interrupted. "We have four to three in favor."

Godfrey swallowed hard and leaned back in his seat without another word.

"Unless there are any other immediate concerns, we should adjourn," Daylynn said.

Hynry hurried over to Godfrey and spoke into his ear. The consul stood and spoke brusquely.

"I'll see you all later. I have a delegation to assemble to meet with the dragon higher king sitting outside our walls. They wish to make peace."

Chapter 64: Lakayre Manor

"There are things to discuss," the man said as he cooked breakfast, "but first, a proper meal is in order."

His long hair fell to his shoulders, and it swayed as he mixed something in a pan.

Miza's eyes went from him to the red-haired woman, Meristal, who sat at the kitchen table.

Though the home they entered was gorgeous and far smaller than Xilor's home, the house was warm and inviting with wood, paintings, and books, a sharp contrast to Xilor's abode of shadows, cold stone, and fires glittering from torches in sconces.

The man cooking her breakfast remained aloof, physically present, but with divided attention. It was somewhat infuriating. His kindness didn't leave her wanting, his attention did. He acted as if pulled in numerous directions. Instead of focusing on a few, he committed to all with partial focus.

Meristal said the council selected her for immediate care, but Miza had the feeling it equated to this man's charge. Perhaps it was his kindness that made her follow blindly, but a part of her didn't fear him. The council, she knew about them, had remanded her to someone's care. If she turned up dead, too many questions would be asked.

It was public knowledge.

The trio retreated to what she assumed was his manor. She ate while he tidied the kitchen, then all moved to the sitting room.

When they were all seated, the man leaned forward, placing his elbows on the insides of his thighs, his fingers steepled and facing the floor.

"Okay, now that we're sorted, it's time to delve into it."

"Like what?" Miza inquired.

She knew her inner worry made its way to her face.

"Your name, for starters."

"Miza."

"Very well, Miza. Let's talk about your uncle."

Meristal arched an eyebrow at him.

Miza revealed her family lineage, and the man's slack face and pale shade bespoke all the shock he felt.

Miza scrutinized him.

"You know him?"

"Yes."

"Where is he? Is he near?"

"I suspect he'll arrive by the conclusion of our conversation."

He evaded, much like his name. But she couldn't help but smile.

"Good, I can't wait to meet him. What's he like?"

"You'll meet him soon enough. First, we must continue our conversation.

What kind of training and treatment did you receive at Xilor's Palace?"

"Not much. We didn't have a curriculum to follow, but someone taught me when he could."

"The Betrayer?" Meristal asked.

Miza nodded.

"He was kind. As far as treatment, it wasn't what you'd call tender, except him. To the rest, I was unworthy of notice."

"This Betrayer, did he use Rumigul magic?"

"What's that?"

Her answer surprised him, but it was one of bewilderment.

"Okay, I'll take that as a no."

"What are you talking about?"

The trepidation and caution snaking through her made it to her voice.

"Where's my uncle?"

Meristal leaned forward.

"Miza, you've nothing to worry about. We're here to help you."

"Why do you want to see him so bad?" the man asked.

Miza noted the shift between the two. He let Meristal be the nicer of the two for the moment.

"He's the only family I have."

"What if your uncle isn't the man you thought? What if he's as cruel as the people you fled?"

Miza snorted.

"I'd doubt that. If he is," she looked pointedly at Meristal, "you're my guardian. I'm sure you'll intervene."

A twitch of a smile came to Meristal then, but the man continued.

"What makes you doubt?"

"The way everyone spoke ill of him at the palace. He must be a decent person for them to hate him. What's Rumigul?"

The man smiled but refrained from questioning her intentions.

"Rumigul's the fifth branch of magic, mages conjuring without incantations. My dear, did you not receive any formal training?"

"I can conjure without incantations, too. Is that good?"

"It's…uncommon. People fear those who use their minds rather than words."

"Well, what do you do?"

"Rumigul."

Miza's eyes slid to Meristal, but she only twisted her lips.

"Why do people fear us?" Miza asked.

"Fear changes people, drives them to strange circumstances and terrible choices."

Doubt flashed through her, and she couldn't hide the tinge of fear coming to her eyes.

"My best, educated guess?" he continued. "Because it gives us a tactical advantage in combat. Another reason is most who use our branch stray to the darker recesses of sanity. Magic isn't inherently pure or evil, only the wielder and how they use their gifts."

"I see."

"Mistakes happen," Meristal offered, "and sometimes our choices become mistakes. Once you start, it's hard to stop."

The man nodded.

"You were around corrupt individuals your whole life. It'll be more tempting for you."

Miza swallowed, holding back a range of conflicting emotions.

"I don't think my uncle would approve of you lecturing me. It isn't your place."

The elderly man rolled his eyes.

"Young people."

He stood and ambled over to his cabinet. Opening the doors, he poured himself a drink. He gulped down the amber liquor, then produced two more cups, filling both, and handed one to Miza and one to Meristal.

The scent of peaches and vanilla tickled her nose. She took a cautious sip. It was warm and sweet and tingled with spices.

"Wow, what is this? It's good."

"Parlaquay," he said, and resumed his seat.

Miza set her glass down.

"Who was the young woman earlier today? The woman with glowing eyes?"

"Er—" he paused, "a former apprentice. You saw her?"

Miza nodded, and she intuited he left some things unsaid.

"Why do her eyes glow red?"

"Physical transformation."

He took another sip.

"In times of great fear, rage, or depression, when emotions are used to amplify power, a toll is exacted. At least, that's what everyone says. This is the first time I've seen it myself. When it advances beyond more than the body was meant to tolerate, the effects are dramatic, and in most cases, everlasting. There are other times when a physical transformation takes place, but those are rare."

"Will the effects ever go away?"

"She's marked for life. Tapping into destructive mystics leaves a lasting impact, but not every blemish shows on the outside."

Her face tightened.

"Are you saying she's like Xilor?"

"No," he said after a moment, then hastened to suppress her sudden qualm. "She flirted with the line; we can only hope."

Miza broke eye contact and glanced out the window.

"When's my uncle getting here?"

Meristal leaned forward, her glass clasped in dainty fingers.

"You never told anyone else your uncle is Judas Lakayre?"

"No. Why?"

"You revealed a name that many want dead, and you by extension."

He took a deep breath.

"Ralloc can be both a safe haven and a dangerous place. Therefore, what I'm about to tell you must remain between a few of my most trusted friends and us."

She leaned back, wary. A sinking sensation settled in her gut.

"Tell her," Meristal encouraged.

He sighed.

"I'm your uncle. I'm Judas Lakayre."

A myriad of emotions danced through her, some as soft as a ballroom waltz, and others thundering like stamping boots in a line dance. Why would he not tell her this from the beginning? How would she discern if he told the truth?

"Why didn't you tell me?"

After she spoke the words, she realized the most obvious answer.

"It was a test."

She glanced between the two.

"You didn't know me any more than I did you. You couldn't figure out if what I said was genuine, or if I was—"

"An assassin?" Meristal finished.

"And now that you know, you've inherited danger. There are many who could potentially harm you. You're my blood, and I'd never forgive myself if you were harmed. I've lost apprentices, friends, and family. Each loss is a failure; each death still haunts me. There's a traitor in Ralloc. We think it's an ally or an apprentice to Xilor. That's why we asked you so many questions about what this Betrayer looked like. We had a suspect, but your description didn't match him."

She swallowed, her breath coming fast. A trickle of sweat rolled down her arm.

"The Betrayer always spoke highly of you to me. And the occasions were rare. Though he never said it aloud, he hated you. A man who demands the respect of his enemies is a man I can be proud to call family."

Both Meristal and Judas smiled at her words.

"But there was another there at Xilor's, his number one apprentice. Krurik. He came and went all the time, and though I was never privy to much, it seems like he spent most of his time in Ralloc. Perhaps this is your traitor?"

Judas's brow twitched up.

"He just might be, and I will want to question you on him and everything else that happened there, but an interrogation isn't the best thing right now. It can wait."

A small grin curled at the end of her lips, and she was grateful.

"What will happen to me now?"

"What do you want?"

"If Ralloc is a dangerous place, perhaps it isn't safe for me here, even with you."

"You're wiser than I gave you credit for."

"Growing up in Gryzlaud Palace will make you sort out your priorities."

Her words made the warlock chuckle.

"You can either live with me, or we can arrange to send you someplace far away, where you can have a chance at a normal life. Whatever you choose, I want you to know, you always have a place here. You're family."

"You mean it?" she asked, scarcely daring to hope. "I can stay here? Are you sure you want me?"

"My dear child, you're my flesh and blood. I'll never abandon you, regardless of the past."

"The past? What are you talking about?"

"A conversation for a later time," he concluded, standing. "I'm sure you'd like a bath and some rest. Let's find you a room."

Chapter 65: Starriace

Starriace dropped her pack and stared back at Ralloc, the city she helped save. Even now, they scurried to put their lives back together.

The pale blue glow of Apor lightened the sky, highlighting the first day of a new age without the dark lord. She hated the title and found it unfitting. A madman, yes, but those caught in the throes of lunacy never knew they were.

Though she didn't witness it, she sensed Xilor's passing. It'd been when Judas came to visit in the pharmacon wing—something small, almost undetectable—and she didn't give it much attention. She didn't want Judas prying further with the revelation. How she knew, she could only guess, but she suspected it had to do with the phantom they'd once shared.

A smile of contentment crept over her face. For the first time since she'd arrived in this chaotic, magical world a year ago, she might find peace.

The people she'd met along the way came to mind, the elyfian, Norek, and Fife Doole. She once thought of them as pawns, but recent events changed her perspective. She'd miss their companionship now, but a new destiny awaited. Being subjected to the elyfian culture helped her gain invaluable experience. The books at Harold's place fell short of capturing their culture.

At least, this particular group.

She honored them and their customs, hunted, ate, and laughed with them. In their time together, they ceased being pawns and became friends.

Lingering beyond those faces were two people she loved dearly: Kam and Lily.

She could do the same with them, but she'd never encroach on their life and impose herself. Her presence would cause more turmoil than good. Contentment filled her at the thought, knowing she made the right decision to leave Ralloc. With the coming of their child, there'd be no place for her. Lily seemed happy, and she couldn't deny her the opportunity.

With a pang of regret, her path lay beyond their home.

Over the last year, all her companions became teachers in unique ways. There was more to life than books and knowledge. Love, friendship, and adventure awaited, ready to fill the pages of her life's story.

Her thoughts turned away from her old journey and to the new one.

Harold was a godsend, a beacon shining in the darkness of her world. He never understood how much he meant to her, how much he truly helped. Judas and Harold were similar in their positions in her life, but the warlock lacked the ease Harold exuded. Judas's presence wound her tight, and she suffocated under his tutelage, hence why she chose to not continue her training.

The memory of Judas's words floated back to her.

Fear will drive people to do shameful things, remember that…

Something else she never considered but now became apparent: she feared Judas.

How would he react if he found out about her search for the brimstones? Would he sabotage her efforts? What if he discovered all her secrets, the flirtation with the line between darkness and light? That she'd committed genocide. Would he destroy the brimstones to undermine her efforts?

She didn't need the agony of worry.

Xilor had been right. There were threats out there, and Ermaeyth needed a strong protector. She couldn't let Judas jeopardize the path with his morality issues.

In the last year, Xilor had loomed like an outstretched shadow. With his downfall, she'd take time for herself, study, and try to find a way to confirm all that Xilor had said. The saddest part about leaving would be without seeing the elyves. She wondered after their wellbeing and the Enclave.

It was better this way.

She'd fade away, no goodbyes to fake, no penetrating questions and evasive answers. She couldn't bear to see the look on Lily's face when Starriace left again. Would she understand?

Her fingers rubbed the piece of parchment in her hand. She turned away from the city and looked out over the war-torn earth. Just the army making camp had torn through the rolling plains of grass. A churn of dark brown marred the verdant pastures.

She looked up and beyond.

The horizon represented her future, fresh, new, and wide open. The metaphor between the calm and beautiful sky and her future couldn't be more poetic. She wanted to live her way. The world was about to change, and she didn't want to be transformed with it.

For once, she was content with herself.

With Xilor dead and his army scattered and pursued, it's going to be a peaceful future.

A faint gust of wind rustled the parchment in her hand. Looking down, she unfolded the creased paper. Judas had offered her a place at his house, but she declined. She had escaped his hospitality and everlasting gaze, but leave it to Judas to get the last word.

While she readied to leave, she found a letter sitting at the top of her pack. How he managed remained a mystery.

Maybe while I was unconscious?

From the contents of the letter, she had to discard that theory. It'd been written after she left the castle.

Judas wrote:

Starriace,

You said you wanted to go off and explore, to discover answers on your own. I hope you find what you are looking for. However, I'd like to meet one last time before you leave.

The young woman who arrived in Ralloc is now in my care, and there are some things you two need to hear. Her name is Miza; also, Meristal will be joining us. I included Norek at Meristal's request, and I find it acceptable. I'd be grateful if you came, and I hope it will shed some light for you on your way.

Please, keep this parchment. Should you ever wish to speak to me and don't want to use a Psimond spell, merely write upon the page. I'll read and respond.

You are ever in my thoughts,

Judas.

For a moment, intrigue tempted her. After the initial shock of the invitation wore off, reason set in, undoubtedly another ploy to talk her into staying.

There's nothing he'd say to change my mind, so why waste my time?

Besides, she already knew what he's going to say, that he's her father. That much was evident when she hovered near his mind in the castle.

And Norek, well, it was evident that he had business with Meristal, and that would be put to rest. Her son had survived. How, Starriace didn't know, but she'd let them figure it out, and when the time came for all the answers, she'd be there to find out.

But no, she wouldn't be attending Judas and honoring his request. Her refusal wasn't meant as a sign of disrespect, or to deny the old man his wishes. She wouldn't bend to his will, no matter how much he pressured. The world tried to define her, to label her and place her in a box.

In her mind, no box existed.

A weary sigh eased out of her. She had a feeling the 'light to shed her way' would be her lineage. And now that she knew, or at least, suspected, it hadn't really changed anything at all.

For him being her father, she owed him respect, but she'd do it on her time.

A breeze kicked up, and she let go of the paper. The parchment flew from her fingers, carried by the invisible courier. She had to break ties, all of them. Clinging to his letter meant she hadn't let go.

Galloping hooves sounded in the distance and drew her attention.

Judas probably sent the palace guard after me.

She resented the idea.

Facing the sound, she waited, surprised by what she saw. The elyfian, her elyfian, rushed towards her with a centaur in tow. They reached her in a cloud of dust. The elyves gave blank and distant expressions; nothing betrayed their inner thoughts.

"Good morning," Starriace greeted.

They caught her escaping and stared in silence for a few moments before Ama Ka dismounted and took a few tentative steps forward.

Starriace was the first to speak again.

"How is the Enclave? Did they welcome you home?"

Their expressions were stoic, solemn, but beneath, a thread of joy quivered through them.

"The Enclave is in shambles," Ama Ka said.

The news rocked Starriace.

"I'm sorry."

"Many died," Cal said.

"Including the king, queen, their family, and the Supreme War

Commander," Fir Fera relayed.

Their saddles creaked as the rest dismounted.

Ari Sha spoke in her soft voice.

"Xilor sent the dragons twice to eradicate them."

Starriace swallowed.

"Does the Enclave still stand?"

"Yes," Iddrial said. "It does."

He came forward and embraced her in a quick hug. The others followed suit, the ones brave enough to get close. Ahn kept his distance, as did Cal, which she found odd.

"Iddrial's been named leader of the Enclave," Mia Ther said. "The king did so before he passed."

This surprised the mage, and her brows perked at the news.

"So, you'll be staying?"

The group nodded.

"But you aren't, are you?" Iddrial asked.

She shook her head.

"We expected as much," he said. "Which is why we've come. Once the Enclave was secured, we set out for Ralloc. We came to aid," he cast his gaze out to the churned earth where Xilor's army had camped, "but apparently you don't need it."

She gave a weak smile. Her eyes darted to the centaur who hung back.

"Who's that, and what's he doing here?"

"Later," Ama assured.

"To business then," Iddrial said. "Where are you off to?"

"Somewhere nice and quiet. Then, I want to travel. Who knows?"

"You weren't going to even say goodbye?" Ari Sha, one of two of the quietest elyves, spoke. She and Mia Ther hardly brooked words.

Starriace regarded her with surprise.

"I figured you'd survive without me. You have for ages."

"Legends," Cal corrected.

"Whatever."

"We'd like for you to take some protection," Iddrial said.

"That'd make us feel a whole lot better," Ama said.

"Protection? I think I'm good. I did fight Xilor yesterday."

"We'll never hear the end of that one," Ahn snickered, and with each passing word, he realized his mistake.

Of all the elyves, she liked him the least. He was too much like her. The elyf grated her wrong. Perhaps Iddrial was right, maybe she should bed him and get it out of the way.

She rolled her eyes at the thought.

"Still, no one can fathom the future," Cal said in reasonable tones. "We'd rather be safe than sorry."

"I'm not going to talk you all out of this, am I?"

"Nope, it's decided," Mia Ther said.

Trepidation filled her stomach.

"Alright, if I'm going to be unlucky, who's the other participant?"

"Well, uh," Iddrial relented, "I can't go, I was appointed the new leader. I'm like the king, but not."

She nodded, then turned her eyes to Ama.

"What about you?"

"Oh," Ama cast her eyes to her feet, "Ralloc has asked for liaisons between the elyves and the council. Cal and I were chosen to represent the Enclave."

"I see," Starriace drawled.

The numbers shrank. Ama would've been her first choice. She glanced at Ru Sol.

"I can't. Fir Fera and Ari Sha are to be military liaisons between the elyves and the Grand Royal Army. The Krey have declared their own sovereignty, and I'm to be an ambassador and open a dialogue with our neighbors."

There went a big chunk of choices for her.

"Uh, huh."

She glanced at Mia Ther.

"What's your excuse?"

"I left a child behind when we were cast out. He's grown now, but I'd like to get acquainted."

Well, at least it was an original excuse and decent at that.

Starriace eyed the last two options standing before her. Both males, one unfamiliar and one she despised. Fir Ki, the brother of Fir Fera, and Ahn Bael.

"You've got to be shitting me!"

The elyves tried to stifle their laughs. Her eyes slid to Ahn, his weak smile held an edge of gloating mockery.

"Why don't I save us all some trouble and me some embarrassment. I guess I'm stuck with you, huh?"

"Afraid so," Ahn smiled gleefully, rubbing his hands together in anticipation.

She rolled her eyes and shook her head.

"I'm never going to sleep with you, so you might as well wipe the smug look off your ugly mug. Set yourself in the mindset for some pretty boring and celibate years."

The others cackled, but Ama Ka looked sharply at her by the revelation.

"Years?"

Starriace ignored the question and pointed to the centaur.

"Alright, what's the deal with him?"

"He's coming with us," Ahn said.

"Why?"

"Because I said so," Iddrial spoke.

Starriace didn't miss the commanding tone in his voice.

"Sedrus has a debt to pay to the warlock, and this is how he'll repay it. Don't be too hard on him, Starriace."

"You know Judas?"

Iddrial laughed.

"Of course, we do. We've been around for a long time, remember?"

"How'd you meet?"

He waved the question away.

"Anyway, Sedrus's debt. He's to go with you."

She sighed.

"What's one more? I mean, it's bad enough with Ahn. Both can equally be a pain in my—"

"Starriace!" Ama cut her off.

"What?"

"You just met him! Don't think so shortsighted. He'll protect you with his life, and when life changes for you."

"Fine."

Does she know? I thought I hid it well, and I haven't been sick in a long time.

She was about to ask Ama to clarify, but Iddrial cleared his throat, snatching her attention.

"And this is where we say our goodbyes," Iddrial said. "May the light of the suns and moons guide you."

He embraced her. The others came forward, hugging, and repeating the phrase.

When they all stepped back, she gave them a small smile.

"Thank you for everything you've done for me."

The elyves mounted. Most turned away then, but Iddrial and Ama stayed.

She eyed both of them.

"I haven't forgotten my promise. I will find a cure for you."

Iddrial nodded, but it was Ama who spoke.

"We know. In time, you'll find us."

Starriace turned back to the open road, shouldered her pack, and began walking south. She glanced at her companions. An elyf, centaur, and herself.

This has got to be the opening line of a joke.

Before they'd traversed more than a dozen paces, Ahn broke the silence.

"Got a plan?"

"Yes."

"Where are we going?"

"South."

"What's south?"

"Our destination."

"Where's our destination?"

"I already told you," she bit her lower lip but couldn't keep from shouting. "South! Beyond the Corridor!"

They had walked a few steps.

"Want me to carry your pack? You shouldn't strain yourself."

She whirled on him.

"Shut up!"

She turned back to Ama and Iddrial. They smiled and waved, and she was certain gold exchanged hands, a bet being paid.

"Thanks a lot!" she yelled before marching off with Ahn and Sedrus on her heels.

"How long do you think they'll last?" Iddrial asked Ama Ka.

"Not long," she conceded. "Until nightfall?"

Iddrial chuckled.

"No, not even that long."

"She's going to kill him."

Ama and Iddrial remained, watching the small figures in the distance. The quiet between the two was thick, heavy with the thoughts of Ama's mistake.

"You nearly messed up again," Iddrial commented.

"It was a slip of the tongue."

"Like before? When you said the word human, and I had to say you meant homugon? That kind of slip?"

"It's hard, okay? It's hard to get everything right and perfect. All this, does she know us yet?—and can we say this to her yet?—and what about that?—it's all very frustrating."

"One day she'll understand," he said, "and then we won't have to pretend anymore. If it bothers you that much, why don't you keep away from her?"

"I can't. I'm attached to her."

Iddrial gave a slow, knowing nod.

"So am I."

The two stood in silence, watching figures fade in the distance.

Chapter 66: Lily

Thirty minutes had passed since Starriace left the elyfian.

Thankfully, the trip remained relatively quiet. Ahn had left her alone and only conversed with Sedrus. Wiping a bead of sweat from her brow, Starriace stopped abruptly when Ava manifested before her.

"Mistress! I've called for you, but you didn't come. You need to hurry! It's Lily! She needs you!"

Starriace looked between the elyf and centaur.

"Go," Ahn said. "Leave your pack. We'll continue south through the Corridor. Find us when you can. Go!"

Starriace dropped her pack, and Ava ported them away. The familiar swirl encompassed them, surged, and then faded.

Lily's gaunt frame filled Starriace's eyes as she laid on her bed. The shock of seeing her like that almost made Starriace collapse. Her breath caught in her throat.

Lily embodied the term sickly. Her once-beautiful skin hung sallow and wrinkled. Healthy, gorgeous features were a distant memory, and a withered shell remained. The term husk came to mind, and bile rose in Starriace's mouth. Lily appeared timeworn, advancing from youth to the end of life.

Her once lustrous blonde hair was now silvered.

How can one so young be so old?

The energy required to move her head tired her. When she finally realized Starriace's presence, a lonely tear rolled down the cracks and crevices of her wizened face.

"You came," Lily breathed.

"I'm here," Starriace whispered in horror.

Just the sight of Lily made her stomach turn. Starriace hurried to her side, sitting on the bed, finding her frail, wrinkled hands.

Starriace spared a moment to glance at Kam, who stood with his arms crossed at the foot of the bed, his face swollen and puffy from the range of emotions he undoubtedly endured. Starriace's heart went out to him, knowing what he must be going through. Did he put up a strong front for her sake?

The mage turned back to Lily.

Lily's lips moved, barely noticeable, and a soft hiss escaped her old, cracked lips.

"We lost Julie."

"No, no, you didn't, I'm right here."

Starriace stifled a whimper. She couldn't cry right now, had to be strong for her. Lily's hand snaked down to her womb, and the realization struck Starriace.

Dear Spirits, the baby.

Her tears came unhindered then, pooling in her lashes, then trailing down her face. She buried her face in Lily's shoulder, sobbing, grieving for the both of them, of all the time missed, and all that was lost. Behind her, Kam's reserve broke, and she heard him crying. He came up behind Starriace, he buried his face in her back, holding her, and he wept.

"Don't cry," Lily rasped.

A sudden wracking cough shook her body. When it abated, and the pain eased from her features, she squeezed Starriace's hand.

Starriace tried to think of something to say, but she couldn't. Nothing came except words that cast blame on herself.

"I should've come sooner; I should've done something—"

Guilt bludgeoned her like a cudgel.

Kam let go of her.

"There's nothing you can do," Kam said.

"Kam's right," Lily muttered, pain filling her voice.

"I'm just glad Ava was able to find you," Kam said. "With the war, the stone walls..."

"It's over. The war, the walls..."

Starriace didn't want to waste time talking about irrelevant things, not when Lily's life lay in the balance.

"Have you seen anyone, is there anything that can be done?"

Kam came to the side, and she glanced up at him, finding him shaking his head.

"Nothing. We've talked to everyone. Lily isn't the only one. The grand maghai of the pharmacon came. Apparently, she's the first reported incident. They don't know how this started. Some are saying it could be to do with the world going dark."

So, everyone saw it, not just me.

"She was the first in the city, but others fell ill, too. I heard the elyfian king and queen are dead from this—aging disease, that's what they're calling it."

"And there's nothing they can do?" Starriace asked.

"Nothing," Kam confirmed.

The word lumped in his throat. Starriace saw it in his eyes, part of him was dying with his wife.

"I love you," Lily whispered.

Starriace and Kam glanced at each other before they both lurched forward to express their own feelings. It was hard to tell who she spoke to, but perhaps to both. They'd never know.

Was it her or delirium talking?

"Take care of each other."

Lily's skin changed, turning from sallow to ashen.

"Lily," Kam choked. "I can't do this without you."

"You must. Love as I..."

Fresh tears rolled down his face, and Starriace caught a new wave of emotions. Seeing her friend dying *withered* something inside of her. Kam's agony destroyed whatever hope and goodwill there was still inside of her.

"I would've liked...some chocolate..."

A deep, rattling breath filled her lungs.

Her last breath eased from her body, her eyes opened, and she stilled.

Kam's anguished wail reverberated in Starriace's chest. It was bestial, like a wolf's howl in the dead of night, filled with sorrow and longing. When he ran out of breath, he slumped forward, holding his wife's lifeless body. Gently, Starriace leaned forward, her head resting on Kam's back.

Indignation filled her soul. Unbridled rage at the cruel circumstances threatened to overcome her. Irritation festered behind her eyes, pulsing red with each passing moment. She wanted to lash out, to destroy the world around her, and find whoever was responsible.

But, to do so would dishonor Lily's memory.

For now, she'd mourn, cherish the fleeting moments they had, and lament the calamity that befell her. And she'd honor her friend by being there for Kam in these coming days.

With halting movements, she reached for Lily's hand. Gasping through sobs, she labored to bring her faltering words to bear.

"You're a part of me and always will be. You found me shattered and broken and made me whole."

Fresh tears trickled down her face.

"My greatest regret is failing you."

Kam heaved a breath, shaking. She placed a hand on his back in reassurance.

"The memory of your smile will remind me of love and hope in life's darkest moments."

Her words lumped in her throat, and Starriace swallowed hard.

"What I wouldn't give to change the immutable. You showed me love when I wasn't deserving. All who follow will live in your shadow, but your light still burns in me."

She took a deep breath, knowing this was the hardest part: saying goodbye.

And she hated them.

"Be free, Lily."

She gasped, and her voice broke.

"Go unburdened and return unhindered."

Starriace fell silent, holding Kam. What more could she say? No mere words could convey what she felt. For now, she'd hold onto Kam, the last piece of Lily's life.

Together, both of the bereaved weathered the swells of despair.

Epilogue: A Betrayer of Many Faces

"Master?" the servant spoke as he bowed.

He put a touch of trembling in his voice.

It'd do wonders. Let Krurik think I'm terrified.

"Yes?" Krurik answered.

The servant acted hesitant, as if afraid to speak.

"My lord, the witch, Miza, escaped Xilor's palace. She's here in Ralloc and with Judas Lakayre. I don't know if he's aware she's his niece."

The servant bowed again, imitating he feared the lashing of anger, but it didn't come.

"I'm aware, Lagelm," Krurik said.

He didn't have to act surprised. It was genuine. How could he know already? This information was fresh, and news wouldn't have traveled that fast unless…The realization came to him.

Krurik isn't at Xilor's palace, he's here in Ralloc!

A finger of worry trembled through him. Krurik lacked Xilor's powers, but could he cloak himself in some way? Complete invisibility was impossible, though many studied it and had yet to find an absolute means. There were ways to camouflage with runes, but that wouldn't work in Ralloc, not with so many people.

Unless he can change his appearance at will?

"Does anyone suspect you?" Krurik asked, breaking into the servant's thoughts.

"No, my lord. They do, however, suspect someone else, someone you might find expendable."

"Do tell."

"Vamor Poplu," the servant offered as a scapegoat. "He's caught the suspicion of the former consul and Judas, but no substantial evidence can be found to bring against him. So, he's in the clear."

Krurik was taken aback by this; clearly he hadn't known. One thing that Krurik prided himself on was knowledge. Knowledge of everything around him.

"Strange that I knew nothing of this."

"Do you wish for me to plant evidence?"

Krurik shook his head.

"No, let this sit and germinate. In time, we may, but for now, keep this for future diversions. You've done well thus far, Lagelm."

The servant allowed himself a grin and bowed. It wasn't so odd to hear praise. Krurik was more generous than Xilor ever thought to be. Krurik believed in giving praise, and his servants would be more willing to do whatever was necessary to please him.

"One last question," Krurik spoke. "Who was the informant before you?

Who served Xilor?"

"On this end, my lord?"

"Yes."

"I don't know."

"Very well. Don't contact me, I'll contact you, if the need arises. In your bed under your pillow, you will find a small mirror. Carry it on you at all times. When I need to speak with you, it will grow warm in your pocket. I realize you can't always answer my summons, but do well to not keep me waiting."

The servant bowed again. When the green swirl faded, the servant grinned.

The fool. He actually thinks I'm Lagelm. I've duped him, the warlock, and the entire council.

Vlad Vikal allowed himself a small chuckle. Since returning to the world of the living, he'd found many of the greatest magicians to be lacking. In the storied past, people like Krurik and Judas would be mere peasants compared to the powers wielded in Hagen's time.

But a tremor of worry rose up in him, remembering the mirror placed under his pillow. Perhaps the former apprentice needed to be watched more closely?

How'd he manage that?

Perhaps he had other servants here in Ralloc? How many of them worked against the council? Was it just a few or a knot of writhing snakes?

He pushed those thoughts aside. The council would be convening soon. He hated holding the facade of Lagelm, but unforeseen actions spurred his hand.

Lagelm, the real goblin, stumbled onto him. At first, the council member didn't realize what he saw, but eventually, the little creature put it together. Instead of presenting the matter to the council, he went to Judas.

Lagelm held his secret close, not revealing his true identity to the warlock. When the goblin returned to Ralloc, he met a swift end, but not before he and Daylynn put a kink in Godfrey's plans. Once he found the council member alone, he killed him.

Now, *he* donned Lagelm's image and took his place.

Stifling a groan, he readied himself to sit on the council. With Kellis under his sway, he'd sow as much discord as possible.

Then, when he could leave, he'd do the same to the Krey.

Epilogue: Krurik

Krurik let the communication between him and Lagelm fade, then used the mirror to call Gryzlaud. Moments later, Sidjuous stepped into view.

"Yes, my lord?" he said as he bowed.

"Call off the search for the girl, she's not there."

"But—"

"Do you question me, Sidjuous?"

"No, my lord, but the palace hasn't been searched fully."

"She's in Ralloc with Judas Lakayre."

"How's that possible? When did she escape?"

"It doesn't matter, she's here. What of the Betrayer?"

Sidjuous took a moment to respond.

"He's nowhere to be found as well."

"I expected as much. He must've fled, too. One last thing, was Miza or Olga privy to the Betrayer's real name and exactly who he is?"

"To my knowledge, no, my lord. Xilor kept the information to himself. Even I don't know his name."

Krurik nodded and let go of his control over the Psimond spell. The green mist swirled once again. He stepped away from the mirror and threw off the dark cloak he used to hide his identity and face. Crossing over to the closet, he folded the cloth and put the garment behind a removable wooden slat in the back wall. He straightened his robes and hair in the mirror, walked out the domicile, and up the street towards the castle.

Krurik had messed up in his first few hours. Instead of hunting down the Betrayer immediately after Xilor's death, the newly-christened dark lord completed the ritual as was expected. Those precious hours had cost him.

If the Betrayer made it to Ralloc and revealed himself, he could name people.

Krurik couldn't let that happen. It was time, as Xilor directed, to scourge his house. And as he did, he'd hunt for the Betrayer.

There's nowhere in Ermaeyth you can run to that I can't find you.

Epilogue: Lakayre Manor

Judas stood with his back straight, gazing out the enormous window in the sitting room; the others, Norek, Meristal, and Miza, sat throughout his sitting room, waiting for him to speak. He let out a disgruntled huff and walked over to the bar behind the couch and poured himself a drink.

"Judas?" Meristal said, "the sun hasn't been up but for three hours. We just had breakfast."

He didn't respond other than pouring himself a glass. He took a slow sip and moved to sit on the long chair with his guests.

"Our fourth guest won't be coming, so we'll go on without her."

He glanced at Meristal, hoping she didn't note the pain in his voice.

"I've called you all here for various reasons. There's much to be discussed, and truth revealed. Truth is a powerful tool, a weapon, and an enemy if wielded so. Hopefully, today you'll find it as a comfort."

The others kept silent.

"It's a long tale and will take time and patience, but I hope all will take some peace from this."

He glanced at Miza.

"This young woman is Miza, and she's my niece."

The announcement was for Norek's benefit. He was the first to speak up.

The young man's smile was sheepish.

"Family reunions are great. What's this got to do with me?"

Judas held up a hand for silence.

"I've never spoken much about my family. I, of course, had a mother and a father, but also a brother. An older, fraternal twin. Twins are in my bloodline, ordinarily identical, but my brother and I were rare for my family, at least. My father was an only child. My mother, however, had an identical twin.

"Because twins are replete in my bloodline, I suspected my brother's wife would have twins when he announced their pregnancy. He surmised the same thing and divulged the names were already picked out for girls and boys. That was one of the last times we spoke. I never laid eyes on his children. My brother only saw them a handful of times before he died."

Meristal leaned forward.

"Really? Josiah was married? What's her name?"

Judas paused. The name had been there, just on the tip of his tongue, and it floated away as if carried on the wind.

"I can't remember."

Meristal's brows shot up.

"You can't remember?"

He waved her question away.

"The truth of his children escaped me, but I assumed they'd died along with their surrogate mother during the war. There was little left of the building.

Their mother died during birth—at least, from what I was told. Who even knows if that's true anymore."

He took a deep breath.

"I was on the frontlines, and my brother refused to have me around him or his family. Then, he was dead, and I felt horrible; he died hating me, and I never knew why."

He motioned to Miza.

"The names for his daughters were Miza and Olga. And this is where she'll take over and explain where her sister is."

Judas shifted in his seat.

Miza cleared her throat.

"I was raised in the dark lord's tower, along with my sister. A long time ago, I was banished from Xilor's presence, but Olga found his favor. But he kept me around. Perhaps he hoped I'd follow my sister's lead and join him. I think I was a tool to use against my uncle.

"There was a man, and no one paid him much mind. He once revealed he betrayed the people of Ralloc but never the reason. Between my sister and me, she turned, but I didn't. I think it was because of this man. He showed me kindness when I was without. His name remains unknown to me, but Xilor and the others referred to him as the Betrayer.

"He taught me whenever he could about magic and how to do it. He tried to teach me not to speak while casting, though he couldn't do it himself. I never learned the proper name until yesterday. Other than that, the rest is guesswork."

Judas nodded.

"Now, you all know why I called you here. I need this to be kept quiet. No one must find out. I would've told Starriace, but she didn't come today. Had she stayed, she would've eventually started asking questions, so I thought it best to share."

"If we're being honest," Meristal said, "I also have a confession. Starriace is absent and isn't ready to hear, so it's perhaps not the best time."

The way she dismissed his daughter, flickered a wave of anger within him.

"Anything you can say in front of us, you can say in front of her."

"Anything? Are you so sure? There's something you're keeping from her, isn't there?"

"That's beside the point; this morning's conversation would've happened if she was here or not. As for the other thing you are referring to, that's a delicate matter."

"And so is this, Judas, it's along the same lines."

She turned her attention to Norek.

"I didn't know this; believe me, I didn't, not until you told me your true name. You said your name is Ethanyul, correct?"

Norek shifted in his seat but nodded. Judas saw a gleam in the young man's eye, but his gaze remained fixed on Meristal.

"My real name isn't Meristal but Merilithiyul."

She swallowed.

"As you can undoubtedly tell, our names are similar. That's because you're my son."

For a moment, no one spoke in the silence. Judas's stomach lurched. Miza let out a long, slow whistle.

"Why didn't you tell me?" Judas asked, his chest tight.

"Did you tell me everything about your life?" Meristal countered.

"How do you know?" Miza asked in a quiet voice, almost as if afraid to speak.

"I chose the name for my child if it was to be a boy," Meristal said.

Miza shrugged but spoke with care.

"That doesn't necessarily mean he's yours. It's possible—"

"Perhaps, young lady," Meristal said with a frosty voice, "you don't realize how children, their magic, and their names come about, seeing as you do not have any."

"Meristal," Judas said in warning.

Meristal nodded, a touch of shame coloring her cheeks.

"Forgive me."

She took a deep breath.

"When an offspring is produced, the magical traits are passed down by the father. This is a fact well known. But a mother names her child before they're even born. When the child is born, they're bonded with the true name of their family through magic. I named him Ethanyul because 'Yul' is a part of my family's name. It identifies us all. Yul isn't a common name; in fact, you'll not find it once among mortals because it comes from immortals."

Norek frowned.

"What are you saying? I can't die?"

"No son, I'm not saying that—"

"Please, don't call me that," Norek interrupted. "Not yet. You can't expect me to call you Mom. Don't take me wrong, I think you *are* my mother. I've searched a long time for you, but don't call me son. It's weird."

"Alright, I can live with that. This must be hard for you to take."

"Not really. I've known for a long time."

"How?" Miza asked.

Norek pulled a crystal orb from within his robes and held it up in answer.

"Alright," Miza said, "so he's your son, but where does the Yul come in? I don't get it, are you half elyf?"

Judas sensed Meristal's gaze upon him.

All those suspicions he had about Meristal, all the little quips, stories, and feelings. They all added up and finally made sense.

"No," Judas said.

He sighed and shook his head.

"Why I didn't see it before is beyond me. It was all right in front of me the whole damn time."

"What are you talking about, Uncle?"

Judas's gaze flickered to Meristal, and she arched a brow in challenge.

"Okay," he said, nodding. "She has violet eyes, not unheard of, but definitely odd. She always appears young despite the years she's lived. And she can change her appearance at will, not enormous changes but eye color, hair color, and facial features. Also, no one had ever heard of her or her family when she first arrived."

He leaned forward, scrutinizing Meristal.

"And there's something else I never let on. I could detect an ancientness in your soul. I dismissed it as something within you changed in the Wizard's War, but now I understand. You're probably legends old. Maybe even fathoms."

"How's that possible?" Miza interjected. "A strong wizard may live to be a legend old, usually less, but several legends isn't possible."

"You're clever, Judas," Meristal said with a coy smile. "But you're also wrong. You didn't sense me. I let you."

He snorted.

"I understand now, but two things elude me, how and why?"

Meristal's lips tightened, then her eyes darted around the group. Her eyes found him, and Judas nodded to her. She stood, and a power trembled within her, something great and ancient. The buzz in his head was vastly different from the Rumigul he called upon.

Meristal's feet left the ground, and she hovered above the floor.

"Okay," Miza said, her voice coming out slow. "I'm lost."

Norek leaned forward, his eyes darting between the floor and Meristal's feet. Judas sensed Norek reaching out with his essence to discern the trick. He wouldn't find one.

"It's simple." Judas's eyes twinkled. "She's an archangel."

He gave voice to the suspicion after all these years. All the pieces were right in front of him, but he hadn't pieced them together. He didn't want to, afraid to lose the comfort he had with her. If he voiced the truth, he feared what she might do, most of all leave him.

"It still leaves the question of why," Judas said.

"I thought that'd be simple, Judas."

Meristal lowered herself back down. Sadness filled her eyes, and she sat with a sigh.

"I left my family, the majority of my powers, the riches, and splendor, to be with you. I loved you almost from the moment you were conceived. You must understand we can see the future—something in motion for mortals—but when immortals are involved, we can't foresee everything.

"Also, as an immortal, your life was a blink of an eye to me, and I knew the beginning and end. Your life was tragic, tormented, betrayed; excelling in magic would've been your only highlight, but without family to share it with. No parents, no wife, no house, no children. That's when I intervened. I couldn't let you fall to despair. I couldn't bear that for you, so I sought to change it, and I have.

"Even before I came down, things were different. Miza and Olga, for instance, never existed. Your brother became consul and set a law to have all warlocks executed. You survived because your father made your brother swear a Blood Oath and bound him with magic. He couldn't reveal the truth about you to the public. In the end, in anger, because he made the oath, he killed you himself.

"That wasn't a future for you, an unsuitable life. Because I interfered in the hopes you'd love me, everything changed."

"So," Judas said with a deep breath, turning his eyes to the young man, "Norek is my son."

Meristal nodded.

"And that also means Starriace is your child."

Her brows frowned.

"How's Starriace my child?"

"Like you, she can fly."

Meristal's mouth opened and closed a few times.

"Er—" Norek started, "I can't fly."

Meristal's eyes went wide, and she paled.

"Oh, gods, this means we had twins! I thought she was Daylynn's daughter!"

Miza's head jerked towards Meristal.

"Wait, how did you not figure it out?"

Meristal's mouth worked.

"Archangels don't perceive pain, not like mortals. They told me it would be painful, but I wasn't prepared. The sensations overwhelmed me after Ethanyul's birth."

She shook her head, her eyes finding his.

"I'm sorry."

"Who told you?" he asked.

A perplexed look came over Meristal's features.

"The elyves."

Judas's brow furrowed.

"What elyves? I don't remember any elyves, just the Time Warden."

"I think I'm going to need a drink," Norek said, standing.

"Me, too," Miza echoed and stood as well.

Meristal's gaze flickered to them.

"What elyves?" Judas prompted.

"They were of a kind I'd never seen before and haven't seen since. They had pale amethyst skin and red hair. But what's this about a Time Warden? What's that?"

"A lady who cloaks herself in shadows."

Meristal inhaled.

"I remember that! I never saw her face, nor did she speak to me. I vaguely remember the baby stopped crying, and they informed me the baby had died. I was never aware of Starriace."

After a long pause, Judas inhaled through the nose.

"I need another drink."

Epilogue: The Time Warden

The Lady of Shadows sifted through the currents of time, plucking each thread, watching the culmination of their journeys. Lost in these moments, something tugged at her, the fracture of a ward she'd put in place a long time ago.

She followed the new sensation, her awareness centering upon Judas Lakayre and Meristal Raviils.

"Ah," she gasped aloud. "So, we've finally come to this point."

She watched for a few moments, their conversation unfurling. They skirted the dangerous topic: their children. The wards fractured more. At this moment, she had but to reach out and strengthen them, and both would veer away from the topic of discussion and forget they ever encroached upon it.

The confusion was natural. She'd placed the ward about them, Daylynn, too. It was to keep all their children safe—those directly related to the warlock, and his nieces, too. The Time Warden had witnessed Norek's and Starriace's birth, and it had been her to confound the events. It was already confounding with all the converging points.

For ages it held, but with Starriace brought back, the suppressed memories tried to resurface. The fissures started to bleed.

The Time Warden reached out a hand, poised to alter events, but she subsided. No, she'd let this play out. With a gentle pull, she let the wards fall away. Judas and Meristal would eventually mull through memories and discover the full truth, at least from what they could tell.

The suggestions implanted within them would remain, but for now, they'd know they brought two children into the world together. It was the others that still remained hidden.

But this brought a flicker of worry from the Time Warden. It'd been a long time since she checked on Daylynn's daughter, one of Judas's other children. He had more children than he realized, and he'd been busy as a young man. And Daylynn herself had three in total, the latter two completely wiped from her memory.

It was better this way. Safer.

None of them realized they were quietly bringing back the nephiliam race.

And that was dangerous, if the wrong type of people found out.

With a smile touching her lips, the Time Warden moved away from Meristal and Judas, turning back to the strains of time, and letting them resolve this hole in their life.

Epilogue: Xenomene

The sword that took Smokey's head was still bloodstained and hung on the wall in the heir's office.

Xenomene's office.

A fond smile graced her lips every time she saw it.

As she promised herself, the first order of business after arming her Krey was to burn the chair Smokey sat in and have a new one built. But she didn't stop there. She burned the desk and the bed, too.

The only furniture to survive the burning purge was Daniel's bureau, the one he kept his choice liquor and other vices in. In accordance with her dramatic changes, Xenomene altered the office, finally walling it off from the outside world, accenting her introverted personality; this, coupled with the fact it gave her undisputed privacy, was also a bonus.

She had a small box seat added on the side of the office so she could still watch the Pit below, but otherwise, it was overhauled. The work was done quickly, and the next day when she awoke for her first full day of being the heir, she walked into her completed office.

After the three squads who fought and bled at Cape Gythmel and Dlad City were armed, the executions began. Xenomene moved swiftly through the ranks, cleansing and culling the disloyal.

In many ways, her ruthlessness was a slaughter.

While customarily considered ill to single out people based upon their birth or status or even physical features, Xenomene did precisely that, targeting all Forgotten Islanders. She didn't kill all of them, in fact, she didn't slay even three-quarters, only the ones who failed her test.

Each individual Islander was shackled, male and female, and brought one by one before her in the office.

She saved Slurp for last and Pint just before him. She promised she wouldn't kill the young man, and she meant it. She wouldn't, even if he failed her test, but if he did fail, she'd watch him all the more.

Thankfully, he didn't.

Xeno kissed him on the mouth before he left—much to Tiny's jealousy—and thanked him for not fucking up her opportunity to kill Smokey. She, and the Krey, were in his debt.

She'd find a way to repay him.

He nodded shakily, his skin white, and his eyes wide. She had a feeling she'd never see the poor boy again, not in the capacity of what they shared in Smokey's room. She relinquished the Heir's chambers as well, not even daring to take them over after Smokey had defiled it with his presence. She left the room open and had plans for it.

When Slurp's beautiful yet terrified features looked up at her from his kneeling position, Xeno sighed in relief.

Last one.

She pulled the execution sword from its sheath, not the same one as Smokey's; that had a special place on her wall. The office remained devoid of others. This moment was for her alone. The tip of the sword rested on the floor.

"What are you?" she asked.

"What do you mean?"

"What are you?" she repeated.

"I don't know what answer you want," he said, baffled. "I'm no one. I'm a sucker, a stooge in the wrong place at the wrong time. I'm a Krey without a people and a person without a home. I'm an exile, an outcast, cursed with the bloodlust, which makes me from the day I displayed my abilities to the day I die, a Krey. I'm stuck here, an Islander with a mad king whose actions put me in an even more sadistic plot. Kill me, I'm tainted. I don't want to live with this blood on my hands."

He lowered his head, readying himself for the blow.

Xenomene picked up the sword and walked behind him. She raised it, tip poised downward. She thrust the blade and severed the rope that bound his hands together.

Suddenly free, he stumbled forward.

He looked at her with questioning eyes.

"You may go," she said.

"Why?"

"Because you said you were a Krey first, not an Islander. Had you said it the other way around, you'd be a head shorter."

He paled.

"I want you to know I don't hold you accountable for Godfrey's actions. I saw the look on your face when Daniel died. You were innocent of their machinations."

She kissed him more passionately than she had Pint. She and Slurp had a history, he deserved more.

"I'm happy I didn't have to kill you."

Once the business of weeding out the threats were done, Xenomene convened the ko-dons to implement her will. She introduced an adjutant, who'd speak in her stead if she wasn't available. The adjutant carried all the weight of her title when speaking in her name.

They were also the first person she'd turn to for advice. They'd also sit in on meetings with the ko-dons, but wouldn't hold the rank. The ko-dons were above the adjutant for command unless the latter filled the role of heir, but the adjutant was also not a subordinate.

They were equals.

Xeno made it clear the adjutant wasn't higher in line for succession, anyone could become heir. Xenomene reinstated the custom of earning the title, creating a tournament each year for combatants to fight for the right to be the heir, or individually, they could challenge within certain exceptions.

If the heir lost the match, they were no longer in command.

This ensured only the best led, and all others had to surpass the heir's excellence to become the leader. The tournament and challenges were all meant to be nonlethal; there was no sense in killing good men and women, especially when so few remained. All accounted, families, children, and Krey, five thousand people lived in the Hive.

They simply needed more Krey.

The Black Tide wasn't as numerous as leaves on a tree. With Ralloc boasting over two million citizens, what were five thousand? A grain of sand unnoticed beneath the heel of a noble. The harsh reality made Xenomene all the more determined to carry out her hatched scheme.

She didn't inform the ko-dons and the adjutant until afterward. She, along with the Mind, Heart, and Hand from the Xenytes, walked the border of Outpost Dire and House Eti until they located all the runes regulating their lust. Bloodlust was magic, just of a different sort. Three hundred sigils were found, and only seventy-five had evaded the purge.

The effects were immediate, small at first, but noticeable.

When they returned to House Eti, she could already see men and women coupling off, talking in hushed tones. Upon returning to her office, the Mind brought up a valid and previously undiscovered observation. With the Krey and A'uri mating together, they may conceive magic-wielding Krey.

The thought was intriguing.

"It's not like it hasn't happened before, and we'll cross that bridge if it comes," she said in answer.

With the potential traitors dealt with, the sigils destroyed, and an adjutant named—she nominated Stallion out of respect for him as an elder, his seniority, and sound, logical thinking.

He declined, so she named Adder instead.

That left a spot on the ko-dons to be filled.

Tiny awaited to be named. As much as he deserved it for services during Cape Gythmel and Dlad City, Xenomene didn't think she could stomach his brooding with what she still had to carry out.

Spectre took the rank. To call Tiny agitated was an understatement. To placate him, she informed him the next seat would be his. Stallion and Chimera were ascending in age. It was only a matter of time before a place turned up vacant.

This went a small way to mollifying the big man. His pride and ego were wounded, undoubtedly because she didn't reward him for backing her edicts as a ko-don. She told him when she made the forthcoming announcements, he'd understand why.

With the ko-dons assembled, her first official meeting as heir began.

"War's coming, gentlemen," Xeno opened. "And lady," she amended. "It won't be like this last one, fought on an open battlefield. Unfortunately for us, the consul isn't stupid. If he engages us on an open field, we'd slaughter his army. This fight will be different. We're now in open rebellion and a state of war with Ralloc. For once, we'll live up to the reputation of being the bad guys. They made the first move with the murder of our heir, I've countered."

"Already?" Stallion asked. "How?"

"Without consulting us?" Chimera barked.

"I'm sorry, when did Daniel ever consult you on something he wanted to do? You may have discussed options, but the final decision was his, always his. I've exercised my own right."

"What did you do?" Panther asked.

"I sent Godfrey the head of his brother. Along with a letter."

"Gods, you've killed us," Craiboar despaired.

"Have I? That was well over four days ago. If there was going to be a response, there would've been one by now. No, the letter tells him how we're going to proceed."

"Pray tell," Chimera groaned.

"As of the moment I severed Smokey's head, we were an independent nation from Ralloc. Outpost Dire and surrounding lands are now part of a sovereign nation, a Krey nation, and we'll never rejoin Ralloc's domain until he's removed from power. Since that's never going to happen, we're on our own."

"Spirits of the Underworld!" Adder blurted. "What are we going to do about food? Money?"

"What do we need of money?" Xeno countered. "What do we *need* to buy that we can't make ourselves? We grow our own crops; we make our own clothing and armor."

"Aye," Stallion spoke, "but the ore comes from Ralloc or from their miners working in *our* mines."

"So, we learn to mine, big deal. Call it a day of exercise."

Stallion spoke, holding up a finger for each of his points.

"No liquor, no mages to teach our young A'uri, no new recruits coming in…"

"We can make our own liquor."

She sighed.

"The gods' hairy vaginas, are we so incompetent? As far as new A'uri being trained, we can train our own, if not, then why have A'uri in the first place? Plus, I may be able to finagle someone here."

"How?" Panther asked. "You've cut us off from Ralloc!"

"This individual has no love for Ralloc, least of all, now."

"Shades!" Spectre cursed, joining the conversation. "You aren't seriously thinking of *him*, are you?"

"What?" Craiboar asked.

"She intends to approach Warlock Lakayre for help," Spectre said.

"And his uh—"

"Concubine?" Chimera supplied.

"Mistress?" Spectre said.

"Whore?" Stallion said.

"Lady Meristal," Xenomene clarified. "Who knows? Maybe they're others who hate Ralloc as much as we do."

"If Daniel were alive…" Chimera began.

"But he's not!" Xeno said, harsher than intended.

A mischievous smile spread across Craiboar's face.

"Still, to have the warlock here, Daniel's rolling over in his grave and cursing you from the Underworld."

Stallion nodded.

"Yeah, but he's also dancing a jig because we're sticking it to Ralloc and that pompous ass, Godfrey."

"We're so few in number," Spectre said. "If war broke out between us, we'd have the upper hand for how long? And when we start losing people in battle…"

"I've been thinking about that, too," Xenomene said and swallowed hard. "I've come up with a solution, and not everyone is going to love it."

Chimera placed his face in his palms.

"What are you planning?"

"We're going to *breed* our army."

The room was quiet for a few heartbeats.

"I can think of several drawbacks…" Stallion began.

"And I can think of several advantages. Look, we get—what?—one recruit every five years? We have the potential to get one thousand or more in a year."

"Not every child born of a Krey has the bloodlust," Craiboar said.

"True, but not every child born doesn't."

"There aren't enough women," Stallion stated the obvious.

His statement also brought her to the hardest selling point.

"Yes, I know, which brings me to the worst part. The women will need multiple partners."

The ko-dons were up in arms with her declaration. They talked wildly amongst themselves and nearly came to blows as they shouted at each other over various points of her proposal. She held up her hands and wrangled them to their seats.

"A reason why I made Adder the adjutant after Stallion's refusal is because he'll now be a record keeper of lineages. He's good with numbers and such. We want to make sure there aren't any close familial ties later down the road."

"Okay, for the sake of the argument that's sure to ensue," Chimera said, "let me play the opposite role. How many times must they be removed before they are allowed to…*breed*?"

"What is it for Ralloc?"

"Depends on how much money they make," Spectre said.

"What do you mean?"

"The nobles are known to marry first cousins every other generation, sometimes second or third. The poorer class doesn't at all."

Xenomene nodded.

"I heard the elyfian sometimes marry first cousins, too, so how about second cousins?"

"Do you know of anyone who would want to fuck their cousin?" Stallion blurted.

"Want to, or would?" Craiboar said with a leering smile.

Xenomene let out a quiet sigh.

"We can ask the A'uri and see if anyone is an expert on lineage, okay? If they say first cousin or seventh, then okay. The point is babies."

The ko-dons nodded, but Spectre spoke.

"What about the women? How many children would they have to bear?"

"Technically, they don't have to have any, but if they're willing, I'd like to try to bear four children from a woman with four different fathers. This ensures variety, and it increases our numbers, potentially four-fold, at least for the first few years."

"What about an age limit?" Stallion asked.

"What do you mean?"

"Do you want to start breeding them as soon as they are able, the Age of Maturity, or the epoch or an age after?"

"Three ages is a good number."

"How convenient," Craiboar grumbled. "You don't have to whore yourself out for another era. I wouldn't be surprised if you changed it before your third age birthday."

"No one said anything of whoring," she countered.

"That's what we're doing now!" Spectre interrupted.

She waved her arms emphatically.

"A breeding whore."

"I have to agree," Stallion said, biting his lower lip.

"Okay, okay! Let's put it this way. Let's share numbers. We're Krey, we train, eat, sleep, drink, and fuck, and that's about it for our whole lives. Stallion, how many have you been with?"

"What?"

"Partners."

"Women? Eighty-five."

"Are you saying you've had more than women?" Chimera asked, a chuckle in his voice.

"Three male partners," he confessed.

"So, eighty-eight?" Xeno said, sidestepping the confession. "And you, Chimera?"

"Counting whores or Krey?"

"Partners."

"One hundred and thirty-four," he boasted.

"Okay, so between the two of you, you've had over two hundred partners. I'm asking for four men. Not a huge number in the grand scheme of things."

"And you? How many have you been with?" Panther asked.

"Including Pint, because I was forced to?"

She did a quick mental count.

"Eight."

Chimera laughed.

"Shades! And you call the Rallocans prudes!"

"It'll change. I'm not exempt from this, and neither are any of you."

"But some of us are married, or old," Stallion said.

"Well, you'll have to find it in your heart to forgive your spouse as she's fucking someone else, after all, you will be, too. You can't get pissed."

They continued debating, but in the end, with slight amendments, most were mollified. She was encouraging sex, and while they'd do it anyway, now she added a birth for the deed—the actual end goal for having sex in the first place. There'd be people who'd refuse, she had no delusions, but the final decision came down to the women since there were about seventy percent fewer women than men.

In short, women could choose their mates.

There were, of course, stipulations. If one particular male was chosen repeatedly and fathered many children, he was to be taken out of the drawing to not contaminate the gene pool. They set the age limit at three ages if women chose to bear children. Xenomene didn't want to take young, strong, and able women out of the battlefield, nor would they be too old to bear children.

If they wanted, a woman could bear children two epochs past the Age of Maturity. While fifteen was adulthood and the age of consent, she couldn't forbid them to have sex, but she would ban childbirth for young women still in training.

Next, they talked about the mining issues and blacksmiths making weapons and armor. By the end of the year, she wanted everyone apprenticed with a blacksmith and miner and to be proficiently cross-trained. At the end of the year, each blacksmith was to take the most promising five students and make them full-time apprentices.

Other duties such as farming, tailoring, cooking, and apothecary were known to all Krey, and they'd continue to rotate through those duties each week.

Once they adjourned, she had all the Krey gather at the footsteps of House Eti and informed them of their course. The Black Tide was a nation unto themselves and no longer accountable to Ralloc, which meant war. Duties and professions were to be learned and later assigned. Everyone, every day, would have to work and train like they always had, but now it meant so much more than feeding themselves.

It meant survival.

To her surprise, they took her breeding scheme much better than the kodons, but perhaps that was because they whittled away all the jagged edges.

She expected an outcry but was surprised by the resounding silence.

Either they understand the stakes involved and agree, or they'll express their displeasure later.

As her speech ended, an explosion rocked the ground, and a barracks was engulfed in flames. The dust cleared enough to see the outline of a dragon.

Liquid fire shot from its mouth again and incinerated a handful of Krey gathered.

She screamed "to arms," and heard her cry repeated. All Krey carried weapons, even in the Hive. Blades cleared scabbards, and the Krey fell upon the dragon, which died in short order. Another two swooped from the sky, raining molten fire upon the unarmored Krey and A'uri.

Xenomene bounded down the steps and drew her own sword.

Fucking dragons! Where did they come from?

But she knew the answer. This was Godfrey's doing. If the dragons made peace with Ralloc, this was probably their atonement for the damage they inflicted.

This had Godfrey's hand all over it.

This is payback for his brother! I'll kill that son of a bitch, I swear!

The bloodlust filled her, and she waded into the foray.

A massive but silent shadow passed overhead. She turned in time to see a gaping maw of diamond teeth swooping down from the sky, closing around her, devouring her.

She felt warmth, and pain…

…and then, she knew only darkness.

Epilogue: Starriace

Starriace stayed with Kam for another three weeks, both lost in grief, but they had each other.

The funeral wasn't a spectacle. Only Starriace and Kam were in attendance, and Kam laid Lily to rest in the backyard with a white marble headstone for a monument. The words scrawled on the tombstone were short and sweet, like her marriage to Kam.

A wife, a friend, a treasure.

Starriace and Kam entered a state of perpetual sadness. They barely had the energy or motivation to pull themselves out of bed each morning. They picked at their meals, turned guests away from the door, and scarcely said a word to each other. In the fog of aching hearts, all they did was sleep and mourn in silence. Kam sent all the hired help home, and the house grew as quiet as a tomb.

They weren't to return until called.

Minutes crept by in silence. For the first few days, Starriace was afraid to break the brittle atmosphere. Their proximity drew closer together as the days went by. At the time of Lily's death, she and Kam held each other, but since the funeral, they were rarely in the same room. As time passed, they eventually ended up drawing together.

Tonight, they sat together in the seating room.

Meager flames burned in the fireplace, the snapping and hissing subdued as if sensing their mood. Starriace hurt, but she found Kam's presence soothing. She broke their longstanding accord on silence in the second week.

"You can't go on like this, Kam. She wouldn't want you to."

"How do you know what she would've wanted?" he retorted.

The look on his face was apology enough.

"She wouldn't want you to throw your life away, wallowing in grief. You hurt, I hurt, too. But you've got to get up."

"Get up?"

"Continue living, one step at a time, but you've got to stand first."

"It sounds like you're getting ready to leave."

She noted the accusation in his tone.

She nodded.

"I am. My leaving isn't a sign of not caring. I loved Lily, you know that."

Her voice broke.

He nodded.

"She loved you, too. You were the friend she never had, or the sister she always wanted."

Starriace paused, and she frowned.

"Kam? I thought she did have a sister."

His eyes went round, and for the first time, a grin split his face.

"She told you that?"

And then it was gone, a fleeting moment.

"It took me years to find out she had a sister. When did she tell you?"

"In Far Point. We were up one night, and we talked."

He nodded.

"She does—did—have a sister, taken away in her youth. Did Lily ever tell you why she started whoring in the first place?"

Starriace shook her head.

"She did it to pay the rent for her and her sister, and to put food on the table. Lily started at fifteen, the Age of Maturity, on her birthday, in fact. Her sister was four, I think."

He swallowed, and it thundered in the quiet home.

"Her green eyes were a plus, but at the time, red-haired girls were not popular, so she paid for a grand master wizard to permanently change her hair blonde. Of course, that set her back more. And not a month after she started whoring did the entire thing blow up in her face."

He stopped, lost in thought. So much time passed, she wasn't sure if he'd continue.

She prodded.

"So, what happened?"

"They came and took her sister away."

"Why?"

"Because she displayed the bloodlust. While Lily was out making a living for them, they took her. It was days before someone told her what happened. She never got to say goodbye. We were planning on going to see her next year, or at least try to. Now that I'm part of the army…They hadn't seen each other for over two ages. Lily doubted her little sister would even remember her."

He gasped, as if about to cry, then he pushed it down, and continued with the tale.

"But Lily kept providing for her sister after she was gone. Each month, she'd send money to the heir at Outpost Dire. The heir tried to return the money, telling her it was unnecessary, but she refused, insisting on paying for whatever gear or training her sister required. There wasn't a day Lily didn't think of her. I wish I would've tried harder."

"I'm sure you did everything you could, Kam. Don't hate yourself; Lily didn't."

She reached out and patted his hand. He held her hand in comfort.

"What was Lily's sister's name?" she asked.

"I don't—something weird. Lily's name was weird, too, before she changed it."

He was silent for a moment, thinking hard.

"I'm not sure, but I think it started with a 'Z.' Zenomene or something."

Starriace nodded, taking in the name.

"It's a pretty name."

"Yeah, pretty weird."

Kam chuckled.

"You should've heard Lily's. Zaeryn."

He nodded to himself.

"Yeah, Zaeryn and Zenomene Kothlus."

Starriace's eyes snapped to him as he said it.

"Kothlus? As in…?"

Kam nodded, then smiled.

"Yeah, the same name of Ralloc's last king. She's a relative, but whether distant or close, who can guess? I don't think Lily appreciates how convoluted her family tree is."

He sighed.

"Of course, they never went by their father's last name but by their mother's. Everyone knew her as Lily Vane, of a minor noble house. If she used her real last name, she could've taken residence in the castle itself, but her family forbade it. With her parents dead, and no son heir to the family name, her relatives took everything. They disavowed them when she took up whoring. Gods! What I wouldn't give to make them pay."

Starriace hugged him.

"I'm sorry, Kam. No one told me the full story. That's terrible."

When she broke her embrace, Kam found her lips.

"Kam," she said when he pulled back. "I want this, the gods know I do, but not now. Not so soon after Lily…"

"I'm sorry. It was foolish. It won't happen again."

"No, Kam! That's not what I'm saying."

She turned his face with her hands.

"I want this, more than anything, probably since the moment I met you, but I feel like I'm dishonoring Lily by doing it so soon after she…was taken from us. Trust me when I say, I'd give up having sex with you if that'd bring her back. But it won't, and I don't want to give you up, but I can't right now. Do you understand?"

He nodded.

"I do. I'm sorry."

"I'm sorry I'm not comfortable enough."

A small, sad smile came to her then. She kissed him softly and pulled away, retreating to her room. Later that night, after she heard the snores coming from Kam and Lily's chamber, she crept to the backyard to say her farewells. She left Kam a note on the kitchen table explaining she'd be back.

I should tell him the truth. But it might be too much for him to take.

She decided to omit some information, keeping it simple.

Outside, Starriace squatted and placed a hand on her friend's grave marker.

I'm going to miss you, she silently said to the tombstone. *I'll look after him, I promise. And if your sister is still alive, I'll find some way to tell her you've passed. She deserves that much. I love you…*

She started to rise, then lowered herself back down.

I don't know if you can hear me from where you're at, or if there's a place beyond death, but please don't hate me for this.

She touched her stomach, lowering her head.

I don't mean this as an insult, but I'm carrying Kam's child. It happened the night I came here, and I was in a rush to leave. I didn't take moon leaf. It wasn't planned.

She didn't know what else to say, if Lily could hear her, or if any of it mattered.

Feeling awkward, she left Kam's mansion, afraid to look back. If she did, she'd never go.

Would that be such a bad thing?

She had two answers, and both required distance from the heartache.

The cobblestone road outside his house threatened to roll her ankles. She stopped momentarily and closed her eyes, reaching out for a familiar presence. She detected him far to the south and willed herself to him, teleporting from Ralloc to Ahn and Sedrus.

They stopped short of the Corridor of Cruelty, once a monument of trepidation, but now, the narrow strip of land held no fear, nor any magic to torment her by.

In a sense, the place had died.

Over the next few hours, the trio made their way south on foot, slipping through the Corridor. Sedrus and Ahn proved to be more or less kindred spirits. Formidable with weapons, stubborn, sarcastic, and borderline insolent or rude. For the most part, they left Starriace alone, knowing she grieved, but not for who.

Despite the dark shadow looming in her soul, her optimism flickered to life. She couldn't let Lily's death stop her. The future was bright and full of hope. Lily would always be in her heart.

A path stretched before her, one laid by Xilor, and she couldn't balk now. Lily's death was the catalyst that hardened her resolve.

Through the journey, she only spoke when absolutely necessary. Ahn and Sedrus tried to talk to her, but she didn't have the heart to. She spent it all on Lily's death, too tired to grieve any more. She thought about her destination, a place where she could go and rest and come to terms with the loss.

Harold's.

Remembering him brought back the words he spoke. Her future.

One of your companions will die. A thing you cherish will turn against you, and you'll lose it forever.

Lily: the companion who died. Or was she the thing Starriace lost forever? The second part didn't fit, but the first half did. Already Harold's prophecy was coming true. It made her heart hurt all the more.

Beyond the Corridor, it took two more weeks to reach Harold's. She could've teleported or flown, but something was soothing about doing things the 'mundane way' as Judas put it. Perhaps she inherited more from her father than she realized.

Sometimes during the trip, she'd become sick and vomit as if the phantom still loomed inside her, but this was different. She'd already gone through the morning sickness before, but perhaps it was coming back? Occasionally, she'd turn food away, the scent making her nauseous.

Sometimes the urge to teleport away became too strong, but she didn't for fear impinging the elyfian's honor by sending one of their own to protect her. The gesture overjoyed her heart, even if she was stuck with the worst in the bunch. Still, when Ahn wasn't trying to be annoying, he was quite pleasant, almost charming. During those times, she could almost see herself bedding him.

Almost.

Ava popped up not long after they started their journey, coming and going as she pleased. The mere sight of her sent Starriace into a deep depression; the melancholy seemed boundless. Ava was a living reminder of two things, the death of every fairy and the bearer of bad news in regards to Lily.

When Ava tried to cheer her up, Starriace would rebuke her and yell that she was a monster, then beg for forgiveness moments later. She didn't have to say any of it aloud, of course. Ava discerned how she felt through their bond.

But there was another bond Starriace could sense, the bond with Rusem. Through him, a sea of risen rose up around him. When she asked Ava how many came forth, Ava shook her head.

"Too many to count, mistress."

"Tens of thousands?"

Ava's lips thinned.

"More like hundreds of thousands."

Starriace sat back, stunned by how many came from the ashes of the dead. It was almost unfathomable.

"That's not the bad news," Ava continued. "More keep coming. I can't stay all the time directing traffic, so I placed a ward around the place. I made it to where they can sense where the others are congregating and are compelled to go."

Starriace looked at Ava in a new light, "Ava, that's brilliant. I would've never thought about it in a million years."

"I know."

Further and further south they went until Starriace announced they'd be stopping at their destination the next day. Sedrus gave a whoop of exuberance that he'd eat a proper meal. Ahn exclaimed he'd be able to check out the local brothel for a woman, and the pub for wine and cards.

As though some gods above looked down upon her proclamation in ill favor, the sky opened up and poured sheets of rain that night. Starriace endured it through chattering teeth and soaked leather. The sun couldn't come quickly enough, so the trio minus Ava started before dawn.

By mid-morning, they passed through the gates of Far Point with more than a few odd stares from the natives.

Starriace glanced around and found the land absent of war scars. Xilor hadn't bothered with these small towns in an effort to close in on Ralloc. The only sign of any military might was the trough they left in their wake going to the northern domain. Starriace trudged through town and came to the edge where a cemetery stood.

"We're here," she said with a smile and a sigh of weariness.

"A cemetery?" Sedrus sneered.

"That eager to die, are we?" Ahn heckled. "They told me to watch you closely. Good thing I listen."

She scolded both with her eyes before rolling them.

"Follow me."

Starriace walked forward with the other two on her heels. When the house and steps manifested before them, they gave a startled yelp of surprise.

An enormous house with one old man alone, but not for long.

"Be on your best behavior," she said, like a parent warning their child.

On Harold's porch, she sensed his aura again, that familiar sensation, and that's when it finally coalesced for her, the place where she'd sensed it before. Earlier, it'd been a nagging feeling, but now, she knew beyond all doubt.

Instead of entering like all the times before, she knocked.

A few moments later, the door cracked open, revealing the sole occupant. With him standing before her, that familiar feeling arose, one she reconciled as Harold's. She'd felt it many times before, but now it was undeniable. Her suspicions were laid to rest now.

The first time she'd truly felt it was shortly after the first battle with Xilor.

His long gray hair on the sides swept back, accenting the baldness on top. His kind gray-blue eyes twinkled with delight, his massive hands resting on the door. A presence of calm, peace, and tranquility rolled off him, like an aroma filling his house.

"You're long overdue, Starriace," Harold said in his kind, warm, deep voice. "I've missed you. The house has been quite lonely."

Starriace beamed with delight, eyeing the elder.

The way he breathed, the way his potbelly giggled when he walked with his notorious limp. The smell of tobacco and coffee wafted in from somewhere deeper in the house. All these things, these memories flashed back in an instant, and she grew confident she made the right choice coming back.

She collapsed into his loving embrace.

"Thank you. It's been a long time, grandfather."

About the Author

Kyle Belote is a prior active-duty Marine, writer, musician, and painter. He's lived in Texas,. Hawaii, and Okinawa, Japan, and has traveled the globe. When not writing, he enjoys sketching, researching companies and investing, and reading and listening to audiobooks. Kyle enjoys a diverse collection of films, books, and shows—just not the abomination called Disney Star Wars.

For more information, visit the author's Substack: https://www.outpostdire.com

Back Jacket Blurb

Ralloc faces inevitable defeat, and all resistance has been shattered. Yet, the dark lord, Xilor, has remained absent on the battlefield.

Two additional squads of Krey mobilize to Dlad City, falling under Xenomene's command. Her enemies close in from all sides, and someone she once called an ally has left her for dead.

And Starriace, battered, broken, and beaten, journeys down a dark path to claim her revenge and unlock the mysteries of the brimstones. But her decisions may bring desolation.

Mark of the Profane is the second installment of the Dark Legacy Series.

www.ingramcontent.com/pod-product-compliance
Lightning Source LLC
LaVergne TN
LVHW050909080826
845145LV00001B/28

9781956180138